"What Do You Want of Me, Marina? Tell Me What?"

"I want to go home to Martín."

"I do not intend to retrace my steps to Mexico. It's a waste of time. The new project begins in Trujillo."

"Then let me go to Martín alone."

"That's absurd. You'll like it in Trujillo. You'll sail there on a fine ship!" He tried a smile.

I took a deep breath, and risked everything. "I want to leave you, Cortés."

He turned his back abruptly and walked away from me to stand some distance off, staring out over the sea. At last he faced me, keeping that distance between us. His voice was calm and resolute. "This life of mine is a hard one for any woman to share. She must live in safety without me or else stay at my side to endure great privations and dangers. And my life will never change. Ahead of me I see a secret strait, an Inca city, the wide Pacific, the South Seas. . . ."

"Your life will never change," I agreed, holding my breath.

He straightened, looking at me kindly. "And so it seems, Doña Marina, that we have come to the parting of our ways."

"Yes, to our parting," I managed to whisper.

LA CHINGADA

BY
JANE LEWIS BRANDT

PUBLISHED BY POCKET BOOKS NEW YORK

POCKET BOOKS, a Simon & Schuster division of
GULF & WESTERN CORPORATION
1230 Avenue of the Americas, New York, N.Y. 10020

Published by arrangement with McGraw-Hill, Inc.
Library of Congress Catalog Card Number: 79-4360

ISBN: 0-671-83494-0

First Pocket Books printing February, 1981

10 9 8 7 6 5 4 3 2 1

POCKET and colophon are trademarks of Simon & Schuster.

Printed in the U.S.A.

To Haven, my daughter, with love:
¡Adelante con los faroles!

Sea route from Cuba to Vera Cruz
March to Mexico and then to Olid's Colony

```
0        300           600 miles
0        100           200 leagues
```

CONTENTS

PART I

▼▼▼▼▼▼▼▼▼▼▼▼▼▼▼▼▼▼▼▼▼▼▼▼▼▼▼▼▼▼▼▼▼▼▼▼▼▼

BEFORE THE GODS ARRIVED
December 30, 1500–March 26, 1519

1

There are those who call me *La Chingada,* who say I was a whore. They lie. A whore sells her body, but I gave mine, and gave my heart and gave my mind until the bitter last. There are those who call me traitoress. Liars. I betrayed no one. I was betrayed. Monstrously betrayed, cruelly betrayed. But from the very hour of my birth I seemed marked for a strange destiny.

I was born at midnight, to the crash of thunder and the flicker of lightning. That I was born at all was due to the bold intervention of my grandmother, Ix Chan. After hard labor lasting from long before sundown, my mother's strength gave out and she sagged, half-unconscious, dangling from the straps around her wrists that supported her in a squatting position between two stone wall brackets in which torches flamed. The old midwife poked and prodded and exhorted, in vain. My mother had no more strength. I was doomed to die in her womb. But my grandmother had one of her visions and saw the solution. She ran for my father, who was waiting with the clan heads and priests in the main hall of the stone palace, and told him what he must do.

He undid the supporting straps, laid my mother supine on a straw mat and, kneeling above her head like a woman grinding corn, he shoved down hard on the bulging abdomen that writhed with futile muscular spasms. Shoving again and again and shouting to her to help him, he finally shoved me out of her body and into this world.

The high priest came in then and the midwife held me up to him and he sprinkled water over me from his sacred staff tipped with seven rattlesnake tails. Chanting a prayer to the goddess of childbirth and eater of dead babies, he shaped on the soft center of my skull a patty of white maize paste. Invoking the benign influence of Ixchel, the moon goddess, he tied around my waist a belt of snakeskin from which dangled a scalloped seashell of gold, symbol of purity, with which he covered my genitals. I would wear this until adulthood, if I lived. My birth merited these attentions from the high priest himself, for I was the first child of the ruler of Paynala.

My grandmother told me all this, and how the wind that night seemed ready to tear the steep thatch roof off, and how it made the torch flames dance wildly, casting peculiar shadows across the tattooed face of the high priest as he stared down at me from underneath his mass of tangled hair, in which blood-red feathers were knotted. And she told me that when my mother learned she had a daughter, she turned her dazed face to the wall and slept, or pretended to. So my grandmother's arms were the first to enfold me with love. "Your mother wanted a son," she said, "but I wanted a granddaughter to warm my old age." My father, having reassured himself that my mother was only asleep and not dead, came over then and looked down at me and wiped blood from my head quite tenderly. It was he who gave me the name by which I came to be known, the name of a great snow-capped mountain to the north: Malinche.

My grandmother was a small, thin widow of fifty, but power burned in her like a secret flame. She had ruled in Paynala until her consort died, and at times still sat with the clan heads and war chiefs in the council house. They were in awe of her because she had the gift of prophecy, and great wisdom. She always wore a long, loose tunic the green of jungle shadows, and there were small bright ornaments in her high-coiled hair—a gold butterfly, a tortoise of jade, a silver skull. Her earrings were dark jade plugs set in rims of silver like round eyes staring from her slit earlobes. Her own eyes were dark and deep, with fans of tiny lines at the outer corners. She had no doubt of the importance of the town of Paynala. "We have been favored by many of the gods," she told me, "because our ancestors scorned to obey evil priests who dishonored sacred symbols." I had no idea at the time what this meant, but it conveyed to me that we were a chosen people.

And so when my father Taxumal had taken as wife the daughter of the chieftain of a little town in the highlands far to the west it had upset everyone, for he had thus spurned several eligible young women of Paynalan clans other than his own, any one of whom Ix Chan would have preferred as a daughter-in-law to my mother, Chituche.

My grandmother conceded that Chituche had been very beautiful at eighteen, with large slanted eyes and a full, rather sullen mouth. She was adept at weaving and at featherwork, very skillful at trapping and catching wild jungle birds for their plumage. She had refused several men who wanted to marry her, and her parents did not press her to get a mate. There were four older brothers to grind maize and weave clothes for, but more compelling than this practical fact was Chituche's stony inner strength. When anyone tried to get her to do what she did not want, she never showed anger or sulked or wept; she disappeared. She had secret hiding places in the jungle and always took with her an obsidian knife. But when my mother set eyes on my father she changed overnight. She washed her blue-black hair with soap bark and put on a new skirt of her own weaving. Kneeling opposite him at the supper mat, she looked up and sent out the strong wish that he would want her. He was instantly drawn to the beautiful, silent girl whose feather tapestry, half finished on the loom, glowed with ancient motifs passed down over centuries from the Old Ones to the south. He believed she must have depths beyond the average.

Handsome, noble, tall, my father was not a man to leap into the tying of the mantles only because of a woman's physical beauty. Political astuteness played a part in his decision to wed a stranger; after the marriage, her town became a satellite of Paynala and several other villages to the west followed suit, which meant that Paynala could count on them for extra warriors if peril threatened. Thus far Paynala had stayed free of Aztec domination; their capital was far to the northwest. But he knew of their recent conquests on the coast; Paynala was only a short distance inland.

And so my mother came to Paynala and at a ceremony held at the foot of the great gray stone pyramid in the plaza, the high priest tied their mantles together —and their lives. To my mother this must have been a dazzling occasion as flutes shrilled and drums thudded and people threw bright flowers. "To Chituche you owe your physical beauty," my grandmother once conceded. "Although it took long enough to conceive you, as the Goddess of the Moon well knows."

My first real memory is of the day the traveling traders came to Paynala in my fourth year. I can still see that small procession filing across the square in the blaze of mid-morning sun, toward the shade of the great ceiba tree by the palace steps where I sat. In the lead were two forbidding men in long, dark capes the color of dung and dried blood, tied on one shoulder. They wore tall black hats with rounded crowns. They were *pochtecas* from the distant capital of the Aztecs— shrewd, hard men who down several centuries had made of trade so honored a calling that a few had even attained the rank of lower Aztec nobles. They boasted that they never lied, never cheated, never spied for their ruler. Traveling vast distances from sea to sea and from the deserts of the north down to Yucatán, they spoke many dialects and effected the exchange of exotic goods, slaves, and news. They were always followed by a file of nearly naked *tamanes,* human beasts of burden bearing heavy loads held onto bent backs by leather straps around their foreheads.

On that day I remember so well, the traders had with them several slaves roped by their necks to a long pole. One was a child. When I asked my mother why those people were tied like that she said they were for sale, and if they were recalcitrant they would end as sacrifices at some temple. Human sacrifice was not practiced in Paynala, so I was unsure what this meant. She said that to the north the priests cut out the victim's heart with a stone knife. To the south the victims were drowned in deep, dark sacred wells. The roped figures took on a tragic aspect and I did not look at them any more, but fixed my attention on some small wares which the *pochtecas,* chatting with my father, spread out on the palace steps. Among them was a curious golden pendant shaped like a coiled snake with a human face, a plume sweeping back from its head. It charmed me.

I had been many times to market day, when people from far away arrived with produce and merchandise, and I understood the principle of barter. So I ran to the rear garden to pick some flowers, then I got the attention of the shorter trader and offered the bouquet for the little snake man. When he turned his head to look down at me, I saw the deep new crescent scar on one cheek that drew up that corner of his mouth in a leer. "The pendant is worth more than a bunch of flowers," he said. "But maybe your father will buy it for you." It was worth a cotton mantle, he said, and I was overjoyed when my father nodded. The trader with the scar put the pendant on my palm and added a thin braided cord, pointing to the hole in the pendant through which it was to be threaded. He called my father's attention to this generosity and remarked that the journey had been long and that he was hungry and thirsty.

I followed them into the palace and knelt on the floormat with my father, my grandmother, and the traders, to whom my mother brought a clay jug of sweetened maize water, which they all sipped formally from small clay cups. I managed to thread my pendant and to put it on, but then I could not see it, so I took it off and laid it on the mat before me, studying my little snake man with delight.

The news the traders brought that day was unusual indeed. First they told us that the year before the Aztec ruler Ahuitzotl the Cruel had died and had been succeeded by one of his nephews, Moctezuma the Second. To us, this was something like learning that one star in the sky had been replaced by another just like it. But their second piece of news was truly astounding.

A short time before Moctezuma's coronation, bizarre strangers had come floating over the sea to the shore of Yucatán, far to the south. They had arrived in several great houses that rode on the water and had atop poles as tall as trees which held aloft great cloth canopies that swelled out with the wind and made the vessels move. A brave Yucatán chieftain who had himself rowed out in a long canoe to the largest of them said that the pale strangers had bearded faces and spoke no language he could understand. He got the impression they did not know where they were; their leader kept pointing landward and repeating the word *India*. The chieftain kept replying *Yucatán*. At last the ships turned and sailed eastward, leaving him puzzled, a little frightened, and glad it was not his land they apparently sought. The description of the alien mariners fascinated me. Indians do not grow beards, so the words were "pale men with long hair on their faces."

"If they *are* men," the older *pochteca* said with a significant glance at my father, "and not, as some suspect, supernatural beings."

Just then I held up my snake man and set it swinging back and forth, fascinated by the way it gleamed in the light from the doorway.

"Look at Malinche!" It was my grandmother's voice, and I saw her finger pointing to my pendant. Everyone was staring at it, so I set it swinging faster. Then someone gave a nervous laugh and my mother commanded me to stop.

My snake man was a representation of the god Kukulcan, the great Feathered Serpent of ancient legend.

Centuries ago he had taken human form as a tall white-skinned man with a dark beard. Kind and wise, he had come across the sea from the distant east to teach people many things, particularly to abandon human sacrifice. After many years he had sailed east again but promised his weeping followers that someday he or his descendants would return, to judge how well his precepts had been followed and to punish the wicked who had disobeyed his commands.

My swinging the pendant depicting this deity had affected Ix Chan because it seemed to her uncanny. Why had I set it in motion at the instant the strange visitors were described? Had it been an omen, suggesting that the bearded strangers might next visit the shore not far to the east of Paynala? Using a little child's hand, had a god whimsically confirmed his imminent presence? "I am troubled," she confessed. "Never in all my years on earth has there been any hint of the god's return. This is the first."

The older *pochteca* nodded. "I can see that you are intelligent people here, so I will tell you that when Moctezuma's couriers brought him the same news, he did not take it lightly either. A priest at the temple of our war god told me Moctezuma spent long hours consulting the stars in order to learn if those strangers were divine beings."

"And what did the stars tell him?" my father demanded.

"I do not know. I only mean that the possibility worried him, as it should any thoughtful ruler." He nodded respectfully to my father, from whom he hoped to make a pleasant profit before the day was done.

2

The *pochteca*'s news brought about a clash of wills
between my father and the old high priest. Ah Tok
argued that extreme measures should be taken to propitiate our gods. Those bearded strangers might re-
appear on the shore just to the east of Paynala or the
new Aztec ruler might decide on further conquests to
extend his wide domain and provide fodder for his war
god. A slave must be bought and sacrificed so we could
offer our deities that strongest proof of abject devotion,
a human heart.

At the council meeting where Ah Tok tried to alarm
and sway the clan heads, my father opposed him. His
grandfather had long ago convinced even the priests
that human sacrifice must be abandoned. To my father,
the very idea of a blood-stained altar was repugnant.
If hearts and blood bought the favor of the gods, he
said, then such sacrifice was useless to protect us
against the Aztecs, since we could never offer as many
hearts as they. As for the mysterious strangers, what if
they had indeed been emissaries from Kukulcan, who
had said that only fruit and flowers should be laid on
his altar? We must continue to obey this gentle deity,
as we had for many decades of peace and plenty. My
father's view prevailed. Ah Tok was forced to forget his
desperate remedy.

Although the cruel sacrifice he had desired would
not have prevented it, a few months later three frightened refugees arrived from the north to gasp the news

that an Aztec army had just swept into their town. Resistance had proved futile; their warriors were dead or captured. The Aztecs might continue southward, to us.

My father had all the women, children, and old men leave for the Black Cave in the hills just to the west of town. Its mouth was cleverly hidden by shrubs and stones and could be reached only by a narrow rope bridge suspended over a deep, swift stream. Nearly four thousand of us filed into the great cave, carrying food, firewood, and blankets. Beyond it were other caves, in one a pool of crystal water in which swam pale eyeless fish. The torches showed gray stalactites from which hideous faces seemed to scowl down at me. My fear vanished after my grandmother told me that centuries ago a little band of our ancestors had taken refuge here after a long journey from an ancient city in the land of the Mayas to the south, a city which gods and people had at last abandoned. Greedy priests had long before taken to selling replicas of holy objects to people in the distant highlands to the west for certain products they wanted. In time those sacred artifacts lost their value, for the barbarians learned to make reproductions of them. The gods became cold; there were earthquakes, disease, and drought. The water supply became scant, receding deeper and deeper in the great *cenotes*. At last a young rebel nobleman exhorted people to follow him from the dying city to a new place. A young priest joined him, and so did several hundred courageous common folk, weary of laboring in fields and quarries to sustain priests and rulers so decadent. "After a long journey they came to the river that flows near our town and found this great cave," my grandmother said. "And here our ancestors camped during the season of rains until the jungle could be cleared and houses built. We will be safe here, too."

The days we spent in the cave were unhappy ones, because we knew we might emerge at last to find our men all killed or captured and our life as a people over and done. At last we heard a familiar voice calling us. The Aztecs had come and gone. Paynala's ruler was now a mere vassal of Moctezuma after a victory both brief and bloodless.

My father had used an old strategy—to leave the town empty, the warriors bivouacking in the heavy jungle nearby. From a tall tree on a hill he had watched the Aztecs enter Paynala from the river road. They were like ants, filling the whole town square and the lanes leading off from it, and still they came up from the seacoast, thousands and thousands, with helmets shaped like eagle heads, or jaguars'. Their drums pounded to the rhythm of one beating heart, and their bone flutes sounded like human screams. Our nine hundred warriors could not hope to prevail against them.

Without his sword or shield or black-and-red war paint but wearing his feather headdress to show his status, my father marched alone into the town and across the square past ranks of Aztec soldiers to the steps of the pyramid where the banner of the Aztecs' war chief was held aloft. He knew only a few words of their language, enough to say "Taxumal bows to the might of Moctezuma." He had to kneel and touch earth and bring that hand to his forehead in humble reverence. He was told that from this day forward to the end of time, Paynala would be visited each year by Moctezuma's tax collectors, to whom we would give whatever portion of maize, cocoa beans, cotton mantles, and other local products they might demand. Failure to do this would end in the extermination of all Paynalans. Luckily for us, the maize crop was only half-grown and unripe. After devouring nearly everything else, the Aztecs took themselves off, leaving in my father's heart and so in mine an overwhelming sense of loss. Our independence was gone forever.

But there was little time to brood, for the immediate problem was to find enough to eat to stay alive until the maize was ripe. Hunters killed deer, hares, and iguanas; our conquered neighbors in Coetzacoalcos on the coast let us catch fish to help feed ourselves. Everyone but the tiny children and the old and feeble worked to clear new fields from the jungle. Fortunately for our survival, our soil was rich and provided two crops of maize a year. Working on his milpa only a few hours a day, a man could feed a family of five. Now he worked longer and harder to produce a surplus for Moctezuma. The easygoing times were over.

It was my grandmother who decided it would be to Paynala's advantage if its ruler could speak the language of our conquerors fluently enough to negotiate with the tax collectors. We all knew a few words of this Nahuatl tongue, but we spoke a dialect of the Mayan language. The two were nothing alike, having been originated in ages past by two very different peoples. The speakers of Nahuatl had come from a region far, far to the northwest, while our Mayan ancestors, legend said, had crossed the sea to the east in a flotilla of small ships from a distant, mysterious island called Aztlán.

When the *pochtecas* visited us a month or so after our conquest by the Aztecs, my father told them we wished to buy a slave who spoke Nahuatl. They had with them two, a young female Toltec who had worked as cook for a noble family in the Aztec-dominated city called Texcoco and her little daughter, who was my age. My father was curious as to why they had been sold. The older *pochteca* said, with a sly look, that he thought the master had become enamored of the pretty slave and the mistress jealous. "I won't charge you much for the child," he said. "I'm being generous because I know your community is somewhat depleted of resources." But he asked the usual two hundred cocoa beans, claiming he could have got much more from a certain rich old cacique of Tabasco who had a penchant for women from distant parts.

The slave woman was named Xochitl, a common Aztec name meaning flower. Plucked rudely from her former life, she feared the same fate again, and was abject and eager to please my mother. The little girl's name was Atotlotl, which means ibis. I shortened it to

Ato. My father and grandmother spent many hours with Xochitl until they had a quite large Nahuatl vocabulary, and they made a habit of conversing together in this tongue, which annoyed my mother, causing Xochitl to tremble. I learned Nahuatl with less effort. At first little Ato was shy and silent, but soon we were babbling away happily, each in her own language. Ato was slow to learn mine and I was eager to learn hers, and before many months had passed my father laughed and said I had casually learned more Nahuatl than he for all his application.

Ato was pretty like her mother, having the same almond-shaped eyes with little folds at the inner corners. From her I learned that the bloodthirsty Aztecs surprisingly included in their pantheon of deities the kindly god who hated blood, for one day Ato pointed to my pendant and insisted that god was named Quetzalcoatl. Ix Chan confirmed that the god indeed had two names. Ato was somewhat bloodthirsty herself, and one day confided a dream she had had, that my mother died and my father married her mother, and we became sisters.

As yet I had no sister or brother, but one day when I was five, my mother said, "You are going to have a baby brother before too long." She had become quite cheerful of late. But time passed and no brother appeared, so I asked when he might be expected. By now the bright gleam was gone from her eyes. She replied sharply that there would be no brother, and when I asked what had happened to him she sent me away.

Crushed, I wandered into the central room of the palace and heard my father and grandmother talking of this very mystery. It was dusk and they did not see me in the shadows by the doorway.

"Chituche has conceived four children since Malinche was born and has lost all of them," Ix Chan said. "Your blood and hers are now enemies. I have seen this happen before. She will not bear you another living child. And so Malinche must be educated to become ruler of Paynala. She must study at the young priest's school with the boys and I will endeavor to teach her what I know. Weaving and featherwork, however exquisite, will not enable her to deal with tax collectors, drought, earthquakes, and Ah Tok."

"But what of my younger brother?"

"Dak Cho is not a leader and knows it. So do the clan heads and everyone in Paynala."

"But what about Ah Tok? He doesn't like women."

"The final decision is not his, but yours. You are evading my suggestion because you still hope that Chituche will bear you a son."

"Ah Tok says she will. He cast the sacred stones of prophecy at her feet only a week ago." My father sounded hopeful.

"As a prophet he is not renowned. Hope must have some basis in reality. Your hope for a son does not." She lowered her voice. "As for prophecies, on the night Chituche miscarried for the first time, I had a strong vision. I saw Malinche, grown to womanhood, addressing our people as the new ruler of Paynala. It troubled me deeply, for I thought it meant your early death. But now I know it meant that you would never have a son to take your place."

A solemn sense of my own importance had stolen over me as I eavesdropped in the shadows by the inner doorway. I saw myself as Ix Chan had envisioned me, and saw the faces of my people looking up as I spoke to them.

My father said, "Certainly no harm can be done if Malinche attends the priest's school."

I walked toward them. "When I rule Paynala, will you both help me?" I wanted a denial of that troubling remark about my father's death.

Startled, they glanced at each other sadly. My grandmother said, "A worthy husband will be chosen for you by the clan heads. But a ruler can expect help only from the gods, and sometimes even they will offer none."

When I told my mother of my destiny, she was unimpressed. "Women are made for other purposes than

to rule a town." Her mouth was bitter and she slammed
down the crossbeam of her big loom very hard, crushing down the rising band of woven cotton as if she
were also crushing down her deep resentment. But she
had not given up her dream of having a son. This I
was soon to learn in a way that overwhelmed us both.

3

I suppose it was natural that my mother preferred to
believe that the goddess of childbirth would relent, the
moon goddess smile at last. She continued to turn
abjectly to the high priest for encouragement, bringing
many offerings to the foot of the sacred pyramid,
which women were not permitted to ascend. Ah Tok
encouraged her to hope and had her eat peyotl and
brew infusions from strange herbs he gave her. He
burned woodpecker feathers under her nose and mixed
the ashes with dog milk and a fermented maize drink
called balche, which made her vomit. The peyotl gave
her visions that frightened her. My father told her not
to take any more of the high priest's remedies but I
think she did so secretly.

It was fortunate that the slave Xochitl was a cook,
for my mother spent most of the daylight hours working on a huge feather wall tapestry depicting the goddess Cioacoatl, whose hideousness awed me. Her head
and body were formed of two thick serpents twined
face to face, their eyes huge and round. Over her
dangling breasts hung necklaces of skulls, severed
hands, and hearts. I wondered why the deity responsible

for the birth of babies should look so fearsome. The loom was in my parents' sleeping alcove, and when I entered one day I found my mother kneeling at an open chest near it. She was holding up a small loincloth she had woven, of a size to fit a boy of four or five, and she stared at the garment with a forlorn expression. I felt very sorry for her and went and knelt beside her, for even if she had no son, she had me.

She turned her head and gazed blankly, then forced a smile that changed to a childish and mischievous grin. "Let's see how you would look as a boy!"

There was something strange about the idea of putting on a male's garment, even in fun, and I took a step backward, suspended between compliance and uneasiness.

"Look, Malinche, I have gilded sandals, too, and a turquoise necklace." She took these new lures out of the basket and displayed them like a vendor. "And a feather headdress!" It was a miniature of the panache of green quetzal feathers my father wore on state occasions. I had always admired it; women were allowed no such headdress, only the small ornaments they pinned into the braided crown of their own hair. Could there be any harm in my mother's little game? Eyeing the little green panache I took off my skirt.

With cold hands my mother quickly dressed me in the garments made for a son. The loincloth's long front panel reached well above my ankles. I felt that I looked not only like a boy, but like one who had outgrown his clothes. But my mother clapped her hands together and burst into shrill laughter while tears flooded her too-bright eyes. "What a tall son I have!" she cried, and clasped around my neck the turquoises set in silver. "And now the noble headdress!" Smiling, she put it on my head, leaned back to stare. "But the hair is wrong," my mother said, frowning. "Come over here to me."

I obeyed, uneasy again. She reached out to the loom beside her and picked up the small sharp knife of black obsidian she used to cut cotton threads to the length she desired. Swift as a striking snake she reached out for one of my braids.

I could not move or speak. The knife came up to my braid. I heard and felt the tiny snicking sounds as some of the hairs were severed. I screamed and tried to step away from her.

"Stand still!" she commanded and jerked me forward by my braid. She wasn't smiling any more.

"I don't want hair like a boy's!" I began to cry, not only for the hair I seemed about to part with, but because my mother had turned into a threatening stranger.

"Stop!" My father was in the doorway and for a confused instant I thought he meant that I should stop crying and let my mother have her way.

His voice arrested her arm in its frantic sawing motion. She let go of my braid and sank back on her heels and looked stupidly down at the knife in her hand. Then he threw it to the floor, where it clattered on the stone, the blade pointing to my feet. She buried her face in her hands and began to sob.

My father came to me, snatched the feather headdress off, tossed it aside and smiled down into my eyes. "Your mother is sorry she frightened you."

"It was only a game," I squeaked.

"I know a better one." He caught me around the waist and swooped me high above his head, laughing up at me. "Fly, little eagle-girl! Flap your wings and fly to the sun!" This always delighted me, and I flapped and flew, smiling down into his eyes. He let me down to the floor with an exciting swing. "Now go to Ix Chan's house. But first put on your own clothes."

As I dressed, my mother's harsh sobs ceased. Still kneeling she looked up at my father who frowned down as though at a puzzling stranger. "What was I going to do?" she whispered. "What am I going to do?"

His words dropped on her like stones. "Stop listening to Ah Tok. Throw out his medicines. Thank the gods for our daughter. Give away these toys." He pointed to the boy's trappings strewn on the floor.

My mother stood up slowly and wearily, and as I

backed out the doorway she bent and began to gather up the husks of the dream she must now abandon.

Ix Chan's house was a stone annex built at the rear of the palace after my father had married Chituche. Ix Chan said she considered it ill luck if the husband's mother and his wife shared the same roof, but I think the truth was that she had been shocked when my father brought home a rustic stranger and had taken that means of avoiding her. To an inner room for sleeping was attached an anteroom with a thatch roof and lattice sides up which green vines had been trained. I loved this bower with its moving leaf shadows, its sweet garden smells.

"Why are you so sad?" Ix Chan asked me as soon as we were kneeling companionably on the floormat. Before I could tell her, a mellow voice called Ix Chan's name, and into the bower trundled a fat smiling neighbor holding out a basket piled high with mangoes and ripe cactus pears. "Here is the mother of Na Chel Cuy to bring you a few humble fruits and news of the day," she beamed. She always referred to herself as "the mother of Na Chel Cuy." After bearing two puny daughters, she had produced an enormous, beautiful boy who became the focal point of her life.

"Perhaps concerning your son?" Ix Chan asked.

"How did you know?" Reaching for a cactus fruit, the mother of the miracle stared in surprise.

"A wild guess," my grandmother said drily.

The proud mother told us then that Na Chel Cuy, though barely ten, had that day speared in the jungle a a large ocelot, had won two games in the ball court, and had found time to scrape the ocelot hide, a lustrous one in perfect condition. "This boy of mine will make some lucky girl the best of husbands," she simpered, and reached forward to pat me on the head, glancing meaningfully at Ix Chan. She was always fawningly sweet to me, always curried favor with Ix Chan and my parents, clearly in the wistful hope of betrothing her son to Taxumal's daughter.

"I fear you have spoiled your son for any wife," Ix Chan said, for his garments were always of the finest, his food the best. His arrogance made other children dislike and fear him.

Denying that she had spoiled her son, the doting mother devoured fruit and regaled us with descriptions of several more of his recent exploits and at last took her sated bulk cheerily out the doorway. My grandmother pointed to the nearly empty basket and we began to laugh. Ix Chan did not question me about my earlier sadness, seeing me apparently happy again. But I doubt that it would have made any difference if Ix Chan had known the truth about the intensity of my mother's obsession. In the loom of time a fatal pattern had barely begun to take shape; some of the threads that would form it were not yet off the spindle.

My father had not lost the respect of our people in bowing to the might of Moctezuma, but rather had gained even more esteem. The Paynalans, sensible folk, agreed with the sentiment he had expressed when he first addressed the populace after the Aztec warriors left and we all returned from the cave. "Survival is preferable to death and slavery. Tribute to Moctezuma is the price of our survival. Working harder to pay that tribute is better than repose in a burial urn. To work!"

Aware that the Aztec tax collectors might prove rapacious, my father decided to hide away a portion of our nonperishable products in the Great Cave in order to build up a reserve that would see us through a drought or some other calamity. He had a secondary motive: our defeat would be a trifle less bitter if we could deceive our conquerors. By the time the lofty and arrogant tax collectors arrived in their royally feathered capes, a great many baskets of dried maize and beans had been concealed. Thanks to his new facility with Nahuatl, my father was able to convince the suspicious Aztecs that the smallness of our year's surplus resulted only from the fact that their warriors had pillaged so voraciously. Warning us that they would expect much more next time the tax collectors departed, their *tamanes* lightly laden. Everyone looked mournful until they had gone.

Over the next few years this hidden surplus grew large and our communal spirit slowly strengthened. It became clear that Moctezuma had no interest in forcing on us his gods or his laws. All he wanted was tribute, not even the living tribute of men for his armies, already vast beyond all need. As for slaves to sacrifice to his war god, that deity was finicky, we learned, and preferred the hearts of brave warriors captured in battle. And if we remembered happier days when the long shadow of an Aztec ruler had not yet touched us, we still enjoyed all our traditional ceremonies and festivities, if on a less lavish scale.

The *emku* was a solemn rite. All the girls and boys who had reached adolescence in the past year were welcomed into adult life, the mother of each girl presenting to the high priest the symbol of purity worn since birth. In a space roped off with garlands below the gods' pyramid, the high priest sprinkled holy water on the initiates and declared them sinless and ready to assume adult responsibilities. After that they were honored with an outdoor banquet to which the parents brought delicious dishes, and all around the plaza other families ate. Some of the very old people drank too much pulque, but in them such rare drunkenness was not frowned upon. Everyone teased the girls and asked them whom they hoped to marry, and they always made the proper answer: "The man my wise father chooses for me."

At nine I was several years from my *emku* or the choice of my husband, a thin child carrying in my head a great weight of knowledge. Among much other lore, I had learned from my grandmother and from the young priest-tutor the story of the great flood that once washed over the whole world, destroying everyone and everything except for Tezpi, who had loaded plants and animals into his huge boat. And I learned that the Age of Water had been followed by the present Age of Fire when volcanoes erupted and earthquakes leveled towns and cities. I knew how to read the sacred calendar, to draw accurately the glyphs of the eighteen months of the year and those representing all the various units of time, from Kin, one day, to Alautun, more than 63 million years in duration. I knew the names of the gods and the feast days of each, and the phases of the moon and when each crop is best planted and harvested, or ears pierced, or honey gathered. I learned to identify a hundred herbs and plants and the uses of each, and which few are deadly poisons, which produce sleep, which give visions. I learned about the many animals of the forest and seashore, and that the barb of the stingray is used by priests to lacerate their own flesh, and that long ago mothers with much milk used to nurse the gentle little coati with its small black hands. I learned that the sacred quetzal bird, with its two long green tail feathers, lives only in the forests of the high mountains and would never be seen alive in our land. I was warned of a small serpent almost as rare, the Snake with Four Nostrils, whose venom is fatal within an hour.

I did not learn of any antidote. None was known. That serpent killed my father.

4

He had gone to visit the chief of the small satellite town to the west which had a plantation of the kind of maguey cactus on which the cochineal slugs feed. Their bodies produce a valued crimson dye and he had to barter for a quantity of it because mantles of this color had been requested by the Aztec tax collectors. Returning home, my father paused at the edge of the jungle that lay beyond our furthest maize fields to admire a strange bird on a branch before him. Large and sky-blue, it had a fan of yellow feathers atop its head. It was as my father gazed up at this bird that the Snake with Four Nostrils sank its fangs into his foot. Feeling the sharp pain, he looked down and recognized the creature and knew he was a dead man. Aware that activity speeds the venom faster through the body, he had the men who were with him improvise a litter from a blanket and on this he was carried to Paynala and into the palace.

They put the litter down just inside the doorway. Below the palace steps a crowd was gathering. Three of the men had gone running to get the clan heads and the high priest, while one who remained told me of the snake. I felt its fangs pierce my heart. I fell to my knees beside the litter; Ix Chan knelt at the other side. At his feet my mother sobbed, her face in her hands, her body rocking forward and back, but Ix Chan and I shed silent tears that ran down our faces. The five priests and four clan heads came in at a run, Ah Tok already brandishing his rattlesnake scepter. He dipped it in an urn of scented water and shook the water drops over my father's chest, and then, eyes closed, head back, he began to intone the customary plea to the gods that they listen to my father's last confession of his sins.

"Be silent," my father commanded in a voice like an echo of his own. The young priest swinging a censer in which tobacco unfurled its purifying smoke was so startled that his arm stopped moving. To die without confession?

"I choose my daughter as my successor," my father said. "Until Malinche's *emku* has been celebrated, signifying her adult status, my brother Dak Cho will sit at her left side on the council mat, and my mother Ix Chan on her right. After her *emku* Malinche herself will rule. I say this as I die."

The last words were whispers. In moments his breathing ceased. His half-closed eyes stared at eternity or at the time-faded mural on the wall, tall figures of warriors, priests, and nobles walking in procession around the room forever. Overwhelmed by my grief, I scarcely heard my mother's wild weeping or the wailing chants of the three old women who came to dress the body for burial. But I saw too clearly the four young warriors carrying in its rope sling the enormous clay urn in which my father's body would sit doubled knees to chest for all eternity, buried on the hillside where our dead formed one mute company, beneath each silent tongue a green jade bead. The interment took place that same day; we buried our dead quickly, I knew, because death was seen as a defilement of the living, corpses as unclean. But I knew too the human spirit outlived the body and that there were many heavens, each suitable to one's manner of life and death. There was a heaven for women who had died in childbirth, and one for dead babies where a beautiful milk tree grew, laden with breasts. There was even a special heaven for suicides presided over by the sad goddess Ix Tab, who had hanged herself. I told myself that my father would attain the bright heaven for brave warriors in the high realm of the Descending God, the sun.

For three months my father's immediate family was avoided by everyone, being unclean until we had performed the rituals of placating the newly dead, who still envy the living, with gifts of food and flowers left at the burial place. We wore old ragged garments and people pretended not to see us when we crossed the plaza to leave offerings at the temple. During this time my uncle Dak Cho had to live with us. He agreed with me that the Realm of the Sun was the proper heaven for my father. This would have been of more comfort to me had Dak Cho been respected for his intelligence rather than liked for his amiability.

Five years younger than my father, he was his opposite in every way: short and solid with glossy skin darkened to copper by the sun, he had a round face and a rather trivial nature. Ix Chan once told me that as a boy he went through his training in martial arts without any belief that it mattered how far he could shoot an arrow or hurl a spear, and had also found every excuse to avoid lessons with the priest-tutor. Yet he was not lazy and worked hard on our family's section of the clan fields. His squashes were the largest, his maize the tallest, his bean and tomato vines the heaviest laden. He would have been happy with the life of any common man, raising his crops and paying his tithes and work hours to the ruler and the priests. He had not yet married, although many a girl had tried to lure him, but he was adept at slipping away. He had once lived in the palace with Ix Chan and my father, but soon after my mother arrived he went to stay with relatives, an old couple glad to have a strong young man under their roof. He worked their field and ours, too, and most cheerfully. But six months after my father's death I learned of the banked fire that had burned behind that amiable façade.

One night when we were all seated around the supper mat Chituche suddenly put down her bowl, looked defiantly at Ix Chan and said, "I am going to marry Dak Cho."

If the roof had fallen in I would have been less surprised. He leaned toward me and confided, "I have wanted your mother since before you were born."

I looked at my grandmother to see if she was as outraged as I. She was staring at Chituche as if she had never seen her before. Her dark deep eyes then moved to her son's face. He said respectfully, as if he had memorized the words: "I will be a good husband to Chituche and a good father to Malinche."

My anger overflowed and I jumped to my feet and cried out "I have a father!"

As I ran out of the room, I heard my grandmother say to Chituche, "You will wait a full year to show respect for my dead son."

"But I am alive," Chituche said. "And so is Dak Cho's child within me."

Stunned, I stood just outside the doorway and knew that my mother had soothed the pain of her loss by embracing kindred flesh. I could not understand such faithlessness.

Only a week later, Ix Chan and I watched the tying of the mantles which made my uncle my stepfather. Kneeling beside Dak Cho at the foot of the pyramid of the gods, Chituche's face was without expression, but he radiated such joy that many people smiled and wished him well despite the general knowledge that propriety had been flouted.

One year after my father's death, Chituche's second child was born, a son.

The season of rains set in soon after his birth and Chituche kept her baby wrapped in so many blankets that Dak Cho gave him the nickname Zub-Zub, saying he looked like an armadillo peeking out of its shell. Two years later the name still suited him, for the small, fretful baby became a timid child, often ill, forever hiding in his blanket or creeping into the shelter of his mother's arms. "Close the door curtain," she would command, "a breeze has risen." Or "Whisper. He is sleeping." Sometimes I wondered if she had ever shown such concern for me, and decided she had not.

But halfway into his third year, Zub-Zub suddenly bloomed. I thought my mother's preoccupation with him would pass, but she could not seem to bear to have him out of her sight. Carrying him on one hip, she boasted of how well he could walk. Nursing him still, she told how many teeth he had grown. Dak Cho began to resent this overabundance of maternal affection. "It's not natural," he said to me one day. "Why does she see this little boy of ours as a remarkable being? It's time for Chituche to face the truth: she has produced no prodigy in Zub-Zub."

I thought I understood her need to believe she had. Could her coupling with Dak Cho have been wrong if it had brought her not only the son she had yearned for but a marvel of nature as well?

Dak Cho summoned up the courage to confront her with the truth. "People are beginning to laugh at you. It is hard enough for me to get the respect of the clan heads and the warriors without that." He had hit on the one barb sure to strike home: Chituche's pride. After that she ceased to carry Zub-Zub with her everywhere and stopped praising him so often. But I soon found that her obsession with him had merely gone underground. Like the brown river that gushed from its hidden source near the Black Cave, it suddenly emerged, a torrent.

One day she and I chanced to meet in front of the palace and she astonished me with words of praise. "How tall you are growing, Malinche." She smiled at me. "I cannot believe that soon you will be a woman." She led me to the stone bench below the ceiba tree. I was flattered when she added: "And you will be beautiful, more so than I when your father chose me." Her next words were so astounding that I did not at once grasp their real meaning. "How fortunate you are that I have given you this little brother! Now you can have a happy life. You can marry the man you want. I have often felt sorry for you, knowing that as ruler you would have to tie mantles with someone the clan heads approved, whether you liked him or not." She leaned toward me with a rapt look and her voice was honey. "But now, if you wished, you could abdicate in favor of your stepbrother, for he, too, is of the royal line. Dak Cho could continue acting as ruler until the boy is of age."

I remembered the day when she tried to cut off my hair and saw the same madness in the black depth of her eyes now. I stood up, shaken by anger. "I will never do that. How can you think I would go against my father's last command?"

My vehemence startled her. "Don't get so angry. To rule a town is hard for a woman, unnatural. I wanted a happier life for you, that's all."

"You wanted your son to rule. My tying mantles with a man I wanted was just the rosebush hiding the snake!" I was the more bitter for having been lulled by her earlier pretense of affection.

Her face grew dark. "Brilliant as you think yourself, you do not know more than the woman who bore you. You have displeased me greatly. I do not want to see your face again today." She turned her head and stared out over the plaza as if I had vanished.

I walked toward the palace with my head high and my back straight. I did not see the little pile of pebbles Zub-Zub must have left on the step when he was playing there. I stepped on one of them. I was thrown off balance and stumbled and fell.

Chituche's harsh laughter appalled me. I got up and looked back at her. She was still sitting under the tree, her head turned my way, white teeth showing in a grin. In that instant I saw that she was not beautiful any more. The bones of her face were too strong and when she stopped smiling, her thick, chiseled lips looked cruel. "One who expects to rule a town should look where she walks," she called to me.

The words would one day seem like a mocking warning.

Even though I was eleven, I took my outrage to Ix Chan. "You must remember that your mother's people are less civilized than we," she said. "Chituche has the ignorant notion that women are not fit to rule a people. But here in Paynala our rulers have been directly descended for twenty generations from that brave young warrior who led us from a dying city, and to maintain this lineage it has been necessary that a woman rule from time to time. As I did. As you will."

Her voice was faint and I saw then that she was not well. The pain she confessed to was intense, as if her bowels had become two serpents, strangling one another. I ran to get the *ahmen*. This priestly healer left behind him a dense haze of tobacco smoke that did not relieve her suffering, nor did his medicine containing powdered moth wings and the ash of red parrot feathers. After he had gone she had me brew a tea of herbs that induce repose, and at last the pain subsided enough so she could sleep. I stayed all night on a mat near hers and lay awake a long time, hearing the sad two-note cries of a bird in the garden. It spoke to me of death. I decided that when my *emku* was celebrated it would be Ix Chan who reached up beneath my skirt to remove the Shell of Purity and she who presented it to the high priest, although this would be unprecedented for one whose mother was still alive. But in the morning when I told Ix Chan my decision, she refused.

"Your mother gave you light, and to her is due this honor. But what is more important, after your *emku* you will become Paynala's ruler. To begin by flouting custom out of mere whim would shock many, and would give enemies the chance to talk against you."

"I have no enemies."

"You have one. Ah Tok."

"Why is he my enemy?"

"For the same reason that he was mine: because you are your father's daughter. Taxumal believed, as my

father did, that the power of the high priest must always
be limited. Ah Tok was still young when I became ruler,
and thought he saw the chance to regain some of the
power the priests had lost since only a woman opposed
him. One day he had the temple drum sounded and
called the people together and told them that unless a
sacrifice of human blood were offered at once to the
gods a great disaster would overtake Paynala. I refused
to sanction such a sacrifice. The next day came one of
those thunderstorms so frightful that the most stolid
people begin to think the gods are angry." Ix Chan
smiled at an old memory. "Ah Tok was struck by
lightning; it burned the soles of his feet and he hobbled
about crippled for a long time. There is nothing less
awe-inspiring than one who prophesies disaster and is
himself struck down, and it was years before he got over
his humiliation. It embittered him and has made him
hunger all the more for the power he thinks should be
his. Be aware: he will prove your enemy."

Even she did not guess who else would be.

5

Three disasters led to my first clash with Ah Tok. A
hurricane roared down from the north, trampling the
young maize. It was replanted but had barely sprouted
when a long heat spell dried the earth and then baked it,
so that fields that normally would have offered stalks as
high as a man's head produced stunted plants with
dwarf cobs. And then the earthquake—which struck

during the festival in honor of the corn god—leveled a dozen farmers' huts and alarmed everyone, dispirited as we were.

Early the next morning, two young boys came to the palace, troubled by what they had seen the night before. Daring one another on, they had stolen up the pyramid steps at an hour when they knew Ah Tok and the priests to be eating supper in their living quarters below and had entered the inner temple. There they had seen that the sacrificial altar of Chac Mool was stained with fresh blood. A heart was lying on a dish before the skull-faced image of Tlaloc, the rain god.

I went at once to the temple and sent Dak Cho to fetch the four clan heads. From the foot of the pyramid I called Ah Tok's name, and he appeared in the dark doorway above. His face had grown gaunter with the years and the cheekbones stood out like a skull's, but his deep-set black eyes burned with his strong life-fire. Today he wore his long white robe, dirty and stained. On one side was a dribble of blood.

"I am told you have committed a human sacrifice," I said.

"Who told you that lie?"

"Prove to me that it was a lie." I started up the steps. I do not think I would have dared to enter the temple atop, but I wanted to hold his attention until Dak Cho arrived with the clan heads.

He spread his arms out wide. "Women cannot enter the temple!"

"Nor can blood be spilled there." My earlier slight awe of him had vanished. I felt shrewd and capable of dealing with him.

"You have heard some rumor of the marketplace." His eyes left mine as he saw Dak Cho and the four clan heads hurrying across the plaza to where I stood.

"Then show them the inner temple," I commanded, triumphant. "Prove that it's clean of blood."

He made no objection, and I watched them ascend. In a few minutes they emerged, and as Dak Cho hurried down the steps to me he nodded and smiled. "It was only a deer," he said. "I saw the head and hooves. Ah Tok said a dream told him that Tlaloc and Chac Mool would be propitiated with merely an offering of deer blood and would send us better weather."

I said, "Blood is blood! Ah Tok is defying us."

Dak Cho frowned. "But a deer is only a deer. We must not make so much of this." The clan chiefs nodded in agreement.

As we walked away I felt Ah Tok's eyes between my shoulder blades and looked back. He stood at the top of the pyramid steps staring after me, the three red feathers in his hair stirring in a slight breeze, the rest of him statue-still. I think that may have been the first time he wished me dead: the clan heads and Dak Cho were malleable. I was not.

Far from procuring any good, it was as though the spilling of that deer's blood ushered in a year of sorrow that climaxed in two deaths. It was not Ix Chan's old malady that took her from me, although it recurred. Much weakened, she succumbed to a plague called *cil* that had already claimed several lives. Blood was vomited, the skin turned yellow, and chills alternated with a burning fever during which strong visions haunted the victim. I was kneeling by her pallet to sponge her hot forehead when she opened her eyes. "I had hoped to see your *emku* and your coronation, but it is not to be," she whispered.

A hard lump of sorrow filled my throat. I took her thin hand and held it and told her she would get well again, that the fever was gone now.

A film came over her eyes as eternity seeped into her. Then her eyes opened very wide. "I see! I see!" she spoke in her normal voice, not to me but to some vision within her mind. Her eyes turned to me in their deep sockets. "Changes. Many changes. You will survive them to rule in Paynala. Do not be afraid." Her eyes closed and I gathered her into my arms.

It was early morning. Gray clouds massing in the north promised rain by afternoon. By noon she had been carried in her funeral urn to the hill of the dead and interred in a narrow stone-lined crypt beside my father's. Standing there alone, unaware of the rain, I believed that no change she had envisioned could be as terrible as this one.

My *emku,* as yet uncelebrated, became a matter of general concern. The people wanted me declared their ruler, not only because they liked me but also because they needed the security of seeing tradition observed and my father's last command carried out, the more so now that Ix Chan was gone from us.

For as long as I could remember I had been friendly with the pretty woman who sold herbs on market days. A month after Ix Chan died, she offered me a bouquet of sweet-scented leaves and asked if there were any sign yet of the arrival of my womanhood. When I said no, she shook her head. "You have passed your twelfth year, yet childhood lingers on in you. But do not be unhappy, for there is an old saying that women whose blood is late are fruitful longer." She smiled and nodded. "It is also said that they are wiser than most."

Ato's early maturing seemed like proof of this, for to her slowness of mind was added a hopeless infatuation with Na Chel Cuy, who brought me occasional gifts of flowers or fruit. He was seventeen now, more arrogant than ever, and certainly not likely to have any interest in a slave girl. But it was Ato's foolish belief that one day he would come to realize that she was pretty, and want her. When she fell ill with the same disease that killed my grandmother, I sat with Ato listening to a rambling confession of her desire, and though my heart was heavy, to make her happy I told her that when I was caciqua I would see that she was allowed to take part in the next *emku.* "And when Na Chel Cuy sees you in new clothes, admired by everyone, perhaps he will take an interest." I thought it unlikely, but what mattered now was to try to lift her spirits above the clutch of her physical misery.

Chituche came in then and seemed very angry to

find me there. "This sickness can go from person to person. You escaped last year when Ix Chan died. Do not tempt misfortune twice, Malinche."

Next day the *ahmen* was sent for, but after he left I disobeyed my mother's warning and looked into Ato's room to see if she were any better. Through the blue haze of lingering smoke her face was wan above her striped blanket and she did not know me. The next day she was worse and Ah Tok came. We met face to face as he entered and he drew back from me in alarm. "Unlucky girl! I see death all around you!" I did not consider that very astute of him, since he must have been told how ill Ato was.

"You will die before I do, Ah Tok." I spoke with arrogance to hide the chill I felt creeping through me.

With a last terrible glance he went to Chituche, who was beckoning him from the rear doorway that led to the garden and the hut where the two slaves slept. Alone in the main hall of the palace, I found myself sad and frightened. The fading murals of priests and warriors on the walls around me offered no comfort. Nor did Dak Cho when he hurried in looking for Chituche. He asked me to tell her that he was going to visit a village that had not yet sent us any tribute for Moctezuma. "It will be two days before I return."

I told him to be careful, for he would be taking the same jungle trail where my father met the snake that killed him.

"You're the one who must be careful, Malinche. Don't keep going to Ato's room as your mother says you have been doing." He hurried out of the palace then and down the steps, the sunlight warming his shoulders and the swinging rear panel of his loincloth, a simple man, unaware of the evil hatching in the room he had warned me from.

That night after we ate our supper, my mother told me that Ato was dead. I had expected this, but I could not keep from weeping. She came to my side and put her arm around me and spoke comforting words. For the first time since his birth, it was not Zub-Zub who claimed her attention, and when he whined she scolded him. He sat stunned, his beady little eyes on me, then crawled over and grabbed a piece of meat left in my stew bowl. Chituche slapped his hand hard and sent him away bawling, then brewed herb tea for me on the brazier. I remarked that the tea had an unusual flavor and she said, "I put in a strong herb that brings sleep, for that is grief's best enemy." Very soon I went to the alcove where my pallet was. I was almost asleep when I felt a presence beside it, opened drowsy eyes, saw her kneeling silhouette against the lighted doorway. "Some things cannot be helped," she said in a dull, brooding voice. I thought she meant Ato's death.

Then, as though from very far off, her name was called. She stood up and went toward the main room, and I heard Xochitl say that the *pochtecas* had arrived. The straw pallet beneath me turned to air and I floated into deep, dark sleep.

6

I woke on a narrow swaying litter and saw above me thick green leafage, bits of blue sky. Ahead was the broad red-brown back of the *tamane* who bore the litter's front poles. I was tied down by hempen ropes around my waist, wrists, ankles. When I tried to cry out only a croaking sound came from my dry throat. I shut my eyes and told myself I was still dreaming, but the flat pat-pat of feet on the jungle trail I knew to be real. "Water!" I croaked. I looked up into the inverted face of the *tamane* who held the rear poles of the litter as he bent forward to peer down at me. It was the face of a red-brown clay statue except that the eyes were human. He said something to the other *tamane,* who turned his head to peer at me over one shoulder. They did not understand me because I had spoken the Mayan word for water. I remembered how to say it in Nahuatl.

"She wants water," the *tamane* behind me said.

"I want water," the one ahead said. "We can't stop."

Now the dryness of my mouth and throat began to terrify me. Was I going to die of thirst between two walking clay statues? The clay feet pattered along the trail, which curved alongside a stream. The sound of water chuckling over stones maddened me, and again I screamed for water.

Then, from up ahead a voice called the procession to a halt. Because of the curve of the trail, I could see the six *tamanes* who preceded mine kneel and straighten, easing their burdens off their backs onto the ground with grunts of relief. I was set down with a slight thud. Turning my head, I avidly watched my two porters go to the stream's edge, each with half a dried gourd. They squatted and drank, and then one filled his and brought it to me. Cool water, filling my mouth and slipping down my parched throat, became the only reality in the universe. Sated, I let my head drop back, content for a moment to breathe without thirst.

But then the truth struck like a spear through the heart. My mother had drugged me. She had sold me to the *pochtecas.* They were not evil people and could not have been accomplices. She must have lied. She told them I was a slave that she was forced to sell because times were bad in Paynala. That was it. But how could she have been so foolish, even with Dak Cho gone and poor cowed Xochitl the only witness to the lie? Foolish? Mad!

"Is she awake yet?" The voice was a commanding one and I looked up at a thin *pochteca* with gray hair who seemed very tall in his high black hat and long red cape. Around his neck hung several necklaces of gold and silver and even one of jade.

I told him, "I am Malinche of Paynala, daughter of Taxumal. You must take me home at once."

To my surprise, he nodded. "She said you would say that." He frowned. "You must never say that again. No one likes crazy people. No one wants them."

Terror struck me. "It is Chituche who is crazy!"

"And is your mother Xochitl crazy too, Atotlotl?"

"Chituche is my mother! Atotlotl is dead!" My heart was beating wildly now.

He nodded grimly. "Chituche told me you'd say that. But I know everything. I know how you and Malinche were raised together like sisters, and how you refused to believe she had died."

"I'm alive!"

"You are, and you are Atotlotl. You are a crazed slave girl who put on Malinche's clothes and paraded about in them claiming the dead girl's identity. You reached such a state of frenzy that the priest gave Chituche a potion that put you to sleep."

"I knew Ah Tok was part of it! He doesn't want me to rule in Paynala."

"Stop!" He bent over me and now his eyes looked cruel. "If you go on telling this lie you will end on some priest's altar. Do you want your heart cut out? Do you?"

Terror became a stone inside my chest and my brain fluttered wild wings in my head.

"Do you?" The *pochteca*'s forefinger prodded my shoulder.

I shook my head.

"Then remember that you are Atotlotl, a slave and daughter of a slave. Hold firmly to that truth. It will procure you a better fate."

"What fate?" I whispered.

He looked pleased at my docility. "I plan to sell you to the most important cacique in all Tabasco. As a palace slave you will have a pleasant life. His city is much larger and richer than Paynala." He smiled down at me. "Now tell me your name."

"Ato."

"Ato?"

"That is what Malinche always called me," I said and laughed crazily. It didn't matter what I said because at the first chance I would escape and make my way back to Paynala.

But after I had swallowed a cold lump of maize paste and a tomato, he put a leather collar around my neck. It had a long rope attached and as I plodded along after him, my heart became more like a stone at every step. When the sun went down I knew that Ato's body had been interred as mine. I shivered and felt the cold jade bead under Ato's tongue. The cries of the birds turned to the laments of my people when they learned I was dead.

Chituche and Ah Tok had planned very well. With such a tragedy occupying everyone in Paynala, who would note that the slave girl Ato was missing? Later, when Chituche said she had sold her, who would care? Would Xochitl dare to tell the truth, overawed by Chituche and Ah Tok? When Dak Cho returned, would he believe what Chituche told him? I decided he would prefer to be deceived, whatever deep doubt he might feel, having left me quite healthy two days before I died.

By habit, my hand stole up to my golden pendant of Kukulcan. It hung next to my skin, hidden under the high square neck of my overblouse. When my fingers touched it through the cloth, a belated shock went through me. Chituche had forgotten to remove it and put it on Ato's corpse! Or else superstition had stayed her hand, since it was a god's likeness. Or perhaps sentiment had moved her. Who can say with a madwoman? Whatever the reason, its presence seemed a good omen and made me able to believe at least for a little while that Chituche and Ah Tok would not succeed with their scheme after all.

Any thought of escaping, of making my way home, left me the next afternoon when we stopped at a town near the bank of the Tonola River. In my ignorance I thought we had reached Tabasco, and then found we were not yet halfway there. But it was not only the distance from my home that disheartened me, nor the snarling of jaguars when we passed through the jungle, nor the night bats that suck blood. The farther we got from Paynala, the more all-enveloping became my dreamy, helpless mood. For I was of Paynala, and of my clan there, the way an arm is part of a body, or an ear is, or a tongue. Far from the sight and sound of my native soil and its people, my sense of identity grew frail. Sometimes it was only by clutching my pendant of Kukulcan that I could get back the feeling of being Malinche, whatever name the *pochtecas* chose to call me by.

I tried to imagine myself watched over by that god. I would stare up at the evening star, which is his star as is the star of morning, and I would whisper to him of the wrong done and try to invoke his help, but no feeling of comfort came. Gods might respond to priests' prayers after suitable elaborate rituals but a person of twelve far from home with a rope around her neck was as remote from their divine concern as if she were a monkey or parrot or lizard. The gods were supernatural participants in the communal life of an entire people. I was a leaf blown from that tree.

We reached the Tabasco River two days later, having stopped at several towns to barter. Men in dugout canoes took us downriver to Xicalanco, the capital city of Tabasco, for although the sun was setting, the *pochtecas* decided not to wait for morning. I shared their canoe and sat in the middle facing the shorter, younger *pochteca*. Suddenly he pointed to my golden pendant. "Where did you get that, Ato?"

For the first time I noticed the faint crescent scar on his left cheek. He had seemed vaguely familiar to me and now I recognized him. Hope stirred. I kept my voice calm so as not to seem crazy. "My father Taxumal bought it from you for me when I was three."

I thought I saw a flicker of recollection in his eyes, then his hand reached out for it. "Malinche told you that, Ato. It's too good for a slave. I'll take it."

"No!" I clutched it and leaned back to evade the reaching hand. "My father gave it to me. You know it. You know I am Malinche!"

My anger only amused him. "You are nothing. I want the pendant."

"No you don't." The other trader spoke. In the light of the setting sun his shrewd old face looked hard as gold. "It's worth more to us around her neck. It sets off her pretty face and gives her status so that we can ask a much bigger price for her." The reaching hand drew back. The old one added, "And there's something else to be considered." Their two heads in the tall black hats drew close together as the old one whispered at some length. I could catch only a few fragments, but these and my knowledge of the *pochtecas'* code of supposed integrity let me guess his message. Just in case I was who I claimed to be, and just in case the plot against me was discovered and I was somehow reinstated in Paynala, it would be best to be innocent of theft of the pendant. At the end he raised his voice and said, nodding wisely, "I have lived a long time. Stranger things have happened than justice prevailing at last."

The trader with the scar nodded and turned to me. "You can keep your pendant, Ato."

My frail hope vanished like smoke blown away, leaving me listless and at last I fell asleep curled against a straw basket. When I woke it was night, and I sat up to watch the dazzling broken reflections of the moon on the dark water into which the rowers' paddles plunged with rhythmic soft splashings. A deep resignation flowed through my veins.

Xicalanco was a great trade center on Pom Lagoon from which a wide brown river flowed east to the sea. There were big thatched stone warehouses for the salt, emeralds, cotton mantles, conch shells, turtle eggs, jade, topaz, alum, bitumen, gold dust, and countless other products and a barracks for slaves, in which the trade was brisk. The town itself was walled, and immediately around it the swampland had been filled in to grow palms and cacao trees. On entering, we crossed a wide plaza where several large ceiba trees cast pools of moonshadow. The palace we approached was enormous, of white stones. Four palaces the size of Paynala's would have fit inside it. We were admitted by a fat, sleepy servant who went to bring the cacique's wife, to whom the older *pochteca* had asked to speak.

The servant came back carrying a candlewood torch; its flame illuminated the ample, elegant figure of her mistress. Her pale underskirt swayed grandly below her square-necked chemise of deep Maya blue. She had weary eyes with highly arched brows, a narrow nose with a curved bridge, and wore a topaz on her pierced left nostril. "The hour is late for bartering," she told the *pochtecas* reprovingly.

"I remembered, respected Kukul, that you said you did not sleep well. I thought it might be a welcome diversion to glance at our merchandise." He pointed to me. "Many have wanted to buy her as we journeyed from her distant town, but I saved her for you, Kukul. She is a rare jewel and worthy of good surroundings." He spoke of my skillful weaving, sublime featherwork.

"Then how did her former owner bring herself to part with this flower of purest jade?" Kukul eyed me with slight interest.

"Poverty, and also a younger husband with a roving eye," he lied smoothly. "Anyone can see that the girl is going to be a beauty."

The cacique's wife spoke to me. "What is your name?"

"Ato," said the older *pochteca* quickly. "A common Aztec name."

"Oh, this girl is Aztec? We don't have any of those. What do you want for her?"

"We can decide that in the morning when I will show you many other rare items best appreciated by the light of day."

By now I was beyond shame or wonder. To be sold like a mantle or clay bowl had numbed me, and when the cacique's wife spoke to me I was not even aware of it and just stood staring ahead.

"Is she a mute?" Kukul asked.

"Say something, Ato," the older *pochteca* commanded.

"I am weary," I said, and it was true.

"Now say it in the Aztec language," the cacique's wife commanded, and I did. A kindly look came over her face. "Poor young thing. Of course she's tired after such a long journey." She told the short, fat servant to show me where I would sleep and I followed her out a curtained doorway, along a passage and across a moonlit courtyard to a low outbuilding with many doors in a row. "The slaves and the concubines live out here," she said.

"Am I to be a concubine?" My voice trembled.

"The old cacique does not take children to bed." She paused at one of the doors and held aside the cotton hanging. "This room was left vacant by a concubine who died, but the priest fumigated it." I saw that she was very cross-eyed, considered a mark of beauty among the Olmecan people. The mothers hang a bead in front of a baby's eyes to make them so. "Sleep well," she said indifferently, and left me.

On the floor was a thick straw sleeping mat with a serape folded at the foot. The sight of it made me realize how weary I was. I took off my skirt, folded it and pulled the cover up over me. Moonlight paled the small square window beside the doorway. In the garden a night bird gave a harsh cry. I remembered my grandmother's last words to me. I would not be afraid. Kukul had seemed kind. Tomorrow after the *pochtecas* had gone I would tell her the truth and ask her to help me. The bird screamed again. It sounded closer.

I dreamed of a large sky-blue bird with a fan of yellow feathers on its head. With a flapping of great wings it settled in the window of my room. The moonlight was so bright that I could see its colors clearly and I knew it was the same bird that charmed my father on the last day of his life. First I felt afraid, but then a great rage filled me. It was clear to me that my father, who had always revered the Feathered Serpent, should not have died because of a snake and this evil bird. Then the bird opened its wings and swooped down to the floor. It turned its head to one side so it could watch me with one blazing yellow eye as it stalked slowly toward me. I knew that it meant to stab its long beak into my heart. I feigned sleep until it reached my pallet and then I seized its neck with both hands and summoned up all my strength to choke its life out. It opened its beak, making a terrible croaking, and flapped its great wings. I held on. Blood came suddenly welling out of its mouth and gushed over me in a stream, but I knew I must not let go until its wings stopped moving. . . .

I opened my eyes on the gray light of early morning, put aside my blanket and got up. It stunned me to look down at a red stain where I had lain. It was not the dream-bird's blood. It was mine. A vision came of that *emku* I would not take part in, of young girls in new clothes, smiling and proud in the sunlight of the plaza in Paynala, and tears filled my eyes. Anger seared them dry. One day, some way, I would return to Paynala and avenge myself. Chituche would grovel at my feet, begging for mercy. Ah Tok would crawl to me in the dust. And I would command that they die!

Kneeling on the mat with its red stain, I tore a long strip from one side of my skirt, and doubled it over and attached it to the belt from which my golden seashell hung. When I put on the skirt I twisted it around so the torn part was at one side. Heavy discomfort in my belly made me kneel again, which seemed to ease the pain. Then, hearing voices and footsteps outside the doorway, I got to my feet so that the next Tabascan to see me would find me standing, unafraid.

7

The short, fat slave woman with crossed eyes peered in. My torn skirt at once caught her attention and she pointed to it, giggling. Several other women appeared in the doorway behind her. A tall one with a kind face and a baby on one hip said her name was Ixlan and asked mine.

"Malinche," I said without thinking.

"Her name is Ato," said the cross-eyed one. "The mistress told me so."

"I must talk to her at once."

"She'll talk to you when she's ready. Who do you think you are?" said Cross-Eyes.

"She's only a child, Chu-Chu," the tall one with the baby said. "She's strange here and afraid. And she's probably hungry." She smiled at me. "Aren't you hungry?"

"Yes," I lied.

"Come on, we'll go to the slaves' kitchen and find you something to eat." Chu-Chu, jealous of her authority, came with us. The baby on Ixlan's hip woke and wailed, and she cradled it in her arms and nursed it as we crossed the garden, beginning to fill with children of all sizes who emerged rubbing their eyes from the many doorways of the barracks. "You'll find it isn't bad here," she said. "The cacique's old and doesn't bother us much any more."

"Doesn't his wife mind his having concubines?" I asked.

"She prefers it this way. She's had six children by him—ten counting the ones who died. The only time she ever gets angry is when the children make too much noise. She can't stand children yelling."

We had reached the kitchen, an open, thatched outbuilding where several slaves knelt chatting and slapping out the morning's maize cakes. A small, rough-coated pig lay under a table watching them. Several white ducks and a tame *guajolote* awaited crumbs. I found myself watching as hungrily as they.

"Now my mistress wants to see you," said Chu-Chu, after I had devoured three maize cakes. "She said to feed you first. She doesn't like liars. You'd better remember your right name."

When we found Kukul in the palace she arched her eyebrows even higher at the sight of my torn skirt and told me I must have a new one. Dismissing Chu-Chu, she took me to a large storeroom where many mantles, skirts, and chemises were stacked and she seemed to take an interest in selecting the proper costume for me. I told her what else I needed and she gave me some squares of soft, unbleached cotton and showed me how to fold one. "I welcome you to the world of womanhood," she said, and gave an enormous, groaning yawn. "I sleep very poorly. It is sometimes dawn before I close my eyes. I do not know why this is. I'm going to my hammock now. You can come with me and swing it."

The hammock, of coarse net striped with many colors, hung between two gnarled pepper trees in an enclosure beside the palace. She collapsed into it with a sigh and I set it swaying. Soon she was asleep and snoring, leaving me alone with my bitter thoughts. When she woke, the sun was halfway up the sky. She rubbed her eyes, smiled, and surveyed me with interest. "You look better by daylight, Ato. The old *pochteca* said you can do featherwork. Is that true?"

"The truth is that I am not named Ato. I am Malinche, the rightful ruler of Paynala. I was drugged and sold as a slave." I stood tall, my head high.

She blinked at me. "Paynala? Where is that?"

"Five days' journey to the north."

"I think I may have heard of it. It's a small place, isn't it?"

"We are over five thousand."

She smiled at me. "Do you know how many Tabascan warriors my husband can summon? Forty thousand."

"The size of my town is not important. A terrible injustice has been done to me and to my people."

"The world is full of injustice."

Her great calm in the face of my momentous revelation filled me with despair. "I would need only a small escort for the journey," I persisted.

"It is never wise for the ruler of one country to interfere in the internal affairs of another. Furthermore, I have just remembered something. Paynala is actually ruled by the Aztecs, isn't that so? Didn't they take over that town and several others up there many years ago?"

"They only want tribute. We still rule ourselves," I said. Bitter disappointment filled me now.

As though she hadn't heard me, she struggled to a sitting position and swung her legs over the hammock's side. Like a big bird on the edge of its nest, she regarded me kindly. "You must learn to resign yourself to circumstances. All women must learn this. Men are made to change circumstances, women to accept. You are much more fortunate than you realize. Xicalanco is no small backwater like your Paynala." She smiled at me. "I am not a native. I was captured after a battle with a town far to the west. At first I was only a concubine, but when the cacique's wife died in childbirth, I became First Wife in her place. Who knows what good fortune may await you here?" She leaned forward, an adult cajoling a child. "Forget the past. Bow to circumstance."

"I will not forget. I will not bow. I will return to Paynala."

She stared, surprised at my vehemence. Her tone was amused when she said "Before you leave us, I would like to see a sample of this featherwork you are said to

do so well. Slaves are expected to earn their keep."
She surged to her feet and moved grandly away, mo-
tioning me to follow, and then paused to deliver a final
blow. "As for this unlikely tale you have told me, I
shall call you Ato."

She gave me a loom and a spindle and cotton and a
basket of feathers of many colors and ordered me to
make a wall hanging showing the moon goddess. In my
little room, with the voices of the children in the garden
for company, my fingers soon remembered the skill they
first learned from the mother I hated. For many weeks
I lived as a recluse, numbing my feelings with the
repetitive task that had been set me. But such a life
was not in accordance with my nature and as Ixlan,
the tall young woman with the baby, persisted in
friendly visits, and some of the others too, I gradually
emerged from my self-imposed loneliness and took part
in the trivial and unimportant life in that small world
of slave women and concubines who were endlessly
spinning or weaving, pounding maize, shaping clay pots
and straw baskets, and sharing the gossip of the palace
and marketplace. Only a few were jealous when the
cacique's wife praised my featherwork and rewarded
me with a bracelet.

Had I been cruelly treated, I would have found a way
to attempt the long journey to Paynala alone, probably
ending as a huddle of bones in the jungle or else as a
captive in one of the small towns we had passed, and
much worse off than in Tabasco. But the kindness I
met with as favorite slave of the cacique's wife allowed
me to be cautious and patient. As months became years,
my present existence often seemed like a dream; at
other times it was my past life that seemed unreal. To
relieve the tedium of endless featherwork, I began to
tell stories to the children of the slave compound who
came to watch me, and that led to my becoming their
teacher. This pleased Kukul, because it kept them quiet
and I think it saved me from despair because I found
a satisfaction when their minds blossomed, and some I
came to love.

Kukul came to my aid when I grew old enough to attract old Nan Chan's attention, though by that time he was nearly blind. She did not understand my disinclination to become a concubine, but humored me, and was able to convince her husband that I was a cold, plain girl best employed in weaving him a ceremonial cape and teaching children how to count. The other women did not enlighten him as to the fact that I was not as she described me, but her lie was useless to avert the sudden infatuation of one of her sons, who could see very well.

Akukum was a young warrior who had been living according to custom in a barracks with the others in training, but he came to the palace to stay when I was seventeen and one morning encountered me as I was swinging his mother in her hammock while she dozed off in her usual morning nap. The next day he came to the slaves' compound to visit me and brought a gift of turtle eggs, just as if he were visiting a person of some importance in her parents' home, and whenever I spoke he hummed politely to show he was interested. He returned the next day, and the next. I was less indifferent when he went to his mother and told her he wished to take me as his First Wife. Had Kukul not liked me, this desire to marry a slave would have caused great trouble and confusion, but as it was, she agreed to ask her husband to free me. Perversely, the old man refused. I think his son's desire for me had made him suspect that he had been duped.

To the other slave women and the concubines, Akukum's wish to marry me was a miracle, and several took to bringing offerings of flowers to the temple where Kukulcan's altar stood, attributing my good fortune to divine intervention of the deity whose likeness I wore and hoping he would provide them also with freedom and a handsome mate. But to me Akukum's infatuation meant much more than freedom and status: my dream of returning to Paynala to avenge myself and claim my proper destiny had not died with time. Now it sprang up fiercely. I saw Akukum as the ally who would make that dream a reality.

Summoning all my art as a storyteller, I told him of my betrayal. Because he desired me, he not only believed me but was incensed. He promised that when I was freed he would gather a group of warrior friends and take me to my birthplace so that justice could be done at last. But until his father granted me my freedom he could do nothing, for that would be to steal his father's property. The old man might even decide to exact the full penalty for theft, which was severe. All he could do was hope that Kukul would find the right moment to wheedle her husband into a generous mood.

This hope suffered a setback after Akukum told her one day of my desire to return to Paynala and the reason for it. I had always thought that she had never believed the story of my true identity. But now I learned from her that the *pochteca* with the scar had whispered before he left that he suspected I might be of high lineage. Kukul's eyes flashed with scorn when she summoned me into the palace for a private conversation after her son had left. "I thought you had finally come to understand that to rule in Paynala would have been a petty destiny compared with dwelling in a great town like this! Akukum might even succeed his father and rule Xicalanco! I will waste no more breath trying to get you freed. I should urge my son to forget all about you. Beauty and intelligence are nothing when they are coupled with a heart clenched on an old grief."

The shock of learning that she had always suspected my true status was worse than her angry words. What would it have cost her to have aided me long ago to return to Paynala? Was her self-centeredness so great that no other hand than mine could have rocked her hammock and woven her feathers? "You knew?" I whispered.

I found then that she regarded herself as my benefactress, believed she had done me a favor keeping me in Xicalanco, for she envisioned Paynala as a rude little town like the one where she had been born. And so I learned the bitter truth, that even affection can be blind to the deep needs of another.

After her tirade, she forgave me. "You are a rare one, Ato or Malinche, or whoever you are. I knew that from the first. I will not urge my son to forget you. I will somehow get my husband to free you. You will marry Akukum. And, who knows, one day you may be First Wife of the ruler of Xicalanco. And then you will thank me and know that you never had a better friend."

But old Nan Chan continued to balk at losing his valued slave. Ironically, the feather cape I had made was now used against me, and he irascibly demanded of Kukul that she show him one other slave who could do work as magnificent. Soon a more important matter claimed his attention.

Word reached him that a small group of pale-skinned bearded mariners had landed on the seashore near the mouth of the Tabasco River. In some anxiety Nan Chan had bravely gone there to see for himself, bringing some gifts to placate the visitors. He returned to say that they were in no way awe-inspiring. "These strangers, though peculiarly clad and possessing an unusual vessel to travel in, are mortal, mere men, unfortunate in being disgustingly hairy. They have now departed for their own land, wherever that may be, so let us give them no more thought and cease concerning ourselves with the possibility of a god's return."

But less than a year after this the strangers reappeared. This time they came in many ships, eleven by the account brought to Xicalanco by some frightened fishermen. From these great vessels they had lowered boats something like canoes, and in them they had begun to row upriver. It seemed to everyone as if the strangers' earlier scouting party had fooled the old cacique as to their peaceful intentions. Five hundred warriors were sent to the river bank and a thousand more lined the shore of Pom Lagoon. But these attempts to discourage the strangers from entering Xicalanco were futile, for they camped that night on an island in the river, evidently planning to land on our shore the next day. Before dawn the city was evacuated, the women, children, and elderly plodding north on the causeway to a hilly jungle area where we could camp. The warriors stayed behind, concealing themselves behind a ridge of land to the west. By this time warriors from other Tabascan towns had converged on Xicalanco to swell our forces, spurred by fear of the strangers.

All of us who were encamped like savages to the north of the city believed our stay there would be brief. We were filled with fear and confusion when a runner came with the news that in a great battle our warriors had been routed. The strangers commanded supernatural weapons that thundered and hurled round stones that killed many people simultaneously. Worse, they had with them huge four-legged monsters, half beast, half human and utterly fearless. Akukum was among the many slain.

His mother wept bitterly, already dazed by this menace to the town she had believed to be as secure as the earth under her feet. I comforted her, but found that even while I grieved for her son's death I was grieving as well for the loss of my only chance to avenge myself on Chituche and Ah Tok and to astound my people of Paynala by appearing among them, risen from the dead.

When old Nan Chan, stunned and humbled, gathered together a retinue that would accompany him when he went to surrender to the gods who had conquered his city and his land, I was among the twenty slave women and concubines chosen to walk behind his litter. Curiosity was stronger than fear; the thought that I was going to see the returned Quetzalcoatl–Kukulcan in all his stern power filled my whole being with amazement.

A first intimation of the utter strangeness of the conquerors struck me when I saw one bizarre figure among those many armed creatures who stood watching us pass. He was beardless, with shining hair, dark gold. His eyes were like emeralds. He fixed them on me. The stare of those jewel eyes sent thrill of fear all through me. I knew he was not of my world or any world I had even imagined, unless it might be Aztlán.

The old cacique descended from his litter and approached the large canopy in whose shade stood the warrior-god, bearded, stern-faced, and covered head to foot in smooth metal with the gleam of silver, but darker. We women were ordered to go forward to where he stood. As we obeyed, I heard my old master say: "In token of our humble surrender we offer these twenty slave women as hostages."

The shock was so great that I only remember looking down at my sandaled feet moving me forward, first one, then the other. The ground seemed to shudder under me as if an earthquake had struck. My head felt very light, filled only with air. Not even on that day when I awoke on a litter far from my home had such terror filled me. That journey had ended among people who spoke my tongue and worshiped my gods. But now, what would be my destiny?

I moved from the known to the unknown. The shade below the canopy both cooled and threatened me, for I stood near the great god's attendants. Some were bearded and helmeted like him; a few wore long brown robes. One of these, I saw, was acting as the god's interpreter. Nan Chan was offering gifts on a tray. The god's hand went out and picked up a small golden animal, holding it high and turning it in the sunlight. He offered a return gift, something he held up and shook so that it rang with a clear tinkling sound. Nan Chan took it and rang it again, looking pleased with the gift as he knew he should. The other women were huddled together, mute with fear, but I moved forward so I could better watch the god and Nan Chan, my fascination stronger than my terror.

The god spoke in a strange tongue which the brown-robed interpreter translated into a Mayan dialect for Nan Chan. It seemed peculiar that a god should need an interpreter; I had imagined that gods are able to speak all human tongues at will. "Last year you gave some countrymen of mine some gifts of gold and now you offer me these golden animals. Do you have more gold?" I wondered why a deity should be interested in mere Sweat of the Sun when he could have asked for jade or emeralds.

Nan Chan showed his cleverness then. "If it is gold you want, what little we have is as nothing compared to what you will find if you go to Mexico or Culhua." I had to praise him in my heart, for he had mentioned the core of the Aztecs' wide domain.

"And where is this Mexico?" the deity asked. Strange, I thought, that a god does not know where Mexico is, or Culhua either.

"Far to the northwest, high in some mountains that I myself have never seen," Nan Chan told him.

"How far?" the deity asked.

"Very far. But in your great vessels you could easily cover much of the distance." I knew how eager Nan Chan was for the gods to depart and leave him free to deal with the problems their arrival had brought down on his poor head, chiefly to try to save his face and lofty rank after having been so wrong in his estimate of the strangers who had arrived last year.

"How many days or weeks would I have to travel to get to this Mexico, this Culhua?" the god asked.

"I do not know," Nan Chan confessed.

Nor did the god! I tried to find some explanation for his ignorance. Only one possibility occurred to me: he might be testing Nan Chan to see if he answered truthfully, in which case I had been wrong in my belief that deities can easily read mere human minds.

Suddenly I felt a presence behind me, and a mailed arm snaked around my waist. I smelled a peculiar stench, the smell of metal armor warmed by outer heat and the body beneath it. A low laugh blew hot breath into my ear. My head and eyes turned in that direction; my body was so tense with fear it could not move. A pair of narrow gray eyes stared into mine. Between beard and mustache teeth showed in an alarming smile. The lips whispered something, and I smelled the creature's breath, like rotten fruit. Then I felt a strong hand caress my hip, lingering on its curve. Outrage overcame my panic. As I struggled to free myself I heard an angry-sounding voice say "Captain!" One of the several brown-robed deities had approached and now spoke sternly to my molester, who at once released me, turning away with a shrug. Shaken, I stepped back among the other women.

I remembered Nan Chan's words when he returned from his encounter with the strangers who came to our shore last year: "They are no gods. Do gods stink? Do they hunger? Sweat? Belch?" Do they lust? I wondered now. Do they subject women to public indignity? Was I a hostage to gods or mere men? Very lustful men, with no normal respect for another's person! But then I recalled their remarkable instruments of warfare which thundered, and their supernatural beasts. I had not yet seen one of these, but had heard a vivid description: they were gigantic creatures like great stags but with human heads and arms covered by metal armor.

As if summoned by my thoughts, one appeared. I heard a thunderous drumming on the earth outside the canopy and saw one of those monsters prancing before it in the sunlight. Poor Nan Chan backed away in horror as the thing suddenly raised high its two front legs, its upper and somewhat human portion leaning forward against a lower, staglike head in which a wild brown eye gleamed and rolled. A terrible sound came out of its mouth. Behind me the women moaned in terror.

The principal deity who had talked with Nan Chan called something to the beast and in a moment it lowered its legs, whirled about, and thundered away and I felt the drumming on the earth with the soles of my feet while hearing it with my ears.

As Nan Chan tried to regain his composure, the great deity again asked through his interpreter, "Tell me, Nan Chan, do you have any more gold to offer me?"

It was clear to me that he had summoned the super-natural beast to impress Nan Chan.

My mind was in chaos. Were these strangers gods or men? The one called Captain seemed no deity to me. But as if to reprove me for my doubt, one of the super-natural beasts had appeared in all its fury and splendor. I was hot and prickling still with the fear it had inspired.

A cool breeze touched me. I turned my head. The rear curtains of the canopy were partly open. Through the aperture I could see the grove of tall palms to the east of the town and beyond them the thick green man-grove jungle in which from time to time an adventurous child got lost.

In that instant I knew that whether the strangers were men or gods or somewhere between the two I was going to try to escape them.

I edged over to my friend Ixlan and asked her to shield my departure by standing in front of me while I backed out. She whispered, "The gods will surely find you and be angry." I shook my head in denial of her warning and again asked her aid. She nodded.

By now the other women were engrossed in discuss-ing the supernatural beast, and all the strangers were intent on the dialogue between Nan Chan and their leader. I reached the rear curtain without being seen, found the opening, and slipped through.

Outside, my fear was to encounter the supernatural beast, but it was gone. No one was in sight in the palm grove, and I hurried toward the mangroves, then began to run. The gray boles of the palms I passed seemed like old friends; far above my head their fans rustled in the breeze that had reminded me that freedom was possible. Soon my life would go on much as it had be-fore the gods arrived, for surely Kukul would welcome me back and hide me until they departed. With a slight pang I remembered then that her son was dead, so that I could never be his First Wife or have any chance of returning to Paynala with his help. But even so the ragged remains of my former life seemed preferable to the fearsome future that awaited me if I had stayed with the gods.

The mangroves were only a short distance ahead when I heard a thudding like distant thunder, glanced back, saw with a thrill of horror that one of the supernatural beasts was pursuing me. It had a human voice; it shouted something in its strange language. But before it reached me I had flung myself in among the twisted slender gray trunks of the mangrove trees, not caring that their branches slashed at me as I plunged deeper in. Soon they were too thick for me to stand upright. I dropped to my knees and crawled, twisting my way deeper and deeper on sandy soil that grew moist under my palms as I neared the little stream that joined the great river to the south. In a deep green twilight I found that I could go no farther; the trees were too close together to pass between.

But of one thing I was certain. The great beast that had followed me could never get in here. Then my heart leaped into my throat. From the direction in which I had come I heard a faint rustling sound. Something was stalking me, coming ever closer. If it found me, what would it do to me? My heart was thudding so hard I was afraid it would hear it. Could the beast have told one of the strangers where I had gone? Perhaps the one called Captain who had molested me? I tried to will my heart to beat more softly, and I listened so intently my ears seemed to move against my head. After a long moment I realized that the rustling was growing fainter. The maize of tangled trees had confused whatever was hunting me. It was moving away from where I trembled.

In the instant of false security this gave me I knew how horrible it would have been if it had pounced on me in anger or in lust. Then I knew this still might happen.

I had a choice. I could wait here like a frightened hare or creep out the way I had come, go back to the canopy, face with what courage I could summon up an unguessable future with those strange gods. I vacillated only a moment and then began to crawl with a growing panic out of the trap in which I had placed myself.

The dimness slowly brightened as the mangroves thinned. I stood and walked out into the sunlit palm grove. I stopped and stared, stunned by the sight that met my eyes: the lower half of the supernatural beast. It stood quietly beside a palm tree to which it was tied. Its large, long head was bent low on the strong arch of its neck. It was nibbling a clump of grass.

In a sudden new light I saw it as nothing supernatural at all, only a large animal of a kind unknown to me. It sometimes carried a god on its back. That was strange, but not alarming.

A sound behind me made me turn. From the mangroves emerged a god; the god who had ridden it. He wore a dark metal breastplate and a helmet that gleamed like gold. As he came closer I saw that it was the beardless one with emerald eyes. He spoke gently in a strange tongue, and then pulled out from under his armor a small silver cross suspended on a chain and held it out for me to see. As the cross swung before my eyes I looked up and saw the design on the side of his helmet. It was a true supernatural beast, clearly half-man, half-stag. It held a drawn bow. Apparently such creatures did exist in the land of the gods.

I knew what to do: I bent humbly, touched earth, and brought that hand to my forehead in surrender.

The god extended his hand toward me. I stepped back. He nodded and smiled and reached for my hand. I saw that I was supposed to touch his. When I did, some of my fear subsided, for I felt only warm human skin, paler than mine but not otherwise unusual. He went to the tree where the animal he had ridden on was tied and released it. Still holding my hand, he walked beside me toward the gods' canopy, the large gray beast ambling after.

PART II

▼▼

TO THE UNKNOWN LAND
January 15, 1519–August 12, 1519

8

On a balmy Havana day, with just a little breeze to stir ragged palms bent by stronger winds, I stood on the cliff where our family land touched the Caribbean and stared west over blue, sun-sparkled water. A distant, unknown land waited beyond the horizon in all its mystery and promise, and waited for *me*. Then with equal yearning I looked to the east toward the emerald curve of the harbor, hoping to sight the fleet of Hernán Cortés sailing west from Trinidad. I was nearly eighteen, eager to risk death and lesser hazards to get a fortune in gold. I exulted in my great luck to be standing at this precise spot at this very moment.

I gave my father Francisco Mondragon too little credit for my whereabouts. When I was seven he had dared the unknown, lured from Spain to the West Indies by rumors of gold and plenty of subdued natives to mine it for him. But when he reached Hispaniola in 1509 he found a devastated island, the good lands gone —and the gold, too, such as there had been. So in 1511, instead of returning home empty-handed, he joined the expedition sent to Cuba by Diego Columbus, son of the Admiral, and led by a tough veteran named Diego Velásquez. Its purpose: to colonize this larger island to the west, overrun by savage Caribs from the north coast of South America. They were fierce cannibals and ate a good number of Spaniards before they were finally defeated. The other natives, Tainos and Ciboneys, were peaceful farmers who raised cassava, maize, and cot-

ton; these were ruled by elected chiefs they called
caciques. After we subdued an uprising and burned
alive their rebellious cacique named Hautey, the island
and its people belonged to Spain.

Velásquez established a settlement called San Cris-
tóbal de la Havana, the original Havana, on the south
coast. My father obtained a large grant of land near the
harbor, where a fortress town began to grow. First my
father had mined a stream bank on his land but got so
little gold that he had his Ciboneys plant cotton for
him; rare in Europe, it brought good money there.
Using native labor he also built a house with an arcaded
patio like that of his childhood home in Spain, then
sent for my mother and me.

We left the safety of her parents' home at Medellín
in southwestern Spain and from Cádiz bravely crossed
the Atlantic in a tossing caravel, bringing with us a
number of things of little practical use in Spain's newest colony. Among these were ten books, six of them
weighty volumes given to my mother's family by a
scholarly Jewish neighbor who had to flee to France in
1492 to escape the Inquisition. But my two favorites
were *Amadís of Gaul,* a prose romance telling of fantastic adventures in strange lands, and *The Celestina,*
whose young hero Calixto fell in love on sight with
Melibea. Chaste and beautiful, she did not at first succumb to his ardor and died soon after the long-delayed
consummation of their passion. Calixto joined her in
the tomb, sprinkled by my young tears. The books
were for me, my mother said, with the Azores just behind us. "For who knows if there's even so much as a
Bible in this place called Cuba?"

My pretty mother, Elvira Flores de Mondragon, had
hair of Spanish gold, sad brown eyes, and knew that she
had married somewhat beneath her parents' expectations. My father was merely the second son of a Castilian who came south to Estremadura with a flock of
sheep and enough money to buy a vineyard which the
older brother would inherit. Whereas my mother's
father had been a magistrate in Medellín since the days

of King Fernando and Queen Isabel, was descended on his mother's side from the famed poet Manrique and was looked up to as a man of gentility and learning. It was my mother's hope that I might one day study at the University of Salamanca and follow in his footsteps.

When we reached Cuba and she saw my father's little house backed by a wide field of cotton and the round straw-thatched *bohias* of his Ciboney Indians, tears of nostalgia filled her eyes and she said in a tremulous voice, "An arcade! At the end of the world!" But I think she sensed even then that our landhold, for all its size, would provide a living for us, no more. Soon after we came, my father sank a second mine shaft in the hills to the south of our plantation. "Let us pray that your father finds a rich vein of ore so that you can go to Salamanca some day, Arturo," she would say, hugging me to her as if this helped her to hold on to his hope. She always smelled sweetly of the pomander she kept in the chest that held her cuffs and collars and shawl of fine lace, her best silk gown.

Due to her praise and prodding, I could read and write both Latin and Castilian by the time I was nine. At ten, sitting high in the sea-grape tree by our house, I composed a sonnet in the manner of the Italian poet Petrarch. She was so pleased that on the Day of the Three Kings I was given a six-string Spanish guitar so that I could set my verses to music for her. But when I was eleven, my father emerged from the discouraging depths of his second mine shaft to suddenly discover that I was far from the son he had hoped to have. "He looks like a girl, with that pretty face, those golden curls," I heard him say. "God forbid that he should sprout breasts!"

His immediate solution was lessons in swordsmanship from an old soldier down on his luck, since my father's lame knee kept him from teaching me himself. He also encouraged my friendship with the son of our Christianized Indian overseer. Rubén was an agile brown child who could swim like a fish, run like a hare, and spit to a distance of nearly four paces on a calm

day. We stalked small animals in the wooded hills inland and fished and swam together, and night after night
I would go to bed filled with shame that an Indian
boy should outdo a Spaniard. But by the time my voice
changed I had attained rock-hard muscles and could
spit as far as Rubén.

So, all in all, I had felt myself just the man Alvarado
was looking for when he came overland with a small
band of soldiers, riding a fine sorrel horse, to announce
in the Havana plaza that in a few days Hernán Cortés
would arrive with his fleet from Trinidad and would
accept enlistments. Eleven vessels! More than six hundred soldiers and mariners, brave-hearted Spaniards all!
Horses, *hidalgos,* arquebusiers, musketeers! Cortés had
been recently empowered by his friend Governor Velásquez to command an expedition that would explore,
conquer, and Christianize that Unknown Land that lay
to the northwest of the peninsula we called Yucatán.

But when I reported all this to my parents and told
them I intended to join Cortés, their lack of enthusiasm
appalled me. "I do not think soldiering would be much
to your liking," my father said, pushing aside his
trencher and pouring himself more wine; his other
hand went to his bad knee. My mother was more to the
point. "No! Never! No!" And my two little sisters, one
so small only her eyes showed above the table edge,
took up the cry of "No. No. No!"

"The answer is still no." My mother's voice spoke from
just behind me there at the cliff's edge, and I whirled,
startled by both her presence and her prescience. "And
it will be the same when his ships sail in, forever *no.*"
I stared at her, standing under a rustling palm in her
worn claret gown, pale, pretty, indomitable. Why
couldn't she understand how much I yearned to lay a
treasure at her feet, make up to her for all that she had
left behind and lost?

Passionately I spoke of the plates of solid gold and
the other rare objects Grijalva had brought back the year
before.

"And he also returned with a severe wound. His reward was censure from Governor Velásquez for not founding a Spanish colony."

"They say there's a silver city high in some distant mountains where the Indians eat from golden dishes set with gems. They even have golden chamber pots!" I did not mention the wild, beautiful Amazons in golden armor told of by Montalvo in a colorful narrative concerning itself with the blank space on the map I wished to penetrate.

"You're too young!"

I abandoned greed and gold and appealed to her piety. "One of the prime aims of this expedition is to make Christians of those poor Indians there. Don't you want your son to help save souls from Hell?"

"Leave that to the Franciscans and Dominicans."

Greed and piety failing, I tried patriotism. "Portugal has dozens of colonies in the New World. Spain must gain a foothold on the mainland Grijalva found!"

"Spain controls the Iberian peninsula except for Portugal, and every great city of Italy except Florence. Your help is not needed." Her smile maddened.

"My father is right! You want me a child forever! So you deny me the chance to serve under a great commander like Hernán Cortés!"

Her voice was shrill. "I can tell you all about Hernán Cortés! His father, Martín Cortés, was an *hidalgo* in modest circumstances and he barely managed to send Hernán to Salamanca to study law. In less than two years, back he came, expelled, the money all wasted. He spent the next year or so climbing into women's windows and writing poetry to them—the women, I mean. He finally disgraced his family with a scandal. To get into a married woman's bedroom he climbed a wall, but it was so old and shaky it collapsed under him and he was half buried under the rubble and got a severe head wound, after which he had to fight the woman's brother, who tried to kill him. Oh, the relief of his family when he joined an expedition to the West Indies at nineteen! He's done well here: good farmlands, a gold mine that produces gold, and a beautiful wife. Governor Velásquez even made him an alcalde of Santiago. But no! All that's not enough for him. He now decides to go roving an unknown sea to an unknown land at the age of thirty-four because of some rumors of quantities of gold. Well, that was the rumor that brought your father here, and you can see how much gold we have!" She paused for breath, staring seaward with a frown as though her anger at Cortés had turned to anger at those waters that now lured her son.

It struck me that she knew a great deal about a man she apparently disliked and I asked how she was so well informed about his early years.

She lowered her eyelids. "You've forgotten how small a place Medellín is. I was friendly with his second cousin, Guadalupe Monrroy."

"And with him, too?"

Her cheeks flushed. "Certainly not!"

"Why not?"

"I've told you! No decent young woman was allowed near him!"

"Even when he was a child?"

"He was sickly and frail. I remember the day his father rode back in triumph from Granada. Dozens of neighbors crowded into the Cortés house to learn how the last Moorish stronghold in Iberia fell to the Christian army of Aragón and Castile. Hernán Cortés was seven, very wan from having been bled with leeches for some ailment. He stood staring up in awe at his father, robust in armor, as if he were seeing the Cid himself . . ."

She was facing seaward, I toward land. I saw a change in her expression and turned. Nearing the harbor was a fine ship with lofty fore and aft decks, pennants blowing back from the three masts, a white bone of wave in her teeth. "He's here!" I cried, and deaf to her objections, I left pell-mell for town.

*　　*　　*

A crowd had already gathered from houses, church, cantina. I worked my way to the forefront just as a file of soldiers, some in full armor, others with none, marched into the plaza from the beach, led by a man on a prancing chestnut horse. As he neared me it reared with bent forelegs and the people crowding around me surged back in alarm. I stood my ground, staring up.

Pale-skinned, with flashing eyes and a short brown beard, Cortés wore his ruby cloak open. His shoulders were broad, his chest deep. At the side of his velvet cap was a short plume held in place by a gold medallion. He wore a gold chain and pendant and a diamond on his forefinger, and looked more like a courtier with the taste to avoid gaudiness of dress than like a commander of soldiers. As he easily mastered his rearing horse someone gave him a cheer; the crowd took it up and he waved airily. The hooves of his horse clashed to the ground only a few feet from where I stood. His teeth flashed as he smiled down at me, and then he was gone and I was staring after the broad shoulders above the shining muscled haunch of his mount.

His standard-bearer followed him, holding high a square banner of black velvet edged with gold braid. Below a red cross rayed with flames of blue and white, a Latin motto was embroidered in gold thread: *Comrades, let us follow the Cross, for under it, with faith, we shall conquer!* As the foot soldiers marched past me, some in armor, some without, their faces shiny with sweat, I envied them and yearned to be marching toward grand adventures. I knew that I was going to follow that banner, with my parents' blessing or without it.

Finally, my brain bursting with excitement and my belly growling with hunger, for it was long past dinnertime, I trudged the dusty road home. As I wolfed cold pork and boiled cassava in the kitchen, the Indian maidservant said my parents had left for town. It was well after sundown when they returned and told me they had attended the reception in honor of Cortés at the home of Don Pedro Barba, commander of the port of Havana. "You were nowhere to be found," my father said, "or you could have come with us."

Sick with envy and frustration, my belly aching from the cold food I had gobbled, I could eat no supper. My father drank more wine than usual, disturbed by his reunion with Cortés, his former comrade-at-arms. "Everything fell out well for him. Other men toadied to Velásquez, hoping for command of this expedition; Pánfilo de Narváez, for one. But Cortés got it. And with his luck, he'll return a rich man."

"And his soldiers, too," I cried. "This is my golden chance, father! Give me your permission to enlist!"

His tone was genial. "Why not? No use wasting your youth on a cotton plantation. By all means, sail to unknown shores!" His wide gesture overturned his wineglass, which he righted and refilled. "I'll give you my blessing, my sword, and my helmet."

"Francisco! He's going to Salamanca!" my mother cried.

"The one does not rule out the other, life of my life. At present I lack the funds to send him to Spain, as you know."

I was both cheered and uneasy. I knew these genial moods the wine induced in my father. Later he often forgot his easy promises. "You won't forget this promise tomorrow?" I asked him. Unfortunately, my eyes went to the wine bottle.

"*¡Sin vergüenza!*" he shouted. "Shameless wretch! Do you suggest that I am in the habit of forgetting my promises?" He had seen my look and had interpreted it all too well. His green eyes glared at me. "For eight long years I've fought and slaved on this miserable island, and all for a son who lacks the least filial respect! Leave this table! Go to your room!"

Past the shocked stares of my two little sisters and past the Indian maidservant, her eyes averted from my shame, I ran down the hall to my room and slammed my door. The frustrating day, the injustice of my father's anger and my roaring stomachache had me bawling like a child for several moments. The shame at this unmanly grief provoked a plan to restore my self-esteem.

Within minutes, dressed in my best russet doublet and hose, I was out the window and on my way to the Barba house, regretting that I had shaved off my tenuous blond beard because my father had assured me that shaving would make it grow in thicker. Barba was well-named: he had an immense black beard.

His Indian maidservant kept me waiting in the tiled hall while she went to an archway to announce that a young man sought General Cortés. "Tell him to wait," Barba's deep voice commanded, and she pointed to the bench near the front door and went away. But I remained standing and moved nearer the archway to listen. In contrast to Don Pedro's burlap growl, the other voice was silken. I was sure it belonged to Cortés.

"Velásquez has grown fat. He's lost the incisiveness he had when he was younger. He blows hot and cold. First he trusts me, then he mistrusts. Now he seems to have the idea of removing me as commander of this expedition, after I have raised eight thousand gold pesos to help finance it. I had to sail from Santiago against his orders, and you should have heard him roaring at me from the dock and waving his fist. 'Is this how you repay my trust?' he demanded, having planned to betray me by putting Narváez in my place. I shouted back that great things have to be done without being too much thought about, or else one loses heart and they're never accomplished at all."

I thrilled as they both laughed. My feeling, exactly!

"And I'll sail without his orders again," Cortés said in a warning tone.

Barba rumbled, "Even if I wanted to obey his orders to detain you, I would be unable to do so against your five hundred loyal soldiers."

"I am happy you see the situation so clearly," Cortés said. "And now, shall we find out who is waiting for me in your hall?"

Don Pedro's bulk filled the doorway as he beckoned

me in. As bad luck would have it, I caught my foot on the edge of a rug and catapulted forward, catching myself with a thump of my worn shoe only a few feet from Cortés, seated at one end of the long table where he and Barba had supped. The ruby cloak and cap were gone and he now wore plain black velvet, a small white ruff, the blazing diamond ring, and the gold chain from which, I saw, hung a medallion of the Virgin holding the Christ Child. By candlelight, Cortés' skin was dark ivory and in either cheek were chiseled deep vertical lines that might once have been dimples. Just below his underlip was a small white scar his short beard did not quite hide. He courteously ignored my bumpkin's entrance, at which Barba grinned.

"This is Arturo Mondragon," he said, "Francisco's son."

Cortés gave me a smile that was, for a leader of men, a gift from heaven. "Your father and I fought Caribs together eight years ago. In the press of people here this afternoon I did not have the chance to find how things have gone for him."

"He raises cotton," I said.

An alert look touched Cortés' face. "With success, I trust?"

Barba laughed. "With more success than he mines for gold."

I said to Cortés, "I believe you also knew my mother once, in Medellín. Her name was Elvira Flores y Sálazar."

He nodded, a distant look in his eyes. "A lovely young lady. Her virtue and reticence were widely praised, though perhaps not by myself." His eyes brimmed with amusement. "But I'm sure you didn't come here to tell me I used to know your mother."

I stood my tallest. "I came to enlist as a foot soldier."

"And what else do you offer me?"

"What else?"

"A horse, by any chance? I need more horses."

"No, no horse."

"Money, then?"

"No."

"Foodstuffs?"

"I fear not."

His smile vanished. "What then do you have to offer me besides your young and inexperienced self?"

Intuition found an answer. "Cotton!"

He leaned back, smiling but sharp of eye. "And what makes you think I need cotton?"

"Your sudden interest when I told you my father raises it."

He nodded. "Now tell me why you think I need raw cotton. Half a dozen large bales, I should say."

I closed my eyes and sent up a prayer to Jesus. There came into my head the picture of Cortés' soldiers that afternoon, some sweating in steel armor, others with none. "Quilted cotton armor, like the Tainos here used to wear!"

My guts jumped as his fist pounded the tabletop. "Good! I have the cloth but no padding. Don Pedro can gather a number of Indian women to do the sewing. How soon can I have this cotton? How much can you give me?"

Only my father could give away his cotton. I felt a blush burn upward from my collar to my forehead and stood mute.

"Well? How much cotton?"

My father's voice spoke from the doorway. "May I enter?" I whirled. His hair and brown beard were neatly combed, his green eyes now as clear as mine. He looked at me without surprise and said to Cortés: "If you need cotton, I offer you mine, at the same price the broker in Sevilla pays me."

I was stunned. He did not yet understand that I had to pay in cotton for the privilege of enlisting!

"Fair enough," Cortés nodded. "As for your son, I have refused a number of beardless boys who don't know a pike from a cannonball. How old is Arturo?"

"Eighteen in a week, and a good swordsman. He can also use the bow and the lance. He is eager to join you."

He smiled. "We men of Medellín have never lacked the spirit of adventure."

We men of Medellín! Blazing with gratitude, I saw that my father had touched a subtle chord. Despite the earlier hopes of Isabel and Fernando to forge a strong sense of national unity in the flames of a triumphant and remorseless Christianity, Spaniards still felt prime loyalty to the region where they were born.

Cortés looked at me musingly and said to my father, "You will outfit him?"

"Certainly. His mother asked me to tell you that Arturo writes a very fair, clear hand. She hopes you may wish to use him as a secretary." He spoke rapidly, in a bored tone.

"I have a secretary."

"I also promised my wife to tell you that he would make an excellent page."

"I have two." Cortés rose and came to where I stood as stiffly as a toy soldier. He dropped one hand to my shoulder; his dazzling eyes probed down into mine. "Always remember this, Arturo: The life of a foot soldier is hard, but great prize was never won without great toil. Glory was never the reward of sloth."

I felt as if I had just been knighted. "I'll remember, General!"

"I prefer my men to call me Cortés."

"Just Cortés?"

"Cortés."

As my father and I walked home under a low yellow moon, I thanked him fervently. He said, "As I told your mother, a boy does not become a man through coddling. I was angry when I found you had run off to enlist, but then it seemed to me to be your rightful destiny to finish the journey westward I have begun."

"I'll make us all rich!" I gestured widely up at the round moon. "We'll dine from golden plates. We'll wear velvet! We'll return to Spain in triumph and dine with King Carlos himself!"

My father's glance was indulgent. "Just take care to keep yourself alive."

"Dying forms no part of my plans."

"At your age, raising cotton formed no part of mine."

"Did you know that when he was young, Cortés wrote poetry, too?"

"Keep a clear head and forget poetry." My father gave a long sigh. "I wish your mother did not have such sad eyes. She is going to flay me with them long after you are gone."

I had expected to use my father's old brigandine, a tight jacket with small plates of metal riveted between two layers of cloth. But when I opened the chest in the storeroom I found that humidity had rotted the fabric. My breastplate, therefore, was of steel, bought cheaply from a huge old veteran with one leg. Leather straps within held the front and back halves together. There were no pauldrons to protect the shoulders and arms; instead, there was a cloth jupon to be worn beneath, the long sleeves and short skirt thickly studded with flat metal rivets. My mother was able to sew vertical tucks in the jupon so it fit, and I had the town cobbler contrive a leather padding which he glued inside the too-loose breastplate. But what a helmet I had! Made in Milan in the days when there were still tournaments, it was gilded and looked like real gold except in a few places where the wash had worn thin. On each side was delicately engraved a prancing centaur aiming an arrow toward whatever enemies I might face.

Looking at me as I paraded about in it, my mother sighed. Yet she now seemed resigned to my going and made me two white cotton shirts. My father gave me a large pouch full of glass beads, small mirrors, and other trinkets for barter with the Indians of that far shore. "Bring it back full of gold," he smiled. Our priest gave me a rosary which had been blessed by the archbishop. On the night before we left I made full confession, except for a few Eros-inspired dreams for which I did not feel responsible.

On the tenth of February 1519 we sailed for Cape San Antonio at the westernmost tip of Cuba, where the vessels would rendezvous before attempting the voyage to the island of Cozumel off the southern coast of Yucatán. As we left the harbor I looked back and saw the little crowd that had waved us off, among them my parents and my two little sisters and my friend Rubén, and I felt a pang of sadness at parting from them. But soon there was deep blue water all around, and my excitement would have had me soaring like a bird except for the weight of my armor. I removed it and stored it in my sea chest and put on my russet doublet instead, for the day was sultry and no enemy threatened. On the contrary, two friendly dolphins leaped from the sea just ahead of my vessel as if joyously leading the way to adventure, plunder, and glory. Our chief pilot, Aliminos, had sailed with Columbus in 1503 on his voyage to Yucatán. We had eleven brigantines and caravels, the largest of a hundred tons burden. We numbered five hundred and fifty-three soldiers, one hundred and ten mariners. We had thirty-two crossbowmen, thirteen arquebusiers, ten heavy guns, four lighter falconets, plenty of ammunition; and we had sixteen horses.

If I could have had any wish in the world, it would have been to own a horse. I deeply envied handsome young Captain Alonzo Puertocarrero when I saw his beautiful gray mare, bought for his use by his friend Cortés—who, I was told, had cut the gold buttons off his own cloak to pay for it. I admired an impulsive gesture even after learning that the Puertocarrero family boasted noblemen with some influence at Spanish court. I equally envied Juan Sedeño, the rich Trinidad settler in whose caravel I sailed: he had a chestnut mare. Horses were still scarce in Cuba, for they weather ocean voyages badly and had to be brought from Spain; to me their noble beauty evoked old heroes: I always imagined Alexander, Roland, and the Cid astride a stallion.

At Cape San Antonio we disembarked. The forces were mustered on the beach and we were divided into companies under the different captains: mine was Pedro

Alvarado. Then the terms of the contract between
Cortés and Governor Velásquez were read by Cortés'
crier, a short soldier with a bull's bellow. As legal documents tend to be, it was elaborately worded, but the gist
was that the purpose of the expedition·was to make
Christians of heathens, get them to swear loyalty to the
King of Spain, and to found colonies. Our monarch,
as was usual, would receive the first fifth of whatever
treasure we got. Another fifth then went to Velásquez
and Cortés, and the remainder would be fairly divided
among the rest of us. The captains, horsemen, priests,
and specialized artillerymen would get somewhat larger
shares than the common foot soldiers, but so immense
a quantity of future gold glittered in my imagination
that I felt rich already. A final stipulation was that, on
pain of severe punishment, no member of the expedition was to cohabit with any woman not a Christian.

After this, Cortés addressed us. It was the first time
I had seen him in full armor. That dark gleaming steel
transformed him and seemed to me his proper garb as
he stood above us on a jut of rocks. In the sky, clouds
sailed like airy gliding ships above our wooden ones
anchored below.

How his voice rang! I still remember his first words
to us: "We now begin a noble undertaking, one that
will make our names famous down the ages. I will lead
you to countries richer and more vast than any yet seen
by Europeans. I hold out to you a glorious prize! But
it will only be won by incessant toil. Great aims are
attained only by great exertions. Glory was never the
reward of sloth."

Startled, I remembered that he had spoken those
same words to me at Pedro Barba's and felt proud that
I had heard them first, and privately. He spoke then
of fame, the noblest reward a man can have, and of
fidelity: "Be true to me, as I will be true to you and
to our venture, and I will make each of you the master
of undreamed riches!" I closed my eyes and saw houses
of silver with furnishings of gold. "I promise you the
support of Almighty God, for we are Christian Span-

iards under the banner of the Holy Cross. Go forth, then, with alacrity and confidence, and carry to a glorious outcome this task which we have now so auspiciously begun!"

The cheers and shouts rang up to the clouds thickening above. As Cortés sank to one knee to receive the blessing of the priests, the rising wind took our banner and blew it wide so the cross showed well, and it seemed to me that Heaven itself was blessing us. I thrilled at my good fortune to be taking part in this venture, and to serve under such a man!

9

The wind that first seemed a blessing turned into a curse; soon a storm howled through the rigging and drove our ship far to the south. It heaved and tossed on great waves and we all left the wet decks to huddle in the hold, crowded with cargo and three stalled horses. I sat wedged between a handsome brown-bearded man named Bernal Diaz and a short black-bearded one with buck teeth and brows that met in a constant scowl above a broken nose. Miserably seasick, I hoped to hide it. But when Bernal said "Your ears have turned green, young man," I knew that I was going to vomit.

I hauled myself up the ladder and onto the tilting deck. Just as I bent forward and retched, a wave swept over the side and tried to knock my legs out from under me, but two hands came up from the hold and seized my ankles. I looked over my shoulder at the smiling face of Bernal, halfway up the ladder and clinging to my legs as if to his hope of Heaven. "Are you a good swimmer?" he shouted above the roar of the storm.

"Not in this sea!"

"Then puke down here in safety!" He backed down, still grasping one of my ankles and I followed on shaky knees.

"I was never seasick in my life," I assured him in as robust a tone as I could manage. "I crossed the entire Atlantic without a twinge."

"It's the damned salt pork," the short buck-toothed soldier said. "Beans for farting and salt pork for the vomits in a high sea, Pollito."

Pollito was a common enough nickname for young men, but to be likened to a baby chicken did not please me. "I am Arturo Mondragon y Flores," I told him with dignity.

"I'm Juan Morla, without a *y* to my name, Pollito," the buck-toothed one said with an exaggerated bow. His friends guffawed. It was little consolation to find that I was not the only one with a nickname: they had dubbed my new friend Bernal Diaz El Galán because of his good looks, good manners, and gallantry. It was more consoling that before the voyage was over, Juan Morla and most of the others were as sick as I.

The storm passed and we tacked in a northwesterly direction and at day's end reached Cozumel, anchoring in clear turquoise water between the island and the low coast of Yucatán, clearly visible across a rough channel. "The flagship's missing," El Galán noted as we strolled along the white beach the next morning to get our land legs back. I counted the anchored vessels: ten.

My spirits sank. Could our best and biggest ship have gone down in a storm the rest had weathered? "What will we do if something's happened to Cortés?"

"For my part, head back to Cuba. Pedro Alvarado would be likely to try to take command, but he's not a man I care to follow into the unknown. No poise. Too impulsive."

"And the other captains?"

"All right, with Cortés in charge. I've studied him well. He's pious, but practical. He's brave, but crafty. He's ruthless, but capable of deep feeling. He can charm birds into the water and fish into the trees and men into Death's jaws." He smiled and nodded as if this grim image were the greatest compliment of all.

"But how could we get back to Cuba if all the rest decided to continue with Alvarado in command?"

"There are nearly a hundred men who feel greater loyalty to Velásquez than to Cortés, and they'd balk at any commander the governor had not appointed. I'd return home with them, not from loyalty to Velásquez but from fondness for my own skin." He pointed to the top of the cliff overlooking the bay where some weathered stone buildings stood. "But why discuss a choice we don't have to make as yet? Come, let's take a look at that town."

I was surprised to find it quite large. A plaza paved with flat worn stones and as big as Havana's was surrounded by stone houses with steep roofs of thick thatch and by some larger buildings I took for temples. The biggest had a pyramidal base with steep steps leading up to an open, roofed structure atop. Going closer, I could see several strange-looking idols within. Over all was an aura of great age, and I stood gaping, caught up in a pleasing sense of mystery. I had just realized that the town was deserted when a man emerged from the temple, but not an Indian. It was blond Alvarado, grinning. He carried in his arms a big clay bowl filled with a number of small objects. "Souvenirs," he called down to us in his high-pitched voice. "No gold, worse luck." He invited us to join him in hunting the jungle for Indians to use as servants. El Galán declined, so I did, too.

We slept on the ships that night, not knowing how safe it was on shore. I was not the only one who felt edgy because of Cortés' absence. But late the following afternoon the flagship sailed in. Mariners waved their caps from the moored ships; Cortés, from the forecastle of his waved back and those of us who had gone ashore cheered loudly with relief.

But Cortés was grim-faced an hour later when he had the captains assemble all of us on the wide beach and then called Pedro Alvarado forward. "I am told you captured two natives and stole from a temple," Cortés said. "We are not here to steal, or to kidnap and terrify these Indians. How can we hope that they will accept our God if we ourselves act like sneak thieves and bullies? You will therefore release at once the two Indians you have in bondage and also give back the objects you stole." Alvarado's face was that of a naughty child pretending to be chastened yet at heart unrepentant. I saw him wink at his brother as he bowed his head.

We had to stay at Cozumel while our shipwright, Martín Llopez, repaired the damage the storm had done to some of the vessels and the next day we saw that many Indians had returned to the town on the cliff. Cortés decided to try to convert them, and we all went to watch as Father Olmedo and a short, surly priest named Juan Diaz sermonized to a large group of Indians through our interpreter, Melchorejo, a cross-eyed Indian who had returned from Yucatán with Grijalva and knew some Spanish. He explained to the natives that God wanted them to remove their idols from their main temple so we could erect there the Cross of Jesus. This attempt took place at the foot of the pyramid, Cortés with the priests and a large white cross standing halfway up its steps, the Indians gathered below, the rest of us filling the plaza or watching from the steps of the other buildings. I was in the forefront and saw that the Indians became agitated after an interchange between their cacique and Melchorejo, who translated into halting Spanish the Indian's words: "He says their gods bring them sun and rain. Make the maize to grow. This is a holy city, very ancient, built to honor Ixchel, moon goddess. If we move any gods from the temple, thunders and lightnings will kill us all." In spite of his Spanish doublet and cloak, Melchorejo sounded to me as if he half believed this himself.

Cortés scanned our faces. He was smiling. "Who is brave enough to dare the wrath of these statues?"

"I am," I called.

"Good. Any more brave fellows to join him?"

Grinning, a number of soldiers came forward. Cortés pointed to me. "Take the lead."

I felt proud as I climbed those steep steps, leading men all older than I. The idols, though of stone, were not so heavy that I could not topple one by myself. It was a serpentlike thing, all coils and scales, with the face of a man and a stone plume on its head. As it crashed and bounded down the steps and came to rest face down at the bottom, it seemed to me I had deposed a replica of Satan himself as he might have looked when he appeared to Eve in the Garden. A great cry of woe went up from the watching Indians below. I felt a little pity for them, seeing their stunned faces. How could they realize that we meant them only good?

No lightning having struck them or us, the Indians stopped their lamenting and stood staring up in wonder at our painted wooden statue of Mary holding the Christ Child, which a priest brought and set in place beside the Cross. Melchorejo assured Cortés that the Indians were willing to embrace Christianity, so our priests went about sprinkling holy water on all their heads from wet mops they swung.

"They'll pretend to be Christians until we sail away," I heard a voice from behind me observe. "For whatever good that will do them, us, or Jesus."

I turned and found myself looking down at Cortés' page, Orteguilla, a young dwarf. Standing no taller than my waist, he had a clever, handsome face, and had mastered the art of looking upward with arrogance. He wore a green velvet cap with a jaunty red feather and his ruby doublet had slashed sleeves. El Galán had known him in Santiago, and now tried to pump him. "Where were you, Orteguilla? Why was the flagship so late in arriving?"

"We anchored off the coast of Yucatán, only a few leagues from here."

"Why?"

"A page does not reveal his master's secrets."

"Why is it a secret?"

"It isn't, so I'll tell you. We were looking for two lost Spaniards."

"In Yucatán?" I asked.

"Eight years ago a ship bound for Darien with settlers and a number of priests was driven off course by a storm and wrecked on some rocks off Yucatán. Most drowned and those who got ashore were slaughtered or carried off by a band of savages. But as Cortés heard the story from Grijalva, who questioned those formerly hostile natives of the beach, two Spanish priests escaped into the jungle and soon reached a city whose ruler decided to spare their lives. So the other day Cortés stopped at the place where this wreck happened and sent Captain Ordaz inland with some heavily armed soldiers, our interpreter, and a rich ransom of glass beads and hawk bells. They returned with the news that the tale was indeed true, and the two Spanish priests were still alive. The old Indian ruler had accepted the ransom and had promised he would release his captives that very day if his gods agreed. Either they did not or he tricked us, because we waited offshore the rest of that day, the following one, and the next morning as well, and finally had to sail without the Spaniards to Cozumel."

"I heard the story of those Spaniards, but I didn't believe it," El Galán said.

"Cortés chose to believe it," Orteguilla smiled smugly. "In part, and I say this with all modesty, because I have warned him that Melchorejo is not to be trusted. Another interpreter, I pointed out, might prove very useful. By now those captured Spaniards must speak the Yucatán language very fluently, or else they're idiots."

His arrogance, as he passed himself off as one to whom Cortés listened respectfully, made me laugh.

He regarded me with cold brown eyes, his face thrust

up at mine. "Callow youth, don't you know that cross-eyed people are naturally duplicitous?"

The dwarf maligning the cross-eyed! I laughed again.

He said to me, "Enjoy your laugh. But you will see I am right. God may have scanted me as to stature, but he compensated with a brain which is subtler than most. That's why Cortés took me off the street in Hispaniola where I made a *toston* here and there polishing boots and running errands. My mother, the poor whore, died of a flux when I was nine. She thought to make a fortune in a place where there were so few Spanish women, but all she left me was a spirit of adventure and the clothes on my back." He strutted a bit in his fine garments. "Beware of those with crossed eyes! You will see!"

The next morning El Galán and I were on the beach when we saw a dugout canoe full of half-naked Indians making its way to Cozumel from the low sandy coast of Yucatán. When it reached shore and they got out, I saw that one was taller than the rest and paler in color. He had no beard, but his long hair was dark brown, not black.

"Do I find myself among Christians at last?" he asked us as we came near. I was so astonished to hear him speak Castilian that I could only nod. He dropped to his knees, bowed his head over his clasped hands, and thanked Jesus, the Virgin, and St. Christopher.

His fervor touched me and I squatted down and offered him wine-and-water from my flask. "Are you one of the Spaniards Cortés ransomed?"

He drank and nodded. "I am Jeronimo Aguilar."

El Galán left at a run to get Cortés, and I asked Aguilar where the other Spaniard was. He returned the flask, looking at me sadly from deep-set brown eyes. "Guerrero took an Indian wife six years ago when the cacique finally offered them to us, and now he has three sons. His face is tattooed and his ears are pierced. I remained faithful to my vow of chastity, even though I had no great hope of ever standing in a Christian church again. And so he will live there as an Indian, and I among my own kind."

"Where is the Spaniard? Show me the Spaniard!" Cortés strode toward us, followed by El Galán and a number of others.

Aguilar stood up. "I am he."

I said, "Permit me to present Jeronimo Aguilar, a very faithful servant of the Church."

Aguilar gave me a grateful smile as Cortés embraced him like a brother and gave him his own cloak to cover his nakedness. Then they walked off together.

Juan Morla, who had been watching, came to me scowling above his buck-toothed grin. "How do you know how faithful to the Church he is? You can't even grow a beard yet."

"A late beard is no crime," El Galán told him with a smile. "And neither is courtesy." Since my friend was a lieutenant to Alvarado and much liked by Cortés, Juan Morla remembered that no flies enter the closed mouth and stopped baiting me.

Like most of the soldiers I found myself among, Juan was originally from Estremedura—stocky, dark, and hardened by poverty. I was the youngest, the greenest, had a steel breastplate and a gilded casque. And, worse, I had made the mistake of letting him know I could read Latin when I discovered he did not understand what the legend on our banner meant. After that, he would lure me into displaying my erudition and then sneak behind me and make the sign of horns over my head while all his friends laughed at me. I saw I had only two alternatives: to become the clown of Alvarado's company or to keep to myself and ignore Morla and his friends. I would have been rather lonely except for El Galán, who took a liking to me and did not share the others' resentment of my literacy.

In addition to his good heart, he had considerable education himself. His full name was Bernal Diaz del Castillo. His father had been a magistrate in Medina del Campo since the days of Isabel and Fernando, and like my grandfather was highly respected. But the security of having a fixed home in a small community did not appeal to the adventurous Bernal. Born in the year that Columbus discovered a new world, his imagination had been captivated by fantastic tales of the shores that lay beyond where the old maps ended. He conceived it to be his privilege and duty to leap an ocean into the glowing future. In 1514 he joined an expedition organized by King Fernando himself, excited by tales of pearls and gold lying about all over the Isthmus of Panama. Reality falling dismally short of such expectations, El Galán decided to try his luck in Cuba, by then conquered by his distant kinsman Velásquez. Too late for luck or good lands there, he had enlisted in two earlier expeditions to that mysterious shore to the west which had beckoned me. While with Fernández de Córdoba he was wounded in the chest with an arrow at Champeton, but soon sailed off again with the luckless Grijalva. Although that expedition got sixteen thousand pesos' value in gold and jewels, the natives attacked them so severely at a place they named Cabo Rojo that Grijalva's men forced him to return to Cuba. "But this time it will be different," El Galán said. "I think fabulous cities lie awaiting us in the interior of this land. I doubt we will encounter El Dorado or Amazons, but I expect to sail home with a tidy little fortune." He smiled. "Who knows, maybe I'll even marry a pretty young woman I know in Santiago de Cuba. At twenty-seven, it's time for me to begin to think of settling down."

Because of the delay while the ships were repaired, it was March before we left Cozumel to sail around the jut of Yucatán. Again stormy weather impeded us; the ships would get separated so that the flagship had to circle back after stragglers. At last, after traveling to the north and west, we anchored at the mouth of a sizable river with a wide sandy delta.

"That's the Tabasco River," El Galán told me, "although Grijalva renamed it the Rio Grijalva. The Indians there were friendly ones. An old, fat cacique came to the beach from his town somewhere upriver and brought us gifts, some made of gold."

Cortés decided that Tabasco merited exploration and ordered Alvarado's men as well as Sandoval's to row up the river with him in ships' boats. At last I was going to set foot on the Unknown Land!

Beyond the delta was a grove of palms, and then mangrove trees waded out into the clear brown water on their slender stiltlike roots. At a clearing where the mangroves thinned, a large troop of Indians awaited us. Friendly they were not but gave harsh, jeering cries and waved their weapons: lances, bows, and wicked-looking double-edged swords toothed with black obsidian. Cortés had Melchorejo call out to them that we were there on a peaceful mission and wished to land and march to their town. They denied us passage, brandishing their weapons more fiercely than before.

Another commander might have turned back to the ships, but Cortés decided to camp that night on a large island in the middle of the wide river. El Galán told me that Indians do not fight at night, but sunrise found the unfriendly Indians again massed on the shore and they hurled blazing sticks of wood at our boats, but soon fell back under fire from our crossbowmen and our muskets, whose noise clearly frightened them.

We broke through the barricade of branches they had set across the trail to impede us and at last reached a large walled town facing a lagoon into which the river debouched. The place was sun-drenched and silent as a tomb. Every man, woman, and child had fled. Cortés went to a large ceiba tree in the square and drew his sword and slashed the trunk twice to make a cross. "I take this town in the name of Carlos of Spain," he announced, and the Royal Notary duly recorded this fact.

But we learned that Melchorejo had been unimpressed by this victorious gesture, for El Galán and I later found his abandoned Spanish clothing hanging from a branch of that same tree. Our Indian interpreter

had deserted. Orteguilla the dwarf happened to be with
Cortés when El Galán and I brought him Melchorejo's
clothes; he beamed with triumph and crossed his eyes
at me. But he sobered abruptly when Cortés pointed
out that the deserter had gone over to the Tabascans
because he thought they would prove the victors. That
night a heavy guard was posted. I drew first watch and
stayed alert and very uneasy with the thought that
Indian eyes were watching me from the thick jungle
of mangroves beyond the tall palms and cacao trees
that surrounded this town we had taken with such ease.

At dawn Cortés sent out a scouting party that came
back with three Indian prisoners. Aguilar learned that
the whole countryside was rising against us and would
probably attack the next day. The old ruler who had
been so friendly with Grijalva was now regarded as a
fool or a traitor by the chieftains of other Tabascan
towns.

Cortés at once sent a detachment to return to the
ships and to have cannons, horses, and reinforcements
sent to us; these arrived by nightfall. Early in the morning, Cortés ordered three companies of foot soldiers to
march out and meet the enemy. Beyond the palm trees
on one side was the mangrove swamp. On the other
were maize fields and beyond was a muddy plain slop-
ing up to a long ridge behind which the enemy was
surely concealed. Full of bravado, I left the maize. I
gasped. A horizon of Indians! Thousands! With shrill
cries they began to move in a mass down toward us.

As we floundered ahead over the muddy ground, a
cloud of locusts appeared from nowhere, whirring and
buzzing while Indian arrows whizzed. Our artillery fire
cut down Tabascans by the dozens, but dozens more
filled the gaps. I felt a blow and heard a thud and saw
to my amazement that an Indian arrow had pierced
my left arm just where my breastplate ended, undeterred
by the rivets of my cloth jupon. I tried to wrench it
out, but the point seemed moored to the bone. Pain
dazed me, and blood flowed down my arm. In the name
of God, where were our horsemen and our cannons?

"¡Santiago y San Pedro!" Our battle cry came from the reinforcements delayed by hauling the cannons across the mud. Now one boomed thunderously. Through the cloud of locusts Cortés suddenly loomed, sunlight bright on his polished armor and the armor of his horse. He rose high in his stirrups, sword aloft, and charged toward the Indians. Several mounted captains followed.

Tabascan war cries ceased as if sliced off by his sword. He never used it. At the sight of him the Indians turned in a body and ran, throwing aside lances, swords, and bows in a total, panicked rout. They had never seen a horse before and thought the horse and rider were one monstrous creature. A centaur!

In a grove of palms near the town, Cortés had a Mass of thanksgiving held. There was cause for it. We had been opposed by five squadrons of eight thousand Indians each and had killed twenty-five hundred. Our losses were two dead and fewer than a hundred wounded. Two dozen Tabascans had died for my one injury, but this did not make the cauterizing any easier to bear: a young priest with a knowledge of medicine seared my wound with boiling oil, having stuffed a rag in my mouth for me to grind my teeth on.

"Now you're seasoned," El Galán said as he bandaged my shoulder. Out on the battlefield I could see through tears of pain some Indians in ragged clothing, their faces painted in black designs, retrieving their dead.

Cortés had granted them permission to do this but had demanded that their principal cacique come to him and acknowledge defeat. When that important personage arrived, I was beside El Galán near the big canopy Cortés had ordered set up at the edge of the palm grove, fearing an ambush within the town. He stood in its shade, joking with Captain Puertocarrero. Aguilar, now wearing the brown robe of his Franciscan order, stood beside Cortés to act as his interpreter. The other priests and many of the captains were massed behind Cortés. I envied them that shade, standing as I was in the sun with the foot soldiers drawn up in files facing the canopy.

The pain of my wound and the dense heat had made my knees weak. I took off my helmet and leaned against the bole of a palm tree and closed my eyes, but then Alvarado's high-pitched voice ordered us to form ranks and stand at attention. Across yesterday's battleground, now cleared of corpses, a long procession of Indians moved toward us. Feather headdresses and bracelets and necklaces showed some thirty of them to be of high rank. Four of these carried the poles of a litter on which sat a very old, fat Indian with the highest headdress of all, its green plumes nodding gently. When the litter reached the canopy, it was gently lowered to the ground and two of the bearers helped the rider to his feet. Slowly and with dignity he approached Cortés.

Then I caught sight of the group of twenty young Indian women, clad in various bright colors, who emerged from behind the other attendants of the cacique; at the sight of them some of our soldiers began to make lewd remarks and a few let out cheers. The women following the old cacique walked past us with downcast eyes and expressionless faces, though a few glanced fearfully around them.

And then I saw her. She seemed suddenly to leap into prominence so that the others faded away. Taller than the rest, she wore a loose square-necked tunic of deep turquoise blue with long, wide sleeves. Below it, a long skirt or petticoat swayed as she moved on sandaled feet. A golden pendant gleamed below her beautiful face, which could have been painted for the Madonna's, though I knew she was only a pagan savage who groveled before idols she thought could bring sunlight and thunder. Her hair shone like jet and hung artlessly down her back and over her shoulders like a little child's. By now the other soldiers had noticed her and were making the usual remarks. "What breasts! What eyes! A real beauty!"

Suddenly, the beautiful one turned her head and

looked directly at me, as if she had felt my burning gaze among all the others. The sun beating down on my head was no hotter than the surge of excitement that tingled through my veins. I saw that her dark eyes were fixed on my hair and I realized that she had never seen blond hair before, as new a sight to her as our horses to the Tabascan warriors yesterday.

Aguilar's voice rang out, translating into Spanish the words the Indian ruler had just spoken: "We tremble and bow in defeat before your supernatural beasts. In token of our humble surrender we offer these twenty slave women as hostages." He turned and motioned to them. They passed into the shade of the canopy and her figure was only one of many massed behind Cortés and Aguilar. Puertocarrero eyed the Indian women with keen interest.

Cortés then solemnly offered the fat ruler the return gift of a brass hawk bell, which he rang. Either bells were new to the old cacique or he was a man of almost Castilian good manners, for he took it and rang it again with every sign of pleasure.

That turned to terror when a stallion, wild to mount a mare in heat, was ridden, neighing, up to the canopy to awe him. The sight of that rampant stallion soon aroused in me an audacious plan to satisfy my own yearning to see that beautiful Indian girl again. I decided to break ranks, slip around the side of the canopy and enter it from the rear. Hand on my bandaged arm, I whispered to El Galán that I had to get out of the sun.

But just as I rounded the rear corner of the canopy, my eyes on the open curtain through which I saw the bright skirt and blouse of an Indian woman, movement caught the corner of my eye. A woman's figure clad in turquoise was running away between the gray boles of the palms, heading for the thick jungle of mangroves far beyond.

I put on my helmet and set off after her, my injured arm throbbing bitterly with every thud of my boots on the ground. Then like a present from God himself, a gray mare came ambling by, reins dangling. I grabbed them and took a moment to speak to it soothingly. Very amiably it let me mount, and in a moment more we were cantering past the boles of palms after the Indian girl. But now the mangrove jungle was only a short distance ahead of her. "Stop!" I called. "I won't hurt you!" But she vanished into the dense grove.

At its edge, I tethered the mare to the bole of a palm and plunged in after her, pausing dead still to hear the sound of her steps. Silence. I moved farther in and peered all around me for a glimpse of that vivid blue. Nothing. It was as though, like a dryad, she had turned into a tree herself.

I had started to crawl deeper into the tangle of growth when a thought stopped me. The clever thing for her to do would be to hide and let me go blundering deeper and deeper in and, when I had gone far enough, slip out and leave me still searching. I turned and went back the way I had come and burst out into the sunlight to find her staring at the horse, which was nibbling a tuft of grass at the base of the palm where I had tethered it.

I closed in on her quietly, but she heard me and turned. For the first time in my life I saw pure terror in a pair of human eyes, midnight eyes, large and slightly slanted above wide, smooth cheekbones. Sweat pearled her upper lip and forehead and she breathed lightly and quickly. "I won't hurt you," I said gently. The words, of course, meant nothing—they were only strange sounds to her. I remembered the rosary I wore under my breastplate and pulled it out and held it before her eyes so the small crucifix could be clearly seen. "Jesus, see? I'm a Christian."

But her eyes went to my helmet, on which the centaurs pranced. Slowly she bent to touch one hand to the ground and then brought it up to her forehead. The look of reverence on her face told me the meaning of this gesture. Not the crucifix but the centaurs on my helmet had convinced her I was a god.

I took her hand and led her toward my borrowed mount. As we neared it, she went rigid and tried to pull away, but I held tight to her cold hand. As I released the tether the mare tossed its head and she leaped back from it and would have been off again if I had not been holding her hand so tightly. But when she saw that the beast intended her no harm, she took one hesitant step toward it and stood looking up at that noble maned head with wonder. Watching her it was as if I myself were seeing a horse for the first time: the size, the gloss, the grandness. It turned its head slightly and looked at her with one liquid brown eye. I bent and plucked a tuft of grass and held it out to the mare, which bent its head and took it daintily, its soft muzzle tickling my skin. I meant the Indian girl to understand that it was only a tame animal and not a deity, any more than I.

The hand in mine seemed less tense as I led the two runaways back to Cortés' canopy, although she stared straight ahead and walked with the slow, tranced pace of one resigned to her fate.

The foot soldier who served as Puertocarrero's groom came pelting toward me, angry and frightened at having found the mare gone. He seized the reins from my hand with an accusing look, and I told him he ought to be grateful to me for catching it, but his muttered thanks was grudging.

As the Indian girl and I reached the rear of the canopy I saw Aguilar speaking with several of the other Indian slaves. When he saw us he strode toward me, his gaunt face stern, his deep-set eyes angry. "What have you been doing with this young woman?"

"Catching her. She ran away."

"And that is all? You did not—harm her?"

Another accusation! "I have also brought back Puertocarrero's horse, which was loose. I suppose I'll get no thanks for that, either!"

He turned to her then and spoke gently in the language he had learned in Yucatán, and she answered in a murmur of words. Jealous that he could talk to her and I could not, I demanded, "What did she say?"

"The old cacique did not warn the women they were to be hostages. She did not want to stay with us, who had killed so many people. But I have assured her that no harm will come to her."

"What is her name?"

"Why do you need to know that?"

"Please ask her!"

He looked at me dubiously but then evidently recalled our first meeting, when I had been kind and courteous to him. His face softened. He turned to her and spoke again. Her shoulders straightened and she stood tall. Three syllables came from her lips. "Mal-een-chay." After a moment's pause, she added something else, curt, chopped-off sounds.

Aguilar turned to me. "She says she is Malinche of Paynala. A cacique's daughter."

I stepped toward her and spoke her name; she turned her head toward me. I pointed to my breastplate. "Arturo. I am Arturo."

"Arturo," she repeated. And so my name was the first word of Spanish she ever spoke.

"Arturo!" I heard my name called by a man's voice. It was El Galán, shaking his head and barely smiling. "Alvarado noticed your lengthy absence. You can expect a reprimand, or worse."

My joyous excitement was undimmed even when Alvarado, hands on hips, called me a loose-wit apology for a soldier in his high, far-carrying voice. When I told him about capturing both the escaping Indian woman and Puertocarrero's horse, Alvarado demanded "Did I command you to pursue an Indian or a runaway horse?" I shook my head and he then developed the theme that the prime duty of a soldier is to obey orders. "This time I will withhold punishment in view of the great value to us of the mare you caught."

How could he have guessed—or I—that an Indian girl would prove of greater value than a thoroughbred mare, one of our best mounts? Who would have imagined then that Malinche would one day change the outcome of our venture? I only knew that she had enchanted me and that if she had vanished into those mangrove trees so that I never saw her again, her face would have been branded on my mind forever.

10

It soon appeared that my meeting with Malinche was also to be our farewell. El Galán told me that when the fat cacique had offered Cortés a number of golden ornaments shaped like frogs, lizards, birds, hares, and deer Cortés had asked him where we could get more gold. The old man, his eyes dimmed by cataracts, had waved an arm in a northerly direction and had said "Mexico. Culhua." Exactly where these places were he could not or would not say, except that they were far to the northwest.

"So you can be sure that we'll be sailing north very soon," El Galán said.

An unpleasant premonition struck me. "But Cortés will bring the Indian women, won't he?"

"I doubt it, in view of our law against fornication." He saw my troubled face and added "You can thank the pen of the good Padre Bartolome de las Casas. He aroused such royal horror with his descriptions of the mistreatment of the Indians of Hispaniola and Cuba that the Royal Council of the Indies was formed to protect them, although I don't know why Governor Velásquez singled out rape over other misdeeds." He patted my shoulder. "If we sail without your Malinche, think of it as your good fortune. Temptation left behind."

When I saw Malinche again after the Palm Sunday Mass which Cortés arranged to impress the Tabascans, it was with mingled joy and sadness. The whole army had marched in procession, chanting in Latin, carrying palm branches high as we made our way across a meadow to a large stone pyramid with thousands of conquered Indians watching us. When Mass was over, I saw that the Indian women had attended in a group, shepherded by Aguilar and the short-tempered little priest Juan Diaz. As soon as I saw Malinche, the pain in my wounded shoulder left as if by magic.

As I ran to her, smiling, other soldiers also converged on the Indian women, and the two priests were soon very busy keeping at bay the most importunate. Malinche's earlier fearful reverence was gone, for she smiled back at me. Her teeth were the whitest I had ever seen; there was a small dimple in her left cheek. Something inside me melted and ran like honey all through my being, and she ceased to be an Indian and a heathen and became a unique being, a mystery, a promise of joys unknown to me. Her skin was no darker than that honey in my veins, no darker than the skin of many a Spanish *morisca* lady. Then I saw that the medallion she wore around her neck was made in the shape of a coiled serpent with a human face, very like the stone idol I had thrown down in Cozumel.

I pointed to it and made a grimace, shaking my head. Her smile vanished, and she covered her idol with one hand and pointed up at my palm branch, her whole face a question. So I gave it to her, and she imitated the way I had carried it, over the right shoulder like a musket.

"No intercourse with the female natives!" It was Father Juan Diaz, scowling up at me. He seized her by the arm and pulled her away with him and I stood sadly staring after her as she stole a glance back at me, the palm branch waving farewell from the other shoulder. I waved back, believing that I would soon be sailing away from her forever.

Sure enough, that evening Captain Alvarado told us as we ate that in the morning we would return to our ships and go north in search of Culhua and Mexico. Sorrow overtook me and with it a reverie in which one day I would return to Tabasco laden with gold to find her again.

An elbow nudged me. "Did you hear that?" El Galán demanded. "The Indian women are coming with us after all."

Alvarado nodded. "Aguilar told Cortés that if we left them behind it would insult the old cacique and would mean that we did not intend to stay on peaceful terms. Cortés wants good relations with Tabasco. We may need a place to fall back to later. Who can tell what lies ahead? So the Indian women are coming with us, on the flagship." My elation was tempered by the fact that on Sedeño's caravel I would have no chance to see Malinche, but still this was better than leaving her in Tabasco. Alvarado added, "And in case those Indian women are giving any of you dogs the scent of sport, you'll get the skin flogged right off your back if you try to lift even one skirt!"

Next morning when we reached the delta and saw our ships at anchor, a surprise awaited me. Sedeño's caravel was one of the worst-battered by the storm and also somewhat worm-eaten, so that half its soldiers and cargo were to be transferred to other vessels. El Galán and I were sent to the flagship. We had barely staked out sleeping places on the foredeck when the anchor jangled up and the great sails filled. Staying close to the curve of the shore, we led the fleet northwest toward waters that had never known a Spanish keel, toward the mysterious land of gold we now called Mexico. A storm that night made me glad to be on that large and seaworthy flagship.

But Malinche, sequestered in the hold with the other Indian women under the watchful eye of Aguilar, was as unreachable as a girl of decent family in Spain. When

I was fifteen I had water poured on my head from a window just for following a pretty girl home from evening Mass and calling her name after I thought the family asleep. I came home dripping. My father was amused, but my mother dwelt at length on the sin of debauching a virgin. My father warned me privately of the buboes I could get if I ever slept with prostitutes, so copulation had not been among my sins of the flesh as I lurked about the hatch that opened onto the dark hold where Malinche was. Far from home, feeling myself a man among men with a wound to prove it, I was torn between the pure wish to ask for her keepsake to wear, like any chaste knight, and the low desire to find some way to pry her away from the other women as soon as Aguilar's vigilance flagged. Her strange beauty spurred me to the poetry that had so pleased my mother, while her low status as a pagan without Christian morals let me imagine her as receptive to my lustful desires. Poetry triumphed.

"Ah, love, let us love while the nightingale sings to the moon . . ." There are no nightingales in Cuba and I had never heard one that I could recall. But what did that matter? I made up a pretty little poem replete with them as well as roses, moonlight, a silvery fountain, midnight eyes, damask cheeks, and a dawn that came too soon. While I sought for rhymes I was pleasantly aware that, at my age, Cortés had done the same.

The dwarf Orteguilla had a guitar and I borrowed it to set my verses to music and finally had a passable little roundelay. Standing by the opening to the hold I began to sing it, with feeling. Malinche would not understand the words, but perhaps the tune would please her and perhaps she would even understand the gesture. I had sung only two lines when a male voice spoke just behind me. "A pretty little song, but this is not the place to sing of love."

I whirled and faced Aguilar. He had let his beard grow, and with his hair hanging to his shoulders and his stern, deep-set eyes, he looked to me not unlike Jesus about to flog the moneylenders from the temple.

"I thought the Indian women might like a little entertainment," I told him with a placating smile.

"You mean a particular Indian woman, don't you? The one called Malinche?"

"May I talk with her for a moment?"

"No. You don't speak her language, nor she yours. If I allowed this, other men would want such 'conversations.' No conversation prior to conversion. Have you forgotten the firm law of this expedition, that no man shall fornicate with a woman not a Christian?"

My blood was set to leaping by the word *fornicate*. Hypocrite, I nodded, "Yes, for some of the men are very lustful, and these poor Indian women don't know right from wrong."

He shook his head. "The Indians in Yucatán taught their children to be chaste until marriage. The girls wore a symbol of virginity hanging down over their genitals."

The word *genitals* created the same reaction as *fornicate* had, and I covered my own with my guitar.

Soft as a dove, a voice spoke from the open hatch behind me. "Arturo." Malinche, halfway out of the hold, gazed trustingly up at me. As a thrill shot through me, a shrill whinny floated up from below and reminded me that several horses were in stalls down there, including the gray mare and Cortés' chestnut. I offered Malinche my hand and drew her up to the deck. What a cruel journey this must have been for her, prisoner in a dark pit with beasts she thought supernatural!

She turned from me to Aguilar and spoke some words of the Yucatán tongue. He looked most concerned. "She says one of the horses is dying. The chestnut. I thought it looked ill."

"Cortés' horse!" I said. "We'd better tell him."

When I knocked on the door of the cabin below the foredeck, it was opened by Cortés' secretary, a tall thin fellow in dusty black whom I had once seen vomiting over the rail into a perfectly calm sea. He demanded to know my business with the general. I was filled with joy at Malinche's nearness but tried to sound properly solemn. "His horse seems to be dying."

The secretary was swept aside by Cortés. Because of the heat, he wore a full-sleeved white shirt. His tone was angry. "The mare is somewhat ill from the sea journey, but who says it's dying?"

"This Indian woman so informed us," Aguilar told him.

"What would an Indian know of horses?" He handed the quill to the secretary and strode to the hold, the three of us trailing after.

As Cortés disappeared into the depths, El Galán called us to the rail, pointing shoreward toward a small isle we were passing. Through verdure we could see the stones of an Indian temple. "We named it the Isla de los Sacrificios," he said. "When Grijalva and I explored that temple, we came upon the slaughtered remains of five Indians. Their hearts had been cut out. One was a young boy. His face, even after such a death, had a strange beauty." I looked at Malinche, staring at the isle yet unaware of the meaning of those words. Her face was an enigma to me and I was reminded that she came of a race of people not only infidel, but often very cruel.

"Dead," said a dull voice behind me. Cortés stood by the opening to the hold, hair ruffled by the breeze of our passage. "Poor beast." He looked down at his gold chain, lifted it, dropped it. "However, there's a fine black stallion called El Arriero. Two soldiers own it jointly. I'll buy it." He started toward the cabin, then paused to call back to Aguilar. "Let the other Indian women out on deck for a breath of air. It stinks down there."

But as soon as the women emerged to cluster at the rail around Aguilar and Malinche, turning their faces up to the sunlight, men materialized from every part of the vessel to encircle them. Aguilar made me think of a brave sheepdog ready to hold wolves at bay. The Indian women were aware of the men's interest; some

shrank timidly behind Aguilar, some giggled and murmured among themselves, some pretended indifference.
Malinche stood with her back to the men, staring shoreward. She turned and said something to Aguilar, and I
asked what she had told him.

"She has been looking for the shore near her home-
land, but she thinks we passed it while she was down
in the hold." I remembered that when I first captured
her she had called herself Malinche of . . . Painilla?
Paynala?

A slim, elegant figure detached itself from among
the men and came forward to confront me. It was
Alonzo Puertocarrero. "I am told that in addition to
catching my mare which was running away, you also
caught a very pretty Indian. Which was it?"

With reluctance I pointed to Malinche. He grinned
at me. "Green as you are, you brought back the only
one worth bedding with."

Before I could think of a reply, Aguilar stepped forward. "I am amazed to hear such words from a Castilian gentleman who calls himself Christian. Do these
poor women arouse in you no pity?"

The reproof put long faces on all the men who had
been grinning and must have stung Puertocarrero. But
with a devilish look in his narrow, glittering eyes, he
only said "They are ignorant savages, one of whom I
graciously complimented by my appreciation of her
pagan charms." Turning on his heel, Puertocarrero
sauntered away and the others followed. For the first
time I was thankful for that law concerning cohabita-
tion with heathen women.

The dwarf Orteguilla came pattering up to me then
to reclaim his guitar, and when I turned from him, I
found that Malinche and the other Indians had followed Aguilar up to the afterdeck where they all knelt
and were soon repeating after him the Lord's Prayer.
But what could those words mean to them? Even
though Aguilar provided a translation in their own
tongue, what could "Our Father" signify, or "heaven"

or "Thy will be done," or "Forgive us our sins as we forgive those who sin against us"?

The next day I got my first gold. North of the Isle of Sacrifices lay another, larger island that Grijalva had named San Juan Ulua. After we had anchored in the lee, a long dugout canoe came paddling swiftly out to the flagship from the mainland, where the beach was thick with watching Indians. The canoe was loaded with flowers and baskets of fruit and when the ship's ladder was lowered, the Indians consulted among themselves and then came up it, hugging their gifts. I had raced to my sea chest to get some glass beads and one of my little mirrors from my pouch. When I saw an Indian boy wearing a golden pendant attached to a round gold wire, I pointed to the necklace and held out my mirror. We traded and he went off happily flashing mirror-light in all directions. The pendant was hammered very thin indeed, but still it was *gold*. Examining it more closely, I was surprised to see it was engraved with the profile of a man with an aquiline nose, a short pointed beard, and a helmet similar to the ones we wore. But how could this be? Indians don't have beards, or such noses, or such casques. I put it around my neck and hid it under my shirt for fear it might be confiscated to go into the common treasury.

Cortés sat in his carved armchair, which he had had brought to the foredeck from his cabin. There he held court, gazing down at a semicircle of squatting Indians and their offerings. Among the baskets of fruit and bouquets of flowers gleamed a few trinkets of gold, mostly small animals like those the old cacique of Tabasco had given us. Cortés turned to Aguilar, smiling. "Thank them for their gifts. Ask them where I can get more gold."

Aguilar rattled off this message in the Yucatán tongue, but the Indians paid no attention. "They do not seem to understand me," he said.

The smile melted from Cortés' face. "Try again."

Aguilar tapped the shoulder of an older Indian with

feathers on his head and spoke to him. The Indian stared back impassively. Aguilar shook his head. "They don't seem to speak the Mayan tongue here."

"What tongue?"

"The language of Yucatán and Tabasco. We are too far north of there. It's as if we had gone from Spain to Austria."

"Bring those Indian women here," Cortés said. "Maybe one of them can talk with these fellows."

They were clustered on the afterdeck, now declared off limits to the men. Aguilar called up to them, and after a moment Malinche descended. She knelt down beside the Indian with the feathers and spoke to him in a strange tongue full of abrupt consonants, hisses, clicks, throaty chuckles. Her hands made many gestures, dancing in the sunlight. The leader of the Indians replied at some length. At last she nodded, stood up and conveyed to Aguilar in the Mayan tongue what she had learned.

He said, "These Indians are Olmec, conquered subjects of the Tenocha, a people they also call the Aztecs. They live a long distance away, high in the mountains, in a beautiful city called Tenochtitlán. Near it are many other cities which it dominates. The whole area is called Culhua."

"Culhua. Where the gold abounds," Cortés nodded.

"The Aztec ruler is named Moctezuma. His power and wealth are without limit, his warriors feared like demons. This conquered coast is governed by a nobleman of his named Teuhtlile." I smiled, because Tay-oot-lee-lay sounded to me like the cry of a small bird of Cuba.

"Mexico," said Cortés. "Ask them about Mexico."

Culhua was within Mexico, a large area originally inhabited by Indians other than the Aztecs but now dominated by them. Cortés held up his hand. "Enough of these strange names. Have the Indian girl tell them that I want to meet their governor."

"They say that to do that we must come ashore."

"Indeed?" Cortés gazed out at the populous coast,

then had Orteguilla go to his cabin and bring some glass beads to distribute among the Indians. Apparently happy with these gifts, they climbed down the ladder and paddled rapidly landward.

Cortés turned his attention to Malinche, eyes fixed on her face while he spoke to Aguilar. "This is the one who said my horse was dying. But how did she know that?"

"She said the light of life was fading from its eyes."

"Very poetic. What is she called?"

"Malinche."

Cortés did not hear correctly, or he did not care for the sound of her Indian name. Wearing a slight smile in which I read a half-reluctant admiration, he spoke to Malinche very loudly, with that innocent belief of most Spaniards that if they shout Castilian, others will surely understand it. "I thank you, Doña Marina, for your help. I may require your services as my interpreter in the future, if that is agreeable to you."

As Aguilar conveyed this to Malinche, I stepped forward. "Pardon me, Cortés. Her name is Malinche."

"Her name *was* Malinche," Cortés corrected me. "I have just renamed her Doña Marina, our lady of the seacoast."

Our lady of the seacoast now had learned from Aguilar what Cortés wanted of her. Did I imagine it, or was there a certain warmth in that dark and faintly tilted eye of hers? There are skins to which the sunlight is kind; hers had the rich flush of some exotic fruit, darker than an apricot, smooth as a pear, ripe and glowing under the gaze of Cortés. Her manner was regal as she answered him in Spanish: *"Sí."*

He swept her a courtier's bow. *"Gracias,* Doña Marina."

Everyone was smiling at the sight of our commander showing such great courtesy to an Indian— all but me. His renaming her had jarred me.

As she returned with Aguilar to rejoin the other women, I fell into step and asked him to tell her that whatever Cortés chose to call her, I would respect her

right to her own true name, but he said, "I do not think
she is disturbed, for I have explained to her that *Doña*
is a term of respect." As though she had understood
him, she turned her head to give me a sweet, dazzling
smile.

Two days later we set up camp ashore. God knows I
had seen places more promising than that wide beach
of high sand dunes the color of dry bones. On the
highest of these Cortés had a formidable battery of guns
set up. On another a tall white wooden cross was raised.

The captains set us to work cutting palm fronds from
the trees behind the beach and chopping down mangroves to make rude huts to protect us from the sun.
Chopping away at a stubborn gray trunk with a hand
axe under the noonday sun that sent sweat running into
my eyes, even though I had stripped down to my shirt
and hose, I gritted my teeth against the pain in my
wounded shoulder. My dread of seeming less than a
man had forced me to make little of my injury, which
was now festered and inflamed, and my brain felt so
too. Suddenly it seemed to me that I could feel my
beard growing very rapidly, brought sprouting out of
my face by the heat and the scent of the tree I was
chopping. I put up one hand to feel my chin, and suddenly all went black.

I opened my eyes and stared straight up into the face
of Malinche, kneeling beside me. My humiliation was
intense. I put the blame where it belonged, pointing to
my bandaged shoulder. "An arrow wound. At Tabasco." She undid my shirt, lifted the bandage, examined
my injury. I saw green pus coming out of it. She motioned me to walk with her a little deeper among the
mangroves where it was shady and indicated I was to
wait there for her. I lay down. My head throbbed, time
passed. It suddenly occurred to me that I could die
and tried to compose an elegy about a wounded knight
breathing his last on a distant shore, but I could not fix
the rhymes in my head.

When Malinche at last returned she had with her

several of the friendly Indians of this coast. They carried straw mats and palm thatch and bamboo poles and, as I watched, they began to build in the sand nearby a crude circular hut. Meanwhile she knelt by me and gently cleansed my wound with water scented with some herb I had never smelled before. Then she put on it something that looked like moss and covered that with large green leaves which she tied in place with a length of slender vine. She had me drink a herb brew with a bitter taste, but it soon brought a pleasant tranquility. Her healing methods were much kinder than the cauterization with boiling oil practiced on me by that young man of God, cruel though her people might sometimes be.

While I lay in a doze, my hut was finished. As I tottered from the shelter of the mangroves, spurning Malinche's aid, I saw that a horde of male Indians had appeared on the beach and that an encampment of rude huts was beginning to rise amid the pale, lifeless dunes. When I thanked Malinche, she surprised me by apparently understanding the words, or at least the sentiment, for with a fluid gesture she made little of her kindness and skill, as when a Spaniard says that an act is of no importance. She left me on a straw mat in the dimness of my hut. I soon slid down into a deep sleep.

When I awoke my mind was clear again, my fever was gone, and my shoulder pained much less. The sands outside were grayed by twilight. For some minutes I pondered on the wisdom this Indian had as to the use of herbs, and then El Galán came in, a clay bowl in his hand, and offered it with a smile. "First, may I congratulate you on fainting where she could find you? Very clever. Women have a peculiar tenderness toward the helpless, natural in them, since they must nurture infants. You could have found no better way to capture her attention."

I took the bowl of soup from him. "There was no need to capture it," I boasted. "She cares about me. I feel it."

He pointed to the bowl I held. "That's called *atole.*

These kind Indians here brought us great clay pots of it."

I swallowed thick maize soup. "It's good."

"As for Doña Marina, tread very carefully."

"Malinche is her name."

"She is now of great use to Cortés, please remember. What is useful to him he regards as his, with God's blessing."

A most disturbing thought kept me from enjoying my second mouthful of soup. "Do you think he has any other interest in her? I mean, as a woman? A beautiful woman?"

"He's had a good many of those, including his present wife in Cuba, so this Indian may not look as beautiful to him as she does to you."

That comforted me slightly, but I was not so innocent as to suppose that the existence of a wife in Cuba would cause a man who had climbed so many balconies when young to turn entirely celibate at thirty-four. And furthermore, Cuban gossip said that although the beautiful Catalina Juarez had adored Cortés and had pursued him shamelessly, he had avoided marrying her until Governor Velásquez, to ingratiate himself with another of the lovely Juarez sisters, jailed him on some pretext until he gave in and wedded her. So it seemed to me doubtful that Cortés loved his absent wife, particularly since she was barren or at least had given him no child.

I lay awake for a long time, tormented by uneasiness. But the law of the expedition said that no member could cohabit with any heathen woman, and that included Cortés. "I will be true to you and our venture," he had said to us on the beach at San Antonio. I slept at last, soothed by that remembered pledge.

Next morning I emerged from my hut into what seemed like a fiesta. Many hundreds of Indians had flocked to the beach bringing fruit, flowers, fish and game, cotton mantles. They gave us the flowers, sold us the rest. They liked my green beads best, for they were the color of the jade they prized far above gold. I had just bought a large striped mantle for my mother when suddenly the captains were calling to us to don full armor, form ranks, and march to Cortés' great canopy, set up below the dune where the cannons were. Followed by dozens of retainers, Governor Birdcall had arrived.

Short and arrogant, with a beaked nose, a pectoral necklace of gold and jade, and a gold bracelet on his arm, he was otherwise naked except for his loincloth with richly decorated panels that hung to the ground front and back, baring his thighs. The presents he brought were even more impressive: bales of fine cotton mantles, a cape of featherwork so rich as almost to take my eyes from the basket heaped with objects of pure gold. A bushel of gold! These gifts, he said, were from his lord Moctezuma, to whom relays of his swift-footed couriers had brought news of our presence less than two days after our ships first appeared.

Cortés had his pages bring gifts in return: a carved chair and a crimson cap with a medallion of St. George killing the dragon. They seemed poor stuff to me in comparison to Moctezuma's rich presents. Perhaps Governor Birdcall thought so too. Staring at my gilded helmet, he came toward me, then said something to Malinche, who in turn spoke to Aguilar. "He says this casque is much like one worn by a certain god of theirs. He wants Moctezuma to see it."

"Give it to him," Cortés ordered me.

Bitterly resenting the loss, I removed it and held it out to the Indian governor. It gleamed in the sunlight as he took it from me. How sad it made me to know that I would never wear it again!

Cortés said to his interpreters "Tell the governor I will be very pleased if Moctezuma will return this helmet filled with the gold dust of his country." He smiled grimly. "For we Spaniards are afflicted with a disease of the heart for which gold is the only specific remedy." Governor Birdcall then asked the reason for our visit to this shore, and Cortés grew serious. "Tell him we are the envoys of a great monarch far across the ocean, and that we bring an important message which I must deliver to Moctezuma in person."

In person! That could only mean that Cortés intended to march up to Moctezuma's city where gold so abounded that the Aztec ruler could offer unknown visitors the precious gifts he had sent to us.

Cortés' proposition shattered Governor Birdcall's arrogant poise. First he showed astonishment, then drew haughtily away from Cortés. This demand to see Moctezuma had shocked him, he said. Who was Cortés to make such an unseemly request? Did we not know that Moctezuma was a divine being? Even the great nobles who served him his food did so with averted eyes, for no one could look upon the First Speaker of the Aztecs except at his express command. And it was not likely that he would so indulge an impertinent stranger from nowhere!

A fierce look came over Cortés' face. He bared his teeth in something akin to a smile, but his eyes were those of a falcon fixed on prey. How vital it was to him to penetrate whatever opposed him! In refusing passage to Moctezuma's kingdom, the Indian governor had only aroused a stronger desire to go there. A flowery invitation might have produced the opposite effect: Cortés might have suspected a trap and decided not to march one league westward. He turned to our interpreters. "Tell this minion that in the name of King Carlos of Spain I insist upon a meeting with Moctezuma in his city."

When Malinche heard this ultimatum from Aguilar, she stared at Cortés incredulously but turned and spoke to the governor. Reluctantly he said that he himself would bring Moctezuma our insolent message. "But I think you had better prepare to leave this shore, strangers, never to return for fear of his wrath!"

When the Aztec governor had gone and we broke ranks, I noticed one of his attendants still kneeling in the sand where he had been drawing pictures of us on a long strip of paper called *amatyl*. His small vivid drawings showed our ships, our cannons with puffs of smoke coming out of their mouths, and our cavalry— which Cortés had had Alvarado gallop up and down the beach to impress Governor Birdcall. The Indian artist used strong, bright colors, men being drawn with large heads and small bodies, but he had a remarkable ability to convey the essential nature of things he had never seen before. When Moctezuma looked at this picture-message, he would know more of us than we of him.

But we soon learned more. As the artist gathered up his paints to leave, I heard the formidable name of his ruler and went over to the canopy where Aguilar and Malinche faced Cortés, still seated in his armchair. Puertocarrero was standing at one side and young Captain Sandoval at the other. Sandoval was tall and muscular with a mop of curly brown hair and an exaggerated Castilian lisp which he said was a speech impediment. I liked him because he was forthright and put on no airs with the foot soldiers. As I approached he said to me, "We are learning things about thith Moctezuma that are thomewhat alarming."

Aguilar nodded. "You are not sufficiently impressed by his enormous power, Cortés. When Doña Marina was a child, her town was invaded by the Aztecs. Her father, the cacique, was a brave man but he surrendered."

"Her father was not Cortés," Cortés smiled.

Malinche spoke to Aguilar in the Mayan tongue. Aguilar continued: "It is not the Aztec custom to kill brave enemies. They sacrifice them to their war god, who likes the hearts of men of courage best. Do you want to die with your heart cut out atop the temple of Huitzilopotchli?"

"Is that the god who wears a helmet like the one Arturo just parted with?"

"No. That god is Quetzalcoatl, the great Feathered Serpent."

"A feathered serpent in a gilded helmet?" Again Cortés smiled. "A remarkable sight, I would say."

But Aguilar remained earnest. "Quetzalcoatl has two forms. He also appeared on earth in the form of a man. A tall man with white skin and a beard who appeared among the Indians here, many centuries ago."

"A white man here, centuries ago? That is most unlikely, since we are the first."

Aguilar ignored Cortés' joking tone. "In a land which had known only the most cruel and whimsical deities, Quetzalcoatl was a force for good. He taught the people better agriculture and architecture and metallurgy. He taught them that human sacrifice was evil."

"Then why did Grijalva find a temple full of dead victims?"

"Are the teachings of Christ followed by all the people of all the countries in Europe?" Aguilar asked gently. "While I was a prisoner there in Yucatán, where this god is known as Kukulcan, I pondered long about this gentle deity. I believe that some divinely inspired Indian priest must have imagined this kindly human god to whom he gave the ancient name of the Feathered Serpent so as to convey to men its transformation into a higher and nobler form. Even to pagans in the grip of fear and ignorance, God is kind and bestows a bright ray of His grace."

Cortés stared at him, then leaned back in his chair and laughed. "A white God! By God, that may prove a piece of very good fortune for us!"

His laughter seemed to puzzle Malinche, who turned and spoke to Aguilar, then walked away. Her angry disdain of Cortés needed no translator.

"What's wrong with her?" Cortés demanded of Aguilar.

"She says that any man who laughs at both Moctezuma and a deity is not only a fool but will soon be a dead one."

Cortés' face darkened and he started from his chair, glowering at Malinche's retreating back, but then he forced himself to sit down and lean back with feigned disconcern. "Aguilar, you must remind this little Indian that she is a woman and a slave and that these do not rebuke their masters." As Aguilar inclined his head respectfully and followed after Malinche, Cortés glanced up at Puertocárrero to remark "These tongues of mine have tongues of their own, it seems."

Puertocarrero shrugged. "Myself, I like a spicy woman better than the milk-and-honey sort. But as for Aguilar, I think his long captivity in Yucatán warped his mind. He seems to liken this Quetzal-cattle to Jesus Christ himself, which, if so, is blasphemy."

I hastily crossed myself, for I had been somewhat moved by Aguilar's compassion. I was sure that the bearded man engraved on my gold pendant was a likeness of the human form of this god. That Malinche so revered him placed her in a different light, and her soul's salvation, too. I had imagined that in order to turn to Christ she had only to abandon some ugly stone idols. But a pagan deity of some spiritual stature had claimed her worship, and to renounce him might prove difficult.

It was also clear that she no longer thought of us as supernatural beings, but whether the good Aguilar's teachings or a dead horse had accomplished this change I was not sure.

11

That day at sunset, Cortés abruptly solved the problem
the Indian women posed, surrounded by lusty men forbidden enjoyment of them by the law against any co-
habitation with heathen females. He had them baptized
en masse. They were assembled below the great dune
where our white cross stood, and our priests passed
among them chanting in Latin and sprinkling holy water
on their heads. Father Olmedo looked sad; he did not
think they yet understood our faith. Immediately after
this ceremony was over, I ran to Malinche and jubi-
lantly took her hands in mine, for she was a Christian
now, and no longer could I be denied the right to be
with her. Having no words of her language to explain
this, I held her hand and brought her with me to
Aguilar, begging his help as translator. But meanwhile,
little Father Diaz and Father Olmedo and some other
churchmen were herding the other Indian women together into a tight huddle. Grinning soldiers circled,
calling to the Indian girls to break away from the
priests. Then Diaz, spying Malinche apart from the
rest, came frowning toward us. "Tell her I'll come to
her hut tonight," I begged Aguilar.

"For what purpose?" he asked with a stern look.

"To serenade her," I improvised. "Just a serenade,
that's all."

As Aguilar spoke to Malinche, Father Diaz reached
us and struck away my hand that held hers. "Lustful
boy!" He placed himself between the two of us. His

fanatical eyes blazed up at me, two black embers. "The holy drops that mark her transformation from savage to Christian are not yet dry before you seek carnal congress!" He hurried her away from me, grasping her upper arm as though she were a felon.

"She said she will await your visit tonight," Aguilar told me in a low voice. I knew he did not like Father Diaz; few did. Ugly and sallow and with a vulture's breath, Diaz had an Inquisitor's soul, alert for the devil in the flesh of men better favored. Aguilar added, "Remember, Arturo, I expect of you a serenade, no more."

I went happily away, my plans now concrete. I would find the dwarf and borrow his guitar again, and then I would wait until the Indian women had supped and retired to their huts, near those of the priests. As I hurried to Cortés' big canopy to find the dwarf, my eyes searched the sky in hope of a lovers' moon and found it floating large and low above the embers of the brief tropical sunset. With anticipation tickling me, I envisioned the charming scene that would soon take place. After I had serenaded her in true Spanish style, she would come out of her hut and we would stroll in the moonlight beside the sound of the eternal waves. And then—who knew?

To my dismay, the dwarf was not to be found. Under the canopy were only Pepe, the other page, and Cortés' valet and his lean secretary, playing cards by the flame of a candle. They said Orteguilla had gone out to the flagship with Cortés a short time earlier. Then I saw the guitar leaning against a tent pole and told them I had come to borrow it. The secretary and the valet didn't care whether I took it or not, but Pepe was dubious. I persuaded him, promising to return it that same night, and stood there strumming and humming until the secretary invited me to practice elsewhere.

By now darkness had fallen, the round lovers' moon was beaming down among the dunes and cooking fires were alight, wafting toward me smells of supper, but it was not food I was hungry for. I decided to sing her a *mañanita,* even though it wasn't morning. She wouldn't know the difference, and I sang it particularly well. My jupon and breastplate seemed unsuitable to the night's dalliance, and I went to my hut and from my sea chest got out my russet hose and doublet and one of the white shirts my mother had made for me. Then I slung the guitar across my back by its strap and trotted eagerly to the row of huts where the Indian women lived, reflecting that one good thing that could be said for Torquemada was that Spanish priests, who had been most licentious before the reign of our Catholic Monarchs, openly keeping concubines and mistresses and reveling in the sins of the flesh, were now very averse to carnal pleasures. So they could be trusted to live in close proximity to the Indian women and to act as watchdogs. When I reached the women's huts, I stood in the moonlight midway down the row, the perfect troubadour, and began my serenade.

But she did not appear, and it had dawned on me that the huts were empty when from the doorway directly ahead of me peeped a short fat Indian woman with crossed eyes. She beamed at me.

"Malinche?" I asked.

Her smile faded and she pointed a stubby finger seaward. I turned and looked that way but could see only the dark shapes of our ships, far out on the moonlit water.

Filled with foreboding, I hurried off to find Aguilar, telling myself that Malinche might have left a message for me. I found him with the other priests sitting in a circle around a small fire. He was eating a broiled fish. "Where is Malinche?" I demanded.

He looked up at the guitar, my ruff, my anxious eyes. His were gentle. "Have you had any food? An Indian kindly brought us these fine fish to grill. They are very delicious, despite their odd appearance." The fish he was eating had large spines along the backbone, very white flesh. "Have one, and then we can talk."

"No fish! Where is Malinche?"

My harsh demand had drawn the attention of the other churchmen, who looked at me reprovingly except for Juan Diaz, who wore a mean, small grin. Aguilar sighed, stood up, brushed a few bits of fish from his cassock and led me away from the other diners. "Try not to be too disappointed, Arturo." His voice was kindly, as if he spoke to a child who had demanded a missing toy.

"Where is she?"

"You must try to remember that man proposes, but God disposes."

"Where is she?"

"On the flagship."

"Why?"

He sighed. "Cortés is giving the Indian women to his various captains. Except for the fat one with the crossed eyes who is to be our servant."

In the rush of agony that filled me I found his calmness infuriating. "God disposes? Cortés disposes! You men of God baptized these women! But now you let him turn them into prostitutes."

My anger did not dismay him or bring me the reprimand I deserved. "No, they are to be *barraganas.*"

"Concubines!"

"A harsh word. Their status is somewhere between mistress and morganatic wife. This is preferable, I feel, to the licentious promiscuity of mere camp-followers."

"And Cortés, of course, got Malinche!"

Aguilar patted my shoulder soothingly. "If you loved her as much as you think, then you would find it in your heart to rejoice if she should find herself under the protection of our general."

"Aguilar, you know precisely nothing of love!" My voice broke on the last word and I turned and ran away across the sands, my borrowed guitar thumping against my back with a hollow sound, the voice of my loss.

I found myself at the foot of the high dune on which our white cross gleamed in the moonlight. I fell to my knees. I prayed that divine intervention would keep Cortés from keeping the woman I loved. "For now she's a baptized Christian, Lord. Cortés has a wife in Cuba. Malinche will only be his mistress. But if you let me have her, I will marry her! I swear it! Indian though she is, I will make her an honest woman!" Far above, the white cross shone serene, and above it the evening star hung brilliant in the sky. As I crossed myself came the fleeting thought of my mother's shocked face if I were to bring home an Indian bride, however beautiful, but I got up from my knees feeling a little better.

A hoarse voice spoke behind me. "He wants his guitar back."

I whirled. The young page Pepe stood there panting. Had he heard my prayer? Apparently not, for he pouted, "I knew I shouldn't have let you take it, and now a mariner just rowed in from the flagship to get it, because Cortés is holding a fiesta there for his captains and the Indian women. He wants Orteguilla to sing and play for them."

Inspiration struck me. "I'll return it myself and I'll take any blame for borrowing it without permission."

"That's only fair," he agreed with some relief.

As I walked to the shore where the mariner waited in a ship's boat, I turned to glance back at the cross. It seemed to me that this chance to go to where Malinche was, coming just after my prayer, was most uncanny. But what, precisely, could I do or say that would change the general's mind?

The mariner at the oars was a cheerful young fellow with a tasseled knit cap. He said, "Well, I guess the captains are all happy tonight, the lucky goats."

"And Cortés, too, having kept for himself the prettiest Indian of all."

"Doña Marina? The general hasn't taken any woman for himself. He gave Doña Marina to Puertocarrero."

Puertocarrero! Of course! The gold buttons from his cloak to buy a horse, and now another mount, my Malinche! In agony I imagined Puertocarrero embracing her. I clutched at the hope of error. "Are you sure?"

"I was right there on deck when Puertocarrero asked for her."

"But didn't she have anything to say about it?" I cried.

"She wasn't there. It was right after that I rowed ashore to bring the priests Cortés' written order for the Indian women. I waited while the priests rounded them up, two boats full, and none for me." Oarlocks creaked while I imagined Malinche's similar journey to the flagship. "How about a tune on that guitar to make the rowing lighter?" he asked.

And so it was to a mariner bending his back at the oars that I sang my serenade intended for Malinche, not without that twinge at life's bitter irony common to even lesser poets. While I sang, my mind was feverishly busy. What could I say to Cortés that might change Malinche's destiny? As I built up in my head a fervent denunciation of him for having baptized the Indian women only to make them concubines against their inclination, I wondered if I could summon up the courage to deliver it. Although Cortés made a point of treating his foot soldiers in a man-to-man fashion, he did not welcome criticism of his decisions. He had put in irons one Velásquez man too loud of mouth. And supposing I did let my anger out, even made Cortés aware that his disposal of the Indian women had been high-handed, was it likely that he would snatch Malinche away from Puertocarrero? And even if he did, would he then give her to a mere foot soldier with his blessing? I sat gritting my teeth so hard my jaws ached. I had set myself an impossible task. But I had to try.

When we reached the flagship I climbed the rope ladder, guitar strapped to my back. Two very different scenes drew my eyes. At the taffrail, several mariners were leaning out to scan the black water by the light of the ship's lantern one held at arm's end, giving the impression that someone had fallen overboard. In contrast, from the gathering on the foredeck came the robust voices of the captains singing with wine-induced sentimentality about the river Duero. Most were seated or recumbent, heads to the low rails, feet pointing inward, their Indian women beside them. I mounted a hatch for a better view, saw neither Malinche nor Puertocarrero. A lantern shed its dim yellow light on

the wine cask at which Captain Olid was filling his cup,
a grin on his black-bearded face. He swaggered back
to his Indian *barragana* to lie beside her and smother
her face with his beard, clutching her breast. I turned
my eyes away as he roughly pulled up her skirt and I
saw her pale brown naked leg helpless under the hand
that convulsively kneaded the captive thigh.

Now, in the center of the cozy group, Orteguilla was
standing on his head, kicking his legs in the air and
singing a bawdy song about the joys of fornication—
written, I happened to know, half a century earlier
by a padre who kept several concubines, one a nun
of the same order. Someone belched loudly. Someone
laughed. Where was Malinche?

Cortés burst out of his cabin below the foredeck; his
frowning face offered a sudden contrast to the carnal
scene just above. He could not have failed to see me
standing there on the hatch with my guitar, but for all
the attention he gave me I might have been one of the
white gulls wheeling overhead. "Any luck, Pedro?" he
called, striding toward midship.

To Pedro Alvarado I was also invisible. He passed
me with a lantern, shaking his blond head. "I searched
the hold, the entire vessel, every nook, every coil of
rope. She's not aboard, and that's for certain." His
high-pitched voice exaggerated his alarm.

Mine was greater. She? Who? Malinche?

I ran to Cortés, stood face-to-face with him. "Who
is he talking about?"

A glance at the guitar evidently reminded him why
I was there. "Doña Marina has disappeared. It begins
to look as if she may have jumped overboard." His
voice rose; he turned to wave a fist in the direction of
his own cabin. "And may God rot the balls of that
hot-prick blunderer!"

Two of the mariners I had seen scanning the water
approached. "No sign of her," one said. "Not a splash.
Not a bubble."

Cortés wheeled abruptly and headed toward his
cabin. I followed, such a welter of emotions churning

in me that my head seemed to be revolving on my
shoulders. Cortés ducked his head to enter; I stood
in the doorway. The small, low-ceilinged room was
dimly lighted, but I saw Puertocarrero getting up from
the floor. He groaned, holding his head, and sat down
heavily on the edge of the bunk, elbows on knees, head
between his hands. Blood still trickled out of his tousled
hair in a narrow rill down his forehead and one cheek.
From his open pantaloons dangled the organ Cortés
had cursed, limp as a sea slug. Becoming aware of what
he was exhibiting, he tucked it away and closed the gap,
moaning to distract our attention. Looking up, he saw
Cortés, fists on hips, regarding him with plain disgust.
"That vixen!" Puertocarrero pointed to the floor.

There, serene face upward, lay a pretty painted statue
of the Holy Virgin. Of wood, and about three handbreadths high, it had stood atop the small altar in the
corner. "The Virgin?" Cortés demanded.

"That's what your Doña Marina tried to brain me
with! She backed into the corner, seized that holy
statue, and tried her best to kill me!"

"And what did you do to her?" Cortés demanded.

Puertocarrero looked up, saw the glare on Cortés'
face, and lowered his head to his hands again, wiping
a drop of blood from the end of his nose with the back
of one of them. "Nothing! I did nothing that a Spanish
countess would take exception to! Doña Marina is
crazy, that's all. Don't blame me for that."

"I know what you did! You dragged her in here
while I was aft with the pilot. You attacked her like a
satyr!"

"*I* attacked *her?* You see me here bleeding to death
and say *I* attacked *her?* You have it backward. *She* attacked *me!*"

"Good!" I shouted, coming at him. "You *pendejo,*
backing her into a corner with your penis waving, what
would any decent woman do?" I whirled on Cortés.
"He treated her like a whore, but she was no whore,
and now you know it! Do you think God wanted a

baptized Christian Indian woman pronged like a strumpet? Do you condone that orgy on the foredeck?"

His face clenched, eyes blazing at me. I saw my doom: weeks in irons and maybe a flogging. But sudden caution shadowed his anger. I knew he had remembered the Royal Council of the Indies and its solemn mandate that Indian women were not to be raped by Spanish soldiers. He knew how swiftly I could spread word of Doña Marina's ill treatment; the Velásquez adherents would make the most of it.

In a strained voice he said, "I understand your outrage. I feel it myself."

"Cortés!" Alvarado's cry made us both turn toward the open door. "Come here, for God's sake."

On deck we found him pointing out over the moon-dappled water. "Look!"

My heart dropped into an abyss as dark as that sea. The triangular fin of a shark passed very near the side of the flagship, moving silent, swift, and deadly across the very patch of ocean into which Malinche might have plunged. "Over and done," Alvarado said. "The woman jumped, the woman drowned, or if she didn't that big *tiburón* or friends of his most likely got her."

Cortés' fist pounded the rail. "No!" He turned to Alvarado, his eyes wild and willful. "Search the ship again! She's clever. She could have outwitted you."

I saw that a very young mariner, most likely a cabin boy, had approached. *"Con permiso,* Cortés, sir?"

Cortés turned and glared down at him; the boy stared up. He swallowed. He tried to speak but his frail voice broke.

"Say it!" Cortés commanded.

"She's not on the ship, Cortés, sir. Doña Marina came out of your cabin, Cortés, sir, with her skirt tore and flying out either side and her bodice all tore open too so you could see her *pechos* all bare and she ran to the rail and went over and I heard the splash."

I heard it too, inside my head. Louder than Cortés' voice saying with terrible control "Why, then, did you not tell me this at the time? Right away?"

Voiceless, the boy stared up. Cortés' arm moved woodenly. His big hand came to rest on the boy's shoulder. He squeezed it as if to press the words out of him. "Why didn't you tell me this when she jumped?"

The boy swallowed. In a voice no more than a whisper he said, "It was *your* cabin she came out of, Cortés, sir."

Cortés released him and the boy backed away, then turned and ran. Cortés looked at me with stricken eyes. "How could he understand that I want no woman while my foot soldiers and mariners have none? That I choose to share their privation?"

"Privation?" asked a merry voice. Captain Francisco Olid had descended from the foredeck, winecup in one hand, an arm around his Indian concubine. Even in my trance of shock and misery I became aware that the incipient orgy on the foredeck had been broken up by the shouting and running about. Most of them were on their feet, the captains looking down at Cortés.

"I want these Indian women treated with decency!" he called up to them, and I saw Olid's arm leave his concubine's waist. "Or you can expect my very great displeasure."

Oh, very late for the warning, I thought bitterly. Too late! "You've locked the door after the loss," I muttered.

Orteguilla had joined us. "Loss?" he asked pertly. "All seems gains here tonight, if not for a somewhat short fellow like myself."

"Doña Marina jumped overboard," I blurted.

Cortés' look silenced further comment. He said, "Captain Puertocarrero was not sufficiently aware of her great modesty. And so I am without an interpreter." He reached out for the guitar; I unstrapped it; he handed it to Orteguilla. Catching his master's mood, Orteguilla at once strummed several brooding chords and began to sing a pavane. Tears filled my eyes as Cortés turned to me and said in a low voice, "Good night, Arturo. I trust your loyalty and discretion." He speared me with a searching glance. I turned abruptly toward the rail to hide my tears.

The mariner who had brought me pulled away from the flagship and began at once asking questions, but I could not have answered even had I wished for the lump of sorrow in my throat. When I turned and looked back at the ship I saw the chastened revelers clustered middeck like mourners at a grave below the dark crucifixes of the masts, their sails furled. Cortés stood alone by the rail staring toward the distant shore. A seagull swept low above him with a harsh cry.

12

As I crossed the wide sweep of water toward the beach where a scatter of campfires glowed no bigger than fireflies, a cruel grief tortured me. I might have passed Malinche after she leaped from the flagship as I was rowed toward it in this same boat. And she, in that black water and in need of rescue, would not have seen it as a source of help, containing as it did two Spaniards. Then I remembered that shark and agony tore at my guts, for I knew she might not have lived long enough ever to have seen the ship's boat in which I had sat trying to think how to get her away from Puerto-carrero.

The shark did not get her, I told myself. That was only Alvarado's idea, but sharks do not attack swimmers as a rule, not unless they are bleeding. I smiled grimly to myself: it was not she who had bled, but Puertocarrero.

While these thoughts tormented or comforted me, I kept scanning the water hopefully, yet also I remembered the drowned woman washed in from a shipwreck off Cuba when I was a child. She had floated face-down, her long hair moving gently in the clear green water. With a thrill of horror I thought I saw a woman floating like that, but it was only a log with a branch like a human arm and seaweed clinging to it and floating like that woman's hair.

"The current's strong tonight," the mariner said, and I saw that the campfires were no longer directly ahead but to the left of the boat's prow. "It's a little arm of the big ocean current that sweeps in south of Cuba from the Atlantic, then around its western tip and out eastward again to the north of the West Indies. There's a couple of oars stashed beside you and I'll thank you to give me a hand, or we'll reach the beach so far north of the camp you'll spend half the night walking back to it."

Aware that he had just given me another reason to believe that I had lost Malinche forever, I did as he asked. We were able to correct our course somewhat after we reached shallower water where the current had little pull, but when I heard the crash of breakers and saw their white manes, the huts and campfires were no longer visible because of the distance and the intervening dunes. "You'll stretch your legs a bit," the mariner said, as a wave lifted the boat and sped it toward the beach.

Wet to the knees on that dark, deserted shore I watched him row away and then started toward camp, walking on the hard-packed wet sand for better speed. Looking landward, I saw above the mangroves that edged the beach the tops of palms and the moonlit *teocalli* atop an Indian temple, and I knew it marked the town of the natives who had come to the beach to bring us food, help us build our huts, and sell us their handiwork. I stopped in my tracks. If Malinche had managed to swim ashore, would this town not seem to her a place of refuge? Would it not be natural for her to throw herself on the mercy of people of her own race rather than again trust Spaniards? I stood pondering this notion to the forlorn and hollow crash of a breaker, the long sigh of spilled waters withdrawing into the sea. The sound reminded me that it had taken two pairs of arms to land the rowboat even at this distance from camp. A swimmer would be taken by the current even farther to the north.

I turned and headed northward, proving that hope can put out a frail blossom even on sand. To keep it from withering I called her name from time to time: her own name, not the one Cortés had given her. Only the waves answered me.

But after I had gone more than half a league, my heart gave a great bound and hope put out a hundred blossoms more. Far ahead on the shining sand at the water's edge a human figure stood. A woman, scantily clad in a few tatters of clothing that did not hide the curve of a thigh, bare arms, a naked breast. She had not yet seen me and bent above the mound of seaweed beside her to disentangle a long strand. My urge was to run toward her, shouting her name, but I forced myself to come nearer so that she could see who I was. As I closed the distance between us, she draped the strand of kelp, thick with flat gleaming leaves, around her neck, arranging it to hide her breasts. I knew then that the rags she wore were rags of seaweed to replace the clothing torn by Puertocarrero as he tried to rape her, and now abandoned in the sea as she swam toward the shore.

"Malinche!" I cried, and ran toward her, my arms stretching wide of their own accord to enfold her. Now I was close enough to see the gleam of the little snake-man pendant and to see the waterdrops still shining on her bare skin. "It's me! Arturo!"

No answering smile came to her lips. A long strand of her wet black hair hung down over the left side of her face. One dark cold eye looked at me. I saw then that she was spent. Her whole body was clenched on itself, knees clamped and shoulders hunched. As I neared, she crossed her fists over her breast and took a step back. She was not looking at me, but at something beyond me. I turned my head and saw the palms of the Indian village, the tip of its upper temple.

I spoke gently. "I only want to help you, Malinche." As her eyes met mine again she raised her arm to brush aside the strand of hair that hid the other, and the curves of that arm and the grace of the gesture belonged to a statue I once saw, except that this arm was not cold marble but warm flesh. With a sudden alertness a lustful imp between my legs announced that it, too, wished to help her in the only way it knew. The urge to embrace her came over me so strongly that I could almost feel her against me, cold seaweed, warm smooth skin, breasts pressed against my russet doublet under which my heart galloped toward hers. "I know what happened on the ship. I assure you that you won't have to go back to Puertocarrero, ever." As I spoke, doubt struck me, but then I told myself Cortés would surely not give her to him again.

Her eyes had left me to gaze again at the Indian temple. I turned my head. The uppermost tip of the white-painted *teocalli* pointed heavenward, quite as though blood had never spilled below it. "Aztecs," she said, looking at me once more.

I dared a step closer. "You don't belong with them. You're a Christian now. You belong with us."

Her voice was low but harsh. "Puertocarrero Christian."

"Cortés is very angry with him." I made a motion of cutting my throat with my forefinger. "Cortés did not know he would do what he did to you. Cortés was very sad when he thought you were drowned. And I—oh, Malinche, my whole world came to an end!"

She appeared to consider what I had said, head tilted to one side. Between the amber leaves tempting glimpses of firm flesh allured me. Battling down the urge to touch her, clasp her, roll with her on soft white sand, both of us joyous and aflame with the desire only I felt, I suddenly thought of the more than five hundred Spanish soldiers encamped to the south. My God, I thought, if any of them were here and saw her like this, they'd probably kill me to get at her! Thus I transferred my own desire to other, evil fellows lacking my own restraint and decency.

The first thing to do was to get some clothes on her. Yes, that is first and foremost, I told myself. She can't run around half-clad in some seaweed. I remembered the striped shawl I had bought for my mother from the Indians here. "I have a rebozo," I said. "At my hut. You can have it." I pantomimed wrapping myself in a large shawl.

She nodded, looking down at her improvised clothing. She raised her head and looked once more at the Indian temple. She looked into my eyes. "I go with you."

My hut had been built at the north side of camp, very near the mangroves. We made our way to it through them to avoid being seen, and I remembered how I had pursued her the day we met, which now seemed very long ago. When I went in to get the shawl, she remained outside; I found it and brought it out to her, bowing toward the open doorway to indicate that she might dress herself within. I stood with my back to the hut and imagined seaweed draperies falling to the sandy floor, leaving her naked as Aphrodite, that goddess who had also risen from the waves. To blot out this image and to subdue desire I congratulated myself on having the strength of will to dominate my carnal nature. Feeling somewhat noble and very pure, I saw a pure and luminous symbol against the dark starred sky: our great white cross on its high dune, bright in the moonlight. It reminded me of the gratitude I should feel to the good Lord who had brought her safely to shore. I crossed myself and sank to my knees.

With this act, a clear light seemed to shine in my brain as if reflected from that white cross. I saw the way out of her plight, a way that would not leave her dependent on the mood of Cortés when he learned she was alive!

A sound behind me made me turn. She stood just outside the hut, the striped mantle tied at one shoulder and wrapped around her body, held in place by a seaweed belt. She looked less like a Christian newly baptized than like a heathen goddess. I took off my rosary, stood up, and offered it to her. "It was blessed by the archbishop," I said. "Put it on." Obediently she hung it around her neck. The silver cross gleamed below her gold snake-man. I took her hand and led her to the dune where our cross stood. I pointed upward. "Wait up there for me." She nodded, and I ran to the huts where the priests slept and called, "Father Olmedo!"

In a moment his long pale face peered out of a doorway. "Yes, my son?" He offered no censure for waking him, just blinked at me with kindly bemused patience.

"Is the dune where the cross stands holy ground?" I asked.

"Holy? Why, yes, certainly."

"Like a church or cathedral?"

"Since we have no other, yes. But why did you wake me at such a late hour to ask me this question?"

"Because a Christian is waiting there to claim the right of sanctuary!"

As we hurried to Malinche I told him everything. She had trusted me; she knelt at the foot of the cross, shoulders wearily slumped, head drooping. When I called to her she stood up, staring down at us. Father Olmedo held out his hand to her, beckoned her toward him, his tonsure like a small moon. She looked at me; I nodded. She descended the dune and trustingly put her hand in the padre's. "Father Aguilar can now explain to her that she is safe, and that the Church will protect the virtue she has suffered so much to preserve."

As they went toward Aguilar's hut she turned her head and looked back at me. *"Gracias."* Her look was soft, and she even managed a little smile.

I went to my hut radiant with triumph and with joy. Triumph over my lower being, the part Satan rules, and triumph over Cortés as well, for now he could not decide the fate of my beloved. Joy came from that one word of thanks, that sweet smile she had sent me over her shoulder. I fell asleep to dream of her.

Alas, I did not wake until the sun was high. No morning trumpet aroused me, nor did El Galán. I dressed myself and hurried to the priests' huts. Too late. Malinche was gone.

Father Olmedo looked pleased as he told me that he had gone out to the flagship at dawn in the canoe of an obliging Indian fisherman, had told Cortés that Malinche was under the protection of the Church; he had censured him on two scores: for having been so hasty in baptizing the Indian women and for not having warned Puertocarrero in advance that his lechery must be controlled in his dealings with Malinche. "Only minutes after the Indian women joined us at Tabasco, Captain Puertocarrero was making lewd advances, to which I put a stop. But Cortés, as I can well understand, is in a difficult position. Puertocarrero must not lose face with the men he must continue to captain. We have reached an agreement, which Doña Marina has accepted: although it will be generally believed that she is under Puertocarrero's protection, she will actually be under the personal protection of Cortés." He nodded at me, pleased.

"Of Cortés!"

He hastily added, "Oh, no carnal knowledge is to be involved in this arrangement. No, no. She is to him his valued interpreter, nothing more."

"And where is she now?"

"On the flagship. She left only minutes before you arrived. Cortés sent for her. He wishes to offer her his personal apology for what she suffered. Captain Puertocarrero will also offer his. Father Jeronimo Aguilar is with her, I should add."

My fury with myself for oversleeping was so intense that I groaned aloud.

"Are you ill, my son?" the good padre asked.

"What makes you think he'll keep his hands off her?" I demanded.

"Córtes?" He looked shocked.

"Puertocarrero! He's a satyr! A lecherous goat!"

"He's also a caballero with noble antecedents. He will keep his word. I must add, my son, that such violent language concerning one of this expedition's captains does not become the young man whose Christian concern for this poor young Indian woman has borne such good fruit."

I took the censure and the praise and went in search of food to break my fast. I had lost the chance to ask her to accept me as her protector due to a delicious dream in which her brief visit to my hut the night before had been of longer duration and had ended less virtuously. But I soon enough came to realize that Cortés would never have agreed to let me have her, even if she herself wished it. With hundreds of woman-less foot soldiers, could he endow one of them with a *barragana?*

But that might change in time. There might, before too long, be enough Christianized female Indians here so that every single soldier and mariner could have one. And in the meantime her well-established chastity would keep her safe for me. I still had hopes of getting her, and at barely eighteen hope is nearly as good as gold itself, or the real embraces of a woman clasped only in dreams.

One thing troubled me. Might she be too chaste? She had violently rejected a caballero with a horse and noble lineage, and I had neither. But there is a caballero more powerful than any other, and his name is Don Oro. The gold I had come here to get became commingled in my mind with the woman I wanted as much. Gold would make of me a future hero called Don Arturo by everyone in Havana. And it would make me equally worthwhile in Malinche's eyes. For, as my father once said, success is a seducer few women argue with, just as failure is a lapse they find hard to forgive. And gold is a proof of success as universal as it is rare.

So far I had only a thin gold medallion of modest value and had lost a helmet worth much more. I went bareheaded under the blazing sun that darkened my skin and paled my hair but could not wither the dreams of gold, glory, and Malinche rooted inside my skull. I would follow our banner; I had faith; I would conquer. Don Oro would one day be my humble servant and Malinche would share my blissful bed.

PART III

vvvvvvvvvvvvvvvvvvvvvvvvvvvvvvvvvvvvvvvvvvvvvvvvvv

FIRE ON WATER
May 7, 1519—August 12, 1519

13

I got back my helmet after all. It was presented to Cortés, filled with gold dust. That, of course, I did not get.

Only a week after he had left us, Governor Birdcall returned with another of Moctezuma's governors from a nearby province. This Cualpopoca looked amazingly like Cortés, although darker and lacking a beard. Among the retinue of lesser Indians were several priests with long, tangled hair and black robes who chanted and swung incense burners to waft smoke over Cortés where he sat in his armchair below his canopy. After the Indians had knelt before him to touch their hands to the ground and bring them to their foreheads, a file of porters with baskets and bundles on their backs came forward to lay their burdens at his feet. It took six men to carry one flat package tied to a litter.

The extraordinary richness of Moctezuma's gifts astounded us all. Spread out on straw mats in the sunlight, a feast for avarice, those treasures drew our awed gasps, our cries of admiration. There was a golden disk as big as a cartwheel, engraved with intricate symbols in a circular pattern. A silver disk, somewhat smaller, lay by it like the moon beside the sun. There were many golden animals, dozens of necklaces and pendants, a large gold bow with a sheaf of golden arrows, crowns of gold and silver with plumes of green feathers and some golden fans. As though for variety there were at least a hundred mantles gorgeously woven of more colors than any rainbow and two curious feather capes that gleamed as richly as gems. But this was a farewell present. Moctezuma would not grant us an audience.

Cortés forced a smile to hide disappointment. "Then perhaps we will visit Moctezuma without an invitation."

Malinche frowned and made a vehement comment. Aguilar turned to Cortés: "She refuses to translate this boast. She says your small army could never enter his city by force. To pretend so is foolish."

Cortés barely concealed his displeasure. "My interpreter has never heard of Caesar: divide and conquer. We may manage to find some Indian allies." He added hastily, "Don't have her translate that, of course. Have her thank Moctezuma for his gifts and say that I return the same warm and friendly feelings that prompted him to send them." This done, he added, "And I now repeat my request for an invitation to visit Moctezuma."

With great reluctance, Governor Birdcall agreed to convey this message to his ruler.

Until an answer came, there was nothing for us to do but wait there on the beach, attacked by mosquitoes, dazed by ferocious heat, none of us knowing if Governor Birdcall would actually keep his grudging promise or how Moctezuma would react to Cortés' persistence if he did. The Indians of the area came to the beach in fewer and fewer numbers and ceased to bring us food, so we were reduced to grubbing for mussels and crabs to augment slim rations of salt pork. Our cassava bread, though it lasts for months, was now full of weevils. Two dozen men fell sick of a fever that turned them, yellow, and six died. A wind rose and blew down three of the wooden crosses that marked their graves. And mutiny was beginning to stir with the blowing sand that stung our faces. The Velásquez men wanted to leave at once for Cuba. The rest of us wanted to wait and see what Moctezuma's answer would be.

Cortés tried to placate the grumblers by sending a ship north under command of a friend of Velásquez named Captain Montejo, with orders to explore the coast to the north for a pleasanter site; he returned in

less than a week to report that there was a good harbor
fifteen leagues away, near a large Indian town. The day
we learned this, Governor Birdcall returned with Moctezuma's final refusal to see us.

The diplomatic wording did not conceal a threat:
"Moctezuma regrets that he cannot enjoy a personal
interview. The distance to my capital is great and beset
with many dangers. You must return now to your own
land with the gifts that prove my friendly disposition
toward you, thus far."

The next day not a single Indian came to our camp.

When Cortés assembled the army below the dune
where the cannons were and told us he wanted to go
north to the harbor Montejo found, his words fell flat.
After a brief silence, a voice shouted "Back to Cuba!"
In a moment it was a thunderous chant as a hundred
voices joined the first. "Back to Cuba! Back to Cuba!"

Young Captain Sandoval started a counter cry: "On
to Mexico! To Mexico!"

Others cried: "North to Montejo's bay!"

Cortés signaled the priests to ring the bell for vesper
service, and its persistent sound finally silenced the
cacophony. We knelt below the cross but this respite
meant nothing. On expeditions such as ours, cohesion
was vital. Grijalva's men had forced him to take them
home. Columbus had to lie to prevent a mutiny. Cortés,
with his divided army, was in trouble.

Nor were the Velásquez men the only ones who took
seriously Moctezuma's request that we leave: soldiers
loyal to Cortés were beginning to agree with them. We
now had more gold than all previous expeditions together. Why not thank God and go, while we were still
alive to do so? "There's no point to squatting here with
empty bellies and sand in our crotches," Juan Morla
said one night as Alvarado's company sat around a
campfire waiting for a cauldron of mussels to boil.
"Cortés ought to divide the gold up fair and square and
sail for home. God knows my woman will be glad to
see my face, and for once I'll be glad to see hers." There
was laughter and grumbling assent.

I said, misquoting the Bible: "Cowards flee where no man pursueth."

"*You* make brave bones here, Pollito. I'll be a rich coward in Cuba."

During the next two days the heat got even worse and five more men died, yet Cortés clung to his desire to maintain a beachhead on this new continent. His captains went among us trying to convince the dubious that our best and only move was northward to Montejo's bay. Above the noise of arguments the stinging wind rose again, the sand blew into our eyes, and it seemed that the very air and beach were hostile to our presence.

Nor was I comforted by even a glimpse of Malinche. Cortés had given her a bed on the flagship, fearing that she might succumb to the fever that raged on shore and leave him without any means of communicating with the Indians of the town near Montejo's bay, assuming he could ever manage to get his army to go there. An angry group of Velásquez's men became so loud in their demands to be sent home that Cortés put them in irons until they cooled down. I said to El Galán: "Why not let them go back to Cuba, and any others afraid to stay? That would leave Cortés with a loyal army, even if a smaller one."

El Galán shook his head. "It would leave him without stature as a commander. He cannot permit dissenters to have their way. He has to hold his army together, although I confess I don't see just how. At the moment, some diversion is needed badly."

A diversion was provided that same day when Cortés had his loyal captains talk with their men, reminding us that we had agreed in the contract with Velásquez to found a colony. If we returned to Cuba without doing this, we could expect the governor's severe censure, no matter how much gold we brought. Pedro Alvarado talked to us in a friendly, persuasive way, the flames of a campfire lighting his frank, open face and his short red-gold hair and beard. "The clever thing to do is to found a colony—on paper. Elect a regular town council and let them choose the town's captain and chief justice. That way a colony will legally exist, even if we don't actually get around to building a city hall." He winked and grinned and we all laughed, for the idea of getting around the letter of the law like this would please any Spaniard.

"Villa Rica de la Vera Cruz!" With a triumphant smile, Cortés announced next day the name he had chosen for our paper colony. All of us liked the sound of it, and soon shortened it to Vera Cruz. Until El Galán pointed it out to me, I did not realize that this Rich Town of the True Cross was a child born of our expedition, autonomous. Founded in the name of Carlos of Spain, it could serve to free Cortés from Velásquez's authority, for Cortés, of course, was chosen by the council as captain and chief justice, whereas the name of Velásquez figured precisely nowhere. Cortés appointed two mayors: Puertocarrero and Montejo— whose loyalty Cortés won when he trusted him with that ship in which he could easily have sailed to Cuba instead of discovering the bay to which Cortés hoped to lead us.

But not all the Velásquez men were as pliable as Montejo. Another diversion was needed, so Cortés named fifty of those dissenters as a special task force and sent them off on a reconnaissance mission along with Alvarado's company. We were to explore to the north five leagues to see if we met resistance or friendly tribes. Although it made me nervous to probe unknown terrain with so many discontented soldiers marching with me, I was glad to leave the sand behind for a while. A march of a few leagues took us onto a pleasant savannah planted with fields of maize and of maguey cactus, hostile-looking plants, each one a silent green explosion of thick, spearlike leaves. We soon came to a deserted village with a large warehouse full of clay pots of honey. After poking his finger in one to see what it contained, Alvarado licked it and reminded us that Cortés had forbidden any looting, but he left that pot open and a good many fingers were licked before we marched to the village temple. Alvarado decided to climb the pyramid for the view it would offer, and I was among the first of the soldiers to reach the *teocalli* atop where the idols were.

In its doorway I stopped, staring. On a blood-stained stone block was a human torso slashed open in a gaping hole below the rib cage, from which had flowed so much blood that it filled the hollow of the altar and ran down its side. The arms and legs were cut off. The heart, torn from the body, lay on a stone dish at the feet of an idol with a grinning skull face of dull gold. Lying all about were large pieces of paper steeped in dried blood, for what purpose I could not guess. The stone walls were layered with blood, old and black, dried and brown, fresh and red. The stagnant air smelled of butchery; nausea crept up my throat. I turned and pushed my way past the soldiers behind me as vomit filled my mouth.

Nausea had spared me another shocking sight. Alvarado told Cortés about it after we marched back to the beach. His face was red with righteous wrath. "Hiding in that temple I found a young boy dressed in women's clothing, and small clay statues showing the priests in the act of sodomy, and the boy made it plain that he had been so used and others like him. Oh, they are truly servants of Satan, those priests!" I did not know what sodomy was, but he showed one of the small clay statues he had brought back with him and it very much astonished me and made the word's meaning clear, although at the time I believed in my innocence that it was an act practiced only by Indian priests.

The news of that bloodied temple spread through the camp in an hour and fanned the fires of dissension to a new heat. The Velásquez minority were against staying even another day, and on learning of the sodomy our little padre Juan Diaz turned livid and went at once to Cortés. "If the rural Indians of that little village are so cruel and depraved, what must the Aztecs be like, whom they serve and fear? The men who wish to leave this place of evil should be permitted to go, in the name of God and all the saints!" And so the diversion of the march Cortés had ordered to keep the grumblers occupied had only intensified his problem. He looked sad that day. His page, Pepe, had been the twelfth man to die of the fever, and was buried with the rest.

This news alarmed me for Malinche, because Pepe had died on the flagship. I went up to Cortés after Juan Diaz had spoken up for the dissenters and asked if she was all right. "Yes," he said. "So far." He sighed. "That was all I needed. Severed limbs, excised hearts, and sodomy. And a Catholic priest who refuses to see that such depravity and cruelty should all the more move us as Christians to rescue these poor Indians from their hideous religion and bring them to God."

I said, "If you had seen that temple, I think you would be less concerned about the salvation of their souls than about saving our lives."

"In Cuba I saw humans barbecued on spits by the Caribs, but Cuba is now a Spanish colony and so, with God's help, will this continent be!"

Cortés' luck changed abruptly the next day. Our camp was visited by five strange Indians, very different in appearance from the half-naked natives ruled by Governor Birdcall. These wore full pantaloons like the Turks' and over them loose cotton robes. In their swaying earlobes were inserted huge plugs of gold, smaller ones in slits in their upper lips. Cortés came running to seat himself in his armchair under his canopy and learn why they were here and who they were. Aguilar and Malinche translated. She was dressed in the same kind of loose tunic and underskirt as when I first saw her, but these were emerald-green.

These Indians were of the great Totonac nation, they said, and came from a city to the north called Zempoalla. Itinerant traders had told their ruler of our great victory at Tabasco and they had been sent to see if we were as powerful and remarkable as rumor suggested. At this point Cortés paused to order several captains to offer a display of horsemanship, which awed the visitors. They revealed that their great cacique had long resented the heavy yoke of Moctezuma's rule, remembering when the Totonacs had lived in freedom and happiness. "He desires very much to meet with you and will welcome you to his capital city. We will escort you there."

Cortés lost no time in addressing the soldiers who had gathered to watch. "Perhaps those cowards among you who were so anxious to scuttle home to Cuba will now be willing to go with me and meet these rich potential allies." Every eye was riveted on the great gold earrings of the five Zempoallans who stood beside him.

Further questioning of the visitors had revealed that the town near Montejo's harbor was inhabited by Totonacs and was ruled by the same cacique who wanted to meet us. Cortés decided that our fleet would sail there with the treasures Moctezuma had sent, the Indian women, and the soldiers too ill to go on foot. The rest of us would march to Zempoalla.

Two days later, without a backwards glance, we left behind the little huts that had sheltered us. Of all the Indians who had once treated us so kindly, none appeared to watch us march away.

One thing bothered me. I had assumed that the village with the bloodied temple and its catamites belonged to Governor Birdcall's Indians. But we learned, to my uneasiness, that it was in fact a Totonac town, at the southern border of their territory.

But Zempoalla was a joy to see, a city of greenery and flower gardens whose civil robed Indians stood aside respectfully to let us pass. A palace was offered to Cortés and his captains, and we soldiers were lodged in its enormous courtyard, which had many apartments opening off it. Its walls were painted with white lime polished so it shone like silver. The plaza in which this palace stood was entirely walled off from the rest of the city and contained half a dozen temples, one with a colonnade of a hundred pillars. All were overwhelmed by a huge terraced pyramid beyond which we could see distant blue mountains, one peak capped with snow. The size and grandeur of Zempoalla was somewhat awesome and I realized that beyond those mountains were other cities perhaps even grander, ruled by Moctezuma. But then food was brought to us by files of servants: maize cakes, beans stewed with meat, fruits, and I forgot everything else, for the march had been made on slim rations. As soon as we had eaten, a group of high officials arrived carrying bouquets of roses and garlands of flowers, and they hung one around Cortés' neck and offered him a big bunch of red roses, smiling cheerfully below their lip plugs, and escorted him to another palace to meet their cacique. The captains and soldiers from each company followed.

The cacique of Zempoalla came down the steps of his palace supported by a noble at either side, for he was very fat. His great pantaloons would have clothed three men and his belly bulged through the front opening of his robe, his navel hidden by a fold of flesh like a thick, winking eyelid. His earlobes with their great golden ornaments hung to his shoulders and his crown with its feather panache was slightly crooked on his head, giving him a rakish air. After a greeting as flowery as the bouquets and garlands Cortés and his captains had been given, he offered him a golden brooch and yet another bunch of roses and called him "Lord of Lords." Then, his bulk heaving with indignation, he told how Zempoallan warriors had been taken to the Aztecs' capital to be sacrificed to their war god, and how Zempoalla's gentle daughters had been insulted and even raped by Aztec tax collectors whose arrogance knew no bounds. "But which one of all the people the Aztecs have conquered dares to complain to Moctezuma of such actions?"

Cortés, in his turn, dwelt glowingly on the great power of our King Carlos across the sea and on the gentleness of our Deity, and on his own desire to put an end to such unkind behavior. "You say none of the conquered nations dares complain or rise up against Moctezuma's rule. An alliance seems strongly indicated. My king has no fear of the Aztecs, nor do I." But at mention of an alliance, the fat ruler backed away with a doubtful look.

That was a grave matter, something he would have to ask his gods about and discuss with other Totonac leaders. "In the meantime, you might wish to visit your great houses that ride on the waves. A runner has just told me that they are waiting in the bay near my other city, Quiahuiztlán. There you will receive a friendly welcome."

After a good night's sleep, we marched to the sea and with no opposition entered that town. It stood atop a fortresslike eminence overlooking the harbor. It too had a large square with many temples, one almost as big as the great pyramid at Zempoalla. Two dozen Totonac nobles bearing bunches of roses came to meet us in a cloud of incense. One of them stepped forward and spoke to Cortés' black stallion in a timid tone and hung a garland around its neck, leaping back in fear when the horse tossed its head but then looking about proudly.

We were surprised when the fat cacique of Zempoalla appeared on a litter, having followed us. He wanted Cortés to tell him more about our king's great power. But before Cortés had more than begun, a messenger rushed up to the cacique to whisper something that alarmed him. With the look of a frightened child he ordered the litter-bearers to carry him away. It was too late, for five Indians in rich cloaks and embroidered loincloths approached us. Their manner was haughty and they ostentatiously smelled bouquets they carried, as though our smell offended them. They spoke harshly to the cacique of Zempoalla, who cringed. Obsequiously, several of the officials who had greeted us led them away to their quarters and Malinche asked the frightened fat cacique who they were. "Aztec tax collectors!" In a quivering voice he moaned that now they knew he was on friendly terms with us and soon Moctezuma would know this, too, and might draw dangerous conclusions.

Cortés strode forward. "Were you lying about your anger at their behavior?"

"No!"

"Were you lying about your desire for freedom?"

"No!"

"Then there is only one thing to do. Take a firm stand. Stop paying tribute to Moctezuma. Arrest these tax collectors, now!"

The fat cacique wavered only briefly. The commanding presence of Cortés, Malinche's ability to translate into ringing terms the great power of our king, and his knowledge that his fat would be in the fire if he let the tax collectors leave and tell Moctezuma of his friendliness to the aliens: all these factors tipped the balance.

Within an hour I saw those arrogant Aztecs tied to a long pole fitted with five leather collars, being led to the main pyramid. The cacique's plan was to offer them to his gods, thus achieving at one stroke their eternal silence and propitiation of the deities whose help he sorely needed. But Cortés sternly forbade this sacrifice, saying it would greatly offend him, our God, and our king. The cacique promised to forego it but insisted that the five stunned tax collectors had to remain in the custody of the Totonac priests.

Then came Cortés' next move. I was one of those he chose to carry out his plan.

I was summoned that evening to headquarters by Orteguilla the dwarf and was astonished when Cortés told me: "I want the Aztec tax collectors secretly freed. I think that if a pretty youth with golden hair were to visit the priests who are guarding them, he might fix their attention long enough so that another man could slip through the window of the prisoners' cell and cut them loose of those collars so they could escape."

I was stunned. It was Cortés who had insisted on their imprisonment. "May I ask why you want them freed?"

He smiled. "I'll leave that for you to puzzle out."

I said, "It seems to me that since I'm taking the risk, I should know the reason."

"Your risk is small. Doña Marina will be with you to interpret and she is too valuable to place in hazard."

He turned and snatched a bouquet of red roses from an

urn. "Take this. These Totonacs love flowers as much as blood, it seems."

"Who's going to get the prisoners out of the cell? How?"

"Yago the acrobat. Through the window. With a grapple. Don't worry about that part of it. Just concentrate on holding the priests' attention."

"But what will I say to them?"

"Tell them a Bible story. Pretend that you have come there in all your young innocence to convert them."

I said that if I were more innocent I would be less fearful and he laughed, giving me the rough map he had drawn which showed the rear of the main pyramid, the small room with one little window where the prisoners were, and the room where the two priests guarding them stayed. "Don't fail me, Arturo. A great deal depends on your success tonight."

I left with the roses and the map, puzzling over his wish to free the tax collectors, then gave it up and instead anticipated my reunion with Malinche.

14

It was a beautiful night with a silver slice of moon from a Moorish fairy tale. Near its tip was one bright star. Malinche's presence at my side was a great joy. I hoped that she might have learned a little more Castillian by now so we could converse. "Are you happy being the general's interpreter?" I asked as we crossed the plaza toward the great pyramid.

"I am happy. I am good. I believe in God, Father

Almighty and in Jesuschristo, only son, our Lord." She
spoke these memorized words of the Catechism in a
gentle singsong. "And I believe in Sainted Virgin, that
Mother good and kind, and to her I pray most often."

"And Cortés, is he behaving well to you?" I wanted
to ask if she shared his bed, but feared it might be true.

"He taught me to ride the horse of Puertocarrero."
She smiled. "I remember when I was very afraid from
horses."

The pyramid now loomed above us. I shivered as I
imagined myself snatched into a bloodied temple like
the one I had seen near San Juan Ulua and told
Malinche, "If anything goes wrong and I have to fight
the priests, you must run away."

She smiled at me. "Don't have fear, Hair of Gold.
I no fear."

I could see that this was true. We might have been
approaching that dread pyramid to visit dear friends
waiting with cakes and wine. The dark bulk towering
above us now hid the moon and star. As we turned the
rear left corner, I became aware of the vast silence of
the night and I was abruptly overwhelmed by the
thought of all the cruelty and evil that had been done
atop this manmade mountain and within its secret
rooms. A dark figure loomed suddenly in front of me
and I gasped.

"Shh! It's me, Yago." In that silence his whisper
seemed very loud. "The grapple is padded, but it will
still make a little noise when I toss it up through the
window. I'll wait until you start to talk. Talk loud!"

Some forty feet ahead faint light spilled out from the
only doorway of the stone prison cells built in a row
against the rear of the pyramid. As we neared, I saw that
the doorway was curtained with a leather hanging; when
Malinche called out something in Nahuatl, it was
drawn aside. A black-robed figure with long, matted
hair made a wild silhouette against the light of a pine
torch stuck into a stone bracket on one inner wall. The
priest smelled like a corpse. Malinche spoke again, and
like a marionette I held out my bunch of roses. He

snatched them, grunted something, stepped back and held aside the curtain for us to enter. It was a small room with two straw sleeping mats on the floor. A black doorway to my right led to the row of prison cells. On one of the mats another priest lay asleep, his back to us.

Malinche's voice made me jump. She turned to me when she had finished her speech. "I said you came here to tell them about a God bigger than any, and that I will put your words in his language." It struck me then that she no longer needed Aguilar, but could translate directly from Spanish to Nahuatl. With the qualm of a schoolboy who has not prepared his lesson, I realized that I had no idea of what Bible story to tell.

The priest was staring at my blond hair. Clearly fascinated, he came closer and put out a hand to touch it. I could see the dried blood around the long nails, and under them. The smell of corruption grew stronger. My throat closed and I wanted to hold my nose. I stepped back. The horrible hand drew away.

I raised my voice to a shout. "Many centuries ago, into a town called Bethlehem, came a pregnant virgin named Mary to find a place to sleep and to bear her child." I paused and Malinche translated. My choice of this story seemed to me a good one, for all men, however evil, know they were born of a woman. I realized that I had left out Joseph, which might leave a wrong impression. "Her husband was with her, but there was no room for them at the inn, so the only place she could find to sleep was in a stable. And after her Babe was born, the only place she could lay Him was in a manger on straw. But Mary did not know that a shining star had led to Bethlehem three kings from afar." The priest now wore a dull, stupefied look.

Malinche nodded. "I know this story." She turned to the priest. With many graceful gestures she rattled out a long speech in Nahuatl. When she stopped talking, the priest seemed confused yet fascinated and had stopped staring at my hair. But a troubling thought had occurred to me. Cortés had forgotten to plan any signal by which we could know that Yago's job was done.

A grunt startled me. The sleeping priest had awakened. He sat on his mat, staring. Then he got to his feet and came toward me. He was taller than the other, more matted, and had an expression of habitual ferocity. He pointed to Malinche and spoke harshly to the other priest. Malinche stepped back to the doorway, drew aside the leather curtain and slipped out into the night. My blood stopped flowing as the taller priest approached me and peered into my eyes and said something which seemed to make the other one angry, for he stepped between us, talking rapidly, and grabbed my wrist. I thought, They are going to sodomize me and the only question is who does it first!

"No!" I shouted, wrenching my arm from that cadaver clutch to leap toward the leather curtain. A clatter of hooves and an enormous cascade of whinnying from just outside the doorway made one of the priests scream in terror. I swept the hanging aside and plunged out, colliding with the forequarters of a horse. "Run!" Captain Sandoval called and backed his mount so I could pass. He did not have to tell me twice. I ran to the corner of the pyramid and around it and clear to the center of the square before I slowed at all. In a moment Sandoval, with Malinche riding behind him, came clattering up to pace beside me as I panted along. "Well done!" Sandoval said cheerfully. "Yago got two of them free."

"Only two?"

"Two will do." He spurred the horse and, mystified, I watched them gallop away.

Having already thanked God for my deliverance, I realized that I could also thank Cortés, who had planned this interruption from the start.

I went directly to his headquarters, determined to learn how the two released prisoners could serve his ends. There I found those formerly arrogant tax collectors kneeling humbly on the floor, their sleek hair ruffled now, without their roses. Cortés smiled at me. "What Bible story did you tell?" he asked.

"The birth of Jesus."

"A good choice. Who could not be touched by that tale?"

"Two sodomist priests of Quiahuiztlán," I said grimly.

The dwarf Orteguilla came in then with a bowl of fruit, which he set before our two prisoners. Cortés looked at them with satisfaction. "I have told them that I was horrified by their imprisonment and I have promised to procure the release of their friends. I will see that these two get safely out of the city this very night so they can return at once to Moctezuma and tell him what has happened here." He looked at me blandly.

I was at first stupefied. Then a great light dawned: I thought I saw his plan. With this one stroke he would absolutely commit the Totonacs to the break with Moctezuma and also convince Moctezuma of his friendliness. He would get his allies and the Aztec ruler's gratitude as well.

When I told him this, he nodded with grim pleasure. "Duplicity is diplomacy's backside, on which even a king must sit."

The next morning the fat cacique, in an ecstasy of anxiety, came to Cortés to tell him about the escape. Cortés feigned anger and demanded that the remaining three tax gatherers be taken to his flagship in the harbor and there safely imprisoned. The cacique of Zempoalla took an oath of allegiance to Carlos of Spain and became our king's legal vassal.

The three Aztec tax collectors on the flagship were secretly released by Cortés the next day and sent on their way to Moctezuma with assurances of our general's friendship, even after our having been ungenerously left to starve on a barren shore.

Oh, the cleverness of Cortés! I myself was not clever enough yet to see precisely why he had schemed to force on Moctezuma this proof of friendship. Cortés' desire to march to that distant city of Tenochtitlán was as strong as ever: he hoped for a welcome there.

His next step was to make Villa Rica de la Vera Cruz more than a paper colony. He chose as the site a pleasant plain on the harbor Montejo had found. To erect a fortified town with a granary, church, city hall, armory, and barracks is a hard feat, especially when using the muscles and technical knowledge of an army divided against itself. After hundreds of friendly Totonacs had brought us load upon load of sun-dried bricks, stones, lumber, and mortar, it was not only the Velásquez followers who stood amid the heaps of building materials in sluggish and disgruntled clumps. Along with a dozen other soldiers from Alvarado's company, I stood staring sullenly at a great stack of adobe bricks. By Cortés' foresight, we had in the ranks an architect, a blacksmith, a stonemason, and a carpenter; the foundation of the city hall was already laid. Out of these bricks its walls would rise. Would they?

It was Cortés who turned the tide when he appeared, trowel in hand. With cheerful vigor he slapped down mortar, lifted one of the big bricks into place, and continued the row, whistling. El Galán and I were among the first to fall to work beside him. "Good, good," he said loudly. "A gentleman who thinks he is too good for this hard labor is no gentleman. This is noble work. I would be filled with shame if some of my own sweat did not wet these bricks. The first colony in New Spain! That is what we build here. More than a town: a gateway for the riches that will flow eastward to make Spain the greatest nation on earth!"

I wet many a brick with my sweat, and so did all of us. My hands grew calluses, and with pain I discovered muscles that marching had not used. We worked through all the daylight hours, well nourished by the good food our friendly Totonacs supplied and aided by many hundreds of Indians who labored cheerfully, as though they were to get the advantages Cortés had envisioned. In a little over three weeks we had built Villa Rica de la Vera Cruz.

We were still working like gentlemen or mules when an embassy bringing more gifts of gold arrived from Moctezuma. It included a number of richly dressed nobles and two of Moctezuma's own nephews. All were very solemn and reverential. The tax collectors Cortés had liberated had arrived to tell Moctezuma how they would surely have been sacrificed but for Cortés' great kindness. "Out of deference to you and your dislike of bloodshed, my uncle will postpone any vengeance against the rebellious Totonacs until after you have returned to your own land. He does not now doubt that you are those strangers whose arrival was announced to him by omens and oracles."

What strangers, I wondered. What omens? What oracles?

Cortés was amiable with these ambassadors, but they left with long faces after he told them that we were not going to return to our own land and still intended to pay personal respects to Moctezuma.

Although Cortés used a low tone, a number of watching soldiers heard this promise and I saw them stir uneasily and glance at one another. The scowling little priest Juan Diaz stepped forward, their self-constituted spokesman. "Are we to understand that you still contemplate this rash journey into Mexico?" He knew he was not loved like Father Olmedo, nor invaluable like Aguilar, but saw himself as the advocate who stood up for the rights of the dissatisfied.

"You are to understand what I want Moctezuma to understand, that he cannot command me or this Christian army according to his whim." Cortés had sidestepped the question neatly.

News of the gifts brought us by Moctezuma's nephews soon reached the ears of the fat cacique of Zempoalla, whose awe of Cortés was increased by this mark of respect. And so he asked Cortés to lend his aid in settling a dispute with a nearby ruler, believing that the mere presence of Spanish horsemen and soldiers would bring matters to a swift conclusion. Cortés agreed, and off we marched just after sunrise, Cortés himself leading us through a lovely countryside of wide rolling plains, groves of cacao trees, and tall palms whose fronds flashed silvery edges in the sunlight. I was feeling joyous, an all-conquering Spaniard in a land that was beginning to treat us with the respect we deserved.

Juan Morla must have felt this, too. When we passed a farm where there were some *guajolotes* in a pen, he ran and managed to grab one of the big birds, whacking off its wattled head with his sword, intending that he and his friends eat well that night. We were all laughing at his speed in getting the bird and catching up with us when a halt was ordered. Hoofbeats thundered toward us from the van and poor Juan Morla, with a big dead bird dangling from one hand, looked up to see Cortés glaring down at him from his black stallion. "You know my rule about looting. I must and will keep the trust of these new allies." Cortés turned and called to Captain Alvarado. "Hang him." Then he wheeled and rode back to the vanguard.

Juan Morla dropped the bird with a thud, not believing his ears. Neither did I. Hang a loyal soldier for one miserable *guajolote* bird? Alvarado ordered a rope brought and in a matter of minutes poor Juan was standing pale as whey under the branch of a large tree, a noose around his neck. I saw it catch on the rim of his steel gorget as he was slowly hauled, kicking, into midair. Even though Juan Morla had made fun of me often, I was very glad when Alvarado, on his sorrel horse, suddenly slashed out with his sword and cut him down, neck unbroken, to sprawl fainting in the dust of the roadside.

Remembering the command of Christ to treat kindly those who spitefully use us, I knelt beside him and gave him water from my flask. He was very shaken, and I put an arm around him and helped him walk until his own legs would hold him, then we double-marched and finally caught up with our own company. There are those who secretly hate one who aids them in a time of humiliation, but Juan was not of that sort. From then on he called me Arturo instead of Pollito. And the moment would come when his affection for me would turn the tide of my fortunes.

The fortunes of the expedition, however, were placed in sudden jeopardy that afternoon, by Cortés.

15

After our presence had aided the cacique of Zempoalla to cow the neighboring chieftain, we returned just before sundown to his city to be met in the plaza by smiling nobles with bouquets. A larger reward was soon offered, living tokens of the fat ruler's friendship and gratitude: eight Indian women, all of high status. One was his own daughter, who was thin and very plain. The other women were for the captains, he said. But his child was to be the wife of Cortés.

Cortés thanked him and said he already had one wife and that his religion did not permit him to have two.

This offended the cacique. Many wives, he said, are the well-known prerogative of power, and he particularly wanted his daughter to be the wife of Cortés.

Cortés ignored this and had his interpreters inform the donor that the women must all be baptized and become Christians before they could be given to his captains.

This greatly disturbed the cacique. "I do not want this done. It would offend my gods."

Duplicity was called for, but Cortés chose this moment to evangelize. "One reason why we came here is to wean you and your subjects away from false gods and from the abominations you perform to please them. You yourself must be baptized in our faith." He was still astride his black stallion, which stood with lowered head to nibble at some flowers that had been reverently placed before it. "Now! This very day."

"That cannot be," the fat cacique said. The man who had trembled before five Aztec tax collectors now gazed up with no sign of fear. "I promised loyalty to your king. I did not promise to worship your gods or abandon mine."

Cortés raised his voice; obduracy in the mound of flesh he had seen trembling with fear of Moctezuma clearly angered him. "Those idols must be removed from your temples! We must replace them with the Holy Cross of Jesus!"

In the brief pause while this was translated, Juan Diaz stepped resolutely forward, holding his silver crucifix high in one hand so that it caught the light of the setting sun and seemed to flame. Father Olmedo joined him, and so did the other churchmen, their faces shining with resolution.

The cacique looked very sad and stubborn. "My gods are good enough for me. For have they not brought me your aid? I will resist any violence to the deities of my people!"

The Totonacs filling the square gave a multiple growl of approval. A wild-haired priest screamed something and I saw other priests moving among the gathering crowd, exhorting them to defend their idols.

"Filthy sodomist priest!" yelled a soldier named Gonzalo, who had seen the same temple as I had. "We'll finish off your idols and you, too!"

Cortés turned his black stallion to face his own soldiers. "We are Christians and Spaniards, and I know that heaven will never smile on our hopes if we do not take a stand against the idolatry practiced here, and the atrocities. To close our eyes and let this people keep to their gods and so face an eternity in burning hell would be a sin, and unworthy of Christians! For my part, I am resolved that the idols shall be destroyed, this very day, this very hour, even if it costs me my life!"

Shouts of assent arose from many Spanish throats, but I stood dumbfounded. Cortés had got what he wanted—strong, compliant allies—and now abruptly he chose to turn friends to enemies. Why? What was the gain? I gawked up at his stern, armed figure and glimpsed another level of his nature: for his successes so far he owed Almighty God His due, and would pay it.

"Arrest the cacique!" Cortés shouted, pointing to him with his unsheathed sword. "Encircle him and the nobles with him!" In only moments, we who were nearest had surrounded the group, our swords pointing outward in a hedgehog. At this moment an Indian priest burst from the watching crowd and came gibbering up to me and I slashed out with my sword blade and lopped off a lock of his long, matted hair, which fell to the ground and seemed to squirm there as though the poor victims' blood clotted on it had given it the power of motion.

Malinche's voice called out Cortés' threat to the fat cacique. "If one arrow is shot at a Spanish soldier, or one spear raised, it will cost you your life!"

The Totonac ruler covered his face with both hands, then lowered them and called out to his people. "Our gods are strong and will avenge any wrong these strangers do them. Offer no resistance."

"Then let us see what vengeance these idols have in store for us!" Cortés shouted. He ordered Puertocarrero's company to march across the plaza to the temple. The watching Indians, obeying their ruler, fell aside like the Red Sea parting for Moses. Our soldiers flowed up the pyramid's steep steps and sent the first of the idols crashing down into the square. With a vast moaning sound, the Totonacs drew back to the margins of the plaza, watching in helpless awe. A second idol tumbled

down, and another, and more. The hollow sounds some
of them made showed they were of wood; later we
burned them in a great bonfire in the middle of the
square, adding ones of clay and stone and smaller ones
from the lesser temples. Night had fallen when the last
of the wooden idols, the height of a tall man, stood
upright in the flames the others had fed, and it suddenly
seemed to me that I was watching an auto-da-fé and
that the ugly thing carved of wood was really a living
heretic burning in this life for having refused the Savior
who could have offered salvation from an eternity in
Hell.

A terrible scream gave an eerie reality to this illusion
and the hairs on my neck stirred, but it was only one of
the Indian priests standing with fists raised above his
head and screaming up at an unconcerned evening star.
He had gone mad and fell to the ground, where he
rolled about with flecks of spittle coming from his
mouth. Finally he rolled right into the fire and his hair
went up in flames, but another priest rescued him, pulling him out by the legs and smothering his blazing head
with his robe, and I saw that his body was crisscrossed
with many gashes and scars. These priests lacerated
their own flesh to feed still more blood to their gods,
now mere smoldering ash and the one charred stalk still
bearing its odd resemblance to a burned man.

But next day, what a reward after these unpleasant
events! The Totonacs had lost faith in their idols, who
had not avenged themselves. Following the orders of
our priests, they cleansed the great *teocalli* of blood,
and it was freshly stuccoed by Indian masons and
painted white with lime. We saw atop that great pyramid
a Christian altar raised, with our high white cross atop;
the altar was hung with beautiful garlands of red roses.
We all knelt at its foot. Led by an acolyte with a high,
clear voice, we chanted a hymn to our sweet Jesus.

Rising from my knees, I felt ashamed that I had
thought so much about getting gold. But then the soldier next to me nudged me and secretively showed me
a flat heavy golden heart, almost as big as his palm;

most of the idols, he whispered, had worn jewelry, and he had snatched this. Sudden covetousness claimed me, dimming my spiritual elevation of an instant before.

Raising my eyes from the heart, I saw Malinche, a Madonna-blue shawl covering her head. She was still kneeling at the foot of the pyramid, head bowed over clasped hands. I hurried to her side and stood quietly until she had crossed herself and risen from her knees. She turned and saw me. The shawl framed the dark purity of her face with the same soft folds as the pale-blue shawl framing the white face of the Virgin far above. The temple graced with Christian symbols had been the pyramid of Quetzalcoatl, and the idols we had burned had been gods she had once revered. What had been her feelings when she watched them thrown down and saw them go up in flames? And then I saw that she wore only the rosary I had given her. The little golden image of Quetzalcoatl was gone.

Its removal must have been a moment of greatest significance in her life. When Cortés had so valiantly insisted on that dramatic enactment of the power of Our Lord he had intended to convert our allies, the Totonacs. That it had so deeply moved Malinche was a benefit unforeseen. I smiled. "I see your pagan snake god is gone."

Her voice was soft and deep. "Now I believe. In the deep of the heart." My mind flashed to the golden heart the soldier had just shown me. How trivial such a heart was compared to the one beating in the breast of this woman now looking up at me with such childlike trust! "I was very afraid when the idols burned. I believed in God and Jesus and Virgin Mary. But I believed in Quetzalcoatl and some other gods too. So I thought a bad thing will come down on the Spaniards. But no. I know those Totonac gods are not real. The gods I had are not real. Cortés serves the true God. I, too."

I had been reminded that Puertocarrero had led that charge that toppled heathen idols from power. Could that have endowed him with a new stature in her eyes?

I had to know. "Perhaps you feel less angry with Puertocarrero now?"

She cast me a glance around the austere fold of her shawl. "You may wish to know my feeling about him?"

"Yes."

She leaned toward me confidentially. "I do not like his smell."

I stepped back, felt the stench of my own sweat enveloping me like a thick haze, and I yearned for one of those bouquets the Zempoallans liked to carry about. "All soldiers smell a bit rank at times."

"Oh, yes. But he has a different smell. It offends me. He cannot help it. But so it is."

Hilarity seized me. Poor Puertocarrero! "And I, do I have a smell that offends you?"

"You smell young and good, like grass."

Like grass? "A million thanks!"

A hard, imperious voice spoke just behind me. "Mondragon!" It was Puertocarrero, who seemed to have grown slightly taller and whose narrow gray eyes were glinting like metal in his tense face. "This is my *barragana*. She is not to be accosted by you when my back is turned! Do you understand? It offends me very much."

The word *offend* reminded me how his smell offended the woman who was not really his *barragana* at all. "To *offend* you was not my intention." I slid a glance at Malinche, saw her barely contain a smile. How rare she was! Another woman would have laughed aloud to show her contempt.

But when Puertocarrero took her arm and tried to lead her away from me she refused to budge, only looked down at his hand. He removed it and walked off alone, his back very stiff. Then she said goodbye to me and went in the opposite direction. I watched her go, filled with pleasure at her true conversion.

We returned to Vera Cruz to find that a privateer from Santiago de Cuba had followed our trail and wanted to join us. He brought two horses, a dozen recruits, and some bad news. Governor Velásquez was publicly boasting that he had just received from Spain a warrant giving him and only him right to establish a royal colony on the new continent. Since we had just done this without his blessing, or that of our king either, I wondered where this left our little town. If not legitimately the first Spanish colony on these shores, then what was it? A mere headquarters, lacking any status with the crown?

This question was being asked and argued when Alvarado told us that Cortés had the answer: he was sending one of our vessels to Spain with a letter to the king himself telling of our gains to date and of the building of Vera Cruz, and pleading for royal approval of what we had so far accomplished, for permission to carry on our exploration of this rich new continent, and also for the reinforcements, arms, and ammunition that would guarantee our success. More impressive than the letter would be the Royal Fifth of our treasures. But fearing that it might not prove adequate to woo the king's favor, Cortés had added to it his share of the booty and had induced the captains to relinquish their shares, too. "Very noble—and smart, too," Juan Morla said. "Gold talks louder than words."

"I'm glad you know that," Alvarado said. His smile was, for him, rather cryptic.

Half an hour later Captain Francisco Montejo appeared with a document, a quill, and an inkhorn to ask the foot soldiers to give up our shares of the treasure, too. "For look," he said, "if what we send back to the king is inadequate to impress him, then all you will ever have is your little portion of what we have so far gained, and divided up into so many parts, your share is not going to look as large as you think. As for the future golden fruits of this rich land, forget them! Velásquez is out for those. It was only by good luck, the arrival of that privateer, that we even knew the governor intended to cut Cortés out. For if he had meant Cortés and the rest of us to benefit from the royal sanction he has been given, wouldn't he have sent us word of his good luck?

We sweated to build Vera Cruz. Velásquez, safe and cozy in Cuba, boasts about his right to do what we have really done. Believe me, Cortés wants to get the king's approval of our efforts as much for your sakes as his own!" Montejo's words had more weight in that he had once been Velásquez's friend. He held up the document. "Those of you willing to relinquish your shares, as Cortés and I have done, sign this paper or make your mark."

Stunned silence greeted his invitation.

Most of us in Alvarado's company were gathered around a large clay brazier where a few of us were roasting in the embers some nuts the Indians called *cacahuates,* which grow underground and have two kernels a little larger than peas. In the silence that followed Montejo's speech, the crackle of a nutshell which El Galán opened was very loud. We all laughed. Having got our attention, he said, "We are on the eastern fringe of a vast new continent. All the riches we have seen are only a few crumbs dropped from Moctezuma's table. We need to buy our king's favor. Any price is cheap." He tossed the nutshells he held onto the coals of the brazier. "I gladly offer my small share. Mere *cacahuate* shells." He took the document and the quill from Montejo and signed with a flourish.

I did the same, and so did all the rest. It took Juan Morla a long time to inscribe the nine letters of his name, printed very large. As he blew on the paper to dry the ink he held it in such a way that I would see he had not signed with an X.

Every single man in Alvarado's company signed away his share, and by the end of the day, every soldier and mariner had done so; the signing urge had spread like a fever and even the Velásquez followers were not immune. Cortés had used the same lure, in a sense, as that with which he hoped to win the support of the king, except that royalty was to be tempted with actual treasure and we soldiers with the promise of it. The hard labor we had expended to build Vera Cruz was also an issue; we wanted it acknowledged as the first legitimate Spanish colony on these shores. I do not know if Cortés had cleverly calculated on this when he came out that day with a fine speech and a trowel in his hand, or whether it was just luck.

When El Galán learned that everyone had signed, he indulged in prophecy. "We are going to march to Tenochtitlán when Cortés is ready to go there, no matter what the cautious may say or do. For I have just found out that not only will we risk our lives for him, we will also unline our pockets of gold at his desire, which is more unusual."

Juan Morla showed his buck teeth through his black beard in a wry smile. "The more I think of my woman's face when I tell her I did that, the more I like it here!"

But El Galán was only a fair prophet. He did not foresee that before we left for Moctezuma's city he and I would take part in an event so extraordinary that only two catastrophes the future held in store for us would impress me more mightily.

16

Before that climactic happening, I played an unwelcome role in a smaller unpleasantness that was to end with two hanged men swinging sadly from ropes. On the sunny morning after I signed away my share of the treasure the page Orteguilla pattered up to summon me into Cortés' headquarters in the city hall of Vera Cruz. Cortés was composing his letter to King Carlos, and since his frail secretary was sick with a flux, he had decided to use me for the moment, wishing to lose no time. He greeted me pleasantly and gave me a folio page to copy.

I dared to comment on one very courtierlike sentence. "Is it necessary to be humble, considering the gratitude our king will feel on seeing the wealth of gifts which will accompany this letter?"

He smiled at my innocence. "One does not expect gratitude from princes. They get their right to rule from God Almighty and do not feel that even He needs to be overwhelmed with thanks. Furthermore, young Carlos is the son of poor Juana the Mad and Felipe the Fair, son of Emperor Maximilian, and was raised at the Flemish court and does not like Spaniards much. I cannot know his mood when he reads my letter. He may have stabbed his finger on a rose thorn. A mistress may have disappointed him in bed, if so Christian a king allows himself such diversion. In other words, my words must bow to him, soothingly. And if I get his blessing and the arms and reinforcements I am asking, it will not be from gratitude, but because he smells more treasure in case I meet with success."

Ashamed of my naïveté, I bent my head to sharpen my quill, only to have it pulled suddenly from my fingers by the thin hand of the pale secretary, recovered from his flux, he claimed in a shaky voice.

As I rose to leave, Cortés said to me, "I have decided to employ you in a special capacity, Arturo." The secretary gave me a cold stare; his devotion to Cortés was absolute.

"In what capacity?" I asked.

"Not secretarial." The secretary relaxed and I heard his quill scratching away. Cortés smiled at me. "It is vital that I know the feelings of the foot soldiers, who do not always confide in their captains. From now on, it is your responsibility to report to me immediately any current of unrest, any remark that hints of insurrection."

"A spy." My dismay must have been evident.

"You will be helping the foot soldiers as well as me. I want to fulfill their needs when I can."

"Soldiers often grumble at this or that," I pointed out, "even the most loyal ones. I'd have no way of telling which grumble was caused by a bunion or gas in the belly and which had real importance."

"Let me be specific, then. I believe some sort of plot against me is brewing. See if you can ferret it out."

"Being no ferret, I do not know how."

"Then I will tell you. You will go about among the men saying you have heard there is a plot afoot. Rumors and guesses will fly. You collect them. I sift." His tone had crisped. This was an order. Then he stood up, dropped a hand to my shoulder, and walked with me to the door. "Do you know why I have chosen you? No? Because you I can absolutely trust. And you are also clever." He gave my back a pat and I grew suddenly tall. I shrank somewhat as I walked in the sunlight past other soldiers from whom I was now secretly alienated.

My first task as a spy was surprisingly easy. The gloomy, dark-skinned young Velásquez adherent named Gonzalo, much troubled by carbuncles and by memories of the bloodied temple we had seen, was one of a group of soldiers gossiping at day's end. I joined them and into their conversation I dropped the comment that I had heard the rumor of a plot against Cortés. Gonzalo stared at me in shock, then loudly denied the likelihood of such a thing. But later that night he sought me out and confessed it was true. The leader of the rebellion was the priest Juan Diaz. He and five Velásquez men had managed, with the connivance of a pilot, to get food and water aboard one of our ships, and they planned to sail it in to Cuba that very night. They believed that if they reported to Velásquez that Cortés apparently intended to march his army westward into great danger, steps would be taken by the governor that would save all our lives. Gonzalo bitterly regretted his earlier enthusiasm for this scheme, for fear of Cortés now outweighed fear of Moctezuma. "What shall I do?" he agonized, rolling his dark Moorish eyes toward heaven.

"You have no choice," I said. "You have to tell Cortés everything you know. If you don't, I will."

He writhed and begged me to go with him when he faced Cortés and put in a good word for his belated fidelity, which I did. Cortés listened to Gonzalo's halting story with an impassive face, but a swollen vein in his temple throbbed.

The other plotters were arrested and tried and treason was established beyond a doubt. The priest Juan Diaz claimed immunity as clergy, but the two other ringleaders were sentenced to death and the pilot who would have stolen the ship was condemned to lose his feet. The rest, including Gonzalo, were severely lashed. Orteguilla was present when the general signed the death warrants and told me that Cortés had cried out bitterly: "Before God, I wish I had never learned to write my name!"

After the executions, Cortés had me summoned and commended me for my part in so speedily uncovering the plot; this praise was so sweet that I did not stress how little I really had done.

We were alone in the room where the letter to the king had been written, standing by the window from which we could see a portion of the harbor and several of our vessels. Cortés was in heavy spirits. With dulled eyes he praised loyalty. "For what is any commander without men he can trust? Only a head full of plans that will never bear fruit. A cipher." He pointed suddenly to one of the ships. "That is the one that sails tomorrow for Spain. The treasure is loaded aboard. I have ordered them to avoid Cuba. Puertocarrero I know I can trust. Montejo, too. Yes, of them I am sure." Brooding there, he seemed to forget me and so after a time I left him. Dusk had fallen, the room was very dim, and he didn't hear me wish him good night.

So Puertocarrero was dispatched to Spain. As I watched the ship bearing him there sail away, all I could think of was what I had just learned from Orteguilla: Cortés had taken back the gray mare he bought for Puertocarrero with the gold buttons from his own cloak and had presented it to Malinche for her use. The dwarf had grinned as he added: "Cortés told Puertocarrero 'You tried to mount Doña Marina against her will. So she will now mount the mare I gave you. I consider this punishment lenient. And a mount for a mount would please even Solomon, I think. Or Moses.' "

"She will master horsemanship as rapidly as she did Castilian," I said.

"As for Castilian, I was of much help to her," Orteguilla said cockily. "She likes me well and we spend much time together. How many times I have corrected her amusing pronunciation! And I have told her the Spanish names of at least a thousand different things." The grin left his face as he said sincerely, "With Doña Marina, I never feel short. She sees that my mind and soul are large."

But the news of the gift of the mare was subtly disturbing. An idea flashed through my mind: from one favorite to another? With so few horses, it had been a lavish gift indeed.

That night I borrowed Orteguilla's guitar again. I was determined to draw her attention with the serenade that had been interrupted on the night Cortés gave her to Puertocarrero. This time, instead of standing outside a rude hut in the sand, I stood below the rear window of the building in Vera Cruz where Cortés and the other officials of the town had their sleeping quarters. From Orteguilla I had found out that Malinche had her own room there, and where it was.

In the moonlight, the window under which I stood with my borrowed guitar could have been somewhere in Spain, or at least Cuba. There was even a grille, though of wood. Once more, my voice rose in serenade. This time no cross-eyed Indian blighted my tender feelings. Looking up, I saw with a thrill of joy Malinche's face at the window, softly lighted by a candle flame. She listened, smiling, while I sang the little morning song of King David.

"Why are you singing a morning song at night?" she asked when the last note died away.

It struck me again how very much Spanish she had learned in less than five months. I tuned a flat string and sang the song I had written for her. "And now, if you were a Spanish lady, you would throw me a rose if you liked my serenade."

She disappeared and a moment later returned and tossed down a ripe mango. "I have no roses. And I am not a Spanish lady. Sing more."

Halfway through the next song I found we had an audience. From the darkness some soldiers and a captain or two had appeared to stand silently watching this ritual of Spanish wooing never before seen or heard on this alien shore. "Very well thung, Pollito," Sandoval called. Juan Morla said: "*Arturo* sings like the birds."

"But the birds are all asleep now," a commanding voice announced from a front window of the house. I looked up and saw Cortés staring sternly down at me. "Go to bed."

Picking up my mango, I waved to Malinche and traveled on air to the open thatched barracks where my company slept, sure that my serenade had touched her heart. I held the plump fruit in my hand for a while, smiling down at it idiotically, and then peeled and ate it with greedy pleasure, sucking from the big seed every drop of golden juice.

A blissful dream was shattered at dawn when Alvarado roused us and told us we were to march at once to Zempoalla in full armor and with all gear. When we demanded why, he said "Because Cortés has ordered it!" At first the rumor ran that this was the start of the march to Moctezuma's city, but that notion faded when Alvarado let us know that Cortés was remaining behind in Vera Cruz, along with several captains, himself one. He placed El Galán in charge of our company. Something unusual was afoot. I knew, but I did not much care when I saw that Malinche had come with us, riding on Puertocarrero's gray mare. Orteguilla the dwarf was perched behind her.

When we got to Zempoalla in the early afternoon, camping in the same enormous white courtyard as before, I rushed over to her and she seemed glad to see me, although more concerned about the horse, stroking its soft muzzle and feeding it maize from her hand until the soldier acting as groom came and led it off to be watered and fed with the rest.

Meanwhile Orteguilla had spread out a large striped serape against the shaded wall of the courtyard where already the men had settled down to dicing, cards, or conversation, waiting for food. He urged Malinche to sit down and rest, absurdly solicitous. She gave him a fond glance and told me he had ridden with her to protect her, and I thought that would have been fine if she had been menaced by a dwarf like himself.

They seated themselves and I sat down, too, and asked if they had any idea why we were here. They both shook their heads. I concentrated on flattering Orteguilla. "I thought that you, being in the confidence of the general, would surely have some notion."

He looked about for eavesdroppers, lowering his voice. "I can tell you one thing. The general was up very late last night discussing a matter of greatest importance with his most trusted captains."

"I don't suppose you would tell me what it was?"

He smiled patronizingly. "A page may have large eyes and big ears, but unless he has a closed mouth, he will not be a page very long."

Though the dwarf stuck close as glue, I gave myself over to enjoyment of the moment, seated close to Malinche on that serape, our little island around which the soldiers moved and talked and laughed, mere shadows in the sun. At last Orteguilla took a siesta, snoring gently on his small bent arm. Warmed by her presence and hoping for praise, I told her that the last song I had sung the night before had been written by me for her.

"Why?" she asked, and I realized she was unaware of this European nicety or its significance.

"Because you are very dear to me."

"Sing it again."

I could not sing well without a guitar, so I recited the poem.

"What is a nightingale?" she asked.

I told her.

"And what is damask?"

"A fine smooth white cloth."

Her hand went to her cheek. "Skin is not like white cloth," she said.

"I was comparing the smoothness."

The page had rolled over with his back to us and began to snore louder. I jumped to my feet and held out my hand to her. "His snoring annoys me. Let's go somewhere else." My audacity pleased and excited me.

"The cacique's garden is pretty." This was a retreat between his stone palace and a pyramid temple. It was his private park, unused by the townsfolk, but as one of the conquerors I had no hesitation about walking there.

It was shaded by a great jacaranda tree that seemed to shut out the rest of the world. Amid its lacy leaves hung clusters of sky-blue flowers like little bells. I sat leaning against the bole of the tree. She knelt on the soft grass. A bell flower fell and lay on her black, black hair. "I love you, Malinche," I said. I used the verb *amar*, which conveys a spiritual love. Honesty and my throbbing body prompted me to add *Te quiero,* the verb of desire.

"And I love you," she said, using *amar*. But did she understand the distinction?

"And from the moment I saw you I have wanted to kiss you." My voice had a tremor in it.

I saw on her face an oblique tenderness. She leaned a little closer to me, just a fraction. The motion made her loose chemise pull tighter against her full breasts. "Would God like that?" she asked with an innocence real or feigned. "Would Cortés?"

My male member rose in defiance of God, Cortés—and Aguilar, too. "Would you?" I whispered, and knelt facing her. The urgent desire to press my mouth against her full lips seemed to be passing almost visibly from my being to hers, a warm current of heat. That scent which was not Spanish answered it and enveloped me. But just as my lips touched hers, footsteps approached; I wavered, recognized El Galán's clean boots, and hated them.

He was smiling down as though he were not as unwelcome as a toad in the water jug. "Poor little Orteguilla is in a frenzy, trying to find where you are, Doña Marina. The soldiers are baiting him by pretending they don't know. He's afraid Cortés will ask for you any minute."

"Cortés is in Vera Cruz!" I cried.

"He *was* in Vera Cruz."

I turned to Malinche, but she was gone. I looked wildly around the garden, saw only the trembling tendril of a vine she had brushed in passing.

"You could hardly have picked a worse moment to come looking for me," I said as I stood up. We left the garden side by side.

"I think I picked a good one. Your ardor was visible from twenty paces. Last night you serenaded her and gathered an audience and a réprimand from the general. Yet today you march her off in full view of nearly the entire army. I have rarely seen a suitor more inept. I am only a simple soldier, God knows, but I did not get the name El Galán for nothing. I can tell you here and now that you must learn to plan things better. First, you arrange to get the young lady to suggest a more private meeting place. If she wants you she will prove adept at this. Only then do you let the little man downstairs rear up his head." We soon reached the steps of the palace that had been given to Cortés as his headquarters in Zempoalla. El Galán turned me around and led me up the steps with him.

"What are we doing here?" I asked.

"Cortés recruited me for a secret mission. He wants you too."

"What mission?"

"I'll let him tell you."

When we reached the palace throne room, Cortés and his captains were talking in low but excited voices, their heads together. When El Galán announced our arrival and Cortés looked over at us, it was with an appraising eye. He beckoned us forward in an informal fashion, dropped his hand to my shoulder. "Here is a soldier fit for our task," he said to the rest. "Like my friend El Galán here, he is totally worthy of our trust."

"Both Alvarado men," Captain Olid said jealously. "I have loyal men in my company, too."

"I do not doubt it, being the captain that you are."

"Tell them. Thee what they thay," lisped Captain Sandoval. The pupils of his brown eyes were large with excitement. All the captains seemed nervous and eager.

Cortés faced El Galán and me, smiling. Again I noted the small white scar below his underlip. "You have no doubt wondered why I remained behind in Vera Cruz. I will tell you. I have just ordered four of our ships scuttled."

I felt my mouth drop open but could not close it. Staring into those brilliant eyes it occurred to me that our commander had gone mad. "Four ships?" I whispered.

"They were quite wormy, unseaworthy. Their pilots have so testified in writing."

"That leaves us only seven ships here." My voice was shaky.

"It is my plan to sink and burn all but one."

"Sink . . . burn . . . ?"

"Do you approve?" His smile would have warmed a serpent; his magnetic stare would have charmed a dragon.

"No," I croaked, and then shouted, "No! Leave us stranded here? No way to get home? It would be the act of a madman!"

Smiling, he turned from me to El Galán. "And do you agree with Arturo?"

He said with a calm I could only admire, "And so will every soldier in the army."

"I said all along we didn't need any foot soldiers, that we can use Totonacs," said Alvarado impatiently.

Cortés frowned. "I wish a few foot soldiers to take an active part. I don't want it later said that only my captains knew and approved of this." Cortés turned back to El Galán and me. "I have determined to march to Tenochtitlán at once. The reward in gold and gems is beyond estimate. We have to trust in God, who has been with us thus far, and go bravely onward." I was beginning to kindle at the old, dazzling promise of great wealth. "But I cannot accomplish this march while a third of my army yearns to crawl aboard the nearest leaky vessel and head home. No general could; not Hannibal or Caesar. I need a united body of men, and I will have it! I will have it, that is, if there are no ships remaining at anchor to tempt their minds and dim what courage they possess. For let me tell you this: someone is going to march into Mexico; someone is going to penetrate this rich continent! Do we want to leave that to others? The English? The French? Or are we going to be the first?" Head high, he raked our faces with flashing eyes.

As always, he had inflamed me with his own passion. "The first!"

He threw back his head and laughed like a boy, joyously.

El Galán said, "You have found the only spur for the balky mules among us: no alternative."

Cortés nodded. "The balky mules cannot be allowed to spoil our venture for gallant and mettlesome thoroughbreds like yourselves." As my chest swelled, his face grew stern. "I now order you both to return to Vera Cruz with me and my captains to aid in the destruction of the fleet." He added, in a matter-of-fact voice, "The sails, rigging and ironwork are to be saved,

of course. Wooden hulls can be built again when the
time comes for our triumphant return to Cuba."

It was true that the wood of certain of the remaining
vessels was well-drilled with wormholes and that others
had suffered dry rot and could be called unseaworthy,
but the caravel I helped to sink after it had been
stripped was sound. To smash with an axe through the
underplanking of the hull and see the water gurgle in
caused me pain, and I felt as if I were killing something
that had never meant me any harm. A tingle of fear
stirred; I was helping to destroy my only link with home
and its safety. As I climbed up and out of the slowly
filling hold, I tried to think of the great adventure that
lay ahead. The cowards could not be allowed to rob the
brave of treasures beyond imagining, of fame that
would ring down generations to come! Cortés was right.
He had to be, or we were all lost.

The sun was low by the time Cortés decided to have
two shallow-draft vessels that were anchored near shore
dragged with ropes into the shallows, there to be stripped
of sails, rigging, and ironwork. This took some time,
even under the supervision of that excellent shipwright
Martín Llopez. Even some nails were saved. Meanwhile, hundreds of astonished Totonacs had assembled
on the beach to watch denuded hulls offshore go down
into the sea.

By this time my initial high spirits had sunk with the
sun, and this was true of all of us, I think, except
Cortés. He had the buoyant air of a man who was
building ships instead of destroying them. But he must
have felt the general mood sag, for he had two hogs-
heads of good wine brought down to the beach from
his private supply in the town. As I filled my clay mug
with rich, cool wine, Cortés cried "A taste of Spain,
from the vineyards of Jerez, to cheer us!" After we
drank a toast to our king, the sherry flowed, and soon
we were all laughing and a little drunk. Suddenly
Cortés was at my side with a torch, a flaming shaft of
pitch pine that the Indians light their houses with. He

thrust it into my hand and pointed out to one of the caravels in the shallows near shore, and I waded out into the water to my waist and fired a sun-parched rail, which shot a flame out at me as if in protest. I waded in up to my neck, torch high, and set the other end alight, too, and by the time I got back to the sand, the vessel was blazing up, as hot as Hell itself.

Some Totonac musicians had appeared with a drum, a flute, and gourds filled with dry seeds to offer their savage music at this strange fiesta. A mariner who had gotten ecstatically drunk began to prance wildly, snapping his fingers like castanets, and soon all the Spaniards were capering in a mad fandango, our grinning sweaty faces reflecting the flames of the burning ships. Our frenzy consumed our regrets.

The fires sank down at last, leaving only poor black skeletons of what had been vessels. Out on the moonlit water of the harbor the prow of a ship that had refused to sink pointed at us accusingly as it floated, hull up. So Cortés had a cannon wheeled to the beach and ordered it fired at the stubborn ship again and again, and at last enough cannonballs had splintered the hull so that it settled slowly into the harbor whose dark waters closed over it and finally were still. Now only one ship was left afloat: the flagship.

The strange celebration had ended, and Cortés ordered us back to town to sleep; we were to march west to Zempoalla early in the morning. After all the others had left the beach, I lingered behind on the deserted sands, haunted by the doleful smell of charred wood and saddened by the black bones of the burned ships. Hugging my knees, I sat near the water's edge and stared in the direction of Cuba, now as unreachable as the moon. Bits of charred flotsam washed up at my feet, no darker than the dismal mood that had engulfed me. A deep and awful doubt of our commander's sanity had edged into my mind. Cortés' reasoning, which had seemed so brilliantly right to me, now seemed only murky rhetoric. He had stranded us all in this alien land where our Zempoallan allies, learning we were at their mercy with no escape at hand, might soon be tearing down our white cross from the temple from which we had hurled their idols. A rat from one of the ships scurried past me, a dark and frantic shape against the moonlit sand.

"Waiting for a mermaid?" It was El Galán, who had missed me and had returned.

"Wishing our ships were still afloat." My hollow voice was funereal.

He grinned down at me and spoke kindly. "You swallowed a great deal of sherry. Come and get some sleep. You'll feel better tomorrow." He held down a hand and pulled me to my feet.

From somewhere down the beach came the sudden mournful wailing of an Indian flute. I looked that way and saw one of the Totonacs kneeling in the sand and staring seaward as if he piped an elegy for all the dead ships. Tears filled my eyes as I walked in silence beside my friend into the silent town.

But wine and sorrow were transformed into desire. I fell asleep yearning to hold Malinche in my arms. The burned ships seemed a boon, for now she and I could not be parted.

17

The march west to Zempoalla next morning was grim. My head ached from the fumes of the wine and my heart ached, too, nor did the memory of the salvaged rigging, ironwork, and other fittings stored in the warehouse at Vera Cruz bring any comfort. That act of preservation now seemed only another evidence of our commander's lack of good sense: did he really believe our fleet could be rebuilt for him whenever he snapped his fingers and commanded it?

As soon as El Galán and I rejoined the rest of Alvarado's company in Zempoalla, I sensed a mood I had never felt before. All over the courtyard men were gathered in angry clots to argue and debate the report of the destruction of the first four ships, spread by a mariner whose emotions had led him to ignore Cortés' command for silence. His ship had been perfectly sound, he insisted, needing only to have the hull scraped; seeing it go needlessly down he had thought that with it went his last chance of getting home alive. But worse than this, someone else had just let out the whisper that the rest of the fleet had also been sunk, or burned.

This news spread like a grassfire. "Cortés has betrayed us!" a soldier cried suddenly. "He's beached us!" My own concern over the lost ships dwindled in importance beside the sudden looming fear of a massive mutiny that even Cortés would not be able to quell. Stripped of power over his soldiers, how long would he command the respect of the Totonac cacique? And if the Totonacs turned from allies to foes . . . ?

It was at this moment that I was summoned into the presence of Cortés by Orteguilla. He moved beside me very fast on his little legs and grinned up at me. His jaws seemed to have more than the usual number of teeth. "I've put in a good word for you with Cortés," he said, "but I warn you, he's very much annoyed."

"Annoyed?" An angry soldier I was passing made a sudden violent motion with his arm which I barely ducked. "With me?" I, who had torched a ship for him? I, his trusted spy, his thoroughbred foot soldier? "Annoyed?"

"Oh, the innocence of Señor Green Eyes!"

My confusion took the form of anger at the dwarf. "I am jealous of no one, manikin!"

"I referred to their literal color. Manikin is a term

I despise, and for obvious reasons. I want you to know that it was not I who told him."

"Told who? What?"

"Of your little ramble with Doña Marina I said precisely nothing, even though you left me asleep on a mat on the paving where I was accidentally stepped on and then got splashed with horse piss."

I stopped dead. "At a time like this he can't be concerned about a thing like that!"

"Correct. What pisses on his page is of no concern to him just now."

"No, no, I mean that little stroll you mentioned."

"You did more than stroll, did you not?"

"We sat under a tree for a few minutes."

"Sat, you say? Just sat?"

"Sat. Just that." For the kiss had missed. "Who told him?"

"Two soldiers. And considering that the entire army saw you take her off to that secluded garden, I would say that you must be quite popular." He added, grinning, "If not with Cortés."

We had reached the door of the palace where Cortés had his headquarters. Suddenly one soldier of a group gathered there pointed to me and nudged another, who stepped forward and blocked my path. "Deny it, you son of the great whore! Deny that the whole fleet is sunk and that you helped him sink it! Toadeater!"

I could not deny the accusation, but drew my sword to deny the epithets. His friend quickly stepped between us and begged me to forgive the remarks because my accuser had drunk too much fermented cactus juice and was not responsible. "And besides, Cortés happens to be waiting," Orteguilla said impatiently. So I accepted an apology, though feeling rather sick and shaken.

Inside the palace room where Cortés sat alone at a trestle table eating a late four-o'clock dinner, the angry voices of the soldiers outside were reduced to a mere hum. He was at his ease in only hose, breeches, and a white shirt that made his shoulders look excessively broad. As he ate, he studied a crude map. At the window some twenty feet away, a group of captains stood looking down at the soldiers in the courtyard below. "Here's that naughty Mondragon," said Orteguilla.

Cortés looked up at me, eyes cold. "You're not going to put horns on Puertocarrero. Stay away from Doña Marina."

I was stunned. Orteguilla's grin stiffened my spine. "How could I put horns on him?" I spoke in what I intended as a tone of respect, but firm. "Their relationship was in name only. It ended when he left for Spain."

"Even so, what makes you think I would tolerate her dalliance with a mere foot soldier?"

Stung, I said, still very respectfully, "I am a little more than that, am I not? Your assistant secretary?" I leaned toward him and spoke low. "Your spy?"

"In your opinion, how deep is the anger of the men concerning the ships?"

"I think they are at the point of mutiny."

He nodded. "To return to the subject of Doña Marina and yourself: she is under my protection, in the sense that a ward would be. In addition to her value to me as an interpreter, there is her stature in the eyes of the soldiery to consider: they have her on a pedestal of sorts because of her great physical beauty and her high intelligence. Many may dream of her, but not as a woman they actually hope to possess. This is good; it keeps them manly and the keener to accomplish our purpose here and return to their women at home. Her conduct must be above reproach. She will bestow no further favors on *you*."

I imagined or heard contempt in his voice, and drew myself up to my full height. "With all respect, let me remind you that I come of good family and am an educated man . . ."

"Boy," he smiled.

"I care deeply about Malinche, and . . ."

"Why do you call her that?"

"Because it's her true name. I care deeply for her. I wish to marry her."

He stared. "Marry her! And how would that sit with the rest of my soldiers? I'll be brief. She is my voice, my tongue. I cannot talk to the Indians without her. I will not have her kissing under trees with you. Forget her. Bow in passing. Goodbye."

Shaken as I was, I stood my ground instead of going. "And what does *she* feel?"

Before he could give any answer but a basilisk stare, Olid and Sandoval had rushed over from the window, and one cried sharply, "It is worse than we believed! Down in the courtyard they're about to burn you in effigy!"

His armchair scraped on stone as he got up to see this sight. I went toward the door, but his voice arrested me. Standing by the window but looking at me, as if the sight of a straw dummy with his name on it were something he saw every day, he said very pleasantly, "I have made El Galán second in command to Captain Alvarado. You I have appointed his aide, which makes you the youngest such in the army." He turned his attention then to the demonstration below.

My wounded spirits soared, though when I emerged into the roar and turmoil of the great courtyard, I wondered if Alvarado would by tomorrow have a company to captain. As I went to look for El Galán, a very cheering thought struck me. Would Cortés have taken the trouble to send for me at such a time and speak at such length unless he knew Malinche cared for me? God well knew the sincerity of my feeling for her, and it was God, not Cortés, who would decide who got her.

The sun had set and the courtyard was in twilight. The crude effigy of Cortés had not been set afire because a squabble had developed over its possession; the Velásquez men lost to the soldiers who did not want to see their general's image go up in flame. Meanwhile, held aloft on the shoulders of a friend, an angry mariner harangued his onlookers: "Cortés said he would be loyal to us and our cause! Is this his loyalty? Leaving us stranded?" My mother's face with its large, sad eyes suddenly filled my mind, and with it the fear that I would never see that face again, or my father's, or ever again close my eyes sheltered by the safe walls of home.

Yago the acrobat bellowed: "Any ass knows how a rumor can spread and grow to a monstrous lie! Maybe Cortés burned a couple of rotten ships! Who cares?"

"More than two! More than two!" someone shouted.

"Where's Cortés?" someone else demanded. "Why doesn't he face us and put this rumor to rest?"

I expected Cortés to appear on the steps of the palace or at the window above to attempt to calm the soldiers, but soon a trumpet sounded from out on the plaza and the braying voice of Cortés' crier called to us to converge at the foot of the great pyramid. I looked up and saw Cortés partway up the steps in full armor. He was flanked by his captains, our standard aloft behind him. Far above his head I could see our altar and the cross. A rumble of discontent from the massed soldiers broke in waves at his feet, but then died away as he waited for our silence.

"Soldiers of Spain," he said in a tone easily heard yet lacking the thrust of authority, "I must tell you that a survey of our ships showed many unfit for service. I ordered them destroyed." Hot murmurs rose; he calmly waited for silence. "This was my great loss, for most of them were my property, all I possessed in the world." A new kind of silence fell now, for no one had thought of that. "But you, my soldiers, will gain an advantage: the addition to this army of the hundred and ten able mariners that were required to man those vessels." The army muttered its dissatisfaction with this boon. Cortés raised his voice up to the level of that ringing sureness I remembered from the speech at Cabo San Antonio. "But even if the fleet were still afloat, what good are those ships to us now? If we succeed in marching to Moctezuma's capital, we will not need them there. Nor

will the ships help us if we fail in that venture, because
we will by then be too far into the interior of this land
to need ships." Cortés took a step down toward us,
arms outspread. "Now I am going to speak to you
frankly: I am glad for the hulls that were rotten, and I
am glad those ships are gone, and I will tell you why.
To be looking back over your shoulder at a means of
escape is a sure way to fail in any venture. It is unworthy of the bravery you have shown me. If you now
go forward yet again, with confidence in yourselves
and in me, our success is certain. Certain!" One arm
gestured upward and we all saw the Cross, our cross,
elevated in this once-heathen land. "As for me, I have
chosen my destiny! I will march westward and meet
face to face with Moctezuma as long as there is even
one man to bear me company!" A faint cheer sounded
and I knew I was not the only soldier who was determined to be that man. "As for those cravens who shrink
from sharing the future joys and dangers of this glorious
venture, then, in God's name, let them go home! There
is one sound ship left. We will let them take it and
return to Cuba. Let them tell there how they deserted
their commander and their comrades! Let them wait
there until we who stayed return in triumph, loaded
with the gold of the Aztecs, the riches of Mexico!"

My heart had soared as he spoke. "To Mexico!" I
shouted, and heard other voices take up the cry. "To
Mexico! To Mexico!"

There was a total reversal of mood. Now enthusiasm
flowed from man to man like a fresh, invisible wind. A
splendid exhilaration filled me. I threw my arms across
the shoulders of El Galán and Juan Morla and the three
of us chanted the names of Santiago and San Pedro,
again and again, and marched singing across the square.
The trumpet sounded, a cannon was fired, and once-
surly faces beamed with smiles and the glow of com-
radeship.

Young though I was, I was aware that Cortés had
achieved a miracle of generalship, using the very act
that had enraged his men to prod them suddenly for-

ward into commitment to the journey westward. And I knew the scuttling and burning of those ships was a crucial moment in history as memorable as any other I could name. In choosing to commit the only act that could keep his army together so he could thrust us onward to the distant land of the Aztecs, Cortés unlocked the continent north of us to penetration. He knew he was doing that. True, this was inevitable: If he had not, another would have, in time. But the fact is, he did. He did, knowing that whatever else history remembered of him, it could never forget this.

And I am not without pride that I took that torch from his hand and used it, though less proud of the wine-sad youth who later sat on the shore mourning the deed to the wail of an Indian flute.

PART IV

▼▼▼

THE MARCH
TO TENOCHTITLÁN
August 16, 1519–November 6, 1519

18

Three days later we set forth for Tenochtitlán: the cream of the force, four hundred soldiers, fifteen horses, seven cannons. Behind us marched thirteen hundred Zempoallan warriors and a thousand *tamanes* to carry the ammunition and baggage. The remainder of the soldiers and most of the mariners stayed to man Vera Cruz, under the command of Captain Juan Escalante, who looked a little like my father. It was the sixteenth of August, six months and six days since we sailed from Cuba. As though to mark my new status as aide, my mustache had turned a trifle darker than my hair, and I let it grow out, though I still shaved my chin. The trials I had passed through merited at least this badge of manhood, I felt.

Orteguilla the dwarf had accompanied us, riding on a litter or on one of the caissons when his legs gave out. I was more surprised to find Gonzalo the traitor among our select number. His carbuncles had disappeared magically after his lashing, and a fervent devotion to Cortés now consumed him. "Our great leader" he called him, rolling Moorish eyes heavenward. "The equal of Alexander, by God!"

Six days of hard marching took us upward from the torrid clime at sea level through a green and temperate zone to frigid mountains thousands of feet high. There an icy rain and hail chilled our bones; a few of the poor *tamanes* were so numbed by cold that they stumbled and fell to their deaths as we made our way along

perilous precipices with steep drops into canyons where
we could see far below us lush tropical foliage instead
of the pines that grew where we were. The breath out of
our nostrils often condensed in cloudy plumes, and
at night we huddled around campfires that kept dying
in the wind and the rain. But Cortés' spirit burned high
as he moved among us when we stopped to rest, as-
suring us that the worst would soon be over. Rain stood
in droplets on his armor; he had lent his hooded black
woolen cloak to Malinche. Marching beside El Galán
in the vanguard of the foot soldiery, I saw ahead, as
our trail curved around a mountain flank, the imposing
figure of Cortés on his black mount, Malinche in his
black cloak riding beside him on the gray mare, and I
thought suddenly of the young French maid of Orléans,
who had so bravely led an army against the English a
century before.

That same afternoon we came to Xocotlán, a fortresslike town whose thin dour cacique, instead of offering
food and shelter to such cold and weary visitors, took
us to view a local monument in which he took great
pride. It was a huge boxlike structure shelved to display
rows of white and grinning skulls: thousands stared out
with their sad, hollow eye sockets, his precious harvest
of the sacrificed, his crop reaped by Death. "But these
trophies are few, compared to the skull rack of my great
lord," he confessed. When Cortés then asked, through
Aguilar and Malinche, if he were a vassal of Moctezuma, he stared in surprise. "Who is not?"

"I am not," Cortés told him. "I serve a king whose
least vassals are as powerful as your Moctezuma."

The cacique of Xocotlán was not in the least impressed. "Indeed? Moctezuma can muster up thirty great
vassals, each master of a hundred thousand men. His
revenues are immense, and his wealth he expends on his
city of Tenochtitlán, which is magnificent beyond any
idea you may have of magnificence. His vast armies
have garrisons in sixty cities. Every year, year in and
year out, at least twenty thousand victims are sacrificed
at the altars of his gods. Many years ago, at the coro-

nation of his uncle Ahuitzotl, more than seventy thousand victims were sacrificed. For days on end they were marched across the city and up the steps of the pyramids in the great central plaza. Priests dropped exhausted from the killings, dripping with blood from head to feet. My grandfather saw this with his own eyes, having gone there as a newly conquered vassal to see his new lord crowned."

As I stood stunned, Cortés asked calmly, "Have you yourself seen the city?"

"I can tell you what it is like. It stands in the middle of a wide lake in the center of a broad and verdant valley ringed by mountains. The only approach to the city is over causeways. There are four, each several miles long. In places these have wooden bridges which can be removed, making it impossible to enter or leave. In the city live a hundred thousand families. Every man, woman, and child reveres Moctezuma as both their ruler and as a god."

In the silence that fell, Malinche said to Cortés, "I will tell him about your victories and of the gifts Moctezuma has sent." There on her gray horse, her hands waving gracefully against the black cloak, she spun a tale which seemed to alter the boastful cacique's disdain of us. He led us to some large stone buildings where he said we could rest, and then sent to us a file of women who made us hot maize cakes on braziers.

We stayed there four days, resting and regaining our strength. The cacique's first hostility seemed to abate, and he readily answered Cortés' questions about the route we should take. We could approach Moctezuma's city by either of two routes. One led to a large city called Cholula. The other passed through the republic of the Tlascalans. This was the route Cortés decided on after the cacique of Xocotlán revealed that the Cholulans were cowed by the might of Moctezuma. The Tlascalans, on the other hand, had rebelled against Aztec domination a century ago and had fiercely maintained their independence: they were civil to everyone but Aztecs. In Tlascala, we could expect a warm welcome.

Our march there took us through a green valley with a lovely little river and many woods in which birds sang sweetly. Along the river were many small Indian houses; their occupants sometimes came out to stare at us, astonished but not unfriendly. The four Zempoallan envoys Cortés sent ahead to take gifts for the Tlascalan ruler and to ask friendly passage through his land would certainly face no troubles en route.

Our journey ended abruptly. Ahead was a stone wall. Nine feet high and with a parapet atop, it looked as if it extended a length of at least a league, buttressed at either end by mountains. We had reached the border of Tlascala, but this barrier did not seem to me to fit the description of a friendly people. The wall had only one opening, at the end of the wide trail we had followed. It was a curious one, formed by two semicircular walls overlapping for a distance of some forty feet and providing a curved passageway ten paces wide, perfectly controlled from the top of the inner wall, empty against the sky. But even though this bastion seemed undefended, Cortés rose high in his stirrups to call back to us, "Forward, soldiers! The Holy Cross is our banner!" I knew then that this formidable wall, which proved ten paces thick, had impressed him, too. I lifted my eyes to our cross for courage, and as I did I saw the long black hair of Malinche blowing back in the wind that had risen. With sudden clarity I realized that our lives were in her hands. Our four Zempoallan envoys had not yet returned with permission to enter this land, so her tongue was our only means to convey our peaceful intentions to whatever horde of Tlascalans might await us beyond the wall. I entered that passageway with my sword half-drawn.

It debouched into a narrow gorge that sloped upward for a considerable distance. No warriors menaced us. We marched along in good spirits, though at first wary about possible Tlascalan arrows and spears from the cliffs at either side. At last our scouts came back with the word that some fifteen Indians were waiting for us ahead where the top of the gorge met a high level plain. Cortés led four of the cavalry forward to meet this welcoming party.

But when we foot soldiers caught up with those horsemen, we found that a furious fight had taken place. To my horror, I came upon the body of a horse lying stiff-legged with blood still gushing from the neck stump; the severed head lay a few feet away. I looked up and saw Malinche on her living mount staring down at it with a horror that seemed to equal mine, and then Cortés galloped up and furiously ordered her to ride back to the rear, out of danger.

In a moment I saw why. Across the open plain, a horde of Tlascalan warriors, three thousand at least, was bearing down on us. But on that open ground, our full calvary was able to maneuver. Within minutes fifty of the enemy lay dead, our musketeers and crossbowmen accounted for a hundred more, and the rest of the Tlascalans ran away across that plain like scared children. Cortés at once ordered the carcasses of our two dead horses buried, hoping to preserve to our advantage the Indian belief that they were mythical monsters. The Tlascalans who had slaughtered them and those who saw it done were all killed now, and could not testify that centaurs can bleed and die.

In low spirits, we camped that night in a wide dry riverbed and supped on some small fat dogs we found in a pen; the Indians breed them for food. Needing oil with which to dress his wounds, one of the men in Alvarado's company, lacking certain sentiments I felt, cut fat from an Indian corpse and rendered it down into oil in a pan over the campfire. I was glad I didn't need to use any, my only injury being a swollen and purple eye for which El Galán advised a poultice of raw dog meat.

As I held it in place, my spirit seethed with rage at the cruel duplicity of the cacique of Xocotlán. I had been there when Cortés had asked him, through Aguilar and Malinche, about the best route to take. And that miserable Indian had said to avoid Cholula and go by way of Tlascala, where we would be welcomed. What a warm welcome we had had! Just below my anger lay uneasy doubt of Cortés for trusting the proud owner of so many dead men's heads. I said to El Galán, "Cortés should have been suspicious when our envoys failed to return. It's clear now that the cacique of Xocotlán deceived us when he said this route was safe."

"Maybe it wasn't he who deceived us," a voice behind me said. I looked around and saw Gonzalo, the former traitor, firelight glowing on his brooding face. He squatted between us and stared at me with eyes both malicious and somber. "Would Aguilar or Cortés have known the difference if that cacique had really said just the opposite? To *avoid* Tlascala?"

In the tense silence that followed, a pine cone in the fire went up in a spurt of flame. Malinche rode across my mind, black hair blowing back.

"A traitoress?" El Galán demanded. "That beautiful creature, so noble in appearance, so gentle-voiced and kind?"

"She's an Indian," Gonzalo muttered. "Just because she speaks some Spanish now and lights a candle to the Virgin doesn't change that. Blood to blood. She's not of our race. Look at how Melchorejo deserted us."

"Melchorejo was Melchorejo!" I shouted. "Malinche is Malinche. She would never betray us."

He gave me a smug and irritating smile. "I am not the only one who has realized that she could have told Aguilar anything she pleased, and like a parrot he turned it into Spanish for Cortés. He wouldn't suspect a thing!"

I suddenly hated this former traitor now relishing his suspicion of treachery in another. "Why are you vomiting this on *me?*"

He smirked. "You are Cortés' eyes and ears, no? You are his spy, no? I'm just giving you the chance to do your job again." A mean triumph gleamed in his eyes. It was clear to me that he had done some brooding and had concluded that it was not by pure chance that I had drawn from him the confession about the plot in which he had taken part. He must also be aware of my high regard for Malinche.

"For a former traitor you're very zealous, Gonzalo," I said with contempt.

His eyes took on a doglike look; squatting there he made me think of a hound, the fawning sort that pants and slavers at the master's feet. "Cortés punished me with a flogging when he could have had me hanged. And when I begged to march with him to Moctezuma's city so as to have a chance to redeem myself, he let me come. And I am going to merit his faith in me. He is going to know what I suspect about this Indian girl." Inflamed by his own loyalty, he jumped to his feet. "I gave you your chance to be loyal to Cortés, and don't be surprised if I tell him you refused it!" He turned and ran in the direction of Cortés' tent.

I stood up, intending to run after him and stop him if I had to knock him unconscious, but then I knew that unless I killed him he was going to bring Cortés his bone of suspicion.

I sank down and sat staring into the embers of the fire and moodily fed them a few twigs and leaves, the voices of El Galán and the several others mere wind to me. Imps and devils leered from the brief bursts of flame, mocking me for my impotence now, in contrast to my nights of secret passion. Ever since Cortés had forbidden me to speak to Malinche, I had lived a secret life with my Indian princess. In reveries and in sleep, she and I became companions of the night, sometimes as innocent as children picking flowers and singing songs together but sometimes locked in thrilling embraces that emptied me of lust. The priest at home had once warned me against those succubuses that fasten themselves onto a man in the night, the Devil's temptresses that make him fornicate against his will. But he had never warned me that one could assume the face and form of a woman who walked by day quite innocent of those dreams I had of her.

Innocent! She was innocent of any treachery! But

would Cortés know that as I did? Or would he believe Gonzalo? I leaped to my feet, furious at myself for having brooded by the fire so long instead of starting at once on my mission: to defend Malinche. El Galán asked where I was off to; I told him; he tried to deter me, saying I had no proof of her innocence beyond my evident infatuation with her. Ignoring him, I raced toward Cortés' tent, wondering what I could say in her defense and whether I could even get past Cortés' sentry.

The tent was large, four-walled, peak-roofed. Lighted from within, it glowed softly. Outside the closed flap of the doorway, Orteguilla was standing beside a sleepy sentry. I had almost reached him when Gonzalo came out looking both pleased (a small smirk) and chastened (a somber backward look). Seeing me, he detoured abruptly.

As I panted up, Orteguilla said, "Do you know what that whoreson just told Cortés about Doña Marina?"

"He has babbled his suspicions. I'm here to defend her."

"Save your breath. When I spoke out in her behalf Cortés dismissed me. There's nothing you can do where I failed. He sent a sentry after her. He's in a cold fury. I think he believes Gonzalo, halfway anyhow. Here she is."

I turned. Malinche was coming toward the tent beside a tall sentry. Her face looked serene. She smiled at me and at Orteguilla as the sentry who had brought her opened the tent flap so she could enter and then hurried away. The other one roused himself for an instant, then fell into his doze again, resting on his pike as sentries do. Orteguilla and I, as one man, moved to the tent flap and laid our ears against it.

I was the luckier. My right eye was a handspan from the crack where the tent flap was not tightly closed. I edged that way and peered through. I could see only part of the interior: Cortés was seated in his carved armchair; much of his armor had been removed; the greave for the right leg lay on the floor where Orteguilla had evidently dropped it on being ordered out. The helmet, pauldrons, and gauntlet had also been shed. At either side of the breastplate Cortés' wide shoulders jutted; his face looked as hard as the metal below it. I knew how much his emotion had mastered him, to let a woman see him thus half-clad. And yet his somber air of authority was such that his appearance did not diminish him. To me the contrast between the vulnerable exposed arms and the armor he still wore expressed his state of mind: somewhat vulnerable to Gonzalo's suspicions, his heart armored against Malinche's defense of herself. He was saying, "A serious accusation has been made against you, Doña Marina. You are suspected of treachery, of sending us here to our possible deaths. The Tlascalans' hostility makes it impossible for me to dismiss this possibility." Parting the tent flap a trifle I was able to see Malinche, facing him.

Something hard prodded my shoulder. It was the butt of the sentry's pike. "Get out," he advised me succinctly. Orteguilla was gazing up at the moon as if he had never eavesdropped in his life. The sentry's crooked nose had been broken. He raised the pikestaff as if quite ready to break mine. "Get out," he said again in the same flat tone. I saw in his small cold eye that breaking noses might be his favorite pastime. I left.

But having disappeared into the nearby grove of plane trees, I quickly circled through them and came to the rear of the tent, unguarded as I had hoped. No doorway there offered me a slit to peer through, but I laid my ear against the tent's fabric. Cortés was saying "You deny any wish to ingratiate yourself with Moctezuma by defeating my effort to reach his city. You tell me the Aztecs are not dear to you. But the blunt fact is that they are Indians and you are an Indian, and most people feel loyalty to their own kind."

Her voice was low but did not sound frightened. "My own kind? At San Juan Ulua that night I swam ashore I did not return to my own kind. Did not choose slavery with them, or death. I stayed with Spaniards. If Tlascalans defeat you, I am defeated. Why would I lie, betray you? If you die, I die."

"By my conscience! You are very cool-headed for a woman!" Did I imagine it, or was there a note of admiration in his voice?

"You are not a fool," she said. "There is another explanation for the hostility of these Tlascalans besides my treachery."

"What?"

"The Zempoallan envoys you sent ahead may have boasted of the gifts Moctezuma sent you. So these Tlascalans see you as friends of the Aztecs."

"I never thought of that, I must admit!"

"I want to leave now. I am very tired."

"You will leave when I give you permission to leave. Do not get above yourself, Doña Marina." Cortés' voice was no longer harsh. "I want you to stay here awhile. There are matters I wish to discuss with you." His light tone changed to a shout. "Orteguilla! Where are you? I want the rest of this armor off!"

Was he going to undress in front of her? Or did the tent have some sort of screen or curtain? What did he want to "discuss" with her?

"You again?" The sentry's pike had preceded him around the corner of the tent as he made his rounds; he thrust it toward me. I leaped away and raced for the grove, my feelings in turmoil. Instead of going toward the pine grove where Alvarado's company was camped, I doubled around and hid in some bushes through which I could peer and see the door to Cortés' tent. The sentry was back at his post, dozing upright. In the stillness of the night I could hear faint voices within the tent. Orteguilla wished Malinche good night. He emerged, closed the tent flap with care, and trotted away.

Kneeling there in those bushes, I waited for Malinche to emerge. At any moment she would, I told myself. The moments passed. I heard Cortés' laugh, the sound of his voice but not the words. More moments passed, a veritable army of moments, as many as the

multitude of cold stars looking down at me, but she did
not come out of the tent. Exhaustion after the day's
long march and battle proved stronger than my urgent
need to clarify my doubts. I woke with a start and
looked wildly about, not sure at first where I was. I
saw then that the tent was dark. Had she left while I
slept? An urge to creep to the tent flap and peer in was
stilled as the sentry coughed.

I plodded to the pine grove, spread out my blanket
beside El Galán, who lay on his back, snoring gently.
The sound was comforting as I lay wide-eyed beside
him, for all around us was the dark expanse of this land
where they hated us. I suddenly remembered what El
Galán had once told me: great danger can be a stimulus
to sexual desire.

"What happened?" he asked me sleepily. "Where
have you been?"

"I didn't feel like sleeping."

"Did you have any luck defending Doña Marina?"

"There was no need to. She defended herself very
well."

"I don't imagine Cortés was too hard to convince."
Now he was up on one elbow, facing me. "I've lived
some and I have eyes in my head. Lately he's regarded
her at times with that look a man sends toward a
woman he intends to enjoy."

The wind of truth howled in my hollow, aching heart.
I knew the look he meant, had seen it, but had chosen
to confuse myself with thoughts of Juana of Orléans,
noted for her purity as much as for her valor and her
voices.

"And there's something else to consider." El Galán
sounded ready to chat all night. "Cortés is a general,
and knows he needs her voice. Gonzalo's accusation of
treachery has sharpened Cortés' awareness of her importance to this venture. To bind her to him with the
tie of physical passion would not be a stupid move. A
well-bounced woman tends to feel a definite loyalty to
the source of her pleasure. I think that before long
Cortés will have her on his wrist like a hooded falcon."

Do you intend to pitch a tent and dwell on this one subject forever?" I cried.

"Poor Arturo. And you found her first." His voice was amused but kind.

Tears stung my eyeballs. I turned my head away; the moonlight might make them glimmer. As I feigned sleep a voice in my head insisted that El Galán was wrong, all wrong. But the hollow inside my chest through which a night wind blew told me he was right.

19

I woke foggy-headed after troubling dreams; soon enough I was as alert as the rest of the army, keenly aware of our peril, ready for another Tlascalan attack. But late in the morning two of our missing Zempoallan envoys were returned to us, brought by polite Tlascalan messengers who said, we soon learned, that we had been attacked by mistake by a border patrol that had been alarmed by our appearance. A cacique named Xicotencatl the Younger sent his regrets for this mistake.

"But nonetheless we'll sleep in our armor tonight," Alvarado said when he told us this, "because Indians are very tricky."

He was soon proved right. Later that same day the other two Zempoallan envoys came back to us, weary and frightened. Because of the fluke of an unlatched door they had managed to escape from a cageful of sacrificial victims where they had been imprisoned after being severely questioned about us. Cortés had the captains tell us what he had learned from them: that our invasion of Tlascala had caused great turmoil and a sharp division of opinion among the caciques and nobles of the various towns when they met in council in the capital. Some were in favor of letting us pass westward unmolested, but the most revered leader in the republic, a blind old man named Xicotencatl the Elder, was convinced that the weight of evidence favored our being friends of the Aztecs and therefore enemies of Tlascalans. The gifts Moctezuma had lavished on us and the fact that a great number of his conquered Zempoallans accompanied us were two indications of this, he said. To tamely let us pass through Tlascala would seem to Moctezuma a sign of weakness of which he would surely take advantage later by mounting an all-out attack on the republic neither he nor his ancestors had been able to conquer. Our two envoys, who had observed a part of this debate before being imprisoned, had no doubt that this blind old man would persuade his namesake and other dissenters to believe as he did.

Nonetheless Cortés and the captains determined that we had to march forward toward Moctezuma's city. Retreat would be a sign to these indomitable Tlascalans of timidity that would release a savage scorn and provoke attacks as savage. Warily we set forth the morning after the return of the envoys. From the high flank of the mountain we rounded we could see what lay ahead to the west: other mountains, among them volcanos like the one looming above us. Behind we could see the white cone called Orizaba; ahead were two stupendous peaks, only their snowy summits jutting above the lower sierra that formed our horizon. The Zempoallans knew their names: Popocatepetl and Ixtaccihuatl. The last meant "Sleeping Princess" because, from the high valley of Anahuac where Moctezuma's city stood that mountain had the form of a shapely woman reclining on her back. A lesser peak far to the south interested me much more when they said it was called Malinche.

I marched forward wondering why a female child had been given the name of a mountain. Later I learned from her that it was only a soubriquet her father had chosen when she was an infant, since among her people it was considered bad luck for a child's birth-name to be bandied about outside the immediate family. But all such idle thoughts were cut off abruptly when we heard drums and shrill flutes and saw on a plateau ahead thousands of Tlascalan warriors running toward us, shooting arrows and hurling spears. The sight of our horses caused a sudden wavering, but the enemy summoned the courage to attack with massed fury. It was lucky for us that they chose this wide level place for their show of bravery, for Cortés could use the Spanish phalanx in which we had been well-drilled, the cavalry driving a deadly opening wedge into the enemy ranks, leaving a great number of them dead. The living retreated, but almost at once thousands more burst out of some woods nearby, all in red and white, armed with pikes, slings, lances, obsidian swords, thick cotton breastplates, and huge shields of wood and leather with bright feather designs. They did not carry their banner to the front as we did, but to the rear—a white crane with wings spread. They yelled like devils. We fought them until sundown and killed eight of their chief warriors, but they managed to kill another of our horses and they dragged the body off the field when they retreated. Soon they would know that it was no supernatural creature, just meat and bone and sinew.

My knowledge of what happened on the large scale in this battle and all the rest was pieced together from what others said after the fighting was over. I entered each encounter with a prayer to God and I assumed that he wanted me, a Christian and a Spaniard, to have a longer life than whatever heathen opposed me, and by this faith and a certain cold exertion of my own will I turned myself into a kind of machine for killing, to make sure that no one killed me. I discovered that I disliked killing even heathens, and I wondered if it had been the same with my father when he was helping to rid Cuba of Caribs.

That night we found a large empty temple which we could use as our fortress and for several days Cortés made brief forays, leaving the main body of his troops to defend this bastion. We left it on the fourth day, thinking the Tlascalans subdued, only to hear their drums and flutes and conch horns and to confront an army of them so vast it made the earlier battles seem like children's play with toy soldiers: later Cortés estimated this Tlascalan army at one hundred forty thousand. But again we fought them on level ground, and again our cannons, musketeers, arquebusiers, and cavalry cut great lanes of dead men in their ranks. After several hours of this there was a division of the enemy, some leaving the field, others staying. But these soon saw the severe losses they had suffered, and disappeared pell-mell, a rout marked by scattered shrieks of fading defiance and the slow drumbeats of defeat. None of our horses was killed, and we lost only one man. About sixty of us were wounded, but I was not among these. We all knelt in prayer on the battlefield and thanked God for this victory.

It had seemingly impressed the Tlascalans, for the next morning when I got up I was startled to see an Indian coming toward me in a cloak tied on one shoulder in the Tlascalan manner. He was holding out a big basket of cherries and urged me with a nod to help myself. I saw many other Tlascalans passing among us with baskets of fruit and tortillas, and I decided they were peace offerings.

I had just popped the first cherry into my mouth, savoring its sweet juice, when I saw Malinche talking to one of these friendly Tlascalans and saw that he looked uneasy. She turned and hurried toward Cortés' tent. I ran after her and fell in step beside her, offering my handful of cherries. She shook her head. "Enjoy them. They may be the last you will ever eat. I think the Tlascalans who brought them are spies, pretending that the younger Xicotencatl now wants to make peace."

In a few minutes I saw Spanish soldiers rounding up the Tlascalans with the cherries. Later I learned that under questioning the smiling visitors first protested their innocence but at last admitted that they had been ordered to our camp to spy out what they could about us. Under further "questioning" at the hands of a fellow we called The Executioner, who had flogged Gonzalo and hanged his cohorts, they confessed that Xicotencatl the Younger planned a night attack on us because their priests had said that Spaniards turned coward after the sun sank. Cortés sent the spies back to Xicotencatl with their hands cut off, punishment for having brought gifts that were false evidence of friendship. I was at first very sickened, for it seemed to me unnecessarily cruel to have treated them so, but then I realized that Cortés was dealing with a savage people who did not understand subtleties and that he was desperate for us, vastly outnumbered as we were, and with retreat down that gorge impossible. I had learned, too, what Malinche had meant when she said those cherries might be the last I would ever eat. She had instantly suspected the worst, as if she had heard the old adage "Beware of Greeks bringing gifts."

Thanks to her suspicion, we were prepared for their night attack as we otherwise would not have been, believing that Indians will never fight after dark. With that day's dusk, some ten thousand Tlascalans moved silently down on us from the neighboring hills, but since they were unfamiliar with night fighting, we routed them by moonlight.

After three days of sporadic battles, Cortés attempted to parley with Xicotencatl through our interpreters. A Tlascalan we had captured pointed the young chieftain out to us, and Cortés had Malinche call out to him that we had come here with only peaceful intentions, had fought because we had been forced to defend ourselves, and now asked only permission to pass through their country. One of the warrior chieftains surrounding Xicotencatl then stepped forward and shouted something at Cortés. Malinche translated his words into

Spanish with no evidence of fear, though I saw some soldiers around me turn pale. "Feel free, strangers, to make your way to our capital city. There we will sacrifice you all to our gods, and strip the flesh from your bones and cook it with chili sauce and vend it in the streets!"

This threat might have seemed merely the ferocious boasting of an angry child had we not learned that these Tlascalans were cannibals. In a town where we had camped for a night on finding all the warriors gone and only women and children there, we had found big wooden cages full of men and women being fattened for sacrifice, after which their bodies would be eaten by the populace, they told us. We had set the poor creatures free; having nowhere else to go, they stayed with us. Such victims had either been captured in battle or had been sold to the Tlascalans by slave traders who procured them in various ways, sometimes from parents facing starvation.

The Tlascalans made a last bold effort to overwhelm us, were decimated by our guns and crossbowmen, and retreated tossing back defiant cries that included the word *chili* a number of times.

The next day, to our surprise, Xicotencatl the Younger arrived in person, along with fifty warrior chiefs, to offer peace. He was a tall Indian with a long, pockmarked face, a high feather headdress, and a toga with a horizontal frieze reaching just below the knees and tied at one broad copper-colored shoulder. He carried himself with royal dignity, acknowledged our victory, and begged us to enter Tlascala's main city. "Either you must kill me now as I stand here or accept my lifelong friendship," he declaimed. Cortés embraced him, said he accepted his friendship and offered his in return. I witnessed this meeting at quite close quarters and I did not have the slightest doubt that Xicotencatl was sincere.

On September 23, having entered Tlascala on the first day of the month, we marched six leagues to the capital, where we were met by a procession of nobles and priests and learned that the city's usual thirty thousand inhabitants were swelled by thousands more, come from near and distant towns to see the white gods enter. We made a fine procession ourselves, three hundred ninety-nine Spaniards and nearly twenty-five hundred Zempoallans, counting the *tamanes*. We foot soldiers behaved like the victors we were, heads high and marching brisk.

And we were treated like victors, given six stone buildings around the main plaza with braziers of charcoal in all the rooms. But the food we were offered tasted flat and strange and we learned that for nearly a century the Tlascalans had done without salt, for that commodity was controlled by the Aztecs. Cotton, too, was scarce; most Tlascalans wore a coarse cloth called *nequen* woven of cactus fibers.

But Cholula, the city lying between us and Tenochtitlán, suffered no such lacks, Xicotencatl the Younger told us bitterly. The Cholulans were abject and servile toward the Aztecs and could be expected to do Moctezuma's bidding. Our Tlascalan ally had now learned that we were proceeding westward against Moctezuma's command, and he said, "Do not go to Cholula! The rooftops will be piled with stones to pitch on your head as you pass. Stay here with us as long as you wish. But do not go to Cholula."

Cortés smiled and said that since he had been told to expect a friendly reception at Tlascala, he would not avoid Cholula on the basis of mere rumor, and asked for further information about Moctezuma, who interested him more than Cholula did.

The Tlascalan said, "He has ruled for nearly seventeen years. In his youth he was a warrior, I have heard. He now lives in idle luxury. But I have been told that from the day of his coronation he has been plagued by many evil omens, and by prophecies of disaster to the Aztecs." He grinned. "Your defiance of his command to leave must disturb him deeply."

That we would ever see the famous Moctezuma was thrown suddenly into doubt, for two weeks after our welcome to Tlascala I found out that a good many soldiers wanted to abandon the march to his city. They had rallied around the Three Moors, brothers we had nicknamed that because of their dark coloring. Rosario, the tallest, fiercest, and darkest, spoke out to at least thirty Spanish soldiers in his deep, hoarse voice. "These Tlascalans treat us good, feed us nice, but how long can we trust cannibals? What we ought to do is thank them for the warning about those Cholulans with the rocks on the roofs and turn around and march back to Vera Cruz and wait there until King Carlos sends us reinforcements. There's too few Spaniards here."

Nods and murmurs of approval greeted this. I said, seeing all hope of my meeting Don Oro go glimmering: "But we have our Zempoallans. And what about the Tlascalan soldiers Cortés hopes to get from Xicotencatl?"

"There's too few Spaniards," Rosario boomed.

"Three hundred and ninety-nine. Only three hundred Greeks held the pass at Thermopylae against the whole Persian army," I said.

Rosario shrugged. "I don't know about any Thermop-whatever, but defending a pass is one thing and marching into enemy territory is another, and I want more Spaniards by me. And I'll wait for reinforcements in Vera Cruz if I have to march back there by myself."

"Be careful, Rosario," Gonzalo called, looking at me. "When Cortés learns you talked like this you can look for a flogging!"

"Yours was well-deserved," I said, reminded of my duty as a spy. I faced Rosario, a good bit taller than I was and twice as wide. "When I tell Cortés that some men want to go back to Vera Cruz I do not intend to mention your name or any other."

I found Cortés in the palace of Xicotencatl the Elder, Malinche at his side. The younger Xicotencatl was there too, and many Tlascalan nobles, gathered in a large stone hall with impressive bas-reliefs of warriors and gods. The blind ancient ruler stood at the center of the group, eyes staring fixedly below the band that crossed his forehead, binding his gray hair which hung nearly to his shoulders. His legs were not withered but still muscular, and his square-jawed face had also retained its strength. Even facing Cortés, he was so impressive that I felt hesitant about interrupting with even so important a message.

But Cortés, knowing I would not intrude except for a good reason, beckoned me forward. I saw that he was elated. "The elder Xicotencatl has just promised me ten thousand Tlascalan warriors to march with us to Moctezuma's city!"

"Five hundred Spaniards would do you more good," I said.

He sobered. "Meaning?"

When I told him his face darkened. "In other words, a mutiny is brewing?"

"It might come to that." My eyes wandered to Malinche. Was her face softer, or did I imagine it? Did she look somehow different? Cortés' voice drew my gaze back to him. "You were wise to bring me this news promptly. By God, I'd make a good muleteer! ¡El Arriero! I have to keep driving balky cowards toward the destiny they want to flee!" He turned to Malinche, told her to make his apologies to the elder Xicotencatl, and strode from the council hall.

A few minutes later I heard his crier call the soldiers to form ranks below the palace steps where he stood. He told us of the huge Tlascalan contingent that would join us, and once again he was able to shame the cowards, inspire every man to march with him to the land of the Aztecs. Smiling, confident, without a fear or a doubt, he aroused in each of us the courage that would not have been there without him. Like a magical mirror he reflected back into us everything we wanted to be as men.

When he stopped speaking all faces were animated, eyes flashing, smiles parting dark beards. And then I saw Malinche. She stood at the foot of the steps, Orteguilla beside her. She was looking up at Cortés as though she saw God himself standing there.

I had lost her. And I could not blame her for this adoration, or him for having succumbed and made her his mistress, for he was flesh and blood after all. But it was bitter to realize that those two would never have known each other except that I had looked up one sunny day in Tabasco and seen walking toward me a vision who embodied all beauty and all desire.

Cortés chose to take only six thousand Tlascalan warriors with us; he did not want to be too vastly outnumbered by our new allies, allies as yet unbaptized, although an oath of loyalty to King Carlos had been sworn. The day before we left, Cortés made Xicotencatl the Younger promise that he would see to it that the Tlascalans did not eat any more people, but this was a promise easily made since we would not be there to see that it was carried out.

On the morning we marched from Tlascala, one sorrowful face stood out to me. It was that of Xicotencatl the Elder, who appeared at the top of the steps to his palace with some old nobles who surveyed the ranks of soldiers massing in the square below. His blind eyes stared at nothingness from deep sockets. At last he shook his head slowly and departed, followed into the palace by the others. His evident sorrow suggested to me that through some rare gift of inner sight he had envisioned many perils that lay ahead of us. Xicotencatl the Younger would remain in Tlascala, but two other sons of the old man were marching with us that morning toward whatever dangers he saw or imagined.

20

The road to Cholula was a dogleg of a little more than twelve leagues, though the two republics were closer than that as the crow flies. We were a dragon with a small body of Spaniards and a monstrously long tail: nine thousand Tlascalan and Zempoallan warriors and above a thousand *tamanes*. In a land without any pack animals or wheeled vehicles it was natural that a low class of human beings should be used as burros or mules are in Spain, but I felt rather sorry for them. I wondered what our toilsome adventure looked like from their eyes. Perhaps it was all as puzzling and incomprehensible as God's ways often are to us.

It was sunset when we neared the city of Cholula. Cortés decided that we would camp for the night on the border of a stream and enter in the morning, rested. We had just settled ourselves there when several Cholulan caciques and their attendants came along the road to the city. They were dressed in a manner quite different from any Indians we had seen, in flowing burnooses of fine cotton.

They offered us a fulsome welcome to their city but balked at admitting our Tlascalans, ancient enemies. Cortés courteously agreed that these allies would camp outside the wall to rejoin us when we left to march on to Tenochtitlán, so next morning we entered Cholula followed only by half of our Zempoallans. Hordes of citizens lined the street to see us pass: tiny children, tottering old men, and every age between. Flowers were strewn at our feet and music from flutes and horns made it all seem like a great public fiesta in our honor.

The main part of the city was in a bowl in the hills overlooked by a vast pyramid of Quetzalcoatl, the base covering forty acres, and there were three hundred smaller temples. The whiteness of the great pyramid in that cool bright sunlight hurt my eyes; it had just been given a new layer of stucco. This was done every fifty-two years, the most significant time span among the Aztecs and the people they dominated, for they believed that at the end of such a cycle the sun may cease to appear in the sky and all things perish. In Aztec cities there was a very solemn celebration of the safe passage through that dread hour: a new fire was kindled in the breast cavity of a sacrificial victim and priests lighted torches from it and brought this sacred flame to all the other temples. But even after we learned this, we did not realize that our approach to Tenochtitlán at just this time added to our dread significance.

We were offered quarters in several large palaces, and in the great courtyard of one a feast was spread by slaves who brought many dishes we had never tasted, among these a chilled and frothy sweet drink made from *chocolatl,* the favorite beverage of the great Moctezuma himself, we were told. Noble Cholulans in burnooses came to our courtyard with their wives to welcome us and again music played delightfully and an air of gaiety prevailed.

We sat on straw mats alongside lengths of fine cotton cloth on which, among the various bowls and platters of food, were scattered flowers. There is an old Spanish saying that too many flowers may hide the stench of a murder, but I truly believed that envy as well as an ancient hostility had made our allies speak so harshly of Cholulans. By opting to stay on peaceful terms with the Aztecs, they certainly had a better life than the Tlascalans—they even had beggars in the streets, a sure sign of affluence. Thousands of visitors came to worship at the famous pyramid and to buy the many wares in the markets scattered through the town, particularly gauzy cottons and delicate pottery.

Watching Malinche sip from a goblet shaped like an open lily, I noticed that the wife of one of the Cholulan caciques knelt close beside her and seemed very enamored of her, if that is the right word for the admiration of one woman for another. This Cholulan woman was much older than Malinche, stocky, with flashing black eyes, heavy gold earrings, and a brooch of carved jade. Before long she and Malinche had their heads together and were conversing intimately and with great animation. Cortés was paying no attention to his "tongue," for his real one was wagging in merry conversation with the captains seated near him. As I watched Malinche and her new friend, it occurred to me that the older woman might have been instructed to strike up this acquaintance for the purpose of learning what she could about us. Would Malinche be wary? I even thought of going to where she knelt to remark, in Spanish, that there was something about this overly friendly woman I did not like. But then Orteguilla, drunk on the pulque served, was urged into reciting some ribald rhymes that took my attention from Malinche, though when we departed from the feast I noted the older woman still beside her.

During the next several days all went pleasantly. I wandered along clean streets, stared at by Cholulans upon whom my blond hair made the usual impression. Along with other visitors, El Galán and I went up the hundred twenty steep steps of the main pyramid to its vast top level, an acre across, where an enormous statue of the god wore a headdress of flames, seen at night for many leagues. With greater awe I looked out at those two great volcanos we had first glimpsed in Tlascala. Popocatepetl was sending up a great volume of smoke or steam that rose in spite of a strong wind straight as a pikestaff far into the sky. As I stared, a priest sounded the hour on a long trumpet; it was a haunting, mournful wail, like the yearning complaint of that fuming mountain which could not ever hope to awaken the serene Sleeping Princess at its side.

On our return to our quarters, El Galán and I learned that in our absence some messengers from Moctezuma had arrived. Juan Morla said they had been very sharp with Cortés; their master was angry at our stubborn approach to his capital and they urged us to retrace our steps to Tlascala immediately. "Oh, but they were arrogant dogs," Juan Morla said, "and they passed by us common soldiers as if we were turds on the pavement, and that's why I made it my business to overhear when Doña Marina translated their words to Cortés. And I hope Xicotencatl was wrong when he said these Cholulans are kissers of the Aztec ass." He gestured at the hills surrounding the city. "Because we're in their pocket, no?"

The change in our hosts' attitude was abrupt. No nobles or caciques visited us that night, and the next evening—when Cortés made a point of sending several captains to invite them to dine—they all pled sudden illness. The slaves brought us only scanty food and left without serving it to us.

That night Cortés sent out some Zempoallans disguised in burnooses to mingle with the populace, and they returned to say that stones and spears were stockpiled on the flat roofs of the buildings overlooking the road out of town, just as we had been warned. Big holes with upright spikes fixed within had been dug at intervals as though in hope of trapping and killing our horses and, even more chilling, they heard that a number of slave children had been offered up as a special sacrifice to the gods, in the hope that these deities would smile on some venture the Cholulans contemplated. That it concerned us we could not doubt. But what was their concrete plan against us?

When I left Cortés' headquarters after learning this bad news, I saw two familiar female figures crossing the plaza together, lost in deep conversation: Malinche and the Cholulan cacique's wife, with whom she had been on such good terms at that first happy banquet. When they saw me, the Cholulan woman abruptly hurried away. Malinche went toward the stone building where she and Cortés slept. I ran forward and stopped her as she began to go up the steep stone steps. "Malinche!"

She turned. New clothing had been provided her in this city of beautiful cloth, and she wore a burnoose of a pale green cotton so fine it floated as she moved. Heavy gold pendants hung from her ears. A hood gave her a mysterious look. Beside her, forming a balustrade, was a great stone serpent head, grinning to show wide-spaced teeth. "No one ever calls me Malinche any more," she said. "Except Indians."

"I will call you Doña Marina if that is the name you prefer," I said stiffly. "I did not mean to offend you."

"You didn't offend me." She smiled down at me, waiting.

I looked up and realized once more that she was perhaps the single most important member of our expedition except for Cortés himself. How could I have dreamed this outcome when I first saw her in Tabasco, stricken with terror at her capture by a god? "Your friendship with that Cholulan lady might be dangerous," I told her.

"Why?"

"She's older than you and has a wily look. She could pry secrets out of you."

"Or the reverse."

"What?"

"Perhaps I can pry some secrets from her."

"She sought you out. I think she had a reason."

"She did. She wants me to marry her son."

"What!"

"I have told her that I am a princess being held hostage and that I am very unhappy. She says that her son saw me at the banquet and liked me very much. She has invited me to come and live at her house. Her husband is an important noble. I will be safe there, she told me. Why, she asked me tonight, should I share the fate of my captors?"

"What fate?"

"That is what I hope to find out when I visit her tomorrow."

My skin prickled with alarm. "It could be a trick! They know how important you are to Cortés. You could be held there as hostage!"

"Then you can come with me as my bodyguard." Her serenity was maddening. "Yes, I must have a bodyguard. For if I were really a prisoner as I told her, I would never be allowed to go freely about the city, true?"

"Does Cortés know about this plan of yours?"

"No. I don't want him to. He would refuse to let me go." She came down two steps so our eyes were level. "No one knows but you. If he learns, it will be you who told him." She paused, eyeing me sternly. "I am sure that Cholulan woman knows the plan they are going to use against us. I think I can squeeze it out of her. At least I must try. Will you help me, Arturo?"

The Devil himself would have agreed, persuaded by those dark, yearning eyes, that sweet voice, and I was no devil, only a very young man trying to forget that I was in love with her. "If you will come to visit me when I am put in irons."

"If that happens, I'll demand that I be put in irons too." We both knew that this disgrace was not the risk we faced. If the Cholulan woman had set a trap for Malinche as I feared, we would both be the hostages of a people who killed little children atop the pyramid of the gentle god who had preached to them of mercy.

We said good night and as I watched her climb the steps, the hem of her full skirt swaying from side to side, I realized that now she spoke Castilian with no more accent than if she had been born a Portuguese. I remembered El Galán telling me that were it not for that miserable law that forbade our sleeping with Indian women, we would all by now be able to speak the Nahuatl tongue with some fluency, as there is no better place to learn a strange language than in bed. I turned abruptly away, but then was cheered at the thought that even if she slept tonight at Cortés' side, a secret would lie there between them, a secret she had just shared with me.

My anxiety about tomorrow's venture took form in a troubling dream of the Cholulan woman, who had hidden Malinche in a big chest and sat on top of it, grinning at me evilly, holding in one hand a knife of black obsidian with which she made curious gestures in the air which I knew were very obscene.

The next day, wearing full armor, I went with Malinche to the house of the Cholulan lady. They sat together on a stone bench in a pretty garden and I stood frowning a few feet away, watching Malinche for the signal she would give me; when she brushed her forehead with her hand I would interrupt them and say that it was time for Malinche to leave. After they had talked quite a while, Malinche made the motion I had been watching for. I stepped forward and pointed toward the street. "Did you learn anything?" I asked in Spanish.

"It is worse than I thought." She turned to the Cholulan woman and said something to her, then stood up. "I told her that I have to return with you now, and that I will gather together my clothing and jewels and escape tonight."

Her hostess stood up, too, and spoke to Malinche in an imperious tone.

Malinche turned an uneasy face to me. "She is coming with us."

They preceded me out of the garden and along the street to the courtyard of Cortés' palace. As we went up the stairs to Malinche's sleeping room she turned to me and said, "I asked her to come into my room with me to help me pack. I'll leave quickly. You keep her there."

I waited outside the room, sword drawn. Malinche ran out, but when the Cholulan woman tried to follow I barred the way with my sword and she stepped back, her face sharp with suspicion as she stared after Malinche's receding figure. I took hold of the woman's shoulder and turned her around and pointed into the room with the sword. She stood there staring about her, trapped. In minutes Cortés, Malinche, and several captains hastened along the corridor and into the room and I watched from the doorway while Cortés questioned her through Malinche.

The terrified woman admitted that Moctezuma had sent bribes to the most powerful of the Cholulan nobles, among them this woman's husband, and had asked their aid in his plan to dispose of us before we came any nearer his city. When we started to march out of Cholula, impeded by the holes in the road, the missiles on the roof, and the barricades, thousands of Aztec warriors now bivouacked a few leagues from the city would march in, dispose of our Tlascalans, and then join the Cholulans in defeating us. Of those who lived, twenty would be sacrificed in Cholula, but the rest would be marched in fetters to Tenochtitlán, there at last to meet Moctezuma and his hungry gods.

"Why is Moctezuma so afraid of our reaching his city?" Cortés asked.

Malinche conferred with the Cholulan woman and then told us: "This is the year Two Cane, the year, according to many omens and prophecies, when a great disaster is to overtake Tenochtitlán and all the Valley of Anahuac."

And then the Cholulan took a step toward Malinche and spoke to her with a look of puzzlement and reproach.

"What is she saying?" Cortés demanded.

"She asked me why I have treated her like this. I told her that I am a Christian now."

Oh, the Madonna sweetness of her face as she stood there in her barbaric finery proclaiming this! I was struck by a kind of awe, for I thought I saw the hand of God and a reward for all those heathens we had baptized and all the idols we had thrown down and destroyed.

Cortés acted swiftly. First he bribed two Cholulan priests with Moctezuma's gold while threatening them with instant death and they confirmed the truth of what

the noble's wife had said. Cortés next had Malinche
instruct a Cholulan messenger to ask the nobles of the
city to come to him to discuss our immediate departure.
Since this was what they wanted, they arrived swiftly.
Feigning sorrow, Cortés told them that since it appeared
to him we were no longer welcome guests, we would
march in the morning to Tenochtitlán. He asked only
the aid of some two thousand men to help us transport
our artillery and baggage out of the city; to this the
Cholulans agreed readily. He then called all his captains and laid the plot for the morning of our exodus.

Before dawn, Cortés on horseback arranged the trap
in the big central plaza where the Cholulans would send
the two thousand men he had demanded. Buildings surrounded this square on three sides, a high wall on the
fourth. There were only three entrances, at three
corners, and these our cannon commanded. Our muskets and arquebuses were ranged along the walls, our
crossbows atop the one. When the Cholulans had all
marched in, most of them mere *tamanes,* Cortés took
aside the nobles who had brought them and sternly
revealed his knowledge of the wicked plot. They were
thunderstruck. Then, at a signal from Cortés, every
musket and crossbow was leveled at the leaders and the
poor creatures in the center of the square, killing at
least half of them, and then Cortés signaled the foot
soldiers to rush in with lances and swords. Hearing the
sounds of this massacre, hordes of other Cholulans outside the square poured in to aid their countrymen, but
were instantly cut down by artillery or steel.

Of all this horror I was not wholly aware at the time.
A terrible thing had happened to me. For the first time
a lust for killing took over my being. I suppose it was
caused in part by fear we all felt because of the trap
we found ourselves in and in part because I had to
steel myself very hard to murder those poor *tamanes*
for whom I had only gentle contempt. The thunder of
our guns reverberating against the buildings that en-
closed the abatoir added to a madness in me as I saw
my blade pierce and slash at flesh I tried to imagine

as a sort of vegetation around me, a vegetation that bled.

Meanwhile our Tlascalans had poured into the city from their camp outside its walls. The Cholulans fled up into the shelter of their buildings, which we set afire, and then were hounded up their pyramids, from the tops of which they poured down javelins and burning arrows, but in our steel armor we got up the steps and set afire the wooden temples at the top so'that enemies in them threw themselves headlong to earth or died in the flames. Then, through the streets, our cavalry pursued others and our Tlascalans killed and looted most savagely; this massacre went on for hours. The clean and beautiful city we had entered was finally a scene of horror, the streets lined with dead Cholulans, white walls blackened by flames. Among their six thousand dead were many nobles, including the unfortunate husband of the woman who had whispered his secrets to Malinche.

By the end of it I was not only physically spent but was also filled with an intense sorrow that alienated me from rejoicing Spaniards and loot-laden Tlascalans. Long after my sword blade was clean I sat on a step, wiping blood from it with a length of blue cotton a passing Tlascalan had let fall. Tears ran down my face, and for the first time I found it strange that such butchery should be required of a Christian soldier. The great white limestone cross that was erected atop the pyramid where the flame-crowned Quetzalcoatl had reigned did not raise my spirits.

I was present when a group of envoys arrived from Moctezuma, bringing Cortés many more gifts of gold. They said that Moctezuma sent his deep regret at the catastrophe at Cholula and disavowed any part in any plot against us. By now, the stupidest soldier among us knew that the great ruler must be trembling or raging at his failure to stop us in our march to his city in the lake.

The day before we left Cholula, our Zempoallan allies left us. Because of their recent rebellion, they feared to enter Moctezuma's city. Cortés sent word by them to Vera Cruz telling of our successful progress and urging Juan Escalante to send us immediate word of the arrival of any reinforcements from the King of Spain or any message from him telling when to expect them. I copied this letter for Cortés, the massacre having almost fatally undone the delicate bowels of his secretary. We left Cholula in the hope that at this very moment a Spanish fleet was already on its way to Vera Cruz and proud that we had come this far without the king's sanction or that of the governor of Cuba, only on the strength of Cortés' imperious will.

It was to take us farther still, up a steep sierra into cold piercing air and through the pass that lay between the great volcanos. Popocatepetl still sent up its column of smoke into the blue sky and now was rumbling like contained thunder. We had learned that this mountain was thought to be the abode of the spirits of the wicked departed rulers of the Valley of Anahuac, and there had been many. When we camped below that tremendous dark bulk at dusk, its snowy peak lost to sight above us, the intermittent rumblings we felt through the soles of our feet sent a thrill along my spine as though at any moment the mountain might send its boiling lava streaming down on me in punishment for the Indians I had killed. I was evidently different from the other soldiers, gathered cheerfully enough around their campfires, cooking an evening meal from the abundant provisions we had brought with us out of Cholula. I could not eat and all night kept waking from horrible, bloody dreams.

In the morning one of the captains, Diego Ordaz, proposed to Cortés that he wanted to climb the volcano and asked for volunteers. I leaped to my feet. Eight others joined, and a few Tlascalans. Cortés smiled on the enterprise and congratulated us in front of all the other men for our daring. To get to the top had a point; from there we thought to look down on Moctezuma's valley.

First we passed through dense forests of fir trees

that finally thinned out and disappeared. In the thin air as we ascended, we grew light-headed and hilarious, even though the going was hard, but at last we were panting and pausing for breath after a dozen steps. Under our feet the rumblings grew louder and more frequent. The Tlascalans turned back when we reached a slope of dark gray pedregal, twisted as it had congealed from its molten state into tumbled and fantastic shapes. Over this I scrambled upward into the perpetual snow of the volcano's utmost peak. All around us yawned frozen chasms. The icy glaze underfoot was so treacherous that at one misstep we could vanish down into one of these forever. To breathe was pure pain, like icicles piercing into the chest, and my legs ached so that I could hardly move them. But we pressed on upward toward the rim of the crater until, all at once, it belched out smoke, sparks, and bits of burning cinder. Our eyes stung and our hair and clothing were charred where the cinders struck. Half-blinded, coughing, and believing ourselves in peril of an even worse explosion at any moment, we had to turn back without peering over the edge of its mouth into the bowels of this monster mountain and without a glimpse of the fabled valley.

I broke off an enormous icicle, one of many hanging in a row off the edge of a rock. To bring it safely down without its breaking became a challenge and I swaggered into camp with the icicle cocked like a musket over one shoulder. Seeing Malinche standing beside Cortés where he had watched us making our way down the final slope of the volcano, I went to her and, with a bow, presented her proof that I had reached the icy summit. "A small trophy for the lady who saved our lives at Cholula," I said, and she thanked me very sweetly.

I saw El Galán laughing at me, and I will not repeat what he said to me privately about the icicle's shape in relation to its recipient; a stubborn imp had not abandoned all hope.

The next morning early we pressed onward and reached the crest of a sierra called Ahualco that rises between the two volcanos, though lower. The night had been bitterly cold; we had weathered it by using some great stone houses built by Moctezuma to shelter his couriers and travelers to his capital. But the morning air was diamond-bright and the sunlight had slowly warmed our bones as we ascended the sierra. Our spirits rose, for we knew that when we descended its other side we would tread on Moctezuma's own land and at last see the city we had suffered so much to reach.

I was in the van of the foot soldiery as usual; ahead were the captains on their horses following Cortés, with Malinche riding beside him. The trail we followed made a sudden turn around a flank of the mountain, and as the last of the horses vanished around it I heard the rider cry out "God save me!"

I rushed ahead to offer aid, but stopped, petrified like the stone from which I had broken the icicle. Below us lay the Valley of Anahuac. Never had I seen such a vista, and never will again. Awe filled me, and that uplifting of the heart that great beauty provokes.

Immediately below us were forests of oak and dark cedars, and beyond these were miles of wide fields of maize and maguey, orchards of fruit trees and gardens of flowers. These all flourished around the rim of a vast basin perhaps seventy leagues long and thirty wide, surrounded entirely by high mountains. In the center of the valley a wide blue lake was shining in the sun, and all around the irregular shoreline stood towns and hamlets, walls gleaming in the bright air, distinct at that high altitude where you could see very far, all details clear and colors vivid, the way things must look in the height of heaven. In the center of the lake stood Tenochtitlán, a jewel on blue water. Its white walls and pyramids caught the sunlight and dazzled it back into my eyes. A horse whinnied and I found that I was crossing myself.

"There!" I heard Cortés cry, exultant. "The promised land, gentlemen! The silver city!"

Behind me other soldiers were pressing forward and we began the descent. We had been nine months reaching this place and hour, and now faced the travail of the birth of that twin expectation fathered by Cortés: wealth beyond any dreams, glory for all time to come.

"I have never seen anything to equal it," El Galán said. "I feel as if I were in a dream, or a tale from *Amadís*." The strange, rapt look of his face and the awe in his voice sharpened the edge of an emotion that was beginning to cut into my marveling wonder. It was terror.

We inched down the steep narrow trail. Behind me murmurs grew. Ahead floated our battered banner. The velvet nap was rubbed off in places and the golden fringe was dulled, which called to my mind the dented armor of the soldiers and our many wounds, some scarred over and others not yet healed. No doubt we were valiant, but valor can have an end, like youth or beauty or life itself. We were fewer than four hundred Spaniards against that formidable city; I felt that I was a fly about to entangle my feet in the outermost strand of an enormous spider web. How many more suns would rise before I looked up at the last thing I would ever see on this earth—an obsidian knife flashing downward toward my supine and helpless body?

Yet I was so young that wonder prevailed, and joy. I had reached the Silver City at last! Now for the dishes of gold, the emeralds, the pearls as big as my staring eyeballs!

Far ahead I could see Malinche, for the trail had curved outward around another shoulder of the sierra. Cloaked against the cold, a silhouette against blue sky, she stared toward Tenochtitlán, turning in her saddle to keep her eyes fixed on it. Very soon, unless we were destined to be killed first, she would encounter the ruler who had conquered her people. What was she feeling now? To hide my awe I began to whistle, a small sound in that bright air above that immense, peopled valley. A moment later a great eagle flew above us, so near I could hear the flapping of its pinions. It headed straight toward Tenochtitlán, as if to bring a warning of our alien presence.

PART V

▼▼

IN THE SILVER CITY
November 5, 1519–May 15, 1520

21

When I looked down at Moctezuma's capital from a mountain pass between two volcanos and realized that I was now riding the gray mare that once had frightened me, I felt for a moment as though I, the real self I had been for nineteen years, was concealed inside the body of a strange woman in Cortés' black cape. How could that earlier Malinche be breathing this chill bright air? How could her eyes be staring down at the vast and beautiful Valley of Anahuac, at Moctezuma's city, that once-distant and legendary place?

It was a long journey that I made after I came out of the mangrove swamp in Tabasco to discover that the beast which had pursued me was no supernatural creature but only an animal called, I soon learned, a horse. The first step was taken when I dared to face that monster and those gods in armor. The next seven months took me not only from a town by the sea to the mountains surrounding Anahuac, but from pagan ignorance to knowledge of God, and from virginity to passion.

An eagle's shadow drew me into present reality, and I watched the great bird sail off over the valley in a long descending flight, its spread wings as wide as a man is tall. I looked at Cortés riding his black stallion beside me, enthralled by those far gleaming towers rising from the wide lake. He turned to me, eyes dazzled, and I saw the same smile of surprise that I had seen in his tent in Tlaxcala when he first saw me naked.

As we descended the wide trail, well-marked by the feet of Moctezuma's many couriers and visitors, recollections of that long journey from Tabasco passed through my mind. I could feel again the silent terror I had felt down in the ship's dark hold when a storm had the vessel groaning and tossing; I could hear once more the moans and wails of the other women huddled around me. I knew that no supernatural beings would keep the ship afloat, for Aguilar had assured us that the Spaniards were not gods: a dying horse confirmed the mortality of our captors. But what a strange race of men they were, and how incomprehensible to me a God who died in agony nailed to a cross! I did not believe Aguilar when he came down to the hold to comfort us with the promise that his God would not let us perish but would bring the ships to safe harbor.

The sunny day when we reached San Juan Ulua seemed to me a confirmation of his faith. How proud I was to find myself Cortés' interpreter, and to learn that "Doña Marina" was a name that showed his respect for me. But at that same place, what anguish I was soon to know!

A secret expectation had filled me when I was rowed with the other women hostages out to Cortés' flagship after our hasty baptism. When Aguilar said we were to be *barraganas,* I believed Cortés wanted me for himself. Because of my feeling for him, the excitement of his presence, my intense awareness of his virility, I believed he must feel corresponding emotions toward me. The shock of being given to Puertocarrero stunned and crushed me so that I let myself be led into Cortés' cabin, never expecting any lewd attack in that place. The first thing my eye fell on was the Blessed Virgin, serene on her stand in the corner. What a contrast to the scene that occurred only moments later! My horror only inflamed the half-intoxicated captain; grinning, he opened his lower garment and I saw the protruding thing reaching out toward me like a blind enraged sea-creature. When he pulled me toward the bed I broke free and tried to reach the door, but he was there before me to seize my tunic and rip it open. Backing away from him into the corner I reached blindly behind me for the statue of the Virgin; as he bent to seize the hem of my skirt I brought my weapon down on his skull. He fell heavily to the floor, a trickle of blood running down the side of his face. I could not think, could only run out of there to the ship's rail and drop like a stone into the black water of the bay. As I fell I heard the loud cheerful singing of the captains on the foredeck.

The cool depths restored some of my sanity. The shore looked a long way off, but I believed that by swimming and floating alternately I could reach it. I shed my torn clothes, which would only hamper me, and began the long swim. The pull of the current did not dismay me; it flowed to the north and away from the Spanish camp to which I had no idea of returning. When I saw a boat coming toward the anchored ships and heard one of its occupants speak in Spanish I submerged: Spaniards I would never trust again.

At last I reached the beach, deserted of even so much as a gull. I flung myself down beside a tangled clump of kelp, flotsam like myself, and lay there awhile, panting and exhausted. I opened my eyes and saw the wide night sky, the evening star brighter than the rest, and I knew it was no god, as I had once believed. The stars were many and far, and the gods too, if there were gods. Neither could help me.

I sat up then and began to consider my alternatives. I could throw myself on the mercy of the Indians of the town near the beach, even though they were Aztec-ruled, or go south to the Spanish camp, tell Father Aguilar why I had attacked, perhaps killed, Captain Puertocarrero. Having lived among the civilized people of southern Yucatán, Aguilar would understand the significance of the golden Shell of Purity, which still clung to me, and might explain to Cortés my terror of the attempted rape. Remembering it I felt shame, then outrage, then anger at Cortés, who had not wanted me.

Two choices I had, and only two. In the town of the

natives here I would be a vagrant without status and would find myself a slave again, or a concubine. And if I proved unruly I might end on a stone altar. If I went back to the Spaniards, one thing could save me from whatever punishment might be in store for me: I was of use to Cortés. Without me he was mute. I began to see I had been hasty in my wish to avoid the Spanish camp. But it was a bitter choice: slavery or even death against a life spent with the Spaniards as interpreter for a man who needed only my voice and had no use for the rest of me.

A breeze from the sea touched my body and I knew that whatever I decided I had to cover my nakedness. All I had was the tangle of seaweed beside me. I stood up, loosened several long strands, washed off the sand in the sea, and fashioned a skirt by looping the kelp's stem through the belt from which my seashell was suspended.

To my astonishment, I heard my name called. Along the beach a man was coming toward me. A Spaniard. Arturo Mondragon. In the distance behind him I saw the upper temple of the Indian town. My alternatives faced me. But even before he reached me and offered me a shawl he had in his hut I had already decided to stay with the Spaniards, although I did not then let myself know why: Cortés.

In addition to the shawl, Arturo gave me his rosary. I thought it clever of him to provide me with Christian sanctuary after Aguilar explained to me what it meant. In the morning, dressed in the clean skirt and tunic I had in my hut I went with Father Aguilar to the flagship when I learned that Cortés wished to offer me his apology. I was cold and formal with him even after he made Puertocarrero, head bandaged, humbly ask my pardon. With lowered eyes I hid my pleasure when Cortés told me that from then on I was to be under his personal protection, no carnal knowledge being involved in this arrangement. I agreed to pretend that I was Puertocarrero's *barragana* in order to save his face. From that day on he treated me with the wary respect a man might give a wild animal that had once turned on him in fury.

My feelings toward Cortés went through many changes. During the time when so many soldiers were sick with the *cil,* twelve dying of it, he gave me his own cabin on the flagship, sleeping outside with the mariners. I would lie there on the high bunk hoping the door would open and he would come toward me, but he never did, and I knew that he had protected the life of an interpreter whose services he needed and who happened to be me. It did not occur to me that he had put himself to some discomfort in giving me his bed. It was only after he gave me Puertocarrero's gray mare, sending him to Spain without it, that I knew I meant much more to him than a voice that spoke Nahuatl. I was secretly amused as he explained at length how convenient it would be to have me ride beside him, ready to parley instantly with whatever natives we met. I knew how few horses he had.

His later anger with me after I went walking in a garden at Zempoalla with Arturo absolutely confirmed my secret conviction that Cortés desired me. I told myself, again, that I was wicked to use that boy's affection in order to enrage Cortés, that such behavior was alien to my real nature. I would always be ashamed of it because from the very first Arturo was good and kind with me. . . .

I was startled out of my reverie by Cortés' voice. "In what dream do you wander, Marina?" I turned toward him. Those dark and often somber eyes of his seemed to glow. Without waiting for an answer he leaned closer, smiling. "See? I did it!" His mailed arm swept out to claim as proof of valor the valley below.

Some of his exultance leaped from his body to mine. It remembered being held in those strong arms. "No other man could have brought us here," I said, and then added piously, "with God's help, to be sure."

He threw back his head and laughed. "You always prick my arrogance when it needs it!" He reached across to press my thigh, then spurred his horse and galloped ahead; a hill now shut off his view of what lay just below. My mind looked back over time past, for that caress evoked his tent in Tlascala and the night that began with an accusation of my treachery but ended so differently.

I defended myself as best I could with what Spanish I spoke then, less aware of Cortés' stern face than of his bare arms, for he was sitting in his carved armchair half undressed. The broad shoulders and biceps were the color of ivory; on the forearms a little dark hair grew. The hands were darker from having been exposed to the sun; a diamond on the forefinger of the right hand sparkled when he gestured. "If you die, I die," I told him in denying the false charge of having betrayed him. But I felt my face flush because I knew I had told a deeper truth. He was as necessary to me now as sunlight, as water, as food.

I knew that he believed me and not my accuser when he ordered me to remain with him and called Orteguilla to remove the rest of his armor. They retreated behind a drawn curtain that parted the tent to make an alcove where there was a cot and a stand holding the Virgin Mary. I stood waiting, my heartbeats marking time, my mind blank. I told myself that Cortés wanted to question me further, and at the same time I knew this was not true.

Orteguilla emerged first. His glance as he wished me good night was roguish and wise. Then Cortés strode around the edge of the curtain, and it was like seeing another man. He wore a long Indian robe of deep red, one of the many sent to him by Moctezuma. By now some of the captains occasionally wore these for comfort and to spare their Spanish clothing, but I had never seen him dressed so. He looked very tall, and less unfamiliar than in armor. He smiled. "Will you take a cup of wine with me?"

I nodded, my mouth dry as sand. He went to the trestle table where a wine keg stood, around it some pewter mugs and also the silver goblet I had seen him drink from more than once. When he turned he was holding it out to me. "Sit down, Doña Marina. And don't be nervous. I have no doubt whatever of your loyalty. Gonzalo once played the traitor, and traitors see treachery everywhere." He turned back to the wine keg and held under its spigot a plain pewter mug for himself.

My knees went weak. I sank onto a camp stool facing his armchair, into which he sank with a sigh of ease. As I tasted the wine I was only aware that his mouth had touched the cool smooth rim now pressed by mine. When he lowered his pewter cup after a long swallow he smiled again at me, lips moist with wine. I wanted to reach and touch the small white scar between his underlip and beard. I could not take my eyes from it, that small evidence of his vulnerability. To disguise my fascination I pointed to it and asked, "In what battle?"

"In no battle. I got this scar when I was seventeen, climbing a high stone wall to get into a lady's bedroom window. The wall was old, the mortar rotten, and it crumbled under my weight. Down I went, and my face met the upturned blade of a garden hoe." He smiled, one eyebrow raised. "I wish I had a more glorious adventure to tell you, Doña Marina."

"The window of your present wife?" I asked, taking the wall-climbing to be some curious Spanish courtship ritual.

"Marriage was not what I had in mind." He tipped his cup and drank again, eyes watching me with crinkles of laughter in the outer corners. "The lady was already married."

I knew what he meant: mere coupling. I also knew that this was what he wanted now, with me. My blood tingled, but I said, "In Paynala what you did is thought shameful."

His laugh was forced; I knew he did not like this reproof. "At seventeen I was an actor playing a role. A very devil with the women, less out of lust than pride. My father sent me to a famous school. But he found he could not afford to keep me there. I had to come home. I did not want people to know my family was that poor. I made up a lie to explain my return. I said I was thrown out of that school because of my many seductions of women. To sustain this lie, I climbed to that window. With very shaky knees, and a wealth of inexperience." He gave another laugh; his eyes were looking at me in surprise. "By my conscience, I've never told anyone this before. I don't know why I am telling you. Did you understand anything of what I just said?"

"I understand pride."

He leaned closer. "Do you know why I asked you to stay here with me?"

"Yes."

"You are under no suasion. I will not command this favor of you. Do you wish to stay?"

Those dark and somber eyes engulfed mine. I saw yearning in them. "Yes."

His hand reached out to touch my cheek. His eyes were half closed; his lips opened a little and I heard his breath sigh in through them. His touch was gentle. I thought how often that hand had held a sword. He opened his eyes, took my hand, raised me to my feet, rising with me. His arms went around me and drew me to him and he kissed my mouth. Paynalans do not kiss, and his lips on mine seemed as alien as his beard. His tongue opened my mouth; his hand caressed me. A haze of pleasure stole over my senses. I did not know time or place, only the sensations his touch gave me. Then I heard the distant mutter of Tlascalan drums. I became aware of the danger all around us, of the night full of enemies eager for our deaths. I clung to him tighter. The kiss ended. He led me to his narrow bed.

It seemed to give him pleasure to remove my tunic, untie my skirt and let it fall. When he saw me naked by the small flame of a candle that burned at the feet of the Virgin his smile of delight was as pleasing as his touch. But suddenly he saw something that puzzled him. My golden seashell of purity. He asked me why I wore it and I told him. Then I took it off.

At dawn when we awoke clasped in each other's

arms, I gave it to him. Propped on one elbow, he looked down at the small gold shell on his palm, then closed his hand around it. He seemed moved. "With this gift I will never part," he whispered. He smoothed my hair in a long caress. "Nor with you." His face was tender and unguarded and I knew how he had looked when he was young.

The thudding of hooves coming up the trail startled me from my reverie. Cortés galloped back from his brief sortie well pleased: in the nearest town below there was no sign of any warriors to impede us. But then Captain Sandoval rode down to him to say that some of his men, overwhelmed by Moctezuma's city, were too frightened to continue toward it. "It's the same in Alvarado's company, and Olid's, and I guess the rest as well, so you had better talk to them." He pointed up to where a huddle of soldiers had sat down on the trail, blocking passage for the others behind them.

Cortés looked from them to the Tlascalan warriors massed at the topmost point between the two volcanos, spears aloft as if in defiance of their ancient enemies. He spurred his stallion and galloped uptrail, followed by Sandoval. He roused the valor of the frightened Spaniards, gold and the Tlascalans' courage his main themes.

We continued down to where the woods thinned out and came to the first patches of cultivated land surrounding a village where the inhabitants came out to welcome us. To my surprise, we learned that this close to the capital there was bitterness against Moctezuma. The rustics of the valley shared none of the affluence of the dwellers in the city in the lake or the others built at intervals around its irregular shores. A villager who was the son of the cacique summed up the plight of his people. He was slender and sad-eyed, his skin a dark copper from working in the sun. "I am not an Aztec. We are of Toltec ancestry," he told us. "Moctezuma takes our young maidens to be his concubines and our young men for his armies, and this is not just." When I translated this for Cortés his face lighted up and he glanced back at the looming bulk of Popocatepetl. "I see that Moctezuma lives in the shadow of more than one volcano." He had me tell the young Toltec that we had come here to redress such wrongs.

"Long, long before the Aztecs came to this valley, the Toltecs dominated it," the young farmer said, "and before us there was a people even more ancient. The Toltecs built great cities, like Tula and Texcoco, and the great pyramids to the sun and moon at Teotihuacan. It was the Toltec ruler of Texcoco who permitted the Aztecs, then only a small band of wanderers, to inhabit an island in the lake." He shook his head in regret. "Who could guess that they would grow in number like weeds? They came here three and a half centuries ago; Toltecs had built cities here for nearly fifteen hundred years by then. But the Aztecs, being ferocious, became allies of Texcoco after only a hundred and fifty years in this valley. A young prince of Texcoco went to them and asked them to help him put down a rebel upstart who had caused a civil war and had killed his father. They did, and the alliance continues to exist until this very day."

This was, he said, of great advantage to the Aztecs, who borrowed Toltec manners, knowledge, laws, and gods. "Quetzalcoatl first appeared among the Toltecs at Tula, not among the Aztecs, as they now claim." Standing beside a field where autumn maize stood taller than he, the young farmer shook his head at life's injustice: ferocity, avarice, and unceasing industry had enabled the Aztecs finally to outdo and dominate their betters. "But for many years now there have been prophecies that foretell a great disaster to the Valley of Anahuac, and in this very year." He nodded with pleasure, as though his village would be spared this general woe.

As we advanced by easy stages toward Tenochtitlán, often along a road lined by curious natives, Cortés asked me several questions about the Aztecs: How had they grown like weeds on only a small island? Would the Toltecs be possible allies? I could only tell him what I had learned about the Aztecs' beginnings from Ato and her mother when I was a child.

In their long southward wanderings in search of a place to settle they had been sustained by their war god, Huitzilopotchli, which one of their priests found in a dark cave. The deity told them that as long as they fed him the hearts of defeated enemies he would always bring them victories. And he told them, through a priest, that one day they would come to a spot where they would see an eagle on a nopal cactus devouring a serpent held in its talons. That was the place where they would settle and prosper. After they came to Anahuac and were encamped in the thick reeds on the lakeshore and eating salamanders and algae, their chieftain went out in his canoe on the lake and came to a deserted island where he saw that eagle and serpent. So he went to the ruler of Texcoco and asked permission to live there. His name was Tenoch, and so the town his people built on the island was called Tenochtitlán, which means "city of Tenoch." They were then called Tenochans.

Hearing this, Cortés smiled. "That has the ring of myth, like the story of Romulus and Remus to explain the founding of Rome. It certainly does not explain how that small island grew into a city now said to hold a hundred thousand families."

An embassy from that city made me postpone the explanation. Several Aztec lords, to judge from their jewelry and richly embroidered *atl* panels, were followed by a dozen *tamanes* bringing Cortés gifts from the emperor: more gold, more feathered capes. They also offered a bribe: if Cortés would turn back now, return to Vera Cruz and embark for his own land, Moctezuma would give him and each of his captains four large loads of gold and would also pay a yearly tribute to his sovereign.

Cortés had me say, with great courtesy, "I could not answer to that sovereign if I were to turn back without meeting Moctezuma in his capital. There it will be much easier to arrange such matters as tribute in a personal interview. We come here in the spirit of peace. We will leave if Moctezuma should find our presence burdensome."

As soon as the nobles left to deliver this message, Cortés showed his elation. "It begins to appear to me that this Moctezuma is a woman, not a man! His superstitious nature makes him fear us very much!"

His people shared his awe of us, as we learned in an Aztec city built on the edge of the lake near one of the causeways. Many houses were on piles extending out into the water, and canals penetrated into the city. We later found that this was in imitation of Tenochtitlán. We were well received and were housed for the night in stone buildings of austere elegance, and there we rested two days.

And there we received a visit from Cacama, the ruler of Texcoco, who rode into the city on a palanquin that was decorated with gold and precious stones. Many nobles accompanied him, and two had brooms and swept the ground before him as he walked toward us. Cacama was a man of about twenty-five, handsome and stately. He acknowledged Cortés as being of high rank when he bent to touch earth and bring that hand to his forehead. Cortés embraced him; this is what European kings do when they meet. "I have been sent by my cousin Moctezuma to welcome you to his capital," Cacama said.

When I told Cortés this his eyes gleamed with pleasure; the gleam was brighter when Cacama then presented him a golden bowl holding three large pearls. In return Cortés hung around Cacama's neck a string of twinkling glass beads called margaritas. When the Texcocan prince left, Cortés said he was very impressed by his noble bearing. "To say nothing of his three pearls!" He told me that any one of them would grace a king's crown in Europe. "As big as pullet eggs!" A pullet, he explained, was a small chicken, but as I did not know what a chicken was except that it must be a bird since it laid eggs, I was little wiser.

The army resumed its march around the borders of the lake, past fruit-laden orchards and fields of waving maize, all irrigated by canals from the lake, although there were many patches of uncultivated woodland. At last we came to the longest and most impressive of the four causeways that connected Tenochtitlán with the lakeshore. It proved to be wide enough for eight horsemen to ride abreast.

And for the first time since reaching Anahuac I felt fear as the hooves of the horses thudded on the planking of a wooden drawbridge some ten paces long; removed, it would leave a gap of water too wide to leap. Ahead I saw another such bridge. I assumed they existed on the other causeways, except for the aqueduct. If ever a perfect trap had been constructed by the mind of man it was this city built on water, its only roads to the rest of the world interrupted by these removable bridges that could prevent invasion from without or the escape of enemies from within. And I suddenly wondered if Moctezuma had really been so innocent as to believe that his lavish gifts would drive Cortés away. Had he rather intended to lure us toward him? The ambush at Cholula having failed, was he now permitting us to enter his city to slaughter us at his leisure, provide hearts for his war god?

"I don't like these bridges," Cortés said thoughtfully. "Still, we must cross to the city. If Moctezuma intends to kill us, he can do it as easily if we retreat as if we advance. Advance has another advantage: If I make as good an impression on Moctezuma as I did on Cacama, then we will meet like two kings, and what king wants it known that he invited another to his city and then slaughtered him?"

I said that Moctezuma might not be as concerned about others' opinions as Cortés hoped. "His authority is absolute, remember. And he is considered a deity himself, or nearly so."

"But don't forget that Toltec farmer! Unless Moctezuma has very lazy spies, he knows that outside his city are many potential rebels. He must keep up a noble front." Suddenly he pointed. "What is that thing out there on the lake?"

I saw my first *chinampa,* a little garden floating along amid the many canoes laden with Aztecs making their way to the causeway and staring up at us in wonder. In the middle of the garden was a small shade tree, under which the farmer dozed. It seemed to me a lovely life, to move over the blue water while one's garden grew. Yet I knew that this *chinampa* was a living relic of the early grim days of the Aztecs. I told Cortés, "What you see is the answer to the question you asked me three days ago: how did the little island the Aztecs settled on grow into a great city?"

And I told him what I had first learned from Ato and her mother, long ago: On that small island, needing to raise more food for a growing population, the Aztecs found a solution. Seeing chunks of earth that had detached themselves from the lakeshore in the rainy season floating along held together by the roots of their verdure, a clever farmer got the idea that large baskets of tightly woven reeds could be filled with mud dredged up from the shallow lake bottom, planted with seeds fertilized with human excrement. Eventually *chinampas* moored to the shore of the island sent roots down through the shallow water to the rich lake silt. The farmers paddled along canals left between them to splash them with lakewater. And so, over more than two centuries, the island of Tenochtitlán spread out wider and wider, a city of canals.

"Such ingenuity merits admiration," Cortés conceded. "I never thought to find a Venice high in these mountains." He lost himself in thought, perhaps wondering how canals might be used to his advantage in case Moctezuma's reception of us did not look promising.

The Ixtapalápa causeway on which we advanced went first due west and then, about a league and a half out in the lake, turned north straight as an arrow to the city. The three other causeways each led out to a different compass point and were of different lengths due to the irregular curving of the lakeshore. There were actually, we learned, several lakes, two being formed by three causeways. Lake Texcoco was the largest. The shortest causeway led to a town called Tacuba.

The nearer we came to the city of Tenochtitlán, the more it overwhelmed me. Now I could see that many of the largest buildings were white, but others were of a rust-red stone, and some were gray. Cortés and I and four mounted captains led toward it the Spanish army, fewer than four hundred soldiers, their battered armor polished to give a brave appearance, Cortés' worn banner floating overhead. Behind them came our Tlascalans, dressed as for battle, their white crane banners held high. Last of all plodded the *tamanes* with their loads on their back, and back there on a litter rode little Orteguilla. I thought how the sights we were seeing must awe that tiny man.

The horses' hooves thudded on yet another wooden bridge. From either side of the causeway wondering Aztec faces smiled up at us from canoes laden with flowers that were tossed to the causeway to make a carpet for our feet. Walking on bright petals I found my earlier fear melting into the pleasant feeling that this was a holiday in our honor. And then I recalled that I had felt the same on entering Cholula.

Ahead a great double gate between two stone towers was opened wide and through it came at least a thousand citizens to greet us, among them war chiefs in the strange costumes of the various military orders, with helmets like jaguars or eagles or serpents. Seeing them I remembered the defeat of my little town of Paynala by warriors like these. A dreamlike mood descended on me for a moment. Was this really happening? Was I really here? I looked at Cortés and knew all this was true. Not only was I here, but I had to translate the formal speeches of welcome delivered by a large number of nobles, one of whom explained that Moctezuma was ill and so had not come in person to greet us. This did not please Cortés, and he accepted the nobles' deep bows of humility rather coldly. At last we proceeded through the great gate to continue into the city itself on a wide avenue that was half stone-paved street and half canal, solid with dugout canoes that had followed us in. I glanced back at the great gateway. When finally it clanged shut after the last of Cortés' army, either a trap would have closed on us all forever or we would be feted as honored guests, all the marvels of the silver city at our disposal. Which would it be?

I looked at Cortés, my mouth dry. He was staring straight ahead. A large palanquin was approaching from the center of the city. It seemed to float on the shoulders of the cluster of richly dressed attendants surrounding it; ornately decorated pillars supported its green canopy, thick with *chalchihuites* and other gems, quetzal plumes nodding at its four corners. Seated on a gold chair in its center was a man as motionless as an idol. From his golden crown a towering fan of green quetzal feathers spread out. His ceremonial cape, open to frame his body, revealed a massive pectoral necklace of gold and jewels. The wide front panel of his *atl* was encrusted with pearls and emeralds. Wide bracelets on both arms almost hid the flesh.

Yet in spite of the color and gleam and glitter of all this magnificence, as the palanquin came closer it was his face that stood out most clearly to me: a delicate face, very pale, with sad eyes and a slight narrow beard cut off square just below the chin. He looked as if he had recently been very ill, yet at the same time seemed above the usual human complaints. All about us humble onlookers had prostrated themselves, faces to the ground. Moctezuma!

His head turned slightly. His eyes looked straight at me. Suddenly I quivered; my throat grew tight, and I was cold with fear. Moctezuma!

The palanquin was slowly lowered to the ground. He

rose from his chair and stepped from the litter to approach us with slow dignity, a noble supporting him at either side. I tried to swallow so as to moisten my parched throat. In moments I would have to speak to him for Cortés.

Moctezuma!

22

Cortés dismounted; I followed suit, looking desperately about me in hope of seeing Aguilar, who had learned some Nahuatl. But at Cholula I had found that I could translate directly from that language into Castilian, and so he had ceased to aid me. I walked beside Cortés toward the advancing Moctezuma knowing how much depended on this first meeting with the ruler into whose absolute power we had so bravely marched. My parched mouth demanded water, and I remembered my thirst on the litter going toward Tabasco. Now that helpless slave child was about to speak to this ruler of rulers! I saw that a length of green cloth was being unrolled before his feet by two richly clad attendants who bent to this task as dextrously as if all their lives their main occupation had been to keep the ruler's golden sandals from ever treading where other feet had walked. The awe I felt was as intense as when I first saw Cortés and thought him a god. This memory was my salvation: Cortés was no god; neither was Moctezuma.

Now he stood directly before us. He was shorter than Cortés, but the green panache, symbol of his power, made him seem to tower over him. Smiling, Cortés stepped forward and spread his arms to embrace him.

Seeing his intention, Moctezuma took one step back; two nobles ran forward to push Cortés away, their faces shocked. One was Cacama, who said, "No one must touch the First Speaker unless by his command!"

Undaunted, Cortés held out a necklace of glass margaritas that was longer than the one he had given Cacama, who took the sparkling strand and clasped it around Moctezuma's neck, being careful not to brush his flesh. I knew these beads had little value in Europe, and so to me they looked strange sparkling against the massive golden necklace of the Aztec ruler.

He raised his arm and a tall, fierce-looking noble, his brother Cuitlahuac, brought to him a golden necklace with pendants made in the shapes of various shellfish. I knew these were symbols associated with the god Quetzalcoatl, who came from across the eastern sea, and I explained this to Cortés. Moctezuma himself hung the necklace on Cortés, who bowed to him to show that he knew he had been greatly honored. Then Moctezuma stepped back. A noble attendant announced: "The great Moctezuma speaks!" His words soon confirmed the significance of the shellfish necklace.

"Our lord, you are weary, for you have come a great distance to your city here in Mexico where you will sit on the golden throne which has so long awaited you. Kings who have gone before me have guarded it against your coming. Oh, if they could see what I see now! It is not a dream! I am now walking in my sleep! I have seen you at last. For many days and nights I have been in agony of spirit, my mind lost in the Region of Mystery as I sought to know the truth of your coming. But now I know you have indeed returned, as was long foretold. Rest now, and take possession of your royal palace. Welcome to your land, my lords." His melancholy eyes left Cortés' face to look up at the mounted captains behind him.

When I heard the sad and hollow voice speaking the flowery words, I knew that he had indeed been in an agony of indecision, and that the legend of the return of Quetzalcoatl or his descendants to judge and punish must have been confirmed as present fact by whatever new omens and oracles he had discovered in his Region of Mystery since Cortés' triumph over the Cholulans. Moctezuma was now resigned to the probability that Cortés and the captains on horseback were no mere mortals.

I thought of the file of Spanish soldiers now halted on the causeway behind us by this ceremony, battered weary men, some scarred in Tlascala, some wounded in Cholula, and very far from being gods or even a god's attendants. And I knew that some of them were afraid. But I also knew that many would march into this city looking all about with eager eyes, convinced as Spaniards and Christians that any land on which they trod was merely a potential colony of Spain.

Cortés thanked Moctezuma for his gracious welcome and the Aztec ruler turned and walked back to his palanquin, the ceremonial cape sweeping the green carpet behind him and forming an iridescent background for the two tapered lengths of quetzal plumes extending downward from his headdress nearly to the ground.

As Cortés and I remounted to follow him into his city a breeze from the lake caught the Spanish banner held aloft behind us, and the blue-and-white flames around the central red cross seemed for an instant to flicker as real flames do.

I glanced at the gold necklace that gleamed against Cortés' steel breastplate: a crab, a nautilus, a scallop caught the sun. Honored as Quetzalcoatl, he would bring to Moctezuma his first knowledge of the one true God, and that seemed to me most fitting, and almost as though the legendary return of that merciful deity was in a sense taking place. But then I knew I was slipping back toward my old idolatry and crossed myself.

As we rode at a slow pace toward the heart of the city following Moctezuma's palanquin along that wide avenue, the houses we passed became larger and grander. At the city's fringes by the lake were only reed-sided homes of the poorer folk built out over the water on piles. Then came one- and two-story dwellings of *tetzontli,* a porous rust-red stone; on the flat rooftops bloomed gardens from which Aztec faces stared down at us. Nearer the city's center temples and public buildings were covered over with a gleaming white stucco against which the colorful clothes of the Aztecs lining the street to watch us pass stood out boldly.

Among the multitude I saw young women with long black hair and full skirts below triangular *huipiles* woven in varying designs, vivid colors. Many wore their hair braided with bright ribbons for some festival. Sunlight gleamed on their bracelets of silver, gold, and copper and lighted their cheekbones, prominent below their jet-black eyes of almond shape. They were squat in build, like the men, whose hair was cut off just above the eyes and below the jaws; many wore narrow headbands. Over their loincloths, the front panels woven in varying motifs, some wore cotton cloaks tied on one shoulder like the Tlascalans', only these were not of coarse *nequen.* Both men and women looked very clean and gave off no smell of sweat because of their custom, I learned, of bathing daily in steam baths attached to their homes or in public ones. But as we penetrated deeper into the city I became aware that it had an odor, which came in part from the canals that crisscrossed it, from the food the people cooked, from incense burning in the many temples, and from the stench of the offerings made on their altars. It was not entirely unpleasant, only strange.

"This city is cleaner than any I have ever seen," Cortés remarked. "Cities in Europe . . ." His voice broke off in midsentence, because at that moment we entered the vast central plaza, thronged with Aztecs who had left a wide lane down which Moctezuma's palanquin and attendants had preceded us. My mare stopped in her tracks as if as stunned as I. Cortés reined in his stallion. Side by side we stared about us.

To the north was a high white pyramid of five levels with stone steps going up its steep face—the temple of Huitzilopotchli, the war god. To the east stood an enormous palace, a high wall enclosing its many buildings of that rust-red stone. It was both imposing and desolate; no curious figures stood on its ramparts or roof garden to stare down at us. We learned that it was the palace of Moctezuma's dead father. His own was even larger and grander, separated from it by a spacious walled garden: above its treetops soared a giant aviary; wickerwork domes emitted a constant bird music. In the square itself, facing the garden, was the temple of Tezcatlipoca, creator of the universe, in whose polished shield he could see all that happened everywhere. The temple of Quetzalcoatl's entrance was an enormous open serpent's mouth, so hideous that the soldiers named it the Inferno. These and the other religious buildings were white and gleaming and the pale stone paving was as clean as though a thousand slaves had scrubbed the immense expanse in the night (which proved true). The southern half of the square was an enormous open market, its stalls loaded with every kind of ware and produce, buyers numerous as bees swarming over a hive. But the huge splendor of the temples and palaces dwarfed them and ourselves, backed by the circular range of distant mountains, snowy tops glistening against the hard blue sky against which a plume of smoke rose from the crater of Popocatepetl.

Cortés was barely able to hide his wonderment from Cacama, who came to tell him that Moctezuma offered us the entire palace of his dead father Axayacatl, unused by anyone for seventeen years out of respect to his memory.

In the first courtyard we entered Moctezuma himself had waited to welcome us, then left us there to marvel at our quarters. The many rooms we saw that day had ceilings of sweet-smelling carved cedar and stuccoed walls adorned with hangings in bold Aztec designs and colors. One hall alone was large enough to sleep a hundred fifty soldiers; this and two others nearly as vast were furnished with thick straw pallets, one for each foot soldier, showing the accuracy of Moctezuma's information as to their number. Evidently his enemies the Tlascalans were to content themselves with the various courtyards. Since it was winter, charcoal braziers on stone tripods gave off a pleasant warmth. Stone wall brackets held unlit pine torches for the night to come.

The sleeping room into which Cacama ushered Cortés was large and low-ceilinged with a narrow window overlooking the main square through which we had just passed. There were many rich hangings, several braziers and wall torches, chests for clothing, tables, chairs, and a raised platform with a large thick sleeping pallet with a jeweled canopy above it. Along the wall by the doorway a row of ten servants waited to see to Cortés' needs. My room, Cacama said, was adjacent. "If there is anything you require, Lord, send word to Moctezuma by one of these servants. For the First Speaker wishes you to be comfortable, with all to your liking."

"Is this First Speaker Moctezuma?" Cortés asked.

Cacama concealed all but a hint of surprise at such ignorance. "Yes, Moctezuma speaks first and last at all meetings of the thirty clan chiefs he graces with his presence. What he says is then law, and cannot be changed except by himself. Even the Council of Four cannot act contrary to the word of Moctezuma, although they may make recommendations to him."

Cortés thanked him and said he was pleased with his room and Cacama departed. We were, for the moment, alone; ten slaves who did not understand Castilian might as well have been furniture and stood as motionless as though they were. Cortés went to the narrow window and stood looking down at his Spanish soldiers now crossing the wide Zocalo between staring Aztecs. Behind them came the first of the Tlascalans; I saw that they stared straight ahead on entering the heart of the city of their ancient enemies.

Cortés removed his casque and rubbed his forehead where it had pressed. "It strikes me as somewhat forbidding that Moctezuma has housed us in a mausoleum." He smiled grimly. "I am pleased that it is walled like a fortress, however." He put the casque on again and started for the doorway. "I must see to the soldiers' sleeping arrangements and to the stabling of our horses. I must also decide on the best placement of our cannons and artillery."

His intended exit was halted by the arrival of the tall, fierce noble who had walked at Moctezuma's left when he met Cortés. He offered only a token inclination of his body and did not touch the floor with his hand. I translated his curt words; they confirmed my immediate feeling that he did not like or revere Spaniards. "I am Cuitlahuac, a brother of Moctezuma. The First Speaker desires an audience with you. He will visit you here, at your convenience." His rigid body and obsidian eyes deplored his ruler's courtesy.

"As soon as I take care of certain important matters I will send for him," Cortés had me say. As I finished speaking, faint cries and jeers floated in through the window, and I knew that the Aztecs were responding to the arrival of Tlascalans.

"Why have you brought our enemies here?" Cuitlahuac asked coldly.

"The Tlascalans are my friends. They have accepted my sovereign and my God," Cortés said. "In this the Aztecs will be wise to emulate them."

"Aztecs do not emulate," Cuitlahuac said flatly, and left us without other farewell.

Before sending Moctezuma word that he could visit him, Cortés assigned his troops to their several quarters, had cannons placed on the palace's front rampart to command the main gate, positioned other ordnance to command approach over the other walls, and stationed many sentinels. It was as if he expected a siege instead of a visit from a generous host.

Moctezuma arrived bearing in his own hands a vase of flowers. He was followed by a cluster of nobles and by servants bringing other gifts. In a large lower hall, evidently an audience room with many benches, Cortés' captains and Moctezuma's nobles all seated themselves, Moctezuma and Cortés apart on a low dais, each in a carved gilded chair or throne. I stood between them, aware that my earlier thirst had returned, although not so intensely. The questions Moctezuma asked Cortés surprised me, and I decided that the reverential speech he made at the causeway had been a mere formality, perhaps intended to impress the many nobles and citizens who heard it. Now the Aztec monarch asked about the government of the country Cortés came from, its distance, size, and the number of vassals its king commanded. Here was no oratory, but an intelligent mind seeking knowledge. "Tell me why you came here," Moctezuma demanded.

"I wanted to meet so distinguished a monarch. I particularly came to declare to you the True Faith as practiced only by Christians."

Moctezuma was not interested. What he wanted to know was whether earlier pale bearded strangers seen by a cacique of Yucatán many years ago, at the start of his reign, had been Cortés' countrymen.

"He must mean Columbus!" Cortés said to the captains after a moment's reflection. "On his third voyage he came to Yucatán." I, for my part, remembered a child in Paynala, charmed by a little gold snake-man. Cortés' voice brought me back to the present. "Tell him I am surprised that he knows of this."

Moctezuma said, "I also have been aware of all your movements since you first came to Tabasco." He explained that rulers before him had perfected a widespread courier system with runners so swift that in relays they brought to his breakfast table certain fish caught the morning before in waters near Vera Cruz. "It is a fish I am very fond of," he said, "although it is spiny and ugly in appearance. But you and I know that appearances can be deceptive." His eyes roved then to the shellfish necklace Cortés had been given, which I had supposed was offered to Quetzalcoatl returned.

"I intend to be open and honest with you," Cortés said, with dignity. "On my part there will be no deception."

Moctezuma withdrew to his palanquin outside the main gate after ordering his servants pass out gifts of fine cotton robes to each soldier and golden chains to the captains. Cortés stood looking after Moctezuma, his face dark. "Yes, appearances can be deceptive. Lavish hospitality is no exception." He turned to me. "Would you say Moctezuma thinks me a god returned now?" I had to admit that his attitude seemed suddenly to have changed.

That night Cortés celebrated our arrival by ordering a discharge of all artillery, including the cannons; the thunderous noise reverberated against the walls of the palace and the air was filled for a while with the stink of sulfur and niter. "Supernatural beings have commanded thunder and lightning ever since Jove's thunderbolts," he told me later. "Let these Aztecs fear me, the sooner to bow to my God and my king!"

Moctezuma's response was to send nobles early the next morning to invite Cortés and his captains to his palace. "Malinche is of course included in this great honor," one of them said, so evidently Moctezuma not only knew my Indian name but preferred it to my Spanish one, although he pronounced it *Malintzín*.

The nobles had been told to show us some of the palace of Moctezuma, and we passed through courtyards and corridors and huge halls filled with strolling Aztec nobles and visitors of high rank, the sweet smell of incense, and the music of flutes. The walls were gorgeous with featherwork tapestries depicting animals, flowers, birds, and butterflies, all glowing with colors both brilliant and subtle. There were three large marble steam baths with pools of crystal water, several vaults for wine and one for chocolate pressed into cakes. In a large annex giving onto the gardens hundreds of pretty concubines passed the day in idle chatter and embroidering. In contrast, the arsenal was a grim, immense room stocked to the high ceiling with racks of javelins, obsidian swords, bows and arrows.

The owner of all this magnificence was seated on his carved golden throne, which occupied a dais at the far end of a spacious audience room, a similar golden chair empty beside him for Cortés. He was surrounded by many nobles, among them Cacama and Cuitlahuac

and a straight-backed eagle warrior named Cuauhtemoc, who eyed us boldly. Moctezuma's humility made
clear to me that the cannonade of the night before had
deeply impressed him. "Thank you for accepting my
invitation so promptly," he said to Cortés while indicat-
ing that he was offering a seat beside his own.

Cortés at once seized the opportunity to speak to
Moctezuma of the Christian Church; the Trinity; the
Crucifixion; the Resurrection; the origin of the world;
the temptation of Adam and Eve by the Serpent in the
garden. "That was Satan who caused the fall of man.
All your idols are other forms which Satan has taken.
They must be removed from your temples. I have come
here to save your soul and the souls of your people
from the eternal flames of Hell. I plead with you to
accept the Cross of Jesus!"

Moctezuma raised both palms outward in shocked
negation. "I cannot be false to the gods who have raised
my land to prosperity and me to great honor! Their
shrines have been entrusted to my keeping. I do not
deny that your God is good, but so are my gods to me.
Your story of the creation of the world is not what I
have been taught to believe. I am sure you are good,
and came here with kind intentions. Once I felt otherwise, hearing about your sending thunderballs to kill
people, throwing down their idols, crushing them under
the feet of your great beasts. But now I think all this
was lies or exaggeration." He leaned toward Cortés.
"I think you are mortals of another race than mine,
wiser and more valiant, and for this I honor you."

Cortés, still wearing the necklace of golden shellfish, stiffened in his chair. "Whether mortals or not, we
are valiant in one cause: to save your soul from Hell!"

"You too have heard lies of me," Moctezuma said.
"You have been told, perhaps that I am a god and live
in a palace of gold and silver. But you can see that my
palace, although large, is of stone and wood like any
other." He held out his arm, touched the bare skin of
the biceps with the other hand. "And my body is of
flesh and bone like yours. It is true that I have a great

domain inherited from my ancestors, and own lands and palaces and gold and gems and receive huge yearly tribute from near and distant places." He stood up; staring fixedly down at Cortés he seemed to be addressing all his watching nobles as well. "But still I accept your great sovereign as my rightful lord. You are his revered ambassador. All that I have you will share. So rest now from your long journey. You are here in your own land, and I will see that your wishes are obeyed as my own."

He spoke calmly. This did not minimize the importance of his concession: Cortés, though probably mortal like himself, was the emissary of a sovereign superior to Moctezuma. This could only be Quetzalcoatl. The legend was still working in Cortés' behalf.

Moctezuma's next words confirmed this. "My ancestors were not the original proprietors of the Valley of Anahuac. We have occupied it for only a few ages. We were led here by a great Being who gave us laws and other knowledge and ruled over us for a time, but then withdrew to the land where the sun rises. He said before his departure that he or his descendants would again visit us and resume his empire here. Your wonderful deeds, and the direction from which you come, all show me that you are this Being's emissaries, sent from him to us."

To my surprise, I saw tears in Moctezuma's jet-black eyes. I knew why. I had seen such tears gather in my father's eyes as he told of his surrender to the Aztecs. I could not help but feel a certain compassion for Moctezuma, and not just because of some tears. It seemed to me that the Toltec farmer had been right; the Aztecs had borrowed the god Quetzalcoatl and made him their own, yet without ceasing to revere their blood-thirsty war god. And so Moctezuma's nature had been imbued from birth with a greater split between good and evil than are most men's; it was as if he revered both God and Satan.

Cortés was quick to seize on Moctezuma's belief that Quetzalcoatl's descendants had entered his city. "Yes, it is true that my sovereign is that great Being you revere. But I promise you he will not interfere with your authority here if you swear to be his faithful vassal. What he greatly desires is your conversion to Christianity, of which I have told you something, and of which I will tell you more."

Seeing the confusion on Moctezuma's face as Christianity was again mentioned, and as he recalled Cortés' earlier and hurried indoctrination into matters very strange and unreal to an Aztec's mind, I recalled how many things had puzzled me when I first learned of them, how I had told Aguilar that Jesus was stupid to have let himself be crucified instead of choosing to live and teach men good things as Quetzalcoatl did in his human form. Nor had I first believed in the Resurrection. I thought it only meant that Jesus had deceived everyone by only pretending to die on the Cross. So I quickly turned to Cortés and whispered that he should avoid any more talk of Christian doctrine at present. "Let Moctezuma ponder what you have already said. And then let our priests do the work they came here to do. They are more skilled than you at getting converts."

He gave me a cold glance, proud of his power of persuasion, but then with a nod admitted I was right. Moctezuma concluded the interview with another display of generosity: a gold necklace for every Spanish soldier, two for each captain. As we left for our palace, they all bowed deeply to Moctezuma, helmets in hand, and on the way back they commented on his gentle breeding and great courtesy. I do not think it was only the golden gifts which had impressed them, because I myself had undergone a great change of opinion concerning him.

I had expected arrogance and had found humility. I had imagined a cruel, proud face and had found a gentle, sad one. None of my one-time hatred of an oppressor had flared up in me; instead I felt some sympathy. His need had been to prove to himself that Cortés and his men were not gods or a god's descendants, just mere men. Everything Cortés had accomplished since Tabasco had proved just the opposite. And so Moctezuma found himself the victim of a legend, faced with a situation nothing had prepared him to cope with. How could he have dreamed when he was crowned at twenty-three that during his reign the long-promised Return would occur? That after seventeen years of absolute authority in accordance with precedents known and changeless he would find himself attempting to comprehend beings so bewilderingly different from any he had known or imagined that they might as well have dropped to earth from another planet?

That night Cortés asked me to share his bed. Head propped on his hand, he lay facing me. " I think I could have done well as an evangelist to Moctezuma if he had only understood Spanish. As it was, my words had to be filtered through you, a neophyte in Christian doctrine."

"You are a commander of men. Do you need to excel as a priest as well?"

He forced a grin at the pricking of arrogance. "What do you think of Moctezuma? Is he a man to fear or a man to love?"

"I think he is sincere, and that we will continue to be well treated by him."

"Have you so soon forgotten Cholula? Do you think he did not order that ambush of us?" He sat up, staring coldly down at me. "Fair words mean nothing to me! Nothing! Has it occurred to you that he could only be pretending to believe we were sent here by that deity of his in order to lull us into a sense of false security? I must proceed as though that were his plan, to disarm us, to make us careless." A sudden crooked grin made his face look sly and somewhat cruel. "When you find yourself in a web, do not look for gnats. Look for spiders!"

When he extinguished the torch and drew me to him I found him in a state of unusual excitement: insatiable, devouring. At last he fell into a deep and sudden sleep, lying prone beside me, sprawled as though flung there by the great hand of the passion that had possessed him. I lay for a long time staring up into the alien darkness. Here, as in Tlascala, Cortés felt danger all around us. I knew that deep within and probably unacknowledged by himself was fear of Moctezuma for his great power which at any moment, and because of some omen or oracle beyond Christian understanding, might be turned against us in all its mighty fury.

And there was reason for fear. The awed Moctezuma was not used to feeling awe for any human alive. After the impact of the Spaniards' strangeness had been lessened by propinquity doubts might arise as to their descent from a deity.

And I was the only link between Cortés and Moctezuma. Through my voice they would come to a better and peaceable understanding—or fail to do so. I dreamed that night that I was a child back in Paynala, my father alive and Ix Chan too. All was golden sunlight there, and no unbelievable future threatened me.

Shortly before dawn the light of a pine torch in a wall bracket awakened me. Cortés, in his red robe, sat at a table near the bed, quill in hand. I was sure he was writing another letter to Carlos of Spain, telling of our arrival in this city, of the warm welcome by a potentate soon to be Spain's vassal, and asking again for reinforcements. I knew by now the long distance this letter would have to travel to reach the king: up the mountains walling this valley, then down the long eastern slope to Vera Cruz, then across to Cuba in the one remaining vessel Cortés had. From Cuba, on another ship, the letter would then have to cross a wide ocean to another continent, then go by land to a place called Madrid where the King Carlos might or might not be in residence at the time it arrived.

Cortés plunged the point of the quill into the inkhorn, then drove it scratching across the page once more. And it seemed to me he was holding the only weapon he could at this moment use against the inner fear that threatened him. Looking at his face in profile, eaglelike with fierce concentration, I knew again that I loved the bravest of men.

23

The next few days passed pleasantly. Cortés and the captains were elaborately banqueted, reverently attended by a swarm of servants. Moctezuma first allotted three slaves to each Spanish soldier, but when Cortés laughingly protested such extravagance he reduced the number to one. The horses were fed maize and bedded down on pallets of flower petals, yet Cortés did not know from day to day when he would ride his black stallion to the lakeshore to find a causeway's first bridge removed and a gap of twenty spans of water separating him from the rest of the world. He was uneasy with the perfect courtesy of Moctezuma, his apparent willingness to have us with him forever, his refusal to embrace the Christian faith. He foresaw clashes between the Tlascalans and the Aztec citizenry, was worried lest a life of sudden luxury would soften his Spanish soldiers, yet could not forbid them to visit the vast marketplace at the southern end of the central plaza.

When he and I went there, I could not believe such plenty, such variety. Each type of merchandise had its regular place: building materials such as stone, lime, and lumber; pottery in all sizes and glazes; cotton cloth of every hue, and cloaks, tablecloths, bedcovers, handkerchiefs, serapes; a feather stall with rare birds in cages and artisans who turned a handful of feathers into a butterfly, a bird, a flower so perfect as to seem real. In the silver market there was a silver parrot that could move its head, feet, wings, and tongue. Cortés bought it for me. He said no Spanish silversmith could better such workmanship. At meat stalls you could buy almost anything that moves: fat little dogs, moles, maguey slugs, mice, deer, hares, muskrats, fish, fowl. There were stalls for fruit, for vegetables, and eating counters where the soldiers bought cooked meats and omelettes and fried beans. A shop sold herbs to cure any ailment, another any color dye. There were barbers, doctors. One shop sold only cooking oil, another pine and candlewood for torches. The paper shop sold *amatyl* in many colors, and every tint of paint and ink. The sweets stall offered honey of many sorts, aloe sugar, candy made from cactus and sweet potatoes. This and the pulque shop were favored by the soldiers: the pulque was flavored like strawberries, cherries, melon, mango. There was a nursery with every kind of plant for sale, even small-sized trees. The air was noisy with bartering, with the piping of flutes and the shuffling rattle of dried gourds; in time to the music a man danced on stilts. Cortés was surprised that cocoa beans, small tabs of tin, and bird quills filled with gold dust were the only money used, the latter carelessly valued by size rather than weight. When he saw a child dragging a toy dog with four small wheels he said he could not understand that a people so clever had never thought of a better use of the wheel; they did not even have potters' wheels, he pointed out, but built up bowls and urns from long ropes of clay.

The busy marketplace offered a sharp contrast to the great five-story temple of the war god. In its forecourt stood a skull rack: tier upon tier of gleaming white skulls formed a wall between two towers built entirely of skulls mortared together and topped by forty poles bristling with pegs, each impaling five skulls. "Is there any spot on earth so soaked with blood, so laden with death as this one?" Cortés asked, and told me that one hundred thirty-six thousand skulls had been counted by one stunned soldier. "And almost in the shadow of this horror these Aztecs buy food, eat it, bargain and chat!" The skulls did not represent human death and suffering to them, he said, but only proof of Aztec power. The hearts of the victims fed the gods; priests and nobles dined on the arms and legs, and the rest was taken home by humbler folk to be cooked into a man-and-maize stew. This cannibalism particularly horrified him, even after I pointed out that it was a religious rite, not mere appetite.

A deep-voiced drum boomed from the top of the temple; Aztecs began to hurry toward it. We returned to our palace, not wishing to view the rite that drum announced.

I was surprised the next day when Moctezuma and a group of nobles arrived to invite Cortés and his captains to inspect the holy of holies, Huitzilopotchli's inner sanctum atop his pyramid. For the first time in my life I, a woman, was to ascend such a temple; as Cortés' interpreter I was indispensable, regarded less as a separate person than as an extra member of Cortés' corporeal being. Sometimes, to his annoyance, Malinche was the name used by Aztecs to address him as well as me.

In the three-story *teocalli,* topped by two elaborately carved wooden towers, were two blood-spattered holy chambers through which flitted dozens of black-clad priests, stinking of the dried blood on their robes. In the larger room the war god stood, fashioned, we were told by a noble, of every seed that grew, ground fine and mixed to a paste with the blood of virgin girls and boys. He was colossal, his face hideously distorted by scowling brows and two fangs. In one hand he held a sheaf of arrows, in the other a bow. A tiny hummingbird was attached to one ankle; a thick snake of precious gems coiled around his waist, and chains of gold hearts hung around his neck. Three fresh human hearts lay in a bowl at his feet. One of his names was The Hummingbird Wizard, but why I do not know.

In the adjacent chamber stood Texcatlipoca in the form of a young man of black stone decorated with ornaments of gold and gems and holding a burnished silver shield in which he could see all that happened in the universe, so his soubriquet was Smoking Mirror. Five human hearts had been offered before him.

These two were the principal deities of the Aztecs, but hundreds of different idols were worshiped at various seasons for various reasons: in homage to the goddess of young corn a virgin boy and girl would be set afloat in a canoe and stoned to death from pursuing boats; to honor Xipe, The Flayed One, a priest would put on the skin stripped from a sacrifice victim and dance wildly to the frenzy of flutes and the throb of the huge snakeskin drum atop the war god's pyramid. In the course of one Aztec year, Moctezuma calmly told us, there were twenty ceremonies to honor various gods. All required sacrificial victims. "One of these is deeply moving," he said, "and I believe would impress you."

After we left the temple, Cortés remarked grimly that blood seemed to be the glue that held the Aztec people together as a political unit. "Remove it and you would have fragments that could be welded together with a purer substance, such as faith in God."

A few mornings later, just after dawn, Moctezuma sent a messenger to invite us to see the beautiful rite he had spoken of to Cortés. We were conducted to the royal box in the *tlachtli* court that adjoined the fore-court of the temple and whose highest tiers offered a good view of the platform atop where the stone altar stood.

Shortly after the sun had risen, a splendidly dressed young man was led by two Aztec priests to the foot of the stone steps of the white pyramid, which he ascended alone. He seemed to walk toward the altar at their top in a trance. He was laid on the altar. The huge snakeskin drum boomed in slow cadence. With a swift downward thrust of a sacrificial knife the high priest slashed open the boy's body just below the ribs, reached in, wrenched out the gushing heart, and held it high in both hands to the morning sun.

I shut my eyes, felt faint, heard the silence as the drum abruptly ceased to beat just as that poor young man's heart now had. Moctezuma's calm voice explained the beauty of this rite. "For one year he has lived as an emperor, known every luxury, slept each night with a different beautiful woman. He had been feted and adored, a national hero." He paused for me to translate this to Cortés, which I did in a somewhat weak voice. "He enjoyed all this in the knowledge that the most splendid of all honors would be the moment when he walked up to the temple altar, the finest gift we could offer our gods." He waited for Cortés to comment.

When Cortés merely shook his head, unable to find words to express his horror, Moctezuma said, "I thought you might see the similarity between our boy hero and your Jesus Christ, who also died for the people of his land, you told me."

"*¡Jesucristo!*" Cortés whispered, instead of his usual oath.

As soon as we left he found Father Olmedo and conferred with him about the necessity of immediately suggesting to Moctezuma that the Cross of Jesus be erected atop the temple where this boy had died. Olmedo counseled patience, but Cortés went without him to Moctezuma's palace. "Our Cross must at once replace that sacrificial stone! And ultimately all your temples will have to be swept clean of your cruel pagan gods! This terrible rite that you insisted I see has convinced me of this as nothing else could!"

Moctezuma's sad face changed as if a mask had been snatched off; the lips thinned, the nostrils flared, the eyes turned to black slits. "What you ask is not possible! Our gods have made us a great people in this land. My five thousand priests would never permit such a desecration. You are foolish to believe that any wise ruler would turn his back on the gods of his nation or let harm come to their places of worship!" He turned his back on Cortés and walked away. Cortés stood looking after him. His face was white, as though sudden recollection of the Spaniards' precarious position here had drawn all his blood down into his still-beating heart.

It was with a show of humility that he went to Moctezuma the next day to ask his permission to build within
our own palace a Christian chapel. Moctezuma not only
agreed to this but also said he would send to us any
wood or stone or masons or carpenters Cortés might
need. After a large room in the rearmost palace building was chosen for our church, it was decided among
the priests that no heathen hands should build its pews
and altar. There were several carpenters among the
Spanish soldiers; one named Nuñez was very skilled.
He said that with half a dozen volunteers to help he
could have our place of worship ready in a week. The
priests had agreed to accept the sweet-smelling cedar
planks Moctezuma had offered to send us; these would
not profane God's house in that trees are not heathen,
having no souls.

I was with the other Indian women who had been
given several rooms near mine while all this was being
decided. I was fondest of Ixlan, who had been given to
Captain Sandoval and liked him very much, but I had
become very friendly with the earnest, slender daughter
of Xicotencatl the Elder, who had been baptized Doña
Luisa. She had no protector; her great desire for Father
Aguilar had been transformed by him into a very
devout acceptance of Jesus. "Jesus be praised!" she
said when Cortés came in to tell me that the wood for
the chapel had already arrived.

"I agree," he smiled. "That Moctezuma has allowed
me to turn one room of his father's palace into a Christian place of worship may well be a first sign that his
stubborn resistance to God is beginning to weaken."

At that moment El Galán and Arturo Mondragon
arrived in haste. Arturo had grown a beard, darker gold
than his hair; it still made him seem like a stranger
to me. Out of boredom both men had volunteered to
help Nuñez build chapel pews. Arturo said, "When
El Galán and I pulled down one of those barbaric
hangings which didn't belong in any church, I happened to notice something odd about the wall where it
had hung. The shape of a bricked-up doorway showed

through the thin stucco that covered it. Nobody closes up a room that way for nothing, and I was all for getting a battering ram, but Bernal thought we ought to tell you about it first."

"It wouldn't do to antagonize Moctezuma by smashing into his father's crypt," El Galán said. "If that's what it is."

"If it is, we will reverently close it again," Cortés said.

He had little trouble opening it, because the two large stone blocks at floor level were not mortared and could be pushed into the hidden chamber, leaving enough space to squirm through. Not wishing to crawl on his belly, Cortés had Arturo and El Galán batter out the two above them, and then entered crouching and holding a wall torch. I followed, Arturo and El Galán just behind me.

The gleam and glitter of the treasures crammed into that small windowless stone vault astonished us all: the most precious objects amassed during a twelve-year reign had been hidden away from all eyes by a miser of misers. There were statues of gold and jade, piles of gold bracelets and necklaces; a chest full of precious stones carved in the shapes of animals; huge disks of gold and silver showing the Aztec calendar; a slit-eyed turquoise mask with human teeth; a gold alligator ten hands long; a large crystal skull on a green onyx pedestal. Dozens of chests and baskets rose to the low ceiling except on the far wall, where a great feather ceremonial cape was hung outspread and seemed like a giant bird guarding this hidden hoard, wings wide.

The crystal skull fascinated Cortés. It was the size of a real one, and he picked it up and held it in both hands, turning it this way and that. "It seems to be carved from one giant crystal," he said. I shivered as the hollow eye sockets caught the light from a certain angle and seemed suddenly to blaze at me, fiery. Cortés returned it to the pedestal and grinned at it. "We thank you, Axayacatl, for guarding all these riches for us!"

Serious once again, he proposed to Arturo and Bernal

Diaz that it would be wisest to replace the stones that closed the doorway and have it plastered over as before. "There's no need for Moctezuma to know that we have found this room. Let it be our secret, except for the mason we will need." He smiled. "And Nuñez, the carpenter. He can make a large pedestal for our biggest statue of the Virgin, and she can guard this crypt for us."

He was elated, and I knew why. The hoarded wealth of a dead idol-worshiper might prove the lever that would finally impress King Carlos. A sudden thought made me cross myself: had Cortés not wanted to build a chapel, it might never have been discovered.

Of all the marvels there, the crystal skull stayed most vividly in my mind; in a dream that night I was tormented by those blazing hollow eyes, that grin.

The next morning a frightful piece of news shattered Cortés' joy at the marvelous find. As I heard the two Tlascalan runners gasp, I could only think of the crystal skull's dreadful smile, as if it had known that good luck would be followed by bad.

There was grave trouble at Vera Cruz.

Juan Escalante, the captain in command there, had recently sent two emissaries to Cualpopoca, the Indian governor who resembled Cortés. They politely requested that he swear allegiance to the Spanish emperor. Cualpopoca refused and had the two Spaniards killed. Learning of this, Escalante at once led a punitive expedition of fifty armed Spanish soldiers and thousands of loyal Zempoallans. The ensuing battle had been fierce; it ended with seven Spaniards killed, including Escalante. His horse, a light chestnut with white stockings, was also dead. And then the Tlascalan messengers delivered a final blow: the severed head of a Spanish soldier had been sent by Cualpopoca to Moctezuma to be offered to the gods as hideous proof of the defeat of the Spaniards, the governor's fealty to his deities and his ruler.

From sorrow over his friend Escalante's death, Cortés went to a state of controlled fury on hearing of this decapitation. The twisted vein on the left side of his forehead swelled and throbbed; the edges of his compressed lips were white. "There's very little doubt that Moctezuma ordered this slaughter of Spaniards, that sly son of Satan!" He called for Orteguilla and sent him to fetch his five most trusted captains: Alvarado, Sandoval, Lugo, Leon, and Avila. "Cualpopoca would never have dared such a thing without his ruler's approval!"

We had been breakfasting in his room when this news came; with a sweep of his arm he sent a bowl of fruit off the table; mangoes, melons, cactus fruit, and cherries went rolling over the floor, the stunned servants staring in astonishment. I too was astonished, for I had never seen him so out of control. "It is not surely known yet that Moctezuma knew anything about what his governor did," I said.

His eyes scorned such innocence: "It will be known. It will be made clear beyond any doubt. I have reached the limit of my endurance. Blood and violence are all these Aztecs understand. Violence he will get!"

I knew I was not welcome or needed at conferences with his captains, yet I lingered out of anxiety. He told them what had occurred at Vera Cruz and said that Moctezuma had to be confronted with this breach of trust. "For days now Moctezuma must have known what Cualpopoca did. His couriers make the run from that coast in a day's time. Yet he has said nothing. He did not come out like an honest man and tell me that to his chagrin a rash governor of his exceeded his authority and slaughtered nine of our countrymen. No! It seems plain to me that he ordered those two Spanish emissaries to be slaughtered, and then the rest followed. For what motive? To test me! To see how we will take it. And I tell you, if we are passive now out of fear of him, we are finished!" He had mastered his anger and spoke with his usual ringing authority.

"But what can we do?" Sandoval asked.

Lugo said, "If we try and question him, he can just lie and say he knew nothing about it."

Alvarado shouted, "I'd like to lop *his* head off, like that Spanish soldier's!"

Avila looked pale and sad. "I hope it wasn't Juan Escalante's."

"Feeding a Spanish head to his filthy gods!" Alvarado shouted, red in the face. He whirled to me, pointing to the servants, who by now had picked up the scattered fruit and waited in a row, looking somewhat uneasy. "Ask them if that's what happened! They'll know!"

I obliged him, and questioned one whose brother not only worked in Moctezuma's palace but served a noble who enjoyed the ruler's confidence. He had overheard a discussion concerning the fate of the Spanish head. It had been brought in a basket by a runner, but it had been so hairy and ugly that Moctezuma had ordered it taken away and buried rather than offend the flayed goddess Xipe by offering her its skin.

When I turned back to Cortés and the captains, they were gathered close and had reached a decision I did not learn of until later that day. They were all grim and tense, and I decided not to tell them about the rejection of the Spaniard's head.

"All right," Cortés said, summing up. "It's agreed. We request an interview with Moctezuma. We confront him with the facts we know. But first I want all soldiers armed. I want thirty or forty to filter into Moctezuma's palace. I want a large detachment stationed in front of it."

When the captains left to carry out these orders he returned to the breakfast table and sat down to eat cold fish. I asked him what had been decided, my anxiety like a cold knot inside me. "To tie up a spider with its own web," he said and would tell me no more.

In his throne room Moctezuma was seated on the dais, surrounded by his nobles, and seemed in a good mood. He offered Cortés a wife from among his concubines, and when Cortés refused he joked about whether one wife was enough. But then Cortés grew serious, and

the captains too. "I am astounded that you, Moctezuma, a valiant prince who had declared himself our
friend, would order your governor Cualpopoca to
take up arms against Spaniards."

Impassive, Moctezuma said, "I gave no such order. I
only recently learned of this."

I felt relief at these words, but when I turned to
Cortés his face told me that he did not believe them.
"Your governor's soldiers have slain a countryman who
was like a brother to me. I wanted to believe that you
did not order our ambush at Cholula. Now I cannot.
Nor can I believe you innocent of this."

"Cualpopoca acted without any order from me. Just
as your dead captain acted without orders from you
when he sent two Spaniards to tell my governor that he
must transfer his allegiance from me to your Spanish
king."

Cortés shook his head sadly. "I would like to believe
you. How can I?"

"I will summon Cualpopoca here and we can investi-
gate the truth of the matter." Moctezuma slid from his
wrist a gold bracelet from which dangled a small jade
image of the Aztec war god. "I will send to the east
coast several of my nobles with this, which gives them
the power to enforce my commands."

Cortés was not mollified. He pointed to the bracelet.
"How do I know that little green fellow has not just
returned from a trip to Cualpopoca when you commanded him to kill the two emissaries of Juan Escalante?" These words, translated into Nahuatl, had a
great many sibilants; Moctezuma drew slightly back
from me, as from a menacing serpent.

"I am innocent of any such command."

Cortés strode forward one step. "Then prove it!"

"How can I prove it, my lord?"

"Come with me to my palace and remain there as
my guest until Cualpopoca arrives to clarify his slaughter of innocent Spaniards."

I stared at him, not believing the words I had just
heard. An impatient nod urged me to repeat them in

Moctezuma's language. When I did his face turned white, then turned red with anger. He straightened his back, staring down at Cortés. "Who ever heard that a great king like myself ever left his own palace to become the prisoner of strangers?"

Now murmurs arose from his nobles; they turned to look into one another's shocked faces. Of this Cortés seemed unaware. He took another step forward, his voice as hard as steel. "Not prisoner: hostage. I cannot any longer trust you. You must be my hostage until the truth comes out."

Moctezuma now looked dazed. "That, of course, is impossible. But if it is hostages you require, I offer you three of my children."

"I want you and only you! Your willingness to comply will tell me much about your innocence as to Cholula or this new aggression against me. Hostage is perhaps too harsh a term. You will be my guest. My men will obey your every command. You will live in whatever rooms of your father's palace you choose. But I insist that you now show me your good faith. If you did not order Cualpopoca to kill my men, then you will feel no hesitance about leaving this room with me, and now."

The murmurs from the nobles were louder now. They buzzed inside my head like angry bees as I respoke these words. Cortés' courage had turned to folly! Here in the heart of this city of several hundred thousand Aztecs all fanatically devoted to Moctezuma he dared to make this demand!

"What is the use of all these words?" Alvarado shouted. "Why waste our lives bickering with this barbarian? Either he comes with us or we kill him, here and now!" And he half-drew his sword. As I stared at the gleaming steel, Captain Juan Velásquez shouted "Yes, here and now!" The other five captains, faces resolute, closed their fists on sword handles.

I said to Cortés, in a low, warning tone, "Surely I am not to say *this* to Moctezuma!"

He did not look at me but kept his eyes on Moctezuma's. "Tell him to dismiss his nobles."

I did so. After a moment's confused hesitation, he
obeyed. He did not seem to be able to remove his eyes
from those of Cortés. With a whispering of sandals,
all the Aztecs who had surrounded their ruler crossed
the room and left. Then Cortés said, "Now tell Moctezuma what Alvarado said about killing him."

Looking up at the Aztec ruler I made my voice
pleading. "Please, my lord Moctezuma, do as Cortés
asks. If you go with him to his palace, he will treat
you with all respect and reverence. If you refuse, you
will expose yourself to violence, even to death."

Cortés raised his arm. Steel rasped on scabbards as
six captains drew out shining blades and held them out
at arm's length, all pointing toward Moctezuma's heart.

The sight of those swords had a stunning impact on
a man never touched except at his own command.
Staring down at them his cheeks seemed to grow hollow; his lids veiled his eyes to shut out what he saw.
The threat of murder had unnerved him as though
from the clear blue sky lightning had pierced through
a palace window to sear him with its white heat. On
that golden throne he seemed to shrink. Cortés grew
taller.

In that moment which seemed like an hour I waited
in terror for the cry of outrage from Moctezuma that
would summon his nobles, then his warriors. But he
rose slowly from his throne, stepped down from the
dais on which it stood. His eyes did not seem to see
Cortés, or me, or anything, but stared inward at
some dreadful vision there, some imperative that drove
him to obey Cortés. "To prove my friendship, I will
do as Lord Cortés wishes." His voice was low and
dazed.

I breathed again. My translation was scarcely necessary: his whole being spoke of his submission. Cortés
gave no sign of the enormous relief he must have felt.
He bowed to the Aztec ruler, then turned to leave. He
and Moctezuma crossed the throne side by side like

dear friends. The captains sheathed their swords and followed. A throng of nobles filled the corridor. I held my breath for fear Moctezuma, seeing them, might be reminded of his great power, tell them he was to be made a captive by Cortés. But he merely nodded at them and asked that his royal litter be brought to take him through the plaza to the gate of Cortés' palace. "There I wish to visit for a time," he said.

There was only one answer: he thought he walked with a god's descendant whom he must at any cost appease. It seemed most fitting to me that a Christian soldier should have been confused with a gentle pagan god who had asked that only fruit and flowers be offered at his altars, and never blood. Then the reality of what had just occurred gripped me, and I looked up at Cortés with something of the awe I had felt for him long ago in Tabasco. Kidnapped! He had kidnapped Moctezuma from his own palace in the heart of his own city in the center of a world that had been his to command. Who else would have planned and dared it? I knew then what his earlier cryptic words had meant: he had entangled Moctezuma in a strand of his own web, superstitious fear of the Aztecs' borrowed god.

24

Tension riddled the next few weeks, though on the surface everything was pleasant. Moctezuma was amenable, the perfect guest. He did not object to the large guard of Spanish soldiers who went with him on his daily visits to the main temple to worship his gods. He seemed pleased when Cortés willingly gave him his own bedroom, for which Moctezuma asked because it had been his father's. When his nobles came to visit him, I had to be present to learn of any orders he might give them to our detriment; he accepted this graciously. He even mustered up a mood of gaiety, as though he were there by choice. One day he ordered three of his canopied pirogues to take Cortés, his captains, and me with him across the lake to Chapultepec, a wooded shore where his other palace stood and where an outdoor meal had been arranged for us by its staff. He took a great liking to little Orteguilla, whose quick mind had enabled him to learn to speak Nahuatl quite well, and Cortés gave him Orteguilla to serve as his page. The two would sometimes stroll together through the palace garden, followed by the usual bodyguard of Spanish soldiers; it was strange to see so great a ruler with a dwarf as his chosen companion.

The underlying tension came from the fact that Moctezuma did not send for Cualpopoca. One day, assuming that this had been done, Cortés saw the bracelet with the jade token of authority still on Moctezuma's wrist, found that he had not yet used it to command his governor's presence in the capital. Charged by Cortés with failing to keep his word, Moctezuma evaded the issue. "I find it pleasant here with you. There is no hurry therefore." He continued to vacillate about the questioning of Cualpopoca, one day promising to bring him before Cortés, the next day refusing to hurry the matter.

"He shows an indecision of mind unbefitting a ruler, or else guilt," Cortés fumed.

Another sore point was Moctezuma's continued resistance to the Christian faith. "I have given my word before my own nobles to accept your sovereign as my own. Do not make further demands on me at present," he said with a cold and haughty show of authority. Nonetheless, our priests and I spent many hours with him, using every power of persuasion to break down Moctezuma's loyalty to heathen gods, to no avail. He was perfectly polite, perfectly unmoved. His occasional remarks reminded me of my own thoughts before the patience of Aguilar and Father Olmedo and the flaming destruction of the idols at Zempoalla made a wholehearted Christian of me. Moctezuma, for example, found the notion of the virgin birth of Christ absurd, since Mary had already married Joseph and therefore was not a virgin at all. Nor did he think it likely that Eve had been made of a rib of Adam, since in that case all men now living would lack one rib, but this was not true. He conceded that the Spaniards clearly worshiped a powerful deity; he denied that it was the only one. "My people, like the Toltecs, have long understood that there may be a One and Unknown God much greater than any represented by our idols. This Force never took the form of a man or died on any cross. This Force is above and beyond mere human understanding. This Force is not your God or your Jesus."

Moctezuma surprised me one day by asking me to walk with him in the gardens of his own palace: perhaps the absence from his wives and concubines had left a yearning for female companionship, although Orteguilla had told me that he had remarked favorably on my appearance and intelligence. "All I ask is that you do not speak of religion," he said in a weary voice as we set forth, followed by the clanking Spanish guard.

"What would it please you to talk about, Lord Moctezuma?"

He paused before his menagerie of wild animals near the great aviary, stared at a caged jaguar, then moved on to the reptile house to watch a rattlesnake coil itself in its feather-lined trough. "You may choose the subject," he said.

I seized the chance to ask about the disquieting omens spoken of by the Toltec farmer. His face grew even more somber. The rattlesnake raised its tail and issued its sinister warning.

"Omens, disturbing oracles, strange happenings have marked my reign from any other," he said. The arrival of the pale bearded strangers at Yucatán had been only the beginning. Ten years before the arrival of Cortés, the waters of Lake Texcoco had become violently agitated during an earthquake, had poured into Tenochtitlán, sweeping away many smaller houses. Then the coldest winter in history iced the whole valley so that thousands froze to death. Not long after this Popocatepetl erupted, its lava burying an outlying temple to the Aztec war god. Then a strange bird with a mirror in its head was found and brought to Moctezuma, perhaps sent by Tezcatlipoca. The bird died. Only a few years before the Spaniards' arrival, a weird crackling blaze of light, broad at the base and tapering to a point and sparkling with tiny stars had appeared in the eastern sky; from it came a wailing as of many voices. At this time one of the wooden turrets atop the war god's temple caught fire from no known cause and continued to burn, inextinguishable, for a long time. All these events, unprecedented as they were, had seemed to the priests of Tenochtitlán and of Texcoco to be warnings of a disaster that would befall the Valley of Anahuac at the end of the Aztec calendar's Fire-Sun era of fifty-two years. "The last day of each such cycle of time is one of great danger," he said. "For the ancients knew that the sun may fail to rise in the sky, and all things cease. But these extraordinary phenomena, clustered in so brief a time and in this valley, indicated a more particular danger than the sun's death which would affect all the earth. My old friend Nezahualpilli of Texcoco was warned many years ago that if this disaster was to be averted an extraordinary propitiation of the gods was required. His priests told him that unless his favorite son was offered up as a sacrifice, doom was certain. But he refused to let this son be killed, saying that he disdained to placate gods so cruel. The fact is that he privately believed only in the One and Unknown God, though he of course rendered the customary public homage to a large pantheon of other deities in which his people believed." Moctezuma smiled sadly. "He was a poet. In his old age he made many songs about the shortness of life and the need to enjoy its roses. One day he and I bet on different players in a *tlachtili* game; the wager was that if I won, the danger that threatened our kingdoms would be averted. But I lost. He died soon after that." He gave me a sad, grim smile. "His city had already declined; chaos followed his death; I chose the next ruler of Texcoco."

"As to the One and Unknown God he believed in: did you never come to believe in Him too?"

"I told you, my friend was a poet, not a realist. He would have been wiser to have sacrificed his son, for he had a great many." His eye met mine in a chill and remote look. "I told you that I do not wish to discuss the gods."

The tranquility of that lovely garden was suddenly shattered by the roar of a jaguar. A flash of fear prickled through me. In great part the strange events Moctezuma had just described had contributed to his present belief that a god had sent Cortés to judge him. But if newer omens caused that belief to waver, Cortés would find that it would have been less dangerous to have brought into his bedroom all the wild animals and venomous reptiles in the garden's zoo.

Moctezuma's next words were like a confirmation of this thought of mine. "The strange events I have just told you of show one thing very clearly. The gods I worship and shall continue to revere gave me many warnings. They will continue to reward my devotion. As of now, they indicate that I am to wait with patience."

We passed then to the House of Freaks, where I saw a girl with white hair and skin and lavender eyes, a boy with skin like a snake's, a creature whose hands grew from its shoulders, a woman so fat she could not walk, a man with a pointed head no bigger than two fists clenched together, a man with a huge round skull, and a number of dwarfs all smaller than Orteguilla. "In these creatures, appearance and reality truly meet," Moctezuma said. "Nothing can disguise their true nature, which is their deformity." His eyes searched my face. "You appear to be of my race, yet you live with people of another and speak their language. What is your true nature, Malinche?"

Taken off guard I said, "I am a Christian and the tongue of Cortés and beyond that of no great importance."

He smiled. "Beauty is never unimportant. At an earlier time I might have made you my concubine."

"At an earlier time, Lord Moctezuma, I was a slave in Tabasco, and before that daughter of the cacique of Paynala and named by him to rule after him."

His interest in me suddenly faded. "I am tired and will rest now, then bathe and change my clothing." Each day he dressed in new garments, all very splendid. As we turned toward the palace he had given Cortés, I knew that even if I had told him of my childhood betrayal, he would have been little interested. Tribute flowed to him from many conquered towns and nations; their internal problems were their own.

Walking through a rose garden he had the wan air of a man whom reality has abandoned. He paused to stare at a red rose; a fish in one of the marble pools then caught his attention. Perhaps these simple forms of life soothed his complicated mind, patiently waiting for his gods to let him know whether he should summon Cualpopoca or defy Cortés.

That night he maintained his royal dignity in spite of the shocking experience of dining in public and not behind a carved and gilded screen so that no mortal eye might see him chew and swallow: Cortés had arranged for a huge banquet in honor of his royal guest. As always, Moctezuma's wine was chilled with ice from the heights of Popocatepetl. His frothy chocolate drink, thickened with honey and spices, he ate with a tortoiseshell spoon from a golden cup. A curious mark of Aztec sophistication was that before the meal and after we had eaten servants brought us basins of warm water and cloths with which to wash our hands. But despite delicious foods—meats with rich sauces; fowl stuffed with fruit; luscious pastries of maize flour, eggs, and aloe sugar—I could not really enjoy the feast. Watching Moctezuma sip from his golden goblet, I was very much aware that for all the extreme luxury and indulgence that had so long surrounded him, the fierce blood of his indomitable ancestors flowed in his veins. Would Cortés be the serpent he at last held in his talons and devoured?

Cortés tried to use the feast as a means of persuasion. "If Cualpopoca were here tonight, and had convinced me that the slaughter of my Spaniards was in any way provoked or justified, then he would be sitting here as my honored guest, second only to yourself."

Moctezuma said almost petulantly, "I have made many sacrifices and have asked the gods to enlighten me on this matter but they have not."

Cortés could not hide his irritation. "There are times when we are expected to behave on our own accord and use the brains we have been given!"

"That may be true for you, Cortés, but it is not true for me." Moctezuma's personal steward knelt to offer him a long pipe of gilded wood and he inhaled the tobacco smoke with pleasure, emitting gray clouds that veiled from him Cortés' urgent face.

The next morning Cortés had another chance to reprove Moctezuma for Cualpopoca's absence. It was reported to him that one of the soldiers of Moctezuma's bodyguard had spoken rudely to him and had urinated in his presence. Cortés had the man arrested, brought before Moctezuma and himself, and flogged. "That is how I treat anyone under my command who does you an injury, Moctezuma. I expect like respect from you. Yet you continue to protect Cualpopoca by refusing me the chance to question him. How long must this continue? Why do you make it so hard for me to believe in the innocence you profess?"

Moctezuma urbanely deplored such a cruel punishment as flogging for so minor an offense, a sentiment flagrantly insincere coming from so clean and elegant a king, in a city whose people were so devoted to bathing, as if to wash away any guilt they felt over all the blood spilled on their many altars.

But rites of sacrifice at one of these altars must have provided Moctezuma with the omen or oracle he claimed to have been awaiting. Three weeks after he became a hostage he announced that Cualpopoca had been sent for and was arriving that very day.

He rode on a litter, accompanied by one of his sons and fifteen other attendants. Entering the audience room where Cortés and Moctezuma awaited him on the dais in two golden chairs, he paused at the door to put on over his fine attire a humble robe of *nequen,* then came forward to kneel at his ruler's feet. Moctezuma spoke coldly and firmly. "You must answer all Cortés' questions honestly." He stood up then and left.

"Are you a subject of Moctezuma?" Cortés asked the governor.

"And what other sovereign could I serve?" Cualpopoca had risen and faced Cortés boldly.

"Did you order two Spaniards killed when they visited you?"

"I do not deny this." Cualpopoca stripped off the *nequen* robe and let it drop to the floor.

"Did you order your warriors to fight against Spaniards, and were seven of them killed?"

"That, too, occurred."

"And was this done at the order of your ruler Moctezuma?"

After a moment, Cualpopoca said, "I have authority in the area I govern and do not always have to ask his permission."

"Then Moctezuma did *not* instruct you to take such extreme measures?"

Now the governor's voice was less assured. "I am trusted by him to a very great extent."

Cortés gave him a smoldering look. "I, too, am trusted by him! In fact, he has placed your fate in my hands! That fate may well be the immediate arrest of you, your son, and your attendants. There is nothing

Moctezuma can or will do to prevent this. So cease all this evasion and give me simple honest answers!"

Cualpopoca paled; his throat moved as he swallowed. "No one had to tell me to remain loyal to my ruler and not swear to obey another king."

"But did he tell you to kill my Spaniards?"

"They tried to tell me to forsake my gods as well."

"I want straight answers! If I tell you this evasion will mean your death this very day, will that bring the simple truth out of you?"

Cualpopoca's bearing changed. His shoulders drooped. He looked at his frightened son. "What truth do you mean?"

"Did you decide on your own authority to kill Spaniards?"

There was a long pause. Cualpopoca stared straight ahead at the empty golden chair Moctezuma had left. "In such an important matter I would not act merely on my own authority."

Cortés' fist pounded down on the arm of his chair. "I knew it!" He turned to his watching captains. "Take this man and his retinue away. Put them all in irons."

I left the audience room filled with uneasiness. All along I had believed that Cualpopoca had acted alone. In sudden fear of his life, and deserted by his monarch, did he lie or tell the truth?

This uneasiness refused to leave me. If Cortés was convinced that Moctezuma had planned the attack on the soldiers at Vera Cruz while treating Cortés as his guest and friend, would Cortés retaliate? Would he forget that Moctezuma's fatalistic patience might snap at last? Finally I sent a servant to find Cortés and tell him I wished very much to speak with him. Before she returned, one of Moctezuma's attendants came to say that Lord Moctezuma wished to talk with me, and at once.

He was alone in the sleeping chamber where Cortés and I had first stayed, and which had been turned over to him. He sat in a carved and gilded chair near the narrow window overlooking the great square. Beyond its far buildings the sun was setting, the sky a blaze of orange light. The glow was reflected on the gold wine cup in his hand. Instead of any panache of plumes he wore only a narrow jeweled headband. His black hair, slightly graying, hung straight nearly to his shoulders. I had never seen him so simply attired. "What did Cualpopoca tell Cortés?" he asked in a rather querulous voice.

"He admitted that you ordered the killing of the Spaniards." I watched his face closely, but saw no hint of guilt.

"That is not true."

"He was in great fear of Cortés."

"What will happen to him?"

"He and his son and attendants have been arrested."

He sighed heavily. "All over my domain people fear my name. Yet I have been powerless to prevent this. I do not think my father or my uncle would find themselves helpless as I am now. I cannot believe what has happened to me in these last weeks." He raised the cup, swallowed wine. "When I was young, I was a very brave warrior. I attained the highest of honors and was made a member of a select military order. I did all this as a means of becoming First Speaker. There were others as eligible: my brother Cuitlahuac, and my cousin Cuauhtemoc, for example. As you may know, succession among us is not from father to son, but from uncle to nephew or brother to brother. Before my uncle Ahuitzotl the Cruel chose another nephew to succeed him, he told me privately that I am unlike our ancestors, that I lack in my nature a certain fierceness which an Aztec ruler must possess. Deeply hurt, I reminded him that fierceness can take horrible forms, and mentioned a daughter of his who married Nezahualpilli, and demanded a separate palace, to which she brought her many lovers, all of whom she killed and had minions make statues around their bodies, keeping some in the bedroom where she reveled. Her husband found out and had her publicly strangled. It was stupid of me to remind my uncle of this crazed daughter. It lost me any faint chance I had of becoming his successor." He drank again, and suddenly he smiled. "But it is surely the gods who rule our destinies. The chosen nephew died suddenly, soon after Ahuitzotl did. That left it to the Council of Four and the thirty clan chiefs to decide on a new ruler. They selected me. It was I, not the fiercer cousin my uncle had chosen, who walked up the steps of the great pyramid to address the people with humility and have the green panache placed on my head." His eyes looked back in time at that great day.

I was in part amazed that he spoke to me so intimately, yet I also knew that he was speaking as much to himself, trying to grasp the threads of his life which had been ripped, unraveled, and tangled by the hand of Cortés.

"As a boy," Moctezuma said, "I thought that if I ever became First Speaker I would inaugurate an old Toltec custom. They used to have Battles of the Flowers, in which no blood was shed. Prisoners were taken as proof of victory after being touched by blunt spears, but then they were garlanded with flowers and released to fight again. And after my coronation I abandoned warfare and turned my mind to the great mysteries, to astronomy and astrology, to the interpretation of omens, to the secrets of the universe. Do you know that the earth, which seems flat, is a round planet like the moon, and also moves through the sky? Do you know that when the heart is taken from a sacrificed person he feels no pain? As his eyes see the knife raised above his body, the god to whom he is being offered sucks out of him all power to feel it so that no screams of pain or writhing of the body can occur to destroy the sacred moment." He nodded. "As a high priest who must order many sacrifices, it comforts me to know that."

"If you are also a high priest, how is it that you can have so many wives and concubines? Christian priests have none, nor did the high priest in my town of Paynala."

My question seemed to bewilder him. "But I am also First Speaker! One of the many prerogatives of such power is the acquisition of wives and concubines. This is expected of me, demanded by precedent. The common people must live monogámous lives. They enjoy the thought that their ruler is able to revel in pleasures denied them. It pleases them that I never wear the same clothing twice, but give away what is once worn. My palace also gives them pride. My palace is exquisite, is it not? I have gone further than any monarch who preceded me in matters of elegance and style. By comparison, my ancestors were as barbaric as the Chichimecas of the northern deserts." He found his wine cup empty, held it out. A steward I had not noticed came and took it from his hand. He straightened in his chair. "No one can say now that we are inferior to the Toltecs. We have outdone them!"

"Your city is very marvelous and beautiful." I felt almost as if I were praising a child for some feat.

The steward returned with the filled goblet. Moctezuma did not notice him, but leaned forward, his eyes filled with woe. "Yet here I am, a prisoner of Cortés!"

I spoke gently. "You are his hostage because you refuse to accept his God. God wants your soul, not your body."

"My soul?" He accepted the goblet of wine which the steward had continued to hold out until his ruler might deign to take it. "I am not dead."

"Those who believe in God will never die. They will live with Him in Heaven, forever."

I thought I saw a gleam of interest in his brooding eyes. "I have listened to a great many words concerning your religion. But for some reason I did not understand that your God offers immortality. Perhaps I turned off my ears. I did that often. Immortality? Or do you merely speak of the long journey of the disembodied spirit to the dark realm of the dead called Mictlán?"

"Heaven is bright and beautiful, filled with angels and with good Christians."

"By Christian standards, I am not good," he said. "Of this I am well aware."

"God forgives all our sins if we believe in Him and confess our wrongs."

"One of your God's commandments is not to kill. I have killed many men. Would this be forgiven me?" He was half smiling, as if he believed I would have to answer *no*.

"Yes," I said.

"I also remember that your Deity can heal afflictions."

"He can heal all ills of the mind and spirit, if we believe in Him."

"And can he make impotent men virile once again?" Our eyes met; I knew what he had admitted. "Since Cortés came here no woman can arouse me."

"I believe that when you kneel humbly and accept Him above any other gods he will remove this affliction." Moctezuma's great candor had amazed me, yet at the same time I felt strong within. Was I to be the one who reached his heart?

"Are you suggesting that I do as Cortés asked and remove my people's gods from their temples?" I could feel his resistance, see it in his frowning face.

" 'You shall have no other God.' That is His first command."

"Again you confront me with this alarming renunciation of all that I have ever believed in!" He stood up; the steward took the golden goblet from his hand. "My priests would never consent! My people would refuse to have their gods taken from them!"

"But you are First Speaker. Your word becomes law. You have the power to save yourself and all your people from burning forever in Hell."

He winced; Christian priests are very effective in describing the eternal torments in store for sinners and heathens. With weak defiance Moctezuma demanded: "As for this Hell, where is it? And where is your Heaven, since earth is a planet?"

I pointed down at the stone floor. "In the realm of

the spirit, Hell is the lowest place, Heaven the highest. It is like the bright Realm of the Sun where I once thought brave warriors go when they die, only Heaven is even more beautiful, and more filled with peace. It is like the loveliest moment of the happiest day you have ever known, stretched out to last forever."

"Peace! I have known very little peace since I first put on the green panache of power. Pomp and luxury and worship, yes. But very little peace." He sank into his chair. "If I were to accept this God of yours, how can I be sure He would not condemn me for things I have done? Send me down to Hell?"

Now a sense of power touched me; it filled me as the wind fills a ship's sails. "God does not want you there! He wants your soul to be with him in Heaven!" I took a step toward him and dared to say again what Cortés had told him. "Your war god is Satan. I beg of you, do not revere him a day longer! Kneel humbly, as I have done, to the only God, the God of Cortés! He will forgive your worship of false gods, for you knew no better. He will remember a little boy who wanted all battles to be Battles of the Flowers. For He is called the Prince of Peace."

When I saw his eyes gleam with unshed tears I knew that God had inspired me to touch a deep chord in his nature. My whole being was tense with hope. I might succeed where wise priests had failed! I knew I must not say another word but let the gentleness at the core of Moctezuma's being flow up in his heart and wash away the now-crumbling wall of his resistance.

Night had now fallen. Through the window behind him I saw the evening star. Suddenly a bright glow was there outside as though the sunset had returned. I walked to the window and looked out. I heard a cry of horror. The voice was mine.

In the Zocalo below the window stood a long row of stakes each amid leaping flames where Cualpopoca and his retinue made living torches. The fires lighted the faces of stunned Aztecs watching their first auto-da-fé and were reflected on the breastplates of Cortés and his captains. The stench of burning flesh filled my nostrils. I heard myself cry "My God!"

"Your God of mercy," I heard a voice behind me say. I turned. Moctezuma's face was lighted by those fires below. "Your Prince of Peace!" A burst of flame leaped up to the height of the window and was reflected in those hard black eyes. "Go from me. Ask your God to explain such mercy as this!"

As I turned and walked numbly toward the doorway, a male servant entered with a blazing torch to light those in the brackets on the wall. The pleasant resinous odor of this smoke did not eradicate the stench of charred human bodies. I turned my head to look back in anguish at Moctezuma. His face was lighted by the torches within the room. Behind was the glare of those other flames. Back straight, he looked every inch a king. And I knew he was lost to God forever except by some miracle God might send.

25

Heavy footfalls thudded on the stone floor of the corridor. Cortés entered with a burly soldier who carried iron manacles: black chains and a heavy ball. At a lope, bent by the weight in his hands, he approached Moctezuma, knelt, and clamped the leg irons shut around his ankles. At a gesture from Cortés he pushed the carved gold chair to a place behind the chained ruler so he could seat himself. Moctezuma bent his head to look down at his fetters. From his throat came a deep groan. The flames of the wall torches and the glare of other flames below the window made him look to me like a man chained in Hell. The staring servant with the torch backed to the door and ran out.

Cortés beckoned me and said, "Moctezuma, your governor has admitted that you ordered the murder of Spaniards. Such a crime merits death for your subjects who were responsible. Even for a sovereign, this crime cannot be atoned for without some punishment."

He waited for me to speak. My tongue refused.

He turned to stare at me. "Speak up! Tell him what I said!"

Nausea from burning bodies clogged my throat; my hand covered my mouth; I held down rising vomit.

"By God, what is wrong with you?" Cortés' harsh voice would have alarmed me if I had had room for any more emotion than I now felt. "Speak!"

I swallowed and repeated in Nahuatl: "The crime of killing the Spaniards merits death for your subjects. For you, this punishment." Moctezuma stared down at the iron ball resting beside his gold sandal. He moaned.

Cortés spoke again. "I want you to reflect on how you deceived me and tricked me after saying you would hold me in honor."

This time he did not have to urge me to speak; like that silver parrot in the market that opened its beak when a wire was pulled, I told Moctezuma what Cortés wished.

"I have never deceived you," he whispered, and sank down slowly on his chair, staring at nothing with dazed eyes.

Behind me I heard the loud and growing noise of many sandals in the corridor and turned as the crowd of Moctezuma's nobles poured into the room, somewhat hesitant about entering without having been sent for. They spread out along the two walls at either side of the doorway. Cortés, the soldier, and I were between them. Others filled the exit. All stared at their chained ruler, awaiting his command.

Cortés turned and faced those in the doorway, waiting imperiously for them to let him pass. The human wall awaited orders from their ruler. It was Cuitlahuac who said, "Do you wish the strangers to leave, Lord Moctezuma?"

I felt my flesh shrink, watched Moctezuma's face for the first sign of his rising anger, reminded by the question of his status and his power. In his pale face pale lips opened. His eyes looked at nothing, or everything. "Let them leave me," he whispered.

Obediently, the human wall parted, flowed aside. Cortés, the soldier, and I passed into the corridor between angry and bewildered faces. The soldier grinned up at Cortés. "That was a narrow one!"

Smiling grimly, Cortés shook his head. "No. I knew the irons would break his spirit if the sight of his governor in flames had not already done so."

A moan like the one that had come from Moctezuma's throat now came from mine. "Lost. We have lost him."

Cortés looked down at me. "What is wrong with you, Doña Marina? You are not like your usual self today."

There was an interval of blankness between walking beside Cortés along that corridor and the moment I found myself in the chapel on my knees before the statue of the Blessed Virgin. Votive candles burned at her feet; her serene white face looked down on me; one pale hand was raised in benediction. High above the altar hung a large crucifix; on Christ's gaunt cheek shone a glass tear. My body was rocking backward and forward as it had the day my father died. Now, too, my tears were silent ones. "Hail Mary, full of grace, be with us now and in the hour of our death," I whispered. But when I tried to raise my hand to cross myself it did not move.

I knew then why I had come here. My faith in the Christian God was in peril. Mere statues of stone and wood had burned in Zempoalla, but now this stench of human flesh was still lodged in my throat so that even the sweet aroma that came from the new cedar pews

could not take it away. I willed myself to be aware of
that smell of the wood of trees first made by the hand
of God and now serving His purpose here, destined by
Him when they were mere seedlings to grow large and
tall and be made into these seats in the first Christian
church in Tenochtitlán. This thought soothed me. I too
was God's humble creature. Humility, Aguilar had told
me, is the first duty of a Christian, who must accept
that God's ways are mysterious, not always to be understood by us. Faith comes from such humility.

A cry went up inside me: but how humble is Cortés?
How humble is a man who burns other men so cruelly?
Chains a captive king? Where is the humility of Hernán
Cortés? What sort of Christian is he? Is he one at all?

The Virgin to whom I raised my eyes had no answer.
Her gentle face and upraised hand seemed to counsel
patience until God chose to enlighten me.

But patience did not come; instead another emotion
began to burn in me: anger. Anger at Cortés. And, for
the first time, contempt. He believed himself so astute,
yet had ordered set alight those flames in which Moctezuma's tenuous rootlet of belief in God had been consumed.

From the chapel doorway behind me came the animal noise of someone retching. I turned. One hand
against the corridor wall opposite the wide aperture, a
Spanish soldier was bent double, vomiting. His helmet
tumbled from his head and clanged to the stone floor.
A gilded helmet. Arturo Mondragon's.

The little figure of Orteguilla, who must have been
following, ran forward; he picked up the helmet. "Well,
at least you didn't do it in the chapel!"

Arturo straightened, wiping his mouth on the back of
his hand. Through the open door he saw me. Orteguilla
did too, and came running toward me. His cocky grin
was gone. "Cortés has put Montezuma in chains. I saw
him. In leg irons. He was weeping. Some of his nobles,
too. They could not comfort him."

"I know," I said.

Arturo joined us, casque under one arm. His voice

was loud yet unsteady. "I rarely vomit. Only once when I was seasick. It was the auto-da-fé. I never saw one before. My father once told me about a Carib cacique in Cuba who was put to the torch for refusing the Christian faith. As the faggots were lighted at his feet he asked if being burned would send him to the Christian Heaven anyhow. No, they told him. He showed great relief and said that was good, as he would not care to go to a place occupied by such Christians as he had known." He looked down at me uncertainly. "I can't help but think that Moctezuma may feel much the same."

"One thing is sure," Orteguilla said. "He must be released from those leg irons. How much can he be expected to endure? Those nobles of his are going to work on his mind, believe me! Cuitlahuac and Cuauhtemoc in particular. I am trying to get up the courage to tell this to Cortés."

The deep feeling of the little man and his desire to reprove Cortés moved me. "He doesn't take rebuke kindly, but he is good at plucking the truth from mere opinion or rhetoric." Many nights beside Cortés seemed now like irrelevant dreams I once had. The daytime man who had laughed when I pricked his arrogance might listen to the dwarf.

"I have my methods," Orteguilla nodded with some of his usual assurance. "Oh, he listens to me, all right. That's what jesters are for, to offer truth with a grin."

"If you can joke about what happened today, you belong at the court in Madrid," Arturo said.

Orteguilla turned to me. "Will you come with me, Doña Marina? I've noticed that he sometimes listens to you, too."

"Well," Arturo said, "I came here to pray and had better do it." He knelt near me before the Virgin, clasped his hands, bent his head. "Holy Mary," I heard him whisper, "help me to understand this thing and then to forget it. Amen."

As we left, several Spanish soldiers approached the chapel, casques in hand, followed by half a dozen more.

We found Cortés in his room, sunk low in his armchair and evidently in a dark mood. His captains were just leaving. They were unusually quiet and said good night to their commander in subdued voices. "Good night, gentlemen," Cortés said. "Perhaps my dwarf can cheer me after this momentous day. Play me a song, Orteguilla. Something on the merry side, if that will not annoy Doña Marina, who appears to prefer a funeral dirge to go with her dismal mood."

Orteguilla sat cross-legged at Cortés' feet, looking up. "As I do not have my guitar with me, I will tell you a fable. It concerns a brave rat-knight who led his band of rats into a sleeping lion's lair. The rat took some jewels, and the lion slept on. He drew his sword and killed a few of the lion's cubs, and still the lion slept. But then, made bold, the rat-knight tied the lion's paws and muzzle. The lion woke, snapped the bonds and gave a roar that summoned a thousand lions, who pounced on the rats and ate them all up."

"I could wish that you had not made me a rat," Cortés said with a forced smile.

"Cat and mouse, lion and rat," Orteguilla said, paling slightly. "The point is, sire, that until today Moctezuma was as docile as that sleeping lion before he was fettered."

"I know the point! But there's much that you do not know! None of you!" He glared at Arturo. "What are you here for?"

Arturo raised his head high and I noticed for the first time that his beard was trimmed exactly like that of Cortés. "I came to say that the auto-da-fé seemed to me excessive punishment, and that other soldiers feel the same."

Cortés stood up, glaring down at Arturo. "Excessive! Rat-knights and lions! Has it occurred to none of you that Moctezuma is playing a feline's waiting game? The murder of those Spaniards was a test of my power! I could not let it pass. If the auto-da-fé is what bothers you, then let me point out that this is the means the Church has long used to deal with heathens. I did not invent it. All Cualpopoca had to do was kiss the Cross. Aguilar made that clear. He refused. If his soul is frying in Hell, don't blame me!"

"And the chains on Moctezuma?" Orteguilla asked.

"I had to cope with his anger on seeing his governor burned! The best way was to humble him."

By now I had seen that Cortés' defensive anger showed that he was uneasy about the chains, if not the flames. I stepped toward him. "You may get more than his humility," I said.

He turned to me, frowning. "More? What more? I want no more."

"If you keep him chained, he may choose to die."

"Die? He has no weapon. Do you mean he could command an adulating noble to kill him? A *coup de grâce?* Is that what you mean?" His voice was urgent now.

"A man who chooses to die can will himself to die."

"Nonsense!" But now Cortés looked both thoughtful and alarmed.

"If Moctezuma chooses to die, because his terrible humiliation makes him believe his gods have abandoned him, another First Speaker will be chosen. Perhaps Cuitlahuac. Or Cuauhtemoc. They do not like Spaniards, and I do not think they are overawed by you as Moctezuma is."

"They are not." Cortés looked grim.

"You need Moctezuma alive, don't you? None of his subjects will make one move against you unless he commands it. His successor's first command might be your death. The death of all of us."

He stood staring at me alertly. Then he went to his writing table and took something from a carved box: a key. The key to Moctezuma's chains! His face was resolute. "I have degraded Moctezuma. But I can also exalt him." I followed him down the stone corridor to Moctezuma's room.

Surrounded by Aztec nobles who looked confused, sad, anguished, or stoic, the ruler sat huddled in his golden chair, head bent low. Cortés crossed the room, knelt before him, and unlocked the leg irons. He unclasped and removed them. Still kneeling, he spread his arms in a gesture that implored forgiveness. "I regret the disagreeable necessity of subjecting you to this brief punishment, Moctezuma."

As I repeated those humble words, the discovery that his legs were again free brought Moctezuma back from his deep trance of sorrow. In a weak voice he said, "I thank you for my freedom." He stood up, walked a step or two, shaken.

Cortés also rose. "I offer you a further freedom. I am convinced that you will be loyal to me, whatever your governor did. So I offer you permission to go back to your own palace to live."

Amazement unnerved me. I knew Cortés had gone too far in his effort to regain Moctezuma's friendship. Once removed from Cortés' personal magnetism, once in daily frequent contact with those nobles who wanted the Spaniards dead or banished, how long would Moctezuma continue to protect us?

As Moctezuma heard Cortés' offer of this freedom, his face had a wistful look; it was replaced by one of resolve. "Many of the nobles in my palace want me to take up arms against you. If I were living among them it would be hard for me to avoid the alternative. But it would pitch my city into a war of great bloodshed and violence. Your weapons would kill thousands of my people. I will not do that to my city."

I felt my tense body suddenly relax. I repeated these words for Cortés in Spanish. But Moctezuma added these: "Nor can I let anyone believe that I purchased my liberty at the price of my governor's terrible death. I must remain here with you, Cortés."

Smiling, Cortés rushed forward to embrace Moctezuma joyously. "I will love you from this day like a brother! Every Spaniard will have your interests first in their hearts!"

Moctezuma stared stoically out, suffering this embrace, he who was never touched. Murmurs of amazement rose from the nobles watching, and I saw Cuauhtemoc stare, mouth open, at Cortés embracing the First Speaker as if the sight would be engraved on his mind to the moment of his death.

As we left, Cortés smiled down at me. "You gave me good counsel, Marina." But I could not return his smile.

A little later, Cortés having gone to tell his captains of the new status of affairs, I removed my clothing and other possessions from the room we shared and took them to the one where Doña Luisa and Ixlan slept. A pallet was brought by servants for me, and it was soft enough for a queen or Moctezuma's favorite concubine, but it was a long time before my eyes would close. I was tense with anxiety, fearing that Cortés would demand my presence in the other bedroom. But it became clear that he was too proud or too angry to do more than ignore my absence. I said a prayer at last and composed myself to sleep among women for the first time in a very long while.

I knew that fear and not repentance had brought Cortés to his knees to remove those shackles. Once again he had created a crisis; once again he had met it with apparent success. His ambition had created all the crises he had overcome. In resolving them with violence or with craft, he had created a new Cortés who seemed more of a stranger to me than that god in armor I first saw in Tabasco.

For many nights my dreams were haunted by bodies aflame, Moctezuma in chains, and by the heavy hand of Cortés on my arm, shaking me awake to come to his bed, and from this dream I awoke with a scream. Yet by day our relationship of commander and interpreter continued as before, except that no intimate words were spoken between us. He was as courteous and as distant as if we had never touched and never referred to my change of sleeping place. After a time I was torn in half between the frightening executioner of my nightmares and the Cortés I saw by day, and within me these two were in conflict; my emotional reaction after the auto-da-fé was on one side of the battle, but on the other was the knowledge that Cortés was in an excruciating position. His letters to the King of Spain had gone unacknowledged. His bold unauthorized march to the Aztec capital would certainly anger Governor Velásquez when he learned of it, for it had placed in jeopardy the expedition in which he had invested much money and much hope. Cortés could not relax his strong grip on the emotions of the Aztec ruler. Was it just of me to blame him for maintaining it by means of a custom to which he had been used since birth, however appalling it might be to me? Even gentle Father Olmedo, even Aguilar, with his fondness for Indians, had told me that the auto-da-fé had been a grim political necessity that might eventually prove a boon to untold thousands of heathens who by that terrible example could more easily be converted to Christianity, fear being a good persuader. Moctezuma, alas, was not one of these.

26

Moctezuma spent long mornings atop the great temple in worship of his gods, lost in his Region of Mystery. Any enlightenment he received must have counseled continued patience. He continued to ignore those nobles who urged that the strangers be forced to leave the city. As though no subjects of his had ever burned, no leg irons ever chilled his ankles, he returned to his former false amiability: he taught Cortés to play *totoloque,* an Aztec game of chance, and ordered a game of *tlachtli* to be played in the ball court, that large sunken

enclosure surrounded by high tiers of stone benches
from which we had watched the boy hero die. The
towers of skulls in the forecourt of Huitzilopotchli's
temple stared down from thousands of hollow eye
sockets at the muscular, agile players who—though
wearing heavy yokes of polished stone—sent a ball of
olli rebounding from walls and finally up into a high
stone hoop. Watching this game, I remembered the bet
Moctezuma had lost to his old friend Nezahualpilli of
Texcoco. It did not surprise me when he turned to
Cortés and said, "We will each choose a player to score
highest. If mine wins, it will mean that you will leave
my city of your own volition."

Cortés agreed, and Moctezuma watched the game
with intensity. When his player won he was overjoyed;
I knew he took the triumph to be an omen. The next
day he took Cortés hunting on the royal game preserve
near the Chapultepec palace across the lake; he killed
a deer but Cortés missed his. The dead stag was
brought back in the pirogue to Tenochtitlán to be
butchered and eaten. "Tonight you will eat the proof
of my superior marksmanship," he told Cortés, smiling. He held in one hand the blood-stained arrow,
glancing often at the obsidian point of his trophy in a
way that made me uneasy. He had bested Cortés twice.
Would a third complete the charm?

But the mood of false tranquility and the days of
playful competition came to an abrupt end; any comfort Moctezuma might have taken from small triumphs
was shattered by the message sent to him from Cacama
of Texcoco. It accused him of abject cowardice.

That same day several nobles who had been in
Cacama's confidence came to Moctezuma to tell him
that the Texcocan ruler was trying to spur a rebellion
against him. He had been going to many neighboring
caciques of the lakeside towns and farther ones to speak
against the Aztec ruler, insisting that he should be replaced by a First Speaker who would either force the
Spaniards to leave or kill them all. I was sure that this
revolt had been ignited by the flames that killed Cual-

popoca even before a sorrowful and deeply disturbed Moctezuma summoned Cortés to his room to tell him of it and to say: "Now you see, Cortés, that your cruel punishment of one of my governors was unwise; it will make all my vassals fear like treatment."

Pale and stunned, Cortés had no answer. He knew that all our lives hung on the outcome of the rebellion. He vigorously urged Moctezuma to summon his army to put it down in its first stages; Moctezuma vacillated, not wanting to destroy the century-old alliance between Texcoco and Tenochtitlán. And such intervention proved needless: few caciques or governors were willing to rise against Moctezuma. Cacama was captured in his city of Texcoco by traitors he had trusted and was brought in fetters to the capital. With him were several Aztec nobles who had conspired against their ruler. One was Cuitlahuac.

Moctezuma chose not to have him or Cacama executed for treason, and they were imprisoned in a cell in our palace. Remembering how Cacama had come to welcome Cortés, I could imagine what he must be feeling now. Cuitlahuac had taken his imprisonment with a stony indifference, showing no gratitude that he had escaped execution by his brother Moctezuma's forbearance.

Knowing how deeply this unprecedented uprising had disturbed Moctezuma, Cortés decided the time was ripe for him to proclaim his allegiance to Carlos of Spain in a formal ceremony. Moctezuma did not object, and called together all his most important vassals, some of whom came long distances. When they were gathered with his nobles before the golden throne in the large audience hall he told them that Cortés represented their great deity Quetzalcoatl and that the time had at last come when he wished to resume his supreme authority.

"For my part, I am ready to acknowledge this authority. You have all been faithful vassals of mine for as long as I have sat on the throne of my fathers. I now expect you to show me this last act of obedience by acknowledging the great king beyond the eastern waters to be your supreme lord. I shall serve him as he commands me. It is your duty to behave likewise. In doing this you will give me much pleasure." The tears running silently down his cheeks belied the words.

Many of the gathered nobles wept with him, for with those words Moctezuma had relinquished the absolute power that had come down to him from a succession of eight rulers. Yet obedience to his authority was deeply ingrained in them; since he thought the sovereign of Cortés to be their ancient god, they believed this too. The oath of allegiance was solemnly administered. To my surprise, many of the Spanish captains and those foot soldiers who were present seemed deeply moved. I saw tears in Arturo's eyes, and in El Galán's and Sandoval's. Cortés looked grave; when he spoke his voice was husky, although his words were resolute. "First my emperor, next my God," he said to Sandoval. So ended a dynasty.

But Moctezuma steadfastly refused to do away with his pagan gods and become a Christian. Nevertheless he complied with a request Cortés had made before the rebellion: to send an expedition to the province where there were many gold mines and bring back this raw gold for Cortés' use. Francisco Pizarro, a distant kinsman of Cortés, and several other Spaniards were placed in charge. When the gold arrived, Moctezuma generously added to it many golden objects from his treasury. To me it was painful to see artifacts of rare beauty smashed to bits and then melted down in the stone crucibles of Aztec goldsmiths, to be poured into clay molds that, broken off when cold, left only squat heavy ingots. It took only three days to eradicate the excellent work of many lifetimes.

But Cortés had decided on a division of the spoils, and this was the only way the value of the gold itself could be measured. After the Royal Fifth was set aside, and Cortés' share and that of Governor Velásquez, and double shares for priests, captains, musketeers, those with horses, the foot soldiers got only about a hundred gold pesos' value each for more than a year

of faithful service amid great dangers. This caused great
anger among them—a small rebellion, in fact, set off
by Arturo Mondragon. I learned from Sandoval, who
was present, that when the modest heap of nuggets and
gold dust was doled out to him, he pushed it right back
across the table to the officer who was doing the doling.
"Give it to Cortés with my compliments! I would not
want our commander to come out of this with empty
pockets!"

"But as he turned angrily away, El Galán stopped
him," Sandoval told me. "He said that except for pain
and the pox, a little is better than none. So Arturo took
his share. But a great many other soldiers imitated his
gesture of spurning so poor a reward, and Cortés finally
went among them and spoke kindly and gave every foot
soldier a gift of gold which he said came from his own
share." Sandoval sighed. "I wish this division of the
loot meant that we could march out of here tomorrow.
But I fear not. Cortés is determined to bend Moctezuma
to his will in the matter of religion. Sometimes I wish
his only interest were gold. Or even glory. He could go
back to Cuba a rich man."

But he had undertaken to Christianize the people of
a land larger than Spain itself. And he had discovered
that Moctezuma could accept Cortés' emperor as his
own ancient deity but not Cortés' Deity as the one true
God. The visits of the Spanish priests were endured with
adamant disinterest and blank eyes.

One day Cortés' patience snapped. Summoning me,
he strode into Moctezuma's chamber and told him that
the devilish rites of the Aztec priests must be stopped
at once. The lengthy thudding of the great snakeskin
drum suddenly ceased. "I command you to order the
removal of your heathen gods from the temples!"

On the same chair where he had sat in chains not
long before Moctezuma was as rigid as one of the idols
he now defended. "Perhaps some of our rites seem
wrong to you, but I warn you that the destruction of
our idols is a sacrilege that neither I, nor the priests, nor
the common people will ever permit."

"Permit?" Cortés looked outraged, as if he were the ruler and Moctezuma the intruder. "Permit it they shall!"

He ordered me to follow him, collected a dozen armed soldiers in the courtyard, and led us at a fast pace to the pyramid of the war god and up the steep steps to the *teocalli,* where he entered the chamber in which Huitzilopotchli stood. The hideous colossus glared down on us; today half a dozen human hearts filled the bowl at its feet.

Cortés clasped his hands and stared up toward heaven with anguished eyes. "Oh God, why do you permit such honor to the Devil in this land? But we are here, God, to serve You, and serve You we shall!"

A number of Aztec priests burst into the sanctum. In a loud voice Cortés commanded: "Bring water at once and wash the blood from these walls!" He pointed to a gory inner altar, the spattered wall and floor.

When I translated this the oldest priest rushed toward Cortés, pointing with a blood-red hand. "This is the house of Huitzilopotchli! To honor him the people of this city hold as nothing their lives, or their fathers' or mothers' or childrens'. They will rise up in arms against you! Take heed, stranger, for they will gladly die for their gods!"

Cortés turned and ordered a soldier quickly to bring more armed Spaniards to the temple. Then he faced the priests again. "And I will fight for my God and if need be die for Him!"

"Our god will eat your heart and we will eat your arms and legs!" the old priest screamed with a sneer.

Cortés turned, seized a long pike one of the soldiers carried and began to smash at the war god, striking high at its face. "Something we must do for the Lord!" he cried to his soldiers. At once they began to attack the idol too. A sword slashed off the little hummingbird on its ankle and it fell to the floor at my feet.

Even though I knew that only an ugly statue was being desecrated, reverence for such idols taught me in childhood surged up in the form of fear. I backed slowly toward the doorway, trembling as if some dreadful retaliation would be sent down by the now-battered war god. There was a more real danger: at first immobilized with astonishment, the Aztec priests came at Cortés and the soldiers with raking fingernails and stone sacrificial knives. More soon joined them. The soldiers had to leave off attacking the idol to protect themselves against the maddened priests. One saw me in my corner and ran toward me with a knife raised high. But at that instant the soldiers Cortés had sent for burst into the room; one felled the priest who menaced me. At that instant Cortés turned and saw that I had been in great danger. He strode over, took my arm, and pulled me with him to the doorway and out. We all but hurled ourselves down the pyramid's steep steps. When we reached its base I was panting, fear still beating in my throat.

"Forgive me," he said, "for placing a woman in such jeopardy. I had hopes of talking with the priests up there, of convincing them to at least make a small beginning toward the end I must attain. And as you know, to do this I needed the aid of your tongue." He amazed me with a smile. In a low, intimate tone he said, "And there are many times when I need more of you than that, Marina. When are you going to stop this game you have been playing? My bed is cold without you."

What kind of a man is this? I thought. How can he leap from righteous fury to carnal desire? But at the same time my body itself responded to his words, to the look in his eyes, that warm bright look that said he desired me. My knees seemed to melt; a languor softly filled the very hollows of my bones while excitement made my blood go hard and fast. My throat wanted to say, "Tonight! Now!" But my mind stayed cool and apart. "It is not a game to sleep among women and not with you," I said. "It is a necessity of my being. I do not want to be touched by you until you can make me understand why you burned seventeen people alive."

His smile turned to a scowl. "I will explain nothing

to you! If you are too dull or to fond of Indians to grasp the necessities my duty forces on me, then to hell with you! You are standing there breathing God's air because I had those heathens burned. Anything less and I would have lost Moctezuma's respect, and with that, all! The news of the blaze you hate me for is going to spread like a wildfire. It may be the one thing that eventually gets us back to Vera Cruz alive, because you can be sure that it will make all Indians very afraid of killing Spaniards. So sleep where you will, Doña Marina! Dream sweet dreams about some other man than Cortés! Some gentle fellow who does not have to control an alien nation of many millions of blood-thirsty savages by means of fewer than four hundred Spaniards and a weak-kneed captive king!" With a last cold stare he turned his back and strode away.

I took a step after him, belatedly realizing how he had left his soldiers fighting the priests in order to be sure of my safety. But had I been saved by the com-mander who needed his interpreter, or by the man who needed me? I felt tears sting my eyes. I wanted to be loved for myself alone by the man I had just sent striding away from me by charging him with inexplic-able cruelty: if the thought had not made me weep a tear or two it might have made me laugh, if harshly, at the miserable knot of confusion that fettered me where I stood watching Cortés mount the pyramid again, sword already drawn. I walked back to the palace, passing below the rack of skulls that silently testified to more than two centuries of cruelty far more terrible than that of Cortés.

Within the hour I was performing my daytime func-tion; for Moctezuma summoned him to an audience and asked as well for the soldiers who had been with him when the war god's temple was so brutally dese-crated. Now the monarch who had wept in chains sat as unapproachable and impassive as when he first rode out on his palanquin to meet us. With a look that combined horror and sorrow he said even he could not save us now from the inevitable results of the damage to the idol and the wounding of Aztec priests. His people would surely rise up against us when they learned of the affront to their gods. "The priests have not made your terrible act public because they do not want it known that they were unable to defend the deities. They offer an ultimatum: you must all leave this city and this land, going back to whence you came."

I saw all self-assurance leave Cortés' face. Yet still he tried to play for time, perhaps in the hope that he would learn at any hour that reinforcements had at last arrived from Spain. With the might of Spain solid behind him, he could try to use Moctezuma's status as vassal of its king to force him to take a stand against the Aztec priests. He spoke quite humbly, for him: "You must tell the priests that we cannot leave this land until a fleet of ships can be built at Vera Cruz. The vessels we came in have been destroyed."

Moctezuma said he would have his subjects on the coast supply the wood needed to build us ships, and would so inform the priests and continue to placate them. "Do not blame me for the situation in which you find yourselves. I do not think it was Quetzalcoatl who inspired in you such foolish savagery." But for all his reproachfulness, I saw on his face a glimmer of triumph. By his own act Cortés had made our exodus inevitable.

I knew our situation was very ugly. Cortés could not know from moment to moment if the Aztec priests might suddenly decide to make public the sacrilege and demand the obvious penalty: our hearts to propitiate the war god whose idol Cortés had all but demolished. The soldiers all slept in their armor. Our palace was readied for a siege. Masses were heavily attended and a special one was held in memory of Spaniards who had died. But Cortés knew well that our only actual strength was his hostage Moctezuma's continued desire and ability to protect us with his hereditary authority.

That was how it was when disaster struck.

Cruelly, it wore the smiling mask of the good news Cortés and all of us had been awaiting.

27

I was picking roses in the palace garden when Orteguilla's excited voice spoke behind me. "Cortés wants you at once!"

I pricked my finger on a thorn. Blood rushed to my face. The words had meaning to that part of me that wanted Cortés.

"I was with Moctezuma when an Aztec courier came up from the coast," Orteguilla said as we walked toward the palace. "A large fleet of Spanish ships has arrived! Eighteen of them! Anchored offshore near Vera Cruz! The King has responded to Cortés' letters at last."

The surge of relief that rose in me was dimmed by a dreadful thought: Vindicated at last and provided with the ships he needed, would Cortés leave Tenochtitlán? Would he return to his wife in Cuba? Or would he be summoned to his emperor's side to be rewarded for gaining him a vast new colony? I found my steps slowing as my spirits sank.

"I can hardly wait to get out of this place," Orteguilla said. "I am reasonably brave, but lately I have to keep telling myself that if I am to die here at least in won't be on one of their hellish altars, for which of their gods would be honored by the heart of a dwarf?"

"Then you think Cortés will leave now?"

"Why wouldn't he? Moctezuma has sworn allegiance to Carlos of Spain. The ceremony was recorded and notarized and went to Vera Cruz the next day to be delivered to his royal majesty. There's nothing to keep Cortés hammering away on that hard Aztec head, I assure you."

Moctezuma, dressed for some ceremony, wore a panache and looked almost cheerful. When I arrived, he beckoned forward the courier who had brought the news; he knelt at the ruler's feet to spread out before his eyes a brightly colored pictograph. Cortés stood at one side of Moctezuma's chair to look down at it, I at the other. On it were painted eighteen Spanish ships, many men in armor on each, and cannons and horses. "Now you will not have to build any ships," Moctezuma said, "and can leave at once."

Cortés bent forward to examine the detailed drawings, then straightened and had me ask the courier several questions. "Are these ships anchored at Vera Cruz?"

"No. They are a half day's walk south of it."

"Have the banners on the ships been correctly depicted?"

"Yes."

"Are all of them shown?"

"Yes."

Cortés nodded thoughtfully, thanked Moctezuma, and left. I followed him, aware that he seemed disturbed rather than excited by the news of a Spanish fleet at last. He walked frowning down at the floor, his feet moving with a slow, heavy tread as if he did not want to follow where his thoughts were leading him.

"You do not seem very happy," I said.

"I'm not." His glance showed slight surprise to find me at his side, but no warmth. At that moment there was the crack of a musket from the courtyard, followed by several more. We were passing a doorway that opened out onto a stone balcony; he went to it and we looked down on the jubilant crowd of soldiers below and at several captains galloping its length, wheeling to gallop back again. *"Viva Carlos el rey!"* one shouted, heartily cheered by the rest.

"One of the soldiers guarding Moctezuma must have

rushed to spread the news," Cortés mused, to himself
rather than to me. "Too bad."

"Bad? It seemed good news to me."

"Indeed? Well, enjoy the illusion while you can." He
turned his back on the cheerful scene below.

"Forgive me, but illusions do not interest me. What
is the truth?"

"It's a matter I prefer to discuss with the captains."

"Forgive me," I said again. As I repeated the phrase,
intending to make it cold and formal, my voice betrayed me. The words sounded gentle, almost a plea,
and I knew then that I wanted his forgiveness for having deeply wounded his pride and his love for me.
How right Aguilar had been when he told me that God
judges us, and that to judge another harshly is not a
mortal prerogative! What right had I to judge Cortés,
and also to punish him for what I had thought wrong?

He must have heard more than the words themselves,
for he looked at me squarely, studying my face. "I sent
to Carlos a detailed map of the coastline from Tabasco,
showing the exact location of Vera Cruz. I do not think
he is in the habit of paying good money to inept pilots
and mariners. Why is this fleet not anchored at Vera
Cruz?" He watched my face as I nodded. "Second:
these Indian artists are wonderfully precise in what
they depict. Yet the flagship did not fly the royal banner of Aragón and Castile, the flag any fleet sent by
the emperor would have flown. Why not?"

"This particular artist might have left it out, not
knowing how significant the banner was."

"I'll allow that. But then there is the third point. If
King Carlos was enough impressed by the treasure and
the letters I sent him to decide to aid me with reinforcements, that good news would have arrived well
ahead of the fleet. It takes time to assemble and launch
such an expedition, but very little to send word it is on
its way. If Carlos had such concern for me as to send
it, he would also want me to know as soon as possible
that he was going to do so."

"If the king sent no fleet, then are you saying there is

none? That Moctezuma is lying? That it is a ruse to get you to leave Tenochtitlán and march down to the coast?"

"I wish that were true. But I think a fleet has arrived. I think it is an expedition sent here by Governor Velásquez of Cuba."

"Velásquez?"

He nodded. "And in that case I doubt very much that the soldiers down there have any reason for rejoicing. I think Velásquez has learned everything: the building of Vera Cruz as a royal colony, the treasure I sent to the king, and my determination to march here without telling him."

"But how could he have learned these things? From the king, you mean?"

"Doubtful. He has been living out of Spain, at the Flemish court, and may not even have read a single letter from me as yet. I think Puertocarrero and Montejo may still be dangling in Madrid, waiting his return. No, there's a very simple way in which Velásquez could have been supplied with all the information I did not want him to have. When Puertocarrero and Montejo left for Spain, I specifically ordered them not to stop at Cuba. I did this knowing that Montejo owns some property on the north coast which he wanted to visit and would be passing, eastbound. I think this order was disobeyed. Probably what happened is that some mariner jumped ship, as they will do, and spread the news of treasure, my letters to Spain, and a projected march to the interior: everything! Such news would inevitably reach the ears of the governor." He gave a mirthless smile: "And I doubt that these ships he has sent are here to render me aid."

"Then why are they here at all?"

"His way would be to first complain of my insubordination to the Royal Council of the Indies, claim I had defied his orders and cheated him as well. If he got no immediate favorable response, he would set about on his own raising the money and soldiers for a second expedition to Mexico. Probably he would put his friend Pánfilo de Narváez in command, the man he came close to choosing to lead this one. And I do not have the least doubt that Narváez has orders to take over this expedition of mine, just swallow it up, and arrest me on sight."

He left me there stunned and went to confer with his captains. Within an hour the entire Spanish army was mustered in the largest courtyard. From the top of a flight of stone steps leading to the front rampart he bluntly told them the worst, much as he had told me, except for heavy emphasis on the greed of the governor who was striking out because of envy that no gold had been sent to him.

Stunned faces looked up; his voice rang out angry and assured. "You all know, and God knows, that the governor's share has been fairly apportioned and set aside for him. You all know, and God knows, the hardships we have endured and from which Velásquez, safe in Cuba, is going to reap great financial benefit. And what is our thanks for making him rich? He has sent out an armada against us!" He waited, nodding in agreement as a low growl of anger arose from the men. Then he smiled down at them, that warm brilliant smile, and cried, "But I say Velásquez has made a great mistake! He does not know the men we are, nor how all our sufferings have strengthened our valor. Did he really think we would let him arrest and punish us for all we have done to his benefit? We are seasoned! We know this country and its Indians, and we have allies among them. Narváez's men may outnumber us, but they are raw, untrained. I say that these ships have brought us arms and horses we badly need. Let us march down to Vera Cruz and take them!" As the first shouts of approval rang out, Cortés shouted over them: "We will swallow Narváez and his men just as they thought to swallow us!" The roar of agreement broke over him like a wave.

And I, I stood there on the balcony where he had told me the truth about the ships and felt the old admiration of him well up in me, as strong as it had ever been. Who but Cortés could have used such evil news to wring from those soldiers shouts of approval? Granted that the tense situation here made the prospect of a swift departure not unwelcome, still his army would march out not as undesired guests who have been asked to leave but as a band of heroes ready to stand up for their rights against a greedy tyrant. And safe in Tlascala, there would be time, I thought, for Cortés to evaluate the situation and make careful plans either to confront Narváez and his army, or avoid them.

That night a more personal problem faced me: how should I now behave toward Cortés if he asked me to return to his bed? For there would surely be an awkward time between us; an estrangement like ours does not mend itself in a matter of minutes, I believed. Would it be best not to refer to the recent past? Or should I try to explain the deep emotional impact of a spectacle I had never seen before, as well as my compassion for Moctezuma, whose nation's history held him in a strangling anaconda grip?

I might have spared myself these questions: Cortés did not send for me. Not that night, nor the next, nor the next. I faced the fact that I had wounded Cortés too deeply for him to forgive and forget with ease. Under other conditions, he might have found time to perhaps make some gesture toward our reconciliation: an hour's conversation, or a meal shared. But as it was, he had problems of much greater import confronting him.

For I had learned that Narváez commanded some twelve hundred Spanish soldiers, nearly a hundred horsemen. And that Cortés had decided to take with him only two hundred men, including horsemen and some seventy well-seasoned fighters whom he considered the most devoted to him. This meant that he was leaving in Tenochtitlán about a hundred forty of his Spaniards, who would have ample ammunition, cannons, and fourteen musketeers and crossbowmen. He supervised the building of additional barricades and fortifications, then announced his plan to the soldiers.

"Against Narváez I need to use a small, mobile force and the element of surprise. The duty of you who will remain here is the all-important one of keeping Moctezuma captive. I believe he is on the verge of becoming a Christian and is already a vassal of the Spanish crown. You who hold this city can do so knowing that both your God and your king will smile on your fortitude." A loud cheer went up when he announced that their commander, to be obeyed as they would obey him, would be Pedro de Alvarado.

An instant feeling of foreboding told me this was a mistake, that a cool man was needed here, not a hot one. Alvarado's tendency toward headlong action was known to Cortés, although his bravery and the love the men felt for him had to be weighed against this, as did his unique status with Moctezuma and his nobles, who called him Tonatiuh, "Child of the Sun," because of his red-gold hair, ruddy skin, and exuberant warmth of manner. I knew the disdain of Indians it hid, and had guessed that under this lay fear of a people whose ways he did not understand.

My doubts concerning him led to others. Suddenly, for all Cortés' assurance when he had spoken of his plans and decisions, the grim reality of his situation struck me with full force, and his decision to maintain his grip on Moctezuma seemed a great folly. Surely a hundred forty more soldiers would be of some help when he was so outnumbered? As for the gold with which, Sandoval told me, he hoped to bribe some of Narváez's soldiers into changing sides, would enough respond to this lure to even the odds, even after the enviable sight of Cortés' soldiers wearing the gold necklaces and bracelets they had taken to putting on out of ostentation?

As if the forthcoming situation at Vera Cruz were not bad enough, the plight of those soldiers ordered to remain behind certainly equaled it for sheer danger if Moctezuma's belief that Cortés was a god's emissary should finally waver. I did not know if I felt more concern for the soldiers who would leave with Cortés or those who were to remain in the city.

I had decided that I preferred to be going to Vera Cruz; at least half our Tlascalans would accompany Cortés, and I knew I would be needed to relay his orders to them as well as to the Zempoallans and Totonacs the fat cacique might provide. Orteguilla spoke Nahuatl quite well enough for Alvarado to communicate with Moctezuma. My spirits rose at the thought of riding once more beside Cortés, his indispensable voice. Under those conditions, surely our estrangement would fade away.

An interview with Cortés which Moctezuma requested made it plain that my concern for those to be left behind was even better founded than I had thought. I went to his audience room feeling happy that Cortés had requested my help when he might well have used Orteguilla's. Cortés was in good spirits too.

Moctezuma's words changed that, abruptly. "I have seen that your captains and soldiers seem agitated. You have not come to visit me to tell me why. I asked Orteguilla. He said you intend to go out against your brothers who came in those ships, leaving Tonatiuh here to guard me. But those in the ships are also vassals of your emperor. Yet it seems they have come here to capture you, even kill you. I do not understand this at all."

After a hard glance at the dwarf, who turned pale, not having guessed that Cortés had told Moctezuma nothing, Cortés assumed a casual air and told me to say: "If I did not come to tell you about this, it was because I love you and did not wish to grieve you, knowing how well-disposed you are toward me. As for the white men who came in those ships, it is true that they are also vassals of my monarch. He rules over many provinces, and their people are very different from one another, some more valiant than others. We here in your city are Castilians, the most brave of all. So do not concern yourself about my well-being, Lord Moctezuma, for I will soon return victorious."

The sad face did not brighten. "They are fourteen hundred in number and have eighty horsemen and twenty cannons as well as seventy of the weapons men hold in their hands to shoot out small thunder. A courier also told me that they possess crosses and images of your God and his Mother and hold Masses. Yet they say you have fled from your rightful ruler, and were not sent to me by him."

Cortés raised his chin and seemed to grow taller. "They are bad people and have come here with a bad purpose. Our God and His blessed Mother will give more strength to us than to them. You will see that we will bring them here as prisoners. So you need have no anxiety about our departure. I beg of you only to stay quietly here with Tonatiuh and his soldiers. He will not allow any disturbance after we leave the city, nor must you."

The crucial instant had arrived. Did Moctezuma believe Cortés? Or did the size of the army sent to capture him seem more convincing? The delicate, mournful face gave no hint of what he was thinking as he stared into Cortés' eyes. The name Moctezuma meant "he of the sorrowful countenance"; for a long moment he epitomized his name. Then he said, "If you should need assistance, I will send you five thousand warriors."

"I am grateful for this offer," Cortés said. "I need only the help of God and my brave companions. I ask you merely to supply my people here with food, and that is all." He went to Moctezuma and embraced him. Moctezuma returned the embrace, his face still sorrowful.

With a daring induced by his earlier amazing candor after his governor was arrested I said, jokingly, "I think you are only pretending sorrow at our departure, Lord Moctezuma. For I know it will please your priests and nobles and reduce their complaints of us to you."

He gave a swift glance but ignored the remark. "If there is anything more I can do to aid you I will do it with all good will, Cortés. I do not want any calamity to befall you." He sounded sincere, and Cortés embraced him again and then we left.

"A pox take the dwarf for babbling," he said.

I defended Orteguilla. "I doubt that he told Moctezuma anything he did not already know or would have soon learned, his espionage system being as it is."

Cortés' annoyance with the dwarf had made him forget our changed relationship, as I realized when he answered me with a return to cool formality. "I am sure that is true. But his spies and couriers have served me too. I did not know that the odds against me were quite that severe."

In as cool a tone I said "Then why worsen them? I cannot understand why you need to leave anyone in this city at all."

He stopped walking, stared down at me as though at an idiot. "You can't, Doña Marina? Then I will tell you. I signed my name to a contract with Governor Velásquez. In it I promised to make Christians of heathens. The fact that he now intends to arrest or kill me does not change the fact that this is what I swore to do. The difference between a caballero and a commoner, as my father told me long ago, is that a gentleman keeps his word, not so much for others as for himself. I will keep mine. But there is an even larger reason why I must keep the foothold I have gained here and refuse to admit failure in making a Christian of Moctezuma. These cruel barbarians must be brought to God! And I seem the one God has chosen for the task." He paused portentously, then added, "Your responsibility is a heavy one. I pray you will show your gratitude for your own salvation by giving of your best in helping our priests reach Moctezuma's heart at last."

My own heart gave a throb of anguish, then sank, aching with every beat. Cortés was leaving me behind! I tried to conceal my feelings. "I thought you would need me to interpret your commands to the Tlascalans and Totonacs."

He sounded pleased when he said "Fortunately, Sandoval has picked up enough Nahuatl to do that."

Part of me wanted to cry out "And can he hold you in his arms? Can you turn to him in the night and forget all dangers and find joy?" But I said "Yes, that is very fortunate."

"Incidentally, I must part you from the mare I gave you. She is spirited, an excellent mount in battle. But do not fear, I will bring her back safely, and she will be yours again, like anything else it has been my pleasure to give you."

Perhaps he did not know the wrench it gave me to part with that particular gift. Perhaps he did not know what it had meant to me to mount and ride the animal that once had filled me with superstitious terror. Perhaps the smile he gave me as he promised to return the horse was not a cruel one but it seemed to me that he knew these things, and also was aware that this particular gift had once conveyed to me that he loved me. Shaken, I said, "Since you have taken back the gift that most mattered to me, I will not weep at losing a mere horse." And with that I turned and left him.

The gift I meant was his affection. I wanted with my whole being to weep for that loss, yet would not let myself. He had his pride; I had mine.

"Marina," he called after me.

I wanted to stop; I wanted to turn. My feet kept on walking away from him. I told myself that never again could I be open with him, vulnerable to such pain as I now felt. Yet all the muscles of my back were tense; my ears yearned for the sound of his footsteps behind me, my shoulders waited for his hand to fall on me and whirl me around. But he did not follow me.

May 15 was the day set for his departure. During all the preceding day I struggled with my yearning to go to him to wish him well and say goodbye; I knew that with the first light of dawn the departure from the city would begin. In the chapel I knelt and prayed to the Blessed Virgin to remove from me this sin of pride, this fear of again being hurt by his cold response. I rose from my knees, went straight to his headquarters, where I was

sure he would be. And I was right. There he was, seated
at a long trestle table, surrounded by his captains, all of
them preoccupied with a large chart spread out before
them and a discussion of Vera Cruz and its environs. I
watched them from the doorway for a moment and then
left, relieved and yet disappointed. This frustration of
my good intention served to stifle it completely. Bitterly
I told myself that to Cortés I had been just one more
woman he had conquered, like the one to whose window he had climbed at seventeen.

Doña Luisa and my old friend Ixlan had long been
aware of the changed situation between Cortés and me,
of course. When Ixlan left us to wish Sandoval, her
protector, farewell she turned in the doorway to say
to me, "He may never return, but we will have had
this hour." Her words pierced me; I started to my feet,
for the first time facing the truth I had hidden from
myself: Cortés might not return.

But Doña Luisa chose this instant to be her most
sanctimonious. "God says to hate the sin but love the
sinner. You are behaving without an ounce of Christian
charity if you do not go to Cortés at once and wish him
well, for the peril he faces is great."

I sat down again.

But not for long. The bell that hung outside the
chapel to call the men to Mass and vespers and to mark
the passing of the hours was tolling nine when a voice
in the corridor asked permission to enter, using the
Aztec tongue. I knew I would see one of Cortés' servants, and the curtain was pushed aside by the one who
had told me what happened to the Spaniard's head.
Cortés was in his room and wished to speak to me.

Doña Luisa was asleep on her pallet; Ixlan had not
returned; I was still dressed, waiting with lessening
hope for some word from him. Now it had come. I
stood up and preceded her down the dark stone corridor
where all but one torch at the far end had been extinguished. Cortés was in his bedroom alone. There
too only one torch burned, so placed that it threw his
huge shadow on the wall behind his chair. He looked

weary, and had on a long robe of deep blue embroidered with disks of gold and silver. "I did not wish to leave without saying farewell to you." His voice was neutral, perhaps because he was so tired.

"Farewell. Go with God, Cortés." No emotion, I told myself as the poignance of parting stirred.

"I debated with myself for some time about taking you with me, Marina." His beard was sunk on his chest, his eyes looking up at me. "And that was a hard decision, because of the great help you have been to me in the past."

The tongue, the voice, the silver parrot that opened its beak when a wire was pulled. "But now you have Sandoval."

He ignored that. "I had to evaluate the relative danger between your staying here and riding to Vera Cruz with me. You will be safer here."

"Then you see no possibility of losing Moctezuma even though you are gone?"

"None. Having treated us as his god's emissaries, he must continue to do so and put a good face on it. As for his priests and nobles, they are placated by the fact that so many of us are already leaving the city." He stood up. "So don't be nervous, Doña Marina."

We stood staring at each other for a moment, and then he turned and went to the table where a wine cask stood surrounded by cups of fine Cholulan ware. He picked up the silver goblet he always used, filled it, and came toward me holding it out. He smiled. "And now, Doña Marina, will you take a cup of wine with me?"

My heart raced back to that August night in Tlascala, and my whole body took command of me and responded to him with all its ardor, heart pounding faster, breasts yearning for his touch. He looked at me for a long moment, then in two strides reached me and put his arm around my waist and drew me to him. His eyes were bright with desire; my finger went up and touched the small white scar below his lip. As our mouths met

I thought of the danger he would march toward in the early morning, and I held him tighter.

"Stay with me," he whispered then.

To feel that strong body close to mine on that soft wide pallet below its jeweled canopy was such a delight I could not believe I had lived apart from him so long. He kissed me gently, many times, and then more fiercely, and whispered the pretty words he used to say, that I was his beloved Amazon, more beautiful than any imagined in any chronicle or legend. I told him that I loved him, and we kissed again for a long, sweet time, my yearning for the consummation growing almost unbearable. But then his body went slack, and although the arms embracing me still clung, I knew he was asleep.

Lying beside him, knowing the stress he was under, I forgave his weariness while I yearned for my girlhood body, chaste and passionless, that did not betray me with this yearning. He suddenly stirred, flung a heavy arm across me. "Marina. My Doña Marina," he murmured, the words slurred. I held his weary body close and was content with that. I fell asleep at last, able to rejoice that our enmity was ended, even though with dawn he would be marching to face Narváez. But for this brief interval, he was almost mine.

When I woke he was gone. I heard the noise and clamor in the palace courtyard; soldiers' marching feet, a captain's loud command, the drummer beating the tempo. A trumpet sounded. I leaped from bed, dressed myself hastily and ran along the corridor to the door that led to the front parapet, filled with soldiers watching their comrades leave. They made way for me, and I looked down at Cortés and his captains starting to cross the main square toward the avenue leading to the causeway across which we had come half a year earlier. It surprised me to see that Moctezuma, on his palanquin, followed behind Cortés. Many silent Aztecs stood in the gray dawn watching. "Cortés!" I cried. I do not know if he heard; he did not pause or turn. "Go with God," I whispered, and tears filled my eyes. I knew I might be seeing him for the last time on this earth: a man in armor on a black stallion riding away to meet his destiny or his doom.

I could not leave, but stood there watching until he had vanished and only the foot soldiers were crossing the square, as if this silent vigil could somehow be known to him. I turned away then feeling hollow, spent of all emotion. For the first time since I had known him I faced the task of women: the waiting. It touched me that in silent sympathy the Indian women had joined me: Ixlan looked sleepy; Doña Luisa was holding her rosary, telling the beads, eyes shut and lips moving silently; Chu-Chu sniveled and wiped her nose with the back of her fat little hand.

"Doña Marina?" I turned. Arturo Mondragon stood a few paces away, in breastplate and helmet. Behind him the sky above the mountains was turning pale and rosy. He approached me, politely removing the casque. "It is a very great honor Cortés has paid me," he said solemnly.

"What honor is that?" My dull voice could pretend no interest.

"I was to have marched to Vera Cruz. But just before he left, Cortés told me he wants me here. He has charged me with the protection of your person in the event of any danger that may arise."

"You?" It seemed a strange choice. Cortés was aware of Arturo's affection for me.

Arturo stiffened. "He trusts me above any other soldier for this responsibility."

I knew then why Arturo had been chosen: his very affection would make him more zealous about my safety than another might be. And I had learned that Cortés' final concern before he left had been my protection. I told myself that this was a better farewell than any last embrace.

The bright arc of the sun slid up behind the mountains. Its light touched that dark gold hair that had once aroused my wonder. "But Cortés foresees no danger here," I said.

"Even Cortés cannot read the future, Doña Marina."

I became aware that now he used my Spanish name. In the square below the Tlascalans were marching after the Spanish soldiers, white crane banners held high. And now the sun had fully risen on the first day of my long waiting.

The voice of the dwarf shattered my self-preoccupation. "We have been betrayed!" I turned to look down at Orteguilla, and in the next few minutes I learned that the odds against Cortés had worsened, though he was as yet unaware of this. I did not guess that the treachery of Francisco Pizarro would precipitate the horror that left me facing Death and my own great fear of dying.

PART VI

▼▼

NIGHT OF DANCERS, NIGHT OF TEARS
May 15, 1520–July 1, 1520

28

I was glad when Alvarado told me I had been one of those chosen by Cortés to fight Narváez. I was proud, too, because I knew it meant that Cortés thought well of me as a fighting man. In the gray light before dawn I stood with El Galán, teasing him about his gloomy mood, yet knowing there was good reason for it. Now we faced battle with well-armed Spaniards who outnumbered us four to one, counting our soldiers who had remained in Vera Cruz, he reminded me—not with superstitious Indians who had never seen a horse or heard a cannon or musket. It was then that Cortés' groom came to tell me our commander wished to speak to me.

He had just mounted his black stallion. I stood at the stirrup, looking up. When he told me I was to stay behind as Doña Marina's personal bodyguard, I thought at first he must be joking, for it seemed like asking the fox to guard the hen coop. But his next words sobered me. "She is in particular danger from being closely identified with me. If another rebel like Cacama should arise, he might well get the idea of kidnaping her in imitation of my coup with Moctezuma. He might believe that he could use a threat against her life to persuade me to evacuate the city entirely, which would guarantee him the favor of the Aztec priests and nobles. And so I need someone who would guard her with his life. The concern for her you have shown in the past convinces me that you are that man." He leaned in the saddle to grasp my shoulder. "You I know I can absolutely trust."

306

Pride outweighed disappointment at suddenly finding myself left behind in the city. I nodded. "You can trust me."

"It will be best that she does not leave this palace at all."

"I understand. But do you really believe another revolt against Moctezuma is likely to happen?"

He smiled. "What has happened before can happen again, as I am going to prove when I frustrate Velásquez in his desire to remove me as commander and put Narváez in my place." The trumpet sounded then; the drummer rattled off a first fast flourish and then settled into a marching beat. The great gate creaked open and the black stallion paced toward it, head high, as if it knew Cortés would lead the army from the city.

I ran back to El Galán to wish him well. He managed a grin after we embraced: "If it so happens that we do not meet again on earth, no doubt we'll be good friends in Heaven or Hell, depending on how God may judge us."

His uncharacteristic pessimism left me feeling uneasy as I climbed the stone steps to the top of the front wall of the palace, a long stone platform with a crenellated rampart, where I stood with other soldiers, their faces wan in the cold dawn, watching nearly two-thirds of our small force march away from us toward the causeway over which we had come. Gazing out over that vast square with its pale pyramids to heathen gods, I saw it with unaccustomed eyes. Once again its bizarre grandeur astounded me, all built and conceived without the help of God, without any ancient Greek or Roman or Moorish examples to copy. And we few Christians held its heart and its ruler. My eyes found El Galán then, and I cupped my hands to my mouth to shout that I would see him soon. "You'll come back a hero!" He turned in the saddle to shout back something I could not hear over the sound of our drums.

As I turned away I saw our Indian women clustered at the parapet's far end. Where they were, Malinche was apt to be. I went to find the woman for whom I had pledged to lay down my life, if need be.

As I told her I had been appointed by Cortés to guard her, I saw the sorrow in her eyes, and that her face was no longer that of a girl. She was no less beautiful, but it seemed clear that her life with Cortés had not been smooth. And then, with a thrill of recognition, I saw that she wore the humble little rosary I had given her, the jet beads, silver chain, and filigree cross barely visible against the barbaric embroidery of her triangular *huipile,* a gift undoubtedly from Moctezuma. The fact that she still wore this gift from me took on enormous significance and suggested to me that she wore it because of affection for the giver until her response to the news that I was to guard her stabbed my pride. "You?" she said, as if Cortés had selected a weakling or a dwarf like Orteguilla.

Oddly enough, he suddenly appeared shortly after I had responded to her in a stiff and prideful manner. There was a stirring among the Indian women surrounding us, and the short fat one giggled as the dwarf pushed his way past her, his small arm holding aside the full skirt of the tall woman next to her like a curtain. Orteguilla's anxious face and staring eyes were a sharp contrast to the women's amusement. "We have been betrayed," he gasped. "By three of our own soldiers!" He paused for breath, one hand on his small, heaving chest.

"Betrayed? How? What soldiers?"

"Francisco Pizarro, for one." He eloquently cursed first Pizarro and his mother, father, and more remote ancestors, then broke off as Malinche, who had been gazing out over the square, its white temples now gilded by the newly risen sun, turned to look down at him. "Pardon me, Doña Marina," he said. "But Pizarro is all I just said, and worse. Here is the situation: Just now several of Moctezuma's nobles came to his apartment to visit him. An ungodly hour, but they knew he had decided to honor Cortés by riding with him to the gates of the city and wanted to be there when he returned. I happened to overhear what they were discussing while they waited. They were much intrigued by a certain message one of Moctezuma's couriers had recently brought him and of which I knew nothing. I tell you, the hair rose on the back of my neck when I realized what Pizarro and the two other traitors with him had done!"

"But Pizarro isn't here! He went down to the province where the gold mines are, sent back the gold, and remained behind to explore the area further," I reminded him.

"Oh, he explored! He went down to the coast and he learned that Narváez's fleet was anchored near Vera Cruz. And he and the two whoresons with him went aboard the flagship, got drunk on wine, and told Narváez he was lucky to have come so soon after Cortés had piled up another fortune in gold. And he also told him how near they were to Vera Cruz, and that there were fewer than two hundred Spaniards there, some of them invalids. And he told Narváez he could easily capture Zempoalla, overawe the fat cacique, and lose Cortés some valuable allies!"

All I could think of was El Galán's unusual gloom; it seemed to me prophetic. Cortés could reach the coast to find Vera Cruz in enemy hands and even Zempoalla an enemy camp.

"But that's not all," Orteguilla said. He lowered his voice to a hoarse whisper. "Moctezuma has known all this for many days!"

I felt the blood leave my face. "That means he thinks Cortés went marching down there to his own funeral!"

"Exactly," Orteguilla said.

A mass funeral was what I saw for us left here, a multiple Aztec sacrifice that would end for me when a stone knife took my heart out and my skull joined the thousands below the war god's temple, just one more pitiful bone pate to grin and gleam in the sun. Malinche's voice made me turn toward her.

"Pizarro's treachery will change nothing as far as Moctezuma is concerned. To him the battle between

Cortés and Narváez is still another game of *tlachtli* on a larger scale." When I said I did not understand, she told me of his bet with the king of Texcoco. "He still believes that Cortés was sent here by his sovereign, as Cortés told him. And that Narváez and his followers are bad people, as Cortés told him. He is awaiting the outcome of the battle between them. If Cortés wins, it will prove to Moctezuma that he is the god's emissary. If Narváez wins, it will prove Cortés a mere pretender."

I tried to think with a mind addled by shock. "So we're safe until news comes to Moctezuma of Cortés' victory—or defeat."

"And Moctezuma would prefer his victory. It will mean that Cortés is all Moctezuma believed, and that in revering him Moctezuma has done the right thing, perhaps the only thing that could avert the prophecies of doom. He is still as fettered by the power of Cortés as if he sat in leg irons."

"But Cortés isn't here," I cried. "And with every minute that passes his personal impact is fading away."

"It is with his spirit that he has overpowered Moctezuma. Spirits are more powerful than bodies, and can remain where the body is not."

"Just the same, I wish Cortés were here in body now," Orteguilla said, glum.

Malinche looked down at him, her face kind. "All Moctezuma can do is wait. I think he must be the loneliest man in the universe."

"Thank God for that!" I said.

She turned to look out over the parapet, and pointed. "He's coming back."

For an instant I thought she meant Cortés, and rushed to look; Moctezuma's green and jeweled palanquin was now heading toward the palace past bowing or prostrate Aztecs. Malinche started toward the steps leading down from the rampart. "Where are you going?" I asked, remembering Cortés' suggestion that she should not leave our stronghold.

She turned. "To beg him to send a runner after

Cortés with this news of Pizarro's treachery." With a whirl of her full skirt she was gone.

Orteguilla was staring after her in admiration. "God sometimes bewilders me, to have placed a mind like that in the body of an Indian!" He turned to me. "I meant to ask her opinion, but I guess you'll have to do. Shall I tell Alvarado about Pizarro?"

"As commander here, I think he should know the worst."

"Now answer this: if I tell him, how can I prevent him from doing something foolish? Such as putting Moctezuma in a jail cell or otherwise humiliating him for having said nothing to Cortés about Pizarro?"

"You've convinced me. Say nothing."

"But if he later finds I knew and didn't tell him, he won't be very pleased with me, will he? My fondness for the idea of sitting in a cell on maize cakes and water is not excessive." Suddenly he clapped a hand to his forehead. "Ha! As God is my witness, I forgot a thing of great importance. Pedro Alvarado hates Francisco Pizarro! As dogs hate cats, he hates Pizarro. Pizarro's treachery will merely confirm this odium. He will rage, but at Pizarro, and it will give him such satisfaction that he won't feel so harshly toward Moctezuma."

"I didn't know Alvarado hated Pizarro. How do you know this?"

"I use my ears for more than holding wax in. It is Pizarro's cold cruelty that Alvarado hates, to be expected of a man who never killed anyone except with his blood at the boil." He gave me a nervous wink. "Come with me, please, to spread over two heads the wrath that can descend on the bringer of bad news."

Alvarado was seated at the long trestle table in Cortés' headquarters. He was eating a mango, of which he was very fond. The juice trickled down into his beard, almost the same color, and he wiped it off with the back of his hand, nodding as he listened to the dwarf's brief summation of Pizarro's betrayal.

"I have a good nose for filth," Alvarado said. "I told Cortés when he decided to send Pizarro to the gold mines not to trust him just because he has some trickle of Monrroy blood in his veins. But Cortés chose to believe that blood would tell. Well, something has moved Pizarro to tell too much in the wrong place, and I suppose it was not his Monrroy blood but that of the great goat-bitch that spawned Pizarro on a heap of dung." He calmly selected another mango from the bowl on the table. "How long did you say Moctezuma has known of this treachery?"

"Oh, a very short time. Doña Marina is asking him to send word of it to Cortés."

"Good." He peeled back the mango's thick skin with a thumbnail. "Continue by all means to spy for me, Orteguilla."

We left reassured by hot Alvarado's cool reception of our news. Evidently it seemed to him that a bad situation had not grown much worse.

I was wrong. Alvarado must have conceived it as proper to his position as commander to conceal his inner fears. Events proved that it had stunned him to learn that Moctezuma had not shared with Cortés this crucial information. He believed that Moctezuma yearned for Cortés' defeat; it did not occur to him that to Moctezuma a god's emissary would not be affected by the information Pizarro had given Narváez. That the Aztec ruler did as Malinche asked and sent a runner after Cortés with the crucial information did not reassure Alvarado because he believed that the courier would have been privately instructed not to deliver that news. That the Aztec ruler continued to be docile did not reassure him either. Although Alvarado appeared so bluff, frank, and outgoing, he secretly saw himself as a man of considerable cunning and subtlety. He confided in no one his conviction that Moctezuma was only waiting to learn the outcome of the unequal struggle between Cortés and Narváez. If it proved to him that we were mere pretenders he would then crush us with a clear conscience. And Moctezuma, because of his many spies and his swift couriers, would learn before we did whether Cortés had met with triumph or defeat. Politely, Alvarado visited Moctezuma daily, hiding his misgivings. He let the soldiers see only his cheerful face, reassuring us in his high-pitched voice that one Cortés was equal to a hundred men like Pánfilo Narváez.

And at last came the night of the dancers.

29

For a week and then another we soldiers, like Alvarado, hid our tension and our secret fear. No news was bad news. And such news as we got was mediocre. After one of Moctezuma's couriers told him that the Narváez fleet had sailed north to Vera Cruz we all became military strategists, devising ways in which Cortés could defend the little town against worse odds. When we learned that Narváez had set up a camp right in Zempoalla and had requisitioned, in the name of the Spanish monarch, the Indian women and other gifts the fat cacique was keeping against our return, we loudly affirmed that the Zempoallan ruler would remain loyal to Cortés. When we learned that he had, and had moreover told Narváez that he intended to complain of such behavior to Cortés, we cheered our faithful ally. We were delighted to learn that Narváez was very stingy, keeping the gifts he extracted for himself. We assured each other that Cortés' plan of bribing away his soldiers with gold was sure to succeed.

An elaborate political development briefed in a short message to Alvarado from Cortés gave us no comfort. The Royal Audience of Santo Domingo, knowing of the treasure Cortés had sent to Carlos, in turn sent an officer called an *oidor* to Vera Cruz to rebuke Narváez, who promptly made him a prisoner. Those who had come with him escaped arrest and joined Cortés, indignant but helpless. Cortés confessed that his letters to Moctezuma, in which he had tried to make him see that the important thing was to keep control of the Aztec capital and urged that they join forces to accomplish this, had not been honored with any answer. What Narváez clearly wanted was for Cortés, overwhelmed by the odds, to give up after a few brief skirmishes. In short, all this news was inconclusive, the first mutterings of thunder before the storm.

I saw almost nothing of Malinche. With Aguilar, Father Olmedo, and the other priests she spent many hours with Moctezuma in fruitless efforts to convert him. It had not been necessary to remind her not to leave the palace; she had become obsessively busy in weaving a large feather tapestry, the loom Moctezuma provided set up in the room she had shared with Cortés where she knelt for hours among baskets of feathers. I thought of Penelope awaiting the return of Ulysses.

Like all the other soldiers, I gambled. We used cards made out of the thin stiff hide sold in the market to make drumheads. Our original cards were long since worn out, and ones made of *amatyl* paper did not hold up at all. My luck was bad; I lost my gold dust and nuggets first, the gold necklace Moctezuma gave me, and even my first gold pendant bought from the boy at San Juan Ulua, although I managed to win back the gold chain Cortés had bestowed the day I rejected my soldier's pay. One gold necklace! That was all I had to show for nearly a year and four months of danger, toil, and frustration. These losses induced a forlornness that rarely left me. Fear lay just under it and would suddenly flare up whenever I heard the booming of the great snakeskin drum atop the looming pyramid of the war god. It was beaten in slow cadence, most often just after sunrise, and for a reason I wished I did not know.

I became very fond of the drink called pulque, and

on many an afternoon I would wander through Moctezuma's beautiful garden with a clay jug of the stuff,
reciting poetry to the freaks and animals and birds. My
deep sense of impending doom intensified.

The single cheerful note was the young slave girl
Moctezuma had given me. She was named Xochitl, but
I called her Sochi. Short, plump, and rather pretty, her
black braids twined with red ribbons, she always had a
smile for me. Most of the other soldiers slept with
theirs, but I did not. She had a little girl, which probably meant that she was married, and that would have
been adultery even though she was only an Indian.
One evening, though, after too much pulque, I found
that I very much wanted to bed with her. She came to
my straw pallet with the smallclothes she had washed
for me, and knelt beside it smiling, waiting. I think all
that stopped me was that her little girl was with her, a
tiny thing with braids like her mother's. I put my arms
around the child instead, and sang her songs from my
own infancy. This served to remind me of home, safety,
another life. Nostalgia was soon stronger than my dark
sense of doom or the urge to escape in a slave girl's
arms.

Abruptly, circumstances merited all my foreboding.

Through Malinche, Moctezuma courteously asked
Alvarado's approval of the annual harvest dance hon-
oring the fruitful labors of the Aztec farmer-warriors
on whose shoulders rested the whole grand hierarchy.
The dance was to be held in the *tlachtli* court just after
sundown. Alvarado agreed that it should be performed.

Unfortunately, at sundown on the day of the dance
Alvarado learned from Orteguilla of the boastful message Narváez had recently sent to Moctezuma, which
the dwarf had translated from Spanish. Narváez had
written that since Cortés had refused to surrender
peaceably, and instead was suborning many of his men
with gold and promises, Narváez was now forced to
wipe out Cortés and his whole army in an immediate
pitched battle of which the outcome was a foregone
conclusion. This battle had probably by now been

fought. We who would be so crucially affected had no way of knowing the outcome except from Moctezuma.

The harvest dance had already begun when a tense Alvarado called together those of his own company still left in the city and some thirty others, making fifty in all. Abruptly, he revealed to us all those doubts of Moctezuma that had been gnawing in him ever since the news of Pizarro's defection to the enemy. "If Moctezuma learns that Cortés has been defeated, then we are dead men, in my opinion! Even if Cortés manages to avoid an outright defeat by a strategic retreat, that will not satisfy the Aztec. As I see it, Cortés will have to capture or kill Narváez. This is unlikely." He pointed toward the ball court, from which a faint barbaric music could be heard. He reminded us that the dancers were warriors as well as farmers and might well be working up their savage spirits for an uprising against us if Cortés did not attain a conclusive victory. "A show of our strength and valor is needed now," he cried in his high, nervous voice. "A show of Spanish arms!" He proposed that we march to the ball court in full armor with muskets, pikes, and swords and surround the celebrants.

The ball court was lighted by dozens of pine torches in stone holders around its upper rim; all the tiers of stone benches were filled with Aztecs, both common folk and some nobles. There were a number of women, undoubtedly the wives and mothers of the male dancers. Alvarado led us into the court itself, where we spread out and stood against its walls. We saw what must have been a thousand male dancers whirling and posturing to the thumping of drums, the blaring of conch horns, the screaming of bone flutes. The dancers overflowed into the temple forecourt. Far above, the hollow eyes of the skulls distantly observed this exuberance of life and motion. The men's bodies, gleaming with the sweat of their exertion, were garbed in the clan jewels, gold necklaces and bracelets, pearls and precious stones, and the plumes that nodded on their heads made them look tall. The beat of the music was simple and repetitive, shrill flutes echoing deep drums: "Dum, dum, *dum*/ dum, dum, *dum*/ deedle, deedle, deedle, deedle/ dum, dum, *dum*." Dancers who moved in a wide outer circle around the rest in the ball court carried rude musical instruments; I saw a notched human femur which a dancer in an ocelot skin scraped at with a stick to make a harsh, rasping noise. Many wore anklets of dry pods and small seashells that clashed together constantly with a soft sliding sound. In the very center, on a pedestal or large drum, stood a young man very splendidly costumed, plumed head back, eyes closed, arms raised to heaven as though he were in a rapt trance.

As the frenzy of the dance and the music intensified, so did the throttled fear I had been hiding ever since Cortés had marched away. And yet the spectacle drew me, numbed my mind, captured my eyes, left me like one enchanted, eyes dazzled by motion and ears by that barbaric music.

I wrenched my eyes away, blinked, and scanned the Aztec faces on the stone tiers above, all solemn and entranced. My heart gave a great lurch. Malinche was seated on the lowest tier to my left. With her were our Indian women. She was leaning slightly forward, her face rapt and childlike. She had disobeyed Cortés' warning that she should not leave the palace.

Then Alvarado's shrill voice rose above the sounds of music and of broad dancing feet. "I want the two entrances blocked at once!" He ordered me and five others to the west doorway near which we were already standing. Other soldiers positioned themselves at the eastern one. Why, I wondered, does he want to prevent the dancers from leaving? For it looked to me as if they might dance until dawn.

I looked up at Malinche; she had noticed the soldiers' movements and looked from one gate to the other, then at Alvarado.

His imperious voice startled me. "We must strike first! This is no harvest dance! This is a war dance! We get them or they get us!" Two muskets cracked.

Alvarado was the first to fall on the bewildered dancers, running one through with his sword. The Three Moors accounted for three more. The muskets cracked again. I stood for an instant frozen with horror. It was as terrible as the ambush at Cholula; worse, because then we were fighting for our lives. In a few moments Spaniards were everywhere, lopping, hacking, stabbing. One slashed an arm off a drummer and then hacked off his head, which went rolling across the smooth stone paving, eyes glaring in surprise. This set the tone; two other heads joined it. Abdomens slashed open leaked entrails. A crossbow's arrow impaled the central entranced Aztec, who toppled forward from his pedestal like a statue, arms wide. Those butchered, jeweled, dead and dying Aztecs I was never to forget, helpless victims of a long-suppressed fear that had given rise to a fury that was scarcely human.

A woman screamed. I looked up. Malinche stood with both fists clenched against her face, mouth open between them in another scream. The women around her were bemused, and that seemed true of the watching Aztecs; they had not had time to believe what they were seeing. At her scream some stirred, rose. And she was up there among them, voice of the absent leader of the insensate Spanish killers in the ball court! All my training as a soldier deserted me. I abandoned my post, ran to a point just below Malinche, raised both arms to her and yelled "Jump! You must get out of here!"

She came to herself, lowered her fists from her face, and lowered herself to the ball court, hanging by her arms and landing heavily beside me. I took her hand and ran with her to the gate I had been guarding; the soldiers let us pass. As we ran toward our palace past Aztecs in the square who did not yet know what was going on, I found I was groaning like a wounded animal. I knew without any doubt that this was the final night of my life. No Spaniard in this city would live to see tomorrow. Even if Moctezuma should want to—and he would not—he could never protect us against his aroused subjects' wrath when they learned how those dancers had died.

I pounded on the great gate and we were admitted. Seeing Captain Lugo, I went to him and gasped, "For God's sake, take command here! Alvarado's gone mad. He's killing all the dancers. Within an hour or less you'll have armed Aztecs storming this place by the thousands!" I could see it as I spoke: wave after wave of Aztecs swarming up over our walls like ants, like monkeys. Lost! We were lost!

A choked cry turned my attention back to Malinche. She was holding out her full skirt, staring down at the splash of blood across it. I remembered the headless Aztec torso that had thudded down at her feet when we started our run for the gate. How unfair her plight: splashed with blood Spaniards had spilled, she would die with us! And how in God's name could I protect her? A thin hope lighted my racked mind. I took her cold hand in mine. "Come on!"

She obeyed me like a child. We ran to the rearmost palace building, to the chapel there, to the secret vault that held the treasures of a dead Aztec king.

30

The chapel was empty and dim, lighted only by one votive candle burning at Mary's feet. Directly behind Her was the section of wall I had helped burst through, now bricked up and plastered over. I moved out from the wall the wooden pedestal concealing the two large floor-level stones which were not mortared in place.

Kneeling, I shoved against one with all my strength.
With maddening slowness it moved inward. I was
sweating with the exertion, but more from fear of being
found before I had hidden Malinche. I lay on my back
when the stone was clear of the wall and with a series
of sharp kicks that jolted my back teeth I sent it far
enough into the vault so a person, if not too large,
could squeeze through. The opening was only about
four handbreadths high and perhaps nine wide, and it
occurred to me, irrelevantly, that to get inside I would
have to remove my breastplate. The way cleared, I
stood up and faced Malinche. "Get in, and quickly!"
I thought then of something I had overlooked: food
and drink to sustain her. And light, for in there it was
dark as a tomb.

I ran to the chest where I knew the priests kept the
necessities for Mass and took the clay olla of pulque,
used for Christ's blood now that our wine had run out.
Beside it were half a dozen maize cakes, very stale,
which served as His body. But now they were just
ordinary pulque and tortillas. I took them and then
stole the votive candle burning in its glass cup at Mary's
feet. Olla in one hand, flame in the other, and the
maize cakes held by one bent arm against my chest, I
turned to the opening in the wall. Malinche had not yet
entered the vault. "What are you waiting for? Get in
so I can close it!"

"And you?"

"I'm finished. It's only a question of whether the
Aztecs kill me before Alvarado strings me up for de-
serting my post." I had meant to sound the hardened
soldier but my voice betrayed me and seemed bitter.

"Would he?"

"What do you think?"

"Hide with me, then."

I realized I had wanted to, all along. "A soldier does
not leave his comrades to die for him," I said. "And
what's the point of my hiding anyway? I'm a Spaniard.
If you can manage to live through the Aztecs' first fury
at us, Moctezuma may well decide to pardon you.

You're a woman, and of his own race and had nothing to do with the butchery tonight."

Her face, lighted by the candle I held, showed no sign of interest in this line of reasoning. "I will not go in there alone."

"You mean you're afraid?"

She nodded.

"But it's out here where the danger is! Get in, I beg you."

She shook her head stubbornly. I thought I saw a gleam of tears, and knew then how badly that sudden slaughter of the dancers had unnerved a woman who had always been brave. After all, I had been ordered by Cortés to protect her, and did that not include helping her conquer her terror at being sealed alone in this crypt? "All right," I said. "I'll stay with you, Malinche. You go first."

She obeyed, and when she had squirmed inside I passed in to her the candle, the olla, the maize cakes. Then I removed my breastplate and shoved it through the aperture, opened out. I moved the pedestal and the Virgin as close to the wall as I could and still leave space behind it to writhe into the vault. There I turned around and wormed back the way I had come until my arms were in the chapel, my hands on the base of the Virgin's pedestal. Bit by bit I edged it toward me, squirming my way backward, until I had it close to the wall again. Inside the treasure room once more I shoved the stone back into place. We were sealed into the crypt.

Malinche stood holding the votive candle high to light the crystal skull that had so fascinated Cortés. He had thanked it for guarding the treasure; now it would guard Malinche. And the foot soldier who still loved her. A bitter thought occurred then: Malinche and I were alone together at last, companions of the night, but not as I had ever dreamed it. "I dreamed of this skull after we first saw it," she said. "It had the power of motion and followed me. I knew if it touched me, I would die." She turned her back on it and looked about her at the other treasures. Even though those made of gold had been melted to ingots, the display was still dazzling. The great gleaming feather cape that hung outspread on the rear wall seemed like a winged symbol of the enormous brooding power of the Aztecs whom we had foolishly thought to overcome.

I saw a pile of folded mantles on a chest and went to them. "We may as well make ourselves comfortable," I said, and took some and made a cushion for her on the floor, another for myself. The floor space unoccupied by treasures, chests, and hampers was quite small; our seats were almost side by side. "And when we get tired we can add more and make pallets to sleep on," I added, and felt a tingle go through me.

She knelt on her mantles in that humble, compact pose Indians seem to find comfortable and set the votive candle on the floor between us. I sat cross-legged, facing her, but in that position the crystal skull behind her seemed to stare right down into my eyes, so I changed position. Her face, dimly lighted from below, had a sudden new aspect, ghostly and mysterious; I got lost for a moment in the midnight depths of her eyes. "You were clever to think of this hiding place," she said. Her voice was low; how had I failed to hear the velvet in it? "And so for the third time you have saved me."

"The third?" I rolled onto my side and propped my head on one hand; from this angle I could enjoy her face in profile.

"From life as a heathen when you followed me in Tabasco. And in San Juan Ulua you brought me to sanctuary."

I sat up; it occurred to me that she was right. "Moctezuma likes you; I'm sure of it. He'll prove reasonable."

She shook her head. "I am linked in his mind with Cortés, and with Spaniards." Above her the skull grinned. "I think this will be my last night on earth."

"Please don't say that!"

"There's only one chance. For me, and for the

soldiers who had nothing to do with that butchery. If Moctezuma were to learn tonight that Cortés has decisively defeated Narváez, then I think he would defer retaliation and let Cortés punish the butchers."

The chance seemed to me so thin as to be almost invisible. "But can Cortés defeat Narváez?"

"He will fight to the death to do it." Her voice was passive, brooding. "I have seen the two I loved most die. My father and my grandmother. She had a gift for prophecy, and foresaw many changes in my life. I wonder if she saw me in this treasure room with a Spaniard with golden hair?" She smiled, her eyes sad. I knew that her faith in those prophecies of her grandmother had faded, replaced by a new Faith.

I spoke staunchly. "Still, we are breathing! And the Sainted Virgin herself is guarding the entrance to our . . ." I nearly said "tomb" but changed it to "sanctuary."

She crossed herself, bowed her head over clasped hands. I knelt facing her and together we said the Hail Mary I had known for as long as I could remember, she for one brief year. "Hail Mary, full of grace, be with us now and in the hour of our death. Amen."

Our candle, burned low when I seized it, flickered and went out. In the utter blackness I heard my heart beating and thought I could hear hers. I imagined, behind her, the icy grin of that skull. But I could not let myself give way to the awful notion that our lives would end in this darkness. "I have heard that flame eats air," I said. "And there is only so much in here for us to breathe."

Creating the illusion of life in that blackness we began to speak of the past, of our short lives, living them again in words to keep from thinking of our peril. Our voices might have been the only sounds in the universe; so thick were the walls around us, so far the chapel from the main buildings that no sound of any conflict reached us in there, not even the boom of cannons. Then it occurred to me that Indians do not fight at night, that dawn would bring these sounds of battle.

The thought brought me to the present; I wondered if Captain Lugo had taken command of our palace-fortress or had believed Alvarado. "Captain Sandoval would have been a better choice than Alvarado," I said. "The men like him as well. But I guess Cortés needed him in Vera Cruz."

"Any captain would have been a better choice."

"Well, Cortés had to take the best ones with him. Without a triumph there, he won't be able to hold this city. With it, he can."

"Even if we're all dead by then, he could come back a victor and still have the respect of Moctezuma."

"Which wouldn't put the breath back into our nostrils or the hearts back into our bodies," I said bitterly.

Her tone was light: "You forget we won't have any bodies. The Aztecs will have eaten them."

A loud laugh burst from me, unlike my own. "And they'll hang our heads up there on the skull rack to dry!"

"We'll see all the *tlachtli* games."

"And bet on the winner."

"And watch the Aztecs bargain in the market."

"But we won't watch any sacrifices."

"No, we'll close our eyes to those!"

Our hilarity abruptly ebbed. We knew that the fantasy of those two skulls observing life in the great square might become, in part, reality. By our laughter we had denied that, tried to make the possibility seem impossible. Men about to be hanged, my father once said, can joke about nooses.

Time flowed with nothing to mark it. We grew thirsty and drank a little of the pulque, melon-flavored and quite good; we grew hungry and ate a maize cake each. At last our eyelids began to close; our voices slowed and there were long silences. We spread the mantles thinner and turned our cushions into pallets. I dozed, then woke to find myself shivering from the penetrating chill within the vault, the cold of stone, of night at a high altitude, of ancient guarded treasure. In that absolute darkness the crystal skull made itself felt to me.

It was a presence that defied mere sight; I fancied that some of the chill in the room was exuded from its smile. I could feel its hollow gaze.

My teeth began to chatter. I imagined the skull as cruelly awaiting my death, I, the last living Spaniard left in Tenochtitlán after the rest of our palace had become one vast charnel house. My mother's face loomed in memory, and I could not bear the sorrow of her eyes.

"Are you cold too?" Malinche asked.

"Yes." My father told me again to forget about poetry, to just concentrate on staying alive. The present was no longer real to me; the golden past claimed me. I swam again with Rubén, I knelt in the little Havana church between my parents, and the sound of the liturgy was sweetest music. In distant Medellín in the vineyard of my father's family I plucked warm purple grapes . . .

I heard footsteps. Malinche was up, moving about in the darkness.

The grapes were sweet. From the cork oak where I climbed to eat them I gazed down like a prince at the workers picking them for my grandfather's wine press. A warm summer breeze made the leaves about me rustle . . .

A whispery rustle filled the cold room where I relived a summer long ago and I heard the sound of something dragging across the floor.

"What's that?" I asked her.

"The feather cape. I got it down. For a blanket."

From cold and sorrow and remembered grapes, my mind raced toward warmth under feathers, and more than that, to the warmth of two bodies giving out to one another their gentle heat. The thought was delicious. I let my hand creep toward Malinche's pallet and felt the soft smoothness of close-woven feathers under my palm. I edged closer and my hand slipped under the cape's edge, into the warmth.

Blessed warmth. Life itself. With a slow sigh, I lay supine on my pallet, intensely aware of her breathing body so close to mine, which promptly responded with a carnal glee; I waited tensely for her command to remove my hand from her bed. Instead, the great cape rose into the air and settled down over my whole body as she shared it with me. I thanked her and lay smiling as I grew warm, willing the imp to subside.

"Are you afraid?" she asked after several moments of silence.

"No," I lied. "Whatever happens, it is God's will for us."

"I know," she said, "but I'm still afraid."

Her honesty shamed me. "I don't look forward to being dead myself." I found that until this moment I had not really believed I would die. I remembered hearing that men walked up the steps of the gallows still thinking that some miracle would save them, and fear gripped me in a clutch as icy as the grin of that crystal skull. Anger came on its heels. "And we have Cortés to thank! How little he really cared for us left here, to give so reckless a man as Alvarado full authority!" I turned toward her, reached out, found her hand, gripped it. "But if I burn in Hell for it, I will tell you this. I have loved you since I first saw you in Tabasco, and I have dreamed of you, and yearned for you! But instead I am to die without you." To the little demon between my legs, Death might have been the most seductive enchantress, for it arose in high anticipation, waiting alertly. "Without you," I sighed.

"With me," she said. "I do not hope for kindness from the Aztecs."

With me? It could have two meanings, that we would die together here, or that I would die after possessing her.

"Do you think God will take us to be in Heaven with Him?" she asked.

That query half-subdued the rampant demon. I knew to what horrible circle of the inferno fornicators went. "We're Christians. We have committed no great sins." I lay for a time like a stone effigy, while every rivet of my jupon ground steel teeth into my flesh. Deciding that the pain of desire was enough to bear, I got up and removed it and put it on the floor with my breastplate, sword, and helmet.

"You said you were cold," Malinche said. "Why are you taking your clothes off?"

"I will never sleep if I don't, and I must try to, because God knows what we will face tomorrow." In only my smallclothes and hose I crawled under the feather cape again. My heart was thudding first fast, then regular, then faster still, trying to beat its way through the wall of my chest and tumble into Malinche's arms. With wild insistence, my male member reared again to attention, throbbing like my heart. All at once, although she said nothing, I knew Malinche was aware of me, of my agony of desire. She found my hand, drew it toward her, and let it come to rest on her breast.

I rolled onto my side, toward her. My lips found hers as unerringly as if the bright sun shone on us. With a moan I kissed a mouth more sweet than even in my dreams of her. From the dark behind me I could feel the icy glare of the crystal skull, chilling my spine. Drawn by her and fleeing it, I escaped inward and upward and outward into the deep warmth of her body, into the ecstasy awaiting me there.

It was over too soon. Lying beside her, I felt suddenly shy. I wanted to say something memorable, words that would express my infinite gratitude. I summoned up one, but *gracias* seemed inadequate to the occasion. I turned my head toward her and listened to her breathing in the dark. What was she thinking?

"I wish I could see you." The words came out of me without forethought. I reached and found her warm hand. "I remember you on the beach at San Juan Ulua. You were like Aphrodite."

"Who is that?" Her voice was low, husky.

"The goddess of Love and Beauty."

She drew her hand from mine. She slipped out from under the feather cape. I heard soft, sliding sounds. She was taking off her clothes! I sat up, blood pounding in my ears. In a moment she lay down beside me. My hand went out and chastely touched her face, traced the line of her cheek, found her lips, moved down her throat. As it followed the smooth curve of her breast and found the nipple a shiver of desire convulsed me and then I felt her shiver too. Her response excited me because before she had lain passive, receiving my blind hungry thrust. I felt a terrible urge to place my lips there. It seemed to tighten and grow firm and her body turned toward me. I felt great wonder that I was doing this and then it seemed quite natural. My hands turned into eyes that had to see every inch of her, and all my manhood saluted her body and the beauty of it that my hands now knew forever. I left her long enough to make myself as naked as she, and this time was as unique to me as the first because my body and hers kissed down all their length just as our lips were doing. When I entered her I was no soldier storming a castle but a welcome guest who gently arrived and moved slowly in the home of her body until the dancing began to a wild beat, all the flamencos in Spain and Portugal . . .

We fell asleep at last clasped in each other's arms beneath the ceremonial cape of a dead Aztec king. For all his great riches he had been a poor man next to me, for I had attained my heart's desire.

I awoke suddenly. The air was stagnant, thick, and it was hard to breathe. My head ached dully and my dim brain knew that no matter what awaited us outside our crypt, I had to let air in. I found Malinche's mouth and kissed it. "Wake up, my dearest, or we'll die before our time." She stirred and murmured something as I got up and put on my jupon and carrying my breastplate made my way through the blackness to the chest by our low doorway and pushed it aside. I could not manage to pull the heavy stone inward by only my fingertips, so at last I lay on my back to edge it outward with my feet. Careful as I was, I heard the pedestal or the Virgin or both topple and crash to the floor of the chapel. Prickling with terror, I crossed myself, said,

"Forgive me, Mary," and shoved the stone the rest of the way out. Along with fresher air a hint of daylight seeped in. Our long night was over. Only silence filled the chapel, and I began to breathe again.

And then a frightened voice demanded, "What thing is that in there?"

I knelt with my cheek to the floor and peered out. I found myself face to face with a young Spanish priest peering in, the same one who had cauterized my shoulder at Tabasco.

"Hasn't the battle begun yet?" I asked, astounded.

"What battle? What are you doing in there, Arturo Mondragon?"

Dumbfounded, I turned and called to Malinche that it was safe to emerge.

With his eyes roving to the fallen Virgin, the young priest told us that even when Moctezuma learned of the massacre of the dancers he had refused to command his warrior chiefs to attack us. Without his orders, they had not dared to proceed to revenge.

Malinche and I shared a lost look. In the shadow of what we had thought was sure death we had committed a great sin. And Death had passed us by. I felt very guilty, as though I had deliberately deceived her with a lie. By now the priest was much more concerned about the damage to Mary than about us, but still I explained to him that Cortés had ordered me to protect Doña Marina. I put on my breastplate and then I helped him right the pedestal and the statue. The end of Her nose was chipped off, and the priest wrung his hands as he wondered aloud if it could be properly mended.

In silence, Malinche and I walked into the palace I had imagined as a battleground. Sudden jubilant shouting reached us from the courtyard, and we hurried down a corridor that led to a balcony overlooking it. Below us men were hugging, shooting off muskets, dancing like fools to the fast thrum of Orteguilla's guitar.

He looked up and saw me and shouted the good news. "Cortés won! He defeated Narváez!"

Elation flooded me; my spirits rose and rode that tide. Alvarado was astride his horse, sword aloft and gleaming, cleaned of last night's blood. He was beaming, roseate, a true child of the sun. Around him soldiers capered in a circle like the now-dead dancers. His horse reared; sword still pointing at the sky he cried shrilly: *"Viva Cortés!"*

"Viva Cortés!" the soldiers shouted with one voice. *"Arriba Cortés!"*

"Arriba, arriba!"

I turned to Malinche. She was in profile to me, staring down. One hand was clenched on the rosary I had given her. She turned her head and looked at me. Her face was impassive. But as one sees pictures in clouds or flames, I saw in her eyes the truth of what I was, and knew with bitter pain that my joyous passage into manhood had made me a man I would never have chosen to become. It did not matter if the Devil had seized his chance while fear of an early death and a desire long felt had weakened me. I, Arturo Mondragon y Flores, had put horns on the great and victorious commander the men below now cheered. Worse, I had marred Malinche's chastity in the name of love. Mortal sin had claimed me. And yet there was a voice within me that defied these desperate facts as nonsense, denied my unworthiness. Shocked by the bloodbath in the ball court, believing death faced us, we had celebrated life. "I will love you, Malinche, until the day I die," I whispered.

Her hand left my rosary, let it fall. "Dying is not the danger we face now," she said. "Only living." She turned and walked away from me and I knew enough not to follow her.

A shouted word drew my eyes to the courtyard below. Alvarado was pointing his sword at me on the balcony. "Coward!" he shouted again. "I saw you desert your post, Mondragon!"

The butchered dancers bled and died in my head, a

flashing series of vivid images. Without Alvarado's command to kill them I would not be the contemptible man standing on this balcony, accused by him of the least of my sins. I leaned far out over the stone rail, pointing my finger down at him as his sword pointed up at me. "Lunatic!" I howled. "Fool! Assassin!"

In the silence that fell I knew I had sealed my fate, and I did not care a *toston,* not a brass peso. I stood there in an arrogant pose, fists on hips, waiting to be seized and jailed, which shortly followed.

In leg irons and manacles in a room with three soldiers doing penance for milder crimes, I was suddenly famished, and asked one of the two soldiers who had arrested me for some food. He reminded me that our food supplies were running low due in part to a severe shortage of maize after a drought, or so Moctezuma had said; they themselves had had no breakfast yet. Hollow, echoing hunger made me curse my mad bravado and deep dejection followed. I saw, in a dim way, that I had, by insulting Alvarado, contrived this punishment, if not for the crime of which he had accused me. It was Juan Morla who came in and shared with me his ration of half a liter of boiled beans and two tortillas. He advised me to drink a lot of water to make the beans swell up and better fill the belly. To my surprise, I found that last night's slaughter had dismayed even this hardened soldier. "I only killed one," he said, "and I did it clean, right through the heart."

With food, my own heart rose slightly. I closed my eyes and sailed out of my prison on memories of love, and then into a lovely daydream, that somehow she would find that she no longer loved Cortés, that somehow she and I would sail to Cuba, man and wife, to live in blissful serenity. I placed our home on the cliff where I first glimpsed Cortés' flagship, never dreaming then to come back with a treasure more precious than even gold or gems: my love, my only love.

31

How totally I, his mistress and his tongue, had under-
estimated Hernán Cortés! That the trusted Pizarro went
over to Narváez must have evoked great anger; Cortés
transformed it into a greater will to win. But Alvarado
gave way to secret terror that burst forth in the mass
murder of innocent Aztec dancers. I saw that horror,
helpless with the shock of it. I was fortunate that
Cortés had assigned a soldier to protect me, even
though I do not now think that the Aztecs watching
the dance would have fallen on me then and there as
Arturo Mondragon believed. Our sanctuary was the
secret treasure room of Axayacatl. When I saw again
the crystal skull, I became as certain as Arturo that
every Spaniard in the city was sure to be killed by outraged Aztecs bent on swift vengeance. His hope that I
might be spared I did not share; I knew that to the
Aztecs I would be surrogate for the absent Cortés, who
had promised Moctezuma that the Spaniards left in the
city would cause no harm.

That long night I spent sealed as if within our tomb
was the strangest I had ever known, and it taught me
once again how wrong it is harshly to judge another. I
came to understand my mother's hasty bedding with my
uncle after my father died: in women Death's near
presence can arouse a deep need to perform that act
that gives life.

Arturo and I left the treasure room the next morning
to learn that Cortés had defeated Narváez: no slaughter

of Spaniards had ever taken place. Watching jubilant Spanish soldiers in the main courtyard as they capered around the mounted Alvarado, who looked as innocent of last night's bloodshed as Arturo, I began to shake inwardly, a trembling I could not control. My body had resigned itself to dying and now knew it would live. I wanted to be in some quiet place where I could collect myself; my footsteps took me to the room I had shared with Cortés. I fell across the canopied pallet where he had last held me in his arms and a storm of sobbing shook me. I wept for my frailty, for the sin of despair that had led to a greater sin. At last I knelt before the same small Virgin that had been my weapon in San Juan Ulua. She brought me clarity of mind. Remorse had not told me by what miracle Cortés had emerged the victor, nor why, even so, there had been no retaliation against at least those Spaniards who had bloodily proven what fifty well-armed soldiers can achieve in minutes against half-naked unsuspecting victims.

I made myself presentable and went to Moctezuma's chamber, but was told by an attendant that he was still at the temple with his gods. I returned to Cortés' room and sent a servant for Orteguilla, who might know enough to enlighten me. He appeared quickly, still carrying his guitar.

Moctezuma's forbearance was swiftly explained. The news of Cortés' stunning and absolute victory had reached him by courier the evening before, a little too late to be imparted to Alvarado in time to assuage his fears, for he had already left with his fifty soldiers for the harvest dance. Moctezuma had not attended, Orteguilla said. He had been under such great tension as to the outcome for Cortés that the abrupt good news had left him weak with relief. He had taken to his bed a little after sundown, ordering his attendants not to allow any visitors to awaken him, for he had slept badly for many weeks. He had assumed that if he informed Alvarado of the good news early in the morning, that would be well and good.

"Cortés has a gift for good luck, and no one can deny

it," Orteguilla said. "Although it was also his knowledge of the climate of Vera Cruz that turned the tide for us. On the morning of that final large-scale battle while Narváez boasted of surely winning, a violent rainstorm from the north swept in. Cortés, of course, had correctly read the sky the night before and was prepared for the deluge. But torrents of rain soaked the enemy's unprotected powder supplies and rendered all their artillery useless. By this time Cortés had got a good number of Narváez's soldiers to defect to our side: mercenaries aren't too particular as to causes, and gold is a good persuader." The dwarf grinned up at me. "In short, it is victory, total victory, against overwhelming odds! Narváez is now in chains in Vera Cruz with a pike wound replacing one eye. Not only has Cortés' triumph saved us here, but it is sure to draw the attention of the Council of the Indies to the justice of Cortés' cause and the injustice of his persecution by Velásquez, a former conqueror now old and fat and jealous of our greater accomplishments in this land!"

He had not answered one question: "But by now Moctezuma must know about the slaughtered dancers, and yet has taken no action against Alvarado. Has he decided to wait until Cortés returns?"

Orteguilla shrugged. "I don't know."

As he spoke, the drum atop the war god's temple began to throb, answered by other drums. Shrill cries and howls arose from across the square, and I ran to the window to look out at the first close-packed rush of Aztec warriors flowing into the Zocalo in full battle dress. They came in from each avenue leading to the causeways, from each quarter of the city, the banners of the war chiefs raised high. I could not see how even the cannons and artillery Cortés had so strategically mounted before he left would possibly stop them for long. Instead of at once storming the palace they massed themselves in the square, confronting it with jeers, with the imposing spectacle of their multitude.

In a frightened voice that tried for nonchalance Orteguilla said, "It would appear that Cortés' victory has not greatly impressed Moctezuma's subjects."

Through the curtained doorway ran one of Moctezuma's attendants to tell me that the First Speaker required my services to translate for Alvarado's ears an important communication.

On his golden chair in his chamber, surrounded by somber-faced nobles, Moctezuma looked like a man who had received a sentence of death. He wore a panache and spoke slowly, solemnly. The powerful Council of Four, representing all the thirty clan chiefs, had just come to him to say that with or without his royal permission the clans had determined that the dead dancers must be avenged. Such a mandate to the First Speaker was unprecedented. "There is nothing I can do to avert this siege," he said without emotion. "Nothing. The Council of Four chose me as First Speaker. This uprising tells me they now regret that choice." His cold, reproachful eyes met Alvarado's. "You have yourself to blame, Tonatiuh, that things have come to this pass. Leave me now."

The child of the sun now looked like the child of the moon; his voice was also pale. "Ask him if he will send a courier to Cortés so I can write and tell him of this siege we face."

Moctezuma nodded, wearily. Alvarado looked more relieved than I felt; even if his letter reached Cortés, what could he do to help us in time? His men would be exhausted from weeks of battle; even with the Narváez defectors his army would be small compared to the Aztecs'; the long march back to Tenochtitlán would take many days.

When Alvarado and I left, he said, "The Devil take these crazy Aztecs! Going against their monarch like this! It's a crime against the very principle of monarchy!"

As he strode off I called to him sharply, and he paused in irritation. I said, "When Arturo Mondragon rescued me from that slaughterhouse last night he was acting on an order from Cortés to protect me."

"Even if he didn't, I can't afford to lose one man. Jesus Christ, woman, I have to man a siege with only a hundred and forty Spaniards to hold the fort!"

They and those brave Tlascalans held the besieged palace for twelve days. Our food supply was cut off overnight. Our Aztec servants disappeared. The conduit bringing water into our palace was severed. The market was closed, so instead of throngs buying and selling I saw only empty stalls, squadrons of Aztec warriors massed down there to kill us, however long it might take. Soon everyone was hungry all the time, such food supplies as we had being doled out scantily. The water in the garden pools made some of the soldiers sick, but then they had a little luck when a well they dug gave fresh water. Seven Spaniards were killed by arrows, spears, or stones that rained in on us over the walls. But Cortés' placement of the cannons he left and other artillery had been shrewd; gunfire kept the Aztecs at bay.

For my part, I coped with constant hunger by weaving the feather tapestry I had begun; on the third day I found a box of camote candy I had forgotten. There were ten pieces left, and I ate one each day for four days, then shared the rest with Doña Luisa, who had become very weak and pale. On the twelfth day I awoke ravenous without any hope for survival, but then became aware of the silence in the great square.

Dazed, I went to the window and tried to move the heavy screen I had placed against it after an Aztec javelin arched in through it, narrowly missing me. I was so weakened by hunger and despair that it was hard to push it aside even a handspan. I stared down at an empty plaza. The Aztec warriors were gone. Over all that vast expanse not a living creature stirred except one small fat dog who ran into the square from the avenue leading to the Tacuba causeway, paused to look around, then turned and waddled back again.

It was hard to believe what I saw, but the little dog made it real and not a scene from a hopeful dream.

Why this sudden cessation of hostilities, just at the point
when the hollow-eyed Spaniards could scarcely have
lasted another day?

Moctezuma soon told Alvarado, through me. Cortés
had been on the march to Tenochtitlán for days. The
news had reached the capital only the night before.
Moctezuma had sent word to the Council of Four that
the invincible envoy of the god was soon returning:
the siege must be ended at once. So unnatural had it
been for the clans to act against their ruler's orders
that they now agreed to do as he wished, their worst
anger against the Spaniards spent.

The soldiers' shouts of joy when Alvarado told them
of Cortés' return were more like hoarse croaks, so
weak were the men from hunger and thirst. But although the aqueduct was repaired and fresh water
flowed into the palace cistern, the Aztec marketplace
stayed closed and bare. Moctezuma had drawn heavily
on the royal storerooms, I knew, considering that the
many people in his own palace had to eat. The ending
of the siege made hunger more bearable; the soldiers
assured one another that as soon as Cortés got back
they would feast as bountifully as before.

The front rampart was thick with soldiers watching
for Cortés. Arturo Mondragon looked older, so gaunt
that his green eyes seemed to have enlarged. I nodded
to him but did not speak. It was a beautiful day, the
June sun benevolent, but the square looked like one
in a deserted city. As I stood there, the recollection of a
dream I had just before waking troubled me. In it
Cortés had returned and seemed fatherly. Like a good
daughter I told him what had happened in the treasure
room. He was at first kind and seemed to take it as a
natural thing of no great importance, but then grew
more severe and said it must never happen again or I
would no longer be his Amazon. Feeling shamed and
ready to cry, I promised him never again to be unfaith-
ful.

"Listen!" I heard a soldier say. I heard the distant
cluttered staccato of hoofbeats on stone paving. It

came from the direction of the Tacuba causeway. My
blood began to race and I realized that soon I would
see him again. The welcome sound came nearer.

Into the vast and silent square rode Cortés. Behind
him floated his worn banner. His black stallion plodded,
head down. The mounts of the captains who rode behind him looked as spent. As Cortés neared the center
of the square the following hoofbeats became a sustained roll of muffled thunder, and I stared down at the
dozens of horsemen pouring in, as though those beasts
had multiplied in battle, budding as plants do. As
Cortés neared our palace, the first of hundreds of foot
soldiers followed the horsemen. Not a single Aztec
lined the way to watch this triumphant return: Narváez had come to take over and swallow Cortés' expedition, but instead Cortés had swallowed his.

When he reached a point some fifteen paces from
the palace gate the soldiers were all cheering him.
Among their voices I did not think mine would be
heard, but found myself calling his name. To my surprise, he tipped back his head and looked straight at
me. His face was grim, but his arm went up in a salute
and I raised mine in answer. A wave of true thankful-
ness that he was still alive lifted me on its crest, and
my hand went up to my rosary. It touched only cloth,
and I remembered that I had taken off Arturo's gift
twelve days before.

Now the soldiers were jostling and crowding each
other on the stone steps leading down to the courtyard,
all eager to be there when Cortés entered. I could not
make my way down to him, for although several
soldiers at the top of the stairs made way for me,
those below were blind and deaf. The gates were
opened and Cortés rode into the courtyard, met by a
solid wall of soldiers, and their cheers and shouts of
welcome.

And then, on the balcony where Arturo and I had
heard of his triumph, I saw Moctezuma, the little figure
of Orteguilla beside him. The soldiers parted to let
Cortés pass. Unsmiling, he looked up at the Aztec

ruler. It was the dwarf's voice, not mine, that offered Cortés Moctezuma's words of greeting: "Welcome back, my lord! We are glad to see you victorious over your enemies."

To my astonishment, Cortés answered in a hard, cold voice: "I have with me ninety-eight horses and thirteen hundred Spanish soldiers. And eighty crossbowmen and as many musketeers. This is not a bad result from a battle you believed would be my death!"

When Orteguilla translated this in halting Nahuatl, Moctezuma seemed stunned, but answered: "Your triumph confirms my faith in you, for which I am glad."

Without an answer, Cortés turned his horse and passed by in disdain. For a moment Moctezuma stared after him, then turned and went back into the palace, Orteguilla trotting after.

I was as shocked as Moctezuma. And I knew that Alvarado in the letter of twelve days earlier when he told Cortés of the siege and asked assistance had distorted the truth to excuse himself. Cortés had to be told at once the facts about the slaughter of the dancers! His contempt of Moctezuma could only mean that he thought an act of Aztec violence had provoked it. This public humiliation of the ruler must be amended, and quickly.

By now the steps to the courtyard were clear, and I ran down and hurried to the far end where Cortés now smiled down at the solid mass of soldiers crowding around the stallion. "Cortés!" I shouted as I neared. "We must talk!"

He turned a little in the saddle and nodded. "Soon, Doña Marina. Soon. First I must talk with my captains."

His smile was echoed on several soldiers' faces. I felt naked. It seemed to me that he had assumed that my desire for him was such that I had lost all pride and propriety. Anger quenched humiliation; I turned and went to the room I had shared with three women during my estrangement from Cortés. I now felt almost as alienated. Let someone else tell him the truth he was blind to!

Sobbing met me. Chu-Chu, considerably thinner, knelt on her pallet, rocking and sobbing. Doña Luisa and Ixlan, standing over her, were trying to comfort her. She turned toward me her cross-eyed face, tear-wet. "They killed him! That nice young soldier who said he loved me! Dead down in Vera Cruz. He was ugly, but good, and he's dead, and he said he loved me!"

I thought of all the other soldiers dead. I knew that if Cortés' insult to Moctezuma proved a last and final straw all of us would join them. My pique vanished. I turned and ran to find Cortés, learned from his groom that he had gone to his headquarters.

All his captains were there with him. It was soon clear that someone had already exposed Alvarado's lie. He and Cortés stood beard to beard, and Cortés was clearly holding down his fury with great effort. "Again I will ask it: What made you order the slaughter of the dancers?"

"Our trouble with the Aztecs started when you went up and smashed the idols in the temple." Alvarado glanced hopefully around at his fellow captains for support; their faces stayed severe and accusing.

"Why did you kill those dancers?" Cortés asked again.

"I knew the Aztecs would attack us as soon as the dance was over."

"And how did you know this?"

Alvarado's eyes sought the ceiling as though the answer might be carved in its cedar. "I think I heard it from an Aztec priest who was talking with two of Moctezuma's nobles when I went to pay my respects."

"You don't understand three words of their tongue! Who translated this for you?"

"I think it was the dwarf."

Cortés turned to Captain Lugo. "Bring Orteguilla here."

"Wait!" Alvarado said. "It wasn't the dwarf. I don't remember who it was."

"What a bad liar you are!" Cortés' rage burst out. "The fact is that the sight of some half-naked heathens capering in their jewels and feathers made you go crazy! You gave into impulse, mere impulse!"

Head down, face red, Alvarado muttered, "You didn't see those pagan devils."

"It was ill done! This terrible error of judgment is something I may never be able to rectify! I can never trust you in a position of authority again!" Cortés turned his back on Alvarado, who stared down at the floor as if he saw his own grave opening there.

Cortés saw me standing near the doorway. He came toward me holding out his hand. When mine came to rest on his palm he bent and kissed it, an elegant gesture which showed respect. "Captain Lugo says you witnessed a part of what happened in the ball court and appeared horrified."

"Yes."

"Could a reasonable man have thought it a war dance?"

"No. The Aztecs had no weapons. They were defenseless."

Alvarado cried, "A woman is no judge! They see things differently! And she left at the very start of the fight!"

I said to Cortés, "I saw enough! Arturo Mondragon got me away, for which I thank God. The paving of the ball court was red blood; blood splashed on me as I ran."

"Mondragon deserted his post," Alvarado cried, eager to deflect attention to another culprit. "If it hadn't been for the siege, when I needed every man, he'd be swinging from a rope for vultures to eat!"

Cortés threw him a look of contempt. "He obeyed my orders. You did not."

As Alvarado wilted, I said to Cortés, "Now you see how wrong you were to blame Moctezuma for the siege. You must go to him at once and tell him so."

The anger at Alvarado was turned on me. "Must? Do not command the commander! It ill becomes a woman!"

As I flinched at his harshness and stepped back from him, two Aztec nobles entered, solemn-faced. In contrast to the steel-armed Spanish captains they looked very vulnerable. "Moctezuma wishes to speak at once with Cortés in his chamber," one told me.

"He can go to Hell," Cortés said when I told him this. "I will not stir one foot to see a dog who won't keep the market open or order food for my starving men!"

I gave the Aztecs a diplomatic excuse, but they had heard the harsh sound of his voice. They looked at each other in consternation; I risked his further wrath. "Moctezuma is behaving very well, considering your insulting response to his speech of welcome!"

"He can open the market! I have to get food for my men!"

It was Captain Olid who said, "Señor! Moderate your anger."

Sandoval added, "Yes, think how good Moctezuma has been to us. How patient. He ordered the siege stopped, Lugo tells me. Except for him, all of those who remained here might now be dead and eaten!"

As though he had not heard, Cortés demanded, "Why should I answer this summons from a dog who was probably treating secretly with Narváez?"

Captain Sandoval lisped, "I think it was the other way around. Narváez tried to treat covertly with him and to convince him that we are no better than felons. But Moctezuma did not believe him, and the proof is that we stand here alive. You were wrong to humiliate Moctezuma. You are wrong now if you refuse to talk with him as he asks."

Cortés turned to me. "Have them tell Moctezuma that I will visit him after he provides food for my men. He must open the market at once. I will give him until midday tomorrow."

I said to them, "Cortés asks only that his hungry

men be fed. As you can see, he is very weary. Perhaps by midday tomorrow, after the market is open, he and Moctezuma can come to a better understanding." But the two nobles had twice heard the angry arrogance in Cortés' voice. Without further comment or any farewell, they turned and left.

The captains were aware that they were offended, and Captain Velásquez said to Cortés, "You are very weary, and you should rest now."

He shook his head, but the other captains all came forward to agree. Even Alvarado, looking slightly reassured since Cortés had done nothing worse than censure him, urged Cortés not to push himself further and got a withering look for it. "I have to find quarters for the new recruits. All the new horses have to be stabled and fed. And I want to check the palace defenses, for who can say how long this peace will last?"

I saw, with stunning clarity, that Cortés would busy himself with these things to escape from giving further consideration to the gravity of Alvarado's offense or to the punishment it merited. I saw too the cause of his unreasonable anger toward Moctezuma: he was deflecting toward the Aztec ruler some of his rage at Alvarado, whom he did not want to punish for his rash cruelty, knowing that it would not have occurred except for his own grave error of judgment in leaving him in command. In other words, to judge and punish Alvarado, he would have to judge himself too. He was not prepared to do this.

Moctezuma's reply came swiftly, brought by the same two nobles. "As your prisoner here I can do nothing. But if you will release my brother Cuitlahuac I will order him to do as you wish and provide food for your soldiers."

Again I was aware of Cortés' weariness. He closed his eyes and covered them with one hand as he thought over this offer. He dropped his hand with a sigh. His gaze roved over his captains' faces. "We have no choice. We have to eat." He turned to me. "Tell Moctezuma I will release Cuitlahuac."

I must have gasped; he gave me a dark and warning look. Having excoriated Alvarado for his rashness, he now made this rash decision as though he had forgotten that Cuitlahuac had been one of the few supporters of Cacama in his rebellion.

He and the captains then left to reorganize the logistics of the entire palace, now packed with the new recruits, horses whinnying in every courtyard.

It was late that night when he finally came into the room where I awaited him. My uneasiness about the release of Cuitlahuac and another more personal matter melted into nothing when I saw him. He moved stiffly, like a man whom only great willpower kept upright. He gave me a ghastly grin out of a gray-white face in which his eyes flashed as if with a fever. "I fell asleep too soon when I left you, Marina. And now it looks as if I'll do it again."

His valet arrived on the run to help him out of his armor, and he gave a groan of relief as the breastplate was removed, sank into his chair for the greaves to be unbuckled. He dismissed the valet, stood, kept his shoulders straight as he walked in smallclothes to the bed, then fell onto it, eyes already shut. I covered him with a blanket, and as if he felt my presence, one eye partly opened. "My Amazon," he whispered, and reached an arm toward me. It dropped like lead to the bed. He was asleep.

I lay awake for a long time beside him, remembering the woman of such a short time ago who had lain here filled with longing. The only desire that filled me now was somehow to prevent him from releasing Cuitlahuac; as far as I could learn he had not yet committed that mistake. Not only did Cuitlahuac hate Spaniards; not only had he already rebelled against his ruler, but he had once been, according to Moctezuma, a contender for the throne. I knew it would be hard to reach Cortés; I had seen tonight a new or earlier-hidden side to his nature: an arrogant resistance to the truth that actions have consequences. Or perhaps he had come to believe that for him this was not true. A hero had come back from Vera Cruz. A hero who knew himself to be one. It would take all his powers to remedy matters here in the city he had managed to hold for a thankless Spanish king. It would also take a touch of humility.

Against all this, my remorse over what happened by chance in a dead king's treasure room seemed trivial indeed.

I said my prayers and told myself that tomorrow, when Cortés was rested and more reasonable, I would express my deep anxiety about Cuitlahuac.

Tomorrow proved, as it so often does, too late. Cortés' last act before he came to bed had been to set Cuitlahuac free.

32

All during the siege with its misery, hunger, and terror I had an inner battle with the recurring fear that my friend El Galán would die fighting the overwhelming Narváez forces: the odds meant to me that Death had about four chances at El Galán for one chance at each of those four enemies. So while other soldiers swarmed around the victorious Cortés as he rode his black stallion into the palace courtyard, I stationed myself by the entrance gate, watching for El Galán. Captains known and horsemen strange to me had passed in before I saw him drooping with fatigue atop a somewhat swaybacked piebald horse. His left leg was swathed in a bandage caked with dried blood, and he looked like his own older brother.

When I ran to him calling his name he looked down at me from eyes set in dark hollows and croaked, "God, what a miserable campaign. We fought the last battle in torrents of rain, but it ruined the enemy's powder supplies and rendered their cavalry less useful, I'll say that for it." With slow care he dismounted, wincing as he tried to stand on his bandaged leg. He put an arm around my shoulders and I felt the dead weight of his weary body. "I am very tired, old friend, and I will sleep a long time now, I think. Will you stable and feed my mare?" He gave her a wry, affectionate glance. "I got her from a Narváez captain who suddenly lost any need for a mount." I went with him to his old pallet next to mine, where he shed his helmet and breastplate and stretched out with a sigh of relief.

After I stabled the horse and found her some straw to eat, which was all the fodder we had, I went back to my friend. He was not asleep, probably due to his pain, so I asked him about that final battle that had saved me from extinction. "Narváez planned to defeat us on a plain near Zempoalla with all his horsemen, crossbowmen, musketeers, and cannons except for two he left in the town, mounted on the first level of the main pyramid where our cross stands. The rainstorm rendered all but the crossbowmen ineffectual. So he ordered a retreat to the town, where the horses would not be slipping and sliding in the mud. What Cortés wanted was the capture or death of Narváez himself. So Sandoval led the charge to take over the cannons on the pyramid where he was, we captains right behind, the fifes and drums beating the charge, soldiers with pikes and crossbows backing us up. And Narváez got a pike in the eye. How he yelled! 'Holy Mary protect me! They killed me and destroyed my eye!' Our soldiers shouted, 'Victory for Cortés! Narváez has fallen, Narváez is dead!' And that began the turn of the tide in our favor, although we had to battle on for a long while after this, and captured Diego Velásquez, the son of the governor, and other important fellows."

"And did Narváez die?"

"No, he was just half-blind and bleeding. With the capture of the other captains, Cortés proclaimed to the Narváez soldiers that they should all join him in victory, surrender themselves to the rightful Captain-General and Chief Justice of Vera Cruz, founded in the name of their sovereign. And this, at last, is what they did. Narváez behaved surprisingly well in defeat; he had asked Sandoval to let his surgeon treat his wound and those of the other imprisoned captains, and Sandoval did. While Narváez was being doctored, Cortés came into the room. Narváez said, 'Señor Captain Cortés, you must consider it a great feat, this victory over me and the capture of my person.' " El Galán smiled. "And Cortés said, 'It was one of the least things I have done in New Spain.' "

"How did you get wounded?" I asked. "Capturing Narváez?"

"After he was captured. There were skirmishes most of that night with those of the enemy too stubborn to recognize defeat. And I got a pike in the leg, but better than the eye. The rain had stopped and there were millions of fireflies, and by their light I saw the whoreson who did it, and I got him. And a captain, too, and commandeered his mare. She doesn't look like much but she's good-natured and plucky."

"It must have been a great day, though, when they all surrendered."

"It was! First the drummers and other musicians Narváez brought all marched into our camp beating their drums and playing their fifes and tambourines and calling '*Viva, viva* the few brave men who conquered Narváez and his soldiers.' A giant Negro beating on a big bass drum roared 'Even the Romans never did a feat like this!' Then Sandoval, Olid, and Ordas rode in at the head of the captured captains. Cortés looked like a king in the long orange robe he wore over his armor. The captains, including the son of Velásquez, all passed before him and bent and kissed his hand."

Now El Galán's eyelids were closing, but he roused himself. "Then Cortés sent soldiers to the port where

Narváez's ships were anchored and ordered the mates and masters to remove all sails, rudders, and compasses to keep them from sailing back to Cuba and told them to come to him and surrender, and they did."

"And then on top of a victory like that came Alvarado's letter about the trouble here in Tenochtitlán."

"Three days later. Cortés was furious when he learned that Alvarado was besieged after some Aztec war dance in which some Spaniards were killed." El Galán's weary lids closed.

The falsity of Alvarado's report stunned me. "But that's not how it was!" A snore answered me. I jumped to my feet. Cortés had to be told the truth!

He strode out of his council chamber just as I reached the door; inside, his captains, Malinche, and a chastened Alvarado stood staring after him. I could see that a momentous scene had taken place while I was with El Galán. Cortés paused to say to me "I know that seven Spaniards were killed during the siege. I am glad you were not one of them, Arturo." He turned to call back over his shoulder to his captains, "Do you plan to stand there the rest of the day?" They thudded past me and I stood looking in at Malinche, now alone. I saw, with a pang, that she no longer wore my rosary.

I went no closer, but called from the doorway, "Does Cortés know the truth about Alvarado?"

"Yes."

"What is the punishment to be?"

"None!"

"I don't believe it!" Our eyes met and I imagined that our thoughts were the same: we had been victims of that crime of Alvarado; our lapse from virtue would not have happened without it.

Yet a wave of guilt and self-despising washed over my stinking body, for we had had no water to waste in bathing. She looked so sad, standing alone in that big room. I knew what remorse she must have suffered. I turned and went silently away, the seducer of this woman whom great fear had made vulnerable to my lust. Cortés' kind words to me of a few minutes earlier now stabbed my conscience like darts.

Yet so perverse was that part of me the Devil uses to his delight and our later pain that it had stirred in excitement at the sight of her, and now stirred again as I despised my own lust. As I pushed my way along a corridor crowded with disgruntled Narváez men asking one another when they would get some food, I fiercely commanded my impish part to get used to relative chastity again.

The next day dawned warm and beautiful and I woke on my straw pallet grateful that El Galán was alive on his. I was sure that with Cortés back I would soon eat a real meal again, not just thin maize gruel or watery bean soup. I went to the front wall to look out and see if perhaps the market might already be open, but no food had appeared on the skeletal permanent stalls that stood as empty as I was, waiting for the abundance of produce that my jaws yearned to crunch, that my belly wailed for.

And then, across the square, I saw a figure come running toward the palace from the street that led to the Tacuba causeway. As it neared I saw that it was a Spaniard and that blood ran down one side of his face. Not until he was at the door below did I recognize Yago the acrobat. I ran down to the courtyard and reached it just after the sentries let him in. "For God's sake, what happened to you?" I asked.

He could only shake his head, panting for breath, and I saw that his eyes were glazed with terror. I went with him to Cortés' headquarters, where we found the general looking more like himself after some hours of sleep. When he saw Yago's bloody face, dismay showed on his.

He poured a cup of water and while Yago drank, Cortés told me that before dawn he had dispatched Yago and several other soldiers to Vera Cruz with news of our safe arrival. Yago put down the cup and told the rest. They had got nearly as far as Tacuba on the shortest of the causeways when they saw ahead a horde of Aztec warriors marching from that town to Tenochtitlán. They had let loose a flight of spears and arrows, one of which had grazed Yago's cheek. He turned and ran for his life. Tears of terror sprang to his eyes. "The causeways to the city are full of those warriors! Thousands and thousands! Spotted like jaguars, hissing like snakes, and with the heads of eagles, or helmets that are great toothed jaws, their own faces peering out. Cuitlahuac is leading them."

Almost before Yago finished speaking, Cortés sent his crier to summon the captains. They conferred only briefly. It was decided that Diego de Ordas, with four hundred foot soldiers and a dozen crossbowmen and musketeers, would go out to reconnoiter. Ordas was ordered to remain calm and avoid any battle if he could.

Moctezuma was still our hostage, but if those approaching warriors any longer intended to obey his command that the siege be ended, would they now be marching on the city? Could he still manage to save us from the wrath of his people?

Ordas and his men were not gone long. They had to retreat almost at once to the main square and fight their way past the Aztec warriors beginning to fill it—and who soon were attacking our fortress with arrows, javelins, and slings. But our cannons, placed by Cortés to command the square from the rampart and roof garden, soon cleared a way for Ordas and his force to enter, although he and almost all his men were wounded, and they left fourteen Spaniards lying dead in the Zocalo.

The battle raged all day. With sunset the attack ceased, but we had to spend part of the night repairing and reorganizing our defenses. At least eighty of our men had been wounded.

At dawn Cortés mounted a counterattack, two forces of a hundred men each. Covered by our cannons and artillery, we forced the Aztecs back across the square, but then we were trapped among the houses and had to retreat under the barrage of stones and weapons hurled down on us from those flowering rooftops we had so admired. Whistling, shouting Aztecs hounded us back across the central plaza. That day we lost another dozen men.

Cortés then conceived a plan of building mobile wooden towers on wheels, horse-drawn and each holding some twenty men. From the tops musketeers and crossbowmen could shoot out at the warriors on the rooftops as they passed, the cavalry meanwhile clearing the street below. It took a day and a night to build them of wood gotten by taking down a ceiling, but they proved nearly useless because the Aztecs put up street barricades to impede our horses. The towers had to lumber back to our palace, damaged by hurled javelins, although no one inside them was wounded.

On the third day of the siege, Cortés decided that if we could get to the top of the war god's temple and destroy all the idols there and set it afire, this might have the effect of subduing our superstitious foes. So at dawn of the fourth day, after commending our souls to God, we carried forth those wooden towers again. With cannons, muskets, and crossbows clearing a way for us, we pushed through fresh squadrons of Aztec warriors to the forecourt of the great pyramid. I was inside one of the towers, which already smelled of sweat and fear. Beside me a Narváez man steadily cursed Cortés, Narváez, and the day he left Cuba. Outside, Aztecs yelled and whistled and screamed, and stones, spears, and arrows rattled against the wood of the tower with fearsome thuds.

Peeping through one of the narrow slits in the tower I saw those thousands of skulls grinning down at our misfortune. A night rain had wetted the smooth paving stones so that our horses slipped and stumbled amid a scramble of attacking Aztecs. Had they massed at the top of the pyramid they could have shot down arrows at us very effectively, but religious scruples evidently kept them from using this elevated battleground. Hundreds of them were massed on the two lower levels, however.

It took all my courage to emerge at the prearranged signal from the safety of that huge shield when it reached the bottom of the pyramid steps. With Cortés himself leading us, we began to fight our way to the top. "Santiago and upward!" he cried to us, and this new version of our old battle cry had the power to move us after him, slashing and stabbing at the Aztecs who hoped to stop us. The angry Narváez man fell dead beside me at the first terrace. Cortés seemed more than human, a figure out of legend, as he hacked his way upward with flashing sword. As I rose behind him, step by step, I saw each enemy through the red blood lust that had come upon me and felt only joy as my sword pierced the throat of an eagle warrior, the bird beak of his helmet framing his final grimace.

We reached the top, toppled lesser idols and set fire to the chamber where the hideous war god stood. Some fresh human hearts laid at his feet began to cook and to send out a greasy smoke, then flames enveloped him. Our damage done, we had to fight our way down again, but now had the advantage that we could shoot down on the Aztecs, and we did away with enough of them to get across the pyramid's forecourt past the wreckage of one of our towers. The cannons and artillery on our rampart cleared a path through the yelling warriors in the main plaza so that we could make our way back into the palace, bringing with us two Aztec priests we had captured.

The grim night was spent in dressing our wounds and burying our dead. We knew that we had done our utmost. If the destruction of their principal gods and the burning of their main temple did not subdue these Aztecs, then all we could do was to surrender, sue for peace, and hope to God to be allowed to leave the city alive.

The idea of surrender roused in me two strong emotions: a yearning to continue living, on whatever terms, but also sorrow at the thought that sixteen months of toil, danger, and battles against great odds would be set at naught.

I was lying on my pallet; El Galán on his beside me was unwrapping the bandage from his leg wound. Despite it he had taken over that day for a wounded crossbowman, being versed in using that weapon. Standing for several hours at the rampart had caused his wound to open. I gasped when I saw it, for the pike had entered behind the greave and gouged a big hole in his calf. He winced as he cleaned it with sherry from his flask. "Wine is good for wounds and seems to keep them from getting pus," he remarked and began to wrap it with a strip torn from a cotton mantle. I helped, holding the lower end in place.

"It's surrender, isn't it?" I asked.

He frowned. "That will come hard for Cortés."

"What choice does he have?"

"To fight on."

"In God's name, how? The food Cuitlahuac sent us is nearly gone; I know that for a fact. The cistern is nearly empty. What happens when our ammunition is gone?"

He shrugged and tied his bandage. "Cortés' victory over Narváez was good and yet bad. It may have gone to his head. Diego Velásquez kissed his hand. The Council of the Indies seems to be on his side now. He expects any day to hear from King Carlos that a mighty force is on its way to aid him. He may believe that he can continue to inspire us to keep at it here until we're all skeletons, fed only by the courage he pumps into us."

I dreamed that night of a fortress full of desiccated cadavers pulling bows and shooting muskets at Aztecs in the square who laughed in derision while Cortés on a skeletal black stallion shouted brave words to inspire his obedient marionettes.

Morning showed the square filling with Aztec warriors fresh and well-fed and yelling for our hearts. Mine sank as my belly rumbled its demand for food. The drum atop the war god's pyramid began to throb and

I guessed that another dripping heart was being held aloft to the morning sun. The thought of rebellion crept into my mind. If we all refused to fight, Cortés would have to forget his swollen pride and sue for peace.

Drearily I got up to take my post and draw my sword and hack at any Aztec who might today be boosted to the top of our wall or climb one of the ladders they used. They were very persistent in these attempts; now one looked just like another to me except for the differences between their strange helmets.

But that day El Galán and I were replaced at the wall by two soldiers who had been guarding Moctezuma. Standing as sentries outside the door to his apartment, El Galán and I could hear the sounds of battle, yet could take no part. I thought then of Malinche, probably busy at her tapestry, hearing the same sounds, able to do nothing but await the outcome.

The thought took me back once more to my early childhood with my mother in Medellín, those years when she waited while my father fought Caribs in Cuba. The lot of women seemed a sad and hard one, their fate forever determined by the acts of a man to whose destiny their own was bound.

33

When I found that Cortés had released Cuitlahuac, I could only hope that my fears were wrong. He kept his promise to Moctezuma and supplied us with maize, beans, and tomatoes, but the price was high: renewed hostilities. After an attack on Huitzilopotchli's temple failed to subdue the Aztecs besieging us, Cortés began to have trouble sleeping nights. I would awake from an uneasy doze to find him pacing around the room in a long orange robe given him by the cacique of Zempoalla. I knew that those captains who counseled surrender were right. On the third night of waking and finding him prowling the room, I sat up in bed and said, "Make your peace with Moctezuma. Tell him you are willing now to leave the city. Plead with him to announce this at once to Cuitlahuac."

He came and stood over me like a tower of flame. "We are not defeated yet!"

"Is that what you are waiting for? Defeat? How much ammunition is left? How much food have your soldiers eaten today? My heart aches for them!"

"Women's hearts were made to ache. Men's were not. I know Moctezuma could have gotten more provisions out of Cuitlahuac if he had tried! Or else he could give us some of the food stored over there in his own palace. The dog has two faces, two hearts! With one he trembles in fear of me and with the other he wants me dead! I will make no peace with him!"

"Why should he let the people in his palace go hungry to feed us?"

"Let these sycophants feel the nip of hunger!"

"Would you take from your soldiers to feed them?"

He glared down at me. "Stop all this sophistry!"

"I don't know what that means."

"It means I am weary of listening to you! Don't get above yourself. And let me think, for God's sake! Let me think!"

I dared a few more words. "Your victory at Vera Cruz may cause your defeat here. It did not make you invincible."

To my surprise, that barb struck home. He stared down at me, then gave a crooked grin. "Pride goes before a fall? Is that what you are trying to convey?"

"With all my heart."

"Do you happen to know that the soldiers of Hamilcar drank their own urine to stay alive?"

"I do not know who Hamilcar is."

"Alexander of Macedon . . ."

"All I do know is that a great leader of men can rise above pride when the lives of men who trust him are in the balance."

He rolled his eyes toward heaven. "May God save and defend me against a woman with little knowledge and a clever brain!"

"God save me from a general who is unwilling to use the good brain God gave him!" By now I was trembling with the intensity of my feelings. I lay back on the bed and crossed my hands on my breast and closed my eyes.

"What now?" he asked.

I did not answer.

He came to the side of the bed, seized my arm and shook it. "What is this? Out of words at last?"

"I am going to die soon. I am trying to ready myself with prayer."

He tossed my arm from him. "By my conscience, for the first time in my life I want to hit a woman!" I opened my eyes to see him looming above me, fist raised above his head, the arm trembling as he held back the blow.

"That will be easier than asking Moctezuma's pardon for insulting him."

The fist was slowly lowered. He turned abruptly to kneel where the Virgin Mary stood. I prayed that She would move Cortés, since I had failed.

In the morning I found that my prayer had been answered. Cortés, armed from top to toe, shook my arm to wake me. "I need your voice. I want you to go to Moctezuma and tell him that I ask his pardon if I was hasty in suspecting him. I want an immediate interview with him."

I was now wide awake. "To what purpose?"

"To tell him I wish my entire army to leave the city peaceably."

I dressed in a beautiful tunic Moctezuma had given me and wore the necklace of gold and turquoise he had also given. Sandoval and Father Olmedo, of whom he was fond, were waiting in the corridor to escort me.

Sandoval was cheerful. "All will be well now, I think. I'm sorry to surrender, but also glad to have the chance to do so."

We reached Moctezuma's quarters to be met at the doorway by a solid wall of nobles. I said, "We have come to offer Moctezuma Cortés' apology for his great rudeness. He was misinformed about the true cause of the siege. He wants an interview."

A noble left the group and went toward a high screen of gilded fretwork at the room's far end and returned to say "Moctezuma will speak to Malinche." I followed him; he halted before the screen. Through the small openings in the elaborate carving I could see someone sitting behind it. Moctezuma's voice was dull and cold. "I refuse to see Cortés. Fate has brought me to such an evil pass because of him that I never want to see his face or hear his voice again."

Hiding my shock, I said: "He wishes to leave the city."

There was no response. I knew further words were useless. I bowed low to the screen and retreated.

Cortés was astonished that Moctezuma, always so amenable, had dared this defiance. "We are the ones brought to an evil pass! And he will see me! Now!" He took my arm and pulled me with him to the doorway.

At Moctezuma's door the same nobles barred the way, but Cortés called loudly above their heads: "Lord Moctezuma! Is this how you treat me when I come in all humility to offer an ending to your troubles and mine? Please, ask your nobles to let me enter!"

In a moment Moctezuma's faint voice said "Enter."

But the screen remained between them as Cortés said, "All I ask is that you go out to the front rampart and address your people. Tell them that this war must cease. All I want is to leave your city in peace."

There was a long silence. Moctezuma said: "I do not believe I can obtain an end to this war. My people listen to Cuitlahuac now. They have made up their

minds not to let you leave here alive. I believe that all of
you must die."

Cortés' power to force Moctezuma to do his will had
failed this last and crucial time! But Cortés, in an
urgent yet humble tone, said, "I beg you to speak to
your people as I have asked. They have revered you for
seventeen years. That will prove a stronger loyalty
than any they may feel toward an upstart like Cuitlahuac. Speak to them!"

There was a long pause. Moctezuma spoke wearily.
"I will do this one last thing you ask of me."

Cortés thanked Moctezuma and left, after bowing
respectfully to the gilded screen. "Thank God," he said
as soon as we were in the corridor. His face was bright
with relief, and I thanked Him too for Cortés' overnight change in perception of our situation, and I marveled at God's power to move intractable human hearts.
Or perhaps it had been the Sainted Virgin to whom he
had knelt the night before who had made him see that
our only hope for survival was a swift exodus.

Within the hour, Moctezuma, Cortés, and I, escorted
by the captains and the ruler's Spanish bodyguard,
made our way to the front rampart. Moctezuma, thinner
than before and with a sadder face, walked slowly to
the crenellated wall splashed with patches of dry brown
blood, and mounted the platform placed there so he
could be well seen from the square below. I stood at
one side, Cortés at the other, but lower than he. Moctezuma stood there in silence, arrayed in the great green
headdress of quetzal feathers he had worn when he
came to meet us. As the Aztecs looked up and saw him
their derisive cries ceased and the conches and drums
fell silent. Aztec chieftains called sharp commands, and
I saw bows lowered and raised lances slowly fall. The
Council of Four came forward and stood just below
Moctezuma, looking up. He addressed them in a firm,
gentle tone, saying what Cortés had asked: that they
must now desist from further warfare, for we would at
once leave the city and go back to our own land.

The oldest member of the Council of Four came for-

ward and bowed to his ruler. I heard his words with disbelief, while putting them into Spanish as they fell from
his lips slowly and with deep sorrow. "Oh, Great Lord
Moctezuma, all your misfortune and injury afflicts us.
But now we make it known to you that we have raised
up one of your kinsmen to be our lord in your place.
It is your brother Cuitlahuac." And Cuitlahuac came
forward to stand beside him, looking up at his former
ruler impassively, wearing a royal green headdress.

I saw Moctezuma's body stiffen. He stood looking
out at the faces of the people who had deposed him.
Such a thing had never happened before in all the long
history of the Aztecs. This moment must have been a
strange and terrible one to bear—and not only for him,
to judge by the awed and absolute silence of the Aztecs
in the square below.

Then Cuitlahuac spoke. His voice was very loud
and had a stony quality. "The war must be carried on.
We will fight until the strangers are dead. We have
prayed to the gods to guard you, Moctezuma. If we
succeed in defeating the strangers, we will hold you in
higher regard than ever before, and you shall rule us
again. We beg you to forgive us."

Thus with respectful words he had refused to obey
Moctezuma's request that the war cease and we be
allowed to depart. There was a beat of silence, then a
high, mocking voice shouted: "Moctezuma has been
turned into a woman by Cortés!" So abruptly that we
could not move fast enough to shield our hostage, a
shower of stones and darts were hurled at Moctezuma.
They came from a little group of warriors surrounding
a tall, bold-faced Aztec. He was Cuauhtemoc, the other
prime contender for the throne. Three of the stones hit
Moctezuma in rapid succession, one on the head. Then
Cortés and Sandoval quickly pulled him down from the
battlement; he seemed unable to move of his own
volition. As they did this, more stones banged against
Cortés' casque and breastplate with brutal, ringing
thuds.

Either the stone that struck Moctezuma's head or

the shock of the attack or both had paralyzed him, for his legs suddenly crumpled beneath him; I reached out to hold him upright. The flesh of the bare arm I grasped was as cold as a dead man's. He stared straight ahead, and I saw a trickle of blood run down one side of his face like a red tear. He smelled of flowers.

We brought him to his private quarters and I told his servants there that he should rest quietly in his bed for a while, and Cortés sent in a Padre de Merced to put salve on his head wound and bandage it. Moctezuma lay immobile while his wound was dressed, then tore the bandage off and turned his face to the wall.

Whenever I looked in, that was how he lay, unmoving. Little Orteguilla, with the tears sometimes running down his face, sat crouched at the foot of the pallet and never left him. He told me that Moctezuma would take no food brought him, or even drink water. He asked that his children and wives be cared for. He never spoke again. On the third day he died.

When I looked down at him my compassion bewildered me. He lay on his wide pallet, raised on a dais and richly canopied. Beside him the great green panache stood on its golden crown, discarded symbol of past glory. His face was pure and serene and untouched by human anguish. Tears dimmed my eyes, for I knew that in his own fashion he had given greater reverence to a merciful deity than to an evil one and had paid a terrible price for having mistaken a man for a god.

Then my heart seemed to become as still as Moctezuma's as I realized that I might soon join him in death, though mine would not be this unbutchered repose that looked so like a deep sleep with no dreams.

"There lies our hope of life" a voice behind me said. I turned; the Spanish bodyguards stood there. Arturo Mondragon had spoken in a voice husky with emotion. El Galán, beside him, removed his helmet. "Heathen he may have been, and dreadful his idols, but he was still a gentleman of great nobility of mind, and I wish to God he might have died a Christian."

Cortés strode in then, with several captains; he was amazed to find Moctezuma dead. They all agreed that the head wound was not enough to kill him. I said it was not the size of the wound that mattered but the source of the stone that had made it, thrown at him by one of his subjects out of hatred and contempt.

"Are you going to tell me he willed his own death?" Cortés demanded.

"He had no people any more. Does a head want to live with its body cut off?"

His own pride let him understand this. He stood staring down at Moctezuma's corpse, shaking his head in amazement that the Aztec's will had proved in its own strange way as powerful as his own. He turned away saying, "However he died, I must find a way to use this misfortune to our advantage."

Misfortune! It was disaster. Total, final, and irretrievable. He knew it. I knew it. Soon all the soldiers would know it. And then the Aztecs.

The priests arrived then to decide what rites should be administered to this infidel who was doomed to burn in Hell for all eternity. They decided to commit his spirit to God's mercy. I looked again at Moctezuma, at those feet pointing outward in their golden sandals, never again to tread this earth. I remembered my father lying like that before his burial. Whatever happened to Moctezuma's spirit, this husk that had contained it merited some gesture of respect. I brought the feather tapestry I had just finished. I had intended it for the wall of the chapel. I covered Moctezuma's body with it instead. It was a nativity scene showing the Three Kings looking down at Mary holding in her arms the infant Jesus, made with tiny flesh-colored feathers, His halo the yellow of ripe maize.

And I told myself that God's mercy would protect this Aztec's spirit as tenderly, knowing as He did how close Moctezuma had come to accepting Him on the night of the auto-da-fé.

*   *   *

After consultation with his captains, Cortés decided on a bold stroke: to lay the blame for Moctezuma's death on his own people. He had me instruct the two Aztec priests he had taken prisoner to go to Cuitlahuac and inform him that Moctezuma had died of the head wound sustained when he was stoned three days before.

The two black-robed Aztec priests, devastated to learn of his death, were brought out of their cell and I solemnly spoke to them Cortés' words: "I will return to his own subjects the body of Moctezuma. He is to be buried like the great king he was. And tell Cuitlahuac, raised to kingly power that was not his by right, to remember and obey Moctezuma's last words to his people: that a peace should be made so we can leave Tenochtitlán." But then Cortés' bravado took command of him. "And say that if this is not done, we will destroy this city which so far we have spared out of respect for the king who is dead." This threat was of course impossible to carry out, but served to remind Cuitlahuac of the supernatural authority Moctezuma had credited him with.

During the time since Moctezuma's ill-fated speech on the rampart hostilities had been sporadic. The deposing of their ruler had subdued the Aztecs' spirits; they had also learned that their attempts to storm the palace were futile because of Spanish artillery. There was a total lull in the fighting when the two docile Aztec priests left to bring Cortés' message to Cuitlahuac. Following them came six captured Aztec warriors who carried Moctezuma lying on his palanquin, the cascading feathers of his green panache trailing in the dust. Cortés had the drummers beat a dead march in slow tempo, and all the Spanish soldiers and captains stood with heads bowed in respectful silence.

Minutes later we heard cries and shrieks and groans of distress arise in the Zocalo, intensifying as word of the death of Moctezuma spread among the Aztecs there. We waited tensely for Cuitlahuac's answer to Cortés' plea for peace and a safe retreat. Within the hour one of the warriors who had left with the dead king came back to say to Cortés: "Now you will pay for the death of our King and Lord, and for the dishonor to our gods. The new king we have chosen is not faint-hearted like the good Moctezuma, and you cannot deceive him with false promises. So do not trouble about how and where we bury Moctezuma. Worry for your own lives, for within two days you will all be dead."

I felt my lips blanch with fear as I translated this devastating response. Cortés stared at the Aztec warrior who had delivered it; his face was stark. He pointed silently to the gate. Walking slowly to deny any fear, the messenger departed.

The sounds of lamentation turned to the whistles and jeers of warfare; a shower of arrows, lances, and stones came over the palace wall. The siege had recommenced. I knew that even if with his superior weaponry Cortés killed twenty thousand Aztecs, another twenty thousand would take their places. And the day was coming when his ammunition would run out. Food, already scant, would be gone even sooner.

I had seen Cortés in many moods and lights, but never before had I seen him as I did then, for standing white-faced in his armor he seemed helpless and immensely vulnerable. As all his army was trapped inside the palace walls, so he was trapped in steel, a walking coffin in which he could die untouched by any weapon except slow starvation. When he spoke I heard only an echo of his old assurance. "Within two days we will not be dead. Nor within twenty days. Cuitlahuac does not realize that he is fighting Castilians."

That night I learned of the decision his captains had all agreed with out of desperation or conviction. Cortés had learned from Xicotencatl's son that there was a little-used route to Tlascala that bypassed the steep sierra of Ahualco and Cholula too. And he had determined that his only strategy lay in leaving the city at night by the short Tacuba causeway in the hope that once we were out of the city itself the Aztecs' fury would be largely dissipated. He sounded grimly confident as he said, "This way I utilize their Achilles' heel: they never fight at night. Darkness becomes our ally, their foe."

Into our room came a soldier named Botello. Small, wise-eyed, and earnest, he was a practitioner of a science he called judicial astrology.

"Several of his predictions in the past have indeed come true," Cortés said. "I have told him I need a night with no moon, and he has offered to read his own horoscope in hopes of also telling me which moonless night will prove most favorable for our exodus."

Botello solemnly stated that the night of the thirtieth of June and first of July was by far the most favorable. "Even though," he smiled sadly, "there are indications that I may then perish."

"And the rest of us?" Cortés asked, smiling a little to show that his credence was not total.

"A triumphant departure," Botello assured him.

The day after the death of Moctezuma Cortés launched a foray with towers, cannons, and cavalry to battle his way to the Tacuba causeway, setting fires to houses on the way and razing some to fill in canals that crossed the avenue leading to it. He found that the Aztecs had already removed the first causeway bridge. He fought his way back to the palace again, which took so long that the rumor went among the soldiers that he had been killed. I would not believe this and denied the possibility to the frightened woman who had heard this whisper. For I knew that whether the astrologer had been right or wrong about the auspicious night, only Cortés could lead us all from certain doom here to possible safety on the other side of the wide lake.

When he returned he was grim. "Our route is now prepared," he announced to the men. "There are not many roofs left for the Aztecs to attack us from, due to the useful fires we set today." He ordered the shipwright Martín Llopez and Nuñez the carpenter to construct a large movable bridge sturdy enough to bear the cannons and horsemen that could be carried forward with us by soldiers and put down to cross the causeway gaps.

The army took well to this plan when he announced it. Even though in such a departure it was likely that some would be killed, each man held the comforting notion that it would not be he. The prospect of decisive action after having been so long pent up enlivened their spirits.

My own stayed at a low ebb. Ever since the night I had in desperation attacked Cortés for the sin of pride he had been distant and cool. To live close to a hero, I had found, is to either risk losing his affection or pretend not to see his flaws, and this I had been unable to do. He took time to advise me carefully to select those possessions of greatest value and leave the rest behind. He found no moment in which to let me understand that he still loved me.

Thus we approached the last day of June and the moonless night of stars said to be propitious. The season of rains had begun. In summer in the Valley of Anahuac they come quite regularly in the early afternoon, last an hour or two, and cease abruptly, leaving a clean and sparkling world for the descending sun to set aglow. But as the sun set and the Aztecs began to leave the square I saw from my window the sullen gray cloud bank rolling in from the northeast and already hiding the crests of the mountains. I knew that Nature was making one of her exceptions. The moonless night would be starless too, and rain would surely fall.

34

In Cuba we have storms called hurricanes, but none of these was ever so alarming to me as the storm that broke on the night all of us who lived through it will always call the *noche triste*. The rain began not long after dark, just a stealthy pattering of large drops, but you could smell all the moisture gathered in the low heavy clouds, dark and dull by last light as unburnished armor. My mother once said that no one enjoys the details of battles so much as the soldiers who fought in them. But even if I wanted to tell all that happened on that sad night, I could not endure the task. It pains me to remember even the small part I witnessed.

On the afternoon of June thirtieth, to confuse the Aztecs, Cortés sent out to Cuitlahuac one of their captured warriors with the message that we were readying ourselves to leave in a week and would leave behind all the gold and treasure Moctezuma had given us if he would allow us free passage from the city. But this was done to put them off guard, for we had readied ourselves to leave that very night, after dark. At sundown the Aztecs regularly evacuated the Zocalo to camp elsewhere, having learned that darkness did not deter us and that they were not safe there from our cannons and muskets and crossbows. A stealthy exodus seemed possible.

Our plan was that four hundred Tlascans and a hundred fifty Spaniards would protect the *tamanes* carrying the bridge we had made and defend it after it was placed in that first gap of the Tacuba causeway, guarding it until the rest of the army and all of our baggage had crossed. Two hundred Tlascalans and fifty Spaniards were in charge of protecting the cannons. Four captains and a hundred fifty Spaniards were chosen to go forward first in case our way was opposed by any Aztecs from the mainland. After them would ride Cortés and a dozen mounted captains to fight to the forward or rear, whichever group might be in most need of help. Pedro de Alvarado and another captain led the rear guard, to protect our *tamanes* with our baggage. Between this rear guard and Cortés' group were to march the soldiers of Narváez, several hundred Tlascalans, and thirty Spanish soldiers charged with the protection of Malinche, the other Indian women, and our prisoner Cacama. I was one of these thirty soldiers, and Cortés said to me: "Guard Doña Marina well."

"I will," I answered fervently, and felt my face go hot as I remembered how I had guarded her before.

Before we left, Cortés had a great amount of gold and silver and precious objects brought and piled high in the greatest hall of the palace. The King's Fifth he placed in charge of two men named as king's officers, who were given half a dozen horses no good for fighting. He then had his secretary and the royal notary bear witness to the fact that he could do nothing about the removal of the rest of the gold. "Since it cannot be placed in safety, I now give it to any soldiers who care to take it. Otherwise, it will be left for these dogs of Aztecs."

I could guess his double intention: to reward us in a way that would raise our spirits vastly and also to satisfy his animosity toward Velásquez by letting his share of gold augment this gift to us.

The soldiers of Narváez were wild with joy, having given up any hope of the rewards Cortés had enticed them with, and swarmed to the great heap of ingots. I went, too, and picked one up. It was very heavy. El Galán cried, "No, no, Arturo! Look!" And he held out to me the wooden box he had, containing six of the

green *chalchihuites* that the Indians prized far above
gold. "Look for these," he whispered, "or any other
gems Cortés and the captains may have missed." I saw
his wisdom and at once found two more *chalchihuites*.
Juan Morla had apparently found another trove of
them, for I saw him secrete something green in the top
of his helmet, which he then strapped firmly under his
chin. But I could not entirely resist the heavy gold
when I found three wide bracelets; I fastened them on
my left arm. My gold necklace from Cortés was already
around my neck. I went pawing feverishly through the
rapidly diminishing mound of wealth hoping to find
more *chalchihuites,* but came upon something even
better lying beside a gold ingot. It was an emerald bigger than my thumbnail. Thrilling with joy at this find, I
tucked it into my pocket along with the two pieces of
carved jade. As I did, a body shoved me aside and a
hand reached down for the ingot. I heard a grunt and
turned and saw one of the Narváez recruits add it to
the stack of ingots he clasped against his chest; he was
bent slightly forward by their weight. "Don't be a fool,"
I said. "We've got miles to march tonight. You won't
even make it as far as the causeway if you load yourself up like a burro." But he only gave me an idiot's grin
and asked me if I were jealous of his luck. A big, burly
fellow, he evidently counted on his bull strength to get
him through. Later I saw he had put the gold in two
cloth sacks attached by a rope slung around the back of
his neck and hanging down like panniers at either side.
This left both hands free, but with the weight of his
armor and the gold he moved no faster than a giant
snail, burdened by a fortune that only speed and a good
sword arm would permit him ever to enjoy.

When we set out after dark for the Tacuba causeway
it seemed to me that the weather was conspiring with
us. The sky had clouded over entirely and the moonless,
starless night was black, hiding the glint of our steel.
Our horses' hooves were padded. No one spoke above
a whisper. Malinche was wrapped in her black hooded
cloak, and little Orteguilla sat on the rump of her gray

mare; thinking he might be called upon to guard her life, he showed me a dirk that he wore in his belt like a sword. I marched directly ahead of them, my more adequate blade ready to serve in the same cause.

When we were halfway across the great deserted square a heavier rain began to fall. We moved in careful silence along the deserted street whose houses Cortés had earlier burned. The Tlascalans with the bridge reached the causeway first, as planned, and put our bridge in place, and the first detachment crossed over safely. Cortés and a dozen captains followed. Suddenly, far behind us, an Aztec conch horn sounded. I had just crossed the bridge, Malinche and the dwarf behind me, when I heard many shrill cries like squadrons of Aztec warriors bearing down on us from the rear. Looking back, I saw that Malinche's gray mare was safely over the bridge. My pace quickened to a run and my heart began to pound. How glad I was not to be burdened by much gold! This race for life would go to the lightest laden. But a rift in the clouds let the moon gleam through for a moment to show me a terrible sight. The lake was alive with the dark shapes of dugout canoes closing in on the causeway from both sides. Then I heard piercing Aztec battle cries on the causeway ahead. We were surrounded.

All we could do was to thrust ourselves ahead toward where the soldiers of the van, led by Cortés and his captains, were battling their way through the oncoming Aztecs. Soon I was slashing out with my sword at the long lances prodding up at us from the canoes.

The moon had been swiftly swallowed by thick clouds. The rain began to fall more heavily, then lightning flared and a clap of thunder sounded in the sky directly above my head. Through these sounds came the mocking cries of the Aztecs and screams of pain from the wounded behind us. As I reached an open gap in the causeway where the Aztecs had removed the bridge, I realized it would be foolish to wait for our movable one, which Tlascalans and Spaniards to the rear were defending against the enemy and over which our forces were still passing. With some horror I looked down and saw that a sort of bridge existed in the gap ahead: the body of a horse, still floundering feebly, a number of bundles and boxes, and two dead men, gold-laden. I turned to tell Malinche she would have to abandon her mare, which could not make this crossing. A shock of horror hit me like a blow. Only the dwarf now rode on the animal's back, flattened forward to escape the arrows now being loosed at us from the canoes. "Where is she?" I howled at him over the increasing din.

"Here," she said, and came forward from the other side of the mare.

"No bridge!" I pointed ahead.

"I saw. What about Orteguilla?" She had to scream the query over the sounds from the enemy and our own soldiers: groans, prayers, curses.

"We'll pull him along between us, but hurry!" In a wave of energy, those behind us were surging forward, away from the pursuing Aztecs. I rushed back and lifted the dwarf off the mare. With Malinche holding one of his hands and I the other, we ran to the edge of the gap, where I let myself down onto the body of the dead or dying horse—which sank beneath my weight but then held firm, so that the water came only to my knees. I lifted down the dwarf and she followed and the three of us blundered forward across the horse, the bundles and boxes, and one of the dead men. The other had sunk, perhaps from the weight of his armor and his gold. At the other side I lifted Malinche and the dwarf up ahead of me and, just as I followed, a prodding lance from a canoe that had closed in on our right grazed my bottom. Once up, I slashed out at it with my sword and it fell in halves that lay on the belly of the dead horse.

As we three hurried forward, pushed from the rear by the others who had crossed the gap after us and stepping on the heels of the ones ahead, the rain came down heavier and thunder rolled our death knell; at last we reached the third gap in the causeway. In this one there were the bodies of many men, Tlascalans and

Spaniards, and to step on them like rocks in a river was terrible to do but my fear was so great that I did, pulling the dwarf and Malinche after me. But the bodies of the men did not give the support the horse had; one tilted under me and I plunged into the water, regretting every ounce of gold and every gem on my person. I found that the fundament of the causeway made the water in the gap less than four feet deep, so my head and shoulders were not submerged. I remembered to pull the dwarf up by one limp hand, and he bobbed to the surface gasping, his cap gone, his hair plastered to his head and his face like a frightened child's. But Malinche had vanished. I heaved the dwarf up onto the causeway and then waded back, calling her name. I submerged to feel about for her underwater, but all I felt was the breastplate of a sunken Spanish soldier. As I emerged for air, a heavy weight suddenly struck my upper back and pressed me forward and under the water again. It was the prow of a dugout canoe that had darted into the gap. I got my feet under me, standing on the drowned soldier, and, gathering all my strength into the pit of my abdomen, I straightened my body suddenly, tipped the canoe off my back and heard cries and splashing as it overturned, which gave me just enough time to wade to the shoreward side of the causeway and haul myself up, gasping and coughing up water. The dwarf was not there, vanished into the jumbled horde ahead. But I stayed where I was, calling her name, jostled by the men who waded the gap as I had, their faces set and eyes blank. But there was no sign of her. Still I tipped my head back and screamed her name out into the rain, again and again. Then a mass of frantic soldiers scrambled up from the water where I had last seen her and pressed me onward with their bodies and their terror, and I stumbled forward streaming rain and tears. I damned the dwarf, for if I had held onto Malinche's hand instead of his, she would have been the one saved.

A fork of lightning glared in the sky and I saw some Aztecs in a dugout canoe carrying off a Spanish soldier with them. As thunder crashed I realized that this is what might have happened to Malinche, and I damned God.

After that I do not remember anything very well, just pressing forward and hacking with my sword at the long Indian lances prodding up over the causeway's wall from the canoes massed below, blindly probing for flesh. My teeth chattered from fear and the cold rain. The next bridge we came to had not been removed, I suppose to give Aztecs on the mainland the chance to get at us. Many of their bodies clogged the causeway, twined curiously with those of fallen Spaniards.

Somehow I finally made it to shore. Just beyond the end of the causeway Cortés and some captains and soldiers were massed together under the dubious shelter offered by large trees. As I plodded toward them through the mud, Captain Olid cried out to Cortés that they must not abandon the foot soldiers still struggling to cross the causeway.

"It's a miracle that any of us escaped," Cortés said in a hollow voice.

My tongue was unable to tell him that Malinche had not. Agony seared through me. I reached the shelter of the trees and sank down onto the muddy ground, gasping. I did not care much at that moment that I was alive.

"Well, come on then, on to the damned causeway," I heard Cortés say, and he and some horsemen galloped down the slope to that accursed place to aid any survivors. I found I was thirsty and tipped my head back and opened my mouth and walked out from under the trees and let the rain fall into my gullet as if it might ease my grief as well as my thirst.

In a very short time Cortés and the captains returned with what was left of the rear guard: Alvarado and four Spaniards and nine Tlascalans. Alvarado was on foot, his sorrel mare having been killed under him by lance thrusts stabbing up into its belly from the canoes. He carried with him a long spear he had wrested from one of the Aztecs and had used to vault over the last gap in the causeway. "He flew right over my head," said one of the soldiers with him, "as if he had wings, and landed on the other side." Blood flowed down his face and Alvarado's was bloodied, too.

"Now," Alvarado said, "the gaps in the causeway are choked with bodies. And gold. And the body of Juan Velásquez de Leon, and many other men from my own company."

"And Malinche," I said, walking toward where he stood looking up at Cortés, still mounted.

"Malinche?" Alvarado said. "Doña Marina? Doña Marina is dead?"

"Drowned, or captured by the Aztecs." As I choked out the words, tears sprang to my eyes. Cortés was staring down at me. Rain streamed down his face. "Let us hope she drowned," he said in a drear, heavy voice. I knew he meant that this fate was to be preferred to her capture, for what would lie in store for the woman who had been his tongue was beyond imagination. Stoically I waited for his wrath to strike me, charged as I had been with her protection. His left hand, wrapped in a bloodsoaked rag, drew up as though to slash backhanded across my upturned face, but then fell. Knowing as he did the horror of our escape, it was beyond him to fix blame. There writhed through my head, straight from Satan's hell, hideous images of Malinche strapped to a sacrificial altar and waiting the descent of a stone knife, her body perhaps then flayed in honor of the idol called Xipe, and her lithe young being all dismembered, legs here, arms there, later to be eaten by the priests and their favorites. "God forgive me!" I cried aloud. "God help me!" Without forethought I turned and ran back toward the causeway, as if by traversing its length to where I had last seen her I might find her alive.

As I reached it I saw something crawling toward me. I ran toward it and knelt down. Juan Morla, his face nearly severed in half by a gash that had taken out one eye, had somehow made it to shore. He inched closer and with a sigh rolled onto one side and rested his bleeding head on my thigh.

"Helmet," he croaked. "Take off." A flash of lightning showed me his one eye looking up just as it froze in the sudden vacant stare of death I had come to know so well. His mouth dropped open, there was a rattling in his throat, and blood came out. "Poor Juan," I said aloud in a voice like a little boy's. Mechanically I obeyed his last request and undid the strap of his helmet and pulled it free from under his dropped bloody chin and the thick black beard that seemed to cling to it. As I removed the helmet I heard something clink inside it and remembered when he had put it there. I reached in and felt something large, cold, and very hard. Another glare of lightning showed me what I held in my palm. It was too clear for jade. It was an emerald, nearly as broad as my hand, carved into the shape of a squatting frog. As thunder crashed I closed my hand around it, numb with awe. I knew I held a king's ransom. Malinche was dead, and God knew how many Spaniards and Tlascalans, and probably my friend El Galán. But I held in my hand a thing of much more value than all the gold I had dreamed about in Cuba.

Kneeling there in the rain, I cried like a little child.

With a dead man's head on my lap I heard a voice from the tomb and saw El Galán limping toward me, bareheaded and streaming rain. I had just put on my helmet, Juan Morla's emerald inside it. I went to embrace my friend, filled with such joy at seeing him alive that it was hard to believe I had been weeping only moments before. He went to where Juan lay, looked down at him sadly, crossed himself, bent, and picked up Juan's helmet and put it on.

The voice of Cortés called us then to form ranks to begin the long march to Tlascala. He had dismounted and stood under one of the dark trees by the lakeshore. We straggled past him, the pitiful remnant of his army, lighted intermittently by those flares of malevolent brilliance the sky provided between rumblings of thunder. He stood stoic at first. But then, just as El Galán and I reached him, my limping friend stumbled on a stone and pitched forward, going down on his hands with one knee in the mud and letting out a groan of pain. I helped him to his feet, and then saw Cortés standing with one mailed arm covering his eyes, his body leaning against the tree trunk, and I heard his sobs.

It made me fearful to see him weep, but in a moment he mastered his emotion. He straightened and came several steps toward us. Lightning glared on his gaunt face streaming with rain and tears, white as if carved from marble, with terrible burning eyes. His voice was loud and hollow. "It appears that evil has triumphed this night, but we must still have faith in God's power." Then meat and blood and hope came back into his voice. "Satan will not have the final victory!" I heard it as a promise he was making to himself and God.

We sent up a ragged cheer; he called to one of the captains and said that El Galán was to ride a lamed horse that was no good for fighting. As I marched through mud with the tatters of our army I could feel the weight of the emerald frog atop my head and tried to comfort myself with visions of future wealth and power, although any future at all seemed very uncertain.

Our Tlascalans led us along the little-traveled route they knew, avoiding the main road where our enemies might look for us. We marched several weary miles along a muddy footpath and at last came to a hill with a huddle of empty houses at its base and atop it a sizable deserted temple. Exhausted as we were, we halted there to rest and care for our many wounded. Climbing the stone stairs, I remembered all the previous temple stairs we had mounted and all the idols we had destroyed. But here there were none. A thick layer of dust showed that for reasons unknown deities, priests, and people had left this place a long time before. In the empty buildings below, our Tlascalans found some stacks of wood and in the spacious room atop the pyramid Sandoval made a good fire in the central hollow of the sacrificial altar. Even if we had had food we could not have eaten, for we had all reached that point beyond exhaustion where the belly's wants do not matter. Kneeling, we wept for our dead and prayed for their souls. I secretly prayed that whatever happened to Malinche, she would not be sacrificed to pagan gods, she who had so sweetly and sincerely turned from them to Jesus.

It was then that the awful reality of her death struck me as it had not before. I remembered her face as I first saw it in the sunlight at Tabasco, saw again the terror in her eyes when I captured her, and the gentle look as she cleansed my shoulder wound. Once again in rags of seaweed she stood like Aphrodite risen from the sea, and then I saw her barbaric figure below the white cross on the dune. In the tent of Cortés she denied betrayal in an impassive voice. I closed my eyes to recapture that sweet passion in the treasure room we thought our tomb, but the pain of that memory was too great and I groaned aloud. To deny the truth that her warm flesh was cold or soon would be, I created a future: again she returned to Cuba with me as my bride, and I imagined a house for us on the cliff by the sea where she slept beside me in my bed and woke me mornings saying, as my mother always did, "God has sent us another sunny day, that we may do His work and ours."

I was roused from this waking dream by the wan voice of Padre Olmedo. He stood at the far end of the room with the friar Casas and Aguilar and several other churchmen looking sadly out over our huddled and recumbent bodies, and he read from the sheet of paper in his hands the names of some of the dead and captured: Juan Velásquez de Leon, Francisco Saucedo, and Sedeño, in whose caravel I had sailed, and Francisco de Morla, Juan Morla, and Gonzalo the traitor, and Yago the acrobat, and the Three Moors, and Orteguilla the page, and Cacama, our prisoner, and the other prisoners with him, and Botello the astrologer, and all the Indian women; oh, the list was long. "And, most sadly, the excellent Doña Marina, who has been of such great help to us." Aguilar, who was standing with clasped hands and downcast eyes, raised his head then to look at me with sorrow.

The pallid secretary of Cortés, shaking like an old man with the palsy, estimated the Spanish dead at nine hundred forty and the Tlascalan dead at two thousand. Of the soldiers who had come with Narváez, almost all had lost their lives on the causeway or been captured, weighted down with too much gold. Of our ninety-eight horses, only twenty-three were left us, some of them wounded. The cannons and artillery and all ammunition were gone. We had a dozen sound crossbows, though not many arrows. These were the conditions under which we had to try to make our way to Tlascala. Even if we managed to, we did not know how we would be received there. They had admired us as victors; now we were the vanquished.

As night paled to dawn additional sentinels were posted on the upper level of the pyramid to watch for Aztecs. I was one. A few clouds to the east flushed to a pale pink. As the orb of the sun rose above the mountains I was thinking how clever I had been to hide my two emeralds inside the leather padding of my breastplate. The frog was pressing hard against my chest, reassuring me that if I managed to stay alive I would go home rich.

A faint sound distracted me from this pleasant thought. It was the insistent throbbing of a distant drum. It came from the direction of Tenochtitlán. I stared at the risen sun in horror. If Malinche had not drowned or been killed, then she would surely walk up the steps of the war god's pyramid. At this very moment her heart could be cupped in the bloody upraised hands of an Aztec priest. This morning sunlight would shine down on it and her dead face just as it was shining on me. I closed my eyes and covered my ears, but still I heard that slow drum beating, beating.

PART VII

▼▼

THE VANQUISHED
AND VICTORIOUS
July 1, 1520–December 25, 1520

35

Of the *noche triste* escape on the causeway I saw little. At the second gap of water where the Aztecs had removed the bridge, our makeshift one was still behind us. I had to abandon the gray mare on which Orteguilla was riding with me, and Arturo took one of the dwarf's hands and I the other. He leaped down onto the wreckage clogging the shallow water, taking Orteguilla with him. I stared down at two dead Spanish soldiers and a dead horse, my steppingstones to safety. But at the third gap as I jumped down I felt the black cloak I was wearing wrenched tight around my throat, choking me, and knew that someone following close behind had stepped on its hem in the instant it lay on the causeway behind me. The hard tug threw me off balance. In the same second I unclasped the cloak, missed my footing, and plunged into the black water. I had glimpsed an Aztec canoe nosing into the gap from the other side, a warrior in it with spear raised. So I swam under water, away from the causeway, for as long as I could. When I surfaced, I saw by the glare of lightning a *chinampa* floating nearby.

Clinging to its edge with my head only far enough out of the water to breathe, I was grateful for its chance presence, but then realized that it might just as well drift back to Tenochtitlán as to the Tacuba shore I hoped to reach. For a long while I was deaf to the Aztec war cries and the screams of wounded Spaniards, desperately scanning both shores to see which seemed to

380

be getting closer. The rain worsened, big drops pock-marking the black water around me and finally agitating it to a frenzy like the one inside me as the *chinampa* drifted away from the causeway but no nearer either side of the lake.

Because of the cold the strength finally left my hands, so I held onto the coarse basketry *chinampa* rim with my teeth, tasting wet earth, smelling green plants growing just above my head. I reached up one numb hand, found a stem and plucked it, a green onion, very cold and strong. I ate it all; it was life I ate, the promise of survival. When I looked again toward the Tacuba shore, it seemed closer.

I lost all sense of time, clinging with numb hands or my teeth. Finally one of my feet brushed lake bottom. Ahead was a thicket of reeds out of which a duck paddled toward me, then veered away. The *chinampa* glided in among the reeds. I was safe.

Pushing my way through the reeds in water up to my hips, I stood at last on firm wet earth, hidden by canes nearly as tall as I. The causeway was a long distance to my right. I did not know how many Aztecs might be rounding up strays between. Their war cries were few and faint. The rain had stopped. In the rifts between moving clouds a few stars gleamed.

Avoiding the lakeshore road above me I made my slow way through the reeds toward Tacuba. After an hour or so I heard, in the thicket ahead, voices speaking Nahuatl with the accent peculiar to Tlascalans. As I neared I distinguished, to my joy, the voice of Doña Luisa praying aloud that God would continue to save them from the Aztecs. When she saw me she screamed; a Tlascalan warrior put his hand over her mouth. She and a few other of the women had been brought safely over the causeway, and the Tlascalans had decided to hide themselves rather than search for those Spaniards who had managed to get across alive. A scout had just returned from the Tacuba end of the causeway to report that there was no sign of any living Spaniard. Certainly the captains had been able to get across be-

fore all the bridges were removed by the Aztecs, and
some foot soldiers too, but where were they now?

My mind was not working well, but I reminded them
that Cortés intended to march back to Tlascala, and
not through Cholula; they decided on the route he
would have taken. And so we set forth, a straggling
band of refugees, fearful of being fallen upon at any
moment by Aztecs still lurking along the shore. Just
before sunrise we saw ahead a small hillside town. The
first rays of the sun glinted on the armor of the Spanish
sentinels patrolling the upper level of its temple. Was
Cortés alive? Arturo? Orteguilla? Aguilar? It suddenly
seemed to me that if I found them to be dead or
prisoners of the Aztecs, the life God had chosen to
spare would have little worth to me. My past anger at
Cortés, my criticism of him, now seemed childish: this
night had proved that he had dealt with a people so
bloodthirsty that even as the Spaniards had obeyed the
request of the Aztec priests to leave the city, the warriors had been unable to resist the urge to kill and to get
prisoners for their war god.

The Tlascalans had one of their white crane banners
and held it aloft so the Spaniards might not take us for
Aztecs and shoot down on us. As we reached the town
wall I heard the faint booming of a distant drum telling
me the grim destiny of prisoners the Aztecs had taken.
Then one of the sentries shouted "Let them enter!
They're Tlascalans!"

As we crossed the plaza to the foot of the pyramid I
looked down at my mud-caked skirt, my tunic smelling
of lakewater and sweat. "Malinche!" a glad voice called.
Arturo Mondragon was leaping down the steep stone
steps, his face alight. "You're alive!" he whispered in
a choked voice.

"And Cortés?" I asked.

"Alive."

My heart beat again. "And Orteguilla? Did you manage to save him?"

"No better than I saved you," he said bitterly.

"God did that." I told him about the *chinampa* as

we went up the steps of the temple. At the top the sun's rays lighted his face; the drum, which had briefly stopped, began its throbbing again. "Poor little Orteguilla," I said. In spite of his clever mind his tiny body had doomed him to die.

Arturo saw my grief. "If he was taken prisoner, maybe Cuitlahuac will pardon him since he was Moctezuma's friend."

False hope. The dwarf had had little chance to survive that frenzied rout on the causeway amid men blind with terror. And a Spaniard was a Spaniard to Cuitlahuac.

Behind me a crow squawked "Madonna!" I whirled. Cortés had emerged from the doorway of the temple. "My Doña Marina!" he cried again in a voice choked with emotion. His face spoke of a miracle and he came toward me, arms outspread. I ran to him. They closed around me. That embrace of cold steel was more thrilling than if his naked body had pressed close to mine. "Thank Jesus and the saints for giving you back to me!" He held me away and his eyes drank in my face as if it were not taut with exhaustion. His hand came up to touch my cheek. He arrested the motion in midair and swiftly lowered it, but I saw the gory bandage and its shape. He had lost two fingers, the smallest and the one next. It was his left hand, his sword hand.

I gasped. Smiling down he said, "A small matter. I can learn to use the other."

By then captains and soldiers had poured out to surround us. With his arm around me Cortés told them, "Doña Marina has been returned to us, and that augurs well for the immediate future. Now I will be able to parley intelligently with the Tlascalans."

I suffered a flicker of doubt that his joy at seeing me alive had been untainted by practical considerations, then scorned myself for the thought. Of course he needed to use anything he could to encourage the men left alive! Proof of his affection soon followed: he delayed the march, risking discovery by Aztec scouts, so that I and the rest who had had no sleep at all the night

before could recover somewhat from our exhaustion
before setting out. A bundle of mantles and robes had
somehow been brought across the causeway by a
dogged *tamane,* and Cortés had a bucket of water
brought from the town's cistern so I could wash the
mud from my body. When I was clean and dressed in
dry clothes I felt less weary. The other women and I
curled up on mantles in a corner of the inner temple to
rest an hour, and Cortés himself came to wake me,
bending to whisper in my ear "In Tlascala we will take
our joy together, and what an end to the journey
ahead!" I opened my eyes and looked up into his and
knew that the last shred of alienation from him was
gone forever, a feather in the wind.

Before we left the temple a small band of Aztecs besieged it, but the dozen crossbowmen made every arrow
tell; those Aztecs who were not killed ran off in fear.

The march to Tlascala took one frightful week.
Cortés gave me one of the horses to ride, though telling me that in case any battle threatened I would have
to give it to one of the captains. It was a stallion,
strong-mouthed and large, and I regretted the loss of
my mare and ached to think of the poor thing abandoned by me on the causeway. I told myself that the
Aztecs would not kill her but would keep her alive as
a curiosity and imagined a pleasant future for her as a
new member of the garden zoo.

That first day we marched until sundown, then
camped and slept with no incident to wake us. The
next day we were harassed by warriors from a town
we had to pass, but this happened on open land where
the cavalry could move freely, and at sight of the
horses our attackers gave up and ran away. A dozen
soldiers were sent out to scavenge for food and found a
field of ripe melons and one of maize, so that night
everyone had food, if not much. The next day Cortés
easily captured a small Indian town, its inhabitants
fleeing as we approached, and we rested there a full
day and ate well. But the next day our Tlascalan guides

kept losing the trail we followed, so we made slow progress, camping that night in the hills at the edge of a wide plain. In the morning we saw some Indians atop a nearby hill; seeing us they quickly vanished. Cortés and several horsemen reconnoitered to see what lay beyond. A large city stood in the plain ahead; Indians were swarming out of it toward us. A Tlascalan said the name of the city was Otumba, long loyal to the Aztecs.

"Oh Tomb?" said Cortés. "But not ours!"

As I watched from a hilltop the encounter that followed, I felt that he was wrong. The approaching warriors had slingshots, which they used very well, wounding Cortés on the face. How could so few Spanish and Tlascalan soldiers, so many of them already injured, hope to battle a whole city full of fresh enemies? Yet I knew we could not go back. Our route to Tlascala lay across that open plain.

Fortunately, the sight of the horses alarmed the first group of warriors enough so that they withdrew, but they first killed one of the horses. Cortés had some soldiers drag it back to our camp, where it was butchered, cooked, and eaten that night. The meat and broth seemed to give the soldiers new strength to face what we saw the next morning. The enemy had decided on a pitched battle there on the plain. Thousands of them were massed around their various caciques, each marked by an elaborate headdress and by a standard carried high behind him.

They had never seen a Spanish cavalry charge.

Cortés had no cannons or muskets, but he had twenty unwounded horses and ordered them prepared for battle. His plan was simple: charge and return, charge and return. Prime targets: the caciques.

I know that the soldiers must have felt that they had come to their last day on earth on seeing that enormous array of warriors, like bees defending their hive, and heard their derisive whistles and cries. But their very numbers told against them. They hemmed themselves in by their sprawling mass so that they could neither maneuver nor readily flee. The Spanish cavalry seemed to believe it was immortal. As the caciques fell, one after the other, under remorseless charges, I saw the ranks that had followed them begin to waver and break. The Spanish foot soldiers at first fought as only the doomed can, defensively, but when they saw Cortés' strategy begin to turn the tide, they seemed to become strong and filled with fresh spirit. They knew that every blow they struck was just and fulfilled God's desire that their dead and cruelly sacrificed Christian comrades should now be avenged. Does not the Bible tell us that God can be a God of wrath?

The Tlascalans also fought like avenging angels, but the son of Xicotencatl the Elder fell that morning; he obeyed Cortés' order and wore no plumes that would distinguish him to the enemy, but he fell anyway. Doña Luisa wept for her brother. As I comforted her she told me that her father would be very sad. "He loved my brother who is dead much better than the son who bears his name." My mood, raised by the extraordinary spectacle of the Spanish triumph over the Otumbans, plummeted. How would Xicotencatl, over ninety and too old to beget more sons, feel toward Cortés on learning of the death of this one? Our only hope was his continued friendship.

But this mood passed in my admiration for Cortés. Even though I learned that the Otumba warriors had been joined that day by others from the nearby town of Tepeyac, Cortés defeated them that July seventh, although he left on the battlefield the blood and bodies of many Spaniards, so that his army was reduced to four hundred once again. After the enemy retreated across the plain the soldiers and all of us knelt and gave thanks to God. But it was clear to me, having observed the whole battle as I did, spread out like a great chessboard, that much though our Saviour had surely aided Cortés, it was the horses that had made so few able to conquer so many. Those brave, magnificent beasts merited all the awe I ever felt for them. To the defeated Otumbans they must have seemed creatures out of the apocalypse long foretold.

The next day, hungry and limping, we reached Tlascala.

My relief was great when three minor Tlascalan caciques came out to meet us and offer food and shelter in a nearby town. The people there received us well enough, but then demanded payment of the soldiers for food and shelter. Cortés was disturbed to learn that El Galán paid one of his *chalchihuites* to their hosts, Arturo giving him a gold bracelet to pay for his share. But they were so glad to have a comfortable place to sleep and bathe and food to eat that they did not complain, and said that the women of the house were washing their clothing and had given them *nequen* robes to wear. Arturo Mondragon, for some reason, had on his breastplate over his, which Cortés said, smiling, made him look like a Roman soldier. But even as he joked I knew he was wondering about the feelings of Xicotencatl the Elder. How would he treat us when he learned that his beloved son was among the devastating list of other dead compatriots? We already knew that the avarice of these townspeople showed that they saw Cortés as no returning hero, which meant that news of the *noche triste* had already filtered over the Tlascalan wall.

When several soldiers ran up to say that Xicotencatl the Elder was approaching the town with his retinue, I took a deep breath and readied myself for the interview that would decide our fate. Cortés looked grim as he and I followed the soldiers to the edge of town to meet the man most revered in all Tlascala.

As he approached us, gray head high, sunlight on his closed sunken eyelids, I marveled at his dignity. Although two nobles walked at either side, they did not support him. He walked alone, a long staff reaching out occasionally to touch the ground lightly. On his spare but still muscular body the simple straw-colored *nequen* toga looked as regal as any of Moctezuma's rich garments had.

His attendants told him that Cortés and I stood before him. Behind us were massed the Spanish soldiers and captains who had followed; I knew they were holding their breaths. The blind ruler spoke.

"How grieved I am at your misfortune, Cortés, and for the death of your men, and for our many Tlascalan soldiers killed with yours! But we do not hold it a small thing that you have escaped with your lives from that impregnable Aztec city. We always knew you were brave, but now we think you even more valiant. And though many women in Tlascala will weep for the deaths of their sons, husbands, brothers, and kinsmen, that is not for you to trouble about. Now you must rest, for you are home. Soon you will come to my city, where we will find you comfortable quarters and where you are welcome as long as you want to stay."

Cortés embraced and thanked him, deeply moved. But then he had to be told about the death of his son. "Tell him he died fighting bravely," Cortés reminded me.

When I did, the old ruler nodded. "I know that."

As the captains and soldiers cheered him, I began to wonder where the younger Xicotencatl was. Once he had sworn to Cortés his lifelong friendship, yet now did not bother to greet him.

The next day we went to the capital where the warm welcome of the citizens showed beyond any doubt that these Tlascalans were truly Cortés' allies and friends. We were housed in the same buildings as before, where sleeping mats were already provided for every soldier. The only sadness that marked our return was the death of the four most severely wounded soldiers, who did not recover from Otumba. "Oh, Tomb for them," Cortés said sadly, "and God rest their souls." But soon he was less sad. Our bone-deep exhaustion had passed and that night we found again the joy we had not known for so long. I knew that God meant us to be together always, for why else would such ecstasy lift us beyond mere earth, mere flesh?

The night after our arrival was a beautiful one, a full moon and a splendor of stars. Cortés and I went walking together, celebrating the unaccustomed peace that surrounded us here. We happened to pass a group of soldiers sprawled under a tree in a small garden or park. Unseen, Cortés paused to listen to them. It was a pepper tree, and its long fronds were like a screen. I heard Arturo's voice say "Cortés will let us rest here awhile, and then we'll march to Vera Cruz. I have hopes of returning soon to Cuba."

El Galán said, "You're hoping for the impossible. Cortés is not going to leave for Cuba until he hears from Carlos. Not a word of thanks for that treasure ship! In my opinion we can blame Fonseca. He rules the Council of the Indies, and he's a friend of Velásquez. I admit it angers me that all we have done and suffered does not seem to have moved our monarch to regard us favorably, but then who can hope to understand kings?"

Arturo said, "Well, at any rate, we will not soon be forgotten in Tenochtitlán. Their remote descendants will hear legends about the time we came and nearly conquered them."

"To me that is worth exactly the dung of a sick duck," another soldier said in disgust.

"Less to me," Cortés whispered. He was staring at nothing. His bitter tone made me momentarily uneasy. I think that was when he began to conceive his incredible plan.

"You should be glad you're alive, Rafael," Arturo said.

"You didn't lose half an ear," Rafael answered.

Another voice I did not recognize spoke of a more crucial loss, and hearing the blunt language Cortés hurried me away. I smiled to myself. After what I had seen and lived through, how could he believe me so delicate as to be offended by a word referring to male anatomy? But I knew then that he wished to believe I was; Spaniards like to endow their women with a Madonna's purity while requiring them to bear children and otherwise accommodate male desires.

"But failure is not a permanent state," Cortés said, more to himself than to me.

36

During the next three weeks I learned that nothing in this life is to be surely counted on, people least of all. The younger Xicotencatl, who had sworn eternal friendship and had helped raise up an army of thousands to march with us, was now going about saying that the Tlascalans should kill us and make friends with Cuitlahuac, the victor. Hearing of this, his old father rebuked him and said it was infamous to scheme against us when we had come back so sorely defeated, but even worse to set at naught the nation's century of independence from the Aztecs. But his son defied him, insisting that the shrewd move was to make friends with them. Then, old and blind though he was, the elder Xicotencatl went to his son and tore his mantle from his shoulder, a great disgrace. The other nobles and caciques present seized Xicotencatl the Younger and threw him down the steps of the palace and would have killed him except that his father forbade this.

Thus it was that Tlascala remained loyal to us, which was fortunate in view of what Cortés now had in mind.

With sleep and good food, the soldiers' wounds healed well in that clear mountain air. After the men had enjoyed three weeks of comfort and abundance, Cortés had his crier call them all together in the main square of the city, and from the steps of a temple he told his plan: to march against the Aztec garrison of Tepeyac to the southeast of us. "For their ruler Moctezuma swore an oath of allegiance to King Carlos of Spain, but they sent soldiers against us at Otumba, and therefore they are traitors and shall be punished."

I could not believe my ears. He had three hundred ninety-six defeated Spaniards—fewer, counting the maimed. Take a town?

"I have already sent back to Vera Cruz for powder, crossbows, a cannon there, and some muskets, as well as the crews of the Narváez ships there," Cortés said robustly. "And Xicotencatl the Elder promises me a strong fighting force." Cries of dissension arose; he waited them out. "But such is the spirit and heroism of my Old Guard, you who have been with me from the start, that I do not have any doubt of the outcome of this little foray. The enemy will meet us in numbers on open ground as at Otumba, and our cavalry will carve up their chiefs, and our staunch foot soldiers will let light into their bellies, and we will have a triumph on our hands." It was Alvarado, face rosy from the summer sun, who sent up a cheer, only faintly echoed.

"And we need this victory," Cortés said urgently. "We need it for the sake of our consciences, our very souls. I cannot feel that Otumba alone has sufficiently avenged our dear comrades whom the Aztecs killed and sacrificed and cannibalized."

I saw that as always he had hit on the right note to move his men as he wished. Any soldier who had lived through what they had could not help but be gnawed by a degree of guilt concerning the dead.

I watched them set out for Tepeyac and was heartened by the turnout of four thousand fresh Tlascalan warriors marching twenty abreast in white and red, drums beating, conch shells blowing, white crane banners bright in the sun. Crossbows and a good supply of arrows had arrived from Vera Cruz, though no cannon.

The Narváez mariners Cortés had promised his men were only six in number.

The dismal feeling that Cortés might not come back to me kept recurring as I waited the outcome of the Tepeyac assault. It had seemed particularly sinister that Cortés had opted not to take me with him, saying that Sandoval would serve well enough as interpreter. This told me that he knew the danger was very great. Doña Luisa's effort to comfort me only revealed her secret certainty that Cortés' ambition had led him astray; she assured me that I was like a sister to her, and that even if the worst happened I would have a home in Tlascala to the end of my days. But this was not to be my destiny.

As Cortés had foreseen, the defenders of Tepeyac repeated the mistake of the warriors at Otumba and came out in great numbers to fight on open ground. Even with only seventeen horses, the cavalry cut their leaders down, and the foot soldiers attacked the demoralized rank and file. Only four Spaniards were seriously wounded and only three Tlascalans were killed. Cortés took the town and named it Villa de Segura de la Frontera. By way of example to other towns loyal to Cuitlahuac, Cortés had all the conquered inhabitants branded on the arm with a *G* for *guerra*, meaning that they were war prisoners and the property of King Carlos of Spain. They were then sold as slaves to the soldiers, the money thus raised intended to be offered to the Spanish monarch as proof of yet another victory.

The auction had the effect of informing Cortés that almost all the soldiers had managed to get some gold out of Tenochtitlán, though not in the greedy and foolish amounts attempted by too many of the Narváez men. And so he had a proclamation read to the effect that all gold must be turned over to him and that three-fifths of it would be returned to each owner after the King's Fifth and his own had been subtracted. I knew that he was deeply upset that a great portion of the share due the king had been lost on the *noche triste,* but still I was incredulous at his daring this. I decided he must be playing a game with himself to see how far he could take advantage of his men and still command their devotion.

Naturally this request aroused the anger of the soldiers. They protested that since Cortés had told them to take the gold on the *noche triste,* any they had was a free gift. Since the captains all had taken gold too, they took the soldiers' side. The proclamation was ignored, and Cortés dropped the matter. He was philosophical, even somewhat amused. "I'm glad to see they've got their spirit back. It proves that Tepeyac had just the effect on them I wanted."

It was as though that triumph had turned the tide of Cortés' luck. He soon learned that two ships had put into Vera Cruz loaded with arms, gunpowder, and other stores intended for the Narváez expedition, its fate being still unknown in Cuba as a result of Cortés' prompt dismantling of all its fleet. The captain in charge at Vera Cruz went aboard one, lured the captain ashore, then arrested him in the name of Cortés. He took the matter gracefully and was brought to Cortés along with his men. It turned out he was an old friend, Pedro Barba, the commandant of Havana. The governor had commanded his services; he seemed not unhappy at this outcome. Cortés embraced him and made him captain of the crossbowmen, a considerable honor. On learning his identity, Arturo Mondragon came to our palace to see him and to ask about his family in Havana. Don Pedro was very much surprised at the change in him and said his own mother would not know him now. The news of Arturo's family was good, I was glad to know.

But Barba brought other news that was alarming; smallpox had been brought to Vera Cruz by a big Negro who had arrived with Narváez and who had died of it. Now it was spreading rapidly, a real plague. Indians, he said, seemed particularly affected by this disease, apparently carried from person to person by some mysterious means. A good many of our friendly Totonacs had died of it in both Zempoalla and Quiahuiztlán. And it was now rampant also among the Aztecs of the coast. "A fair return," he said, "for the syphillis Spaniards got from the Indians of Hispaniola and Cuba." Cortés debated this point, saying he thought it was the other way around.

The arrival of the smallpox proved another piece of good luck for Cortés. He soon learned that it had reached Tenochtitlán, perhaps with one or more of the captured Narváez men. The reign of Cuitlahuac proved a very short one: he died of it. The new Aztec ruler was Cuauhtemoc.

This meant little to me, for I thought that the triumph at Tepeyac had assuaged Cortés' bitter humiliation of the *noche triste*. He had struck a last blow at the forces of Satan, and when he next wrote to the Spanish monarch, as I was sure he would, he could report a victory wrenched from total defeat.

For the first time since I had known Cortés, our life was without immediate stress. No danger surrounded us on all sides, unacknowledged yet omnipresent. Used as I had been to that dark ambience, the sunlit present as honored guests of admirable people found me creating a worry to replace the past ones I evidently missed.

That worry was that Cortés would grow weary of waiting for word from King Carlos and would decide to return to the West Indies and present his case in person to the Royal Audience at Santo Domingo. This soon extended itself to the idea that he might even decide to cross the ocean to Spain itself, seek out his ungrateful sovereign, convince him of the great value of the new colony he had founded in his name. But whether he went to the one place or the other, was it likely that he would take me with him?

I was sure now that he loved me well, that my usefulness as interpreter took second place to my importance to him as a woman. On the rare occasions when I thought of that one strange night in the treasure vault, I could recall it only dimly, like a dream that has nearly faded away. My strongest feeling concerning it was gratitude that the urgent matter of his dangerous insult to Moctezuma had taken immediate precedence over some possible selfish desire to clear my conscience by confession, forcing him to share the burden of my sin. I knew that it was not likely that he had always been faithful to me, either. During the Narváez campaign he might well have eased himself with one of the Indian women the fat cacique had given him, for—as I knew—danger always aroused his desire. But these were small matters now. All we had been through together had made us very easy with one another, as a husband and wife can be, I thought.

His actual wife in Cuba was unreal to me. I knew by then that like many Spanish husbands he viewed her as a bond he could not shed but which need not too much inhibit him. But with my hidden fear that he would decide to leave New Spain, Doña Catalina assumed large proportions in my mind. I did not believe that he would choose to bring back with him to the West Indies an Indian mistress. My nagging worry that he might soon leave me, and for a long, unendurable time, began to invade my dreams: I, like a luckless *soltera* no man had ever loved, draped in a black rebozo like Doña Luisa's, walked in the marketplace and bought food I would eat alone. Or awaiting Cortés in Tlascala I learned from a sad-faced Doña Luisa that he was never going to return.

On the day I revealed to Cortés my secret fear, he and I were alone in the garden of the palace where we lived, I with my embroidery, which he liked to see me do because that was what Spanish ladies like his mother did. He had on one of the *nequen* robes Xicotencatl had given him. We were taking our ease before our afternoon siesta, a Spanish custom in which he could now indulge. I was kneeling on the grass, which he did not like but which was more comfortable for me than the stone bench on which he sat. We had spoken idly of a number of small matters, but for all his appearance of indolence, I knew he was preoccupied; at such times his left leg, crossed over the right, would swing in small impatient jerks, while his eyes roved over objects around him, not really seeing them but rather his own inner visions. With the forefinger of his maimed left hand he began to smooth one of the lines across his forehead again and again, as if to erase both it and all memory of the past anxieties that had put it there, and which might, if remembered, overload him with caution.

All these signs made me sure he was planning to leave me, and suddenly I could not contain my anxiety any longer. I pushed the bone needle through the square of cotton cloth, completing the last stitch in the blue wing of a bird. "When you go, will you take me with you?" I raised my eyes to catch his surprise that I had guessed his thoughts.

"Of course," he said, surprised. "I will need you there."

"In the West Indies, or in Spain?" I was filled with a sweet relief, yet pleased to let him know how well I knew what he had been thinking.

"Spain? The West Indies? What are you talking about?" He straightened and made a sweeping gesture toward the west. "I'm going to Tenochtitlán."

The needle stabbed my finger; I dropped the embroidery to the ground. And then I learned his ambitious plan: to send Barba to Jamaica to buy more horses. And to send to Spain yet another letter, pleading for Carlos' belated support. And to march once more to the Valley of Anahuac. And to build there a fleet of a dozen shallow-draft sloops to use on the lakes when he attempted to conquer Tenochtitlán!

The horror I felt was like pain. I gaped up; he smiled down as if he could already taste that triumph. He had gone mad! All virtues in excess become vices and can destroy: his excess of courage would now kill him. I stood up. "Do you want another *noche triste?* Or worse?"

He stood too, his smile gone. "With those ships I can dominate the lakes and besiege the city. I can cut the aqueduct."

"What ships? Ships of air? Do you think the Aztecs

will stand by and let you build a fleet on their lakeside?"

"First we will dominate one of the lakeside towns."

"Oh, a simple matter! And reeds are abundant. Reed ships? *Chinampas* with sails?"

"Xicotencatl will supply all the wood I need, and thousands of Indians to haul it to Anahuac. I have safely stored in Vera Cruz all the ironwork, sails, rigging, even nails from the fleet I sank there. Martín Llopez is an admirable shipwright. I have talked with him at length. He can train enough soldiers to turn out a dozen hulls, given the wood and the time." My resistance aroused his resentment. "Why am I justifying my plan to you? It's going to be done!"

"You cannot do it. No one could. The Aztecs are too powerful. You will have to fight your way there. You will not be able to hold one lakeside town against the might of all the rest."

"Listen to me! The Aztecs up there and the towns they have dominated, such as Texcoco, are undergoing upheavals they have not known in two centuries! The deposing and death of Moctezuma began it; the repercussions from such a momentous event don't die down in a few months or even years. Then their Cuitlahuac died of smallpox. To a superstitious people two such events are shattering. Omens! God knows what prophecies now abound. I tell you, those Aztecs are afraid they have slaughtered and driven out godlike beings: us!"

"All four hundred of you!" I cried derisively.

"Three hundred ninety-three. But I can count on Xicotencatl for thousands of Tlascalans, and they are brave men!"

"But why? Why? Even if you should succeed, do you imagine that even that would nudge awake your stupid, ungrateful king?"

He smiled at me coldly. "I did not conceive this idea to please Carlos. I am doing it to please Cortés! Defeat is defeat only if it is acknowledged as final. That is why the sun rises: to remind men that each day is new and full of promise if they will forget the night. *Noche triste* is now months in the past. And I swear to you that God's Holy Cross is going to stand atop that Aztec temple of sacrifice, and God's sun shine down on it!"

I knew that nothing human would stop him. Moving slowly and without conscious knowledge of where my steps were taking me, I found myself kneeling before the simple wooden cross on the wall of our sleeping room. The little Virgin I had often prayed before had been a casualty of the departure Cortés was now determined to redress. But I closed my eyes and imagined Her there, and prayed that Cortés might be restored to sanity. "Do not let him attempt this! Do not let his courage kill him!"

"Praying, Doña Marina?" His hard voice spoke behind me. "For me? Better pray for the Aztecs. Even better, come to bed."

His hand fell on my shoulder. I looked up at him. He raised me to my feet and enfolded me, burying his lips in my throat. To be taken so suddenly from pain of mind and prayer to the edge of ecstasy numbed my protests and soon my fear. I remember how, after he was sleeping, I lay looking at the ray of sunlight that slanted into the room from a window and saw how motes of dust danced in it. I knew I had no more volition than one of those specks. My destiny was not mine any longer, and would never be again.

When we left for Tenochtitlán on the twenty-fifth of December I was all but certain that I was going to bear his child. I did not tell him this. I feared that he would insist that I stay safely behind in Tlascala. I preferred to face with him the dangers ahead. I knew I would endure those better than long months of waiting for word of his triumph or his death.

PART VIII

▼▼▼▼▼▼▼▼▼▼▼▼▼▼▼▼▼▼▼▼▼▼▼▼▼▼▼▼▼▼▼▼▼▼▼▼▼

THE FALL OF TENOCHTITLÁN
December 25, 1520–August 14, 1521

37

One night shortly before we left Tlascala I had a bad dream in which an Indian who looked like Cuauhtemoc stole my emerald frog. The next morning I went about the city until I found a stonemason and got from him some wet mortar of a very fine consistency. I took it to my room in the building where I was staying and when no one else was there I used it to fix my emeralds to the inside of my too-large breastplate, covering them first with a layer of fine cotton so they would not get scratched, then covering the whole with the mortar, packed firm and solid into the breastplate's central concave trough. The stuff dried like rock and stuck well to the metal. For the first time I knew that my gems were secure against any contingency but my death, and even then might be buried with me.

Only El Galán knew about them. I told him during our last steam bath in Tlascala so that if I were killed he could pry them out and eventually take them to my parents. He cocked an eyebrow at me and said, "Here I am at the end of my third campaign in this New World, about to begin another which may prove even more disastrous, and all I have to show is five *chalchihuites,* two gold necklaces, and a gold bracelet. And you, green as you are, come out of your first venture with an emerald as big as your fist! With luck like that, don't talk of dying." He added. "And trim that beard; it has a shabby look."

I remember that my hand went up to it and that

growth of hair felt strange to me. I had once yearned for its belated appearance, proof that I was as much of a man as any. Well, I had proved that often enough by now, and in another way. A curious sadness came over me as I thought of how much Indian blood I had spilled to write the affirmation *Arturo Mondragon y Flores is a man among men.* But did blood make a man? Did a beard? Or entering a woman? What is manhood? I looked at El Galán. Whistling through his teeth, he was briskly scrubbing his arm with a pad of cactus fiber. I found another and did the same. As I luxuriated in the herb-scented steam the pleasure of being alive inside a whole skin transcended my fleeting and unreasonable mood.

As we marched out of the Tlascalan capital the next morning I saw old Xicotencatl standing on the same stone balcony as before. Then I had marched toward Tenochtitlán as an innocent. Now I knew what we faced. Yet here I was, risking my skin again. Drums beat, fifes played, and I put one foot in front of the other in time with all the rest. Again an army of Tlascalans followed us in hope of defeating their ancient enemy. Cortés had enchanted us all.

Some soldiers thought—or pretended to think—that the birthday of Our Saviour was an auspicious one to begin our campaign of vengeance against the Aztecs, but to me that was foolishness. No day is a good one to attempt the near-impossible.

It was after we reached Anahuac and had conquered several of the lakeside towns that Cortés' luck changed dramatically for the better. From Spain . . . *Spain* . . . came ships to Vera Cruz bringing arms, men, *hidalgos,* and horses! At long last, Carlos, now crowned Holy Roman Emperor, had apparently shifted his favor from Velásquez to Cortés! And so now we had a cavalry of eighty-six horses, a hundred eighteen crossbowmen and musketeers, more than seven hundred Spanish foot soldiers, and also three cannons, fifteen field pieces, and half a ton of gunpowder!

Nonetheless, the conquest of all the Aztec towns and

cities bordering the lakes took four long months. At Xochimilco, Cortés was nearly killed when his horse faltered; enemy warriors dragged him off its back and into the reeds and mud of the lakeshore, but several of the Old Guard managed to fight them off and save him. By this time we had taken Tacuba, and it was deserted, At a place called Chalco, which we took after hard fighting, we were saddened to find in the main temple the flayed faces of several Spaniards, the beards still on and the skin tanned like leather for gloves. Written on the stone wall of one of the prison cells was the message "Here miserably died Juan Yuste and his unfortunate companions." I had reason to remember Juan Yuste well; it was to him I had lost at cards my first little gold necklace. God knew who wore it now, but I wished him ill luck with it and prayed for poor Juan's soul.

God had spared the life of Martín Llopez the shipwright. It was after we took Ixtapalápa that we learned Cortés' astounding plan: this skilled craftsman, along with a work force of thousands of our Tlascalans, and with the aid of Nuñez the carpenter and another old lame carpenter named Ramirez, would build us a fleet of small, light-draft craft at the edge of Lake Texcoco. Cortés had already ordered sent up to us from Vera Cruz all the ironwork, rigging, sails, and anchors he had preserved from the ships he sank and burned there. Old Xicotencatl had readily agreed to supply us with all the wood we needed, which was being transported to us on the backs of some ten thousand Indians. By the time this wood was brought to us, we had marched and fought our way completely around the vast lakes.

We had expected most resistance at Texcoco. We were astonished when half a dozen messengers arrived in our camp, their banner lavishly adorned with shining disks of gold, bringing the news that Texcoco was surrendering. We marched there wary of a trap, but there was none. In the largest palace a group of nobles met us, dressed almost as grandly as Cacama had been. They revealed that they felt no further allegiance to

Tenochtitlán, and none to their own king. Malinche questioned them and learned that this ruler had murdered his brother, the former ruler, and with the support of Cuitlahuac had usurped his place. The man they wanted as their king was the youngest son of their late ruler, Nezahualpilli. He was quite willing to become a Christian and was baptized forthwith; the Christian name he chose was Don Hernán Cortés. Our commander was godfather at the ceremony.

The new Texcocan ruler offered us all the assistance within his power and also sent out messages to the surrounding peoples with whom he was friendly, telling them to accept our friendship and to become, as he, loyal vassals of our Castilian king. And he offered us many buildings in his city, where we established our headquarters.

Some of the Spaniards who had joined us were very young; with them I acted the hardened veteran. To one wide-eyed fellow with a wispy excuse for a mustache I boasted outrageously, but my pose as one of the heroes of a campaign that was now being talked of in Castile, Aragón, Cataluña, Granada, Andalusia, and all the not-yet firmly welded regions of Spain collapsed unexpectedly. The Church of Rome sent out to us a Franciscan with papal bulls offering to us soldiers absolution for all sins committed during our long struggle against the heathens. That night, in a palace of Texcoco, a most beautiful Mass was held and we soldiers entered singing, each holding a lighted candle. When the Host was passed and I tasted the bread and the wine and realized that now in the eyes of God I was clean of all the Indian blood I had shed, a dam broke behind my eyes and the tears cascaded down my cheeks and I could not hold back my sobs. And when the good father laid his hand on my head and said "God has forgiven you, my son," I took that to mean that the sin I had committed with Malinche was forgiven, too. And when at last I raised my head, all the candle flames were blurred by my tears and were glowing like flowers or stars.

I saw the young recruit I had boasted to regarding me strangely, but I did not care. I am glad I did not know what lay ahead.

Our little ships were launched, flags flying, after a Mass on Sunday, April 28. Thirteen sloops. With a fierce joy the soldiers and mariners on them went scudding across the wide lake after rowing a bit to catch the wind and overtook many dozens of Aztec canoes, which they sank, killing most of the occupants. Watching this first naval victory from the shore, we could see the causeway of Tacuba over which we had fled that bitter *noche triste,* and we cheered. Like a magician, I thought, Cortés had caused those ships he had destroyed to rematerialize here, just when and where he needed them. To the thousands of Indians and Spaniards who had labored to build them, and to the soldiers who had guarded them day and night, I am sure their presence did not seem miraculous at all.

Coming ashore elated, Cortés made one of his speeches to us. We now needed only to dominate the causeways and we could besiege and defeat Tenochtitlán, avenging our dead comrades and regaining all the treasures we had been forced to leave behind. He was sending messengers to Tlascala and also to Cholula and certain other regions, summoning their warriors for an all-out attack within ten days.

In five days the Tlascalans arrived, fifty thousand of them. It took them three days to enter the city of Texcoco, plumes waving, their white crane standards flying high. As they marched they chanted "Castile, Castile, Tlascala, Tlascala!" It was a very moving sight, a vast proof of loyalty.

Less than five weeks after this, Cortés had more than seventy-five thousand Indian warriors assembled at Texcoco, and two days later he paraded his army and issued battle orders. We would advance in three divisions: First, Alvarado with thirty horses, eighteen crossbowmen, a hundred fifty Spanish foot soldiers and twenty-five thousand Tlascalans. Then Captain Olid, with thirty-three horses, eighteen crossbowmen, a hundred sixty foot soldiers and twenty thousand Indian warriors. Then Sandoval with twenty-four horses, four musketeers, thirteen crossbowmen, a hundred fifty foot soldiers, and thirty thousand Indians. Alvarado and his force were to march around the lake and occupy Tacuba. Sandoval was to camp at Ixtapalápa and later advance into the city on the same causeway by which we had entered nearly a year and a half before. Olid would occupy Coyocán. That would give us command over three causeways. The fourth was an aqueduct. Cortés intended to command the ships, manned with archers and musketeers.

His master strategy was simple. The wooden aqueduct would be severed. Commanding the three other causeways, we would prevent food being brought in. Our vessels would patrol the lakes, preventing Aztec canoes from carrying in provisions. As we had once been besieged in the palace of Moctezuma's father, so we would now besiege the whole city. "Without food or water they cannot last long," Cortés told us.

He decided to send eight Aztec prisoners with a message to Cuauhtemoc, begging him to sue for peace: "I do not want to be the ruin of your great city. I will pardon you and your people for the losses and deaths we have suffered if you will surrender now." He reminded Cuauhtemoc that nearly all the peoples of the area around the lake that the Aztecs had once dominated were now on our side.

When the offer of peace had been made, Malinche spoke long and earnestly with the Aztec messengers to be sure that they understood well and that they were convinced that Cortés would keep his word. One was a handsome young eagle warrior, and his eyes never left Malinche's face; whether it was her eloquence or her beauty which held him spellbound I do not know. She had never looked more lovely, not even on the day I first saw her. A soft radiance glowed from her skin and eyes, and I believed it was because she saw hope of an end to the fighting, a victory without further bloodshed, and a long peace.

After the eight messengers had left on their errand, she turned and saw me where I stood watching and smiled at me, so I went to her side. "I am sure you convinced at least one of them," I said. "That is, if he listened as hard as he looked."

"I am praying that Cuauhtemoc will be convinced. He is no gentle mystic like Moctezuma. He is a warrior. He took a strong stand against Moctezuma's temporizing with us. It will be hard for him to offer his people the counsel of surrender now."

I heard a hard laugh. Cortés joined us. "What choice does he have? He knows that as soon as we capture all the causeways his city is lost."

"But you haven't yet captured all the causeways," she said.

"If we must, we shall." He turned away from her to Sandoval.

Malinche said to me, loud enough for him to hear, "It takes courage to surrender. My father had that kind of courage. But does Cuauhtemoc?"

Cortés turned on Malinche. "You are not a man, not a warrior, not the leader of a people. Perhaps you should not presume to know the mind of one who is."

"You are angry because you fear just what I do, that Cuauhtemoc will choose to fight to the end."

They faced each other in silence for a moment, then Cortés nodded. "But in that case, history will record that I offered him the chance to save his city from annihilation." His tone was triumphant.

Days passed with no word from Cuauhtemoc. It finally became clear that the Aztec ruler did not even deign to answer Cortés' offer of peace. Instead we saw evidence that he was readying his city for battle. He sent a large force to defend the aqueduct. We had to fight desperately before we could break the large wooden pipes it supported. We found that the long lances of the Aztecs were now even more dangerous, because they had fastened to their ends those steel swords scavenged from our dead on the *noche triste*.

The day after we took the aqueduct we set out in triple force to make ourselves masters of the first bridge of the Tacuba causeway. A swarm of Aztecs defended it. Despite our ships, their canoes paved the shallow lake around it. Our cavalry was useless because of barricades the Aztecs had built. We made no headway at all. Pressed by our pikes and swords, the Aztecs merely threw themselves into the lake, too shallow that near shore for our ships, and continued to hurl their javelins and arrows at us nearly as well as on land. Jeering, the ones on the causeway threw at us five severed Spanish heads, all flayed and streaming blood. At last we had to fall back with as many losses as they, maybe more. I was glad to hear the order to retreat. That accursed causeway, soaked once more with Spanish blood, made my knees as weak as the water on either side.

Although Cortés was disappointed at our failure to take the causeway, to him his thirteen ships were the real key to victory. The next day, when he sailed against the canoes of the Aztecs, the wind failed and his fleet stood dead in the lake. With at least five hundred canoes of yelling, whistling Aztec warriors converging on his ship with raised spears, it looked as if our next disaster would be the death of our commander. But a gentle land breeze suddenly arose, the sails filled, and our ships bore down on the canoes, overturning and wrecking them. Sailing on through water littered with broken canoes and with Aztecs swimming desperately away or floating dead or stunned, our ships fired muskets and crossbows left and right. We were masters of the lakes from that point on.

With the cooperation of two ships of the fleet sailing at either side of the Ixtapalápa causeway, Cortés was able to take it bridge by bridge. As each was taken, we sent up shouts of joy. Our Indian allies then followed, using the causeway's ramparts, which they smashed, to fill in the gaps to make a solid path for our cannon and horses and also to give us an escape route if we needed it. And so at last we reentered the city on the same broad avenue by which we had first approached it to meet Cacama and Moctezuma.

This much gained, we all believed that the end was near for our foes. But the Aztecs fought for two long months from that day. With no regard for death, they defended their city canal by canal, house by house. If we managed to tear down their barricades by day, they built them up by night. Whenever we razed a building we used the stones to fill in the nearby canal so they could not stand in it and stab up with their lances at our horses' bellies. But by night they would reopen the canal, using the stones to build another barricade. For a time they were able to bring in food and water by canoe, for the lakes were so broad we could not patrol the whole surface, but with the ultimate total defection of all their allies, this meager supply ceased. Long before the end of the siege they were suffering hunger and thirst. By then the city stank from unburned and unburied corpses. How the living fought so long under such conditions I do not know. Somehow they existed on such brackish water as could be got from wells they dug, and they ate water reptiles, and algae and weeds and plants and leaves and bark of trees and roots they dug from the ground. Finally they ate their starving prisoners.

Meanwhile, building by building, we destroyed the city, but they fought atop the debris and took refuge behind such walls as still stood. They fought until they were gaunt and starving skeletons with almost no weapons left but the ancient two-sided *macahuitl* they were almost too weak to brandish.

And so we did not take over a city so much as the shattered corpse of one, a disemboweled cemetery, a nauseating awesome scene of annihilation. My eyes refused to believe the things they saw, and I found it hard to grasp the fact that the Aztecs had not chosen to be vanquished on any lesser terms than their own total destruction as a people. But I began to see that in no other way could they show their contempt for us and for their powerless gods than by this contempt for their own lives. And in no other way could they avenge themselves than to leave their city in smoking ruins without a man, woman, or child to serve as a sacrifice to our more potent deities.

Of all the many more terrible scenes I saw, one has stayed always in my memory: the emaciated body of an Aztec mother clasping in her arms the frail, thin body of her child, a little girl. Both were powdered with dry mortar and lime dust from the wall that had collapsed over them and then had been removed, evidently to form a nearby barricade. Flies, fat on cadavers, crawled over their dead faces and open eyes. Even in death there was something familiar about the woman's face and the faded red ribbons in her braided hair. When I bent over to look closer, I saw she was Sochi, the little maid Moctezuma had given me, who had kept my clothes so neat and always smiled . . .

And I say now what I felt then, that the defense of their city by the Aztecs was an astonishing feat and worthy of being placed beside any in history. It fell into our power only after contagion and disease made the last weak efforts of the few survivors futile. And it fell without a whimper.

On the day I came upon Sochi's body we leveled a barricade and found one eagle warrior who stood atop a heap of rubble strewn with the dead. We thought he would surrender, but he raised his obsidian sword and charged down on fifty of us. A musket bullet took him in the chest and he fell and rolled to my feet. Framed by the open beak of his helmet, his mouth was still wide in that last cry of defiance. His cheekbones were like a skull's. He was a small man, in size.

38

It was on August 13, 1521, that Cortés led us for the last time across the fire-darkened ruins of the fringes of the city to its central heart, where a remnant of the Aztec fighting force still defended Cuauhtemoc's palace and the war god's temple. Cortés sent ahead messengers to Cuauhtemoc, asking him to appear for a conference and promising him personal safety. But the messengers soon returned with an Aztec noble who reported with dignified sorrow that Cuauhtemoc preferred to die rather than meet with Cortés. Aguilar was the interpreter of this message, for Cortés had left Malinche safe in Texcoco, wishing to spare her sights and smells we soldiers were more able to endure. "It is for you to work your will on us," the Aztec noble finished in a resigned tone.

"Then go and tell your countrymen to prepare for annihilation," Cortés said sternly. I could see that he did not like the task before him; to cut down the feeble remnants of the Aztec fighting force was not a very glorious enterprise.

We launched a final attack on the last of the Aztecs huddled together in the core of their shattered city, all ages and sexes in garments stained and tattered like the poorest of beggars'. Some could not even stand alone, but had to support themselves against the walls of buildings still intact. Nonetheless the men sent into flight a feeble volley of their last arrows, most of which fell short, and a flight of lances that wobbled to earth.

This show of valor was answered by the rattle of our

artillery, and with shrill and terrible whistles and shouts our Indian confederates fell upon their victims. The sight sickened me, but I told myself that it was the re-enactment of what Aztecs had done down centuries in the many dozens of cities they had conquered. A message came then that some Aztecs had got away in canoes and were crossing the lake, but that our sloops were intercepting them with gunfire.

One of our ships gave chase to a large pirogue with many paddlers, moving rapidly shoreward. The wind being in his favor, the captain of our vessel was able to overtake it. Suddenly there arose in the middle of the canoe a young Aztec warrior armed with a shield and two-edged sword he raised above his head as if to beat off his enemies. But then his arm dropped to his side. "I am Cuauhtemoc. I will go to Cortés. Now I am his prisoner." He gestured toward the woman and the others with him. "Do not let harm come to my wife or these faithful ones who have followed me." The Spanish captain guessed he was surrendering from his gestures; his words were explained by a Tlascalan on the vessel who had learned some Castilian.

It was from him that El Galán and I first heard of this crucial capture, shortly after the royal prisoner was brought back in fetters to Tenochtitlán. "Thank God," El Galán said fervently. "With their prince our prisoner, it is finally over at last!"

Late that afternoon El Galán and I went with Alvarado and other captains to the rampart of the palace of Moctezuma's father, where Cortés was to meet with his royal captive. The great square looked very different now, for Cortés had systematically razed or wrecked buildings hoping to break the spirit of the people, though the war god's temple still stood, defended to the last. In the Zocalo much of our army was encamped; beyond them the ruined buildings on the west side of the square were like snaggle teeth reaching up to chew the orb of the low sun. Flanking Cortés, who faced the stairs leading up from the palace courtyard, were captains, lieutenants, aides, and priests. Beside him stood Aguilar and Sandoval to interpret. To me it struck a wrong note that Malinche should be absent at this historic moment of final triumph.

Cuauhtemoc came up the stairs to the roof with straight back and steady tread, dressed as an eagle warrior. He faced Cortés. In a low but firm voice he spoke a number of words in Nahuatl. Aguilar's voice translated into Spanish this formal speech of surrender.

"I have done all I could to defend my people and myself. You will deal with me now as you wish." Then Cuauhtemoc pointed to the dagger at Cortés' waist, spoke harshly. "Rid me of my life!"

Cortés had quickly turned his body so Cuauhtemoc could not snatch the weapon. "Do not fear," he said. "A Spaniard respects valor in an enemy. I will treat you with all honor."

Cuauhtemoc, again impassive, inclined his head. This sentiment he apparently understood.

After this, Cortés sent soldiers to escort Cuauhtemoc's young wife to him. A long trestle table had been set up; platters and bowls of food were brought to it for a victory feast, though really to feed the hungry royal captives. I turned to El Galán. "It seems wrong, in a way, that Sandoval and Aguilar were the interpreters at this moment of final victory."

"Instead of Doña Marina, you mean?"

"I realize that Cortés did not want her to see the hideous sights here or smell the stench of so many corpses."

"Especially since she is about to give birth to their child."

"Their child?"

"I thought you knew."

"No." The foolish hope I had clung to had crashed finally to earth, this arrow of truth in its heart. Now she and Cortés were to be bound together by the closest of ties, especially since his wife was apparently barren. I watched Cuauhtemoc, like a statue with the power of motion, walk beside his small wife to the victory table.

My eyes swept over the stinking ruin of the city he had defended. The smell of food was wafted toward me. My throat closed. That laden table, Cortés, the genial captains, the stricken guests seemed the strangest of sights. El Galán had joined them. I turned and left, to find myself wandering forlornly toward the remembered trees and flowers and fountains of Moctezuma's garden.

Once so lovely, now it was grassless, leafless, like a stripped devastation locusts leave behind; I knew that human locusts had swallowed the verdure. The great aviary—that airy, graceful structure of bamboo—we had burned; near it the ground was strewn with bright feathers from the royal birds the Aztecs had plucked and eaten: the dry basin of one of the pools was nearly filled with plumage. The zoo cages were empty, too, the rare animals devoured. Had jaguar warriors eaten the jaguars, eagle warriors the eagles? The stone house of the freaks was empty now; one latticed door stood half open, hanging by one hinge. I turned away, sickened by the thought that perhaps those poor creatures had been eaten like the birds and animals. Then I heard a squeaking sound and through the wooden lattice saw something tottering out from an inner cell toward that open door. I went closer, staring at the starved face atop the body of a tattered child: it was Orteguilla the dwarf.

After I lifted him down he was at first too weak to talk, but I gave him some wine and water from my flask, sitting beside him and holding it to his mouth. That sustenance, or the great relief of being found by a friend, made him able to speak in a weak but valiant semi-whisper.

Caught in the rush on the causeway on the *noche triste* after I thrust him up to safety from the water, he had the wits to see that he would be trampled to death in the increasing panic of our fleeing soldiers, and so he lay down beside the bulk of a dead Spaniard and when Aztecs came later and looted the victim, Orteguilla played dead. There he stayed until late morning, hearing the temple drums. When he believed that the

Aztecs' blood lust had been satiated by many sacrifices and saw that no more were scavenging the bodies, he began to make his way toward the Tacuba shore but was found by a small troop of Aztecs coming from there to the city and was captured. Talking fast in Nahuatl, he had convinced them that he had been page to the late Moctezuma, was a favorite of one of his daughters, and knew Cuitlahuac. So they brought him to their ruler. He refused to have a Spaniard in his palace and ordered him taken to the House of Freaks. Those poor creatures were fed, if meagerly, until two weeks before the end of the siege, then Cuitlahuac ordered them freed. Almost all of them had been foolish enough to leave. "I stayed," Orteguilla said. "I knew there was no food elsewhere, and here at least there was a little brackish water in some of the pools. And with my dirk I killed a rather large snake that had escaped from the reptile house of the zoo, and I dined on a slice a day, keeping myself well hidden in a small inner room of the Freak House in case some starving Aztec should get the idea of dining on me."

I realized that, against all odds, this little fellow had come through the grim night that had taken the lives of huge men like the Three Moors and soldiers even braver. "God must really love you, Orteguilla."

"And also I learned to speak Nahuatl," he grinned.

I told him then of Cuauhtemoc's surrender, and that we had finally taken the city. "Malinche will be happy to know you are alive."

"So will Cortés." His old arrogance had at last returned, full force. "Though I admit he seems to have done quite well without me. I suspected a Spanish victory when I heard some battering rams at work but, frankly, felt too weak to reconnoiter." He looked down at his small legs dubiously.

So I offered to carry him on my shoulders to the rooftop where our victory was being celebrated.

"Thanks. And you will have to find someone willing to carry my companion." He turned his head toward the Freak House and called out something in Nahuatl.

From an inner room there emerged, walking slowly and timidly, a tiny dwarf with large dark eyes. She wore a child-sized skirt and *huipile* and her hair was braided with ribbons of green and pink. "Her name in Nahuatl means lovely little jade butterfly," Orteguilla said, "but I call her Blanca. I cannot say that she is highly intelligent, but she has a sweet nature and is most accommodating." He gave a wink.

That under such conditions he had found a paramour was too much for me, and I burst into laughter and went to find someone willing to transport Blanca. There was no one in the garden, but in the forecourt of the war god's pyramid some Spanish soldiers with a battering ram were attacking the skull rack while others watched and offered instructions; one of these men agreed to aid me. Just as we started back to the gardens there was a loud splintering sound and a tower of the skull rack crashed down. A loosened skull rolled and bounded a great distance to come to a stop before me, grin upward, to remind me of the death that day of my sweetest hope.

When we reached the crowded rampart of Moctezuma's palace, the dwarf riding on my shoulder and waving right and left at grinning acquaintances, his paramour just behind us, the sun had set. Its brief embers glowed below the bright spark of the evening star and a gloomy furl of purple-gray clouds that covered all the rest of the sky. The victory feast was finished; the smell of rain was in the air. Cuauhtemoc was leaving for Texcoco escorted by a number of captains, his wife beside him. Cortés stood looking after him, well pleased. And why not? He had it all: the last Aztec king, Malinche, and soon a child by her. With the ironic sense of putting the final drop in his full cup I presented him with his returned page.

Orteguilla had asked to be let down to his own feet, and he approached Cortés with a parody of his old jaunty trot, his head tilted back arrogantly. Cortés smiled down at the dwarf over whom he towered as he towered in courage and will above us all. "By God, it's my jester!" Cortés shouted, and tipped his head back to laugh.

"At your service, Your Majesty," Orteguilla replied with a courtier's bow.

We evacuated that ruined city in falling rain, driving before us the last of its citizens, reduced now to the status of slaves. Long before we reached Texcoco we were wet to gooseflesh.

That night a terrible storm burst over the Valley of Anahuac. The lake waters rose in waves to hurl themselves against the ghastly ruins of the Aztec capital, revealed by flashes of lightning to us on shore as a terrain that might well have burst up, smoldering, from Hell itself. The thunder, like ten thousand cannons, reverberated all over the valley from its ring of mountains, loud enough to awe the spirits of the evil monarchs said to dwell in the bowels of Popocatepetl. It seemed to me that Nature herself, expressing the wrath of the one true God, had risen up in frenzy against what was left of that proud city to cleanse it of the last taint of the last drop of blood spilled on its altars over three long centuries and more.

But I did not feel like a victor.

The next night in a palace in Texcoco where Alvarado's company was quartered, where braziers warmed the air, where food and drink were brought us by scurrying Indian servants, I stood aloof at a window watching the falling rain and drinking strawberry-flavored pulque as if it were water. The other soldiers gambled and joked, wild with relief that it was at last over, this long and terrible campaign. But not Arturo Mondragon y Flores, who got morosely drunk and conceived the notion that he should go to Cortés' mistress and offer her his hand and heart and name in marriage so that her child would not be born a bastard. Fortunately I confided this plan to El Galán, who persuaded me to wait until morning, plying me with more pulque until I collapsed into sottish unconsciousness and was hauled off to my sleeping mat, where I awoke next day with a headache to which death seemed preferable.

The severe chills that set in later I attributed to my indiscretion, likewise the fever which followed, and I tried to cure myself with more pulque, a remedy suggested by several more experienced drunkards than I. As I vomited up this anodyne, the depressing thought occurred that this adventure that had begun for me with seasickness on Sedeño's caravel was ending in an even worse nausea on dry land. Would poor Arturo Mondragon y Flores be remembered as the luckless soldier who had vomited his life away after the last battle had been finally won?

PART IX

▼▼▼

FAREWELL TO GLORY
August 15, 1521–January 22, 1522

39

I had smallpox. Sequestered in a cell at the rear of a
Texcoco palace, I lay with throbbing head, aching in
every muscle, while hideous pustules spread all over my
face, neck, chest, legs—even the palms of my hands.
I insisted that my armor be placed on the floor beside
my pallet, which was taken as delirium by the Padre de
Merced, though not by El Galán, who looked in on me
frequently. Chills and fever came and went; at times my
brain was quite clear, at others so muddled that I barely
knew who I was or cared. In dreams Malinche brought
me herb tea and told me she cared; at other times it
was my mother who bent above me and spoke of sunny
days when I would be well again. But in reality I
opened my eyes one day and saw Aguilar's face looking
down into mine. He had come to administer the final
rites, but I refused to make any last confession, for it
seemed to me that if I did my soul would fly out of my
body. "You are ill to the point of death," he said gently.
"I will not deceive you as to that."

"To hell with Death," I said. "I have emeralds to get
to Cuba." He shook his head sadly at this fantasy.

The worst moment of my long illness, worse than the
fever, the aches, the delirium, or the damnable itching
and stinging of the pustules, was the lucid moment
when I awoke and found myself in an Indian robe with
my gold necklace around my neck and my gold bracelets on my arm, but my armor gone. Cursing and rav-
ing, I got up from my pallet and yelled for the poor

Tlascalan slave girl who acted as my nurse. I made her understand what I sought, and she led me to the next room where she slept, and where she had been polishing my armor with pumice. I snatched up my breastplate, found the mortar that concealed my emeralds still intact, and carried it back to bed with me. Men have taken very strange bedmates, but few have slept hugging a battered breastplate as I did from then on.

My first hints of recovery were a perfectly clear mind and a pang of hunger. After that I improved amazingly. I was not left very pockmarked either, and knew myself much luckier than the late Cuitlahuac. When El Galán saw that I was over the worst, he told me that two weeks before Malinche had given birth to a baby boy.

For a moment I was numb. Then came a fierce pang, as if my heart were being cauterized, and my hand went to the scar on my shoulder.

I was fortunate to have my emeralds and my gold, for the booty found in Tenochtitlán had been far below all our expectations, only something like a hundred thirty thousand gold castellanos' worth. This was much less than even the amount the Aztecs must have recovered from our dead on the night we fled the city. We all believed that our enemies had buried the greater mass of treasure in various secret places around their island or sunk it in the lake, or both, rather than ever let it fall into our hands. But if the harvest of gold was much less than we had expected, the terrible harvest of dead foes was much greater. Cortés estimated it at one hundred seventeen thousand, just from the start of the siege. The smallpox at least had spared me from taking part in the nauseating task of burning and burying the wealth of Aztec corpses.

"The Aztecs never grasped the concept of empire," El Galán said of our foes on my first day out of that small room, as I walked shakily beside him in the sunlight of a palace garden where the trees and flowers looked like things out of Heaven itself, very bright and beautiful. "Unlike the Romans, they never extended the rights of citizenship to the peoples they conquered. They never offered down laws and justice to the vanquished. They merely extracted tribute, giving nothing in return. Without the hatred of them this aroused in the Totonacs and Tlascalans, we could never have triumphed. I say this with all due respect for the military genius of Cortés and our own valor."

I nodded, smelling a red rose, watching a spider mend its web. I knew El Galán was trying to engage my long-torpid mind in one of those conversations with which idle soldiers distract themselves, but I was not bored. Everything that grew or crawled had the charm of novelty.

"But I regret our near-annihilation of the Aztecs of the capital," he continued somberly, also watching the busy spider restore its gossamer world, made with such labor from its own essence. "And I fear that it may prove the unfortunate paradigm for later conquests of other Indians of this continent." He smiled somewhat ironically. "Yet given the circumstances we had to face, and being Spaniards and Christians, we could not have done differently, as God well knows." He added, "And Satan."

The torture of Cuauhtemoc to make him reveal where the Aztec gold had been hidden went against Cortés' true inclination. For a time he resisted the demands made by disenchanted soldiers that he learn where the gold was, refusing even after they had covered the outer walls of their barracks with cruel and scurrilous graffiti aimed at him. But finally Alderete, the Royal Treasurer, acting as their spokesman, openly accused Cortés of having made a secret agreement with Cuauhtemoc to defraud his soldiers and his king of their fair shares, and he demanded that Cuauhtemoc be turned over to him for "close questioning."

It was a dangerous ploy, for Cortés by this time was full of a rankling anger at having received no answer to the last letter he had sent to Carlos telling of the final defeat of the Aztecs and laying at his feet all the vast realm of Mexico. But chagrin at this royal procrastination rather than the accolade merited had left Cortés very vulnerable to the accusation that he was defrauding the king who had treated him in a way to deserve just that. Alderete's accusation seemed to him to be irrefutable except by turning over Cuauhtemoc and thus proving his own innocence of any preference that the Aztec's lips stay tightly closed. Impulsively he handed him over to the Royal Treasurer and his clique. In short order they set about roasting the former ruler's feet over a slow fire, and did the same to the cacique of Tacuba on the chance that he, too, had some hidden gold. I know that Cuauhtemoc did not groan or cry out even once during this lengthy torture. Alderete himself admitted his courage: when the Tacuban cacique moaned in his agony, Cuauhtemoc reproached him for it and said "Do you think I lie here on rose petals, or in a cool bath?"

Cortés swiftly repented of having broken his promise to treat Cuauhtemoc with honor and rescued the poor man before Death did. Later a little gold was found by dredging the lake where Cuauhtemoc told Cortés some had been thrown; and a large golden calendar wheel was found under the muddy water of one of the ponds in Moctezuma's garden, but that was all. Where the rest of the treasure was hidden might never be learned.

Slowly, inevitably, the first luster wore off our victory in the absence of the vast loot hoped for or any approbation from our monarch. Cortés told us that we could expect royal grants of land, but as this hope was deferred long month after long month our commander's popularity slid into eclipse. Respectful Indian rulers came from far and wide to render homage to the conqueror of the Aztecs, but from Spain came nothing.

El Galán guessed correctly that Carlos was in Germany. Moreover, he had empowered an ascetic and inept churchman named Adrian to rule Spain in his absence; Adrian believed all Velásquez's claims against Cortés, because they were sustained now by Fonseca, the bishop of Burgos, the highest power in Spain's colonial department. But somehow Cortés managed to convince himself that all would be well and became engrosssed in his plans to rebuild a capital city, finally deciding to utilize the spot where Tenochtitlán had stood. This task would give employment to his idle and disgruntled soldiers, from whom all sense of triumph was slowly draining, our high hopes of wealth mocked by that stark and ruined island from which by now even the vultures had departed.

To that devastation was added the rising smoke of the bonfires our priests were setting. Under the fanatical suasion of a churchman named Landa they were rooting out and burning every scrap of picture-writing they could find in the lakeside cities, having already burned all the codices they could discover in the ruins of Tenochtitlán. It seemed to me a terrible waste but to Landa they were the work of the Devil himself, and his hysteria prevailed. I began to feel that my narrow escape from a squalid death by smallpox had been my warning that this ghastly place might yet prove my grave if I stayed much longer. I wanted urgently to get my gems home, and myself with them, and soon I yearned for Cuba as intensely as I had once yearned for the Unknown Land where now I languished.

The other soldiers in my company, taking the baptism of the ruler of Texcoco to have christianized his female subjects as well, were bedding with young women there. Hoping to cheer me, El Galán told me that the younger sister of the girl he liked had shown great interest in me. "A woman might be just what you need now," he urged me, "and you need have no fear of the buboes, for these girls are very clean and virginal and come of decent folk."

So I met the sister, a pretty girl with deep dimples in her cheeks and a musical laugh, and I took her walking along the streets as the other soldiers did with theirs. One night when we found ourselves alone in the small garden of her parents' house, she drew close to me, but when I embraced her I felt no excitement. My male member, which must have risen stiff as a pole at least a hundred times sleeping or waking while I had throbbed to lustful or romantic dreams of Malinche, now stayed dolefully flaccid. This girl might have been a purring cat or little friendly dog. After a while she gave me a strange look and stood up and walked slowly toward the house. I felt ashamed, unmanned. Self-dislike turned to superstition. Was Malinche a witch who had enchanted me? Would she hold me in thrall forever?

When El Galán asked me how I was getting along with the sister, I said coldly that she did not appeal to me. "I wouldn't worry," he told me. "Very likely your illness left you temporarily unfit for gambols with girls. I've heard of this happening." I saw then how unfair I had been to blame Malinche, and soon she returned in dreams after our long separation in the unreal land as well as in reality. I had not seen her or her child because I was unwilling to have her see my marred face, and had been told by an earlier victim that time and sunlight would make the pockmarks less noticeable.

There was great excitement when the rumor spread that a Spanish ship had arrived in the harbor at Vera Cruz. Could it have brought a message from the king at last?

It had brought a man named Tapía, the Royal Inspector of the gold foundries in Santo Domingo, sent by Fonseca to arrest Cortés and bring him back to trial for breaking his pact with Velásquez.

At Vera Cruz the intrepid Caballero and the other officials had received Tapía coldly, had disputed his credentials, denied the truth of the charges against Cortés, and refused him passage to the Valley of Anahuac, a delaying action meant to give Cortés time to find a way out of this contretemps, if a way could be found.

I learned all this when Alvarado sent for me, explained this new threat, and told me Cortés' plan: to send down to Vera Cruz an outrageous price for some horses and Negro slaves Tapía had brought with him. "Cortés has decided that you and El Galán are the right ones to take this bribe to Tapía. If you are successful, Tapía will sail back to the West Indies a richer man and ruefully report his failure to capture Cortés," he grinned.

My reply sprang from my lips without forethought: "If I am to go to Vera Cruz, I ask your permission to leave on Tapía's ship." With the words I saw a vision of my mother's face. Home!

Alvarado stared in amazement. He had gained some flesh and now was ruddier than ever. When he laughed at me he looked so jovial it was hard to believe he had ever ordered that massacre of the dancers. "Don't be a fool. And don't lose faith in Cortés or our king. When he learns of our total conquest of this land, Carlos will reward us all handsomely. A veteran of the Old Guard like yourself will get the pick of the most valuable property. You'll end up a *haciendado,* even a *hidalgo.* Think of that!"

I thought of it. I had no wish to live any future years of my life in this afflicted valley, but I was unwilling to sacrifice any land grant due me. "Surely a leave to visit my family would not mean that I would sacrifice any rewards justly mine?"

He shrugged. "Cortés will have to decide that. I have no authority to tell you that you can skip off home. As for my part, I am staying where the luck is. Cortés is loaded with it, like a rich mine with ore. I don't understand you. You suffered through all the hardships and now you want to leave just when the fruit is about to drop in your mouth!" We were at the Texcoco palace where he and a number of other captains lived, and at this point an Indian servant came in with a basket of mangoes. Alvarado's hand went out and closed on a blushing fruit. To my surprise, he tossed it to me with a grin, then grabbed an even bigger one for himself. "Stay for the windfall!" he commanded.

I left determined to disobey. The wind had blown down the fruit here, and it was mostly corpses.

Cortés was on the island of Tenochtitlán, where I found him in the ruins of the central square. With the architect who had laid out the plans for Vera Cruz he stood at a table made of planks on two sawhorses, scanning the drawing of a façade with two towers. All around him were piled the dark gray stone blocks from the pyramid of the war god which was being razed by sad-faced Indians under the supervision of Spaniards. He pointed to the drawing before him and asked the architect, "Considering the occasional earthquakes they have here, what is the highest the towers can be?"

Then he looked up and saw me. How the handsome face that had smiled at me from Don Pedro Barba's supper table had changed! Every battle, every sleepless night, every doubt and anxiety was marked there, like the plan on which a new face would be constructed. With the easy arrogance of great power he said, "Well, Alonzo, I'm glad to see you've recovered from the smallpox."

Should I have been flattered that he called me by the name of his former favorite? "I am Arturo."

He nodded. "Arturo Mondragon of Havana. Your father sold me cotton." He pointed down at the drawing. "Look what I'm going to do here. A great cathedral is going to rise where that damned pyramid was. Built of the same stones. And along there, to the east, a governor's palace. And where the House of Dancers used to be, an embassy for visitors of note from Europe." I stared across the bleak, rubble-littered expanse toward where the thriving marketplace had been, with its colors, its profusion of wares, its throngs. He eyed me shrewdly. "Not interested? Then why are you here?"

"You want me to take gold to Vera Cruz to bribe Tapía, or so Alvarado said."

"Correct. But I don't have it here," he smiled.

"I came to ask your leave to return to Cuba."

He stared as if I had asked his leave to go to Hell. "Cuba? What do you want to go to Cuba for? There's nothing more in Cuba. Don't you realize the extent of this land? I've been visited by caciques from Oaxaca, from Tehuantepec, from all over. Northwest of Michoacan there's a narrow inland sea that produces huge pearls. A cacique brought me some. Here. Look!" From his pocket he drew a small pouch of soft leather, and with the thumb and forefinger of his claw hand that lacked the little finger and the one next to it he drew out a tremendous white pearl and held it up before my eyes, watching my face as I stared at it. "And to the south in the jungles of Yucatán and Honduras are many magnificent Mayan cities. Where so many people flourish, natural wealth must exist, and we'll find it! Olid will command my first expedition there. You should stay and join him. Hard marches, and toil, too, but I can promise you a new adventure and riches as great as any we've seen!" He glowed at the prospect.

"Still I ask to return to Cuba."

His face assumed a hard and shrewd look. "Now why would he want that?" he asked as he put the pearl back into its pouch. His gaze pounced onto mine. "Why? A jewel or two? A little trove of loot? Mere baubles, soldier."

My heart turned over and my emeralds seemed to be visible through my breastplate. "I feel a great need to see my home and my parents again. I do not know how things have gone for them. They may need me much more than you do, who have so many soldiers now."

"Filial love? Then make them rich for their old age. Join Olid or Alvarado and subjugate the Mayas. The journey may be arduous, I grant you that, but riches were never the reward of sloth."

"For most of us they have not been the reward of bitter toil and brutal battles, either."

He glowered at me, then laughed. "But don't forget the glory!" I thought I saw the glint of mockery in his eye. His was the glory. A few of his captains might also be remembered as heroes. But Arturo Mondragon y Flores and many hundreds of dead Spaniards who had helped to make that glory possible might just as well never have been.

"Not being a greedy man," I said, "I'm content to go home with only whatever glory I've already earned."

He gave me a hard look, but he had decided he had use of me. "I have selected you and El Galán to take a small fortune in gold to Vera Cruz because your look of innocence and El Galán's fine manners will nicely garnish the lie Tapía must pretend to swallow. To wit: that I need or want his Negroes or his horses. There will be given into your custody ten gold ingots to buy them with."

"Ten! How many horses and Negroes does the man have?"

"Irrelevant. I am not buying horses or Negroes, but Tapía. Let him see only five ingots to begin with. Be sure to let him feel the weight of one. I need to place him in such a position that returning rich without me he can only give the bishop of Burgos a glowing report of my fine efforts here, do you see? I hear Tapía is a little fellow. You and El Galán must make him feel a giant. Butter him. Soothe him. Force a few grudging words of approbation of my efforts here into his mouth and then praise him for his acumen. Let him understand that Velásquez wanted me to do all the hard work while he reaped the lion's share of the credit and the profit. I have already spoken to El Galán and he understands me perfectly. Take your cues from him. Smile often." Cortés looked suddenly grim. "This bribe could turn the tide for me. These ingots you are bringing to Tapía can work magic. Their cold gold can give birth to warm words of praise of Cortés that will travel from Tapía to Fonseca to Carlos and perhaps make me the first governor of New Spain."

I said I understood him perfectly. "But you have not yet given me permission to leave on Tapía's ship."

His eyes roved back to the architect's drawing. From it he gazed up at blank air where the war god's pyramid had once loomed. "Go, then. You have my leave. I think you will live to regret it, but go with God, Arturo."

I said farewell to him and crossed that great square

that once had awed me so, and in my mind's eye I saw it as it had been then and heard the sweet remembered singing of a hundred thousand birds that had filled the aviary of Moctezuma the Second. And I wondered if it were possible for even Cortés to build a city as fair and beautiful as that one, forever gone.

40

The gold ingots were brought to El Galán and me the next day, and horses for the journey. The gold was divided between our two saddlebags. We would leave at dawn.

I could not go without saying farewell to Malinche. As I made my way toward the Texcoco palace where she and Cortés lived, along streets where humble Indians stepped aside to let me pass, the bright November air would have been exhilarating if I had not been saddened by the knowledge that I would soon be seeing her for the last time. The far snow atop Popocatepetl and the Sleeping Princess was as white as wedding cake.

The Spanish guard admitted me; inside the courtyard another went to see if I were to be allowed to see Doña Marina. Orteguilla came trotting out with him, all his old cockiness as evident as his plumed cap and red doublet. He had the grace to apologize for not having visited me while I was ill with smallpox. "The truth is, I was afraid of getting it. My sense of logic told me that to visit you would do you no real good and might do me great harm." He hung his head. "Maybe that snake I ate gave me the caution common to low creatures that live near the ground." With a return to his self-importance he told me that his little Blanca was now one of Doña Marina's serving ladies, and he her majordomo. When I asked what that was, he said that princes and nobles all had them. "I see to the smooth running of the house." He added: "She will see you, by the way."

She sat by a sunny window in a stone room. Her hair was braided atop her head, and she wore a Spanish dress of deep red trimmed in black velvet. She held her baby in her arms. Wrapped in a blanket and sleeping, it could have been a doll.

She smiled at me so sweetly it hurt. "I am glad to see you well, Arturo."

"I came to say goodbye."

"Goodbye?"

"I leave tomorrow for Vera Cruz. Then I sail for Havana."

"May God go with you."

"And may He be with you always." The double banality had me racking my mind for something better to say; something memorable. On her lap the baby made a grimace. She saw it, smiled, and held him up. "Look! Martín is offering you a smile." The grimace as suddenly vanished. Fat-cheeked, he looked self-contained, dreaming of milk.

No unforgettable remark had occurred to me. I, the erstwhile poet, stood tongue-tied. I blurted "I will never forget you!"

She smiled. "It would be most unnatural if you did not, in time. But I will remember your kindness."

"It was nothing." We could not speak of the night we had shared. I felt as though I might cry. With a last *adios* I turned and started across the room to the door. The baby wailed, and I looked back. She gave it her breast and I went out into a world without her.

Tapía was very little, and scrawny too, and rooster-fierce with self-importance. El Galán and I had a wonderful time using our wiles to tame him into a sweet little bird that gratefully gobbled up golden ingots and sang out praises of Cortés. Over a glass of wine to seal the bargain he even apologized for the decrepitude of two swayback horses, and I remembered when the worst of these would have looked to us like the Cid's great stallion.

On the night before I was to sail with Tapía, El Galán tried to persuade me to stay on and later join him in the expedition Cortés intended to send to Honduras, but he understood my refusal. "If I owned your emeralds, I might want to go home too. But as things are for me, I must try to change my luck down there in those fabled Mayan cities."

To say farewell to my friend made me very sad, for who knew when we might see each other again? I told him he would always be welcome to visit me in Havana—"If you should ever want my company after having had so much of it." He smiled down into my eyes, his frank and handsome face marred by a scar from the siege livid on one cheekbone. He said, with that grace that marked him from all others, "To some few men God gives the great boon of a friend one can absolutely trust, and you have been that friend to me." His words made me feel very humble, for it was really the other way around. Mine had been the boon. He had been that to me.

Before I left I sold my *chalchihuites* to a Totonac noble for two dozen large quills of gold dust, since the carved jade would have much less value in Cuba. As Tapía's ship sailed on the morning tide, I stood aft looking back at the little town of Vera Cruz. A man's tall figure stood on the flat roof of a building that overlooked the bay. I thought it looked like El Galán. Then he raised one arm and waved it slowly back and forth at my retreating ship. I waved too, and found that I was smiling yet had a large lump in my throat, and as long as I could see him we both continued to wave.

When the once-unknown land had vanished from sight, I went to the foredeck of the caravel just as a school of dolphins sported by, leaping in shining curves from the sea. The sunlight was brilliant, and to the north a bank of high white clouds sailed a blue sky, grandly remote from human farewells. I stood staring eastward across the Gulf of Mexico, toward home.

As I walked toward the door, I was amazed at how the house had shrunk, at how the sea-grape tree I had climbed as a child seemed to have grown downward instead of higher with the years. When my mother saw me, she laughed and cried both at once and hugged me to her despite my breastplate, and said that if I had not been wearing the gilded casque she might not have recognized me. My father embraced me, too, and my little sisters stared up at a conquering hero, which in fact I was.

At first I showed them only my twenty-four quills of gold dust and my gold necklace and bracelets. I could tell, for all their exclamations, that these were less booty then they had hoped for, having heard of the fabulous treasure Cortés had sent to King Carlos. But that night I brought my breastplate to the supper table along with a small wooden mallet. They stared as at a madman while I carefully tapped the edges of the mortar that held my emeralds in place. As I removed the cracked and loosened mortar and came to the cloth which protected the gems, my heart stood still. The moisture from the mortar when it was wet had made the cloth adhere to them, so I dampened it well with wine and peeled it away. First I put the smaller emerald on the table, and it made them all gasp. Solemnly I set the emerald frog beside it. By candlelight it looked even larger and more glowing than it had when I first saw it by a lightning flash. My parents' astonishment gave me great joy. My mother picked up the frog and held it on her palm, staring. Her brown eyes were not sad now, but like a child's, filled with wonder. "It's so large. It's so heavy. Is it really an emerald?"

"It's all but priceless," my father said flatly.

"Now Arturo can go to University at Salamanca!"

He caught my eye and smiled. "You will certainly have to go to Spain to sell this gem. In Valladolid I can ask the aid of a cousin I trust, a maritime merchant who has connections wth wealthy families in cities like Sevilla and Venice and Florence. He will know who collects such rarities, and who can afford this one." He pondered. "The Medicis, perhaps."

"And after the jewels are sold," my mother said to me, "you can remain in Spain and begin your studies at Salamanca."

I did not dim her pleasure by revealing that I had no intention of studying at Salamanca or anywhere else, feeling myself too old and too experienced in dealing death for schoolrooms, although I would certainly go with my father to sell the emeralds for fear that on some unlucky night the wine might take his senses so he would boast and be robbed, or lose the gems in some other way. "To Spain, yes."

"But you must not leave too soon," she said, and reached out to touch my hand. "It has been so long since I have had my only son at my side." Her sweet smiling face glowed with pride in me, quite as though she had never forbidden the journey that had brought us this treasure.

My father wrenched his eyes from the emerald frog and raised his wine goblet to me. "I salute my son, the *conquistador!*" Our eyes met, and in his I saw both pride and the knowledge, conveyed as well by the wry quirk of his lips, that his status in Havana had just changed to hero's father. The gold he had hoped to mine I had found. I told him then of Juan Morla to show the part pure luck had played, and this was good for his self-esteem and my humility.

My father's second cousin Enrique Mondragon was an aging fat man with oyster eyes. My gems overwhelmed him. We went with him to a rich merchant he knew in Sevilla who would value them fairly and not cheat me. For the emerald frog I got fifty thousand gold ducats.

I got thirty-eight hundred for the smaller emerald, and eight hundred for my gold. I was rich beyond all my hopes.

In my new clothing made in the latest style I could only approve my image in the mirror of my room at Enrique's villa in Valladolid. Guests flocked in to meet the rich young *conquistador* who had served under Hernán Cortés, a name now widely known in Spain, thanks to periodicals like that of Sevilla. So rich men's greetings to me were very courteous; women's willing eyes smiled over fans at Don Arturo of Havana. It was January 22, 1522, my twenty-first birthday. I had got the gold and the glory—and, if I had lost Malinche, a dazzling future beckoned, and many pretty women awaited me there. Yet as I told myself this, her image arose in my mind more vivid than any of the actual faces around me. And I knew that the greatest prize of all had eluded my grasp. Not even Don Oro had helped me attain her.

A girlish voice spoke my name; I looked down into the pale, adoring face of Don Enrique's daughter Amalia. The only child of his middle years, she would inherit the bulk of his fortune and his fleet of six trading vessels that sailed down the west coast of Africa for Negro slaves and north as far as London. Those ships intrigued me more than his villa or his heiress. Whenever Amalia looked at me her soft little mouth was slightly open, her gray eyes wide. Her father had told me he was not long for this earth and wanted above all else to see his one child married to a worthy young man, safe from fortune-hunters. He had dwelt then on my many sterling qualities: courage, intelligence, perseverance, a good wit, a pleasing appearance, and worthy forebears. The gold I had banked was not mentioned.

I smiled down at Amalia, was rewarded with a blush and a giggle, and felt no urge to embrace that slender body. "Happy birthday, dear cousin," she said, and stood on tiptoe to offer my cheek an impulsive, girlish kiss.

PART X

THE RETURN TO PAYNALA
November 14, 1522–November 28, 1524

41

My son Martín was born the day after Cuauhtemoc surrendered. While I was in labor in the high Spanish bed Cortés had ordered built he came in to tell me of that final moment of victory. Even in my pain I had been moved by his promise to treat the defeated ruler with all honor. What a rosy picture that had given me of a brutal conquest!

Not for another three months did I learn how total had been the destruction of Tenochtitlán. Soon after Arturo Mondragon left for Cuba, Cortés took me across the lake in a canopied pirogue belonging to Cuauhtemoc to show me the plans of the new city he was already beginning to construct. I could not believe what I saw: canals filled with rubble, houses and temples razed, and over all the faint sickening smell of the dead. I became ill and asked to return at once to Texcoco.

Then I remembered the gentle, doomed Moctezuma, his nobles, his hundreds of humble servants, those thousands in the marketplace, now swept into eternal darkness like a hundred thousand more. And I, within a cocoon of self-preoccupation, had been sheltered in Texcoco to bear the child of that pitiless conqueror.

As we crossed the lake toward Texcoco, seated side by side in the canopied boat sent smoothly over the blue water by the paddlers standing fore and aft, I turned on the bench to look back toward Tenochtitlán and then I began to weep. I found my body rocking back and forth in funereal grief, my arms hugging my belly.

"What you weep for cannot be changed by tears," Cortés said.

I stared at him in outrage. "Do you feel nothing? No shame? No grief? No remorse?"

"I cannot afford the luxury of remorse. Great problems face me now. The first is how to protect the conquered Indians here from Spanish exploitation, from the inhumane customs practiced in the West Indies."

I pointed toward Tenochtitlán. "More inhumane than that?"

He kindled. "Do you dare to blame me because the Aztecs decided on suicide? I pleaded with Cuauhtemoc to surrender at the start of the siege. I did so again! And again! His obdurate refusal has killed many Christians. So weep for them, too! Weep for my dear friend Pedro Barba of Havana and for his widow and his children! I have!" By now the two forward paddlers were casting glances back at us; we were speaking Spanish, but the sound of anger transcends mere words. Cortés gave them a cold stare that turned their attention instantly toward the Texcoco shore. "But all the grief on earth will not help either the dead or the living Indians of this land. I and I alone must find a way to protect them from cruel exploitation by Spaniards. So I will leave the tears and the rocking and wailing to you. Enjoy your pain!"

His words had dried my eyes. I turned to him, saw the back of his head; he stared across the lake at the fire-darkened walls of one of the lakeside towns he had taken early in the siege. "What exploitation do you mean?" I asked in nearly my normal voice.

His head turned; his eyes explored my face; he wiped a tear from it with the forefinger of his maimed hand. "There are two customs I deplore; at least when used in conjunction. *Repartimiento* and *encomienda*. The first grants to Spaniards land on which to settle. Since a colony cannot be held without colonists, it is a necessary evil and cannot be avoided. But *encomienda* gives to the colonists the native people on the land—serfs

who must work for their Spanish masters without rec-
ompense and often under inhumane conditions. The
Indians of Hispaniola and Santo Domingo and Cuba
died by the tens of thousands from the abuse of these
two customs. I will not have that here. I want the size
of land grants limited, and I want *encomienda* declared
illegal. I have written King Carlos to this effect. As yet
I have had no answer. I have also asked that my loyal
Tlascalans and Totonacs be treated with the honor due
them."

The pirogue had reached the Texcoco shore and was
being poled flush with the stone jetty we had embarked
from earlier that day. My ignorance had been left behind somewhere in the lake, between the ruins I had
deplored and my understanding of Cortés. That he had
already written Carlos reminded me that thus far that
uniquely ungrateful sovereign had not yet acknowledged
the letter informing him of the defeat of the Aztecs and
the acquisition thereby of their vast domain. "I will
weep no more," I said. "Forgive me."

He rose to help me from the boat, and when we
were both standing on the stone jetty he smiled down at
me very kindly. "Your momentary weakness was very
unlike you, and I think was caused in part by your new
condition of motherhood." And as we walked toward
our palace he told me, again, how proud he was of his
fine, strong son.

As we entered the main courtyard we came face to
face with Cuauhtemoc; he and his wife had been given
an apartment in one of the palace buildings. Cortés
nodded to him pleasantly and had me ask if there was
anything he required, and I was thus reminded that the
victor was treating the vanquished with honor, as he had
promised to do. Cuauhtemoc's feet were still in ban-
dages, for the greedy Royal Treasurer had seized and
tortured him to learn where more Aztec gold might be
hidden; Cortés, on learning of this, had gone into a rage
and ordered the flames searing the Aztec's feet put out
and that Cuauhtemoc be returned to his personal
custody. It was typical of Cuauhtemoc that he had

attempted to walk in the courtyard before the surgeon believed this possible, and Cortés reproached him for this, but Cuauhtemoc shrugged and said the pain was not much and the sun and fresh air good medicines.

During the next ten months the profile of the island of Tenochtitlán slowly changed; sunlight glinted on new walls, proof to me that Cortés was no mere destroyer, but a builder as well. By October 1522 one gray stone belltower of the cathedral at the north side of the Zocalo pointed toward heaven and the nave was nearly completed; to the east the nearly completed governor's palace rose two stories high where Axayacatl's palace had been, and now a busy marketplace spread out where the old one had been, though not so large. Fringing the central plaza and lining the main avenues leading to it, Spanish houses like stone fortresses had risen or were rising, the proud homes of captains of the Old Guard, although other colonists had begun to populate the city of Mexico, some from families of high category in Spain, drawn by hope of land grants.

But the natives were not forgotten by Cortés. Tatelolco, where the Aztecs had made their last stand, was now a district boasting many new houses occupied by former nobles; Cortés was going to build there a smaller cathedral, several churches, a school where native children could learn Spanish, and a hospital. But as if to remind these Aztecs and other natives of the Valley of Anahuac that Spanish power was an ever-present reality in their lives, a fortress called the Matadero was being constructed overlooking the dockyard where the ships that had served in the siege were preserved as memorials to the conquest. The fort had seventy cannons, made in part from copper mined in Taxco. They fired stone balls, and gunpowder was made with sulphur mined on Popocatepetl. Because the fort, the cathedral, and many other buildings were made of volcanic pedregal, the city of Mexico had an over-all gray look, but this would be modified when the trees Cortés had ordered planted grew taller.

By the time Martín was learning to take his first steps,

I had no more sorrow in me for the city that was gone; the new one rising in its place assured me that the whole wide land called New Spain would surely emerge into an era of peace and prosperity where Spaniards and Indians would mingle in friendship, Christians all, their enmity forgotten.

I had become fond of Cuauhtemoc's wife, still living in our palace with her husband and his small retinue, which included the former cacique of Tacuba, who had also been tortured by the wicked Royal Treasurer. She told me once that Cuauhtemoc's scarred feet still gave him pain if he walked on them too long. I believed that another and greater pain accounted for his aloofness and his look of stern sorrow: he knew that his staunch refusal to surrender had brought about the decimation of the Tenochas. When I told his wife I understood his grief, she merely shrugged. "Our gods abandoned us and that is why our city fell." As soon as she had been baptized she always attended Mass whether Cuauhtemoc did or not. By now his preference for a solitude first imposed by his burned feet had given him the air of a man who is alone even in a crowd.

To Cortés the long hours Cuauhtemoc spent within his apartment suggested the possible hatching of some plot against the conquerors, maybe an Indian uprising. To the surviving Aztecs, the few in the city of Mexico and the many in the other Anahuac cities and towns, Cuauhtemoc was, as the last Aztec ruler, a figure commanding respect—nor did his hopeless stand against the Spaniards reap their disapproval, rather the opposite. I became aware of Cortés' change in attitude toward his prisoner when he began to take Cuauhtemoc with him when he went to the city of Mexico, even when he walked out in the streets of Texcoco. Thus he kept an eye on him and also showed that he was treating him with honor. I think Cuauhtemoc served as an illusory shield as well, for once when Cortés was ill with a fever he awoke in the night and told me of an evil dream: a deranged Aztec, willing to lose his own life if by doing so he could kill the conqueror of his people, tried to assassinate him, hurling a javelin at him in the street. But Cortés was walking close to Cuauhtemoc; the spear pierced the Aztec's heart instead. This dream seemed to Cortés to portend a very real possibility, even though I told him this fear was foolish, for how could any Aztec fail to see that Cortés now lived only to make their land a better place?

In this he was impeded by lack of royal recognition, but at last, in October 1522, Emperor Carlos V finally acted with astonishing generosity. He made Hernán Cortés the governor, captain-general, and chief justice of all New Spain, a territory reaching from the Pacific to the Gulf of Mexico and from the isthmus of Tehuantepec to the distant northern deserts, an area somewhat larger than Iberia. Along with these titles went a liberal salary, honors, and land grants to all his captains with smaller discretionary grants to his foot soldiers as well. In addition, the emperor sent a letter in his own handwriting thanking and complimenting Cortés' soldiers for their great service to Spain and himself.

Cortés was exultant when he told me this news: the royal commission had exceeded his wildest hopes. "Do you realize what this means? I am at this moment the most powerful and important man in the Spanish Empire, second only to the emperor himself!"

Nor was this all. The royal messengers bringing to Cortés the king's commission had stopped off at Santiago de Cuba, where the news of Cortés' vindication was publicly proclaimed. Governor Velásquez learned that all chance of redress against Cortés was gone and with it the fortune he had spent to equip the Narváez expedition. He fell at once into a deep melancholy, Cortés was told. Of this he was to die the following year. "If only he could have trusted me," Cortés said on learning of his illness. "But from the first he gave in to doubts of my character. And so he is today ill and penniless instead of happy and rich."

Because of the Royal Commission, I suddenly found myself in a position of great prominence: I was like a queen in her palace surrounded by her ladies-in-waiting, my faithful Indian women. Orteguilla capered and clicked his heels in the air with glee as he pointed this out to me, and finally did a somersault that ended with his kneeling at my feet. "You are now sitting on top of the world, my lady! How does it feel up there? Is the air too thin? Forget it. Your lungs will soon become accustomed. There is nothing easier to get used to than a higher social status, as I learned when Cortés turned me from a street boy into a respectable page. And you deserve it all! I know, and every Spanish soldier knows, and soon the whole world will know that your loyalty and cleverness were of inestimable value to the Royal Governor of New Spain. You share his glory." The grin left his face, and I knew why: he had remembered that Cortés was married and could not change my status from mere *barragana*. Moreover, I was an Indian. But he instantly brightened. "And you have given the governor his only son. So hold your head high and learn to deal with the sycophants who will besiege you with gifts and flattery."

In this he prove right; from Spaniards who came in hope of choice land grants offerings flowed to me: a music box made in Austria, a Bible bound in Morocco leather, a black lace shawl, and other pretty gifts. In thanking each giver I made it clear that I had no power to persuade Cortés to favor one person over another; such frankness shocked them and they denied any such notion.

My own elevation in status meant nothing to me; what mattered was that Cortés at last had the necessary authority to carry out his humane ideals regarding the conquered peoples. Carlos had accepted his evaluation of the Indians of New Spain as being in all ways superior to the natives of the West Indies so that the abuses of *repartimiento* and *encomienda* would here be particularly cruel and unnecessary.

The month of November 1522 opened mildly enough with a visit from Father Jeronimo Aguilar. For many months he had been in Oaxaca, where a Christian church had been built; I had missed him. When Orteguilla announced my guest I was kneeling on the floor encouraging Martín to walk the whole length of the bedroom toward me: he had spoken early but still preferred crawling to walking. As soon as I saw Aguilar's face I knew that something had deeply disturbed him.

He nevertheless smiled and complimented me on my new Spanish dress; Cortés had just given me two new ones, of rose brocade and deep green velvet—he had sent to Spain for them. The waists were constricting, the cloth rather heavy for comfort, but it pleased him to see me wear them. I was wearing the brocade today because I expected him to return from a visit to Vera Cruz. I also had on a small brocade cap that came to a point in front and had a pear-shaped pearl that hung down over my forehead. Orteguilla had assured me that in this costume I could pass for a *dama* of highest category anywhere in Spain, although at that moment I might not have, for I was wearing native · leather sandals. Along with the gowns, petticoats, hose and cap had come a pair of brocade shoes too narrow for my feet and two instruments of torture called *chopines,* a kind of shoe made with wooden supports below heel and sole so as to give added height to the wearer. These I had worn once and put away.

Aguilar, having complimented my appearance, smiled down at my son, who was walking wide-legged toward where I knelt with outspread arms to receive him. "A beautiful boy. His face seems to combine the best features of both parents." Martín, as if overwhelmed by this compliment, lost his balance and sat down hard. I picked him up and swung him high over my head just as Doña Luisa came in to give him his supper. When they left, I offered Aguilar a glass of wine and aloesugar cakes and we sat down in two chairs by the window to visit like old friends. "I can see something is worrying you," I said. "Is there any trouble in Oaxaca?"

He looked at the small cake he was holding as though it had turned bitter in his mouth and set it down beside his wineglass. "I am afraid that Cortés is going to perpetuate here the execrable system of *encomienda,* a high-sounding word for making slaves of indigenous people."

He had amazed me. "You are wrong! Cortés has written to the king deploring this practice."

"I know that. But the needs of Spanish colonists could easily prevail with Cortés over his concern for Indians. To continue to hold this land for Spain, Cortés needs more Spanish settlers. To get them he promises landholdings. But to work this land they are going to need and demand native labor. The temptation Cortés therefore faces is to permit *encomienda* on a temporary basis. Once established, it will become permanent." He gave me one of his sad, probing looks. "You could intercede between him and this temptation. You could point out to him that few evils are content to remain temporary, for evil thrives on itself and grows the stronger through practice."

"But the king himself has forbidden that evil, and on Cortés' own recommendation!"

"The Crown may forbid, but the Crown has also given Cortés absolute power in New Spain. The colonists in Oaxaca are already claiming that without the help of Indian labor they cannot survive. The last thing Cortés wants is for discouraged settlers to return to Spain and the islands claiming that land grants without *encomienda* are like empty promises. He will temporize, I fear. The fate of the conquered will prove secondary to the needs and desires of Spaniards."

This conclusion grated on me harshly. I pointed toward the distant island across the lake where the city of Mexico was rising. "Have you seen what Cortés is building there? A Christian city! And in all the towns and cities of this land churches will rise so that heathens lost to God may kneel to Him! Their voices will sing hymns to Jesus and his Blessed Mother, and all the saints and angels of Heaven will smile down on them, and no one will ever burn in Hell again. Their children's children will bless the name of Hernán Cortés!"

Aguilar was unmoved. "That city on the lake or any

other such cities, however many churches they may boast, cannot compensate for the crushing of the lives and spirits of the native people." He leaned toward me, earnest. "It is Cortés I am also concerned for: his political future. He has enemies, some powerful ones such as Fonseca, the bishop of Burgos who for decades has determined the policies of the Council of the Indies. He was on the side of Velásquez, and would not delay in grasping any pretext to make trouble for Cortés with the king. To condone Indian slavery here would put a powerful weapon in the hands of Fonseca—and others."

"You don't understand Cortés. What he wants above all else is to Christianize the native people of New Spain. He has just petitioned Carlos to send him many, many holy men. Not bishops and pampered prelates, but good, humble men of simple devotion to God. Friars of your Franciscan order, and Dominicans, padres who will found missions, gently teach and uplift!"

Aguilar nodded. "To replace the rituals of the native religion with the rituals of Christianity on the one hand, and yet on the other to doom those same natives to the misery of serfdom is not beyond Cortés. He could justify slavery by the opportunity for spiritual enlightenment also offered the victims."

I stood up, stared down at him in outrage. "To do that he would have to hate Indians, and you cannot claim he does!"

"We hate whom we have hurt," Aguilar said calmly.

"That makes no sense at all!"

"Why are you so angry?"

"You don't know Cortés. The discontent of some Spanish colonists in Oaxaca or anywhere else will not make him change in his hatred of *encomienda!*"

"I hope you are right."

After he left I was faced with the fact that Aguilar was not given to exaggeration and had not reached his conclusions on inadequate grounds. I knew, too, that he loved Cortés and was truly concerned for him. And he believed that I, better than he himself, might be able to point out to Cortés the danger of compromise.

I walked to the new mirror and saw what might have been a Spanish lady of highest category, although perhaps with a touch of Moorish blood. I stood on my toes, for the rose brocade skirt was a little long. I went to the chest where the *chopines* were and took them out. At supper I might find the right moment to bring up the matter of *encomienda* without letting Cortés know that Aguilar had doubts of him. Or that I did.

Sitting on the closed chest I inserted my feet into the *chopines* and again practiced walking in them. From the mirror as I passed my reflection stared back at me, a stranger. I faced her, smiled, and offered her the bow Orteguilla had taught me and with which I planned to greet Cortés.

But he did not return in time for supper; I was in bed and nearly asleep when he arrived, vexed and weary. When I asked what troubled him, he spoke bitterly of Fonseca. "For thirty years this malignant creature has used his power to work against all Spanish explorers, from Columbus to Cortés! Now, one would think, the great honors Carlos has bestowed on me should give him pause. Not at all! In his chagrin over my glorious vindication, which just may finally end his great influence over the Council of the Indies, Fonseca has managed one last sting. He accused me, I have learned, of extending both *repartimiento* and *encomienda* to New Spain!"

His anger brought me great relief. "You would never do that!"

"By my conscience, no!"

When I fell asleep I was dimly aware that he was still tossing and turning, as though conscience troubled him.

He had already left for the city of Mexico when I awoke to learn from Doña Luisa that Martín was ill. She had become his nurse; Cortés did not think it suitable that I attend to all our son's physical needs, for a Spanish lady of all but the lowest category always had a nurse for her infants. When I went into the room where Martín and Doña Luisa slept I found his forehead like fire. With a finger I explored his mouth, but he was not teething. He had caught a catarrh in the brisk November weather, but even after I washed his body to cool it the fever raged on. I was rocking him in my arms and singing a Paynalan song about a little boy who threw a rabbit so high it landed on the moon, which is why we see the shadowy shape of a rabbit on the moon to this day, when Orteguilla said Alvarado was waiting to speak to me. I asked that he wait and stayed with Martín until he was sleeping. But by that time Alvarado had left.

Orteguilla looked at me reproachfully. "You should have told me. Do you no longer trust your majordomo? Plans must be made, you know."

"What plans? What are you talking about?"

He stared at me, stricken. "I thought you knew."

"Knew what?"

"While Cortés was in Vera Cruz he received a letter from his wife. She intends to join him here in his hour of glory. She will embark from Santiago de Cuba in a ship bringing a number of new colonists. She has asked that a suitable entourage be sent to meet her and escort her to the capital."

The true cause of Cortés' troubled mood the night before was now clear. Not Fonseca's malice, but Doña Catalina's imminent presence had darkened his spirits.

Orteguilla was already full of plans: "We must be prepared to entertain her with elegance. Perhaps Cortés' godson, the king of Texcoco, may be persuaded to stage an entertainment in his palace in her honor— some amusing barbaric ceremony that will dazzle her and reflect well on us." But he at once saw my disinterest in entertaining Doña Catalina and discreetly retired.

I was puzzled and angry. Why had Cortés been evasive? Why had he left me to learn of his wife's arrival from someone else? Had it been by chance? Or had he preferred that Alvarado break the news? The day passed slowly for me. Martín grew worse and whimpered almost steadily. The remedies I knew did not help him, and so in the afternoon I sent for the Spanish physician, recently arrived and residing with colonists in the city of Mexico. The many hours before he arrived seemed endless. He recommended leeches and bleeding, but I could not bear to have the ugly things attached to my son's body, nor to let the doctor cut the veins in his wrists. The surgeon departed in anger. It was after he left that a message came from Cortés saying that he was going to stay in the governor's palace overnight because certain furnishings had just arrived from Spain and he wished to see to their placement in the morning. By this time my concern over Martín made anything else seem a minor matter. The threatened arrival of Catalina, anguish over Cortés' lack of candor, Aguilar's fears as to *encomienda,* all were mere flyspecks. That night I could not sleep but kept going to Martín's bedside. But by midmorning the fever had broken and he was hungry and I knew the worst was over.

It soon occurred to me that the angry doctor whose aid I had requested, then spurned, would surely state his grievances to Cortés, so I dressed myself in rose brocade and *chopines.* Now my care with my appearance was not because I wished to do what Aguilar desired and express my concern over the enslavement of Indians: I wanted out of pride to look my best when I charged Cortés with his lack of candor about his wife's visit.

He returned at the supper hour, very much concerned about Martín, for the doctor had been gloomy about his survival without the leeches and bloodletting, which in his opinion would have assured it. I was able to show Cortés our sweetly sleeping son, his head now cool, his breathing regular. We supped, as we often did, at a table in our bedroom, now on white damask brought us by a hopeful colonist. He used a silver fork, an eating novelty among the noble folk of Europe.

I watched him consume a meat pie and then I could

contain myself no longer. "I did not like learning of your wife's visit from Alvarado."

The fork clattered to his dish. "I did not intend you to. He happened to have been with me in Vera Cruz when I got her letter from the captain in charge there. I didn't tell you at once because I wanted time to think the matter over. My first intention was to send word asking her not to come at present. But then I realized that this would be a stupid letter, sure to cause anger on her part. She has a large family, none of them famous for keeping their mouths shut. There would have been scandalous whispers all over Santiago in a day's time. So I slept on the decision and came to the conclusion that I will have to let her come."

"Why did you rage against Fonseca instead of telling me the real reason why you were disturbed?"

He poured wine, spilled it on the white damask cloth, stood up angry. "I see that I must explain certain facts to you. You are my mistress and enjoy my affection and my protection. But Catalina is my legal wife and is entitled to my respect. She has learned of you by now, without doubt. I will courteously refuse to discuss you with her. I do not wish to discuss her with you. I have decided that the two of you will never meet. You will remain here in Texcoco with your child. She will reside with me in the governor's palace the length of her stay. I want no malicious gossip, no Spanish colonists in the capital sending back to Spain tidbits about the two women of Hernán Cortés. A mistress is permitted a man of high category, but with so Christian a young monarch as Carlos, that man must be discreet." As he spoke and paced, some of his anger had evaporated. He nodded down at me, pleased with his own decision. "I count on you, who have always shown such concern for my happiness, to forget from this moment that my wife is to visit me. Her existence made no difference to you while she was in Cuba and should make no difference now, for I was no less married to her then."

"When she was in Cuba there was no chance that she

would share your bed." The unintended words sprang out like toads.

He stared at me. "Are you trying to extract my promise that I will not sleep with her? My legal wife? What I do with her should be of no concern to you. She is barren and cannot give me a child. So do not trouble yourself with so trivial a matter as whether or not I choose to perform a certain conjugal duty."

Filled with the bitter knowledge that fidelity demanded of a woman may be dispensed with by a man, I suddenly remembered a night in a dead ruler's treasure room; it struck me that the stone vault was now mere air the birds flew through and the boy I had been with in Cuba or elsewhere or dead.

Seeing me mute and with downcast eyes, Cortés assessed my mood as having no taint of sullenness, only dejection. "You have a very particular place in my life and always will, Marina." Smiling, he held out his hand to me. "So come to bed."

I felt for the *chopine* I had kicked off under the table and wedged my foot into it. Discomfort gleaned me a compliment when I stood and took his hand. "Those clothes become you well! You look taller, and height has its own elegance."

I smiled as though two added inches of wood and leather did not squeeze my toes in vises. His lips were moist and his eyes had that bright gleam of desire, and Doña Catalina was a long way off. Perhaps, I thought as I walked carefully toward the bed, perhaps her ship will sink in the Gulf of Mexico!

But it did not. Sandoval was dispatched with a dozen soldiers to meet her in Vera Cruz. I took what comfort I could from the fact that Cortés himself did not go to welcome her. Less comforting was his departure to take up residence with her in the governor's palace. Not only was he gone, but most of his clothing vanished with him. His *ropero* now gaped emptily when I opened it; the stand for his armor was a skeleton stripped of its metal flesh. And the high canopied bed had grown very large.

Emptiness was all around me. No longer did the palace echo with his voice and the voices of captains, colonists, or caciques from distant places. Sometimes I felt as much a captive as Cuauhtemoc, yet at the same time knew this was only in my mind. The only wall that curtailed my freedom was the one Cortés had raised between his wife and me.

42

A sudden change in my relationship with Cuauhtemoc took place a few days after Cortés left. Martín eluded Doña Luisa, toddled down a corridor, crawled down a flight of steps, and went across a courtyard to the apartment of the last Aztec ruler. There, exhausted by his bold effort, he sat down on the steps and wailed for me. I, meanwhile, had begun my search with Doña Luisa. I found my child in tall Cuauhtemoc's muscular arms, sucking a thumb and looking well content.

As I took him into my own arms, my eyes and Cuauhtemoc's met. His, to my surprise, held a hint of amusement. He spoke a Nahoan aphorism: "Like father, like son." Just as Cortés had come a long distance to encounter him, so had Martín. This first friendly remark I did not want to let pass and so I told him how well I liked his wife, how much I would welcome a visit from him as well.

He took a step back from me; amusement left his eyes. To my surprise, the next day Orteguilla announced that both he and his wife were downstairs. I told him to invite them up to the large bedroom-sitting room and to bring refreshments. Cuauhtemoc's eyes kept wandering to the high bed with its canopy. He asked me whether Spaniards like to sleep that high up in order to be nearer their Heaven in case they died in their sleep; I said I did not think that was the case so much as rats and told him what Cortés had said about their prevalence in European cities, due in part to the sewers. Cuauhtemoc was amazed to learn that the Europeans did not utilize their own excrement as a fertilizer or their urine for tanning leather, but allowed them to be wasted in open sewers in the streets. What, then, did they use to fertilize their fields and gardens? he asked. I told him they used the dung of horses and cows, and then explained what a cow was, and how Europeans drank the milk. His face showed that he found this somewhat repulsive, but he only remarked that this seemed a strange drink for a people so fierce. His wife was clearly pleased that he had come so far out of his shell of isolation. Everything went well until he asked how soon Cortés would return.

Animosity filled me; I stared hard at his eyes and mouth to find if the remark had been intentionally cruel. "I do not know," I said coldly. He was at once aware of my change of mood and very soon thanked me and left.

The following morning he and his wife returned my hospitality: she said that in the market their servant had found some excellent iguana meat and also a fresh mojarra fish, and I would dine with them that evening? They still had not adopted the Spanish way of eating the largest meal of the day in the afternoon; I had, but was delighted to change my usual routine for so good a reason. Soon, I thought, Cortés' nagging suspicion of the Aztec ruler would be a thing of the past. For although Spaniards can break their bread with someone they intend to harm, that would not be possible to Cuauhtemoc.

That bread was never broken, nor did I taste iguana or mojarra. Cuauhtemoc himself came to cancel the invitation. "Cortés has sent for me to come to his palace and remain there with him." His face was expressionless, but I knew he knew the reason: Cortés had decided it was unwise to leave Cuauhtemoc unwatched by him in Texcoco, for fear he might perhaps succeed in enlisting in his own cause some of the nobles who had not taken too kindly to their ruler's passionate conversion to the true faith. A slight smile curled Cuauhtemoc's lips. He added an Aztec cliché: "Below the green panache bad dreams occur." I could not defend Cortés against this truth. We parted, Cuauhtemoc and I, with friendly words, and later he and his wife left with the escort of Spanish soldiers for the governor's palace.

That night, alone in that wide bed that no longer smelled faintly of Cortés, I felt the truth burst over me like a crashing wave. I and I alone was forbidden to see Doña Catalina; even a conquered Aztec would be presented to her, while I was left in my isolation to wonder what she looked like and if she were really as beautiful as I had heard.

I had pumped Orteguilla and knew that although very lovely she was of no family whatsoever, had no connections, and thus was actually something of a detriment to a man in the high position Cortés now enjoyed. The dwarf's philosophy of eminence was simple: getting to the top of the heap is hard, but staying there is harder. Kings can be fickle, envious friends dangerous, outright enemies lethal. Thus marriage for reasons other than social and political advancement is a luxury not often indulged in by the elite of Spain or any other nation, he said. Cortés had finally agreed to marry Doña Catalina to maintain his good relationship with Governor Velásquez, who had championed the lovesick young beauty's cause out of his own infatuation with one of her equally lovely sisters. "Had Cortés defied the governor, he would never have later got command of the expedition to Mexico, so to that extent Doña Catalina has been of use in the advancement of Cortés' career." When I asked him if they had been happily married, he rather reluctantly reported that she and Cortés had spent three apparently amiable years together, marred not only by her inability to conceive a child.

When I said it struck me as odd that she and Cortés' mother had the same name, Orteguilla was surprised at my ignorance. "Catalina is a very common Spanish name," he said. "And her present situation is just as common. One of the functions of priests is to comfort abandoned wives and get them resigned to their lot."

"Except that she is not abandoned," I said. "I am." With those words it became a fixed truth. All Cortés' talk of a brief separation to prevent gossip and scandal I saw now as the first wedge in a gap that would grow wider and wider. Orteguilla's denial did not alter this belief.

My need to see my rival and form my own opinion of her became unbearable. But how?

A visit from Captain Gonzalo Sandoval gave me the information that caused me to hatch a plan as underhanded as it was childish. I had liked Sandoval from the first. He was twenty-six; his exuberance was tempered by good manners and a kind heart. His curly brown hair and heavy Castilian accent seemed to me to match well; by now I could understand his lisp with little difficulty. I at once began to query him about Doña Catalina. He reported Cortés' public courtesy to her, and that in private he was less constrained. Yes, she was as beautiful as I had heard, and dressed with great style, favoring black and deep blue, which showed off her pale skin to advantage. She was quite vain of her complexion and never exposed herself to sunlight. There had been a fiesta in her honor after her arrival. Another entertainment was planned, a daytime feast by the lake in the pretty forest of Chapultepec near the ruins of Moctezuma's summer palace. Indians would dance for her, and swing from ropes attached to high poles. "They hang by their teeth," he said, "and the wheel atop the pole is so adjusted that they swing out very wide and seem to be flying."

I instantly formed my plan to see my rival. I knew that Indians would cluster in their canoes along the shore to watch these festivities and I decided to be one of those Indians. I would abandon my Spanish gown for a skirt and triangular *huipile* such as the Aztec and Toltec women wore, and let my hair hang down loose again.

Orteguilla, though dubious about my defying Cortés, was also excited by my scheme and arranged for a dugout canoe to be paddled across the lake by one of our male Texcocan servants. Doña Luisa was reluctantly willing to accompany me. For additional disguise I used a black rebozo which I could hold across my mouth and nose as Aztecs do in crisp weather.

It was a brilliant, sparkling day as we crossed the wide blue lake toward Chapultepec, but the sunlight could not charm away my inner knowledge of wrongdoing. I smothered this uneasiness with righteous annoyance. Why shouldn't I see Doña Catalina? Was I expected to live forever with a figment of the imagination, a nebulous Catalina made up of mere words? Cortés had been blind to my need to see with my own eyes the woman whose existence was a bane to me. Well, I would remedy that!

As I had foreseen, a hundred or more canoes filled with gaping Indians already crowded the lakeshore facing the dining area with its tables on trestles draped in cotton cloths of various colors: a tall rack held a spit on which a big pig slowly turned and sizzled in the Cuban manner, *barbacoa*. Our boatman had just managed to nudge a place for us between two canoes when the first of three large canopied pirogues arrived containing the visitors. I drew my black shawl across my mouth as I saw Cortés in the first of these, seated beside a woman in dark blue, her back toward me. A stretch of beach had been staked out for the boats; the one in which Cortés and Doña Catalina and a dozen others rode pulled to shore only one canoe away from mine. When the flat prow grated on the beach, Cortés disembarked first, then held up both arms to lift his wife down. Laughing, she landed lightly close to where

I sat in the canoe, my face half hidden. She turned to call something to the other people in the boat.

And, oh, but her skin was white! Her brown hair had red-gold glints and was curly. With a dainty gesture she raised her full blue skirt and I saw a tiny pointed slipper of brocade. Her eyes were green or blue, and they caught light as gems do, gleaming. On her very pale bosom glowed a huge pearl set in a pendant of gold, one of those a cacique from the north had brought to Cortés a year before. She cast a look of worry up at the beaming sun. Cortés laughed and held his ruby cloak out above her head like a protective wing so that its shadow shielded that white face, that pale bosom. She cast up at him a look of adoring gratitude and he smiled down at her.

In that instant I felt a pang of most awful jealousy, and with it, despair. I had seen too clearly the difference between her and me. They were Spaniards. Of a different race, a different world. I could easily lose him to that Spanish world, in which I had no place. I could easily lose him to her. My eyes stripped silk and velvet from her body. I saw it white as her pearl in the arms of Cortés.

In a voice that did not sound like my own I asked to be taken back to Texcoco, and with dull eyes looked over my shoulder at the figures of Doña Catalina and Cortés, now mingling with other Spaniards who soon surrounded them completely, their voices and laughter mocking my misery.

I nursed it for weeks as carefully as I had tended Martín when he was ill. Daily I hoped for some reassuring word from Cortés; daily I was disappointed. In my dreams he sailed off with her to Cuba and did not even say goodbye. All other concerns became unreal: Aguilar came one day to report that in one colony the natives were being misused by Spaniards in the mines, working long hours without remuneration. This seemed to me of little importance compared to my own overwhelming pain, rooted in rejection by Cortés and my helplessness. What could I do to change the bitter truth? She was his Spanish wife; I was his Indian mistress. I could not cause him to unmarry her. I could not bleach my skin, pale my eyes, become a Spanish *dama*. One night, lying alone and imagining him with her, I desperately thought of taking my child and disappearing from Texcoco, going somewhere he could never find me again. Let him worry if I were dead or alive, and where his son might be! The next day, looking down at Martín, I knew he was my strongest hope of winning Cortés back, and I searched my son's face for its resemblance to his father. I confess all this with shame; I was a woman of nearly twenty-three, and such childish rebellion against the facts of my existence did not become me.

It was Doña Luisa, aware of my anguish, who reminded me that I was a Christian and should turn to God for comfort. I could not confess my jealousy to any priest, but I did kneel alone and ask God's forgiveness for my unworthy emotions. "Thy will be done," I said, and then hoped His will would be that Cortés would send her back to Cuba, soon.

Evidently God or the Sainted Virgin took pity on me, for the next day a message arrived from Cortés; a dozen lines in his own hand said he had been very occupied in raising funds for his new maritime campaign to the north shore of Honduras, to be headed by Cristobal Olid. A second reason he had not been able to visit me in Texcoco was that Doña Catalina had fallen ill with a catarrh or asthma and had pleaded with him not to leave her alone in a strange land until she was better. "Alvarado will soon be leaving to lead the expedition of exploration and colonization in Guatemala. I trust Martín is well, and you also."

Even this brief communication cheered me. I told myself that only a very heartless man would leave a sick woman in a strange city among servants little known to her. At the same time I felt that Doña Catalina could have managed to bear her illness for a day or two had she not chosen to use it to play on Cortés' sympathy and thus keep him from seeing me.

It was about a week later that I was awakened late one night by voices in the hall outside my bedroom. Orteguilla sounded excited. The other voice was Sandoval's. In a moment Orteguilla appeared in the doorway, his face lighted by the candle he held. His eyes popping with surprise, Orteguilla cried, "She's dead! Doña Catalina is dead!"

Behind him Sandoval nodded his curly head. "Poor soul," he lisped, "it was a congestion of the lungs, very common at this altitude. The Spanish physician who attended her said she was of a watery humor, shown by a long history of catarrhs and asthmas."

Dead. I rose to compassion, thinking how hopefully she had journeyed to her husband's side. "Poor soul," I repeated. "She was very beautiful." A sharp glance from Orteguilla made me add "Or so I have been told."

And so my rival was buried far from home, and a Mass was said for her soul, attended by every Spaniard in the area. I, of course, did not attend, but I prayed for her.

While I wondered how soon Cortés would think it proper to return to me, a question arose in my mind. Had she lived, would Cortés have found that he cared more for her than for me? Might he have found it expedient to abandon me? Remembering our nearly three years together, the disasters, the triumphs, the passion, and looking down at the fruit of that passion, little Martín, I told myself "No never!" Yet I also remembered Cortés' outspread cape sheltering the fair skin under which flowed the same Spanish blood as his own.

That sight had a result unexpected by me: I had found it impossible to put on my Spanish garments again. For I had seen such clothing worn by a woman born to wear it. After her death I had several new Indian cotton skirts and tunics made in strong beautiful colors, exquisitely embroidered.

A week after the funeral rites Cortés returned to me, arriving one gusty evening. I was ready for his sorrow, ready for his desire to speak of his dead wife or to remain silent. I was not ready for his rage. It was in him, throbbing, as he gave me a perfunctory embrace. He hurled his cape to a chair, threw his cap after it, and burst out: "There is no end to the indecency of those enemies my fame has hatched! There is nothing they will not stoop to say against me!"

I thought of Aguilar, of *encomienda,* of Fonseca. I was a long way from the truth. I learned, to my shock, of the whisper now running from mouth to ear in the capital: that Cortés had murdered his wife or had this done!

"Some are saying it was out of my love for you. Some say it was my pride and ambition; that I wanted to leave the way open for a later advantageous marriage to a Spanish lady of noble birth. You should thank me for making you stay here in Texcoco. If I hadn't they might have named you as my accomplice!"

"What are you going to do to stop this slander?" I asked.

"Absolutely nothing! Nothing! I will not dignify it with any comment at all. Her physician is furious; he is implicated too in that he attended her. He has issued a public statement of the true facts of her disease, in brief, a severe lung congestion, the water at last filling them so she could no longer breathe. So far above the sea, she drowned!" He gave a bitter laugh, then sobered abruptly. "Well, God rest her soul. When I married her she believed her prayers had been answered. And that marriage proved the death of her. We must be very careful what we pray for. I prayed for fame. And got it. And am now called a wife-killer." He was sprawled low in his carved armchair, like the one lost on the *noche triste.* I went to his side, where I had stood so many times. I touched his shoulder; he looked up at me.

"Those who admire you will never believe this lie. Those who hate and envy you will believe anything at all. This slander means nothing more than that, which you already knew."

His hand came up to cover mine. He looked then from my face and down the rest of me. He stood up, holding me at arm's length. "Where are your Spanish clothes? Why do I find you in these native garments?"

I could not tell him the whole truth, that ever since I had seen his wife at Chapultepec I had never once worn the Spanish dresses he had given me, that the sight of her had shown me a truth that came of both my pride and my humility: I was not a Spanish lady and could never be, and dressing like one I was only a poor imitation. I said, "The shoes pinch my feet. The tight waist keeps me from breathing. And I am tired of masquerading as what I am not."

I was prepared for irritation, even anger, for I knew those clothes had been costly. But he laughed, and in his eyes I thought I saw a certain respect. "To tell the truth, I think I like you better this way, after all." His lips, thin with anger when he first returned, now softened, and the hard look left his eyes. "By my conscience, I have missed you, Marina!"

"And I you," I whispered.

He smiled. "In that case, will you take a glass of wine with me?" He gave me the silver chalice, as he had in Tlascala, but it was not wine which took us from pain to joy. I went to sleep happier than I had been in many months.

It is part of the human condition that our happiness is usually brief: the next day mine was shattered. For the moment came—I do not remember the precise opening his words gave me—when the ending of my selfish personal anxiety made me remember Aguilar. I told Cortés of rumors I had heard concerning the fact that some Spanish colonists now had Indian slaves.

"And where did you hear this rumor?" he asked, very alert.

There was a look in his eyes that made me sure I did not want to mention my friend Aguilar. I was vague: "Oh, in the Texcoco market one hears people talk."

"And since when do you go to market?"

I was telling the truth when I said "During your absence it became one of my diversions. I would put a basket over my arm and mingle with the people here and buy little delicacies for the table or a toy for Martín."

I had briefly deflected him. "You must not forget who you are. Trotting around market stalls with a basket on your arm like one of our servants does not suit your rather exalted position in life. Do you realize that your name is now known in Spain? That a poem has been written about you?" He smiled. " 'Noble Indian woman, beautiful peregrine, like an Indian princess, a spirited Amazon.' "

It was astonishing news to me, but did not make me forget about Indian slaves. "Aguilar also heard this rumor I mentioned. I told him of your letter to King Carlos concerning the superiority of the natives of Mexico. I said you would never allow them to be so abused."

We were at breakfast, a meal he enjoyed when time permitted. He looked down at the broiled fish he was eating and pushed the dish aside. He heaved a heavy sigh, yet also looked rather proud. "One of the heavy crosses borne by those in absolute authority is this: one's heart may yearn toward the ideal, yet one's mind is sometimes forced to accept an expedient dictated by grim reality."

The ornate words seemed to have no meaning. "Does that mean that you now condone *encomienda* here?"

He looked across at me with hard eyes. "It means that I have to get more Spanish colonists! It means I am going to counteract Fonseca's efforts to discourage settlers from coming here! I am going to hold this land for Spain, and that means settlers, settlers, and more settlers! I cannot permit the blood of the brave Castilians who died here to be shed in vain! If the colonists need local labor to work their land grants, that they shall have! Naturally I will see to it that the Indians are decently treated. Of that I assure you."

He sounded as if he were addressing a large audience. Or perhaps it was his conscience, by which he so often swore. "How?" I asked.

"What?"

"How will you enforce decent treatment of the Indians?"

He jumped to his feet. "Do you know how many Indians there are on Anahuac and the areas just around it? Something like twenty-five million! Do you imagine I can hold this territory with a mere trickle of Spaniards? And now, for the love of God, stop interfering in matters that don't concern you!" He turned and strode from the room.

I was left to face a new discovery: Aguilar understood Cortés better than I, at least in this matter. All I could do at present was to pray that Spaniards by the thousands would cross an ocean out of the desire to own land but not the people on it. I did not then know how deeply Cortés' abandonment of his humane earlier stand on slavery had dismayed me.

On the day I learned that Aguilar had been right in his doubts of Cortés I took Martín with me to visit Cuauhtemoc and his wife; I brought them gifts and flowers. Their apartment was pleasant, a number of servants saw to their needs, and it was very little like a prison.

43

During the next year Cortés was intensely, if not joyously, busy. He continued with the rebuilding of the capital; he established five major settlements, from Zacatula on the Pacific to Antigua on the Gulf of Mexico. In Antigua he established the Board of Trade and because of its fine harbor predicted it would become the greatest commercial capital of New Spain. Vessels coming into the country, and there were many, were required by royal edict, petitioned for by Cortés, to bring quantities of seeds and plants: European fruits and vegetables, sugar canes, and mulberry bushes for the raising of silkworms. He made it a condition of land ownership that new settlers cultivate these various plants; only after eight years of such husbandry would final title to the land be granted. Cortés felt that this plan not only prevented the impoverishment of native plantations which he had seen in the West Indies but also bound the settlers to the new soil with plants that reminded them of home. A Spaniard able to bring over within eighteen months a wife might lay claim to as much land as he could traverse on horseback between dawn and dark, and some clever fellows used relays of horses to stretch the distance. But except for Tlascalans and Totonacs, too many natives knew the burden of serfdom; their lands went into the possession of colonists and they went with the land. The most fortunate Indians were those living in their towns and villages under their former caciques, on land not tempting to the Spaniards because of poor climate or soil, lack of precious ores, or for being in an area subject to frequent earthquake. Although Cortés made many stipulations limiting the power of Spanish master over Indian slave, these were too often disregarded, particularly in the mining districts.

Even with all these concerns, Cortés could not forget his need for discovery and conquest. Alvarado had gone southward with an army to subdue the chieftains of Yucatán and Guatemala. Captain Olid had embarked on a maritime expedition to Honduras.

Our private life suffered from all the various projects Cortés had involved himself in, but at the end of 1523 I found I was again pregnant. My faithful friend Aguilar noted a change in my eyes and face, and on learning my condition said, "It is time for Cortés to legitimize Martín and this new child you are going to bear him."

Privately I felt the same. Doña Catalina's death was

more than a year in the past. The scandalous whispers concerning it had lost their novelty and had apparently died too. But I said, in an offhand way, "That would be well and good, I suppose." Cortés had never spoken of marriage to me.

"Does he know that you expect another child?"

"No."

"Perhaps when he does it will suggest to him a change in your status."

When Cortés returned from Zacatula, where he was building a small fleet to explore the Pacific coast northward, I told him I expected another child.

He eyed my belly, still flat. "Considering how little time we have had to spend together, this argues well for my potence. Do you wish for a girl or another boy?"

"Whichever I have, it will still be a bastard," I said calmly.

His eyes flinched. "That harsh word I do not like to hear from your mouth, Marina! You are not a Catalonian to use such blunt language. Boy or girl, the child will be mine. I have freely acknowledged paternity of Martín, and will do so again." He winked. "Even though I have been much away, I have no doubt as to your chastity." He sobered. "To be the natural son of Cortés is to have a better start in this world than to be the legitimate heir of just any man. Martín will receive the education he needs to fit him for a high position in this land. There's a lovely valley to the west of here which the Spaniards have named Cuernavaca. The climate is admirable, and I am going to build a summer palace there. From that palace I intend that one day Martín shall rule as governor."

"For the son of a *barragana* that is a fine prospect," I said, eyes lowered.

With great earnestness he leaned toward me and took my hand. "I cannot subject myself or you to the instant scandal our marriage would launch. If you believe that my enemies would hesitate for a moment to bring up the suspicions concerning my wife's death, think again! Our wedding would only prove to them the truth of that evil lie." He reached out to stroke my cheek. "You have a very lovely glow. Are you glad for your state?"

"Not glad, not sorry. What is, is."

He thought a moment. "I'm really quite pleased."

That was unfortunate, for early the next year I miscarried.

It happened on the January day that twelve Franciscan friars in worn brown robes reached the city of Mexico. The emperor had generously responded to Cortés' plea for more priests to Christianize the natives. The bell in the cathedral's one tower pealed a welcome, echoed by the bells in the smaller churches. Cortés headed a cavalcade of caballeros and important citizens who went out to honor the arrival of these men of God. Later Sandoval told me that Cortés dismounted and humbly knelt to kiss the hem of the robe of Father Martín of Valencia, and this amazed the many Indians who had gathered to watch, and taught them at once to regard these poorly dressed servants of Christ as persons of greatest importance.

I did not see this myself, for I was in the canopied bed, very sick and bleeding copiously, which did not prevent the Spanish physician from bleeding me further. I was too weak to resist, but after he had gone I had Doña Luisa bind the dripping perforations in my wrists. Despite the arrival of the padres, Cortés found time to visit me and brought me flowers and several of the Spanish oranges that they had brought all the way from Valencia.

I continued sick for many days, sleeping little and very feverish. Just as I decided I had better make my final confession a great weariness overcame me and I slept a day and a night without waking. When I did I felt myself again.

The loss of this baby made me all the more grateful for little Martín, and I spent many hours with him that spring and summer. At Cortés' command I spoke to him in Castilian, which Martín learned quickly. I became somewhat heavier, taking great pleasure after my illness in fruits and honey and the thick frothy chocolate drink Moctezuma had preferred above all others. The only shadow on my bland comfortable days was that Martín had no knowledge of his grandparents; neither of Cortés' parents in Spain nor mine, one dead and one who, if still alive, undoubtedly ruled Paynala until her son would be old enough to sit in the council chamber with the clan heads. I realized that nearly eleven years had passed since I had been spirited out of Paynala by the slavetraders; my half-brother's *emku* would be celebrated when he was fourteen, and after that my mother's scheme for his preeminence could be fulfilled. I knew this should be no longer of any importance to me, yet the deep anger, the desire for justice and revenge I had harbored in secret all during my years of slavery in Tabasco caused me to frown, to clench my hands, to sigh.

When Martín asked me why I was angry with him, I smiled down at him and denied it. In that instant some trick of light made his little face look less Spanish than Indian. I saw him as the future cacique of Paynala, grandson of my father Taxumal. But how absurd, I told myself. I told him, as I stroked his cheek, "You are the son of Hernán Cortés, destined to govern the province of Cuernavaca, an honored liege of the greatest monarch in Europe!"

That day saw the end of one period of my life and the start of another. The Spanish captain named Cristobal Olid was the cause of this great change.

I liked Olid even less than Alvarado; he had great contempt of all Indians. He was black-bearded and swarthy; more than a few drops of Moorish blood probably ran in his veins. He had always treated me with elaborate respect, saying *"Doña* Marina" as though to convey that I was an exceptional Indian and so he was prepared to overlook my unfortunate origins.

To Olid Cortés had entrusted one of the two expeditions southward. The ultimate objective of both the maritime force he commanded and the land army under Alvarado was to search for a strait between the Atlantic and Pacific. The discovery of this suspected secret westward passage was of greatest interest to King Carlos, for at present the only way from the Atlantic to the Pacific was Ferdinand Magellan's dangerous route around the southern tip of our continent. In a letter Cortés had promised Carlos to postpone all interests and projects, if need be, for the fulfillment of this great objective: to find that strait if it existed.

Alvarado, penetrating southward from Oaxaca, had succeeded in subduing much of Guatemala and had sent back Cortés full accounts of the country, its resources and its people. Of Olid's expedition, with orders to found a colony on the north coast of Honduras and then to cruise southward along its shores in search of the secret strait, nothing had been heard at all. Cortés' fear was that Olid's ships had been wrecked in a tropical hurricane. This, following the accidental burning in the shipyard of the Zacatula fleet, would have been the bitterest of blows. To finance these two expeditions Cortés had spent royal revenues, had extracted tribute from caciques just as the Aztecs had done, and had incurred huge debts of his own for which the Crown would in time remunerate him. "Particularly if I am successful," he said grimly.

It was a great shock to learn in that summer of 1524 that Cristobal Olid had betrayed Cortés. A few loyal soldiers brought the news. Having reached Honduras and established a colony, Olid's power had gone to his head. The great distance from Mexico gave him the idea that it would be safe to assert his independent jurisdiction. It occurred to me that in this he evidently felt as Cortés once had toward Velásquez: all the suffering and toil and danger fell to Olid; Cortés would reap the benefits. The difference was that Cortés had financed half the cost of that first venture to Mexico; Olid had not put up a peso toward this one.

Olid's silence was now explained. On learning of his rebellion, Cortés dispatched to Honduras a vessel with a complement of soldiers led by a kinsman named de las Casas, who had orders to arrest Olid. Within weeks word came back via a Cuban vessel that the ship had been found wrecked off the Honduras coast, leaving the rebellious Olid still flaunting his autonomous power.

Not for years had I seen Cortés in such a state of mind; he could think or talk of nothing else but Olid's rebellion. "I cannot risk the example of such unpunished defection! As captain-general I must maintain my absolute authority! Already Carlos has sent to my capital several pompous functionaries, ostensibly to aid me in administering colonial revenues, but also to spy on my activities. I do not want any news of a successful insurrection to reach the Court. By taking the administration of revenues out of my sole hands the king has already curtailed my power, and more of the same will follow if Olid succeeds in defying me."

I knew him well enough to see that these reasons, however good, covered a deep personal anger that a trusted captain had betrayed him.

"But in addition to King Carlos I must consider the effect of such a rebellion on the Indians here. Any breach in my absolute authority will see a dozen insurrections hatching overnight. There is only one thing for me to do. I myself will lead an army down to Honduras! I will hang that traitor!"

The expedition of vengeance was quickly organized. The army would march down the mountains through Oaxaca and Coetzacoalcos Province, and thence to Honduras overland across the western end of Yucatán. Of Spaniards Cortés planned to take a hundred horsemen and fifty foot soldiers, augmented by three thousand Indian auxiliaries: Tlascalans, Toltecs, and some Aztecs. Among these would be Cuauhtemoc and the cacique of Tacuba who was tortured with him, for Cortés was fearful that if left in the city these two former rulers might spearhead an uprising, though I told him that was doubtful.

Cortés also decided to bring a personal retinue to make the journey less tedious: several pages, a butler, a steward, some musicians, a juggler, and a few young gentlemen of good family, drawn to New Spain by glowing reports of gold, silver, and large land grants to be had, but unseasoned as soldiers. Among these was one Don Juan Jamarillo, caparisoned like a knight of old, Cortés told me with a smile. Young, blond, and innocent-eyed, when I first saw him I suffered a slight shock before I realized that Arturo Mondragon had not returned on horseback in shining armor.

The governor's palace had a pretty garden-patio in the Spanish manner planted with a number of the trees of Spain: orange, lemon, and a grapevine on a trellis. There was also a round central fountain where Martín liked to sail his paper boats. We were there together one day, and as I sat on the fountain's rim and watched one of his vessels float away from us, I found myself struggling against low spirits. I knew the expedition against Olid was necessary, but I also knew that the secret strait to the Pacific was as heady a lure to Cortés as Moctezuma's gold had once been. Moreover, from Alvarado in Guatemala had just come an exciting rumor: in the southern continent, far below Panama, there was said to exist atop a high mountain range the rich and fabulous land of a people called Incas. The gleam in Cortés' eye when he spoke of this told me that his lust for exploration had not been sated. And so, though he assured me that he would be gone at most a few months, I believed I might be facing as much as a year without him.

Martín leaned far out over the rim of the fountain to puff his cheeks and blow the paper boat farther on its course, and as it sped away, I knew that the thrust of Cortés' ambition would as surely send him away from me. I saw myself as I really was to him: not the most important figure in his life, but merely a companion during the first of his grand adventures. And in a few more days he would be gone; the departure of the expedition southward had been set for October twelfth; this was the ninth.

Footsteps sounded on stone paving; his footsteps. I turned. He looked exuberant; I could not force a smile.

He looked down at my woebegone face and said, "Have you packed your clothes and other necessities?"

My heart leaped up. I jumped to my feet. "You want me with you?"

"Why else would I ask you to pack? May I suggest one of the Spanish gowns for ceremonial occasions?"

"But how can I leave Martín?"

"With Doña Luisa and the other women and Orteguilla and the tutor I have employed. A few months without his mother will not harm the boy."

Martín's voice was shrill. "But I want to go too!"

"I want you here," Cortés told him. "I need Martín Cortés in this palace to remind my friends and enemies that I will soon return."

After pondering on this responsibility, Martín nodded. "I will tell them that. And I will have chocolate and camote candy whenever I want." He returned to his paper boats.

Although I already felt a pang at parting from Martín for even a few months, the pleasure of being needed by Cortés was greater. I went to him, looking up to search his face. "Why did you decide to take me with you?"

He looked down. "I will need an interpreter to talk with the Yucatán caciques."

"Aguilar would serve as well as I, speaking Mayan as he does."

"But he is not my Amazon." He reached out his hands and held me by the shoulders in a tight grip. "He is not my talisman. You will bring me luck, just as you did before."

And, oh, I wish that had been true!

As I was folding clothing in our bedroom, trying to decide between a chest or a large straw hamper, with Doña Luisa recommending the chest in case of rains and Ixchel sure the hamper would serve as well, my mind was not on the skirt I was holding. It was on the projected course of the journey just ahead. Oaxaca to Coetzacoalcos, the province where Paynala stood.

Vividly I remembered the place of my birth, saw

again the stone palace with its steep thatch roof, once more gazed up at the gray tiers of the sacred pyramid. Happy days of my childhood fluttered through my mind like butterflies. Again I splashed and paddled in the slow brown river while women pounded clothes clean on the rocks; again at the seaside town of Coetzacoalcos a fisherman's son taught me to swim to shore with the waves as they broke. I saw my grandmother Ix Chan's wise old face, my father's, and then my mother's face on the day she tried to cut off my hair.

The garment I was folding had dropped from my hands to the floor. I ran from the room in search of Cortés.

I found him in the main *sala,* talking with several captains. My heart was so full of the past that without ceremony I said, "I must talk to you at once. It's a private matter of great importance." Between concern and irritation he excused himself and followed me outside into the empty patio. There I faced him. "You must stop in Paynala when we go through Coetzacoalcos."

"Your birthplace? I understand this sentiment on your part, but . . ."

"Sentiment? You are mistaken. The great wrong done me by my mother and Ah Tok must be righted. This I demand of you in the name of justice!"

To my astonishment he laughed. He quickly said "Forgive me, but your great emotion surprises me. I thought you had forgotten the matter, or at least given it a place of minor importance in your present life."

"I have not forgotten." The sound of my own voice startled me. It was cold as stone.

"I'll try to humor your wish," he said easily, and turned to go back to the captains.

I seized his arm. "Not good enough! Olid's betrayal of your trust is about to send you on a march of hundreds of leagues to punish him. Do you believe that I was any the less betrayed when I was sold as a slave? Betrayal is betrayal. In God's eyes, surely. And I do not think Spanish law condones kidnap, treason, or the theft of a child's patrimony. But you, Chief Justice of New Spain, could inform me if I am wrong."

All amusement left his face as he stared at me. "The punishment for those crimes is death."

"Death," I repeated. "Yes. So I thought."

He regarded me now with a wary respect. "We will stop at Paynala. I will see that justice is done."

He returned to the captains, and I stood there by the fountain. What had happened to the mournful wife who had brooded here an hour ago? The woman who now stared at the water where one soggy paper boat floated on its side held one hand clenched against her heart that throbbed fast with the fierce emotion that had burst like blood out of an old wound. I was going to return to Paynala at last, risen from the dead!

44

At dawn on October twelfth, 1524, an army set forth to punish two traitors. The hundred horsemen made a brave sight when the sun rose to shine on brightly polished armor. El Galán rode in the vanguard; he had a fine chestnut stallion now. I was also glad to see that Aguilar had joined two of the Franciscans who had arrived in January from Spain. In contrast to their worn brown robes, the motley assortment of persons making up Cortés' personal retinue looked garish, except for the Spanish gentlemen; Don Juan Jamarillo's casque had a plume as blue as his eyes; he rode awhile beside my litter, looking down at me from time to time. He had a Castilian accent, though not so strong as that of

Sandoval; Cortés had told me he came of a very fine old family and was pure Castilian on both sides.

In addition to the litter, I had been provided with a mount, a graceful mare, black with white stockings and white blaze. It was ridden by my groom when I chose to take my ease. The *tamanes* who carried my litter poles reminded me of the two who had removed me secretly from Paynala so long ago.

The journey down the slope of the *cordillera* to Oaxaca was without incident, a march of easy stages along a well-marked jungle trail, the trees providing shelter from the sun while our bodies grew gradually used to the heat of the lower altitude. When we reached some cleared farmland we were met with jubilance by Spanish colonists who reported to Cortés that the Indians there were sweet-dispositioned and tractable, their women very pretty. Cortés firmly reminded them that they needed Spanish wives. "I want *criollo* children here, not *mestizos*," he said. Later I reminded him that Martín was a *mestizo,* and that even Cortés would find it hard to prevent the flowering of this new branch on the tree of life. He said, "Still, families only half-Spanish might suffer from split loyalty in case of an Indian uprising." He glanced toward where Cuauhtemoc rode a piebald mare which had been provided because of his burned feet.

Cuauhtemoc was an impressive figure, dressed as an eagle warrior. The cacique of Tabasco was always looking up at his square-chinned, proud-nosed face, and I knew this was not only because Cuauhtemoc's body was taller, but because his spirit was too. The former Aztec ruler had accepted the "invitation" to ride south with Cortés with a calm resignation, knowing the reason.

From Oaxaca we descended farther toward sea level, and came at last to Paynala, sleeping beside its shallow meandering river. We did not approach along the river road as the Aztecs had when I was a child, but by the less-traveled route leading us over the hill to the west of the town. From its top I looked down, my whole being very alive and my mind rushing ahead to the moment when I would at last encounter my unnatural mother and the cruel priest, her ally. But how small Paynala was! How it had shrunk! The pyramid of the gods was no bigger than a child's toy.

As we descended the hill I saw that a religious ceremony was in process; the plaza was filled with townfolk, all facing toward the temple. Was it possible that we had arrived on the very day of my half-brother's *emku?* How fitting that would be; how well it would show the precision of God's hand! As we came still nearer I could make out the figure of a white-robed, white-haired priest standing now at the mouth of the *teocalli* atop the pyramid. Ah Tok! I was sure of it!

I was riding beside Cortés and asked him if the horsemen might make a sudden, dashing appearance. He nodded, turned in the saddle, raised his arm and ordered a charge. There was a thunder of hooves as a hundred Spaniards spurred their mounts and rode past the maize fields and into the narrow street that led to the town square. I followed them; immobilized with fear, the townsfolk stared at awesome figures in armor gleaming in the late rays of the sun as they deployed themselves around the sides of the plaza. On the highest level of the pyramid Ah Tok stood like a statue, sacrificial knife upraised. And then I saw on a stone altar that had not been there in my childhood the bound victim our arrival had spared from death.

Ah Tok swayed. The knife dropped from his hand and he melted back into the darkness of the temple.

At a gesture from Cortés, El Galán dismounted and went up the steps to cut the bonds of the supine figure on the altar, which was made in the terrible likeness of Chac Mool whose cruel, half-open slit of mouth was stained with blood. El Galán brought the intended victim to Cortés and me. The boy was no more than twelve, very thin. In a whisper he said he came from a village far to the west. There had been a pestilence, everyone was dying, and when his parents died he made his way for a long time through the jungle and over hills until he came to Paynala. It was sundown, the people were eating supper, and the first person to see him was Ah Tok. He had dropped a hand to the boy's shoulder, claiming him. The child was in a state beyond mere fear. Looking about him at the silent horsemen he asked "What will you do to me?" I said we would feed him, as soon as possible.

By now some of the townspeople had fled, others were still staring about them, uncertain of our intentions but realizing there was no place they could hide from such apparitions as we seemed to them. Among the ones who remained I saw several familiar faces, but none of these people recognized me, for to them I was a child who had died of the *cil* more than eleven years ago.

As soon as the fifty foot soldiers and some of the Indian warriors and the *tamanes* had trailed into town, packing the few streets leading from the plaza, Cortés ordered his canopy set up at the foot of the pyramid. Because he wanted the plaza to be filled with townspeople during the ceremony of surrender to the King of Spain, he ordered the Indian warriors and foot soldiers out to encircle the town. The horsemen remained. I pointed out the council house, and Cortés sent Aguilar there to demand of the clan heads that the citizens who had left the square return and that the cacique be brought before him. "Tell them Cortés is here."

He was in his armchair-throne, I beside him, behind us the priests and the gentlemen of his entourage and some captains. The sun had lowered in the sky and its rays fell on Cortés and me at the tent's edge.

The townsfolk stepped aside to make a lane for the two figures coming toward me, walking just ahead of the four clan chiefs who had been told to summon them: I saw my mother Chituche and my half-brother, slender except for a round belly, no doubt stuffed with good things by his doting mother. He looked as frightened as the sacrificial victim had, his beady eyes so wide the white showed all around.

Chituche looked much as I remembered her; slightly heavier, with a few gray hairs in the black braids topping her head. A look of discontent pulled down the corners of her mouth as though her duties as acting caciqua of Paynala had been less than pleasing, yet her solid figure had a look of monolithic authority. Her eyes were humbly lowered.

"Good evening, Mother," I said. A shocked murmur came from the Paynalans who were nearest.

Her eyelids flew up. She stared at me as if she did not believe her own eyes. Then she tottered a step back as if to run away. Suddenly she threw herself at my feet, and there she groveled. A moaning came out of her mouth.

Until that instant I had not known how I would behave to her. My prayer for God's guidance had not been heartfelt, for the old wound had trobbed stronger than any prayer. I looked straight ahead at the low orange sun. Poised just above the hilltop, it stared at me like some powerful, benign deity.

Abruptly, all that I had learned of Christianity seemed to burst into flower within me. My body felt irradiated by the light of that setting sun and by a larger light, unseen but felt as a radiance that lighted all my being. I knew what Christ's great message to the world had been: love is greater than justice. Justice balances good and evil; but love creates greater good, as a seed becomes a tree.

I looked down at my mother's dark head, now rolling from side to side as if expecting a fatal blow to fall on it. I bent over her and touched her shoulder and felt her whole body stiffen in terror. "Let me help you to your feet, Mother," I said. As I did she stared at me in wonder.

I do not clearly remember the words I spoke to her, but Aguilar wrote them down, so impressed had he been. I embraced her and said, "Do not fear me; I forgive you. God has been good to me. He has freed me from the worship of idols and has let me bear a son to this great lord beside me. And I would rather have served him than been caciqua of all the provinces of New Spain." These words came out of my mouth without forethought. I was intensely conscious of the poor heathen woman before me, the caciqua I would have been had her betrayal not sent me from Paynala and onward to my better destiny. With this insight I encompassed all my life: all twisted resentments and unanswered questions were as neat and compact as a nut inside its shell.

"Ah Tok," my mother whispered. "I knew that if you stayed in Paynala he would kill you with magic or poison."

And that may have been true, I thought. Her justification, at any rate. But even this hint of some concern for me moved me to take a ring from my finger and put it in her hand, and then a gold bracelet. Cortés put out an arm to stop me. "Enough. Such love as she is capable of you have already bought."

Ah Tok had been found by then. His fate, which I suggested, was acceptable to Cortés. So I went from the canopy to the sacred pyramid and stood near the top to command every eye. Two Spanish soldiers brought Ah Tok and held him beside me. His dirty robe was stained with daubs and trickles of blood. Below the long rags of his white hair his eyes glowed in their caverns like a demon's. I had asked a third soldier to go into the *teocalli* and find his sacred wand with the seven rattlesnake tails. When he brought it I held it up for everyone below to see, then I held it out and told the soldier to slash it in half with his sword. He did, and the snake tails fell to the ground. I held up the stump in my hand and then threw it contemptuously aside. "You are nothing, old man," I said to Ah Tok. "Your power is broken." The two soldiers led him away.

To the people below I said, "I am Malinche, daughter of Taxumal. Now I am ready to be crowned."

The elder of the clan heads came forward with the ceremonial panache my father had worn and mounted the temple steps and placed it on my head. There was a great sigh from the people below, and I saw one old woman begin to weep. I said to them, "You saw my mother kneel to me in fear. I tell you now to kneel in awe. Not to me, not even to Cortés, but to the God whose servant I am and who brought me back to you!"

And there, in the last rays of the sun, those thousands of Paynalans knelt as one being. A Franciscan monk climbed the temple steps with the Cross raised high, singing a hymn to the Lord. The soldiers and the mounted captains joined in. Some of the Paynalans looked about in startled pleasure at the lovely sound. It was a beautiful moment as I gazed down on my people, saved from eternal damnation.

Cortés had mounted the temple steps to stand facing me. "And now, Caciqua of Paynala, do you swear fealty to Emperor Carlos V, ruler of Spain and the Holy Roman Empire? Do you swear to love and obey him as his faithful vassal from this day forward?" I waited until Aguilar translated these words so my people understood, and then I said "This I swear."

The sun slipped down behind the hill and it was dusk; looking down at those kneeling Paynalans I felt that the opposite had happened for them; their sun had risen on a new and better day. Great emotion filled me; tears came to my eyes.

Cortés said in a low tone, "You surprised me, Marina. You are more politically astute than I thought." His look of admiration was so pleasing that I did not try to explain what had happened.

Early the next morning I appointed the eldest clan head to act as cacique in my absence. Spanish soldiers removed the stone altar of sacrifice; a white wooden cross was set up in its place. It pleased me that Aguilar wished to remain in Paynala to instruct and baptize the people. Ah Tok was banished, perhaps a crueler fate than death would have been, but the half dozen other priests were given the chance to embrace Christianity. These problems disposed of, Cortés allowed me an hour to talk with people who had known me as a child and who came flocking to the canopy to embrace me.

Ato's mother, I learned, had not lived long after her child died. Dak Cho had left my mother and was said to be living in Coetzacoalcos with a young widow who had three children to raise. The mother of Na Chel Cuy came simpering up with a large bowl of fruit, her son beside her. A handsome man now nearly thirty, he had not yet married, although his mother assured me that every girl in town wanted him. His skin was a dark copper from his fondness for hunting, and his *ati* was made of the skin of a deer he had speared in the uplands; a snakeskin headband gave him a fierce look. When his mother spoke of his bachelorhood his narrow eyes went boldly to my face and he said that he had not yet found a woman worth the trouble of tying mantles with. His mother nodded, looking up at her rare son.

The voice of Cortés broke into this chatter; he had returned to the canopy where I had been receiving my guests. "On to Honduras! Say goodbye to your subjects, caciqua! We have a day's march ahead."

PART XI

▼▼▼

THE CEIBA TREE
November 28, 1524–November 8, 1529

45

Córtes had earlier sent to Tabasco asking for a map of the area we had to cross and had received from Nan Chan a chart that showed the principal towns where traders stopped. A straight line of march south from the Coetzacoalcos River would take us across the base of Yucatán and part of Guatemala to the north coast of Honduras. He said we could pick up Indian guides to take us from one town to the next.

The journey to the headwaters of the Tabasco River went smoothly, although the land became increasingly marshy. We soon had to cross many streams and rivers. At first we encountered only small streams, easily forded. Then came deeper ones which the horses could swim, though getting equipment across was troublesome and slow. But then we encountered wider and deeper rivers over which the soldiers had to build bridges. Cortés estimated that to cover seventy-five leagues, fifty bridges had to be constructed. The weather had worked against us; heavy rains before our arrival had swelled the streams; progress was very slow and discouraging. I had hoped to return to Martín by the Day of the Three Kings in early January with luck. This hope began to fade. Luck was what we lacked.

The rivers were bad enough, but in addition, the lands between did not supply us with the food we had counted on to augment our supplies, because the natives, in evident fear of us, had fled after burning their villages to the ground. Laboriously crossing yet one more river and yearning for food and rest and comfort, we would come upon smoking ruins, not a human in sight. Our Indian guides seemed as confused and surprised by this phenomenon as we were.

This disturbed Cortés for a reason other than the great inconvenience. To his knowledge, as to mine, vacating a town ahead of an enemy's arrival is a widespread custom; burning it down is not. The third time this happened, he said, "It is as if these separate village chiefs are acting in concert, inspired by some master plan to harass us. But who could get them to act against us at the cost of their own dwellings?"

Our immediate destination was the town of Iztapan, on the bank of a tributary of the Tabasco; Nan Chan had said that the people there were friendly, the cacique fond of visitors. It took us three weeks to reach it. After floundering so long over marshes and rivers and finding only charred ashes where villages had been, it was a joy to see that sizable town still standing surrounded by wide maize fields. The soldiers let out shouts of delight.

After having been welcomed and fed, and after persuading the cacique to swear allegiance to King Carlos, we rested some days during which the priests evangelized, then set off again, to find that we faced yet more marshlands. I found the sound made by horses and foot soldiers struggling across mud into which their feet have sunk dispiriting. It is as if the wet, slavering earth reluctantly lets go of its prey while yearning to swallow it whole. When we saw a thick forest ahead I rejoiced; my horse was so weary I could feel it trembling. To our misery, the marshy soil continued below the tall hardwood and cedar trees. There was another discomfort added; the foliage above was so dense that we crept along through a constant gloom like early night. It was hard to see where we put our feet, and since there were patches of quicksand this was dangerous. The cries of invisible birds in that humid shadowland were eerie, like the shrieks of disembodied spirits, but insects, reptiles, and snakes were plentiful.

The second morning in the forest we woke to find that our Indian guides had deserted us. When Cortés sent a soldier up to the top of a tall tree to spy out the terrain ahead he came down to report only more forest, endless treetops. It was now clear that Alvarado could not have taken the same route we had, although ours had seemed the better, being the most direct. I think I was sorriest for Cortés' little private retinue: the pages, steward, musicians, clown, juggler, and the fine gentlemen. The clown forgot his jokes, the juggler caught such a catarrh that he could not juggle for coughing, the young pages seemed in need of a mother's care. The musicians, however, were something of a boon, for when we camped on coming to less swampy ground their songs and tunes broke the dismal stillness. Of the Spanish gentlemen of Cortés' little retinue, Don Juan Jamarillo proved, to everyone's surprise, undaunted. Well-versed in legends of the past, he would remind us of terrible marches of Alexander or Hannibal or Caesar to make us less depressed by our own difficulties.

One day an excited soldier descended from his treetop observation post to tell Cortés there was a city only a few hundred paces ahead. A large one, he guessed, because the *teocalli* atop its sacred pyramid stood even taller than the treetops. The prospect of reaching civilization made us all cheerful, for by this time our supplies of food were used up and we had been subsisting for days on roots, nuts, and berries scantily supplied by our imprisoning forest. But when we reached that city, cheer vanished. We found it deserted of all but snakes and lizards. Forest vines and creepers hid whole buildings and crawled up the pyramid the soldier had seen, only its summit still free of this green shroud. We had found not a city but a tomb, deserted by all its people and left to crumble away. I wondered if it might have been the home of my remote ancestors and whether others had later followed their lead in leaving forever behind them the corruption of the noble and priestly classes. The clown at that point managed a sort of joke:

"Small wonder the people left a climate like this one!" His painted smile was trickling down his face along with his sweat; in addition to our other troubles the air had become even more humid; moisture from our own bodies ran down to mingle with the marshwater that soaked our feet.

Lacking Indian guides now, Cortés had only the map Nan Chan had sent us and a compass. After a long day's march before reaching a place dry enough for a night's slumber, he decided to give the army a full day's rest and time to gather enough roots and berries to make a meal that would really fill the stomach. By now a number of the Indian warriors and *tamanes* had died from hunger and from the heat, humidity, and low altitude to which a lifetime high up in the mountains had not accustomed them. One of the pages had also perished. After a supper of hot water, Cortés tried to conceal his gloom and disappointment as he spread out the map by the campfire and studied it. Sandoval, El Galán, and the other captains crowded around him, peering down in search of some landmark that would inspire hope. "Although this chart won't tell us if a town's still standing," El Galán remarked.

Cortés lifted the compass from the chart and nodded. "I can't forget those damned burned villages," he said. "I have to fight the suspicion that even if we come to a place of human habitation it will be only chars and cinders. By God, there has to be a malign unifying force behind this kind of warfare!" He turned to me, for I had joined the group, unable to sleep for hunger. "Tell me, Doña Marina, could it be Nan Chan? Could he have deceived me with pretenses of friendship? Could this chart be false and designed to lead us into this wilderness of trees and muck where at last we'll leave our bones?"

I did not have to ponder. "What would that gain him? He is in a good position as your friend and first ally on this continent. That is what keeps him in power in Xicalanco, his friendship with Cortés."

Cortés stared down at the point of the compass, turning it in his fingers. "What about Cuauhtemoc?"

"Cuauhtemoc?" His old suspicion had reclaimed him; the compass had become the spear of an Aztec assassin in a nightmare he once had.

He frowned. "Could Cuauhtemoc have managed to communicate with a chieftain of these parts, perhaps by night when we thought him sleeping? Could he have suggested to them this sabotage of my venture?"

"Not without an interpreter," I reminded him. "He does not speak or understand any dialect of the Mayan language."

Cortés gave an abrupt laugh. "I forgot that."

Sandoval offered his theory. "Maybe the natives here all went crazy in unison, having heard that we defeated the Aztecs and were marching toward their own villages."

El Galán rubbed his old leg wound and shook his head. "No. I think Cortés is right. A clever leader could have risen among these Indians of Yucatán. He realizes that we were counting on living off the towns and villages of this miserable land."

The compass in Cortés' hand stabbed down into the center of the chart. "But who? Who is this enemy? Who?"

"That is something we may never learn," El Galán said. "So for my part I think we had better study the chart and figure how much farther we have to travel before we come, by God's sweet mercy, to another town."

"Four months of this!" Cortés announced without any need, for we all knew that. "I planned in this length of time to reach Honduras, hang Olid, and return to the city of Mexico!"

With gallows cheer El Galán said, "Well, since we cannot hope to live through another four months like these last, let us assume that the end of our journey is near."

At this point Don Juan Jamarillo joined Cortés and the captains somewhat tentatively. "When Hamilcar's soldiers were trapped in a desert pass after a grueling march . . . ," he began.

"They drank their own pith," lisped Sandoval, "but lack of water is not our problem."

"Aculán!" Cortés announced, pointing to the map. "It's a large province, directly ahead, apparently not more than a week's march. Or ten days, allowing for fatigue, hunger, and this hellish forest. Nan Chan indicates its capital city, called Petén. A smaller trade city is still closer." He pointed to the chart, and we all looked at the X on the map he pointed to and tried to imagine a town with a bursting marketplace and a friendly cacique eager to feed us everything in it.

The days somehow passed. Spirits sank as if the swamp pulled them down into slimy depths. In lofty branches above our heads parrots screeched and unseen birds sang mockingly.

By now I was thinner than I had been even after the first siege at Tenochtitlán, and thought of it as providential that I had eaten so well after losing my second child. We had discovered that a certain bark, boiled, was edible.

When at last the trees about us grew more sparse so that real daylight filtered down upon our faces, I scarcely dared to hope we had reached the forest's end.

We ran out from under the last trees, spirits soaring. We found ourselves on the bank of a river far wider and swifter than any we had passed, or any I had ever seen. Dizzy, I looked out over the rushing waters.

Louder than the river's steady muted roar was the great groan that rose from the throats of the foot soldiers. Many of the horsemen echoed it as they realized no horse could swim that mighty flood. I heard one say "This is the end of our journey! That river cannot be crossed. All that's left us is to try to return the way we came or find a better route back to Tabasco."

"Yes, another route!" a soldier cried. "And here I sit until Cortés decides on one!" In total agreement, the foot soldiers all sat down along the narrow beach.

Ignoring this, if indeed he had heard, Cortés continued to eye the sweep of water. He turned. "We can build a bridge," he said matter-of-factly, as if the feat were of no great difficulty. He waved an arm toward the lowering forest we had left. "Plenty of wood. Lianas for ropes. A floating bridge is what we'll build, anchored to this shore and extending outward, log after log, until it touches the other."

The soldiers' earlier groans turned to shouts of disbelief. "We're done in, Cortés," one rose to yell. "You might as well ask us to build a Spanish galleon! Or the city of Madrid to camp in while we do it!"

"A bridge can be built," Cortés told him. "And will be, if not by you." He asked El Galán to bring Cuauhtemoc and the cacique of Tacuba to him. The Spanish soldiers waited alertly. Cuauhtemoc listened patiently as I explained what Cortés wanted. He said he would urge the nine hundred Indian warriors to volunteer their aid.

"I can do no more than ask them; I cannot command, having no more power over them," he said.

"Then add to your persuasion the fact that Cortés commands this of them," Cortés ordered. "And point out that it will be to their great advantage to reach Aculán, since many more Indians have died than Spaniards."

The response of the Indians was swift; within the hour came the sound of a hundred hand axes attacking the nearest trees of the forest. "Those Indians respect Cuauhtemoc, whatever he may say," Cortés remarked to his captains. "I doubt if they would have responded to me any better than my Spanish soldiers did, yet Cuauhtemoc could persuade them."

"And lucky that he could," Sandoval nodded.

Shamed by the good spirit with which the Indians had fallen to the task, the Spaniards soon joined them. For three days the thudding of axes on wood drowned out the river's sound. The bridge Cortés had conceived ultimately required a thousand trees, each log of wood as thick as a man's body. When after four days the bridge was done, I had to marvel at it. So did the men who had chopped and hauled the trees and labored to lash log to log. "Nothing but fire can destroy it!" Cortés exulted. It was a monument to his refusal to acknowledge defeat. That tough, undaunted spirit of his had communicated itself to his soldiers, who now showed each other their raw blistered hands with jaunty pride.

It was devastating to discover, with that river finally crossed, the river which had seemed the final barrier before we saw ahead the towers of the first trade city of Aculán, that still another swamp had to be crossed, worse than any yet. Horses floundered ahead up to their bellies in muddy water. Sometimes, whinnying with terror, they sank into deep quagmires from which the soldiers and riders got them out only with great effort, covering the muck around these treacherous pits with the boughs of trees onto which the poor muddy beasts desperately floundered.

But when at last we struggled through this enormous swamp we came to solid ground that rose in a gentle slope upward. At the top we could see the first cultivated fields of Aculán, the tall ripe maize, hundreds of yucca plants, many pepper trees. It seemed to the padres a very good sign that we had reached this land of plenty on the first day of the Lenten season.

That night when we camped the air was full of the good smell of roasting ears of maize or baking cassava roots, for Cortés could not forbid the starved men from plundering these wide fields. After food, everyone became cheerful. The musicians, listless for some time, began to play their tunes, and soon some of the Spanish soldiers were singing. The Indian camp, apart from ours, was silent, but they went to sleep earlier than the Spaniards.

Cortés had lost his look of constant anxiety and was laughing at his juggler, who skillfully kept four gnawed maize cobs in the air at once. But his merriment was short-lived—and mine. A converted Aztec wearing a silver cross on his bare chest came to Cortés' campfire

outside his tent to whisper an accusation of Cuauhtemoc.

I, of course, served as translator. The accusation was
that a conspiracy had been set afoot by Cuauhtemoc
and that the cacique of Tacuba and other Indian nobles
were privy to it. Cuauhtemoc had decided that before
we reached Honduras, at some moment when the army
was again bogged down in a morass or handicapped by
some other obstacle, the Indians, greatly outnumbering
the Spaniards, would suddenly fall on them and kill
them all. Then Cuauhtemoc would lead the Indians to
Olid's settlement, conquer it, and take command. News
of this successful revolt would be sent to the capital. It
would foster an Indian uprising there, and after that
in other Spanish colonies. Vessels in the ports would
be seized by Indian rebels to prevent news of this general insurrection from crossing the sea to Cuba or
Spain. The Spaniards' overlordship would thus be ended
forever.

While the informer narrated this wild plot his eyes
roved crazily and his voice became higher and higher,
finally only a squeak. He seemed to me to be a man
impelled to tell some nightmare he had dreamed, or
some fantasy of his own, and so rid himself of its bane-
ful effect.

Knowing Cortés' slumbering suspicion of Cuauhtemoc, I volunteered this opinion, and others. "Would
any sane man dream of such a scheme? A venture certain to fail? Even if Olid's settlement fell, even if this
provoked a general uprising, which is very doubtful,
any intelligent mind can see that if just one Spanish
ship escaped eastward, the entire might of the Spanish
Empire would be flung against him!"

"Let Cuauhtemoc defend himself," Cortés said
brusquely, the two frown lines between his eyes deep
and harsh. "If he is innocent, he does not need your
help, and if he's guilty you're wasting your breath."
He turned to Sandoval and El Galán. "Get a complement of soldiers and bring Cuauhtemoc and the Tacuban cacique and those other Indian nobles here to me."

While we waited in silence, I noted that his face, like my own, was very thin from the hunger we had undergone. I said, "You are weary. That makes you impatient. But remember, Cuauhtemoc is weary too. If he shows anger at this accusation, or is sullen and refuses to defend himself, remember how he got the Indians to help you build the bridge."

He ignored me, staring into the fire. "I think my famed luck may have run out in this accursed land. Lachesis seems to have taken a hand in my affairs of late."

"Lachesis?"

"The Greeks of long ago believed there were three Fates. One spun the thread of a man's destiny. One cut the thread. One wove the shroud. Lachesis was the Fate who cut the thread. Yes, that great whore Lachesis is clicking her shears and laughing at me."

His face as he spoke looked flushed by more than the firelight. Two patches of red glared on his cheekbones. I reached out and put my hand on his forehead. It nearly burned me. "You have caught that fever that killed so many in the swamps," I said.

He put a hand to his own head and nodded. "Yes, I am ailing. Just one more way my luck has turned bad."

"Luck never made Cortés. Luck won't break him," I said.

"Your faith is touching, but I still hear Lachesis laughing."

Cuauhtemoc and the Tacuban cacique appeared, the latter looking up at the former as usual. Behind them were half a dozen nobles of their two cities. "Tell him what the informer said," Cortés ordered me.

I did so, but added that I myself believed this accusation to be untrue.

What happened then was most unfortunate. Several of the noble Tacubans, eager to ingratiate themselves with Cortés out of fear of him, came forward and admitted that, yes, they had indeed heard Cuauhtemoc speak of some sort of uprising against the Spaniards, but they had refused to take any part in it. Reluctantly I conveyed this information to Cortés.

"Well?" he asked Cuauhtemoc, standing up to face him. "What do you say to that?"

Cuauhtemoc showed no fear. He tossed those Tacubans a look of contempt and drew himself taller, staring at Cortés without anger. "I was a fool not to have taken my own life before surrendering to you. I was perhaps also foolish to have told you where you could find a quantity of gold after you saved me from having my feet burned off, for that made you think the pain had cowed me. But I am not such a fool as to imagine I could succeed in fomenting such an uprising. Even if every warrior with me joined in such a conspiracy, I would have to reach Honduras without any idea where it is. Even if I reached it, I would not be likely to succeed against Spanish weaponry; but even if I did, this could not cause a general uprising of native people from sea to sea. But even if that came about, there remains the final impossibility—that every Spanish vessel in every port could be kept from sailing to your ruler Carlos with news of this uprising. And what that would bring down on the heads of all the native people of my land of Anahuac and elsewhere does not even bear thinking about. Can you really believe that I would subject my race to a second conquest even more terrible than the first? I am not a fool. I am not a madman."

By now Cortés was nodding, unable even in his feverish state to resist the logical progression of Cuauhtemoc's defense. He caught himself in this silent act of agreement and turned sharply to me. "He argues well. Or did you put the words into his mouth?"

"You have admitted in the past that I have some powers of logic. I merely said what any rational mind would conclude."

Cortés turned to Cuauhtemoc. "Then these Tacubans who said they heard you conspiring are all liars? And the informer—a liar too?"

Cuauhtemoc stared straight ahead. "One of them

brought up the idea of a rebellion against Spaniards. I said this idea was foolish, and why. The informer may have eavesdropped and heard only part of what I said, and so assumed I was outlining the plan of a rebellion instead of denying its feasibility. He may therefore have believed what he told you. But as for my planning any uprising, the Tacubans who said so are liars and cowards."

Cortés' maimed hand was pressed to his burning forehead. "What it comes down to is that I can believe them or you."

"According to the code I live by my surrender was absolute, final for all time. I cannot take it back or change it. I have given myself over to you as conquered. No rebellion could ever change that act of mine. The last Aztec ruler was Cuauhtemoc. He now rules only himself. He is not a foolish king."

Seeing him standing there immobile as a tower on his scarred feet, I felt admiration and great compassion. The rock he once hurled at Moctezuma had rebounded against him a thousandfold, but he was not broken and would never be.

Cortés' face showed that he, too, had not been unmoved by those words. "I am impressed by what you say, Cuauhtemoc. I also respect the former cacique of Tacuba, who did not shelter himself from my anger by turning against you."

"When two have burned together side by side it creates a close bond," Cuauhtemoc said.

Cortés blinked. I could see he did not like being reminded that he had not prevented that act of torture. But he said: "Then I hope that the perils of this journey may have the same effect on you and me" and dismissed Cuauhtemoc and the others with him.

His fever grew worse that night; unable to sleep, he left his tent to prowl through the camp—looking, he said, for spies sent by the cacique whose borders we had reached. He returned in an excited state, woke me from my half-doze to whisper that the truth about why those towns had been burned had dawned on him.

"You remember I said this clever schemer had to know something of our ways? Who could this devil be but a Spaniard? Eh? Yes, a Spaniard. He learned somehow the route I planned to take and moved ahead of us, inspiring the natives to burn their towns. But what Spaniard, I asked myself? An answer came to me: Guerrero!"

"Guerrero?"

"The Spanish priest who was with Aguilar in Yucatán! The one who would not leave because he had an Indian wife and sons. He has turned on his own countrymen!"

I sat up. "But the town where he lived was a great distance from here, on the west shore near Cozumel!"

He ignored geography. "Yes, Guerrero has become an Indian, but one who knows our methods and our ways. He can think as we do. Oh, if I had guessed such a thing would happen, I'd have hauled him out of there myself by the hair of his head! I'd have laid him dead at the feet of his Indian wife!"

This fantasy frightened me more than I dared to show. "It's only your fever talking. And even if you had such an enemy, he failed to stop you, because here we are at Aculán."

His eyes burned below his burning forehead. "But a long way yet from the north shore of Honduras. The Spaniards who first found it called it the Golfo Dulce. I wonder if the seawater is sweet there? Could such a thing be?" As his mind wandered from sweet seawater to the existence of mermaids, I knew how sick he was and went for cool water to bathe his head, urging him like a mother to go to his bed, to rest, to sleep. As I sponged his hot body as well, he suddenly seized my arm in a steel grip, but spoke gently. "You are a good Indian, my proof that such exist."

He fell asleep then, and slept heavily until dawn. I waited by the tent for his valet, to tell him not to wake Cortés. When he woke and dressed he seemed better. The flush was gone from his face and his words seemed normal and rational. The captains were by then waiting to confer with him, and I left them talking of the day's march while eating boiled maize the quartermaster had cooked.

Don Juan Jamarillo surprised me with a present: he had been very kind to me during that long and terrible journey, bringing me berries he had found, and once some orchids, apologizing that they were not edible. The gift he brought me that morning was a baby parrot; he had found it on the ground, one of its wings lamed or broken. He had made a little cage for it out of a basket. I named it Orteguilla because its bright coloring and way of cocking its head to one side reminded me of my dwarf friend.

Because the morning was a lovely one, less warm than usual, Don Juan and I walked a little distance from the camp together, enjoying the sun and the pretty landscape with its pepper trees. There were some ceibas too; a large one marked the beginning of the wide roadway that would lead us toward Petén. When we reached one of the pepper trees, the spot where he had found the parrot, he pushed aside the dangling feathery branches to point to where it had lain on the ground. I looked up into the tree for the nest from which it might have fallen, for it was very young. Seeing the clumps of small red pepper berries, I wondered if parrots ate them. I tasted one. Only the black seed had a strong flavor; the red hull was tasteless. But should such a young bird eat pepper berries, even if older ones did?

The dangling leaves beside me were suddenly parted. I stared at El Galán's bearded face, the skin pale and beaded with sweat. His eyes were anguished. "For God's sake, come with me. Cortés is going to hang Cuauhtemoc! You must try to stop this thing!"

I thrust the parrot cage at Jamarillo and ran down the road beside El Galán toward the great ceiba tree I had seen earlier, around it a great clot of Spanish and Indian soldiers, their backs toward me. "Let us through!" he commanded. I stopped dead at the inner edge of the crowd, staring up in shock.

From a great dark branch of the ceiba tree Cuauhtemoc was hanging, head tilted sharply to one side, neck stretched long by the rope around it. His body dangled limp and dejected, the morning sun burnishing his dead flesh, his golden necklace and bracelets. Near him, on a lower bough, swung the cacique of Tacuba.

I could not scream, I could not weep, I could only stare at the last Aztec king. I closed my eyes, opened them, and only then was aware that Cortés stood directly opposite me across a short space of dusty roadway. He raised his maimed hand and with a sudden slashing gesture indicated that the bodies were to be cut down. A soldier's sword severed the rope that had hanged Cuauhtemoc, and his limp body fell with a thud onto the dust of the road.

I think I made some sound; Cortés turned his head and saw me. Our eyes met like those of strangers above the corpse of the man he had promised to treat with all honor.

Into his came a startled look, as if he had read mine and seen my deep revulsion. We stared at each other for an instant longer and then I turned and ran down the road, away from the disillusionment I knew I would never outdistance or forget.

I had slowed to a walk when I heard the voice of El Galán behind me; turning, I saw that he and Sandoval had also left the group around the hanging tree. As they fell into step at either side of me Sandoval said in a troubled voice, "I can't forget Cuauhtemoc's last words. When the noose was put around his neck."

"What were they?" El Galán asked.

" 'I knew I was wrong to trust in your false promise to honor me, Cortés. I knew I was destined for a fate like this at the moment I surrendered instead of taking my own life.' " There was a pause. "And then he said, 'Your God will demand to know why you kill me so unjustly.' "

"Unjustly," El Galán repeated, somberly.

"And then the cacique of Tacuba looked up at

Cuauhtemoc and said, 'I ask no better fate than to die beside my Lord Cuauhtemoc.' "

"Is Cortés going mad?" El Galán asked. No one replied. The three of us who had admired Cortés and loved him continued in silence away from the murder of two brave men. The last words of Cuauhtemoc haunted me: if he had known that Cortés would surely kill him, why had he endured this perilous journey to the final moment when a noose snapped his neck? He could have escaped a hundred times. Did his code of absolute surrender prevent him? Was it his belief that his gods had deserted him? Was it his razed city, gone forever? But all these were just ideas: it seemed to me that he had not valued life enough, just life itself, the sunrises and sunsets, the starred nights, the beauty of trees or the sea, and the little daily pleasures of food to eat, a friend to talk with, the sound of music, a child's smile. Why had he remained a docile prisoner of Cortés, his nemesis? Such fatalism was beyond my understanding. "I knew you had destined me for a fate like this . . ."

I was shivering in the warm sunlight. I knew that my life with Cortés had come to an end under that ceiba tree. We were six years from the day I first saw him and thought him a god.

46

All the rest of that day I was like a woman suffering
from a fatal illness. When the march to Aculán began
I could not mount my mare, told the groom to ride her,
and took to the litter. Despite the heat I began to shiver
with a chill and hid under a blanket. The sun hurt even
my closed eyes; I covered them with my bent arms.
The pat-pat of the litter-bearers' broad feet made me
drift back in time; I thought of myself as going not
toward Petén but toward Tabasco. In fantasy I escaped
the Spaniards by staying hidden among the mangroves
until darkness fell and I stole out late at night and
found Kukul, who hid me until the gods had sailed
away forever.

I found I was very thirsty and again remembered an
earlier journey on a litter much like this. I heard the
slow clop-clop of a horse's hooves. A shadow fell across
my covered body; I felt the sun's heat leave me. I
stiffened under the blanket. Cortés?

"Doña Marina?" a gentle voice said. I lowered my
arms from my face and looked up at Don Juan Jamarillo. He held the horse's reins in one hand, in the
other the little parrot in its cage. His expression was
compassionate. "That was a terrible sight for a woman's
eyes," he said. "Is there anything I can do to bring you
comfort?"

"Yes. Get me some water."

"Water? Surely." He fumbled a bit at the other side
of his saddle, then bent to offer down his flask. I drank.

The water was cool. Some spilled. I did not care. Water is life, I thought. I am drinking life. I am not like Cuauhtemoc.

Those few words shocked me with the deeper meaning implicit in them. Don Juan Jamarillo became determinedly cheerful. "This poor little parrot seems to miss you. Look how eagerly he is watching you now." He lowered the cage, smiling in his neat blond beard.

I looked. The parrot's yellow round eye met mine. The caged bird seemed a symbol for Cuauhtemoc. And me. I sat up and reached for the cage. As soon as the parrot's wing is healed, I thought, I will set it free. "Thank you," I said.

Jamarillo nodded. Pleased and believing he had somewhat cheered me, he spurred his mount and rode forward to rejoin the other horsemen.

I lay back. Holding the parrot cage in the curve of one arm, I put together the meaning of the fragments of thoughts and feelings I had just experienced. I knew I had to escape Cortés. Not because I feared for my life; because I feared for my soul. Painfully, I went back to the beginning of our time together, and I saw with utmost clarity that while Cortés had been busy creating a new colony for Spain he had also been creating a new Cortés. He had overcome every obstacle that stood between him and the achievement of his ambition, and in doing so he had turned from a man of unusual courage into a monster with new ambitions yet unsatisfied.

That one single act, the hanging of Cuauhtemoc, had opened my eyes to what I had been willfully blind to before. Every other action he had been able to justify to a woman who yearned to continue to love him. But this act he could never justify. I knew the fear that had inspired it, a fear that had waited only for the moment to spring like an adder on its victim. "Below the green panache of power bad dreams dwell." The conqueror hates the conquered, however much he tells himself his own cause was just. Humans do not become the greater by subduing others, but by serving them with love.

As to how I could manage to leave Cortés if he did not wish me to, I did not know. Nor did I see how I could also manage to claim my son in doing this. All I knew was that I would. Somehow. Someday. In time.

From the day of Cuauhtemoc's execution, Cortés was moody, irritable, and unlike his former self. His fever continued, burning like a low fire, although his mind became clear of fantasy. Our friendly welcome at the large trade city of Aculán, which we reached late that day, did not seem to remove from his mind the shadow of that dark ceiba tree. We were given pleasant quarters and ample food, yet he slept scarcely at all. His tossing and turning gave me an excuse to ask for a separate room. "This terrible journey has wearied and weakened me very much. I am only a woman, after all, and am suffering great anxiety about my child whom I have not seen for so long."

He gave me a hard, probing look as if he half-suspected my aversion. That maimed left hand, the claw with which he had signaled the cutting down of Cuauhtemoc's body, had become particularly horrible to me. I could scarcely believe that on the morning of our reunion after the *noche triste* the blood-soaked bandage that covered it had filled me with compassion so that I ached for him and his pain and the loss of his fingers.

"Very well," he said. "You can sleep in the antechamber to this room if you wish. I admit this fever keeps me restless."

The next day I learned, with horror, that Cuauhtemoc had not been buried beside the cacique of Tacuba as I had assumed. Cortés had brought the body with him, slung in a great sack which two of the soldiers carried on a pole. "His reason was strange," El Galán told me, troubled. "He said he did not want Guerrèro to find the grave and know our hostage was dead. He has told the cacique there that the last Aztec monarch is still with him, though unwilling for company, which God knows is true. Cortés did a wrong and terrible thing in hanging him. He should have cherished him like a precious jewel, proof of his victory over the Aztecs and his noble treatment of a vanquished foe."

I did not trust even El Galán, in my desperate state of mind, and did not tell him I agreed. I shrugged. "Cortés was ill with fever. Perhaps in his right mind he would have behaved differently." But I knew that the fever Cortés suffered from was no passing one caught in the swamps; it was a fever that would burn in him until he died or had explored and conquered all the unknown lands of the world and then, perhaps, would have him eyeing the cold far moon and wondering if it might be made of silver.

A few nights after we reached the city of Aculán, when Cortés went out to walk on the upper level of the temple near our dwelling place, perhaps to see if any spies or other interlopers were skulking in the garden of our palace, he slipped and fell many spans to a stone paving on which he injured his head. When he came into the anteroom where I slept, I screamed on seeing the fierce face pinched with pain, one glaring eye staring at me, the other hidden by a curtain of blood. For an instant I thought one of the Aztec soldiers with us might have tried to kill him in revenge for Cuauhtemoc's death. But as I dutifully wiped away the blood and bandaged the wound I learned of his misstep on a high place, and I knew his enemy within had caused the fall: that conscience by which he so often swore had risen up against him and seized the chance to hurl him down to the earth.

But remorse he would not admit, and insisted to me and others and later, in a letter to King Carlos, that the former monarch of Mexico, by the ascendance of his character and his former high station, had maintained an influence over his countrymen that would have enabled him at any instant to rouse their smothered animosity into open rebellion against Spanish rule.

I did not try to reason with him; even if I had wished to it would have been fruitless, for it soon became plain to me that he was not in his right mind. One evidence of this was his great sensitivity about the fall he had

and the head wound it had left him with. He tried to
conceal this injury from his soldiers, a futile effort since
the gash refused to heal firmly and would suddenly
open and let blood run down his face. But I knew his
reason for wanting to preserve the illusion among the
men that he was all but invincible against common
injury. We were still a long way from the Honduras
colony where Olid maintained his stolen authority, unaware that his nemesis was inching closer.

From that first Aculán town we went to Petén, a
pretty city built on islands in a lake and so reminding
me of Tenochtitlán on a much smaller scale. There
again we were well received, and there the priests in-
troduced Christianity and again the ruler of Spain attained another vassal. There, too, Cortés' smoldering
fever abated at last, leaving him gaunt and somewhat
yellow, the lines at each side of his mouth gashed very
deep. He soon regained something of his old assurance.

This was fortunate, because after we left Petén,
further hardship and peril confronted us. Instead of
sucking swamps we had to make our way over a mountain of flints some nine leagues across. It took twelve
days; the flints cut the horses' feet to pieces, and so
many slipped suddenly down into deep crevasses that
when we reached the other side there were only thirty-
two mounts left out of more than a hundred. There, at
last, Cuauhtemoc was buried; by then the stench was
so terrible than no soldier would carry the sack containing his corpse.

The flints left behind, the season of rains began to
deluge us, swelling rivers to torrents that we crossed
with great danger and further loss. For my part, I
marveled that I had once considered the first journey to
Tenochtitlán an arduous one; now it seemed like a holiday. My clothing was shabby and travel-stained except
for that one Spanish gown of green velvet, which I had
worn only once—in Petén—to impress the cacique there.
It had dressed a marionette who stood beside Cortés
and performed her well-known duty.

But at last we neared the Golfo Dulce and Olid's

colony at the eastern end of the north coast of Honduras. The salt smell of the sea first told us our journey was nearly over; from a thickly forested hill we looked down at the distant little town, surrounded by a wooden stockade, poor and shabby-looking under the glare of the tropic sun. Weary and shattered as we were, the only hope was to take the colony by surprise. Camped amid trees that hid us from his objective, Cortés was in consultation with his captains about the strategy to be employed when the hand of tragic irony struck him.

Scouts sent ahead to sniff out the terrain and the strength and weakness of the fort came running back with grins and the astounding news that they encountered some people from the settlement who were friendly and talkative. "Olid is dead!" the flushed soldier said. "It seems that Casas was not drowned in that shipwreck you learned about. The mariners who reported the wreck to you saw the vessel on the rocks and assumed the worst. But the fact is that Casas and most of the others got safely ashore. Armed with his orders from you, they marched right into Olid's settlement, got the majority of the Spaniards there on the side of the law. And then they hanged Olid!"

Looking at Cortés' stricken face, all I could think was that our terrible journey had been for nothing. All for nothing! "Then God is good to have saved me from that disagreeable duty," Cortés managed to say.

I saw then the great irony: he had set out to hang Olid; instead he had hanged Cuauhtemoc. Punishing a traitor like Olid would have gained him only respect. Hanging Cuauhtemoc had already brought him reproach from such men as El Galán and would surely bring him more, elsewhere. And it had lost him the admiration of his Amazon. His talisman. His tongue.

Cortés entered the little settlement at the head of his dispirited army, and at once sent for de las Casas to demand why word had not at once been sent to him of Olid's capture and execution.

"It was!" de las Casas protested. "I dispatched a small troop overland to Coetzacoalcos. They either died en route from the dangers of the journey or else were killed by hostile natives. You cannot blame me for that."

Cortés indeed could not, remembering the obstacles our large expedition had barely survived. But then he said one word which chilled me: "Guerrero!"

De las Casas did not understand, and Cortés explained to him his theory of the renegade Spaniard.

A terrible despondency settled over me, for I knew that it was hopeless to try to appeal to Cortés' kinder side, to try to make him understand how desperately I yearned to see the son I had thought I was leaving for only a few months at most. This dreadful expedition with its ending that had turned all the pain and loss into a grim joke Cortés was unable to deal with except to believe that an unforeseeable enemy accounted in part for the great fiasco. If I showed him my true feelings, would he decide I had been in league with Guerrero?

My low spirits were not helped by the fact that the little colony was in a state of near famine so that even the modest comfort of sufficient food was denied us. Having no other challenge to face at the moment, Cortés took this as one. Since the land offered nothing, he said, the sea would have to be made to feed us. Finding that on the rocks of a natural jetty near the town there was an abundance of crabs, he inspired the making of dozens of crab nets out of lianas plucked down in the jungle and woven into a mesh tied to hoops of wood. Of crabs there seemed no end, large juicy ones, and in a few days simmering kettlesful had turned the tide of listless near-starvation. We had some fishhooks with us, dugout canoes were made, fish were hauled up in quantities ample enough to lead to merriment.

Hunger coped with, Cortés and a party of soldiers set out to explore the area farther than the desperate colonists had, but reported only dismal swamps and venomous insects. There were also alligators; he brought a dead one back as a trophy, hopeful that it might taste somewhat like iguana, but it did not.

For my part, I disliked the ugly little settlement,

which felt too much like a prison with its surrounding stockade, and took to wandering along the beach near it. There I would gather seashells, of which there were some pretty ones. It became almost a passion with me, and when I found a shell unlike any other it seemed like a piece of great luck that betokened good fortune in the future. This inane occupation temporarily assuaged my feeling of being forlorn and friendless. This was merely self-pity; I deeply hurt poor Don Juan Jamarillo when I refused his offer to accompany me on one of my walks.

One day I wandered farther from the town than I ever had before; it was out of sight behind dunes of brownish sand. I stood there with a seashell in my hand gazing southward. I knew that somewhere beyond the ocean before me lay the vast continent of South America, and on its western side the fabled mountain cities of the Incas. Somewhere to the west, perhaps, was the secret strait to the Pacific Cortés hoped to discover for King Carlos. Would I find myself one day ascending high mountains toward the Inca cities? Or would I sail through that strait to the great ocean to the west? Was I fated to journey with my captor endlessly? I looked back in wonder at the self I had once been, filled with pleasure when Cortés told me he wanted me with him in Honduras.

Alone on that beach, I was the first to see the Spanish ship and ran back to the town to spread the news. Very soon two brigantines arrived, stopping off en route to the principal Spanish colony on the Nicaraguan coast, Trujillo.

With something like his old enthusiasm, Cortés told me he had decided to embark with the major part of his force on those ships. "From Trujillo I will plan and launch a new expedition, to search for the strait to the Pacific. I also intend to explore and subdue the entire province of Nicaragua. The emperor, I know, will look on this with favor and send the needed vessels and supplies." He smiled down at me. "In Trujillo you will find things more to your liking, Marina. It's a large colony now. There are some women there for company, and other pleasures and conveniences."

I could not speak, only nodded mutely. I turned and went out to my lonely refuge, the seashore. Another expedition, and after that another. And I the faithful Indian mistress at his side, his good-luck piece, his comfort on some nights, his possession, as useful as his horse. With an infinitely somber sound waves broke and slid back into the sea, dragging pebbles after.

Cortés spoke behind me. "Why do you wander out here alone? What is wrong with you, Marina? Why do you look so sad, now that our troubles are over at last? Oh, it was a hard journey for you, and I admit it. Had I guessed the misfortunes ahead, you would have remained safe in the city of Mexico with Martín. But here we are, alive after it all, at a new beginning. For my part, I am looking forward to the journey ahead." He gestured toward the wide blue sea. "If that strait exists I'll find it! That will please our sovereign more than all the gold and silver I've sent him from Mexico!"

I felt no response. Not pride in his renewed spirit, not fear for the dangers he would face: nothing. It was like being partly dead. Perhaps this is how dying feels, I thought.

His smile vanished. "What do you want of me, Marina? Tell me. What?"

"I want to go home to Martín."

"I do not intend to retrace my steps to Mexico. It's a waste of time. The new project begins in Trujillo."

"Then let me go to Martín alone."

"That's absurd. You'll like it in Trujillo. You'll sail there on a fine ship!" He tried to smile.

I took a deep breath, and risked everything. "I want to leave you, Cortés."

He stepped back, gave me a cool, probing look. It told me that he knew and would always know that I had seen him at his worst, knew that I would never forget Cuauhtemoc hanging from that ceiba tree.

He turned his back abruptly and walked away from me to stand some distance off, staring out over the sea.

At last he faced me, keeping that distance between us. His voice was calm and resolute. "This life of mine is a hard one for any woman to share. She must live in safety without me or else stay at my side to endure great privations and dangers. And my life will never change. Ahead of me I see a secret strait, an Inca city, the wide Pacific, the South Seas. Before I go there, I want to explore the Pacific coast of Mexico northward. I'll build another fleet at Zacatula."

"Your life will never change," I agreed, holding my breath.

He straightened, looking at me kindly. "And so it seems, Doña Marina, that we have come to the parting of our ways."

"Yes, to our parting," I managed to whisper.

He nodded, took one step closer, paused. "There remains the matter of your future. I have given it some thought. I do not intend you to live it alone, a woman abandoned. You need a husband. I suggest Don Juan Jamarillo."

This abrupt arranging of my future left me numb. I said that I needed no husband, only my son.

"For the sake of that son, as well as your own, I prefer that you marry a Spaniard. Don Juan is of a fine old family, which would give you the status you well merit. Martín would benefit from a stepfather able to set him an example of the manners and morals of a Castilian of high category."

I found my voice, even tried to smile. "But surely Don Juan has something to say about this arrangement?"

"It has not escaped me that he is in love with you. He will say yes and thank me from the bottom of his heart. As a wedding gift I intend to endow him with a handsome grant of land. You I will also endow, and to a much greater degree. I intend that you shall have an estate encompassing your little town of Paynala and many leagues of land around it."

"You are very generous."

"I wish also to make you a gift of a number of

jewels beyond those I have already given you. Despite the heavy financial cost of this failed expedition to Honduras, I have the faith that I can retrieve the loss elsewhere, and so I will be able to muster up some gold as well."

Our eyes locked. In his I thought I saw a yearning, as if perhaps he hoped that I would run to him across the space of sand between us and tell him that no grant of land, no jewels, no gold, no Castilian husband could ever compensate me for the privilege of continuing at his side. I said, "Then Martín will live with me?"

He nodded. "With you and Don Juan Jamarillo. As for Martín's future, he is my son and heir. The plans I have made for him will remain unchanged except for the better, depending on what capacities he develops as he grows older."

"May I request one thing more?"

He nodded. I pointed to the brigantines anchored offshore.

"Could you have one of those ships take me to Mexico at once?"

He shook his head. "No. I need them both to take me and my men to Trujillo. I will see to it that another ship is sent here for your passage to Vera Cruz." He smiled. "And that will allow time for your wedding to Don Juan."

Thinking only of returning to my son, I had considered this marriage a future event. "Surely the marriage can wait."

He frowned. "No. I intend to embark for Nicaragua knowing that you are the legal wife of a knight of Castile and that this much of my arrangement for your future well-being has been complied with." Now he had struck his most arrogant pose, head high, one fist on his hip. It occurred to me then that his enthusiasm for Don Juan Jamarillo concealed a fear that his son might end with an Indian stepfather.

Looking at him there, backed by blue sea, I remembered Cortés as I had first seen him in Tabasco. It seemed to me that just as I had been wrong then in thinking him a god, so I might have been wrong now in thinking him a monster. Yet I knew that since escaping him meant marrying Don Juan Jamarillo, marry him I would. Perhaps in the green velvet Spanish gown, if that was what Cortés desired.

I bowed my head in assent. "He is a kind gentleman and will be good to Martín."

He nodded, relieved at my compliance, and came toward me. He held out his hand, not the three-fingered claw but his right whole hand, and seeing what he wished I rested mine upon it. He bent and kissed it as he would the hand of some fine Spanish lady. He straightened and looked deep into my eyes and his face assumed an expression combined of affection and regret. He pressed my hand, then released it; it slipped from his. "Know this: Cortés will never forget you."

"Nor I Cortés," I said, truthfully, and saw Cuauhtemoc hanging. In that instant I knew he was the symbol to me of all the native people of Mexico. The promises Cortés had made concerning them had all been broken too.

And so we parted, Cortés and I, and the only sound of mourning was the cry of a seagull passing overhead toward another shore. That cry, and the hollow crash of a breaking wave. We turned and walked sedately toward the crude buildings of the little town and my wedding day.

Cortés kept his promises to me. And so because of him I became not only the caciqua of Paynala but also the entitled owner of the land on which it stood, and even of the great cave, ancient refuge of my people. It was in Paynala that I chose to live, Don Juan being graciously anxious to please me in this as in all things. For Martín the change seemed for the better; he ceased having the colds and fevers that had sometimes plagued him in the drafty stone governor's palace at that high altitude, and as his tutor formed part of our household, his education did not suffer. His beloved Doña Luisa also joined me there. At first we lived in the stone palace where I had spent my childhood, my mother and her son having long since been removed by the clan heads to a more modest dwelling, but soon Don Juan became engrossed in the project of building us a Spanish house of adobe bricks on the corner of the plaza opposite the site chosen by Aguilar for the mission his Franciscan order was constructing there.

On the day Don Juan declared our new home finished to his satisfaction and took me proudly through its rooms, I learned that Cortés had not been wholly mistaken in his wild fantasy concerning Guerrero, the Spanish renegade. A letter came to me from Orteguilla, who sometimes wrote to me, although he could not bring himself to leave forever the aura of pomp and prestige enjoyed by a page of the governor, chief justice, and captain-general of New Spain.

Captain Montejo had been sent to Yucatán by Cortés to carry out the subjugation of all Yucatán, which proved a hard task. The various caciques there, already bound together by the same traditions of more than a thousand years' duration, had been formed into a strong coalition against Spanish conquest, inspired by Guerrero, whose knowledge of the Spanish mind and whose great personal valor offered Montejo a challenge he had not expected. "Imagine this renegade turning against his own people in such a fashion!" Orteguilla wrote indignantly. "What will history say of such a traitor? How could he betray the land that nursed him in order to aid another, inferior race?"

That night I dreamed I met Guerrero, and in my dream he looked like an Indian warrior and was the age my father would have been if he had lived. His tall, well-muscled body seemed to glow as he emerged from among the trees around us, for I was going along a trail through a deep jungle. He spoke to me in Spanish, with that mournful intensity that people in dreams sometimes have. "I am Guerrero, that Spaniard who went over to the Indians, and whom my former countrymen call traitor and hold in contempt. You are Malinche, an Indian who went over to the Spaniards.

Will you, too, face contempt from the people you were born among?"

I said, "Still, I will live in Paynala."

"That is either very brave or else a great folly."

I became angry with him, in this dream. "My people will never hold me in contempt!"

He looked at me with pity. "That is what I once thought," he told me, and turned and vanished among the trees.

Most dreams fade, but this one has remained with me, for I already knew when I dreamed it that many millions of Indians had come to hate Cortés, and that with him they must hate me. There are those who call me *La Chingada,* as if I were a whore. But a whore sells her body and I gave mine. There are those who call me a traitoress. Liars, too. The Aztecs were never my people, but their oppressors, and it was the Aztecs Cortés set himself against and fought and conquered. And so I betrayed no one, I who had once been so monstrously betrayed, so cruelly betrayed, and by the woman who bore me. If there was a betrayal on my part, then the one person I betrayed has been myself. I knew long before I acknowledged it that Cortés was ruthless but I called it courage. I knew he was cunning but called it cleverness. And I knew that shedding Indian blood did not seem to him like murder, but I assured myself that the many souls he would save could wash it all away. Passion against reason was the battle that I lost. And if I call passion love, it does not change defeat to victory.

But there is a Power greater than Cortés. And so I believe that wrongs done by him will be made right at last. This I must believe. I must trust in God, walk humbly, and do whatever good I can.

PART XII

▼▼

THE FIST OF SATAN
January 1, 1530–June 30, 1530

47

At the start of the year 1530, my twenty-ninth birthday just ahead, I was able to look upon myself with satisfaction and to consider the past eight years of my adulthood well-employed. I was the most important man in Havana, nor was the name of Don Arturo Mondragon unknown in Santiago, even Spain. If anyone had told me that within a few months my life would be abruptly changed forever, I would have laughed and denied the possibility.

The decisions I made as a veteran of twenty-one who had just acquired a modest fortune from the sale of two emeralds and some gold proved wise ones. I had to weigh three alternatives. My father took up my mother's cry of "Salamanca!" He told me that wealth and the study of law go hand in hand. Cousin Enrique had other plans for me. He owned a fleet of vessels and now was eyeing New Spain with avarice, enthralled by what he had learned from me of the many products aside from gold and silver which could be imported into Europe at good profit: chocolate, vanilla, cochineal, tobacco, tomatoes, potatoes both white and sweet, cotton cloth, and even *guajolotes,* that large delicious fowl, unknown in Europe, which soon came to be called "turkey birds." A partnership was what he saw: my knowledge of New Spain and his ships. But my marriage to his daughter of sixteen, Amalia, was also in his mind. It would have been an advantageous marriage, since she would one day inherit the bulk of his fortune, but having known with every fiber of my being what real love felt like, I could not imagine myself embracing that pale thin little body, and for the rest of my life at that. But how to get the partnership without getting a wife I did not want?

A third alternative faced me: should I use a portion of my money to exploit better the Mondragon land adjacent to Havana, which was clearly destined to become the major port of the Caribbean? I had learned that sugar cane throve in a tropic climate with heavy rainfall, and sugar in Europe was worth almost its weight in gold, a luxury enjoyed only by the rich. It was this project that lured me most; my old fantasy of bringing Malinche to Cuba as my bride had not perished, for I knew Cortés could never marry her. I wanted to create a small self-contained world where a boyhood dream could come true.

Among these three choices I vacillated. The hard benches and drafty lecture halls at Salamanca did not appeal to me, yet I suspected that any future dealings with the shrewd Enrique would make some knowledge of the law a necessity. But a huge plantation of sugar cane with some Negroes who knew how to plant, harvest, and mill had such allure that I made a trip to the south of Spain and the meager cane fields there to get the plans for constructing a sugar mill. I learned to my delight that canes planted horizontally and watered well produce plants that tower to three times a man's height or more within eight months. I imagined Enrique's ships' holds bursting with ingots of Mondragon sugar.

On my twenty-first birthday I was still vacillating at Enrique's villa, honored by a fiesta. Amalia, as usual, was beside me. Her father, in conversation with a plump widow in black, glanced fondly at the two of us, and the widow, seeing this, smiled and nodded her approval of the pair we made, Amalia and I. "Happy birthday, dear cousin," Amalia said, and stood on tiptoes to place on my cheek her impulsive, girlish kiss.

I had been thinking of sugar cane, and she took me by surprise. Her lips were as cool as her gray eyes; a

moth's wing might have brushed my cheek for all the
response I felt. On second thought, the kiss did not
seem to me impulsive but rather calculated; with it she
claimed a right to that tiny sector of my body. And,
strangely, it evoked a memory of Malinche, by contrast.
Amalia's pale, adoring presence was a mere shadow;
Malinche's dark and vital beauty remembered seemed
more tangible. Amalia represented life's reality: an advantageous marriage. Malinche stood for the dreams
men live by which inspire heights of effort merely
practical considerations do not.

"What are you thinking of?" Amalia asked—one of
her more annoying habits.

"An Indian princess."

She hid annoyance with a look of innocent amazement. "A princess? Really? A real Indian princess?"

"As real as dreams," I said, to her confusion. And
then my mind seemed to brighten. I saw with immense
clarity that I did not have to choose among three alternatives; I had to embrace all three! I would learn
enough law so Enrique could not cheat me; I would get
his ships without getting his daughter; I would plant
sugar cane in Cuba. All three were possible; all three
I would accomplish. By shrewdness and hard work I
would use my small fortune to attain in time a much
greater one. And so the Indian princess as real as
dreams ruled the realities of my existence, dictated a
life shaped as though by getting richer I would get her
too.

It was fortunate that I did not know that Doña Catalina was destined to die in less than a year, leaving
Cortés free to marry Malinche. By the time I learned
of this, I was well embarked on my triple plan: my
brain was stuffed with a year of law; the canes to plant
my first field were en route to Cuba in one of Enrique's
vessels, which would return to Spain loaded with goods
from Mexico; and Amalia was destined to meet on
my return to Valladolid a young veteran named Rafael,
whom I had reencountered in Vera Cruz and who was
more than willing to marry an heiress.

It was he who told me that Doña Catalina had died of a lung congestion in the city of Mexico. I concealed from him the shock I felt at the news; how cruel of Fate to deal the one blow I had never expected! With gloom I watched Rafael's meeting with Amalia a month later, saw the round O of her mouth pointed toward him, not me, by the evening's end. My not marrying Amalia cost me a land grant in Mexico; Cortés wanted only colonists who would remain there and bring wives.

I decided that Cortés would not marry Malinche for at least a year after Doña Catalina's death, but after that I expected to learn at any moment that Malinche was his. By now she was somewhat famous. A history of the conquest of Mexico, written by one who had taken no part in it, had made the name of the beautiful young Indian woman who so nobly served the Spanish cause almost as widely known as that of Cortés himself. It was as Doña Marina that she had been so honored; the lavish description of her raven tresses and form divine rivaled for banality the poem I once wrote to her. This portrait bore little resemblance to the Malinche I had loved, nor was her past life before she encountered Spaniards even touched upon. Full-grown, she arrived in our midst to graciously aid us, a goddesslike aborigine without a past worth note. Since fame always stirs some to malice, there was a counter image as false: she was the enamored Indian female of whom a virile and clever Cortés had taken every advantage, to Spain's benefit and his own.

So I knew that their marriage would be no secret long and after a time got used to the idea that I had lost her. But the good thing about ambitious plans is that they have their own momentum and carry one along to new concepts; I decided that I wanted to possess a ship of my own, for in this way I could make a number of short trips to Mexico and stockpile in my Havana warehouse nonperishable goods which Enrique's vessels could then pick up when they brought to Havana the European goods I would later sell in Mexico. I returned from Spain to Cuba in my own caravel, as proud as if it were a galleon, only to find that I had missed seeing El Galán.

On his way back to Mexico from Cortés' disastrous campaign to Honduras and Nicaragua, a storm had struck and his ship was driven clear to Cuba—in fact, to Havana, and so he had decided to visit me. He had acquired, my mother said, a new scar, a recurrent fever, a hatred of lush green forests, and little else. Moreover, Cortés' intention to search for a strait to the Pacific had been abruptly terminated when he learned that his funeral services had been held in the city of Mexico, word having arrived and been spread wide by his enemies there that he and all the other members of his expedition were dead. There had been no choice for Cortés but to return and prove he was very much alive, if battered, fever-ridden, and impoverished.

"I must say I like your friend Bernal Diaz del Castillo," my mother said. "He stayed here for several days, but then could wait for you no longer as his ship was repaired by then."

"Did he happen to mention Doña Marina?" I asked.

"That Indian woman? Yes. He said she is married."

I had known that this was inevitable, but still the words brought a pang. "Yes, I was sure Cortés would marry her at last," I said with admirable calm.

"Cortés?" My mother was astounded. "Why would a man of his fame, a man any number of rich and noble women would give their hope of heaven to get, why would he marry a penniless Indian woman?"

Her lengthy rhetorical query had left me confused. "Cortés didn't marry her?"

"Of course not. She married quite well, though. A Castilian gentleman named—let me think—named Don Juan Jamarillo. In Honduras, it was. Or Yucatán."

Jamarillo? Who was this Jamarillo?

"What is wrong with you?" my mother asked. "Your face is white as cotton.

I turned away, saying I was going to the cane fields. Staring up at those green lofty stalks that towered above me, I saw instead the green forests of Yucatán which

El Galán had told my mother he hated. If I had gone there with Cortés, would I now be in lucky Jamarillo's shoes? The thought was unbearable; that night I got very drunk.

In the morning, sad and sober, Malinche's marriage continued to puzzle me. I thought of the years she and Cortés had spent together, the child she bore him. Had Cortés really turned his back on his faithful Indian mistress so as to marry some noble and wealthy lady? But, even so, why had she married this upstart, this Castilian gentleman who came galloping to Cortés' banner after the conquest had been won by braver men? Where were they now? In Spain? In the city of Mexico? Where?

It was El Galán who at last told me. A letter from him said he was for a time in Santiago, where he had married the woman he told me of when we first met. I sailed there in my caravel with a wedding gift.

In the eight years since I had last seen him his brown hair had receded; the look of youth had quite vanished. His wife was buxom and pretty and left us to talk while she went to see to our evening meal; they were living in a modest house belonging to her parents. He was full of information about Cortés.

"After we returned to Mexico in twenty-six, pretty well battered by that damned Honduras campaign and knowing we had been declared dead, things looked up for him. In the towns where we stopped on the way to the capital the colonists entertained us royally, and since word of our resurrection had preceded us we got a wonderful welcome to the city of Mexico: flower-decked canoes on the lake and a big feast at the convent of St. Francis, built just about where Moctezuma's palace was. In a few days, Cortés had his hands firmly on the reins of government once more.

"But would you believe that within a month the Court at Madrid sent over a resident justice to take over the actual governing of Mexico? It seems that Cortés' enemies got Carlos to believe that Cortés intended to establish himself as an independent sovereign, cutting

Mexico off from Spain. This was a bitter blow to Cortés, but he took it in stride and welcomed the resident justice, named Ponce de Leon. He turned out to be a fair-minded fellow and he and Cortés got on well. But then he died in a month of the same lung congestion that killed Doña Catalina. On his deathbed he appointed the Royal Treasurer to succeed him. This Estrada happened to hate Cortés, inflicting on him and his friends every annoyance a petty mind could think of and ignoring all his recommendations. When Cortés finally protested the theft of some land from one of Sandoval's men, Estrada ordered Cortés to leave the city. Think of it!"

"But did Cortés go?"

"He didn't want to be the cause of a civil war that would have Spanish blood flowing in the streets. He was bitter at heart, but he and his loyal followers left for Texcoco where we stayed until another blow fell. Cortés learned that a Royal Audience planned to examine a large number of charges against him—charges made, of course, by Estrada and his cohorts. This Audience would have the power to send Cortés to Spain for sentencing and punishment."

"Punishment for what, in God's name?"

"Lies and calumnies, mostly. And a few misfortunes and mistakes, to be sure. This final blow was too much for Cortés. He left at once for Spain to plead his cause in person with the King. He took quite a retinue; it included Sandoval, now his closest friend, myself, a son of the elder Xicotencatl, Orteguilla and his wife Blanca, and four amusing Indian jugglers. He also brought two hundred thousand gold pesos and some jewels of great value; I myself saw some emeralds of remarkable size." He winked. "No frog among them."

"I guess he was wise not to meet the King looking poor."

"Face, face; he had to save face!" He frowned then. "But for all this pomp, he crossed the Atlantic very much saddened, for en route, in Vera Cruz, he got word that his father had died. We landed at Palos—the port,

you remember, where Columbus returned thirty-seven
years ago after discovering a new world for Isabel,
only to die at last in poverty and neglect. 'And I may
end no better,' Cortés said to me. Only a week later, in
Rabida, Sandoval died in Cortés' arms of the disease he
contracted on that Honduras march, a recurrent fever.
And in that same town, as if to prove that loyalty dies
and treachery flourishes, Cortés encountered Francisco
Pizarro. With an abominable aplomb, Pizarro flatly
denied any past betrayal of Cortés, then boasted that
he had high hopes of soliciting royal financing for an
expedition to the land of the Incas." He grinned. "I
said to him that I wished him soldiers as loyal as he
had been to our commander in Mexico, and the look
he gave me would have felled an oak."

In spite of the questions I had come here to ask
about Malinche, Jamarillo, and their whereabouts, I
found that I wanted to know how Cortés had fared with
the king, and asked El Galán about that.

"In spite of his sorrow and bitterness, Cortés wrote
a brilliant letter to Carlos, denying all charges against
him. It brought an invitation to Court. The magnificent
welcome surprised us, and the king was very gracious,
and appeared at Cortés' side on all public occasions.
In other words, he accepted Cortés' appraisal of himself. I must say that I enjoyed the flattery and attention
of a number of ladies of the court, having been long
estranged from women in silk and velvet and perfume."
He smiled blandly, "Although I was truthful and told
them I had lost my heart to a certain faithful young
woman in Santiago."

As one who had also lost his heart to a certain young
woman, I asked about Malinche. "I know of her marriage to this Jamarillo fellow. But where is she now?
What has happened to her? Do you know?"

"Still living in peaceful obscurity in Paynala, I believe."

"Paynala? The place where she was born?"

"After their marriage in Honduras she returned to
the city of Mexico with her new husband to reclaim her

son, and they left shortly for this little town; Cortés gave it to her. After all, in the course of her years with Cortés she had endured several lifetimes of excitements and danger, quite enough for a mere woman."

"Mere she was not."

"Agreed. But still a woman. Now, after such perils, she has attained what most women want most: a nest. She has her son to raise, an adoring husband, and, for all I know, other children by him."

"But why this Jamarillo? What happened between her and Cortés?"

He was silent for a moment; I could see loyalty to Cortés struggling with candor. He gave me a long look. "Well, as to precisely what passed between them, I do not know, of course. But I must admit that Cortés showed a very strange side of his nature during that long march across Yucatán. For one thing, he hanged Cuauhtemoc, you know." I nodded. "This seemed to affect Malinche very deeply. And then, for a time, Cortés was somewhat crazed. I would guess that she could not bear the change in him. Women, you know, like to look up to their men. And there was Jamarillo, very handsome, very loving— and, I must admit, very brave though mostly out of a certain innocence of the fact that heroes can die. To give Cortés his due, after he recovered his senses I think he realized that since he had no intention of marrying Doña Marina, it was unfair to keep her from a decent life with a very worthy husband."

Stricken, I saw again that if only I had been there in Honduras, my boyhood dream might have come true. That night I dreamed of my emerald frog, the proud possession that had more than anything else inspired me to return to Cuba while I still had it. It was of giant size, and hopped toward me, mouth open as if to swallow me, but it had very sad eyes.

The next day as I was leaving I thanked El Galán for having shared with me his wealth of information. "You seem to know so much more than I about the destinies of these people who once shared ours."

He smiled ruefully. "I have a peculiar quirk, Arturo.

People and events in themselves seem to fascinate me much more than whatever wealth I might extract from them. My fear, now that I have started a family, is that I may depart this earth with nothing more to leave my wife and children than a thousand tales of the Conquest which they will have already heard."

Memories of Malinche haunted me on the journey home, and I relived those days of romantic idealism when I could see a Madonna in an Indian girl's face and could feel more ecstasy in dreams of her than any flesh under mine has brought me since. But I would not have voyaged to Paynala had it not been for what I learned from Cortés when he stopped at Havana on his way back to Mexico with his bride.

48

"A welcome must be arranged at once," the commandant of the port of Havana told me, having arrived at my door in a state of great excitement. The news had just reached him that Cortés, his new wife, his old widowed mother, and a large retinue had stopped in Hispaniola on their way from Spain to Mexico and would undoubtedly come to Havana when they continued westward. A small, excitable man with a wispy beard, he was in all ways opposite to Pedro Barba. "We must plan a reception of style and elegance, worthy of the Marques of the Valley of Oaxaca. That is the newest of Cortés' titles, conferred by the sovereign personally."

It seemed to me that in raising Cortés to the height of titled nobility with one hand, King Carlos had pushed him downstairs with the other when he appointed someone else to govern Mexico. I said as much.

"Still, Cortés is overlord of more than twenty large Indian towns and has something like twenty-five thousand Indian vassals," the commandant said. "This is in addition to his large estates in the city of Mexico and Cuernavaca.. And he's still captain-general of New Spain. Wealth, high honor, and none of the hard work of governing a huge territory. Do you think a mere reception will seem an adequate welcome? I think a procession and a band should meet him at the dock, with pretty children to present him with bouquets, that sort of thing."

"Do as you will."

The real reason for the visit to me then emerged. Would I be willing to defray some of the expense? "There must be a barbecue for the whole town. The wine must be the best we can get. There is not just Cortés to consider, but his noble wife. Doña Juana de Zuñiega is the niece of the Duke of Bejar, who defended Cortés so well at Court. We don't want her to think that Havana is just a rude, backward colony, do we?"

I agreed to pay half the costs, for the sake of the honor of Havana. Week after week passed with no word of Cortés' imminent arrival. The news that finally reached Havana was almost unbelievable. The Royal Audience in the city of Mexico had attacked Cortés again. A lengthy document charged him with many crimes and malfeasances. A copy of this Secret Inquiry had been delivered to him in Hispaniola, another had been sent to the king.

I told the commandant that we might as well shelve the idea of a splendid reception: before a royal investigation of these charges could be completed, the wine bought to toast Cortés in Havana would have turned to vinegar, the plump pigs for the barbecue would be ancient sows. He glumly agreed.

My disappointment was keener than his; because

their son Martín was with Malinche I believed I could learn more about her from Cortés than El Galán had known. Was her marriage a happy one? Did she have other children now? Was she still living in Paynala? Or had her Castilian husband taken her to Spain? And so the Secret Inquiry that had prevented Cortés from coming to Havana had a personal significance to me. Would he be pardoned or found guilty? If guilty, he would probably be arrested and taken to Spain for punishment or reprimand by Carlos. But if the charges against him were refuted, then he would most likely continue the journey westward from Hispaniola as he had planned.

A privateer arrived from Hispaniola to tease me with half-news. Just before he had sailed, a galleon had arrived from Spain, flying the royal banner. He thought it might have brought to Cortés the king's decision as to the Secret Inquiry. But what it was, the stupid fellow had not waited to learn.

The humid heat of early summer had settled over Havana. On a sweltering afternoon in late May I was standing on the cliff where I had sighted Cortés' flagship more than eleven years before. But now I was watching for my partner Enrique's brigantine from Spain, long overdue. I saw instead a splendid galleon sailing grandly toward Havana's harbor, sails full and white against the lowering cloudbank that promised the rain my sugar cane needed. As the ship came closer I saw that it flew the royal banner. By the time it dropped anchor within the protective arms of the bay, I was on my horse headed for town, the first raindrops pelting me.

But no boat left the galleon for shore. Sailors climbed the rigging, furling the sails. The ship floated serenely on dark emerald water, prepared to wait out the storm. Was Cortés on the vessel? And if so, did he plan to come ashore or merely take refuge in the harbor until the tempest had passed?

Impatience seized me; I went to the cantina and there found a fisherman willing to row me out to the galleon.

The ship's hull loomed as high above me as a palace. The rain was heavier by now, and a crash of thunder drowned out my first hail. But then a mariner peered over the rail far above. He confirmed that Cortés was indeed on the vessel, lowered a wide rope ladder and took me to the aft cabin. As I neared it, the wind blowing my cloak wide, excitement gripped me at the realization that in moments I would see again that hero of my youth who last wished me godspeed in the dismal ruins of Tenochtitlán.

Cortés, his hair and beard grizzled, was pondering the chessboard on a small table between him and a fair young lady who wore on a gold chain around her neck a large emerald carved in the shape of a flower. Her little white hand fondled the jewel as Cortés played his knight and then looked up. The grooves in his cheeks were very deep, like old wounds. Seeing me, he was at first blank-faced, but then smiled as gladly as though I were an invited guest. He came to me, embraced me, and presented me to his wife. "Doña Juana is inclined to seasickness," he said then, smiling down at her. "This harbor was a welcome sight."

She had an exaggerated Castilian lisp, like the late Sandoval. "Thith ocean ith much bigger than I guethed."

Cortés gazed down at her as fondly as though she had quoted Aristotle. He clapped for a servant, ordered wine brought, and himself drew up a chair for me so we were three around the little table. When I told him how the commandant and I hoped that a proper reception could be arranged in the morning, he said he had already planned to sleep aboard and glanced with satisfaction around the cabin, quite sumptuously appointed, with walls of polished teak, bedcover of dark red velvet, and even a carpet on the floor. "Now tell me, what can I do for you, Arturo? If this visit concerns claiming land in Mexico, I stand firm about the need for permanent colonists."

Although I knew he must be often pressed for favors by the greedy or the needy, I was still annoyed. "My visit lacks so practical a motive, Cortés. Does your arrival in this fine ship mean that you stand cleared of the charges made against you by the Royal Audience?"

His face darkened. "Can you believe that those knaves hatched a document a hundred folio pages in length?" I saw the old signal of his anger, that distended vein throbbing in his temple. "I read it with astonishment and disgust. The testimony was vague and contradictory. The witnesses to the crimes attributed to me were either obscure persons who could have had no firsthand knowledge of anything I did or else were known enemies of mine." The vein had subsided; he shrugged. "The same old charges: that I withheld revenues due the Crown, hid Aztec gold, and so on. For novelty, two new crimes were added." He smiled crookedly. "But then, fame always attracts human maggots looking for a corpse to inhabit."

"What were the two new accusations?" I asked.

His eyes met mine levelly. "That I murdered Ponce de Leon, the first resident justice of Mexico. And that I murdered my first wife, Doña Catalina."

Astonished, I cried, "But what motive could they find?"

His sharp glance accused me of feigning innocence. "Of Leon, that I resented his power. Of Doña Catalina, that I loved Doña Marina and wished to marry her." He reached for Doña Juana's hand, which left her emerald pendant. "Since I did not do so, one would think this a poor motive, but such limping logic was typical of the whole absurd and venomous document. After my first anger abated, I saw that it had no legal weight whatever. I chose to scorn it as a monument to the petty malice of my enemies. I so wrote to the king." He smiled. "Did you happen to hear that when I fell ill in Madrid last year he personally visited my bedside and remained more than an hour?"

Doña Juana nodded solemnly. Blonde, gray-eyed, and lipped like a cupid, she lisped, "And then he thent a jugged hare hith own cook prepared, and a thoup!"

I said to Cortés, "And yet you will no longer govern Mexico."

His graying beard jutted toward me as his head went back, proudly. "Our sovereign told me he was removing that burden from me so as to throw open the door to my ambition for new conquests. I will soon explore and map the entire western coast of Mexico, and perhaps the shore of the great continent I believe lies to the north. I will later journey to the South Seas that Magellan found, where the king has promised me I will personally rule over any lands I conquer." He leaned toward me, his dazzling eyes fixed on mine. "First I will go to the north of Mexico, sailing up the west coast to that narrow sea where the great pearls are. I intend to circumnavigate it, find if the land mass to its west is an island or peninsula. You should come with me! How would you like to bring a bucket of pearls home to your wife?"

"I have no wife."

"Well, to your pretty mother, then."

"I have a sugar plantation and a small thriving enterprise which I cannot abandon to go looking for pearls." I smiled.

"Small enterprises do not interest me." He leaned back. "To complete our interrupted discussion of that Secret Inquiry, on writing Carlos that I did not deign to defend myself against accusations so scurrilous and false, I also said that I would not sail one league westward or embark on any new venture until the charges against me were dropped, my name cleared. I also asked that the present Royal Audience be dismissed and another appointed. I said that I would wait in Hispaniola for his assurance that this was being done." He smiled shrewdly. "Only three days ago he so informed me, and placed this galleon at my disposal. So now I will take my bride and my mother to my new governor's palace in Cuernavaca, where the weather is mild and pleasant. There I will begin to make arrangements for my expedition to the Sea of Pearls." His eyes evaluated me. "Did you know there's an Indian legend that says that to the north of that sea there is a city with walls of gold? El Dorado! The land to the west is located more or less where the legendary Isle of California is supposed to lie, rich in gems of all kinds. You should join me, Arturo! I'll buy you a horse and make you a captain."

"I have a horse."

He warmed. "What has happened to your spirit of adventure? Where is that brave young man who would have gone with me to Mexico against his parents' wishes and in only the clothes he stood in?"

"He was seventeen. A city of silver could lure him. But I am older now, and golden cities do not. The less so since I have learned all about your disastrous and unrewarding campaign in Yucatán and Honduras."

He leaned back from me, looking older. "I finally sent Montejo down there, with a fourth expedition. He had some severe difficulties before his ultimate success. Do you know who his worst enemy was? Guerrero, that Spaniard who chose to stay behind when I rescued Aguilar. He became an Indian in mind and body. Under his leadership, those Yucatán Indians nearly won." Anger heated his voice, and then he shrugged. "But who can read the future? It is always a dark land toward which we must march with courage, expecting triumph."

I saw the gray adoring eyes of Doña Juana gazing up at him, and I remembered midnight eyes that had once looked up with just such admiration. "I am told that Malinche is now married to a gentleman called Jamarillo," I said.

The abruptness of this remark, for he could not know the thought which had prompted it, took him off guard and erased his smile. "She was."

"Was?"

"Jamarillo is dead."

My heart stopped beating. "When?"

"Last December. In Spain, where he went to visit his ailing parents." Cortés shrugged. "A foolish duel. He was never much of a swordsman—"

"And Malinche? Where is she?"

"In Paynala. She has a large estate there, my wedding gift to her. She preferred that place to any other, although I consider it a wretched area—heat, humidity, storms, and earthquakes. Only last week a mariner I talked with in Hispaniola said he had just come from that area and had experienced three temblors in as many days. Slight ones, he said, but still I am beginning to wonder if Paynala is where my son should live."

His indifference to Malinche jarred me. "What about the boy's mother? How slight were those temblors?"

"No one was injured, or so I was told."

But I had to know this for myself. Jamarillo's death had filled me with wild hope. Yet anxiety for Malinche tore at my heart. I asked if a ship's boat might row me ashore.

"But the storm's not over yet," Cortés said, glancing at the aft window streaming with rain.

"No matter."

Crossing the dark and agitated waters of the harbor, I whispered a prayer for Malinche's well-being. Twice I had lost her. But now, at last, my chance had come.

Cortés was welcomed to Havana, but not by me. I alerted my pilot and crew that night and sailed with the early morning tide.

49

A winding river road led from the port to Paynala. Five leagues had never seemed so endless by the time I reached the town in the late afternoon. On the south side of the paved central plaza stood a Christian church of whitewashed adobe, buttressed and boasting a bell-tower. To the north loomed a gray-stone pyramid to the ancient gods. They faced each other like adversaries. All around the square were thatched stone Indian houses, except at the southeast corner, where a flat-roofed adobe dwelling in the Spanish style held shadow in its arcade. The enormous poinciana tree beside it flaunted brilliant orange blossoms, as if proclaiming the triumph of local verdure over the alien dwelling.

Evidently Spanish visitors were few. In the middle of the plaza an old Indian woman with a basket on her arm stopped to stare. Several dark little boys in loin-cloths came toward me to look up shyly, ready to flee. I smiled down at them and pointed toward the Spanish house. "Señora Jamarillo?" One of them, after a pause, pointed in the other direction, toward the church. My relief vanished when I saw the small cemetery to his left, behind a black iron fence. But surely the child would have told me if she were dead. On my ship I had dressed with care to look affluent but not pretentious: hose of indigo, doublet of pale blue, the sleeves lined with ruby silk. Hope had made me dress for celebration, to deny anxiety. As I took off my flat velvet cap to wipe sweat from my forehead, a choir of young voices sounded from the open door of the church as piercingly sweet as though a flock of the Pope's castrati had been magically transported to this backwater Indian town on the Isthmus of Tehuantepec.

My black mare's hoofbeats were loud on the paving as I headed for the cemetery fence to tether her. I had just reached it when the voices ceased and in a minute more Indians began to trickle out onto the steps and down, the women with shawls over their heads, the men in loincloths and some in shirts of unbleached cotton cut full-sleeved in the Spanish mode. At the sight of me they all stared, but no one greeted me or smiled. I walked toward the church steps, eyes on the entrance for first sight of Malinche in her widow's black. The steps were empty, the Indians making their ways home across the plaza.

Then from the dark mouth of the wide doorway she came into the sunlight. She wore a mantilla of black lace but her cotton skirt and loose chemise were like those she had when I first saw her, only of a deeper, richer turquoise. Beside her was a little boy in a ruffled white shirt and short dark pantaloons, Indian sandals on his bare feet. She paused to speak to him and to drop the shawl back onto her shoulders. Her black hair was dressed high on her head and the strong column of her neck was the color of honey. When she saw me, her face lighted up with the beacon of her smile. She held out her arms to me. I ran to her, and our outstretched hands clasped. We were both laughing. "Arturo! My dear Arturo."

"Malinche!" As we briefly embraced, no moment I could remember had ever contained the joy of this one. My head was light with it. Why had I tormented myself with foolish anxiety, lost the pleasure of anticipating this reunion?

"Mother, who is he?" The boy at her side was looking up at me with dark, unsmiling eyes.

She stepped away from me to put one arm around his shoulder. "This is Martín," she said to me. And to him:

"This is Don Arturo, a dear friend of mine from long ago."

I smiled at him. "When I last saw you you were only three months old."

"Only three months old?" He looked up at me dubiously. "Then that is why I don't remember you." Above his head I saw a tall, thin priest in the brown robe of a Franciscan, and recognized Jeronimo Aguilar.

He stared at me intently. Nodding and smiling, he came to where we stood. He carried a little more flesh now, but his eyes were still cavernous. "You have been often in my thoughts and prayers, Arturo." His eyes went to something behind me and I turned and near the steps saw a group of Indians watching us. "Come inside and let me show you our church." I looked at Malinche, one eyebrow raised. I did not wish a church tour moments after our reunion, but she turned toward the door she had just left and I obediently fell into step, telling myself it would be good to get out of the hot sun.

High in the wall above the altar was a stained-glass window of the Virgin holding Jesus. Aguilar pointed up. "That was made in Europe, and to pay for it Doña Marina gave jewels that a vain woman would have kept to adorn her own body." In the soft light falling on her face from the holy scene she glowed with such loveliness that she needed no gems. When would I kiss those lips?

Aguilar was indefatigable. "She also built a school behind the church proper. The children learn to speak Spanish and to read and write. Doña Marina teaches them, aided by my young acolytes." He must have seen that the school did not interest me, for he smiled and changed the subject. "But you have had a long journey. Come, I will take you to your room where you can rest and refresh yourself."

A bed at the church, like any casual wayfarer? I glanced at Malinche, expecting that she would insist that I be a guest in her home, but she only asked us both to take an early supper with her at seven and hurried out, the boy beside her.

I was being offered everything I did not want—a bed, a nap, a good supper, instead of what I desired above all else: an uninterrupted private hour with Malinche. No boy, no Aguilar, no observant Indians. As I followed Aguilar to a monkish cell overlooking the church's inner patio with its central fountain, a slight resentment nagged. I had the feeling that he had guessed that Malinche was about to invite me to her home and had deliberately interposed his own invitation. But why had she so passively permitted this? Her house was quite large, so there could have been no lack of room for a guest. And she had been overjoyed at my sudden appearance. Of that I was sure.

I turned to Aguilar. "I would welcome a glass of wine, after my horse has been watered and fed."

He must have caught the cool undertone, but ignored it. "Yes, I must see to your horse. It must not be left unguarded in the plaza a moment longer."

He hurried out and I followed. "Surely you do not mean it could be stolen? In such a Christian town?"

"Paynala is only half Christian. You will understand that the old pagan influences have not been eradicated in only the few years since this church was built. There is a faction here that resents Spaniards and everything Spanish, including our Faith." He turned his head to regard me severely. "You were foolish to make the journey from Coetzacoalcos alone."

"I hired two Indian guides in the port."

"Well, your horse is all right." He sounded relieved. From the church steps I saw that it had drawn a modest crowd of a dozen children and as many adults, among these a tall, muscular Indian of perhaps thirty-five, dressed with ostentatious simplicity in a loincloth that reached only to his knees and was made of brown leather, perhaps deerskin. He wore a snakeskin band around his head and a necklace of dark green jadeite and silver. As I passed him to untether my mount he made a harsh remark in his native tongue, staring at me with beetle-black hostile eyes.

"Guilliermo is the leader of the unregenerate hea-

thens here," Aguilar told me as we led my mare through
the cemetery gate and around the church to a small
stable at the rear. "He prefers his pagan name, Na Chel
Cuy. He is a thorn in my heart, an obdurate creature
whom the grace of God has not yet touched. It was his
hope, apparently, to take Doña Marina as his wife
after she returned and became cacica. In his rage when
she came back from Honduras as Señora Jamarillo he
has done all he could to undermine our efforts to Christianize this town wholly."

We were crossing the patio toward the front wing
of the church. As he finished speaking, I felt the ground
under my feet shift, a very slight, uneasy motion that
seemed to arouse a tremor inside my body. "Did the
earth move just then?" My voice sounded less calm than
I would have liked.

"These temblors began again recently after many
years of calm. The old exiled priest Ah Tok tells people
they are signs of the anger of the ancient gods of this
land. He was banished half a dozen years ago and lives
now in the depths of a cave in the hills, where I know
he holds secret heathen rites to which some of the
townspeople steal away, out of their superstitious fear
of their old deities." He must have seen that my interest
in these two thorns of his was not intense, and forced a
smile. "But now I must offer you the refreshment I
promised. It is a wine made here at the mission, from
our own grapes." As he poured it I saw a few broken
veins on his cheeks and noted that he drank with
eagerness.

The dim refectory with its long dark table and
benches was pleasantly cool, and the wine was welcome, yet I would infinitely have preferred to be drinking plain water with the woman I had come here to see.
I decided to speak bluntly. "I feel that in offering me a
bed here you discouraged Malinche from inviting me to
stay at her home. Why?"

He refilled his glass. "Perhaps she also preferred that
you sleep here. She is recently widowed, still young,

still beautiful, and the caciqua of Paynala. Her every action is scrutinized by many eyes. A male guest . . ."

I put down my goblet with a crash. "I came here to marry her!"

He stared. "Then you already knew of Jamarillo's tragic death?"

"I sailed from Havana as soon as I learned of it."

"You are widowed too?"

"I never married."

In their caverns his eyes left mine to glance at nothing, or the past. Was he remembering a heartbroken youth with a borrowed guitar, serenade unsung? He surprised me then by saying, "I would not be sorry to see her leave Paynala. She does not owe these people here her whole life. God understands all she did, and forgives it all. But she must now forgive herself."

"For what, in God's name?"

He reached for the wine carafe, saw my half-empty glass, filled it and then his own. "You are a Spaniard, and you see her with Spanish eyes. But can you for a moment imagine yourself an Indian of this land—freed from the Aztecs only to find yourself a serf under the heavy yoke of Spanish rule? I tell you, hers is a heavy cross. To thousands—no, to millions—of Indians in New Spain, Doña Marina is their betrayer. What matter that in Paynala there has been no slave labor for an unfeeling Spanish landowner? These Paynalans know that she rules them not just as a hereditary caciqua but as a sworn vassal of Carlos of Spain. And they have heard what Spaniards have done to Indians in other places. Oh, they have heard! And so she is hated by hundreds of her Paynalans. And feels guilt, at times, as though she had indeed betrayed her own kind instead of having helped Christians to overthrow the cruel Aztecs and so bring Christ to pagans." His rhetoric had so moved him that tears stood in his eyes.

I was dumbfounded. "But surely the Catholic Indians here must respect and love her?"

"To more than half her people she is almost a saint. But to perhaps a third she is merely Cortés' former

mistress who then took another Spaniard as husband.
And as this town is split, so is she. Only her faith holds
her together. She knows herself to have been God's
servant when she aided Cortés, yet at times she suffers
dark hours because of much cruelty the people of this
land have suffered at the hands of Spaniards. With
great courage she stands firm against acts of enmity
done to her and hers, and continues with her Christian
duty here. Of late, she has begun to worry about
Martín's well-being. Only yesterday, she spoke to me
about Cortés' promise to educate the boy . . ."

"She deserves a better life than this!"

He nodded. "But does she think so?"

When I went with Aguilar at seven to the Jamarillo
house, all that he had told me of local hatred did not
prepare me for what met my eyes as I stepped under
the arcade. Beside the front door, bold against the white
wall, the vile epithet was smeared with what looked like
brown excrement: *LA CHINGADA*. The whore, the
degraded victim, rumped and left in the dust to crawl
away or die!

Stunned by anger and outrage, I bent my arm and
tried to erase the words with my sleeve. The stink told
me what had been used to print them. The stuff was
dry. Some rubbed off but the whitewash below was
stained brown. Aguilar took my arm and stopped me.
"I'll see that this is scrubbed clean. You go in. Say I'll
be a little late."

"Who did this filthy thing?"

"Na Chel Cuy, probably, or one of his bravos. I was
afraid your presence in her home would bring on some
act of malice. Now it seems that your mere presence
in town has sufficed."

"An Indian did this?"

"I told you we've taught some of them to read and
write."

"How can you be so calm?" I cried.

"This is not the first time, nor the worst."

"What could be worse than this?"

"A poisonous viper. Twice these have been found in the patio of her house. They are quite rare here. Once might have been chance. Two, no."

"Then her life is in danger here!"

"So I have told her. Knock and go in." He turned away.

The door was opened by a figure both familiar and strange. All in black relieved only by a large silver crucifix, the woman had a sad, serene face and looked like a Spanish widow until I recognized Doña Luisa, the daughter of the cacique of Tlascala. She greeted me pleasantly, with an apprehensive glance at the thickening twilight outside, but did not see the words on the wall. "Welcome, Don Arturo, to our house of sorrow." She closed the door, slid in place a large bolt, led the way to the *sala,* and said that my hostess would join me immediately.

Against whitewashed walls stood dark carved furniture from Spain. A lighted candelabrum on the table relieved the dimness. Shutters at the two small windows were closed and the air was hot and still. A vase of roses caught candlelight. There seemed too many empty chairs.

I felt Malinche's presence before she spoke and turned. She seemed to light the room. Now she wore earrings of gold filigree; a few small ornaments gleamed in the dark crown of her braided hair. I suddenly wondered if my stained sleeve stank. Would I still smell to her like young grass? "Aguilar will be a little late," I said.

"Sit down, my dear Arturo. There are so many things I want to ask you about your life now." As she gestured toward an armchair with her left hand I noted for the first time the absence of any ring. This, and the simple blue-green native dress instead of black intrigued me. Had El Galán been wrong in supposing a blissful domestic life with Jamarillo? She sat in a chair angled toward mine, the curve of the table with the candlelit roses between us. Suddenly her head turned and she glanced toward the arched doorway that led to the small entrance hall. "What is that sound? Do you hear it?"

I did, though barely: a mere whisper from the other side of the dark paneled front door. I knew what made it: a scrubbing brush cleaning the filth from the wall just outside. "I hear nothing," I lied. If the faithful Aguilar wished to protect her from such a sight, so did I. "As for my life, I am a sugar planter and a trader and own a caravel, and without much doubt will be the next alcalde of Havana."

She nodded. "Are you happy? Do you have children? What brought you here to Paynala?"

"I came here to see you. I have no children. Because I have no wife. As for happiness, I would say that I am busy rather than happy." It was the first time I had put my condition into these words: they sounded true.

"You mean you lost your wife?" Her eyes were wells of sympathy.

"I never had one to lose." I leaned toward her. "I never wanted a wife, because . . ."

The door knocker hammered. Doña Luisa admitted Aguilar. The tatters of interrupted intimacy hung on the air, but he did not notice them as he apologized for his tardiness with the grim look of satisfaction that attends a dirty job well done. Her eyes kept straying to my face, and I was sure my long bachelorhood was the reason. Good! Before this night was over I was going to spend time alone with Malinche, and in the meanwhile she could puzzle about my single state and perhaps come to the right conclusion.

At supper she sat at the head of the table, I at the foot. Aguilar was on one side, Martín and Doña Luisa at the other. Bowls of soup were placed before us by an Indian servant girl. The bowls were of red-brown clay but the spoons were silver. "As you can see, Don Arturo, we are a house of women now," Doña Luisa said, and cooled her spoonful of soup with her sigh.

"Except for me," Martín said.

"Except for you," Malinche agreed. I saw the motherly pride as she looked at him. The absence of other children told me that Jamarillo had given her none, for which I was deeply grateful. I wondered then about Malinche's absent mother and half-brother, and asked if her mother were still living. "She and her son Lazaro live in the little palace where I grew up." Her tone was cool. "Both are Christians. Her baptismal name is Marta."

Doña Luisa sounded even cooler. "Marta tries to seem devout, but she does not convince me. And why is she still friendly with Na Chel Cuy after he spat upon . . . ?"

"Enough!" Aguilar was firm. "I know your fondness for the late Don Juan, but we must be patient with Marta and Lazaro. They lead sad lives and have few friends."

"She is very nice with me," Martín said. "And she gives me camote candy."

"She is very fond of you," Malinche said.

"But Lazaro is stupid," Martín offered. "He thinks Spain is a city in Madrid. He thinks some god named Tlaloc brings rain to make the maize grow."

"But his Spanish vocabulary has improved greatly this past year," Malinche said.

The front door knocker sounded, a loud repeated battering, but no one showed interest and in a moment the Indian servant girl appeared to say "No one. Again."

I had become aware of a peculiar atmosphere, hard to put into words. It was as though a plague raged outside in the town, all over Mexico, and the people around this table were aware of it but chose to act as if it were not there. It was very hot and I wished the windows were open for the sake of whatever evening breeze might be astir, but knew enough not to suggest it. The yearning I felt to be alone with Malinche made me less appreciative than I should have been of the fine supper. At last it was over and Aguilar left and Doña Luisa took the boy to his bed. When I remarked on the authentically Spanish ambiance the house had, Malinche showed me through it in a truly Spanish gesture of intimacy.

The sala and dining room occupied the front or main building. In the right wing were her bedroom, Martín's, and a third which had been, she said, Jamarillo's. Malinche's bed had four tall carved posts but no canopy or curtains because of the heat here. When I remarked on the contrast between her Spanish home and her Indian clothing, she smiled. "I have some Spanish dresses Don Juan gave me, but they are very warm for this climate." Her rejection of that clothing, however practical the reason, pleased me. I found that I felt more kindly toward Jamarillo. Many hints had suggested that theirs had been a companionable but not ardent marriage. "But perhaps the contrast you mention tells a truth about me. I am a spiritual *mestizo*. Part Spanish, and part what I was born," she said.

We had returned to the *sala;* the heat within that shuttered room was now nearly intolerable, and I wished that I had chosen comfort above elegance when I had dressed that morning on the ship for this reunion. Worse than physical discomfort was the dismaying fact that since dinner my brain had grown torpid; I could find no words with which to make my way back to that moment of intimacy Aguilar had interrupted. "Might it be cooler in the patio?" I asked.

A cautious look reminded me of two vipers found there. I would have faced two dragons for fresh air. She nodded and rose.

Outside I was at once struck by the immense silence of the night. Even the cicadas were quiet now, although they had been chirping their lulling chorus loudly enough when I had crossed the plaza with Aguilar at sundown. In Cuba such a humid calm precedes a storm, but the sun had set in a clear sky, an orange orb that had slowly disappeared behind the high hills to the west of the town. Now a humpbacked moon shone down from a sky of stars. I found that I was nervous as we sat on the wide rim of the fountain. We both started to talk at once, laughed and broke off, and waited politely for the other to speak. I had to break the constraint between us.

I leaned toward her. "You were wearing this same color when I first saw you in Tabasco and fell in love with you." I was surprised that my voice trembled and tried to read her face, lighted by the gibbous moon. "Before supper I had started to tell you why I never married . . ."

A harsh scream cut off my words. I started, flesh prickling, and looked wildly about. A caged parrot hung from a hook on the patio wall. "Santiago and onward!" it cackled.

Malinche stood and went toward it. "When Orteguilla says that he wants to be let out of his cage." She opened the little door, and the parrot hopped to her wrist, wings wide to attain balance. Even by moonlight I could see its vivid coloring. It walked up her arm and settled on her shoulder, turning its head to regard me with a round eye. A malevolent eye; a possessive eye, its bright body brushing her hair. Was I jealous of a parrot? "I see the likeness to our dwarf friend," I said. "Who taught him Cortés' battle cry?"

"Don Juan. He gave me Orteguilla in Yucatán." The sorrow in her voice, the haunted look on her moonpaled face transferred my jealousy from a parrot to a dead man.

"Mother?" Martín, naked except for a small pale loincloth, emerged to stand beside his mother and to regard me with sleepy dislike.

"It's late, and you should be asleep, Martín."

"I just came to get Orteguilla. He likes it in my room."

"But you must put him back into his cage."

The parrot had other ideas, fluttered from Malinche's shoulder to the rim of the fountain. Martín stalked him halfway around it. The mother watched him fondly. I watched her. At last the boy and the parrot departed. By then I had the desperate idea that at any instant another interruption would occur: Doña Luisa would emerge to admire the hunchbacked moon; the servant girl would decide to water the plants; Aguilar would return on some pretext. Malinche had seated herself on the fountain's rim; I reached for her hand and held it firmly. "May God forgive me for it, but I envy a dead man. If I had been in Yucatán, maybe it would have been me you married. Lucky Jamarillo!" The laugh I attempted was a mistake.

She stared as if at a cruel idiot. "Lucky? You think he was lucky?"

Confusion made me hate my tongue, which stuttered. "F-forgive me! That was an outrageous remark. May God rest him, poor fellow." The last sounded false as a brass gold piece.

"Do you know how he died?"

"A duel, Cortés told me. Last January. In Madrid."

"Yes. He went there on the pretext of his mother's ill health. It enabled him to escape for a time from his existence here."

"The Castilian gentleman grew bored with life in a backwater Indian town?"

The remark made her back go rigid. Her voice was both hard and sad. "Did Aguilar tell you nothing of his life in Paynala? That Castilian gentleman endured three years of misery, of contempt, of malice. He was an alien even to the true Christians here. His blondness, his clothing, his home, his language, all these marked him as a Spaniard and set him forever apart. To the heathens, to Na Chel Cuy and his followers, he was the little husband of the whore of Cortés. And knew it. So do not speak of him with contempt again."

"But why in God's name did you stay in this place?"

"Where were we to go? To Spain? He knew that to return to his family with an Indian wife would put me in the same position as his here. Our hope was that time would prove our friend, that as the Christian faith prevailed in Paynala, the enmity would diminish and fade away. Here our home was, here my people were, and here we stayed. I cannot blame him that he took to drinking too much, and badly. I concealed this fault as best I could from Martín; Don Juan was good to him and Martín loved him. I was glad when he decided on the trip to Spain. I believed that being there and surrounded by his family and by people who respected him would be good for him and restore his self-esteem." Her voice broke; she bowed her head, I think to hide tears.

"Poor Don Juan Jamarillo," I said softly, and reached for her hand again.

She snatched it from mine, raised her head. "He died in a cantina—in a swordfight with a man who called me *La Chingada*."

The church bell began to toll the hour; ten iron tones. "But you are not to blame for that!"

"His mother told me the way he died in a short, cold letter. And said I had taken ruthless advantage of her son's romantic nature when I married him." The last iron note died away. She stood up. "Forgive me for speaking of such sad and bitter things. I did not mean to ruin our reunion. Now we must say good night."

I stood too. "Do you really think that I will allow this night to end on the dismal misfortune of your late husband? Or his mother's cruelty in her grief? Guess again, my dear. You have had enough of sorrow. I came here with one intention: to ask you to marry me. In Havana, as my wife, you will be treated with respect. This I can promise you."

"Your wife?" Her eyes were wide. "In Havana?"

"Why do you think I never married? I wanted no one but you!" I went to her and took her in my arms. At last, after so long! The sudden warm aroma of her body enveloped me, and with it the past we once shared. I kissed her mouth, and after the first amazing instant of feeling her lips melt into mine, the man I now was excelled the fumbling young Arturo. My hands caressed and fondled her and my shuddering sighs breathed my passion into her mouth, and we stood locked together, one ardent creature. I will swear that there was never a kiss like that before on earth. It stopped time; a little eternity passed like an instant; I was carried up into a realm where there was only us.

When at last we parted we stood staring into each

other's eyes and I knew that not just our lips but our souls had kissed. Joy brimmed in me. "We belong together," I whispered, holding her hands tightly, kissing the back of each one. "Everything else that happened was just a mistake. Marry me! Tomorrow! Yes, tomorrow morning!"

Her eyes longed; her voice was desperate. "You cannot live here. I cannot live in Cuba."

"Marry me tonight! Aguilar can perform the ceremony."

"No."

"I do not hear no! I can only hear yes! I give you a choice. Tonight? Or tomorrow morning? Which?"

"No, Arturo. No." She tried to pull her hands away. I clung. "You do not understand. I will not desert the faithful Christians here. And I must stand firm and hope to help the others, no matter how they hate me!"

"They have Aguilar!"

"I will not desert my people!"

The desperate inflexibility and all that Aguilar had told me of her made me realize I was now on risky ground. I spoke calmly. "Then I have the perfect solution. We will live part of the year here and part in Cuba. I own a ship, so transportation is a simple matter. You will not desert your people here, and I will not abandon my obligations there." I secretly believed that her pleasant existence in Havana would soon make her see how foolish it was to immolate herself in this place.

But she was shaking her head as though at a dense child. "Do you really think I would let you live here after what Jamarillo faced? Do you really think I would be regarded any differently in Havana than in Madrid? Do you think there is any place we can escape what I am? Do you imagine that I want you shamed as he was? Harmed, as he was? He died because of me!"

"I am not Jamarillo!"

"Neither was he, at the start!"

Again I remembered what Aguilar had told me of her. Only she seemed in a more extreme condition than he had believed. I took her shoulders in my hands and gently shook her. "Listen to me! You are not responsible for what he became, or for how he died! Or for what Cortés has done to Indians! You cannot punish yourself any longer. I won't let you! And I will not let you punish me by refusing the happy life I know I can give you."

She spoke as primly as a saint. "My happiness concerns me less than your future misery."

"For the love of God, stop confusing me with Jamarillo! I am not a fragile Castilian knight with my head in the clouds! I've worked, and schemed, and been clever. I am Don Arturo of Havana. I can offer you another world, my world, where you will forget the petty local conflicts here in Paynala!"

"The conflict would always be in my heart. We cannot change that."

"We can, and we will! The fact is, you love your misery! It is your penance. You act as if you are here by God's will. It is your own will that keeps you here. But my will is the stronger. And I tell you, you will marry me!"

She surprised me by saying "You have a ship."

"Yes!"

"Then when you leave here, take Martín with you. To Cortés. He wants to educate his son. It is time. I must not keep him here with me any longer."

She had astounded me. "Are you saying you would give up the son you love before you will leave this place?"

"He has a certain destiny as the son of Cortés. I will not cheat him of it. That is not love."

"And what will that leave you with, other than martyrdom? I see it now. You are unbalanced. You have had more grief than any woman could bear. You must rely on other judgment than your own. On mine. On Aguilar's. He wants you to leave this place."

She nodded. "He thinks my life may be in danger. I do not believe that. But even if I did, I would stay."

"I am taking you to Havana. To safety. Martín too."

She smiled at me tenderly. "I wish I did not know what I know. I wish I were not as I am. I wish I could share your life in Cuba. But . . ."

I flung my arms around her, pressed her tight against me, silenced her refusal with my lips on hers. The last words between us this night were going to be hers, just spoken. She would sleep with them echoing in her head. I took her hand and kissed it, back and palm. I broke my resolve and whispered, "I will never leave Paynala without you."

The household was asleep as we walked through dark rooms to the front door, our way lighted by the candle I carried. "Until morning," I said as I left her in her doorway. I looked back as I reached the arcade and she stood in the dark doorway beside the white wall cleaned of its ugly epithet, and I saw her as one standing on the threshold of a new life, her life with me.

Crossing the moonlit silent plaza to the church, I knew that this reunion with Malinche had given meaning to all my striving life since I last left her in Texcoco. In my cell on my boardlike cot I stared up at the darkness, smiling. I knew I would rescue her from this troubled place. For if God wanted her here, I would never have learned about Jamarillo's death, would never have come to Paynala. As He had shaped her path so it crossed ours in Tabasco, so He had shaped mine so it had brought me here. On this serene and heartening thought I let sleep close over me, deep, dark and dreamless. . . .

. . . To awaken and sit bolt upright to the sound of the world ending. Under me the earth stirred and heaved in slow waves to a low, grinding roar. Nausea trembled in the pit of my stomach. I tried to cross to the door but was flung to my knees. I heard the water ewer crash down and shatter, and the water ran to where I knelt on hands and knees like a dumb animal. There was a last small shuddering under me, and then uneasy quiet.

I got to my feet and ran through the church, past Aguilar who emerged from another doorway, shielding a lighted candle with one hand, his face elongated with shock. Far above our heads the temblor had set the church bell ringing wildly. I hurled myself out of the church and down the steps. Across the plaza the Jamarillo house stood serene in the moonlight. I started toward it.

The second temblor was worse than the first. I struggled for footing as though on a pitching ship. The terrible underground noise was louder, and to my horror I saw a chasm open the paving only a few paces ahead of me; first a small crack, it yawned jaggedly to a width of nearly an arm's span. I told myself this was earth's last hour. It was splitting into fragments, and next would come Judgment Day. I was flung to my knees and began to pray: "Be with us in the hour of our death . . ."

The crevasse started to close with a great grinding noise from below. Ahead, the Jamarillo house began to shudder in the moonlight. The front arcade fell slowly forward; the crash as it struck earth and broke into rubble was unheard in the rumble of the earthquake itself. The entire front wall fell outward and added itself to the broken arches, while at the same time the right wall fell to the north side of the house. By now the earth had stopped groaning and so I heard the awful thud as the roof of the right wing dropped to the floor. Dust arose, silvery in the moonlight. I got to my feet and ran across the seam where the crevasse had just yawned and to the edge of the fallen rubble of Malinche's house. Now I could hear moans, cries, and screams from all around the plaza. The great church bell was still tolling crazily: the church still stood.

I climbed over the jumble of adobe bricks and looked down at the broken roof of the right wing, the wing where Malinche and the boy slept. The water had splashed out of the patio fountain, leaving the basin empty. The servants' wing still stood. Someone was screaming within. I struggled over wreckage to the place where I thought Malinche's bedroom was and saw jutting from the rubble a dark bedpost, broken off jaggedly. I frantically lifted and heaved aside broken chunks of mud brick that had paved the flat Moorish roof.

By the time Aguilar and some others arrived to help me, I had excavated down to the corner of her bed, my hands already scraped and bleeding, my lips repeating my litany: "Let her be alive!" When we got the rest of the roof off the bed, she was not in it. I paused, panting, full of a wan gratitude.

I uncovered her bare foot a little later. We all worked silently and grimly to lift a fallen roof beam and found the rest of her on the floor between bed and door. She lay on her side, profile toward me, legs wide like a runner's, one arm reaching forward. She had slept naked and the sight of that body pierced me with a longing even as I became aware that the thick dark tendrils across her cheek were her blood.

I touched her shoulder. It was warm. Aguilar said we should carry her to the church, in case another quake leveled the rest of her house. We carried her on a litter we made from a blanket one of the stunned, tearful servants brought, and we laid her on the cot of a monk's cell like mine, and covered her nakedness. Her eyes were closed and she was breathing faintly. One side of her head was badly injured, crushed. For the rest of the night I stayed by her cot, dozing briefly. Sometimes I poured water, drops at a time, through her parted lips. Her closed lids had the same look of mystery as a statue's orbed blind eyes. I kept touching her hand, and it was cold, but not with the chill of death. Sometimes I softly kissed her unwounded cheek and whispered that I would always be with her and that she would heal and be well again and come with me to Cuba. Once I lifted the sheet and looked at that brave body, so finely made, so generously breasted. I prayed, and prayed, and prayed that she would live. At dawn a troubled Aguilar came in to say that the body of Martín had not been found. This seemed a strange but unimportant piece of news.

The sun had risen when I nodded off to sleep, but I awoke with a start, looking all about for the strange presence I felt in that room. What I had felt was the absence of life in her. I touched her hand. She was gone.

50

"Her spirit is with God and all the angels of heaven," Aguilar said.

But I had yearned for her flesh on earth.

"God's ways are mysterious, and as a good Christian, you must bravely accept this loss."

But what of her loss, the loss of her life? What kind of God would permit an earthquake to kill a woman who had brought so many souls to worship Him?

"Remember that she has now attained life everlasting."

And a grave. In my heart the worm of heresy gnawed and became a serpent.

I was scarcely moved when Aguilar told me that Martín was alive. "It seems that he was eavesdropping and heard his mother ask you to take him with you when you left. So he ran to the garden of his grandmother's house, carrying his parrot with him, and he was hiding there when the earthquake struck. One could say that his mother's concern for his future saved him from a death like hers."

The serpent within me stared at him with cold eyes. It coiled cold as a stone at the Mass held for her soul, and when I stood in the churchyard while her coffin was lowered into the grave, and while earth was spaded onto it. The simple stone cross did not please me, and I told Aguilar "I want an angel in white marble, wings half spread, and it should have her face." I made a sketch of the angel. "Is there a stone cutter here who is enough of an artist to carve this?"

He nodded, and I gave him money to pay for it. His sorrowful face was more cadaverous than ever now, and in a remote way I recognized that his loss had also been great. He said, "This earthquake has been more than a physical disaster to Paynala, even though twelve died in it. The most terrible effect has been on the minds of the Christians here, because it killed Malinche."

"There is nothing I can do to stop that, or you either, perhaps."

"But I will try."

"I wish you well. For myself, I cannot bear to stay in this hellish place another day."

"You are thinking only of yourself and your own grief. What about Martín? The grandmother has taken him to live with her, a fact you would know if you had not been so preoccupied with your own suffering. Should a Christian boy, half Spanish in blood, be left to live among Indians of dubious faith? But Marta is possessive of her grandson and says she has the right to him now. And it is true that she is his closest living relative, except for one."

"Cortés."

He nodded. "Martín may not wish to go, but it's the best solution."

"All right. I'll take him to Cortés."

"Do you know which house is his grandmother's? Come, I'll point it out to you. I'm sure you can persuade him."

"Why should I persuade him? You're the one he loves and trusts."

He spoke gently. "My task here will be hard enough without Marta wailing to everyone who will listen that I kidnapped her grandson from her."

I grinned. "You devious men of God!"

Seeing the steep thatch roof of the palace where Malinche's mother lived, the thought occurred to me that if Malinche had been sleeping in such a house on the night of the earthquake she might still be alive. Her Spanish house had buried her. I went up the stone steps, calling Martín's name.

For minutes there was only silence, and then in the doorway there appeared a short, stolid aging Indian woman in old and ragged clothes, her hair hanging in two braids. She looked like a madwoman or a beggar, and then I realized she was mourning in the ancient Indian way. On her stony face hints of a savage beauty still lingered. "What does the Spaniard want?", she asked in heavily accented Castilian, standing in the doorway as if to bar me from entering her home.

"To speak to Martín."

"He plays in the garden."

"Then find him and bring him here."

"He will not want to see you."

"Bring him." Under my hard glance she wavered.

"Enter, then."

The walls of the main room were decorated with faded, bizarre figures that marched in endless procession, some with high headdresses, some carrying spears. A small green lizard sitting very still on the shoulder of a warrior sped suddenly across the wall and vanished.

Marta returned with Martín beside her. He wore only a loincloth. On his bare chest lay a necklace of large flat turquoises set in silver. When I asked him if he would walk outside with me, he nodded. Marta started to follow us, but I told her sharply I wished to speak with the boy alone.

In the shade of the ceiba tree was a stone bench, and it was far enough from the doorway where Marta stared out at us so she could not hear my low voice. "Are you happy here with your grandmother?"

Martín looked up from under thick black lashes. "I am happy nowhere."

"Forgive me. I did not mean 'happy.' I mean, are you contented living here?"

"I am not contented, either." He bent his leg, knee to chest, and picked at a scab intently.

"Would you like to go to live with your natural father?"

"With Cortés?"

"Yes. Do you remember him?"

"I think not. Maybe so." He removed the scab from his knee. A little trickle of blood ran down his shin. He spit on it and rubbed it away with his palm. "Why should I live with him?"

"Because that is what your mother wanted for you." To my horror, with those words a lump of pain filled my throat and tears blurred Martín's sullen face.

"Well, don't cry," he said.

I tried to deny that I was crying. No words would edge through my throat. I turned my head away from him, staring across the plaza until I had mastered my emotion. His face was gentler when I looked back at him to say, "I have a ship anchored in the harbor at Coetzacoalcos."

"Martín!" called a woman's voice, seductive. It was Marta, still in the doorway.

He looked at her and stood up. She beckoned him toward her, smiling. He faced me. "Let's go, then. To Cortés."

As we started side by side toward the church, Marta called his name again, her voice sharp now and imperious. He turned and looked back and gave her a very Spanish salute of farewell.

Enough of his clothing had been retrieved by the servants so that he could be outfitted in Spanish garments for the journey. A mournful Doña Luisa trimmed and combed his hair while he assured her that he would come and see her, something she clearly doubted. Against my arguments, he pleaded to bring his parrot, so I contrived a cloth pannier to hold the birdcage which would hang by his left foot when he rode behind me. In the other pannier I put the small flat locked chest Aguilar gave me just before we parted. It was beautifully inlaid with various woods and a design in mother-of-pearl. He said, "This contains a document I wish Martín to have, and which you may read at your leisure. I will leave it to your discretion whether to give it to the boy now or at some later time." He gave me the tiny key that unlocked the chest.

I left him on the steps of the church, standing where I had seen Malinche after so many years. Turning in the saddle to offer a last wave to that indomitable robed figure, it seemed to me that if any churchman could keep the Indians of Paynala from the dark cave into which the old high priest was trying to lure them, it was he. And I knew it would be not only a duty to his God, but an expression of the love he had felt for the woman now lost to both of us.

Martín was delighted with my ship, and I saw his sullen sorrow lift for a moment when he saw his first dolphin. We had fine weather for the run to Havana, where I would outfit myself and get money for the long journey to Cuernavaca and Cortés. I had intended to read on shipboard the document Aguilar had given me, but found that I had lost the key to the chest that held it. Rather than mar the wood by prying it open, I decided to wait until we reached Havana, where a key could be found to fit.

My mother welcomed Martín kindly, although even after I explained his presence she seemed perpetually astonished to find the bastard son of Cortés sleeping in her home. Martín was as astonished at our six Negroes, for he had never seen a black man or woman before. Rubén took him to see the sugar plantation and the mill, and my father showed him the site of his last mine up in the hills and told lies about the gold he would extract from it. The night before we left for Vera Cruz, Martín came into my room and asked "If Cortés doesn't want me, can I live here with you?"

Somewhat touched, I said, "What man would not be pleased to have such a fine son?" But I lay in bed debating in my mind the wisdom of this venture. How would Doña Juana behave, finding herself suddenly confronted with his natural son, and half Indian at that? How would Cortés feel about this fruit of a liaison now so many years in the past? It was one thing to have promised the mother that Martín would be given a position of importance when he was adult, but another to rear him. Lying sleepless, I suddenly made up my mind that if I saw that the boy was not welcome, I would raise him myself. More and more I had seen in him sweet traces of Malinche. Their smiles, now that he sometimes smiled, were almost identical. The very fate that had wrenched her from my arms might well have given me her son, the flesh of her flesh. This was not the flesh I had yearned for, but I had learned of late that destiny is a hard bargainer, and to snatch back any small portion of the lion's share it demands is not a small feat.

How strange was the journey to the plateau of Anahuac, which we had to cross to get to Cuernavaca! I passed along the same route I had traveled long before, but now the child of the woman I had loved then rode behind me. We were part of a caravan that included several mounted Spanish soldiers from the garrison at Vera Cruz and a coach full of Spaniards with business in the capital. We passed the edge of Lake Texcoco and I saw the new city of Mexico on its isle, and though many buildings had risen, they were not to be compared to those that once had gleamed like pale silver. I had no curiosity to enter this city.

The mountain trail to Cuernavaca led us so high that for a time we rode through clouds, but then we descended into a pleasant valley, much lower in altitude than the vast one we had left. The town was small, but the new governor's palace was built as for all time of dark gray volcanic stone and overlooked a park shaded by trees and lighted by flowers. The anteroom to which an Indian serving woman admitted us showed signs of very recent residency: several large wooden crates stood as yet unpacked, and the room was furnished with only a rude bench by the door. Martín and I sat side by side, the parrot cage on his lap, while the servant went to tell Cortés that Don Arturo awaited him.

He entered smiling, a smile that dimmed to a look of puzzlement as he saw the boy beside me. I rose and Martín followed suit, putting his parrot down on the bench. I said, "Cortés, allow me to present to you your son, Martín."

Flicking me a question with his eyes, Cortés looked down at Martín and said pleasantly, "It's been a good many years since last I saw you, Martín. Do you remember me at all?"

"No, Father." Martín looked up calmly.

"And how is your mother?"

"Dead."

The smile vanished. Cortés looked suddenly old and hollow-cheeked. Lifeless eyes met mine. "Now I understand the reason for this visit."

A pretty little voice called "Hernán?"

He did not seem to hear it. "How did she die?" he asked me.

"An earthquake."

"Hernán?" Into the anteroom came Doña Juana, dressed in pale blue and her emerald. She stopped to stare at Martín, then at me, then back at Martín again.

Cortés went to the boy's side and dropped a casual hand onto his shoulder. "This is my son, Martín. He will live with us now."

And that young gentlewoman smiled down at the boy without the flicker of an eyelid; she might have been anticipating this visit for weeks. "You are motht welcome, my dear, though I muthst warn you, things are in a meth. We only got here yethterday."

I found it in my heart to be glad that no rejection faced him here, yet at the same time a feeling of loss cast its fleeting shadow.

We supped very well and afterward Cortés declined to play a game of cards, of which his old mother was very fond, and he and I walked together into the garden, sweet with the smell of flowers. I admired the naked white marble nymph he had unpacked and set in place only that morning. He had bought it in Rome, where he went to bring the Pope a gift of four Indian jugglers, pleasing him greatly. Faintly from within the house came the voices of Martín and Doña Juana and Señora Cortés, playing their card game with a childish amount of delight at a win, loud moans at a loss. "Santiago and onward!" the parrot called, to laughter.

Suddenly realizing that I had not seen Orteguilla the dwarf among the household, I asked what had happened to him. "He and Blanca are enjoying an extended visit at the home of the Duke of Bejar, my wife's father. The pair created quite a stir at Court. The elegance of his wardrobe dazzled all beholders. He now wears two-inch *chopines,* like an actor, and towers as tall as Martín." The smile left his face as he mentioned the boy, and he thanked me for my kindness in bringing his son to him. "I will of course repay you for the costs of the journey."

I spoke rather brusquely. "I can well afford what it cost. It was a kindness I did in memory of his mother, and because the boy could not be left to be reared by the Indian grandmother who had treated her own daughter so cruelly."

"Your good qualities showed themselves to me when you were a green youth, and they seem to have grown with the years," he said politely. There was a silence in which crickets chirped their cheery yet lonely a capella chorus. "An earthquake," he mused. "I gave her that town to reward her, and in it she died. Sad. Very sad."

"Sadder for me. If she had lived, we would have married." I remembered her refusal, her renunciation, but I brushed them aside. I would have won her!

He was looking at me with amazement. "Married?" For all his praise of a moment before, he sounded as if he did not believe it.

Fury gripped me. "Married! To me, Cortés! Me! You

were the first, I don't deny that. First in her heart. But I would have been the last, if she had only lived! Because she loved me, too. Didn't you ever understand that?"

"I knew she was fond of you," he said calmly. "But with you she would have been nothing more than a little foot soldier's camp follower. I made her a legend. You cannot argue the truth of that, nor will history."

I could not argue with that. As Doña Marina and as La Chingada she would be remembered as long as there were Spaniards and Indians. But he had had her and I had not, except for one brief night. My voice was cold as I said "I think a chill is falling, and I confess to being weary. Perhaps you will forgive me if I retire early. I wish to leave early in the morning for Cuba." I moved toward the lighted doorway.

His laugh after my coldness astonished me. "Cuba again? Always Cuba! Why not stay here as my welcome guest and go with me to the Sea of Cortés?"

I turned. "Where?"

"That northern sea I told you of where the pearls are found. Surely there is someone you can entrust to manage those little enterprises of yours? My God, you're not yet thirty! You're too young to tie yourself to sugar cane and trade and miss the chance to meet an Amazon." He nudged me, full of good cheer. "Remember those tales of the big-breasted wild women, laden with gold and gems and hot for love?"

"Having already tempted me with a golden city, you now offer Amazons. What else among your wares? Don't mention fame or glory, and for the love of God don't talk of the salvation of heathen souls, for in my present doubt of either a heaven or a hell I consider the heathens well enough off as they are."

In the sudden silence I decided I had shocked him, and cursed myself for revealing my heresy. I must learn to keep my present state of mind to myself, for the Inquisition was busy and widespread, and for words like mine men died in flames.

He spoke softly. "I offer you something else. Not

glory or fame or riches or saved souls. Something else. Something that you want more than you ever wanted any of these, something you secretly yearn for, something you have missed, something you need without knowing that you need it."

"What?"

"Danger."

"Danger?"

"Great peril. The whisper of Death's black robe passing you by inches. The full taste of the mystery which is being alive, alive and far out on the edge of the known, all that lies ahead a vast surprise."

There was a sudden pang inside my chest as though a gong made of my own flesh had been struck there and still reverberated. I knew that he knew me, and that we were alike. We had been forged by conquest into other creatures than most men are. A wild urge filled me to abandon caution, leave the gains of the years, follow him once more. With an effort I shook my head. "No."

"Danger," he whispered again. We had reached the lighted doorway; our faces were no longer shadowy masks. His eyes were fixed on mine, gleaming, glittering, a wizard's eyes, or a siren's. I saw that for all his fame and glory and wealth and noble wife and fine bastard son, he needed to know he had not lost his old touch, could still lure men to follow him to an unknown sea.

But it was as important to me to know he could not lure me. I smiled. "Danger is a whore I no longer frequent."

He blinked, recoiled slightly. The luster faded in his eyes. I doubted that any other man had ever implied that he was a whoremaster, his trulls Danger and Death, Gold and Glory, and felt a kind of elation at my daring as we entered an empty *sala,* cards still scattered on a polished table. Cortés went to a sideboard and poured a glass of wine for himself and another for me. He watched me over the rim of his glass as we drank. In a gentle voice with just a tinge of mockery under it he said, "On second thought, I wonder if I want you with me after all. You're reasonably brave, and you're clever. But one thing about you puzzles me. A certain lack of awareness, shall we say? Yes, a tendency to take matters at face value."

"I don't understand what you mean." Pretending to sip wine casually, I felt myself grow tense.

"Has it never occurred to you to wonder why I always treated you differently from the rest? With particular kindness and concern? Why I made you my spy, my confidant, my secretary on occasion, giving you knowledge of privy matters?"

"How many of your soldiers could read and write?" But my voice sounded unsure.

He shook his head slowly from side to side. A smile parted his grizzled beard and his eyes pierced mine. "You could have been my son."

After a stunned instant, I knew he was not my father. My resemblance to Francisco Mondragon was too great. But he had not claimed that. He had only said he might have been. I remembered the blush on my mother's cheeks when I had asked her at seventeen if she had known Cortés intimately, and I recalled her vehemence in denouncing him as a womanizer. Had hers been the married woman's balcony he had climbed, falling from the wall on the way down? Or had he seduced her before she knew my father, when she was a very young girl and he a stripling? I would never know, but I knew what he was telling me with his cruel hint. He had seduced her.

"Ah, now I think you are aware," he said, eyeing my face as his earlier words echoed in my head: you could have been my son.

An answer to his attack rose in my throat like a scream: and Martín could have been mine! Oh, that would tent him, prick him deep in, rob him forever of his faithful Indian mistress who had loved no other man until their last farewell in Honduras. I felt the veins in my temples throbbing as his used to, and I clenched one fist, but I throttled the gush of words in my throat before I told him I had cuckolded him in the treasure room of a dead Aztec king. I could not be so faithless to my dead love.

So his was the last thrust. But mine was the victory. For as my anger ebbed I knew that his need to hurt me was a weakness and my silence a strength.

He had a servant come to lead me to my bed, and in going I passed the open door to the garden and saw the white marble nymph chastely covering her private parts with a spill of stylized drapery. I wondered if my white angel yet graced Malinche's tomb.

In Cuba I at last opened the little carved chest Aguilar had entrusted to me, which I had put away in the rush of preparation for my departure to Cuernavaca. A small key to a chest where I kept private documents fitted the lock, and on a stormy night in the privacy of my room I read the story of Malinche's life until her parting from Cortés. Sometimes it seemed as if I could hear her voice speaking, and I looked wildly around the room. Sometimes I felt her presence. I marveled at her ability to remember the very words people had said.

It was after midnight when I sat beside a last guttering candle, shaken by the power of her mind, the depth of her feelings, she, one of those Indians Europeans had regarded from the first as an inferior race. The senseless waste of that mind to death now aroused in me an anger as great as that I had felt at the waste of her beautiful body. The candle flickered out and I went to bed. The wind was howling around the house, and for me the universe reverberated with the shrieking, mocking laughter of a dark power that might be Satan but surely was not God.

There might be a God somewhere out there amid the distant spheres of the planets of this universe, but he had never been with us on our march to Tenochtitlán, nor had we ever been the fist with which He had smashed idols and killed men to save heathen souls. Where men kill in God's name, there God is not. That is true whether the weapon is a Spanish sword or an obsidian sacrificial knife.

During the next month this island of Cuba shrank to a paltry place, and my sugar mill and my ship turned into toys for a child. All my enterprising years seemed just a silly game played for petty stakes, and if a hurricane had flattened my cotton and young cane and the house with me in it, it would have been all the same to me. For hope a man must have, however unlikely, however much it is a secret, unacknowledged except in dream or reverie. And the source of mine lay in earth below a marble angel.

I wrote to my partner, Don Enrique, charged my faithful Rubén with the care of all my property when my father was indisposed, and told my parents I was leaving them for a time. Then I went to the storeroom and got my old breastplate and the gilded helmet with the centaurs.

I might encounter pearls, perhaps, or Amazons, or the rediscovery of my old faith in God, or the bone-faced gentleman in black with the lipless grin, or even the golden city of El Dorado. But very surely I would find what Cortés had last promised me.

ACKNOWLEDGMENTS

The author wishes to express her indebtedness to the works of Bernal Diaz del Castillo and William Prescott and the many Mexican histories which were rich sources of fact and inspiration; her gratitude to Ellis St. Joseph for criticism, suggestions, and encouragement, to her friends Vera Caspary, Irving and Susan Niemy, Wolfgang Nebmaier and Ramona Stewart, and to her agent, Jay Garon, and her editor, Beverly Jane Loo.

sounded through the front door of the room as she